M000105336

Beyond
KNOWING

IT'S JUST A CHIP... RIGHT?

Cynthia Pavlicek

ISBN 978-1-0980-3743-7 (paperback)
ISBN 978-1-0980-3845-8 (hardcover)
ISBN 978-1-0980-3744-4 (digital)

Copyright © 2020 by Cynthia Pavlicek

All rights reserved. No part of this publication may be reproduced, distributed, or transmitted in any form or by any means, including photocopying, recording, or other electronic or mechanical methods without the prior written permission of the publisher. For permission requests, solicit the publisher via the address below.

Christian Faith Publishing, Inc.
832 Park Avenue
Meadville, PA 16335
www.christianfaithpublishing.com

Printed in the United States of America

PROLOGUE

Curfew sirens are beginning to sound. People from all over the city begin to scurry into their homes. Fear is the main motivator. Although it is merely a rumor that some of the offenders of the curfew have been shot, rumor is enough to convince the people of this new nation to heed the sirens and make sure that everyone is tucked away for the night.

While most of the world is secure inside the closed walls of their homes or shelters, there exists an underworld. A group of people known only as the Knowing. They are people who no longer stand by to wait and see what happens but now stand for what they believe to be right. These are the people of yesteryear that were too busy to get involved but now find it necessary to risk their lives in order to help stop the remaking of their faith. They risk their lives to help keep the knowledge of the one true God alive in this world they now live in.

The Knowing choose not to follow the way that the government had decided the world should go but instead to hold fast to the teachings of their Bible. Since the signing of the One World peace treaty, a lot of changes have taken place. The least of which is a New World religion, regulated not by God but by the government. In the beginning we (the Knowing) were excited. One world united under one God, our one true God. A dream come true. Then the truth, as it somehow always does, started to show its face. It was not the face of our God, but was an image of a controlling system, a system used to keep the masses under control, in the name of God.

3

As the last few notes of the sirens sound, Sandy Smithson hurries to find a safe place to stay for the night. Almost everyone has an assigned place to go, but for the few who refuse to adhere to all the new laws, there are very few shelters left. To go to some of the shelters that do exist, there could be a great risk of being singled out and arrested as an enemy of the State.

During the fifty-two years of Sandy's life, she had read and heard about people of the past having to hide and keep secret the activities in their lives in order to fight against tyranny. In all of those stories, she never believed that her life could ever come to such a crossroads. She had heard about the Underground Railroad that was set up for the slaves seeking safety during the Civil War and then later stories of the Jews of Europe. She had heard of Corrie ten Boom and Anne Frank, just to name two who choose peacefully to stand for a cause. Stories of how they had been able, with the help of others, to hold to their convictions and to keep doing what was right in the eyes of God.

Tonight, Sandy's refuge would be like one of the hidden places they had. They had tunnels, Sandy would have a space under a house, the crawl space to be exact. The type of places you go to when you wanted to check the plumbing or such. Now these crawl spaces serve as secret survival shelters.

Many a late night, the crawl spaces of some homes were found and dug into. It had become a fact of the underground that these spaces could not only provide refuge for the believers in the night, but some also could provide heat in winter and meeting places that no one except the Knowing knew about. To this point in time they had not been discovered by the government officials.

CHAPTER *1*

Date: December 27, 20XX
Order: #1610
Name: Jacob Allen Singleton
Status: Confidential
Note: Above mentioned is to report to government office headquarters 16 ASAP

Jacob sat in the waiting room of government headquarters reviewing the orders that had been delivered to his apartment a few hours ago. He was trying hard to recall anything that he might have done in the last few days or months that could have warranted him being called up to the office of the top brass, but for the life of him, he couldn't think of a thing.

As he sat waiting for what seemed like an eternity, he looked down at the badge in his hand. The face on the badge (his own) was looking back at him.

The face in the picture was looking incredibly confident. Not at all how he was feeling at the moment. His dark eyes and hair were almost a perfect match in color. He had thick wavy hair that would at any time turn to a curly mess, unless properly maintained.

His looks had always been a problem for Jacob. Since he had graduated from the government academy a year ago, he had found it difficult for others to take his position as a government officer seriously. Not only the people he served but his coworkers as well. From the very beginning of his career, no one would believe that he was old enough to be an officer of the state. Jacob had what they would call a baby face, complete with dimples that framed his mouth. These dimples would show themselves at the most inopportune moment or at the least amount of emotion, often giving up whatever chance of a straight face he was trying to pull off. Not that keeping a straight face was ever a plan of his. One of Jacob's biggest problems was his temper. How many times had he reminded himself that he should keep a professional attitude, keep his cool, only to find himself flying off the handle at the least little thing? But not this time. As of late, Jacob had not done anything that could have caused him to be called up to the main office. Not that he could remember anyway. What would become of this young man looking at him from his badge? What indeed?

Jacob was deep in thought about how unfortunate he was for having such a baby face when he realized with a start that his name was being called out by the secretary.

"Jacob Singleton? Well, isn't that you? Please do pay attention. There is too much to do around here without adding a daydreaming, pain-in-the-system boy!"

Jacob caught only a part of the rampages of this "overseer type" of secretary and jumped to his feet to answer her.

"Oh yes. I am Jacob Singleton." *Oh, great way to start*, Jacob thought. Jacob could think of one hundred other ways to have started this conversation.

"Come with me." Speaking as she turned to show Jacob the way, the secretary's heel got stuck in the strap of his backpack. Almost falling and then catching her balance, she turned and gave Jacob a look of distrust. All he could think to do was to smile and say a quiet "I'm sorry."

Expressing words not clear to Jacob, she steamed off motioning for Jacob to follow.

Going down a long hallway of this office, Jacob couldn't help but notice its decor. It was very much like the home he had grown up in. It was decorated tastefully and very modern. Not sterile, but not warming either, practical. Somehow a thought of thanks came to his mind. Having been raised in very much the same surroundings as this might help him to be more comfortable in this situation. Whatever this situation was.

Finally reaching the last door at the end of the hallway, the secretary stopped and gave such a soft tap that Jacob was truly surprised to hear a voice offering entrance.

As the door swung open, Jacob could see a very large man begin to rise from his chair behind an overloaded desk.

Extending his hand toward Jacob, the man began to ramble on. "Come in, young man. I am so glad to meet you. I have heard so much about you. Oh my, but you do look very young indeed. Just as I was told. Are you sure that you are telling the truth about your age?"

After the rush of words, a very deep laugh came from this man. Not knowing what was so funny, Jacob tried to laugh along with him.

Taking Jacob's hand and giving it a good shake, he introduced himself as J. B. Diggings, head of undercover operations for the government.

Odd, thought Jacob, that he had never heard of this man before.

Jacob had been raised in a prominent political family. A lot of his family members were on the government force. His father and grandfather were both in management. He was the youngest of five. His two oldest brothers were upper-level officers, and his only sister was in intelligence. The oldest three had all found their way onto the government force way before Jacob had finished growing up. Jacob had one more brother who was older but closer to his own age. His name was Mark. So far Mark had not found his way into the family business, as it were. Not yet anyway. Like Jacob, Mark had been to all of the right functions with all of the right people and connections. Everyone knew that it was only a matter of time until the last of the Singleton brothers would join up in the cause of changing this new world. It would be said that it was just simply a matter of finding the right spot. But for now, Mark did odd jobs and went to college. Jacob was not sure what it was Mark was majoring in at this time, he thought it might be something to do with computers or counseling, but that was anyone's guess. Mark didn't stay with any one thing for very long, but that did not matter to Jacob. Although Jacob had a great relationship with all of his family, he and Mark had a closer one somehow. Jacob always wondered if it was because they were so much closer in age or if it was that they were so much alike. For whatever the reason, they were close, and Jacob was glad of it.

From the oldest brother to Jacob, there was a span of over twelve years.

For as long as Jacob could remember, he and his siblings had been taken to all the political functions, and he was sure that he had met almost everyone in this service, but he was equally sure he had not seen or heard of this man before.

With a face and a name so very unusual, this was not someone he had met or could recall hearing about. So who is he? Where did he come from? What did he want with him?

It was as though this J. B. Diggings was reading his mind when he spoke to Jacob. "Bet you are saying to yourself, 'Who is this J. B. Diggings? Never seen him before.' Well, son, that is the whole idea behind this program. And, Jacob, you are about to become one of the most special tools of this unit, that is, if you decide to take this offer that I am about to extend to you. Young man, come on in and have a seat." Looking to the secretary, Mr. Diggings addressed her. "That will be all, Kim. Please see to it that we are not disturbed, do you understand? No matter what comes up, okay?"

"That is fine, sir, I understand." Giving Jacob one final look of disgust, she left the room with a huff.

"Oh, don't mind Kim, she takes her job way too seriously. She thinks that everyone is a spy or something." Mr. Diggings gave a wink to Jacob. Somehow insinuating that they had an inside secret between the two of them.

Mr. Diggings looked to see that the door was completely closed before he resumed any more conversation about this new unit.

"Now, son, let's get down to business. What do you know about why you are here?"

Jacob, totally confused, now gave a questioning glance to Mr. Diggings. "Sir, I have absolutely no idea what you are talking about or anything about what I am doing here."

Mr. Diggings was looking as though he were trying to decide if he believed Jacob. He pursed his lips and rubbed his face. Jacob could see that Mr. Diggings had finally decided he could trust him. Mr. Diggings leaned back in his chair. "Good. Young man, this is going to be very good. I was just checking to see if there had been any leaks in the office, what with you being in the Singleton family and all."

Now Jacob was getting angry. He was feeling as though this man was somehow insinuating that he had gotten his position in the government department by using family ties. "Sir, I don't know what it is that you have heard about me, but I want to make it clear that I received my position on this force by my own means. In fact, sir, most people know me as Jacob Allen and *not* Jacob Allen Singleton. Per my request might I add?"

Mr. Diggings raised his right hand as if to motion a cease-fire.

"Whoa, young man. I am not sure what it is that you are thinking I was trying to say. And I have no idea at all about how you came to be on the force, nor do I care. All I want to do is to make sure that this new unit has not been compromised before we even get it started. Now let's start this whole conversation over again, shall we?"

Jacob took a deep breath and sat back into his chair. Not believing how quickly he could get riled up when it came to his family. What was the matter with him? Why couldn't he just behave like everyone else? Why was he so defensive? After all, he had a good homelife and he loved his family. Perhaps that was it. Perhaps he had too good of a homelife.

Mr. Diggings began to speak and brought Jacob's attention back to the moment. "Now, Jacob, you, young man, have been selected by several high-ranking officials to work on a special unit. It is going to be undercover, very deep undercover. The program, or unit as we are going to call it, is going to be tagged Find the Leader." Mr. Diggings stopped for a second or two to see if he could find any reaction in Jacob's face. With none detected, he continued.

"The goal is going to be to find the leader of a rebellious religious group called the Knowing. For several months now, since the signing of the world peace treaty, there has been a growing group of religious crazies calling themselves the Knowing.

"Have you ever heard about them, son?"

Jacob shook his head, indicating Yes. "But not much. They are chipless right?"

"Well, you will know more by the end of this assignment. It is known that from your family upbringing that you don't adhere to any such teachings, and that is a good thing."

"What such teachings, sir?" Jacob had been raised religious. But it was more of a benign religion. Yes, there was God. But He was someone you could go to in a time of great need. He wasn't an every-day part of life. The world was way too big for God to care about the little things of life.

"You will see some crazy religious teachings. Yes, Jacob, you will be running into some real religious fanatics. These people have it in their heads that God needs to be served every day. You know like the people from history used to do. They call meetings on a regular basis like they used to in the heathen days, and they make decisions for their lives based on what they call the Word of God. You know what I mean, don't you, all that Bible stuff."

Jacob had heard of these things, of course, but he himself had never studied or really seen any of it. His family safeguarded him from such disruptive influences.

"So as far as we can tell, we know that you of all people will be safe from being sucked into their craziness. It was hard to find someone like you. Someone with a strong family background that is well educated and has a strong, balanced, passive religious upbring-ing. When you were selected, it was unanimously decided that you should be the one in this position."

"Are you sure I am the one, sir?" Jacob was feeling irritated again. The idea of being selected for anything because of his family made him uncomfortable.

"Yes. You, son, are going to become one of the Knowing. You will get deep into the organization and uncover the identity of the leader."

Jacob began to smile. "Sounds like a spy movie, sir."

"Son, this is no laughing matter. This group has single-hand-edly undermined many programs that this government has tried to establish. How, you ask? Well, I'll tell you how. They do it by putting ridiculous questions in people's heads. Instead of people doing as they are told, they question everything. What's the government's motive? Why should we obey? What would God say about it? And so on. Just for example. Take the chips. Everyone should have received one, right?"

The chips were known well to Jacob. His family was one of the leading families to promote the program. The chip contained all the important information about the person who had them. It had their financial, health, family, education, and job status all in one place. The amount of paper and time saved from these chips was immeasurable. The fact that they were a safety tool was something that needed to be accounted for too. When someone had a chip, they could be monitored to within about three feet of their exact location. Many people were allowed out of jail because they could be tracked, thus lowering the cost to the government and ensuring public safety.

"The chips are a great thing. A great way to save trees, land-fills, and so on. Everyone thinks this is a great idea, right? But no, not these people. They act all crazy with their doomsday attitude. The mark they called it and refused it for their family and children. They are absolutely ridiculous. Why, just the other day, a child was kidnapped. He did not have a chip, so we have no way of recovering him. If he were *chipped*, as they call it, then the child would have been found just seconds after the satellite had come into range. And they call us the bad guys, the enemy, the marked, the sold out."

This Mr. Diggings was really getting himself all worked up. "Anyway, let's get back to you and the matters at hand. Now your job, if you accept, will be one of great danger. These people are real crazies. I am sure a well-raised boy like you can't even imagine how crazy. They somehow have an ability to get into people's heads. We are not sure of exactly how this cult works, but we have seen several of the finest people won over to their side. Strong even minded people who, for whatever reason, will simply choose to give up every-thing they have—their status, their families, their jobs, even their very lives—to go over to this Knowing group."

"Sir, how is it that I have heard so little of this group or their activities?"

"Well, son, I'll tell you that has not been an easy task. Keeping a lid on the publicity about this group has been an ongoing and time-consuming endeavor."

At this point, Mr. Diggings got up and began to pace around the room. Realizing that he was about to disclose some very important information to this young man he had only just met, he gave Jacob another thorough inspection. But then if Jacob were going to get this job done, he needed to know everything. It was a risk that he was going to have to take.

"Due to the new government controls on the media, we have managed to delete a lot of the outgoing information on them. On the grounds of group hysteria, you understand. We don't want to give them any unnecessary attention. Not giving them a chance to sound like heroes or, worse yet, martyrs. But somehow this group continues to grow. They keep showing up in the strangest ways. We find printed materials in all of the official offices. Bulletin boards have to be monitored constantly for propaganda flyers. They are on the Internet. Even in our government computer system. Why, just the other day, a virus was placed in the system spreading their crazy ideas. They were telling everyone that the one true God loves them."

Jacob was getting excited as he thought over this opportunity. It was obvious that his opponents were not going to be easy ones to take down. If he would be the one to do it, his life would change for sure. He would have a place in the government that was of his own doing, and everyone would know. This might be exactly the chance he needed to prove himself. This could be his way to prove his status as more than just a kid from a rich, political family. This could be his way to finally be recognized for who and what he really was, and that's a good government officer.

"Sir, this does sound like something I would be interested in doing, but there is one thing I can't figure out. How is it that you haven't been able to catch this leader? He has to live in this area. He would have to have a job. And would need to have a chip, right?"

"Well, son, this is where your lesson on these people begin. You can't think of them as being like us. They don't have the same goals or standards that the average person has. In addition, they somehow have a hold on the people who work for them. These people are loyal like I have never seen, as I said before, even unto death. As for not having the chips, well, not all of the people have them, it is our guess that the people who went over to the Knowing after already getting the chips are somehow working with them and helping them out. Real crazies, I tell you."

"Sir, to date, how many of these leaders have you captured?"

"Darn it, son. You are just not getting it, are you? To date, we have not gotten a single one. Just when we are getting close to what we think is a breakthrough, poof, they vanish as though they had never existed, only to pop up in another area. All the time recruiting new members and spreading their lies. So as you can see, this is not going to be an easy job. Not to mention the risks you will be taking?"

"Risks, sir? Exactly what are the risks you are talking about?" Jacob wanted all the information he could gather.

"Well, it is obvious that you are interested in taking on this assignment, so I guess that there is no time like the present to fill you in. Time is of the essence. The first thing we have to do is get you into the Knowing, and that should be relatively easy."

"You think getting in will be easy?" questioned Jacob. "How can getting me into a group that you can't even find be easy?"

"Don't get smart, son, you're getting ahead of me. Well, these people have one great flaw. They seem to trust anyone who doesn't have a chip."

"Well, that leaves me out. I have had my chip from the very beginning of the program." Jacob was a little glad of this fact. He liked the idea of this job, but he wasn't sure if he truly trusted Mr. Diggings. There was something about him that made Jacob feel uneasy.

"Not exactly, Jacob. We have a way around that problem." Mr. Diggings was smiling at Jacob.

"Are you telling me that you want to deactivate my chip?" Jacob leaned forward, stunned at even the thought of such an important part of his life being tampered with. Why, from early on in his life, he had been warned of the importance of the chip and how the information on it could be considered life and death. The very thought of going by a demagnetizing device sends horror through him, but here sits a man wanting to erase his very existence by suggesting he delete his chip.

"Well, son, it isn't quite that easy. You see, this Knowing group are very smart and not to be taken as backward in any shape, way, or form. In fact, some of us have begun to think that the people in this group may even have scientific backing. At any rate, what I am trying to say is that we could not just delete your chip. The Knowing would be able to detect that, but it would be removed altogether."

"Removed?" Jacob jumped to his feet looking as though Mr. Diggings had said he was going to shoot him.

"Yes, removed. Now don't get yourself all riled up. It would be only a temporary thing. And as soon as this case is closed, you will be rechipped."

"But, sir, I don't get it. What would happen to me without my chip?"

"Son, it will be like starting a new life, a life of the Knowing. We are not sure how it works. It seems that as soon as a nonchipped person hits the town, they are somehow detected and taken into the fold. That's exactly what we are banking on to happen to you."

"At that point in time, you will become a part of their group. With your education and background, I am sure that they will find need of you, and eventually you will work your way up into the system and find their leader."

Jacob sat back down very slowly. He began to think about what he had been told. All of it acceptable, except the part about losing his chip. That thought had never even entered his mind, until this moment. Jacob wasn't usually one to get ruffled. Angry yes but not ruffled. But life without a chip?

As soon as Jacob could think clearly, he began to consider the steps of what would have to happen for this plan to take place. The chip would have to be removed, this was as good a place to start as any.

"Sir, if I understood you correctly, you plan to remove my chip?" He took a deep breath. "Well, the only time I ever heard of that being done was when a crazy man cut off his hand trying to remove his chip by himself, and unless you know something that I don't, I don't think that worked."

"Well, like I said, that with the media under government control, there is a lot of information that the average person would not and does not have access to. One of those safeguarded facts is that a chip can be removed, if need be. Although we can adjust, update, and even delete chips without removing them. There was a need a while back to remove a chip from an upper government official's son. He had an allergic reaction to his chip, and it was becoming life-threatening. So a lot of effort and expense was used in developing a way to remove a chip. So, young man, you would be the second of only two people in this world who would have had his chip removed, and might I add, one of only a few select individuals who even know that it can be done."

"Okay. Let's say that I do have this done and I do get into the Knowing. How on earth do I ever get out? How will I contact you?"

"Well, you don't really just get out. We have a plan to remove you on a timetable. At a designated time, we will come in and get you ourselves. Whatever the information you have, well, that is what you will have. Hopefully, it will be exactly what we need to get this group we are after. You will not report to anyone, and the only records you will have is going to be a handwritten journal. We understand that is one of the ways that the Knowing have escaped us. We can't tap into the computer system in order to get them. Well, because they are not using the system. Brilliant, isn't it? Beat them at their own game with their own game."

Mr. Diggings was feeling quite smug with himself. Telling this young man about his plan had gone even better than he had hoped. Most men would have not inquired any further once they had heard about losing their chip. Obviously Mr. Diggings had made the right choice when he had chosen Jacob, who was a man from such good stock. And he, Mr. Diggings, had the good sense to choose him.

"Well, son, I need your answer now. We are on a very short timetable. And if you do take this job, I have a lot more to explain to you. But not another word until I know whether you are committed to this project or not?"

Jacob's mind was racing. This could be the chance of a lifetime. This could be his chance to prove himself. His chance to prove himself once and for all to his family and friends who Jacob felt up until now only thought of him as the "kid."

On the other hand, if things went wrong, it could mean hurting his family, and that notion didn't sit very well with him. Especially the thought of hurting his mother or causing her distress. Jacob's mother was a proud woman. Her place in society as well as the family name was very important to her. Jacob loved his mother, but he knew that along with being her son came the responsibility of keeping up appearances. What if things did not go as planned and Jacob was found out to be one of the Knowing? It would devastate the whole family, but it would be much worse for his mother. On the other hand, if things did go as planned, then Jacob would be a hero and in his own right. He would then help place the family name in even better standing. Well, there was a risk either way you go. A chance like this might only come along once in a lifetime. Jacob couldn't pass this chance up. There was no doubt in his mind.

With his chin set and head held high, Jacob held out his right hand. "Mr. Diggings, I would be honored to accept such an assignment. I do still have a lot of questions, but I am looking forward to bringing down the Knowing."

Newspaper article:

> Today a new law has gone into effect. The law will require all persons of the New World to adhere to an all-alert curfew. Curfew will be from sundown to sunrise. The curfew is expected to help stop crime that has gone to an all-time high during the last six months. The law was passed by the council of the State leaders and was met with only one opposing vote. Severe penalties will be applied to anyone not obeying this law. There will be no exceptions.

CHAPTER 2

Curfew sirens are blaring. Everyone who does not have authorization to be on the streets after dark was running to take refuge in whatever place there was for them to go.

Some would seek the safety of their own homes, others would be tucked away at their workplace, and yet others would have to find shelters to stay in. Everyone in their place and a place for everyone, or so it was to be.

There is however an unexpected exception that the powers that be had not counted on. There was a small, but strong and very well-organized, group of people known as the Knowing. This group is made up of people of the everyday variety. They are not easily detected by anyone as being special. It was this group of people who had decided that the way of the world was not the way in which they wanted to be going with their lives, neither by action nor by thought. The new laws that were being put into practice were, and continue to go, against what their faith in God and in country had taught them.

Under the new government, there was a worldwide peace agreement along with a New World religion. At first glance this religion was thought to be a dream come true, but as with all things that are not right, slowly and almost without notice, the differences started to appear. As the new laws were passed for the good of the government, it became apparent that there were problems for those of the Christian faith.

Due to economic reasons, there were people who had lost their jobs and money resulting in many becoming homeless. There were many homeless on the street, too many for the government to take care of. So it only seemed to be the right thing to do, to support the new law that allowed the government to take over the church buildings so that they could house some of the homeless. What else could good Christians do? Giving up the buildings was to be a good thing. At least we still had the ability to use other meeting places for our church services.

After a very short while, that all changed too. Then there came another proposal for a new law restricting religious groups from using the government buildings. It was passed, so the meetings had to be moved to private homes. The size of these meetings became a problem, and parking was a nightmare. Then there came yet another new law, restricting any group larger than ten to meet together at any one time. Soon many people got tired of the hassle and gave into the new idea of self-worship and not being tied to any one group. The government really (for the good of the whole) encouraged this and publicly thanked the religious leaders for supporting such actions.

Soon to follow was a law that drastically changed their lives. This law was to rid the nation of the radical religious cults, as it was proclaimed. Never in our wildest dreams did we suspect that the Christian religion was listed as one of these groups.

Oh, how we rejoiced when we heard the news that this law was passed. Oh, how we praised our God that no more cults would be allowed to mislead any of the flock down the path of destruction. But then it happened. They released the list of groups that would not be allowed to legally have any meetings. There it was in big letters. It was number three on the print out.

3. ANY RELIGIOUS GROUP CALLING THEMSELVES CHRISTIANS.

We all thought that there must have been a mistake. Someone was perhaps playing a joke on us. Hadn't anyone read the fine print on this law? How was it that we all, without even knowing it, had been added to the list and voted out our own faith?

As the days passed, we tried to get verification on this. No one seemed to have any answers. Word on the street was that several

Christian groups had been arrested and put in jail for having Bible studies, but even that was only a rumor.

The newspapers, radio, and TV stations had been taken over by the government and were undergoing changes that were to help keep the community securely under control. It seemed to be the right thing to do at the time. Questions were beginning to increase.

Who did we need to have security from? We had a worldwide peace treaty. With us not being at war with anyone, who was the enemy?

As we were soon to find out, the enemy was us. The enemy was the believer, the follower of God.

It was no longer accepted that God, Jesus Christ, and the Holy Spirit could meet our needs. Instead we were to look to the government for all our requests.

Even our religion was to be regulated by the government.

Yes, there was to be a god, but it was a god of the government, taught by the government. It was even directed by the government for the needs of the government.

At this point, we started to question the things that were happening, and almost overnight we became the enemy. We became the Knowing, the secret followers of the one true God.

*****

With the curfew sirens blaring, Sandy had only a few minutes to find refuge before she risked being arrested. In this day and age, that wasn't a very good thing to have happen to you.

Curfew had been established by the government to help the law control the crime taking over the streets after dark.

Although many were to blame for this crime, it was the people who had not received chips that were being singled out to be the culprits. Most had received the chip, but many had also declined the offer to become one of the future people of the New World order, to become someone in the New World of government technology. To date, no one could make you take the chip, unless of course you were found to be one of the "high risk" individuals needing to be followed or tracked. Then as soon as everyone let their guard down, it was no longer your choice but for the good of the whole, a chip would be implanted in everyone thought to be high risk.

Being arrested for anything or even getting a ticket could place you into this high-risk group. And being chipped would forever keep you from doing and being what you wanted unless the government approved of it. Not at all a situation Sandy was looking to find herself in right now.

Realizing that she has only a few minutes before curfew and that she needed to find a safe place to stay, Sandy started looking around. She was talking to herself.

"Don't panic. Use your head. There must be some place or someone you can go to."

Sandy spied a safe haven, or rabbit hole as it was called by the Knowing. Quickly, but trying to not draw any special attention to herself, Sandy walked toward a yellow house on the road she had been walking down. She did not take the walkway up to the house but cut across the yard along the right-hand side of the building. Along the house wall itself, large evergreen bushes were growing thick and tall. Sandy walked up to the evergreen looking as to admire its beauty and then kneeled down. She gave one last look around to see that she was not being watched. No one else was around. Sandy gave a strong tug on the plants, and down toward their roots, the branches slightly parted. There before her was the entrance to safety.

Sandy had to pull a few rocks and some dirt away, but now it would be easier to go through this entrance and down into the crawl space under the house.

These spaces were safe but often rather small and very dirty. They were especially dirty if it had been raining, and wouldn't you know it—this day was no exception; it had been steadily raining all day. After looking around again one last time to make sure no one was watching her, Sandy took her coat off and turned it inside out and put it back on. She did the same to her stockings and hat. This was so that when she got ready to leave and walk down the street in the morning, she wouldn't look, as though she had a mud bath. Although people were used to the chipless walking around in a different mode of dress, being one covered in mud would definitely call even more unwanted attention. With this routine of reversing the outer clothing, all she would have to do when she got ready to leave was to dust off and then turn them right side out, and off she would go. She took off the shoes she had on and placed them into one of the plastic bags she always tried to carry in her coat pocket. This was a practice of the Knowing. Keeping as many supplies on you as you could without drawing attention to yourself. Plastic bags and some dried foods had almost become a clothing accessory.

These past few months had taught Sandy one thing for sure, and that was to be as prepared as she could. Always carrying a few extra things with her just in case the unexpected happened has become her new way of life. Many of the things she liked to carry were things like extra socks and some food. Nothing big, pieces of bread or fruit, but the plastic bags had always been the winner. They could protect you in the rain and could be used to carry things picked up along the way. In this case, they could be used to help keep things dry and clean in a rabbit hole.

Quickly, Sandy plunged feetfirst into darkness. For a moment, while she waited for her eyes to adjust to the dark, she sat there thinking to herself what an awful mess she had gotten herself into these last few years.

Here she was in her early fifties. Not at all doing what she thought she would be doing at this age. By now, Sandy's youngest daughter should have been going off to college, not hiding out with her older sister. This year, Sandy had sent her youngest daughter, Vicky, off to Africa to be with her older daughter Janet. Janet had been working out of the country as a missionary. Sandy wasn't sure exactly what it was that Janet was doing now, but she knew she was happy and safe, and that was all that mattered. Thank God, Sandy's two girls were safe in another country.

How funny that sounded. Sandy remembered when she thought of our country as being the safest place on earth. Things sure have changed, and in such a short time too.

Sandy's eyes started to adjust to the dark, it was still dark, but she could see at least enough to move around some.

"Great!" Sandy said to herself. Not only did she get herself caught out after curfew, but the rabbit hole that she had picked wasn't one of the good ones. This was a safe place yes, but not at all a good one.

She was laughing to herself about having such a funny thought. A good rabbit hole versus a bad one. When all the government changes started happening, Sandy remembered thinking how crazy and paranoid everyone was getting. Back then, to even think of making a hiding place or rabbit holes seemed crazy.

She had been at the meeting where the idea of digging under homes around the area in order to make handy hiding places came up. "In case there was ever a need they would say?" Sandy went along with what she initially called a harebrained idea just to keep the peace.

Many a late night was spent making these places. Under the dark of night was the only way most of them could be set up. Some of the homes had people in them who were sensitive to what was going on and welcomed the chance to help. These houses were easy to set up. But for the neighborhoods where none of these sympathetic homes existed, the Knowing had to get a little more creative.

Great pains were taken to get at least one crawl space opened up and then set up on almost every street. Free landscaping was offered to elderly families in neighborhoods where a safe haven was needed. This offer was almost always accepted, and thus the opportunity to dig, cut, and chip into the crawl space was provided. Then follow-up planting helped to camouflage the entrance. This was a great plan, and it really worked well.

Never in Sandy's wildest dreams did she think that she, a by-the-book, go-with-the-flow kind of lady, would ever be found hiding out in a crawl space for any reason. Never in a million years would Sandy ever think she would be going against the government and for sure not because of her Christian faith. But here she was doing just that. Not only hiding out but also rating the places that she had to stay in. Yes, now let's see, a good rabbit hole, which is one where the people know that you are using their crawl space is considered a five-star. They often feed you, might let you shower, and had even been known to give you a bed for the night.

The next best rated four-stars was one where no one in the house knows that you are there, but they are clean and dry, and there are water pipes running under the house. Hot water pipes in the spaces are an advantage here in Washington State. Although it rarely gets cold enough for a person to freeze to death, it does get cold. All you had to do was to loosen up the insulation around the pipe, then when the people of the house ran the hot water, the water running through the pips often heated up the crawl space. If you curled up around the pipe just right, there could be enough heat to at least help you fall asleep. You might wake up cold, but at least part of the night could be spent in heavenly slumber.

But a one-star rabbit hole, like this one, had no help, no heat, nothing good about it except it was a place off the street. Because the rain that had been falling for the last few days had run into the space, most of the ground underneath her was wet.

Sandy began to move around. She started to reach out with her hands to see if she could find a dry spot to curl up on for the night. All at once, she realized that she was not alone.

Oh, God. Had it finally happened? Had they (the government officers) found out about the rabbit holes?

To date, none had been discovered, but then Sandy had always thought that it was simply a matter of time. In fact, Sandy often thought that it was a major miracle that they hadn't already figured out how it was that the Knowing could just disappear and not be found during shutdown or curfew, as the government called it.

Regardless, here it was, the moment of truth. What was to happen to her now that she was found?

Not wanting to delay the inevitable any longer. Sandy called out, "Okay, who are you?"

"Shhh! Are you crazy? The people are home, and in case you don't know, they are not of the Knowing!"

Sandy backed up as far as she could. She was trying hard to focus on the figure in front of her.

"My name is Sandy," she said, trying to hide the shaking of her voice. Often when Sandy got rattled, she would shake, and when she talked, her voice would give her away. No matter how brave the speech was, the quivering in her voice sold her out.

"Oh wow, it's you, Sandy? You scared me to death. The way you dropped yourself down in here, I thought the government had found me for sure."

"Victor, is that you?" Sandy called out, this time remembering to whisper. "Thank God, it is you. I thought that this place might have been compromised. What on earth are you doing here? Last time I heard, you were on your way out of the state."

"I know," replied Victor. "I almost made it too."

"Was the border closed?" Sandy questioned. "We haven't heard of any closures?"

"No, the border wasn't closed!" Victor scooted back closer to the wall away from the opening.

It was obvious to Sandy that Victor was irritated, but at who or what, she wasn't sure. Lately he had seemed upset all the time. If it wasn't the border being closed that kept him here, then all she could think of was that Victor had changed his mind about going. That wasn't such a far-fetched idea to Sandy as it might have been to anyone else.

Often Sandy had thought about leaving this place, maybe joining her daughters. She thought about going her own way and never looking back. Getting out and leaving these people of this country to their own fate. Aren't these the same people who are now being misled the same ones who voted this new system in? But then, the same old thought always came back to haunt her. That she too was one of those people who didn't see this New World coming; she never thought it could really happen. Not that initially she would have had the courage to do anything about it anyway. Just the same, Sandy felt that the call on her life from God was to stay and do what she could to help change things, or at the least to help keep things from continuing to change for the worse. Perhaps she could stop this world from going toward the way of no God other than the one the government had put into place.

After Sandy had made the decision to stay in Washington, there was a short period of time that she was angry. First she was angry at herself for doing what seemed to be so foolish, and second at God for calling her to do the job she felt so unqualified to do. Sandy suspected that this was how Victor might be feeling right now, and so she sympathized with him, but she also knew that in time, as it so often is with God, a real peace about your decision comes, and then nothing, or no one, can change your mind. (Thank God.)

Sandy decided not to pursue this area of conversation with Victor any further. She changed the tone of her voice to one more of friendship instead of one of interrogation. "Do you have any dry spots to share with a friend?"

"Yes, fortunately for us, these people placed some plastic by the drop space in the upper room."

This was not the best place to be in case the people should have reason to go under the house, but necessity won out. The thought of spending the night on the dry ground outweighed the danger in Sandy's mind.

Sandy moved toward Victor. Walking was a rare treat in rabbit holes. In most of these spaces, you would be lucky if you could sit up straight, much less walk.

Now that the light from the streetlight filtered in, Sandy could catch a glimpse of Victor's face. He had aged tremendously, but hadn't they all. His once dark thick hair had now given way to a thinner, graying look. It came to Sandy's mind that on most of us, this look would have been a tragedy, but on Victor, it seemed somehow fitting and dignified. Sandy, from early on in their acquaintance, had always thought of Victor as the stern hero type. Always standing up for what he thought was right no matter who was on the other side of the opinion. In fact, he usually did more than stand up for what he thought was right. He was even known to fight for it a time or two.

Sandy remembered the first time she saw him standing up for something he believed in. His fight was over, of all things, the right to have large public Church meetings. Sandy thought he was nuts for making such a big deal about limiting the number of believers that could be together at one time. What did it matter? God wouldn't care how many, as long as we came together.

Sandy couldn't remember for sure if she has ever told Victor that she wished she had been one to support him way back then. But, oh how she now wished she had. Back when there was a chance to really have done something about what was happening. And now, here they were, two very different people hiding under a house in the cold, damp Washington winter. Hoping to share a safe place, and if they were of a mind to, perhaps they could take this time to worship together. Silently, in the dark, alone, yet together with God. Perhaps they could even find praise for the safety they were now experiencing and for the gift of time with a friend. Not another word was spoken that night, just a peaceful feeling of sharing a common goal and a common belief. A belief, that a few years ago, was a way of life that people took for granted. Faith in God was now being tested as it had never been tested before, and by so many.

The next morning, the all clear siren woke both Sandy and Victor up with a start. No matter how long that thing was in effect, most of them would never get used to it. It was another typical Washington State day—wet, foggy, and raining again.

"Good morning." Victor was the first to speak. Not looking at Sandy but looking outside to see if anyone was around. And of course, as it usually was, the streets were full of people excited to be out and about. The people felt free, even if freedom were for only a few hours, until the next curfew.

Many a day was spent continuing to hide because the coast wasn't clear enough to get out of the rabbit hole. Keeping these places a secret was not just important but for some a matter of life and death.

"Good morning, Victor. I am glad to see that your mood is better with a good night's rest in you." Sandy gave a half smile as she winked at him.

"And I am glad to see you too," Victor said, trying unsuccessfully to mirror Sandy's facial expressions, only looking like he ate a sour lemon instead.

"Sandy, if I might be so bold as to ask. What are you doing on this side of town, and how on earth did you get caught out after curfew?" Victor had known Sandy for a long time, and he knew that she was not usually one to take any unnecessary risks. Being out after curfew though was definitely one of the craziest things Victor had ever seen her do. The Sandy that he knew was a very special lady. She had great faith in God. She truly believed that with prayer she could do anything no matter how hard. Her faith was childlike and almost always seemed too simple for Victor to understand. Sandy would often decide that they needed to do things that Victor knew would be impossible, but most of the time, he could be talked into whatever it was she wanted to do. Sandy had a great track record for getting things done. She gave very little thought as to the how, just that it needed to happen. Then with total faith, the things would work out. Although her childlike faith could make Victor crazy, he always noted that she had kept a level head about herself. This wasn't like her to be so reckless. There had to be more to this than he currently understood.

"Oh, Victor, you know me. I never did know when to come in out of the rain." Sandy was trying her hardest to make humor out of such a dumb and dangerous mistake.

"No, Sandy, I am serious, what are you doing here?"

Sandy, getting somewhat irritated at Victor's line of questioning, decided that this was one man that she could be straight with regarding her activities. He was someone she could trust in any situation.

"Well, if you must know, I had a meeting with an informant last night. Someone who is on the inside."

"Someone from the inside of what, Sandy? Do you mean on the inside of the government?"

"Well, yes, Victor, and he was to have had a lot of very important information to pass on to us, but he never showed up. And well, I waited a little too long to see if he was going to come."

"Sandy, I can't believe that you would go out by yourself to meet up with such a risky informant. What if it had been a trap? What would have happened to the people at your shelter then?"

"Victor, you can't expect me to send someone else out on a trip that I wouldn't go on myself. I wouldn't feel right about it."

"And I suppose that you would feel better if you had been caught? Who would have gotten you out? Who would have led the way then? Well, I can see now that it was a good thing that I came back when I did. I see that this extended period of resistance has weakened your mind."

Sandy was getting mad at the words and at Victor's tone of voice. Who was he to criticize her? She was doing the best that she could. She was about to let Victor have a piece of her mind when he looked her straight in the eye and said, "How is your prayer life?"

Like a ton of bricks, Sandy stopped dead in her tracks. Prayer life. How was her prayer life? Well, things had been so crazy, and yes, she and God had daily time together, but to be honest with herself, her prayer life and her alone time with God had somehow taken a back burner. If there ever were a time that she needed God's guidance, it was now, but somehow until this moment, she hadn't even noticed she had slipped in that area of her life.

How did she forget the importance of time alone with God? She needed to always be seeking his advice. How long had she been heading out on her own? How long had she been meeting her own agenda?

Thank God that Victor was a good friend and not just there for her in the easy things. Thank God that he had the courage to address the spiritual things of her life as well as the everyday things. Not too many people Sandy knew would be willing to risk a friendship by being be so bold as to call it as they saw it. She thanked God for making Victor who and what he was, a good Christian man who cared about her spiritual life as well as their friendship. And now without a doubt, Sandy knew that God had a plan for Victor's return to this area.

Perhaps it is the help that she knew she needed, and again, perhaps it was a much greater happening than any of them could understand. For whatever reason, at this moment in time, Sandy was grateful for God's call on Victor and for his coming back.

"Sandy, do you have any idea what information the informant was supposed to have for you?"

"Well, Victor, it was not clear, but it was something about a new government project. Something called Follow the Leader or something like that, but he never showed. So, I guess that either he changed his mind or it was just gossip."

Their conversation came to a halt. Victor motioned to Sandy for her to follow him. As soon as she realized what he was doing, they both scrambled out of the hiding place and into the daylight, taking all their things with them. They threw their bags containing their shoes onto the ground, turned their outer clothing to its right side, placed their shoes on, and started to walk out to the main street.

They both walked away together going down the street as though they were continuing a morning stroll.

The only difference here was that they were both covered in dust. Taking a good look at each other, they both broke out in laughter at the sight. Each helped the other to brush off as much dust as possible. How very strange it was to be walking on the same street that only last night brought such horror to them both, causing them to scurry for shelter. And yet here they were walking brave as can be, right out in the daylight, for the whole world to see. What a difference the daylight can make.

Victor and Sandy chatted as they walked along the road. So much had happened since she had last seen Victor. "You know that they have closed several more shelters? We are getting so crowded, and the food supply is dwindling. We can hardly keep the doors open." Sandy hated to complain, but Victor was someone she could talk to that would not take the things she said personal. She needed to bounce things off someone, and Victor was truthfully one of the safest people she could confide in. They had known each other for years and were truly very good friends.

CHAPTER 3

Only a few days had passed since Jacobs meeting with Mr. Diggings, and yet Jacob's life had already changed so much that any history of his existence was gone. It was as if he had never been born. Once the chip had been removed, there could no longer be an apartment, no checking account, and no educational records, not even a car. If you did not have a chip, you were not allowed to drive because of the fact you couldn't be tracked, and even if you did somehow have a car, the limited gas supply always went to the chipped.

What a strange feeling it was to be without a chip. For as long as he could remember, his chip had been a part of his life. His family was one of the very first of the families in the country to receive their chips. It was a great way for his father to show the government how supportive he was of them and the New World order that was coming. Jacob did not understand what all that meant back then, but it was what his older brother had told him his father had said. No matter what the reason, the whole Singleton family had their chips and were very proud of that fact.

Jacob could remember how safe he felt after receiving his chip. No one would ever be able to take him anywhere without someone being able to track him. He even thought about running away once but then realized that it would never work. Just one scan of the satellite, and they could know where he was within three feet or so. Not much use in running away. The only attention he would get from running away was a bad spot on the family name. And that would never do.

But now this was different. This time he could run away, and no one could find him. That thought scared Jacob, but deep down he couldn't help but be a little excited about the thought of this new kind of freedom. It was not like anything he had experienced before. He was feeling fear and excitement both at the same time. What an odd combination to feel together, and yet if he were to describe his feelings right now, it would have to be...fear and excitement.

During the time before his chip had been removed, Jacob underwent major training in the areas of religious fanatics. He was briefed on all of the information the government had on the Knowing. At the end of the training, the only thing Jacob knew for sure was that there was very little information on them.

During Jacob's training, he could not help but be amazed at this new enemy he was learning about. How was it that they would choose such an awful way to live their lives? How could they all believe in someone that they couldn't even see?

Although Bibles had been outlawed for over a year (having been labeled propaganda material), Jacob was able to get his hands on one. How very strange it was for him to read the history of his very own enemy. What was the fascination about this book anyway? Several groups had been jailed for refusing to give up their copies. After all, the government had offered to replace the old ones with a new and updated one. All he could come up with was that they wanted to be known for something special, like not giving up their Bibles.

Jacob could remember the headlines in the newspapers. It had commented that the group of crazies had refused to give up their Bibles "in the name of God." Not really knowing or caring what it was all about, he did not pay much attention, until now. It took him some time and a lot of persuading to get a Bible out of the "special interest" supply room. But he got one. Here it was, one of the old books, a Bible. For the life of him, Jacob could not figure out what all the fuss was about.

After spending many hours thumbing through this Bible, Jacob did not feel any closer to understanding these people than he had before.

Whoever had owned this particular Bible was named Gary. This Gary had taken a lot of effort and time to mark, underline, and date several places on the pages.

In fact, it seemed somewhat strange to Jacob that in reading this Bible, he seemed to be learning more about the man who owned it than the people in it.

Jacob then went on to read several articles on the Knowing group. With having learned some of the history of this group, he then went on to learn about the street life and rules for the chipless. This was going to be a totally new lifestyle for Jacob.

The way he was expected to dress was less than appealing to Jacob. Buying clothing these days was not only expensive, but if you didn't have a chip, new clothing was out of the question. There were several secondhand stores still open for the chipless, but there were slim pickings most of the time.

The mode of travel was usually on foot. Riding a bus cost. But most of all, it could be dangerous. Many reports had been filed about chipless being attacked while using the bus. The prejudice against the chipless was almost too overwhelming for Jacob to read about. He had been given a computer file that contained entry after entry of infractions done against chipless street people of all ages, colors, and status. Why this was a prejudice that was an overall blanket against the chipless. As far as Jacob could see, nothing had been done about stopping it either.

Jacob did not spend too much time thinking about why the government did not have any interest in doing something about helping the chipless. After this assignment was over, Jacob would make it a point to ask his family if they knew anything about it, but for now, the question was put at the back of his mind. The cases that were listed in this file were not assigned to anyone. How strange, Jacob thought, and how uncomfortable this made him. But he had too much to do to get caught up in this matter now. So the decision to put it out of his mind was a good one. This would be something he could bring up after he had closed this case.

Living arrangements were almost more horrible than the clothing problem. There were too few shelters to accommodate all of the chipless people in this area. But again, no effort was being made to find out where these people went during curfew. The government did not care. Perhaps this was a government method to persuade the people to conform to the new ways. By making their daily lives as miserable as possible, they might be persuaded to get on with real life and get their chip. This was yet another thought to put on the back burner.

Then he came to the information about the food supplies. There were none. Jacob thought that this part must be a mistake. But nowhere in all of his reading material about these chipless street people were there provisions for feeding them. Convinced that this must be an error, he decided that once he found out the truth, he would come back and update this area of the training.

Then he went on to learn about the public washing facilities. The money that had gone into setting up the shelters was very limited. There weren't enough funds to put showering and laundry facility in each shelter, so the government made it mandatory that the fire stations in each of the areas were to be open for four hours a day. Here people could shower and do laundry regularly. Laundry had to be done by hand, but ample water was available here, both hot and cold.

Jacob was relieved to read about this. Being clean was of major importance to him, and this would make doing his job easier, physically anyway.

The way the chipless made their living was hard to imagine for Jacob. They all had a number that gave them a place in the workforce. It was on a card though and not a chip. These cardholders could work for money, but the government restricted the jobs in which they could work. For security reasons, they would be allowed to hold all maintenance jobs in the chipless areas and any of the dangerous or unwanted jobs as well. There were no rules to speak of about how these people needed to be treated or how much they were paid. The working conditions were also left up to the employer. This did not sound like a good arrangement to Jacob at all. What a risk these people took to even have a job, but then at least they were still able to work.

Jacob had skimmed over the rest of the paperwork and had run out of time, so he did his best to learn as much as he could and then went on his way. His list of things to do was getting shorter and shorter.

Before getting his chip removed, Jacob had gone to visit his family. The Singleton family always set aside one day a week, Thursdays, for the whole family to be together for a dinner. From time to time, someone would have to miss this event, but as a rule, everyone would try to be present. Jacob hoped that would be the case that evening. He had really wanted to see everyone that night to tell them that he would be leaving for a special assignment. Mr. Diggings had been very direct about not telling anyone about his mission, not his friends or even his family. This was hard since telling the truth in his family was held to be of great importance. Surprisingly, it was not as hard as he thought it was going to be since it was really telling half-truths and not complete lies.

Jacob had arrived that last Thursday night, and his hopes had been answered. All of his family was there, even Mark, his favorite brother. If anyone was to miss a family dinner, it was usually Mark. Although Jacob wanted to see him most, it was from Mark that it was the hardest to keep the truth. Mark was still in college and so was removed from government work unlike the rest of his siblings. Jacob always found it good to talk with Mark about things going on in his job. Another point of view.

Jacob and Mark shared almost everything together. Over the years, they had shared their room, friends, their thoughts, and even their deepest secrets.

Jacob had thought a long time about telling Mark, trying hard to decide what he should do. It would feel really good to confide in Mark, to have someone he knew he could trust know about what was going on, someone on his side. But on second thought, Jacob wondered about this Mr. Diggings; he was supposed to be on Jacobs's side, but something did not feel right, and so he was still not sure. If things went wrong with this mission, it could cause trouble for Mark if people found out he had known about it. He could get blamed for information getting out. After mulling it over in his mind, Jacob decided it was better to not tell Mark the real story of his mission but to tell him along with the others that he would be going away for some special training.

As Jacob had arrived at his parents' home, he could see that he was not the first to arrive. His two older brothers' cars were there. Ben is the oldest and Marcus the next in the family line. Jacob searched for the car of his one sister, Sally; she was born in the middle of the two sets of boys. Her car was out on the street. All three of the older siblings worked for the government department in some way or another.

Jacob parked his car and was getting out when Mark pulled up into the drive. To Jacob's surprise, Mark was on a motorbike and not in his car. Jacob wanted to ask Mark where his car was. But from the look on Mark's face, Jacob could tell that he was the first to know about Mark's riding a motorbike instead of driving a car. All Jacob said was, "Really?" Jacob and Mark both knew that their mom and dad were not going to be happy about this new arrangement. Jacob only hoped Mark's explanation was going to be a good one. Mark's face had always given away how he was feeling about things, and that night had been no different. As hot tempered and quick to judge as Jacob was, Mark was the opposite. Mark was supersensitive, always the last to want to make waves, and yet lately somehow, he seemed to be the first to do so. Jacob usually had been the one to hold that position; being the youngest in the family, it just seemed natural somehow. Having four older siblings always watching you made it easy to always be under some judgment or other about what he was doing. But lately Mark had taken that focus most of the time, and quite frankly, Jacob was glad.

Over the years, Mark had been known to give his things away. To whom Jacob was not ever sure, but it always seemed to cause friction between their parents and Mark.

Jacob knew that his parents loved Mark just as much as they did all of the others, but they had a hard time right now understanding how Mark thought and looked at things. Mark was part of the family, but at the same time, it seemed he thought nothing like they did about anything.

One day years earlier, Jacob had overheard his mom and dad talking. His dad was saying that he thought Mark was more like his grandmother. "The religious one," he had called her. Jacob thought about it, but for the life of him, he couldn't see anything wrong with Mark or his grandmother for that matter. So he decided that his dad must have been in a bad mood. After all, Jacob's dad had always loved their grandmother even if she was "religious," as he had put it.

As Jacob thought back to his conversation with Mark about the bike, his brother had said that he had sold his car and bought a bike in order to save money on gas. Mark also said that he had decided that it would be best for him. He would get better gas mileage and much better insurance costs as well.

Jacob had decided to go to bat for Mark and suggested he mention about how much cheaper the maintenance would also be. Jacob had smiled as he was trying to give Mark as much ammunition as he could to help out with the battle that was to come when his parents saw the bike.

Jacob wasn't sure of what Mark's real reasons were for getting rid of his car, but he respected Mark and knew that since he made the choice, there had to have been a real good reason.

Jacob also thought it odd that Mark had not come clean with him about the whole truth, but perhaps this was part of grown-up games. For a man, some things might need to be kept private. Thinking that was the case had helped Jacob keep his story about his mission to himself. Anyway, Jacob knew that it was only a matter of time until Mark would tell him what was really going on with his car.

As Jacob and Mark entered the house, it was a wonderful feeling for them both. No matter what else went on in their lives, it was always nice to go home for a visit.

Jacob's oldest brother, Ben, was telling a story about something funny that had happened at work. Mom and Dad and the other siblings were all listening and having great fun as his story was unfolding. When their dad had seen the two boys walking in, he gave a motion with his hand for them to come in and join them all. Each in turn went in and kissed their mother and then their sister on the cheek. Jacob remembered thinking about how he was going to miss

Thursday nights for the next six months. But then he found great assurance in the fact that as soon as his mission was over, he would go home, and it would be the same.

If things went as planned, it would be him telling the exciting story of his job. That would feel really good. He would not be just the little brother but then a fellow officer.

The evening went well. They all had a turn at giving a story or two, and then it was Jacob's turn to tell of his future adventure. Jacob had shared how he was to go off for special training.

It was Sally, Jacob's sister, who pointed out that she had not heard of any special programs, but it was also Sally who remembered that she had been away for some special training herself and that perhaps the paperwork had gone through while she was out of her office. She was in intelligence, and those orders would have had to go through her office. Jacob was surprised that Mr. Diggings had not picked up on the fact that Sally's working in that department could have been a problem. Perhaps Mr. Diggings was not as good at this kind of thing as he was letting on. But at the end of the story, there had been a quick save by Sally, and so Jacob's story was evaluated and accepted, then they went on talking about the next family event.

The whole evening went easier than Jacob had thought. Somehow, he thought that lying to his family should have not been so easy. Maybe he would be good at this undercover stuff after all.

Then came what Jacob knew Mark was dreading. The evening was over, and it was time for everyone to leave. As tradition had it, when they all decide that it's time to leave and everyone walked outside together, down the walkway to the driveway, there they would say their goodbyes, but not that night.

As the family walked to the cars, it sounded like they were all talking at once. One by one, the voices stopped speaking as they each in turn saw the bike. With quick evaluation of the cars, it quickly became apparent as to whose car was missing and to whom the bike belonged.

All eyes were on Mark. It was Mom who was the first to speak. All she had said was, "This had better be good, young man." She had kept her voice very level. She was really good at keeping her emotions intact. Jacob decided that if he had not known any better, he would have thought his mother was so okay with this new bike thing that she might have even been the one to suggest it.

Mark didn't say a word but instead looked to Jacob for help. It was not just because Jacob was the youngest and that he could usually get by with a little more than the others but more that Jacob had a way with words, and over the years, he would better express how Mark was feeling to the others than Mark could himself. Jacob was used to this, but he never thought that Mark would expect him to explain something that he did not know anything about.

But that was his cue. The first thing that came to Jacob's mind was that Mark was doing an experiment for one of his classes at the college. Their dad had asked Mark if that was right. Jacob looked at Mark and thought for a moment that he might not be breathing. Mark didn't move, he didn't even blink.

Jacob had shoved Mark by the arm so as to get his attention. He needed Mark to confirm the excuse Jacob had made up.

Jacob could see that Mark had not planned on lying to get out of this situation; it wasn't in his nature. But there it was, a lie. It was well on its way, and there was not a thing he could do about it. Mark only nodded his head in agreement. Jacob could not believe he had lied, but all he knew was that he did not want this last night together to be one of fighting and of being upset.

Jacob was not sure about what had happened exactly or as to why no one questioned the story, but they all gave a laugh. Someone said something about how only Mark would do such a crazy thing, and then they said goodbye and headed out for the evening.

Mark motioned with his eyes for Jacob to stop and have a talk with him. Jacob knew exactly what Mark was going to say even before he said it. Mark was not happy about Jacob's explanation, but then, what had he expected? Mark had not done any better; he had just stood there. Jacob did not want to get into it with Mark, not that night anyway, so he used the curfew as an excuse for not taking the time to talk about it. Hopefully Mark would get over it. After all, he would have six months.

After arriving back at the station, Jacob had gone to get his new wardrobe, if you could call it that. His outfit consisted of oversized pants and shirt, one black belt, three pairs of sox, undershorts, and an undershirt. Jacob got to choose his own shoes, but the choices were very limited. Finally, after a time, he decided on a pair that he considered the least offensive of the lot. It made him sick to think that people were choosing to live this way. In the past, Jacob had thrown out clothing that looked better than this.

The last of his outfit that had been selected for him, was a backpack and a coat that did not have very much stitching left to hold it together. But it would keep him warm. Or so he thought.

In the backpack were some papers that gave him evidence of being who he said he was. He found a pencil and the two notebooks that were for him to keep the records that would help him take down the Knowing.

Now here it was, Jacob's last meeting with Mr. Diggings. It was scheduled to take place in about fifteen minutes. This would be his last chance for six months to have any contact or help from the department.

Jacob took this time to review what his orders were for his assignment. In three months, Jacob was to make a drop in an old bus locker over on Front Street, in locker #363, to be specific. He had been given the two paper notebooks, one for each set of three months. In this book, he would place names, dates and locations of those of the Knowing, those who would later be picked up and arrested for being enemies of the government.

Once they were arrested, they would be questioned then chipped, and most would be released into a new relocation program that had been set up. They would be brought back into society as best could be managed. At that point, the world would be a safer place because these people could now be tracked. "Whoa," Jacob said to himself. Getting a bit ahead of ourselves, aren't we? First you have to find these people before you can save the world from them. He gave a smile at himself, full dimples and all.

Jacob had waited for a long while. Finally, there he was, Mr. Diggings himself, walking right out in the open street. He was coming straight toward Jacob. How strange this seemed to have an open meeting like this. Up until this point, all of their meetings had been very private and very secretive. Jacob stood and waited for Mr. Diggings to come over to where he was standing.

As Mr. Diggings got within arm's length, Jacob extended his hand out expecting a handshake from the headman himself.

But what he got instead was a government officer baton hitting against his arm causing a sharp pain to radiate through what felt like his whole right side. "Hey, what in the world do you think you are doing?" Jacob was yelling.

Two officers took him one by each arm and held him. The third scanned him for a chip. Of course, none was detected.

The officer was speaking to Mr. Diggings. "I am sorry, sir, it is just another one of those radicals." Mr. Diggings gave a look of disgust at Jacob. Throwing his head back in the air, Mr. Diggings walked over to the other side of the walkway.

Jacob looked close at this big man and could not help but feel betrayed. Why didn't he tell the officers that they were going to have a planned meeting? Why didn't he do something about them being too rough to a regular guy? Just because he didn't have a chip didn't make him a bad guy. All he wanted to do was to shake his hand. What was this action all about?

All at once, Jacob got it; this was a test of some sort. Perhaps it was a show so that the Knowing group might see him being mistreated by government officials, and they would want to take him into the fold. Oh, brilliant, simply brilliant. Or was it?

After some discussion by the officers, it was decided that Jacob was to be let go. So with a warning from one of the officers, Jacob was sent on his way. How strange it seemed to Jacob that these total strangers were so angry with him. Of course, they did not know of his assignment, but there was no reason for all the anger he felt from them.

Just in case having the Knowing see him being treated like this was the plan, Jacob took this opportunity and headed out on his own. This was his first time out on his own—no chip, no friends, and no backup. What was to come next?

Jacob walked down the street for about an hour, not sure what or how he was going to get in touch with the Knowing.

He stopped in front of a department store and caught a reflection of himself in the window. Oh man, no wonder the officers had taken such offence to him. There he was—dressed like a street person with baggy, old clothing that was more than slightly used. Unfortunately, not as warm as he had thought they were going to be either. His hair had done its old trick and had gone to full ringlets all over his head. He was not even sure if his own mother would recognize him.

That was a thought. If things did not go as planned, he could always go find his family.

But they lived in a high security part of town. No one without a chip was even allowed on the streets there.

This was something he most likely should have thought of beforehand, but now it was too late to think about anything except figuring out what he should do next.

As those thoughts were racing around in his head, Jacob heard a voice talking. He guessed to him.

A man had come along behind him. This man was facing so that his back was to Jacob. "So, you must be new around here?"

Jacob could hardly make out all the words, but he got enough of them to know that his answer was to be "Yes."

The man spoke a little louder this time. "So, what's your name?"

"Jake!"

"So where are you from?"

"Oregon State." As he spoke, Jacob started to turn around, but the man backed up and pressed Jacob to the window. Not real hard as to be mean but enough so that he could not turn around without making a scene.

"So, why?" He went straight to the point.

"Why what?" Jacob had a tone or attitude in his voice.

"Why are you here?"

"Oh, I kind of got into some trouble and had to leave or be chipped." Jacob had toned his attitude down some, realizing that he might need to get to know this man.

"So, what kind of trouble did you get into? You aren't some kind of a bad guy, are you, kid?"

"No, but what is it to you anyway? Are you some kind of sidewalk monitor or something?" Jacobs's attitude was back. Jacob was getting irritated by this kind of questioning, and he didn't like being referred to as a "kid."

On second thought, this was not someone he wanted to get to know. He was thinking not to get into a verbal fight with this crazy man. So Jacob decided that he should just slip away, go to the side, turn, then walk away and not even look back.

As he was going to make his first move to the side, he heard some noise coming from a group of people down the street.

The voice behind him started to talk in a slow but very steady and monotone manner. One that even Jacob took seriously.

"Whatever you do, don't look at them. They are the government officers, and they do not like you if you are not chipped. I do not know how it was in Oregon, but the officers here are not to be messed with. So now, kid, I want you to walk away. Do you hear me? No matter what happens, just keep walking the other way."

The first thing that came to Jacob's mind was, how did this stranger know that he didn't have a chip? The second thought that Jacob had was that he had never walked away from a fight in his life, and chipped or not, he was not about to start this new life by doing any different. So he stood watching in the reflection as the officers approached. Jacob could see that they were looking for a fight. If he had not seen it for himself, he would not have believed the way that they were acting. And to top it all off, if he were not mistaken, he might even know some of the officers personally. Geez, this could get sticky.

Jacob and the stranger were standing there out in the open. They were doing nothing wrong, and now they were to be the participants in an officer-involved showdown.

As the officers were about to reach the two of them, three men seeming to come out of nowhere had walked between Jacob and the stranger. Two of them sandwiched Jacob between them on either side, and the third walked directly behind him. Where they moved,

Jacob moved. Not that he had any choice in the matter. The way they had surrounded him, there was not anything else he could do but move with the group around him.

It took a moment for Jacob to realize that the stranger had been left to the officers. He began to object and tried to turn back to help him, but it was of no use. The three men were determined to get Jacob out of the area. And out of the area he did go. Yelling at them this time, thinking that they must not have realized what was happening between the officers and the stranger. "Hey, you guys! You don't know what it is that you are doing? You left that guy all by himself!" Jacob was told to keep quiet, or he would cause trouble for them all.

They led Jacob down the street and around the corner to a dead end. Jacob was taken to the very end where he was met with a final shove that found him face-first against a solid wooden wall. What was it with these people, always being at his back? At this rate, he would not be able to recognize even one of them. Jacob realized that he was no longer being guided, so he stopped and turned around so as to finally meet at least these three men face-to-face. But when he turned around, they were gone. Just like that. It was as though they had vanished. Not before his eyes but before he could see them leave.

What was this craziness? Jacob, for the life of him, did not even begin to think that he knew where they had gone.

Oh no, he remembered the stranger. What about the stranger? With that thought, Jacob turned and ran back to the street that he had originally been on.

There was no stranger. He was not with the officers.

He was not anywhere. As Jacob looked over to where the officers were now standing, it was obvious to Jacob that they had received a call and were off to do their Job. But what had happened to the stranger?

Jacob stayed there on the street for a short time and then realized that curfew would be coming soon. The only thing for him to do was to get off the street, and the only place for him to go was a shelter. Going to a shelter was bad enough, but this was worse than that, the shelter he needed to go to was one for people who did not have chips, a chipless shelter.

Thinking back, he could not remember if he had ever really seen a chipless shelter, much less been in one, not even as an officer on the job. Well, there was no time like the present.

Jacob knew from his briefing that there was a shelter over on Front Street. He also knew that he had to get there before the last siren had sounded.

It was the rules of the street that at the last sirens call, the doors would be locked, and no one would be allowed to enter until the all clear sounded in the morning. This seemed like a harsh thing to Jacob at first, but now he was realizing that this was one of the only ways to protect the people in the shelter. Perhaps not from the chipless so much as maybe from the radical chippies that he had encountered earlier who had taken offence for whatever strange reason.

So off he went to find a new home for the night. As Jacob was walking to the shelter, the fifteen-minute warning siren went off. Jacob's heart was beginning to beat hard, but he wasn't sure if it was from his walking so fast or from the anticipation of what was ahead.

Odd how different the sirens sounded to Jacob tonight. Somehow the old "inconvenience" had become a new sort of fear.

Jacob arrived at the shelter door as the final siren began its howl. Jacob slipped in through the door as it was being closed. The first thing that he laid eyes on was a young man with keys in his hands. Following Jacob's entrance, the door was closed tight and then locked.

As Jacob walked into the room, he was amazed to see how many people had been fit into this small building. There were people everywhere. Most of them were dressed very much like he was. All of them seemed to be looking at him, but then he realized that could not be true, there were just too many people for everyone to know everyone else. He was being paranoid.

There was a long counter over to his right. On the counter were very large soup kettles and what looked from where he was standing to be a pitcher of water.

A pile of clean dishes was stacked up on a table at the end of this counter.

Jacob saw people in a line patiently waiting their turn at helping themselves to the simple dinner that had been made available. What he was seeing was nothing at all like what he had read or heard about with regards to these people and places. He had been told that they were loud and unruly. They were supposed to be frantic and completely out of their minds and acting crazy. Not so. They were all so much like regular people he knew. In fact if he had not known that they did not have a chip, he would have not been able to tell. Other than their clothing and the food they ate, they looked like regular people.

Jacob looked again at the dinner and was still shocked at how simple it was, there was not even any bread. Perhaps it just had not been put out yet.

Jacob continued to observe the room some more. Over to the left side and toward the back wall was a door marked Bathroom. About three feet or so from that door was another marked Kitchen. So this was a shelter—one main room, a kitchen, and a bathroom. Not much to speak of, but it was safe and warm. No, on second thought, it could have been warmer than outside, but it was not warm. Jake looked over to see what the source of heat was in this place. As he looked around, he realized that there was none. There was only a spot marked by the floor and an old pipe still hanging from the ceiling where a stove had once been. Someone had sealed it off so the outside air did not come in, but the stove was completely missing. Jacob had come to the conclusion that they most likely removed it to make room for more people. So the only real heat in this building was the overflow from the cooking in the kitchen. Body heat could also account for some of the warmth; there were so many people in here, Jacob could hardly believe it.

Jacob felt so tired that he could not stand the thought of waiting in line with these people for even the most wonderful of meals, much less for this stuff. Jacob decided he would wait and eat in the morning.

He continued to look around the room; Jacob half expected someone to say something to him, but to his surprise, no one acted as if they even cared that he was there. It seemed as though a stranger showing up was an everyday occurrence, but then perhaps it was.

As Jacob looked toward the back wall, he found a corner off to the very left of the room. Jacob took himself a seat with his back to the wall and tried to wrap his new, old coat around his legs. Man, he could not remember the last time he was this tired, this hungry, or if ever this cold.

How strange it was that his life had made such a change with the simple removal of his chip. He watched as the people got their dinners, ate, and returned the dishes to the kitchen. They gathered together in groups, some looked like families, and bedded down for the night. Some had blankets they put down to lie on. The blanket served as a sort of divider for their sleeping area.

It was hard to believe that anyone would give up his or her life in order to be a part of the Knowing. Mr. Diggings might have been right. Although these people appeared normal, they must be real crazies, total nutcases to choose to live like this.

Some of the last thoughts to go through his head before sleep took over were the thoughts of the stranger and of the three men he had seen on the street earlier that day. What had become of them? And what was this new name Jacob had taken? That was not planned. "Jake," he had told the stranger. Since when had he decided to become Jake?

He had very few answers; he had a lot of questions. Tomorrow was going to be a busy day for gathering information. Then without another ounce of energy left in him, he fell asleep.

CHAPTER 4

It was very unusual for Sandy to be late. But then so far this week, everything had been unusual, and the hardest part of this story was to think it was only Wednesday.

Already this week, Sandy had been caught out after curfew. She had lost a whole night's work by being caught in a rabbit hole. Had run into someone that she thought was gone out of the area long ago (Victor). Which if she really thought about it was one bright spot in her week so far. But now she was having a morning to beat all mornings. Everything seemed to be going wrong.

She needed to reset her thinking. She needed to forget about all that had happened and think about how it was behind her now. She needed not to dwell on the past but to focus on the days to come. So much energy had been wasted on worrying and fretting about the past. It was a new goal of hers not to let herself fall into the trap of what-ifs. Instead, she would put her energies into today and the tomorrows.

A smile came to Sandy's face, as she was feeling much better now.

Sandy was almost to the shelter where she worked. She knew that if she worked really fast, then she would be able to make up some of the lost time from the morning.

Sandy rarely stayed at this shelter, but she had remained one of the main organizers of this one here on Front Street. It was one of the few chipless shelters left, so making sure that it stayed open was a real important job.

A lot of laws had been passed trying to shut down all of the chipless shelters. It was a miracle and also a lot of work to keep it from happening to this one as well. It was up to the people who ran the shelters to make sure that every effort was made to never be in violation of any of the rules. One of the ways this was accomplished was for everybody to be an enforcer of the rules. No one person was the watcher of the shelter, but each and every one was to be accountable for not just themselves but each other as well. This was the plan, and so far, this plan seemed to be working great.

As Sandy rounded the corner of the street, she saw the shelter, and she was met with an awful surprise. There right outside the door was an officer. Sandy did not see the other one, but she knew that he must already be inside. The officers almost always travel in at least a party of two.

Her heart was beating so fast that she was sure the officer would hear her coming. Not being sure of who was in charge of the shelter this morning, Sandy was anxious about even approaching. But approach she must; after all, this was just another part of her job.

With a deep breath, Sandy walked right up to the officer outside and asked if there was anything she could do for him.

The officer took at least two steps backward, acting as if he might catch something from her. Sandy did not mind this kind of reaction, seeing how she did not want much to do with him either. She figured that the less time she spent with these officers, the better. Too much time spent with the officials, the more chance of being found to be in violation of something. She needed to get on with this.

The officer did not answer Sandy but motioned at the doorway for her to see the officer inside. Then he continued to inspect the outside of the building. He was taking way more time than he needed to in order to see if the lids were on trash cans and such. For sure, it was a sign that he wanted to spend as little time inside as he could.

Without further hesitation, Sandy went to the shelter door, opened it, and walked inside to meet whatever it was she was to face.

When she entered the room, the officer inside had his back to her. He was startled for a moment by her entrance but quickly regained his composure. *Funny,* thought Sandy, *they almost seem as afraid of us as we are of them. And to think that they are the ones who hold all of the cards.* She wondered what it was exactly about the chipless that made them so afraid of them.

"What can I do for you, officer?" As Sandy spoke, she started to unload the things she had in her arms onto the counter.

Today was her day to do the cooking or at least to get it started. Vegetable soup was to be the menu. Vegetables were a lot easier to come by than anything else. They grew them themselves in the summer and put them up for this time of year. It was far better than depending on others to supply all their needs.

As she waited for the officer to answer and wanting to look as confident as she could, she took the bag of frozen peas, opened them, and started to place them into a bowl.

The officer spoke to her. "This is a State inspection," he said as he raised his eyes to meet hers.

At first glance, she thought she might have known him. Quickly she glanced at the name tag that hung from the pocket of his shirt. It had *Officer Hansen* stamped on it. But no, she could not recall knowing a Hansen. There were so many of the officers, and they all looked so much alike in their uniforms. Yes, that must be it.

As she continued to look at him, it was as if he were trying to tell her something without words. He would catch her eyes and then raise his eyebrows and shake his head back just ever so slight. If she hadn't been looking straight at him, she would not have even noticed.

"Yes, State inspection. I understand. What would you like to see?" As Sandy was answering, she stepped a little to the right of the officer, and then she could see past him over in the corner.

There in the corner was a young man sound asleep. *God help us!* was all she could think of. This one broken rule could shut the shelter down for good. No questions asked. And definitely no second chances.

She had never seen this man before, but she could tell he was young, and judging from the way he was dressed, he was probably new to this area. His clothing was not nearly warm enough for these streets. No cap, no gloves, and for sure, he must not have known the rules.

No one was permitted in the shelter after the all clear siren sounded in the morning, unless of course they were working. And it was clear to anyone who could see him that this young man was not working.

Fear swept over Sandy along with a mixture of anger and disappointment. Where were the people who were supposed to be taking care of the shelter today? She even had disappointment with herself for being late. But couldn't they have carried the ball just this once? Well, there wasn't time for blame right now, for herself or for anyone else. What was she going to do? The life of this shelter depended on how this came out right now. What should she do? What could she do? All she could think to do was to pray. And pray she did. She said a prayer that was sweet and to the point. "GOD, HELP!"

What happened next, even Sandy wasn't too sure of. The officer from outside came into the shelter with a loud banging of the door. Officer Hansen, standing across from Sandy, reached out and knocked the bowl of peas from her hand, spreading them across the room; they slammed to the floor short of hitting the young man who was still asleep in the corner.

But now he wasn't sleeping. Now he had jumped to his feet with a total look of surprise. You could even go so far as to say he was also ready to fight.

Oh, great, Sandy thought. First, he was a sleeper, now he was a fighter. Who was this kid? Was he determined to ruin everything here at the shelter?

The officer from outside was not too sure of what he was seeing, and neither was Sandy for that matter.

With only a short pause, Sandy then called out to the young man, "Please do be more careful, will you? This is tonight's dinner you are throwing around."

Sandy walked around the counter and began to pick up the peas.

As she got near the young man, she bent down and said in the softest voice she could conjure up, "Help me pick up, will you?"

As he knelt down and started to help pick up peas, their heads were close together. Sandy said, "Quick, tell me your name?"

"Jake," he replied as softly as she had spoken to him.

"Where are you from?"

"Oregon," he answered, not daring to look up at her for fear the officers would hear them.

The officer from outside walked over to Officer Hansen and gave him a questioning look. "What in the world is going on here?"

"I am almost done checking things out. It all looks good so far as I can see." As he said that statement, he gave a glance over to Sandy and the young man. "They are the workers getting the evening meal started. That woman over there, her name is Sandy. She is in charge."

Sandy stopped picking up the peas when she heard that statement. How on earth did this man know that she was in charge, and how did he know her name? He had not asked, and she had not told him.

Sandy stepped forward and placed her right hand out in order to shake the outside officer's hand. But all he did was give her a disgusted look and turned his back to her. He walked over to the young man and kicked a pea over toward him.

"And you. Who are you?" The outside officer was rudely staring at the young man, trying hard to get him to be afraid. But instead of inciting fear, he began to stir up an attitude of defiance in Jacob. Not an attitude that would fare well in this situation.

Sandy chimed in from back by the counter, "Oh, this is Jake. He is a helper for me today."

"I have not seen you before." From the way the outside officer was questioning, they could tell that he had something on his mind, and not something good either.

Sandy answered again, "He is here from Oregon. He just got here. And look at us, we have already put him to work."

Sandy, acting as though she and Jake were alone, began to talk directly to him. "You know, Jake, we really should go and get you registered right away. I know that we have seven days, but we do not want to put it off too long. Don't you think?" Not being able to help herself, she added, "We would not want to break any rules now, would we?"

Now the attitude showing was Sandy's.

Jacob looked at Sandy and raised an eyebrow at the fact she had verbally teased the officer some. He thought he might actually like this lady if he had a chance to get to know her better.

Still not sure what was going on, the officer from the outside gave Officer Hansen a motion with his hand, calling him over for a private conservation.

"What do you think? Is there anything here?"

Lowering his voice, Officer Hansen answered, "Nothing wrong here, unless you can give them a ticket for being unorganized and clumsy, other than that, I can't find anything."

Having ended that conversation, both officers laughed and decided together to get the blazes out of here and have some breakfast. They were both laughing as they walked toward the door. Officer Hansen gave a parting glance toward Sandy.

In turn, she sighed and nodded her head toward him. She was not sure why he had helped them out, but for whatever reason, she was very grateful.

The door closed. And for the moment, things were all clear.

Sandy sat down on the floor right where she had been standing. A feeling of gratefulness overwhelmed her and then anger. She had a lot of close calls, but nonetheless, she didn't like them. Especially since this one could have been avoided.

As soon as Sandy had recovered enough to speak, she called to Jake. "Jake from Oregon, do you have any idea what you almost did to this shelter? What on earth were you thinking? Don't you know the laws?"

Jake's head was also spinning with thoughts of what could have happened. The whole case could have gone up in smoke, and it was only the second day of his assignment.

As soon as Jake could get a word in edgewise. "I am sorry. Yes, I do know the rules, but I guess I was so tired. I did not hear the all clear. I am sorry."

In Jake's whole life, he could not remember ever having slept so sound. Never in his wildest dreams would he have dreamt that he could have even slept here at all, much less overslept.

Jake began to look around. Now that daylight had come, the shelter looked different but not any better. It was a little warmer and a lot less crowded but definitely not any better.

Paint was coming off most of the wood surfaces; and the furniture, what there was of it, was old, very old. Almost everything in the place had been repaired or needed to be. Not a single thing matched. How very unlike the furnishings from his other life, and yet there was something about this place that let Jake have one of the best night's sleeps he had ever had. This was crazy, real crazy.

With Jake's answer about not having heard the all clear, Sandy's thoughts went on to the fact that someone had not done their job. Who had dropped the ball?

This was not getting them anywhere, and for sure, this was not getting the dinner ready.

"I am sorry, Jake, but you see, this is only one of five shelters of the chipless nature left open in this area. And it is really important to the people of this area that it stays open."

Jake kept looking at this woman trying to figure out what on earth would convince her to live like this. It was obvious that she was a healthy and intelligent woman. How was it that she could choose to give up all opportunities she could have had and instead become a cook at a chipless shelter?

"Oh, yes, ma'am. If it were not for this place last night, I might have ended up in a jail somewhere, seeing that I have no chip and all."

"Well, let's not dwell on this, and let's do get on with the day, okay? And for the record, now that we have told the officers that you work here, you will have to be a worker for a time anyway. Is that going to be okay with you?"

Jake didn't answer but nodded his head.

Within a few seconds of their new agreement, a young girl came running in the front door of the shelter. She hit the door so hard that at first Jake thought one of the officers had returned.

But to his surprise, there stood a very small-framed young girl, or lady. It was hard for Jake to decide at first just which she was. The way these people dressed, it was really hard to tell their gender sometimes, much less age if you even took the effort to find out. Her wavy red hair was pulled back with a hair tie. Her clothing was less than to be desired, baggy and dressed in layers. She had gloves on, but the fingers were worn out of them. Her shoes—well, if you could call them that—were old and had more tape on them than actual shoe. She was clean, but that was just about the only good thing Jake could find to say about her. Jake could see it now. She was a very beautiful—yes, a beautiful young woman.

Totally out of breath, she ran on into the room and straight over to Sandy, who was now getting up from the floor.

"Are you okay? I passed two officers, and I saw that they had just left here?"

"Calm down, Peggy. We are fine."

"Oh my, did they shut us down?"

"No. Peggy, would you please slow down and let me introduce you to our new worker, Jake? He is from Oregon."

Sandy stopped short with that. All she knew about this young man was that he was named Jake, from Oregon, he didn't have a chip, and until this moment, he had shown no common sense when it came to his surviving on the streets.

But common sense or not, he had to be their new worker since Sandy told the officer he was. She now had to follow through with that idea; God must be up to something with all of this. So for now, she would carry on with the idea of Jake being here and his working for them.

Turning to Jake, Sandy took a really good look at him, and she asked, "Jake, what brought you to this shelter?"

"What?" Jake was surprised by the question. With what they had just gone through together, how was it that she now questioned his being here? Hadn't he just proved his need?

"I heard on the street that this was a safe place to stay." Jacob tried to not have a tone in his voice.

"Where on the street did you hear this?" Sandy began to reorganize the things she had brought.

Thinking fast, Jake replied, "Yesterday, on the street, there was a ruckus. There was this stranger, and he was confronted by the officers. I am sure that you heard about it, yes?"

Yes, indeed Sandy had heard of the happening on the street. And she had heard of a young man who almost caused a riot too. Boy, this kid could be more trouble than he was worth. Perhaps keeping him here with her was going to be doing more than giving him a place to stay, but it could be doing the rest of them a favor too by getting him of the streets and keeping and eye on him.

"Okay, Jake, I get how you found us now. I am glad that it was one of us who told you about the shelter. And now that you have found us, would you confirm that you will stay here and work with us, for now anyway?"

Jake wasn't sure if this was his way into the Knowing. But at least it was a place to stay, and a place to learn the way of life on the street.

"Yes, that would be nice. Thank you."

With that out of the way, Sandy looked over to Peggy. There were other things that needed to be cleared up.

"Peggy, do you know what is going on here? When I got here, there was no one to make sure that things were in order. Who was on duty last night? And why aren't they here?"

Peggy seemed a little uneasy talking in front of Jake. So Sandy reached over and took Peggy very gently by the arm and led her over to the corner out of earshot of Jake.

Sandy looked at Peggy. Straight in the eye. "Now what's going on? What happened?"

"Well, last night, there came word that an undercover informant had been sent out. They think that it might be someone high up in the government. And so Victor, he was the one on duty. Did you know that Victor was back?"

"Yes, Peggy, I know that he is back, now what happened?"

"Well, for some reason, Victor thought that you might have somehow been involved with this government guy. Any idea of what made him think that?"

"No, Peggy, I don't. Now, what happened?" Yes, Sandy did know what made him think that, but this was not the time or place for confessions of being caught out past curfew. She had not said it very nicely, so she restated it with a better tone. "Now, Peggy, what happened?"

"Well, he went."

"He went where?" Sandy was getting so exasperated with Peggy she felt that she could shake the rest of the information out of her. But not being patient with Peggy was one of Sandy's shortcomings, and on more than one occasion. She had to go to God about it. Sandy took a deep breath.

Slowly and very exactly, she asked, "What did Victor do?"

"He left."

"He left?"

"Yep."

"Left where?"

"Oh, he mumbled something about you getting in over your head. He told me to stay here while he went to find you."

A look of worry came over Sandy.

Peggy noticed the worry in Sandy, and right away, she quickly spoke to reassure her.

"Oh, it was real dark out, and I am sure that he wouldn't get caught. Don't you think?"

Sandy reached up and rubbed her head. Oh, what a day. And what a headache she was getting.

"Yes, Peggy, I am sure that you are right. If anyone can take care of himself, Victor can, but, Peggy, that does not explain why you were not here?"

"Oh, that's easy, it wasn't my day."

With that answer playing back through Sandy's mind again, she decided to let it go for now and to get to work. If she did not end this conversation, it could make her crazy.

"Okay, for now, let's get things back in order. Will you please show Jake here what it is that we do? Can you do that for me?"

Peggy looked over her shoulder to get another good look at Jake.

All Jake could think to do was smile.

He hadn't heard the conversation. And for all he knew, she had been told to throw him out. But to his relief, she was going to be his new trainer.

Peggy and Jake were heading off to the kitchen when Sandy called out to Peggy.

"Peggy." Peggy and Jake both stopped and turned to look at Sandy. "Please, in the future, if you are asked to stay here, please do so until someone comes to relieve you, okay?"

"Okay, Sandy."

"Come on, Jake." Peggy motioned to Jake, and off they went to get things started in the kitchen.

Sandy, taking advantage of this time to be alone, began to continuing picking up the peas. A thought ran through her mind that while she was down on her knees getting the peas, she might as well pray.

Wasn't that what Victor had reminded her of the last time they were together? And pray she did, again for help, but also remembering to be thankful for the extra saving of the shelter that had happened this morning.

Who was Officer Hansen? His name still did not ring a bell, but that was not what was important. What was important was that a need arose and a need was met, again. "Thank You, God."

The day went on much better than the morning had gone. Sandy kept herself busy with the daily chores. But her mind often wandered off to what was going on with Victor. Still not sure if he was all right. She would send up a quick prayer. She would then remind herself and remember how many times he had not only saved himself but others as well. She was sure that he must be okay, but then to actually know for sure would be great.

As the day continued on, many people had dropped by. Usually, the word about what was happening on the street was quick to reach them. But today there didn't seem to be any news of the happenings of last night.

It was just minutes before the curfew sirens were to start. There was always a warning siren and then a fifteen-minute break, and then the real siren for shutdown would sound. During the fifteen-minute warning period, a very large number of people would file into this small shelter. Along with them would come the stories of what had happened on the streets that day. This was better than a newspaper but often incomplete and came with personal opinions about what had happened. But at least it was something.

Jake had worked all day. Cooking, cleaning, and doing anything that needed to be done. It was good work. Jake felt somehow complete by doing it; even though he wasn't sure what it was that made him feel this way, he liked it.

Peggy had proved to be a wealth of information. Not anything he could use on his assignment about the Knowing, but she made sure that Jake knew about every "important member," as she called them of the shelter.

The first siren was in full blare. One by one people filtered into the room. All commented on the wonderful smell coming from the kitchen.

Jake couldn't help but feel proud of being a part of the upcoming dinner. But at the same time, he made sure to keep his head and his ear in tune to any conversation that might pop up about the Knowing.

Each time Peggy saw someone that she thought was "important," she would call to Jake for him to come over and meet them. One by one they each became a part of his new life. How strange it was to feel such a part of a group. And yet he had only been here for a night and one full day.

This was unlike anything he had ever encountered. What was it about these people that they would accept him so openly? Why? Didn't they have any idea how other people felt about them? Didn't they realize how dangerous it was to take in strangers? Well, strangers like him anyway.

The sirens had stopped, and the dinner had been served. So thankful were these people for such simple foods. Jake and Peggy along with several others were picking up the last of the dishes and getting them washed when all at once there was a tap on the door. It sounded as though something metal was being hit against the wood of the door, so the sound was a very clear one. Almost at once the lights were shut out. Jake was caught off guard by this happening. Jake was trying hard to focus his eyes, but it was of no use. He had looked directly at the lights as they were going out. Even though he couldn't see, he was sure of one thing, that the front door had been opened. He thought that he had heard it open, but when he felt the cold air come over him, he was sure of it.

The lights came back up, and people went on as if nothing had happened.

How strange this was to Jake. Why put the lights out and then open the door? For what reason would they do this? But then there was his answer. There was a new man in the room. This man still had his coat on, and Jake knew for sure that he had not seen him before. They had opened the door in order to let this tall gentleman in. His hair was graying, and he had very distinct features.

Jake was sure that he hadn't seen him in the shelter at all tonight. So who was he? And what was he doing coming in after curfew?

One thing was for sure: he was either really brave or really dumb. Time would have to answer that one.

In a short period of time after this man's entrance, the people of the room began to rumble with excitement. They were excited. But there wasn't anything Jake could see that should make it so.

Jake could hear Sandy's voice above the crowd. "Victor, where on earth have you been? Are you crazy coming in after curfew? You could get arrested and get us written up for a violation."

Jake thought that this was a strange reaction from a woman who was truly worried all day about Victor. She had asked everyone she saw today if they had seen or heard from Victor. But then perhaps this wasn't the Victor that they were all worried about?

"Victor, I can't believe that you would risk this shelter for your crazy running around. Do you know what happened this morning? Why the government officers held an inspection first thing, and it was by the grace of God that we made it through it."

No, this was the man that they all had been worried about. What a crazy group of people.

Victor didn't say anything but stood there looking at Sandy like she was a crazy lady. Jake was pleased to see that at least one person here had some common sense. Then he realized that he was staring at the two of them, so he went back to wiping off the counter that was in front of him. While he was looking down, he heard Victor begin to talk to Sandy.

"Would you please lower your voice?"

Jake's head jerked up at once. That voice. That voice, he couldn't be mistaken. It was the voice of the stranger on the street yesterday. He was sure of it. So he was Victor. Jake finally had a name for his notes. His first contact on the street was from Victor.

Lowering her voice, Sandy continued talking to Victor. "Do you know how worried I—I mean we—were about you? Couldn't you have gotten word to us somehow?"

"No, Sandy, I couldn't get word to you. I was caught in a rabbit hole. Again." He gave her a raise of the eyebrow and a bit of a smile.

"Well, thank God you had enough sense to stay there. But how could you move at night, are you out of your mind?"

"Sandy, I had to get to you before you left here. I have some information that you may need to know about before you do any-thing—" Victor let his voice trail off and stopped short as he looked over at the counter.

Victor saw Jake. Victor looked back at Sandy.

"How long has he been here? Do you know who he is? He is the kid on the street yesterday."

This was going to be great, thought Jake; this would be his first and last day on the job. He could tell that this man recognized him as the one on the street that may have gotten him in trouble.

But then a strange thing happened. Victor had a genuine smile on his face. This man was actually happy to see that Jake was at the shelter. This was truly one of the strangest things Jake could ever remember happening to him. This man had every right to be mad at him. Jake had obviously fouled up something important on the street yesterday, but instead of being angry, Victor said, "Thank God he made it here. I was really worried about what had happened to him."

Victor began walking over to where Jake was standing. Victor extended his hand out and offered him a welcome. Not at all what Jake thought should have happened. What a strange thing for a man to do seeing that he had somehow caused him trouble the only time he had seen him before. "Jake, Jake from Oregon, right?"

Sandy followed Victor and added into the conversation, "Yes, this young man found us and almost closed us down in a single night. No thanks to you." Under her breath, she expressed that she would explain it all to Victor later. "Jake here is one of our new workers, and a real good one too, might I add." Sandy truly was happy with Jake's work, but she was still upset with Victor, so it was hard for anyone to really tell.

Victor and Jake said quick hellos, and then Victor and Sandy went off to be by themselves. As by themselves as you could be in a room full of people. Off to one corner anyway.

There was no way that Jake could get close enough to overhear them talking. So having all his work done, he said his good nights and a big thank-you to Peggy and the group. He found himself another corner and settled himself down to sleep. But sleep did not come before he had a chance to think through the things that he had learned on his second day out on assignment.

No Knowing. No secret group. And no last names. Until this very moment, Jake hadn't realized that they did not use last names. How very strange. All he had found out for sure was he now had a new life with new friends and a new job. The strangest part of all was that he liked it. What was it about this new life of Jake's that felt so good? It sure wasn't the wonderful surroundings. Jake laughed to himself at such a thought. And once again, sleep took over.

CHAPTER 5

Jake had been at the shelter for a week now and was starting to get discouraged about the lack of information he was getting.

So far, all he knew was that Sandy, along with Victor, seemed to somehow be in charge of the things around here. There were others like Peggy who rotated in and out of this shelter. But the one and only constant at this shelter for sure was Jake.

He stayed here almost all of the time.

The only real outing he had was when he and Sandy went to get supplies for the shelter. This was exciting to Jake because in his briefing, there was no information about the provisions for getting food to these people.

So surprised was Jake when they took empty bags with them and merely walked the streets. In and out of stores and in and out of homes they went. But not once did Jake see Sandy really talk to anyone or buy anything. She would just walk in and lay the empty bags down on the counter or whatever space was available. Then she would walk around as though she were shopping. After having spent some time looking, she would pick up another bag that was placed somewhere in the store. It would be full. With what, Jake didn't know at first. Most of the day was spent wearily going in and out of places. Just one bag exchange after another, an empty for a full.

Jake went to way too many places to keep track of who and where he had been. In fact, most of the time, Jake felt lost. His time on the streets in the past had been by car. Not in and around town on foot like this. On that day, Jake found more back doors, side doors, alleyways, and walkways than he knew existed.

Sandy never once looked at a map or a list. Each of the places had expected her, and the parcels were ready.

Shortly after they had started on this "gathering," as Sandy had called it, Jake found out why it was that he had been invited along. As a packhorse—yes, he was a packhorse. But then he didn't mind. He felt sure that sooner or later, someone was going to slip up and tell him of the Knowing and perhaps even of its leader. Jake almost felt sorry for these people. They were so trusting and innocent. They did not suspect anything, and that almost made Jake feel bad about how he was using them to get information.

Finally, with the day almost over, they headed back to the shelter. When they arrived at the shelter, several people were waiting for Sandy, all of them having similar parcels. Apparently, Sandy and Jake were not the only ones collecting that day. Everyone had waited for Sandy before going through the sacks. Without a doubt, Sandy was a leader of some sort.

As they started unloading the bags, Jake was amazed at what was inside. Foods of every kind; most of the foods were the kind that could be stored easily, but some were perishables—meat, milk, cheese, even some real butter and eggs. What a treat this was going to be after one week of nothing but vegetable soup. He was ready for anything that was different. Jake could not believe his eyes. The things people would just give away.

In some of the other bags, there was clothing and even cleaning supplies. Jake knew that these people had always kept things and themselves clean, but until he had seen this, he hadn't thought of how they had accomplished it. One of the bags had hats, gloves, and socks in it. When that bag was opened, Sandy stopped what she was doing and picked out and gave Jake a pair of gloves and a hat. "Now, you will be warmer," she had said, and then went back to her duties. Jake was surprised that with all that needed to be done, Sandy would take the time to notice that he needed something and then to fulfill the need herself.

Jake was excited. He had never been so happy for a gift in his life. But then he couldn't think of a time in his life when he needed anything more. He had decided that this had to have been one of the coldest weeks he had experienced.

The people who were there with the bags were not the regular people who came to the shelter each night, but for sure, they were chipless. Jake could tell now, somehow these people had a special way about them. Nothing he could write in his journals, but something other than just the way they dressed like he used to think. The Gathering, as it was called, had taken place two days ago; and since then, nothing seemed to be going on, until this morning that was.

Jake was getting things ready at the shelter so they could start the dinner, and the main shelter door opened. Expecting someone Jake knew, he was very surprised to see a middle-aged man coming in. This man was chipped for sure, his clothing screamed of it. He had a fancy hat on, business type, and it was pulled down quite low in front so as to shadow his face.

He stopped as he entered, looked around as if looking for someone or something. Then his eyes met Jake's, and he walked directly over to in front of the counter where Jake was now standing.

In his hand was a large paper sack. The top was rolled down, and it made a loud thud as he placed it on the counter. "Sandy wanted this. Tell her that things are not good. The information about the *leader* was correct."

Jake's heart almost leaped out of his chest. At last, perhaps this was what he was looking for, some information on the leader of the Knowing.

The man had turned and was walking away.

Jake knew that if he was going to get any more information, he had to talk to this man. So Jake seized the moment and called out to him. "Can I tell Sandy who it was that brought this to her?"

The man stopped short and swung around as to make a connection with Jake's face.

Jake was not sure what was on this man's mind, but he could tell that he did not quite trust him.

"Sandy will know," was all he said as he turned and walked away.

Jake stood for the longest time looking at the bag on the counter. To open it and look inside it would make him a good officer, but to do so was also to betray a trust. Sandy had trusted him so completely that Jake had almost felt sorry for her. Didn't she realize what could happen if the wrong people got into the wrong areas of their business? But then that was what he was supposed to do. Wasn't that his job? Having reminded himself of what his job was, Jake didn't hesitate anymore. He took the bag, opened it, and to his surprise, he found the strangest things. In the bag was a frozen can of grape juice. The juice was beginning to thaw and was starting to get everything else in the bag wet. Along with the juice was some very unusual bread. It was very heavy and very flat. Jake thought to himself that if someone cooked like that for him, he would give it away too. But all laughing matters aside. This was just about the strangest thing Jake had seen yet. This very proper chipped man had risked coming into a chipless shelter to bring such a crazy thing as grape juice and bread, bad bread at that. But what then of this strange message for Sandy? "'Things are not good. Information about the leader is true'?" Whatever could that mean? Perhaps when he told Sandy, he would be able to get some more information from her.

As Jake was standing there holding the bag in his hand, obviously looking its contents over, the door of the shelter opened and in walked Sandy and Victor.

They both stopped short at the sight of Jake going through the bag. The look of concern, not anger, was on both of their faces. At that moment, Jake began to realize how things might look, like he was snooping or, worst yet, that he might be stealing from them.

Flustered by this thought, Jake went to place the contents back into the bag so as to give it to Sandy along with the message, but when he did, the bottom of the bag broke through, and the entire bag of stuff fell crashing onto the counter and then onto the floor.

Victor turned to Sandy with a smile. "So, Sandy, are you hiring your own demolition crew now?"

Sandy gave Victor an "I'll deal with you later" look and turned to Jake to talk over matters.

"Jake, what's going on? Where did you get that stuff?"

Jake quickly picked up the things that had fallen out of the bag and placed them onto the counter. He placed the paper bag under the juice so the moisture couldn't do any more damage. Oh, how he wished that Sandy and Victor had not seen him snooping. Part of him was worried about his case being exposed, but another part of him did not want to let down these new friends of his. The fact that they trusted him felt really good, and he was not ready to give that up yet.

"Sandy, a man dropped this stuff off and said that you would want it."

"Did he say anything else?" Sandy walked on into the room.

For a moment, Jake thought that maybe he ought to withhold the message so as to create a gap in the communication. Perhaps that would rattle things up so as to bring on some more of the data that he needed. But then again it could somehow cause some trouble for the shelter, and that would not be good either. So thinking it best, Jake told Sandy and Victor what the man had said.

Jake added, "He didn't leave a name or anything. Do you have any idea who he was?"

Sandy just smiled and answered, "No, no idea at all." With a smirk on her face as if she had a secret that she really wanted to share but had not planned to yet. Sandy picked up the bread and the grape juice and, almost giving them a hug, walked off to the kitchen.

Victor stood there in the room watching Jake carefully. Jake thought that he might have drilled a hole in him if he had looked any harder.

"Jake," Victor called out to him, "tell me now what was it that you did that made you have to leave your hometown?"

Jake was taken aback by Victor's question. He thought that they had cleared that up on the street on the first day of their meeting. But on second thought, they had been interrupted before he had told his whole cover story.

"Well, I had a few curfew problems." Jake had to think quickly on that one.

"Why?" Victor's voice was neutral.

"What do you mean why?" Jake did not like being questioned like this.

"What were you doing that made you stay out past curfew?"

Jake was thankful as Victor was remaining calm and did not show any sign of mistrust but was showing simple curiosity.

"I had friends, you know. And well, we just did things, you know." Jake felt like he did when his own father questioned him. He did not like it any more now than he did back in his old life.

"No, I do not think that I do know. Please tell me?" Victor was still as calm as he could be with the most peaceful, and irritating, look that Jake had run up against.

Jake was getting really uneasy. "Why, what is it to you why I left? I just left, okay?"

Victor, being actually concerned about this young man, walked over to where he was standing and looked directly at him. "Jake, I do not know if you know it or not, but all of us here at the shelter care about you and are worried about you."

Panic overtook Jake like a wave. These people cared about him. They are worried about him. Why, if things were what Jake thought they were going to be, in a very short time, Jake was going to be taking these people down. And they are worried about him? Really what they should be worrying about right now was themselves. With Jake's help, these people were all going to be arrested and were going to be chipped. Their lives were going to be changed forever, and they were worried about him. These people are nuts. Even the ones who seem most balanced obviously did not understand the real truth of how dangerous things could be.

Victor could see the turmoil building up in Jake, but Victor thought it was from something from Jake's past. "Jake, I am sorry if I have brought up bad memories. I was just trying to help. Consider the matter closed. I will try and not ask another thing about you. You will share when you are good and ready. I just want you to know that we care, okay?"

Jake was confused by this whole conversation. This very strong community leader was sensitive to the fact that Jake was upset. First of all, how was it that he even noticed? People seldom noticed or cared if he had been upset in the past. He did not think that even his own family would have seen that fact, and they were close to him, they were family. And second, how was it that this man could share these kinds of feelings with another man? Didn't he realize how weak that made him look?

The more that Jake thought about it though, he really did not feel that this man was weak, but somehow rather that he was actually brave. Yes, that was it, brave for being willing to go out on a limb like this with his emotions. Wow. What a novel idea, it was something to consider later on.

Then a most wonderful idea came to Jake. Perhaps these people, his new friends here at the shelter, were not the ones he was looking for. Perhaps these people would not turn out to be a part of this Knowing group at all. That very well could be true. Hadn't he been here for over a week and not seen or heard anything that could confirm or even hint to the fact that they were Knowing? Perhaps Jake had just found some nice new friends, and perhaps the people of the Knowing were in an altogether different location. That thought sent a warm peaceful feeling running through Jake: these were just new friends, and they were all chipless yes, but really good caring new friends—THAT HE WAS LYING TO DAILY. His warmth now turned to distress. This new life that Jake was living had him off-balance somehow. He did not like the way he could not settle in on his own thinking. He had always thought of himself as a very levelheaded person, but his feelings right now did not seem to be like that at all. He was not sure of anything right now, much less about anyone.

Coming from the kitchen, Sandy returned into the room with a water pitcher in her hand, but this time it contained the grape juice all mixed and ready to drink. Under her arm was a plastic bag that had some kind of white linen in it. In her other hand, she had a silver platter, beautiful in design. How out of place it was, considering the decor of the shelter. Sandy placed the bread on the platter; it almost covered the whole thing. She set all the other items down. She began cleaning up the left end of the counter. With the top shining to her satisfaction, Sandy carefully unfolded the white linen. It was as beautiful as the platter was. Then getting the linen laid out ever so carefully, she placed both the pitcher of grape juice and the platter of bread on it just right of the center.

Then she called out to Victor, "Would you please get me the two glasses, two napkins, and a towel from the kitchen?"

Victor went off on his search as Jake stood and watched Sandy put together the layout.

Sandy was happy. Yes, truly happy, almost giddy, and over what? It was a pitcher of grape juice and some hard bread. What craziness this was, for her to be so happy over something so simple? There would not even be enough bread to feed more than a few people, much less the whole shelter. But for whatever reason, Sandy was happy. And in a funny sort of way, that made Jake happy too.

Victor came back with the whole order filled—two large glasses, nothing special, two napkins, and an old dishtowel.

Sandy received them with a great big "thank you" and then placed the glasses on the linen left of the other things. With great fulfillment in her face, Sandy covered as much of the setting as she could with the dishtowel. Sandy took three steps back and looked at the overall creation.

"What do you think, Victor, will that do?"

"That will do great, Sandy. Do you plan dinner first, or will we have it after?"

Jake was lost in the conversation. What was before or after dinner? What? Jake was desperately trying to figure out what on earth these two seemingly normal people were talking about. And again, what on earth were they so happy about? Hadn't they just received news of something of a bad nature? The man had said, "Things are not good." Jake had heard it himself, and yet these people were acting as though they were planning a celebration or something.

"Jake. Are you all right?" Sandy was looking at him as if he had told her how confused he was about all of this. He was so deep in thought that he had not heard all of what she was saying.

"What?" Jake questioned Sandy.

Sandy just laughed, reached up, and tousled Jake's hair a bit in jest. "You remind me so much of my older daughter. She always was a pensive and thoughtful one. Sometimes I thought that she was off in thought more than she was with me. Keeping her attention was

BEYOND KNOWING

hard to do, but it was easily overcome with bribery. You do want to eat, don't you, Jake?"

Jake couldn't help but love this lady. What a warm and vibrant woman she was. Jake had never thought of her having a family. An older daughter, she had said. What of her? Where was her family?

"Sandy. Where is your family now?"

Sandy's look of happiness somehow softened into a little sadness. "Well, Jake. They are safe out of the country."

"Safe, Sandy, what are they safe from?"

"Oh, you know, from the way that this crazy world has gone. I thought it best if I did not endanger my girls because of my choices. You know each one has to decide for themselves who it is they will serve, don't you agree?"

Sandy looked up at Jake and realized that he hadn't any idea of what she was talking about. A small amount of fear landed in the pit of her stomach. How was it that this young man did not know what she was talking about? If he was what they had thought him to be, he would understand the having to make choices, the not receiving the chip by choice. If his not having the chip was not by choice, then how was it that he was choosing to live here?

Thoughts of what the message left earlier that day had meant suddenly came to mind for Sandy. "The Leader" was the codename for some supposed new program the government was planning on putting in place. Or so the story went.

What was said about the leader was true. Isn't that what the message had said? But then wasn't it Jake who had delivered the message? If he was the secret undercover officer said to have been sent out to find them out, why would he have given her the message?

Sandy looked back at Jake; she laughed at herself. Why, he is just a boy, and a "not so easy to have around" boy either. Although he had hardly any street savvy at all, and his being an officer could explain why, it just did not seem to fit somehow. That thought sent another chill down her spine. *No, not Jake. Not in a million years.* But then what was it about him that kept her on guard? Why, he had been here for more than a week, and this was the first time she felt she could share something personal with him. She was usually more

70

open than that with people. Perhaps it was not her intuition at all but all of this stuff about an undercover officer who was to infiltrate the Knowing that was making her feel on edge.

Sandy needed to rethink her facts. First of all, Sandy remembered that this story of an undercover officer was only a rumor. And second, that the information was not received by Sandy firsthand, and not to forget that the informant on the inside never showed up at the meeting. All that put together brought a big question as to if an undercover officer could even be true at all. The information she had been told had been filtered out through the street people. Although that form of information was usually reliable, there had been times that things told were not true. Perhaps this was Sandy's imagination going overboard, but then it would not hurt to be careful.

Sandy hated it when she was divided in her thinking. To trust Jake or not would prove itself out in time. She would pray about it and give it to God. God knew what was going on, and other than be careful, she would trust God to take care of it.

Everything was in place for the night. Sandy, Victor, Jake, and several of the other workers sat down to have a rest before the evening was to begin.

Jake still wasn't sure what was making these people so happy, but tonight, without exception, everyone was happy.

It was almost an hour away from the fifteen-minute siren going off when Peggy came running into the shelter. She hit the door so hard that everyone jumped at the sound. As she continued on into the room, her eyes caught the view of the setup on the left end of the counter. The biggest smile came across her face. Her eyes widened. And she at once looked over to Sandy. "Tonight?"

Sandy gave a little chuckle. "Yes, Peggy, tonight."

Peggy almost did a little dance right where she was standing.

Jake's heart nearly broke when he looked down at Peggy's shoes. When Jake had first met her, Peggy's shoes had been held together with tape. But now with all of the rain that they had been having, the tape was letting go. Truthfully, she might as well of been barefoot.

71

For sure, without having to say it, this young woman was having a real hard time. And yet here she was dancing over grape juice and bread. Now that is crazy.

Sandy remembered something. She asked Peggy to wait for a minute as she went into the kitchen.

Sandy returned, and she was holding one of the bags that they had picked up the other day. "Peggy, what size shoe do you wear?"

"What?" Peggy stopped and looked down at her feet. Then she realized that the question was waiting for an answer. She replied, "Oh, anything would do, but six and a half is best."

Sandy, with a big smile on her face, reached her hand into the bag and pulled out a brand-new pair of lace-up type of work boots. She then looked at the tag that was still hanging from them. "Yes, just as I thought, these must be for you. They are a size six and a half."

Peggy didn't move but stood there with the look of disbelief on her face. She reached up with her hand and covered her mouth. Then tears ran from her eyes and rolled down over her fingers and then onto the floor. No true sound came from Peggy's mouth, only a few gasps.

Sandy's eyes also started to tear up now as she walked over toward Peggy. When she reached her, Sandy placed her arm around her and handed her the boots.

Sandy then gestured to Peggy for her to try them on. As Peggy looked at the shoes, she noted that there was another gift inside the boots; someone had put two pairs of new socks to go along with the boots. What a blessing this gift was, and whoever the giver was had even sent socks, making it the perfect gift.

Jake was standing by Victor and leaned closer to him in order to ask a question in a very low voice. "Victor, did you order the stuff for Peggy, and if you did, how does that work?"

Victor smiled. "Sort of, I am not sure that *order* would be the right word though," was all that Victor said, then he went back to watching Peggy try on her new boots.

Peggy sat down right there on the floor and took off her old shoes. She looked down at her feet, and then she stopped moving.

Without a word, Sandy knew what the problem was. Peggy had new socks and boots, and damp, dirty feet. Without any hesitation, Sandy reached up and pulled the dishtowel off the setup she was so proud of and began to help wipe off Peggy's feet.

This was an act of love that Jake had never seen the likes of. Having done this to the satisfaction of Peggy, then and only then did the socks and shoes find their new home on her feet. Peggy was sure that her life could never get better than this, what with having new boots and even socks. And they were really new and had never been worn by anyone else.

Jake stood there and watched as this whole thing unfolded. What a wonderful sight to see someone have a real need met. Jake felt proud of the fact that he might have been the one who got to carry the bag the boots came in. What an honor. What a pleasure to be a part of all this.

But what happened next was a conversation that would haunt Jake for a long time to come.

Peggy leaped to her feet grabbing Sandy in a hug. She was shouting, "Thank Him for me, Sandy, thank Him for me. Will you? Please, Sandy, will you?"

Jake froze. Thank Him. Him who? It had to be the leader. Who else would be able to get new anything without a chip? Sandy will be telling the leader thank-you from Peggy.

Then it happened.

Sandy smiled, looked at Peggy getting her attention, and said, "Peggy, why don't you thank Him yourself?"

Peggy stopped short. Bright-eyed. Her face, and I mean her whole face, broke into a bigger-than-ever smile. She wiped the tears from her eyes and said, "I will. I'll tell Him myself."

With that thought in mind, Peggy decided to give her new boots a trial run. Or one could say a trial dance. Again, Peggy just gave a little dance of sort right where she was standing. Then off to the kitchen she went to do her assigned work.

With so much excitement welling up in this young lady, it just seemed to overflow to everyone there, even Jake.

But Jake's excitement was mixed.

There was the excitement of the grape juice and the bread. There was the excitement of the new boots for Peggy. But for Jake, he now might get the chance of meeting the leader. All he had to do was stay close to Peggy, and sooner or later, she would lead him to their leader. Finally, he could get down to business. This plan was going to work.

With all the excitement, they had lost track of the time and were surprised to find people beginning to filter into the shelter.

Jake could not help but notice how the people would light up when they saw the setup on the counter. They would often look to Sandy for confirmation. She would simply smile and nod her head yes. They would give a smile back and then resume their usual routine. Jake was getting even more confused as to what was going on with the setup but was sure that he would find out soon enough.

As usual, most people had their blankets and had stretched them out on the floor. He had now confirmed that this was a way of setting up a boundary for their family. After setting up home as it were, they filed over and waited in line for their dinner. Jake had noticed that as a rule, there were rarely families with younger children at the shelter. They did come to the shelter, but at most they would be there for a night or two. Jake had wondered where the children had gone, but he had not had the opportunity to date to ask anyone about what he had noticed.

For some of these people, this would be their only meal of the day. Some had workplaces that provided lunch, but very few if any ever received breakfast.

Because this truly was for some the only meal of the day, it often struck Jake odd that they all remained so patient for the food. As was usual, they would all wait until everyone was served. Then, when everyone had their meal and was ready to eat, they would all look down at their food for a moment and then dig in as most would expect. The patience of these people was, to say the least, strange to Jake.

Tonight, the shelter was completely full. The final siren was beginning to do its job of setting the night's routine in motion. It was now time for the closing and the locking of the door.

As the door was being closed, Jake could not help but notice the look of concern on Victor's and Sandy's faces. As Jake watched these two, he followed their gaze as they both turned and focused on the door.

With only inches away from being totally closed, the door came to a halt. A hand and then an arm and then the whole man came through the door. As his entrance was complete, the door was closed and then locked behind him.

This man still having his back to the crowd, leaned his head forward, and began to shake the water off his jacket. The rain must have really been coming down for him to have gotten this wet.

Shaking as much moisture off himself as he could, he began to remove his jacket, followed by his hat and gloves. Several people jumped up to help him with his things.

A look of relief came over a lot of the people in the room, but most of all Sandy and Victor.

Having said greetings to several of the people, this man saw Sandy and Victor over by the kitchen door and headed that way.

Victor was the first to make a move. "Cutting things a little close, aren't we?" He extended his right hand toward this man, then with his left arm, he was reaching around him giving him a type of a hug greeting.

Then it was Sandy's turn. No handshake for her, just a full-out embrace. "Hello, sister," this new man said.

Jake was confused now. Hadn't Sandy only today told him that her family was not anywhere around here?

Sandy's reply to him was simply, "Hello, David. Thank you so much for tonight. It was exciting to get word that you were coming. It has been a long time."

David, Jake thought, *this new man is David. And he must be important too, the way that everyone was acting. This could be the leader perhaps?* Well, if he was, there was nothing Jake could see that would make this man so special.

David smiled at Sandy. "It feels like it has been too long."

Having finished their conversation, David looked over toward Jake. Then he brought Victor's attention to who he was looking at. "Is that Jake, the one from Oregon?"

This man knew of him. And that freaked Jake out.

"Oh yes, let me introduce you to him. He really has become a great help to our effort here." As they spoke, Victor brought David over to meet Jake.

"Hello, young man. It is really nice to meet you. I have heard a lot about you, and I am looking forward to getting to know you better."

Jake was at a loss for words for a moment. How had this man heard of him? Until now, Jake had not heard even one single word about this David.

"Hello, sir, nice to meet you." Jake extended his hand for a handshake and was surprised by the sincere warmth that this man extended him.

As he shook Jake's hand, he placed his left hand on Jake's forearm. He looked at Jake giving him his total attention, acting as if they were the only two people in the room. No fake emotion here, this man really was glad to meet him.

But why would he care about Jake? Of what value could Jake be to this man or his group?

From Jake's point of view, the only value to this man's group was as a dishwasher and perhaps as a packhorse from time to time. Why, to these people, Jake was nobody with nothing, and yet they had treated him better than most of the people who knew that he was from the rich Singleton family.

One of the women, a regular at the shelter, came over to offer David a serving of the evening meal.

David looked to Jake and asked if he wanted to join him for dinner. Jake stood looking at this man trying to figure him out.

But no way, there was not a thing Jake could figure out about this man. So far all he knew was that there was something about him that stirred things up in Jake's head. He was finding more questions than answers. He could almost say he felt it in his heart, but that sounded strange to Jake.

Victor interrupted, "No. I think that Jake here needs to get on with his work, right, Jake?"

Great save, thought Jake. He needed some space to think things through, and Victor had given him his way out.

"Yes, that's right. I have work in the kitchen." Jake went off to the safety of the kitchen. This was a place where he could be more alone, where he could think. Jake was feeling strange right now. He was feeling emotional. Not at all like his normal self. He was used to being out of control of his emotions when he was angry. But not like this, he was used to having to try to control anger, not emotional feelings, not happy ones, not like this at all. Perhaps this was his reaction to Peggy getting new boots and socks, but it seems so out of his ordinary. In his past, he would have been ticked that she had needed the shoes at all. But to be this happy at someone he barely knew getting a gift?

As he pushed through the kitchen door, what he saw was all the more disturbing. There on the floor, off in the right-hand corner was Peggy. She was down on her knees, with her hands clasped together, and she was talking to the air.

Yes, even with a second and third look, she was talking to the air. What she was saying, Jake wasn't quite sure of, but those same tears that had shown up earlier when she got her socks and shoes were back again.

What was going on around here? For one week, nothing happened; and now in one day, the whole bunch had gone crazy.

Jake stood there watching Peggy as she talked to the air. What else could he do? He wasn't about to go back into the room full of crazy, happy people. Not yet anyway.

Boy, when that Mr. Diggings had said "crazy beyond your thinking," he was right. These people were not so much dangerous as they were just all nuts.

Jake stopped himself in midthought. Why was he so off his game? What was it that was making him so frustrated with these people?

Perhaps, just maybe, it was the fact that these people who had nothing were happier than Jacob had ever been while he had lived with everything. That did not make any sense. And the thought of that just plain scared him.

Jake went on into the kitchen and found a place in the opposite corner from Peggy. His head hurt. His mind was racing. He was confused. He was tired. Yes, that must be it, he was overly tired. Perhaps eating nothing but vegetable soup could be causing this confusion. He had read somewhere that diet could be a part of brainwashing. Perhaps someone was spiking the food. No, that was nuts. After all, he was one of the cooks.

Never in his whole life had Jake lost control of his emotions like he had lately. He needed to get himself under control. So settling himself down on the ground, Jake leaned back in the corner, pulled his knees up, and placed his head down to perhaps get some rest. There would be some time before they would be done with dinner and the dishes would have to be washed. So now was a perfect time to take a quick break. As he laid his head down, a feeling of perfect peace flooded over him. Yes, this was exactly what the doctor had ordered.

It was only a short while later when Jake woke up. He could have only dozed for a few minutes, but he felt much better now, more in control.

He raised his head to see what was going on now. There in front of him, completely back to normal, or back to herself anyway, was Peggy. She was all smiles. "Thank you for praying with me, Jake. I always love it when others join in while I am praying. My mom used to say that where two or more are gathered. Well, you know the rest."

Praying? Peggy thought he was praying? Not in Jake's wildest dreams would he have guessed that was what Peggy was doing. And why on earth was she thinking that he was praying too?

All of Jake's life had been spent with government people who really shunned religious anything. Praying was mentioned, but he had never really seen it done. Even Jake's friends were raised like he was. So the closest he had ever gotten to a religious experience was when his grandmother had died. At the time, he thought it was odd that some of the older people at the funeral had talked the way that they did.

He could remember some of the things they said like "Let's pray as God is waiting for her." and "Only God knows the why of these things."

But later when Jake had asked his mother about God, she only brushed it off as the crazy ravings of a bunch of old people.

Jake remembered too that before she had passed, that he was not allowed to be alone with his grandmother. A quote he remembered his father having said once was something like "I don't want Grandmother teaching our children the religious things," something about how it would not be safe for any of them. Jake did not understand then and even less now.

It was funny, thought Jake. That until now he had not even thought about his grandmother, one way or the other. But thinking back, he remembered how she almost had the same kind of happiness that these people do.

But they are not all old, or even all crazy for that matter. Or were they?

He remembered his grandmother once saying to him as she was getting ready to go back to her home that she prayed for him. She had wanted him to know that for some reason. Now he wished he had asked her about it.

But this was not some old lady praying for him, but instead he was being accused of praying himself. This was thought to be totally barbaric by the people of his upbringing. What if they got wind of this later on? Why, he would be the laughingstock of everyone he ever knew or met. This had to be put to an end right here and now.

Jake moved over next to Peggy. "Peggy, I need to explain something to you about this praying thing."

"I know, Jake. It was no big deal to you, but it was to me. So, thank you." She leaned over and gave him a kiss on this cheek.

At that very moment, Sandy entered the kitchen through the doorway. "There you two are. We really could use some help. Okay?"

Getting up from the floor, they both came as soldiers called to action.

"No problem, Sandy. Jake and me, we were just praying."

Sandy stopped midstep and looked at Peggy with one of those disproving motherly looks.

"Peggy. You were in the asking. Got it! You and Jake were in the asking."

"Oh, right. Sandy, we were in the asking. I knew that." And out the door she went.

Peggy's leaving the kitchen left Jake alone with Sandy. Sandy looked at him with the same disciplining look she had given Peggy, and Jake knew at once that this was not the time to state his case about not praying.

In fact, he could feel that this was not the time for anything but getting down to the business of cleaning up and doing dishes. Or so he thought.

As Jake reentered the main room, he was surprised to see that everything was picked up. All of the dishes were stacked over to one side. Each family's blanket was folded up and had been placed away.

This for sure was not going to be a usual evening. By now, most of the families should be bedding down for the night, but not tonight. Tonight, things were different.

Victor was standing with David over by the layout on the counter.

As Jake was coming closer to see what was happening, someone handed him an unlit candle.

Jake took it. "Thank you." He wasn't really sure what he needed it for, but he was sure that he was going to find out.

Sandy could see Jake's confusion and noted that he was uncomfortable about what was going on. So she took Jake's hand, pulled him to one side of the room, and whispered to him, "Perhaps you would rather stay in the kitchen tonight. You can get a start on the dishes if you would rather not do this." Sandy's statement had startled Jake, and she could see it in his face.

Then Jake's reply even surprised him. "But why can't I be a part of this?" He was not exactly sure what *this* was, but he did know that he wanted to be included all the same. After all, it was his job. He even had to admit to himself that a part of him did not care about the job but needed to see what could create so much happiness in so many; he wanted to see and learn about what it was that had such a hold on these people. And perhaps a little hold on him too.

Sandy wasn't to be put off so easy. "Jake, we really need you to get the cleanup started. Now please go and do your job." By making it more of a command she was trying to give Jake a way out of this situation without him feeling bad. He really did look uncomfortable.

Jake was angry. How dare Sandy decide to exclude him. Who on earth did she think she was? Jake, feeling more like a little kid than a man right now, began to lodge another complaint.

"Sandy. What seems to be the problem?" Victor had moved closer, unnoticed by either Sandy or Jake. He was standing right beside them both and was now a part of their conversation, if you could call it that.

"Victor, I was just telling Jake here that perhaps he should spend the rest of the night getting things ready in the kitchen. There are a lot of dishes that need to be done, and if he gets a jump on them, well, it would make things go a lot easier later. Don't you suppose?" From Sandy's way of speech, any fool could tell that she was wanting Victor to side with her in her decision about not including Jake in whatever it was that was about to take place.

To both Sandy's and Jake's surprise, Victor did not do that. Instead, he turned and looked at Jake while he was talking to Sandy. "Sandy, don't you think that Jake here knows what is best for him? And don't you think that he deserves a break from work for a little while?" Not once did Victor blink or look away from Jake. "And I am sure that Jake here is fully aware that along with knowledge comes a responsibility. Isn't that right, Jake?"

Along with knowledge comes a responsibility! What on earth was Victor talking about? Quickly Jake mulled it over in his mind. Yes, this was a statement that he could accept and that he could live by.

"Yes, Victor, I understand there is a responsibility that comes with the Knowing."

Like a flash. There it was right off Jake's own tongue, "The Knowing."

With total awareness, Jake looked first at Sandy and then at Victor. Both had a half smile. They had not said it, but he had. This was a part of the Knowing.

Victor looked over at Sandy. Although she was showing a slight smile, a show of concern was still on her face.

Victor leaned over and placed a very light kiss on her frowning forehead. "Don't worry, trust God. This is bigger than all of us."

Sandy wasn't sure of what that had meant, but over the years, she had learned to trust Victor when it came to Godly situations like this. So based totally on trust, Sandy decided along with Victor to let Jake make his own choice.

There was no other choice for Jake to make. He chose to stay.

After speaking his choice, Jake looked to Sandy to see if there was going to be any anger toward him for not doing as she had told him. But to his amazement, there was nothing but a look of peace and happiness over the whole situation.

Then a look back to Victor brought him a slap on the back. "Good choice." For a moment, Victor sounded more like a proud father than a new friend.

With this decision made, Victor walked back to join David by the counter where he was still standing.

As Victor approached David, he reached into his pocket and took out a candle and a book of matches. Victor lit a match and then placed the flame to his candlewick. Then blowing out the match, Victor motioned to a man over by the light switch, and all at once, the lights went out. The only light in the room was the light coming from Victor's candle.

David then reached over with his candle and lit his. Then both men turned to face the crowd that had surrounded them.

Only a hand length of space was between them and the first row of people. One by one the people in the front row lit their candles, and then each in turn lit the ones behind them, who in turn shared their flame with the next.

How quickly the light passed from person to person. As each man lit his candle representing somehow the family there with them, a glow began to fill the room.

And now the lighting of the candles had gotten to where Jake was standing. How wonderful and nervous this felt to Jake. As each row was lit, it somehow became a part of the whole. And now he was to be a part of this whole himself.

He liked it. It felt right.

As Jake received his light, he in turn twisted around to give light to another.

As he did so, he caught a glimpse of Peggy's face coming out of the shadows. She was beautiful. She had a special glow, and yet as the light in the room grew closer to her, the glow remained.

Jake shook his head a bit thinking for a moment that his eyes were playing tricks on him, but no, she looked radiant, not from without but from within.

With all the candles lit, the entire room turned back around to look to Victor and David.

David handed Victor his candle and then turned to the pitcher of juice. He placed his hand over the opening and lowered his head. Without hesitation, the entire room lowered their heads also.

Everyone, that is, except Jake; he couldn't take his eyes off David. Jake could not make out the words at first. His heart was beating so loud that he was having trouble hearing.

Then David picked up the bread, broke it, and then the words that David said were like nothing Jake had ever heard before.

"Do this in remembrance of Me."

Jake wasn't sure what these words really meant, but from the way David had said them, he knew that they were important.

Again, there was another wave of happiness.

Victor let candle wax from each of the two candles he was holding drip down onto the counter. Then he placed the lit candles into the wax so they could stand alone.

David took both pieces of bread and gave one to Victor. They both turned to the circle edge and broke the bread into as many pieces as there were people in the front row. Jake guessed about four each. Before giving the last piece of bread out, each tore a small piece off and held it in their hand then passed the larger piece on to the next row.

Row by row, each man, woman, and child old enough to be a part, took a piece of bread and then passed the larger piece on. Now it was Jake's turn to pass on the bread; as he turned around, he could see Peggy. She was still looking just as radiant as before.

When the bread reached the last row, all of the leftover bread was brought back to the front and was given to David, who in turn placed it back on the platter. Jake had been wrong, there had been enough bread for the whole shelter, and even leftovers.

Having finished that part of the goings-on, David turned to the crowd, held up his piece of bread, closed his eyes, and again he repeated, "Do this in remembrance of Me." With that statement all at once, everyone ate their piece of bread.

That being done, they then went on to the grape juice. David again lowered his head and spoke words that Jake again really couldn't hear and then poured two glasses full of juice. Then David said it again. "Do this in remembrance of Me."

Both David and Victor had a glass full of juice and a napkin that Jake had seen Sandy lay out earlier.

One by one each person would go forward and take a sip from the glass. Each waiting and then taking their turn. Like clockwork, each person took a sip, and Victor and David would wipe the edge of the glass and speak to the people and then continue to do the same for the rest of the people in the room.

As each person drank from the glass, the words "May God be with you" were said." This was the very first time Jake had clearly heard the word *God* used by these people. But somehow hearing them speak about God did not excite him the way he thought it was going to when he caught them saying it.

Then something incredible happened. Somewhere behind him came a voice so beautiful, so clear, and, well, yes, one could say it was heavenly. A voice was singing. It was a woman's voice. All by herself, with no music, and yet it was music in and of itself. Jake had never heard this song before, but it did not matter. The words of *grace, love,* and *peace* all seemed right, and somehow he knew they were important to everyone here. The words rang through Jake.

Now Jake was getting closer and closer to the front of the group. Jake was able to see more and more of Victor and David and of what it was that they were doing.

Now was his chance to get the list of those who participated in these religious goings-on. But for the life of him, he could not focus on anything but the words he was hearing sung over and over again. "Love, peace, happiness, joy, provision, and protection."

Now it was Jake's turn to take a drink. And as fate would have it, Victor was the one who was to give Jake his serving.

As Jake took his drink, he heard for the very first time in his life.

"Jake, may God be with you." These words almost knocked the breath right out of him.

As Jake turned to walk back to his place, he could for the first time clearly see who it was singing such a wonderful song in such a beautiful flowing voice.

It was Peggy.

Jake looked closer to be sure, and yes, it was Peggy all right.

What a wonderful discovery he had made. Why, she could be famous with that voice. She could be rich. Why, with his family behind her, he could offer her the world. Why, she could buy herself a whole shoe store with the kind of money her voice could make. All he had to do was to make her the offer. But what could he offer her?

He stopped and looked back over at Peggy, new boots and all.

Then it came to him there was nothing he could offer her that would be anything of value to her.

There was nothing that his old world could offer her that could make her any happier than she was right now, at this very moment. His family had it all, and yet this kind of happiness wasn't a part of the package he could offer.

Jake realized that he was now happy. For the first time in his whole life, he was truly happy. He had no money, no family, and nothing to base his new happiness on, but he was happy. No, not just happy, but he had found pure joy.

It was all over in less than an hour, but Jake's life had been changed for good. Jake was not exactly sure what had happened, but these people let him be a part of their life, a part of their life that they hold very special. And he was thankful.

It was decided by all the kitchen group that the cleanup could wait until morning.

One by one each family put out their candle after bedding down for the night in their allotted space.

Jake didn't want to put out his candle just yet. He wasn't ready for this night to be over. As all good things do, sooner or later they must come to an end, but not yet. Just a few more minutes, and then he would blow his candle out.

Sandy and Victor had bedded themselves down in separate parts of the room. There was a rule for single adults. Each had separate sides of the room; in this shelter, single women were on the right, and single men on the left.

But both Victor and Sandy could see Jake from where they were bedded down. Both had to agree that the choices they had made tonight concerning Jake were good ones. The choice of letting Jake make his own decision was a good one, and Jake had done well by choosing the knowledge and responsibilities of being a part of the faith.

Finally, Jake decided to blow out his light. He was hoping that someday he could return to this feeling that he had experienced.

Odd, Jake thought, *I still feel all lit up, even without the flame.* Sleep then won the fight.

CHAPTER 6

In the middle of the night, Jake woke with a start. It was as though a bolt of lightning had gone through his body, and now its energies were causing his brain to work over time.

What on earth had he done? How on earth had he let himself get so caught up in the craziness of these people?

Jake could remember what it was that he had done, but for the life of him, he could not figure out why. This was some sort of a ritual, and he had become a part of it.

Victor and Sandy had all but admitted that they were of the Knowing, although they had somehow tricked him into saying it. For sure, that information would never hold up in court. It would be considered a form of entrapment without a doubt; besides that, he did not have any witnesses.

Of course, everything last night looked extra mysterious; they were in candlelight for goodness sake.

Then there was David. If not the leader, then he had to be really close to him judging from all of the attention that he had received. He must have some clout with someone from higher up.

Well, this was it; no more Mr. Nice Guy. He had a job to do, and he was going to do it.

No more of this touchy, feely, emotional stuff either. He did not need all of this sensitivity stuff before, and he sure could do without it in his future.

Well, no use crying over spilt milk. Jake was sure that he was not the only one to have been lulled in by these people. Mr. Diggings had already told him at one of their first meetings that even some of the most level-minded people had been led astray.

Well, not this man! They were never going to get to him again, never. Those thoughts and others kept running through Jake's mind, over and over and over again. It was truly hours from when Jake had awakened to when he finally fell back to sleep.

Jake woke up again, only this time he could tell that the sun was up even before he had opened his eyes. Jake was thinking that for a winter day in Washington, it sure was sunny, when he heard a voice calling his name standing right in front of him. It startled Jake; he jumped a little and opened his eyes. There standing in front of him was David. He was wearing a white apron tied around his waist. In his hand was a cup of coffee. Yes, it was a cup of real coffee from the smell of it. Jake had not seen a cup of coffee since the first day they removed his chip. Until now, he had not realized how much he had missed it. But for sure it would be accepted with great pleasure.

"Good morning, sleepyhead." David was speaking to Jake, and he had that great big "really happy to see you" look on his face.

Jake, who was now determined not to be drawn in by their goings-on, reached out and took the cup that David was holding out for him. "Thank you. Where on earth did you get coffee? I swear I could smell it in my dreams."

Taking a sip, Jake had not been wrong. Yes, it was coffee, good coffee at that. Not too strong and not too weak. Just the way he liked it.

After getting over the pleasure of having a cup of coffee, it came to Jake that it must be later in the day than he had originally thought. Everyone had cleared out. Darn, he must have slept through the all clear siren, again.

With good mornings having been said, David walked back over to the sink where it was obvious that he had been doing dishes. He must have been doing them for a long time. Out of all of the hundreds of things that need to be washed, there was only a very short stack of plates left to be done.

"David, did you do all of those dishes yourself?" Jake was thinking it odd that this obviously high-ranking leader in this group was stooping so low as to be a dishwasher, and worst of all, it was Jake's job that he was doing.

"Yep, but I do not dry." He swung his hand over to the side just enough to get dishwashing soap all over the counter.

Jake looked over to where David had pointed to see Peggy with a towel in her hand doing the drying. "Let me introduce you to my assistant." At that point, both David and Peggy laughed.

Peggy, who was still laughing a bit, spoke to Jake. "Good morning, Jake. I hope you slept well? How is the coffee? I have good news. I didn't make it." Again, David and Peggy started laughing.

What was it with these people? How was it that they were having so much fun, doing dishes—of all things? Jake had been doing dishes for days now, and he didn't see any such pleasure in it.

"Jake, are we a little grumpy this morning?"

Jake turned and looked at Peggy. "No, Peggy, I am not grumpy." *What are they, mind readers too?*

"Okay, you are not grumpy, but please do tell your face, it hasn't gotten the message of happiness yet." Laughter erupted again. Only this time a water attack broke out from David's direction, hitting Peggy right in the middle of her forehead with a splash of water.

"Peggy my girl, do leave the poor boy alone, will you? Not everyone is of good cheer so early in the afternoon."

"Afternoon!" Jake leaped up to his feet to find out what time it really was.

What David had said was true. Jake had slept the whole morning away. He must have been more tired than he thought. That could also account for his "problem" last night, being sleep deprived.

But now it was afternoon. He had slept away the morning. Someone else was doing his job. He was served coffee in his bed. And he had snapped at Peggy. Not the best way to start a day.

This was a new day. And Jake had determined with himself that he was going to stay on track from now on. He had a job to do, and he was going to do it.

The notebook that Jake was to be keeping had only one entry in it. From the first day, all Jake could really come up with were questions, but after last night, Jake was finally starting to get some answers.

First, there had been a religious meeting. That alone could do enough harm to shut down the shelter. But shutting the shelter down was not what he wanted, that was not the goal he had been sent to do. He needed to find the leader.

Second, now Jake had a new potential leader in mind. This man named David had come into first place as the possible leader. Up until now, he had only suspected Sandy and Victor. Neither of them had really met the profile of a leader. But they were the best suspects he had found, until now that was, but then looking up again at David having a water fight with Peggy and doing dishes like some kind of servant, he realized that David was not much for the profile of a leader either.

Jake decided it was time to get started with his day. He drank every last drop of coffee in the cup and walked over to the sink. "I'll wash this myself."

"Okay, young man, I will hand this job over to you." David's voice was lighthearted and sounded as though he had not a care in the world.

The door of the kitchen swung open and in walked Sandy. "Good morning, sleeping beauty, it is nice to see you up and around." Sandy patted Jake on the back as she walked past him.

"Is there any more of that coffee left?" Sandy enquired as she looked around the room. As Jake looked down at the sink full of soapy water, he saw the empty coffeepot soaking ready to be washed. Oh no, Jake had drunk the last of the coffee. Sandy should have been the one to have had that cup.

"Oh, Sandy, no there isn't any more, sorry," David called out as she was searching around.

"Oh well. Thank God. I really do need to be cutting back on that stuff." Sandy's voice was so dramatic and said with such flair that the whole room broke out in laughter.

Each went on with what needed to be done. Waiting to clean up last night's dishes in the morning was going to put getting the dinner ready for that night a little behind, but somehow, they all knew that the dinner was going to happen and that with everyone's help, it would be on time.

The rest of the day went no different than any other. The only true exception was that David was there to help. And no one could miss the happiness that seemed to be radiating from everyone at the shelter.

It was about two hours before curfew when David and Victor sought out Jake.

"Jake, can we see you for a minute?" The look on Victor's face was one of concern but not one of anger or mistrust.

Jake, without a second thought, answered, "Sure, what can I do for you?" Jake placed the last of the dishes on the counter, getting them ready for the dinner that was soon to come.

Then he walked over toward the two men and stood leaning up against the wall, trying hard to see if there were any hint in their face of what they wanted.

"Jake, what do you think about what happened last night?" David asked him straight out without any hesitation at all.

Finally, thought Jake, the whole day had gone by without any-one talking about the ritual that had gone on. Perhaps this was his opportunity to find out more information and about *who* this David really was. And then there was the other part of him that was inter-ested in someone telling him what it was that they really were doing last night. Why something so strange had made him feel so good inside. "Well. I am not sure what you are asking."

It was Victor's turn to speak. "Well, we wanted to know if you had any questions. It is not quite clear how much of a religious upbringing you have had. And, well, if you are lacking in any area, or do not understand anything, it is one of our jobs to help you out with it."

The first thoughts that came to Jacob was to note that one of their jobs is teaching. Good, that was something for him to report.

David added, "The world has gone so crazy that not everyone has had an opportunity to study the same. And, well, we want to offer you the opportunity to ask any questions if you should feel the need. Not that we are saying you do, mind you, but just asking."

Sandy was across the room from where the men were talking, and she could overhear what was being said by all three men.

Hearing how David and Victor were handling this situation was one of the reasons that Sandy so admired these men of faith. They were not overpowering but genuinely concerned. They did everything they could do to offer help, and at the same time, they were making sure that Jake's dignity was left intact.

Jake was taken aback by these two men. They cared. They truly cared not only that he knew what was going on but that he would know it correctly.

After taking a few moments to gather his thoughts, Jake decided that his keeping up appearances was too important to become a student now. If he was going to find out who the leader was at the top of this group, he needed to be more than a student at the bottom. So he decided that he should give an appearance of one who had his religious practices well in hand. "Well, I am grateful for the offer you two are making, but I can't think of anything that I need to know right yet. But I will let you know if I do."

David accepted Jake's answer as confirmation of his being on the right track.

But Victor was not so easily put off. "Jake, you realize the importance of what you are saying. This is a sacred thing we do. It is a privilege not to be taken likely. Communion is something we do as a profession of faith, and it is oh so important that you understand what it is you are saying when you do it."

Communion, so that is what they were doing. Jake had read about it in the footnotes of the Bible he had scanned. Boy, did he wish he had given more attention to that part of his preparation. For the most part, Jake had only read what had been highlighted. One thing was for sure, and that was that the man who had owned that Bible and study book had thought communion was important too. He had highlighted many pages. And yes, Jake was sure that was the stuff about the blood and the body. That part of his study alone gave Jake an uneasy feeling right from the start.

Jake hoped that he was right in what he was going to say, but he had to say something to convince these people that he was at the same level as them. "Yes, I understand. I know, the blood and body stuff, right?"

David had never heard it put so bluntly, but he agreed that yes, that was what it was all about.

With Jake's answer, Victor should have been convinced too, but something inside of him did not feel right, he did not think that it was that easy. But what could he do, test this kid on the scripture? And if he doesn't know about it, what on earth would keep him from seeking the help that they were offering? Pride perhaps. Yes, that could be it. Pride has stood in many a man's journey to walk with the Lord, and most likely Jake wasn't any different. He was young but still a man.

Regardless, Victor couldn't just leave it at that and felt compelled to say something. "Jake, all I want to say is that emotions can be cheap, but commitment is something that can really cost. Remember that, and you should do fine. Okay?"

Jake looked at Victor somewhat out of breath; he did not have the foggiest idea as to what Victor was talking about, and yet the words seemed strangely comforting. "Thank you, Victor, for caring, and you too, David."

Victor and David said their goodbyes. Sandy came from across the room and got a hug. Everyone was acting as though this was to be the last time they would see him. David did not seem concerned about anything. So Jake decided that these people were being a little overdramatic.

Now it was Jake's turn to say his farewells to David. But when he went to shake David's hand, David reached out to him and pulled him in for a hug. The thought of what a contrast this was to the time on the street when he had gone to shake Mr. Diggings's hand, the difference was drastic. The pain then, the unconditional acceptance now.

"Thank you, David, for doing my dishes—oh, and for the coffee too." With his statement, Jake expected David to let him go. But instead, David leaned to Jake's ear and whispered, "Keep the faith! And it will keep you!" Without another word, he let Jake go, turned, and picked up his things then gave a wave and a smile, and he walked right out the door.

Jake was overwhelmed to say the least. Both Victor and David had said words that he didn't even half understand, and yet somehow, they brought comfort to him. They made him feel good, kind of. Well, different anyway.

Several days had passed, and there had been no sign of David or any words spoken of him either. It was almost as if he had never been there. Things had gone back to the way it was before what Jake now called the big night. There had been no mention of God, communion, David, or anything even hinting of religion or of the Knowing. How was it that they could be religious and not talk about it?

*****

Jake was almost to his three-month drop-off, and as far as having any real information about the Knowing and its leader, he had nothing to tell. The only information he really had was that they did some kind of religious acts. He could report that, but then it would not tell them anything about finding the leader. It would not help them find the leader, just affect the lives of his new friends. Friends? Jake thought it odd that he should call these people that, and yet that was how he was beginning to feel.

If only they weren't religious fanatics. But then perhaps that was one of the things that drew Jake to them. The excitement of living on the edge. Jake looked around the room. No, that was not it. There was no excitement here. Just dishes, food, people, and more dishes.

CHAPTER 7

It seemed like forever since Victor and Sandy had found a chance to get away alone together. There were a lot of things that needed to be discussed and a lot of decision that had to be settled on and real soon. Today was to be the perfect opportunity to do so. They had plenty of extra help at the shelter, and almost everything was ready for the evening.

The weather was exceptionally warm for this time of year, so they decided that a walk to the park would be a wonderful way to have their meeting. Finding a picnic area, they found a table and bench that were perfect for a private conversation.

"Did you notice all of the new people in the shelter last night?" Sandy spoke as she raised herself up from the bench onto the table-top, giving her a better view of Victor while they were talking.

Victor had his eyes closed turning his face to the sun enjoying the warmth it gave. "I sure did, there wasn't hardly any walking room. I could hardly get to the bathroom without stepping on some-one." Victor was remembering back to the last few weeks. "You know we have been growing by a few people every day. So far we have been able to take care of everyone, but at this rate, it is just a matter of time until we won't be able to."

Sandy seized the moment. "You know, I was thinking that we should rethink the idea of sending some of the overflow off to one of the farms." Sandy knew that Victor wouldn't be very happy with that idea. Like Victor, she knew that it could come at a risk, perhaps they might be sending a government spy out to one of their farms, a well-kept and guarded secret. She was not at all surprised when she saw the look on his face.

The past had brought about many changes for many lives. A few years back, when things started getting difficult, several of the families who used to live in the town had made the decision to move to farmland on the outskirts of town. These people had chosen not to get chipped and were being bothered by the government. They decided that this was not the way they wanted to live, so while it was still possible to buy land without a chip, they did so and moved their family out of the city.

Later, these farms became additional safe havens for many. These farms accepted many of the overflow from the shelters. In addition to taking overflow, they also had become a main source of food supply for the shelters.

It was determined early on that generally families would be sent to the farms where they could live together and be safe. In turn, for being able to live on the farm, they would work. The men and young boys worked the fields and tended the animals while the women and young girls baked, canned, cooked, and did the sewing. They had set up schools for themselves and became a society of their own.

It had now become a fact that without the help from these farms that the Knowing would no longer exist.

So far, the government had not paid the farms any attention. It would have been just another area for them to patrol. But everybody knew that it was a matter of time until someone started to snoop into the fact that the shelter had a seemingly never-ending supply of food. Some of the local people were sympathetic to the cause and would supply a few things by way of what the shelters referred to as "the Gathering," but one real look at the number of people who used these shelters, and anyone could figure out that there had to be additional outside help of some sort. So keeping a low profile for both the shelters and the farms had to be a priority in the leader's mind. Too many people staying at either location could draw unwanted attention.

"Sandy, I know that you think that it is a good idea, but I think it is too big of a risk right now. As it is, the farm is starting to look like some sort of a commune. But then I really don't have any better ideas either." Victor looked up at Sandy's face expecting to see her ready for a debate, but instead she had one of her "Oh wow, I have an idea!" looks. This as a rule usually meant that Victor was going to have to do something that he really didn't want to do. "Okay, Sandy, let's hear it, what are you thinking?"

"Victor, I have an idea that would help us with the entire problem. All we need is new shelters." Sandy was looking at Victor to see if he might get the idea without having to be talked into it.

There she went again just like that, we need new shelters. Victor thought he would be used to her way of thinking by now, but no, she never ceased to amaze him. He sat there waiting to hear her out. "I know that sounds a little nuts, but I have an idea that I think would work." Sandy looked at Victor to see if he was still listening, and he was, so on she went. "Well, in the last three months, two chipless shelters have been shut down, right?"

"Yes, that's right, but what does that have to do with getting more shelters opened?" Victor was almost afraid to ask, but ready or not, here it was.

"Don't you see, the shelters are just sitting there empty? When they shut them down, no one put together a relocation plan for the people who used to live in them. All we have to do is get the word out and advertise that fact. Then when the local people hear about all of 'those people' living on their streets, they will want something done about it. The people themselves will be the ones who demand the shelters be reopened. The very fact they have already paid for the shelters to be built and that it would cost them even more to relocate the people. Well, do you see? They do the work for us." Sandy was really excited. She thought right away that it was a good idea, but it wasn't until she heard herself say it out loud she realized just how good it was. God truly got the whole credit for this idea.

Victor had to agree it was a good idea, but it had one flaw. "Sandy, are you forgetting that we no longer have our 'helper'? The last time we used him, he almost got caught, and now it is too risky for him to help us."

"Oh, is that all you are worried about? That part is easy. We can ask around, and sooner or later, someone with computer experience is bound to show up. Then we will have us a new 'helper.'" Sandy gave Victor another look. That was when she noticed a look of disbelief written all over his face. "What?"

"Well, Sandy, it is that you always look at everything as being so simple." Sandy's hand was resting on her leg. Victor laid his hand on top of hers. He spoke softly now. "I don't mean to be hard about this, but we must face facts. Some things are just out of our hands."

"Okay, Victor, here is the deal. I will do it simple, and you do it the hard way, but for now, let's ask around for a new 'helper,' and let's bring it up at the prayer meeting tonight. How does that sound to you?" Sandy kept her voice light, not wanting to get stuck on this one subject. There were too many things to go over today and too little time to do it in. Getting no answer, she asked again, "Victor, how does that sound?"

"Simple." Victor raised his hand in retreat. "But it works for me."

"Now onto another subject, what do you think about this kid Jake?" Sandy looked up at the sunlight now hitting on her back; it felt good, really good. It was warming her to the core. She shook her head getting her thoughts back on track. "You know there is something about him I don't trust. Do you know what I mean?" Sandy didn't know why she even asked the question. She already knew that Victor had a special interest in this kid. But she guessed this was the easiest way to let him know that she still wasn't sure of him.

Victor stood up, put his hands into his pockets, and kicked at a small stone in the dirt. "Well, when it comes to Jake, I have great hope. I am not sure that he really knows as much about God as he professes, but I don't think that he is up to something bad. I rather think it is more of a pride thing. And you know, I have confidence that with a little more time, he will open up and own up to the fact that he's just not as trained in Bible teachings as he lets on."

Sandy and Victor rarely argued, they would often disagree but almost never argued. Except that is when it came to this kid Jake. The night of communion when she had not wanted Jake to be a part of the service, Victor had overruled her. Up until that night, Victor had never done that before.

Then again Sandy decided that she didn't really have any real evidence to support her feelings of distrust. So for now, as not to cause any more tension about this, she decided that her telling him how she felt would perhaps be enough. "Victor, I know that you trust this kid, but all I am saying is that perhaps we might want to keep him out of some of the major details of our program."

"Sandy, I don't think that would help him to feel he is a part of us. Do you? I think that he needs to feel a part of us so that he can begin to trust us."

Sandy didn't have any proof but only a feeling that something was wrong when it came to Jake. For now, she had done what she could to warn Victor. "I know that what you are saying is true, but could we be careful at least? Please?"

Victor looked at Sandy, and he knew her enough to know when she was serious about something, and this was one of those times. He still felt that she was wrong, but he also knew that she usually had good instincts. Usually. "Okay, Sandy, I will tell you what. I will make him as much a part of everything as I can, but I will be careful not to let him in on the major details of who or where. Okay?"

Sandy conceded but added in, "And not about the rabbit holes either?"

Victor smiled. "All right, not about the rabbit holes either."

It felt good to Sandy to have that conversation over with. She did not want to question Victor about his thoughts on Jake, but she couldn't ignore her own inner feelings either. This was a great compromise, definitely one she felt good about. "Now that we have that over with, I was wondering who you are planning on bringing to the asking tonight." Sandy had stood up and joined Victor slowly walking back to the shelter. They did not need words. They were close friends and worked well that way.

Now that Victor knew how Sandy felt about Jake, it was going to be hard to explain it to her, but he wanted his choice tonight to be Jake. "Well, Sandy, I had planned on asking Jake. I think it would be good for him to see how it is we go to God for our needs. I am sure that he had never had communion before, I would stake my life on it, even though he said otherwise. I think that he could use the experience of seeing how an asking goes. And not to worry, I will see to it that he will not know where it is we are having it."

Sandy wasn't sure how it was that Victor was going to pull that off, but if anyone could get someone, somewhere without them knowing where they were, it would be Victor.

Sandy could see from the look on Victor's face how important he thought it was. "Well, I guess if you are going to take Jake, I think it would be a good idea for me to ask Peggy. After all, she is one of the only true friends that Jake has made here."

"Yes, I know what you mean. Jake hasn't let her out of his sight since the communion night." Victor leaned into Sandy and gently kissed her on the cheek. "Thanks, Sandy." Victor truly was grateful to have a friend like Sandy. They could agree to disagree and still be friends. In Victor's past, he had people that he considered friends, a lot of them, but somehow Sandy was one of the best he had ever known.

"No problem." Sandy still felt uneasy about Jake but was feeling better just knowing that Victor was aware of her thoughts on the matter.

Victor and Sandy verbally decided that they should get back now, but they agreed that they would take the long way back and enjoy as much of the sun as they could. This had been a great meeting, and the rest of the day was going to prove interesting as well. But for now, they had this moment of peace and wanted to enjoy every single minute of it they could get.

While Victor and Sandy were having their meeting, the only people left at the shelter were Jake and Peggy. All the other workers decided, like Victor and Sandy, that they had to take a break. Everything was ready to go, and the weather was so good.

Jake had not let Peggy out of his sight all day long, and if things went as planned, it was just a matter of time until she would guide him to the leader. "Hey, Peggy, I have a great idea. As soon as someone comes to relieve us, let's get out of here for a while. What do you think?"

Peggy was checking everything over one last time. "That sounds great, Jake, but what do you want to do?"

Now this was Jake's chance. "Well, do you have any errands you need to do or anyone that you want to visit?"

Peggy stopped and looked up into the air for what seemed an eternity to Jake. "No, I can't think of a single thing I need to do. So why don't you choose."

"Okay." Jake was thinking to himself. That did not work. "I have it, Peggy. Why don't we go and thank that man for your new boots? What do you think?"

Peggy was giving Jake one of her funny "like I haven't a clue as to what you are talking about" looks. "Peggy, you do know how to get in touch with him, don't you?"

"Jake, you are so funny. You know that I already have."

"Have what?"

"Have thanked him."

Jake was lost in this conversation. He knew that there was no way that she could have thanked him. Jake had been with her every single moment since the day she had received the boots. "Really, Peggy, I am serious. We really should go and thank him properly."

Peggy's eyes teared up. She walked over to where Jake was standing and gave him a hug. "Jake, you are so sweet. I can't believe you."

"What?" Jake asked, perhaps a little louder than he should, but he has had other conversations like this with Peggy where he didn't understand her, but in this one, he absolutely needed to know what she was talking about. "There is no way you told him thank-you, Peggy. I have been with you all the time. And at no time have you left to do so." Jake's voice was steady but definitely irritated. *Great,* he thought to himself, *now why don't you tell her that you are spying on her?*

"Oh, Jake, that's so sweet. You want to thank him again, don't you?" Peggy clasped her hands together and made such a happy type of reaction.

Jake was getting so frustrated that he was running his hands through his curly hair, slightly tugging at his curls. "Now, Peggy, let's take this slow, okay? What do you mean, I want to thank him *again?*" Jake was speaking very slowly. One word at a time, and very exactly.

Sandy and Victor walked in totally unnoticed. Sandy had heard Jake's last words and could hear and see the frustration radiating out of him. She knew that look because she herself had conversations with Peggy that brought her to that very same level of frustration.

"Hi, guys, what's going on?" Sandy walked over to Jake and laid one hand on his shoulder hoping to help relieve some of his tension.

Peggy was the first to speak up. "Jake here is so sweet. Do you know what he wants to do with some of his only time off in a long time?"

Oh no. Jake's head was spinning. What if she told them that he had asked to go and see the leader? That could be trouble. "Peggy, it was no big deal." Turning to Sandy and Victor, Jake asked, "How was your walk?" Perhaps, if he could change the subject.

Everyone was ready to change the subject. Except Peggy, that was.

Victor started to speak. "Oh, great, the weather out there is—"

Peggy interrupted, "Don't you want to know what wonderful Jake here wanted to do with his time off?"

Jake, Victor, and Sandy all stopped and simply looked at Peggy. She didn't wait for anyone to answer yes or no. But just blurted it out. "Jake wanted to pray again."

At those words, Jake jumped. Sandy, still having her hand resting on Jake's shoulder, noted his extreme response to being accused of praying.

Jake's head was screaming. What was it with this crazy girl that she always thinks that he is praying or wanting to pray? Who mentioned prayer anyway? He hadn't heard that word, not even once.

Sandy, noticing Jake's reaction, thought it was Peggy's choice of the word *prayer* and chimed in, "Wanted to be in the asking. Remember, Peggy?"

"Oh, yes, that's it. He wanted to be in the asking." Peggy was overflowing with joy. "About my boots again. Isn't that just so sweet?"

Victor, teasing Jake, looked over to Jake. "Yes, isn't that just sweet."

Sandy, thinking that this was as good of a time as any, decided now to ask Peggy to go to the asking with her. "Peggy, would you like to go to the asking with me tonight?"

"Oh, Sandy. That would be great. Thank you." Peggy was excited and could hardly stand still.

"Okay then, we will go together. But for now, let's get to work, okay?"

Victor, seeing that this was his cue, asked, "And, Jake, would you like to go as my guest?"

Jake wasn't sure just what he was saying yes to, but if it got them off the subject of him praying, then it would be great. "Yeah sure, why not? Where do we go?"

"I'll come by and pick you up right before curfew. Okay?"

Jake thought that was about the nuttiest thing he had heard since he had moved here. "I'll pick you up right before curfew." Why, was he nuts leaving around curfew?

Victor could see that Jake was trying to figure the curfew part out. "Don't worry, we will be off the streets before the sirens go off. It will be okay."

"Yeah. Great. I'll see you later then." Jake was not too sure of what Victor was up to, but then there was really no other way but to trust him.

"Okay then, later." Victor turned to walk away. "Oh, and, Jake."

"Yes?" Jake was looking at Victor now.

"Don't worry so much, okay?" With that he gave a confident smile to Jake and a nod to Peggy. Then telling Sandy he had some things to do, Victor left.

As Victor walked out the door of the shelter, Sandy could not help but notice how different she felt about things when he was not around. Perhaps this is what it is like having a big brother. Victor somehow always made her feel surer of herself. She did fine on her own, but she felt better with him here. What a strange thought to be going through her mind. Why now of all the insane times would she develop a needing of a man in her life? Dismissing that thought as another one of the craziest she had ever had, Sandy decided it was time to get started on the last-minute things to be done for the night.

Besides, if things went as planned, in a few short hours, she would be seeing Victor again.

*****

Everything was ready for the evening meal, even the group that was to take over the cleanup for the night was on the job. All they needed to get on with the night was for Victor to show up at the shelter. But to Jake's puzzlement, Sandy and Peggy got their things and started heading out the door. Jake took their lead and started to go out with them. At seeing this, both Peggy and Sandy stopped. Peggy giggled. Sandy spoke, "No, Jake, you need to wait here for Victor to come. He will be bringing you."

"But, Sandy, why don't I go with you, and we could save Victor a trip." Jake was confused now, especially since Peggy was still finding this whole thing so funny. Turning to her, he said, "Peggy, I don't see what is so funny?"

"Oh, Jake, it is you. You really do not know anything about how things go, do you?" Peggy was feeling kind of glad now. She was usually the one that was getting told how it was and was not to be. For the longest time, it seemed to her that she was the only one who didn't know how things were run around here. She was more than happy to give up her status as learner and was oh so happy to become a teacher to Jake. "Jake, don't get so mad at not knowing things. It will just take time for you to get it all." Peggy leaned into Jake and gave him a quick little hug, pulled away, and headed off in the direction she had originally been going.

Sandy walked over to the door. She and Peggy were still getting ready to leave and without Jake. "Jake, wait here until you see Victor, okay?"

"Sandy, I still think that it would be better if I went with you. It is late, and what if Victor does not come in time?" Jake's voice was giving off a little nervous anger.

"Jake, Peggy is right. I do wish that you didn't get so upset every time you do not know what is going on. Just ask when you don't know, and someone will be glad to help you out."

104

"Okay. So, I am asking, what do I do if Victor doesn't come?" Jake was totally frustrated with this whole evening. He needed to get to this meeting, and it had to be tonight. His official report was due in two days, and he needed something of value to put into it. All his instincts were telling him that this was his chance, and if these two left without him, perhaps his last chance was going to slip away with them.

Sandy stopped again. She turned and walked up to where Jake was standing. With her face merely inches away from his, she looked him straight in the eye. "Jake. Victor said that he would come for you, and if there is one thing I know for sure. If Victor said he would come, he will be here. Do you understand? You do not have to doubt anything that Victor tells you. If he said it and it is in his power, he will come through. Now wait here for Victor, okay." With those words said, Sandy and Peggy pulled up their coat collars and continued out the door. Jake stood there. A blast of cold air hit him, which made him realized that he needed to be doing something other than standing there looking at the door. Although the day had been an extra beautiful one, the night without its usual cloud cover had become an extra cold one. As it sometimes is in the northwest, the days rarely give any hint to the kind of weather the night will bring. Any more than the goings-on of these people could give you any idea of what has happened in the past or of what was to come in the future. Jake truly had not a hint of how to read these people, and not wanting to look any more overanxious than he had already done, began to go over the setup for the night. The fifteen-minute siren was beginning to sound, and still no sign of Victor. People were coming in the front door now and were beginning to settle in for the night. Jake was standing behind the counter keeping watch as each person filtered in through the door. Sandy had said that if it were in his power, then Victor would come. Perhaps this was not going to be in his power. Most likely he had gotten caught up somewhere and forgot about picking him up. As Jake kept his eyes on the door, a large hand came down heavy on Jake's right shoulder. "Are you ready to go?"

Jake swung around, and there standing right next to him was Victor. Jake's heart was beating fast. "Victor, you like to have scared me to death. Where in the world did you come from?"

"Jake, didn't you remember that I was to pick you up?" Victor was the one who was confused now. He thought that Jake wanted to go. That was what Sandy had told him only a few seconds ago.

"Yes, of course I remember. I just did not see you come in. How on earth did you get into the shelter?" Jake had been watching the door and knew for a fact that Victor had not entered the shelter form that direction. But then that did not make any sense either since there was no back door to this place.

"That doesn't matter now, we had better get going if we are going to get there in time." Victor motioned for Jake to follow him out through the door.

Jake was noting the time. "Victor, are you sure? There is not a lot of time until the last siren is to go off?"

"Jake, trust me, will you? We have plenty of time. Now let's go." With that he headed out of the door with Jake following close behind. As they were walking down the sidewalk, they continually picked up speed until they were at a steady jog. They had gone along about three blocks or so when three other men joined them, one on each side of Jake. Victor was directly in front of him, and then the last man joined in right behind him. This formation somehow seemed familiar to Jake, but for the life of him, he couldn't recall. Then all at once, it came to him. His first day on the street. This setup was much the same, only this time, instead of Victor being left all alone on the street, he was the leader of the group. Down the street and around the corner and to the very same dead-end street where he had last time lost the three strangers. But not this time, this time he would be on his guard. Perhaps they had found him out, and they were going to leave him stranded on the street after curfew. What a fool he had been. How could he have trusted Victor? He had a choice not to leave the shelter so close to curfew. What had happened to his common sense? Well, he would have to deal with this mess he had made for himself. Perhaps he could at least find out who these three men are before he lost them to who knows where. Last time they just seemed to disappear, but not this time. He would be watching for them to do their disappearing act. As Jake's thoughts were coming to this conclusion, Jake, Victor, and the three other men had come to that very same dead-end wall in the alley. Now what? Victor and Jake were standing side by side; both had turned and were now facing the three men. Victor definitely knew these three. He was looking at each to see if they were ready. Jake could see it in their eyes. But ready for what? That very second the final siren was beginning to sound. Jake looked up to where the sound seemed to be coming from and then was looking over toward Victor to somehow seek reassurance of what to do. Being caught out after curfew was the very last thing Jake wanted to have happen. Even if he were found by Mr. Diggings, it could mean at least three months of being in prison or, worse, until things got straightened out. Not to mention that his assignment would be over. Not only without success but with total failure.

Victor also hearing the siren, noted the look of concern in Jake's eyes. This was going to be a hard thing to do to Jake, but it was necessary in order to keep everyone safe. Jake trusted him. He was questioning him at this moment with his eyes, but he had trusted him enough to risk going out so close to curfew. Victor was sure that someday Jake would understand the precautions that they are now having to take. Even if it did mean alarming Jake at this very moment. The blasted siren wasn't going to keep sounding forever, although at this time, it seemed as though it might. Jake was just about to say something to Victor when all at once one of the three men shoved Jake by the back of his head face-first in Victor's direction. Victor, now taking this as his signal to make his move, grabbed the collar of Jake's coat and lifted it up over Jake's head in such a way so that his vision was now obstructed. As the coat was lifted halfway over his head, Jake's arms were naturally lifted as the arms of the coat also moved up. Another shove should have found Jake face-first into the wall that had been behind him, but to his relief, he was instead caught by several hands who helped him to regain his balance. The sound of movement and Victor's voice were the only things that Jake heard. "Okay. We are here." But Jake noted that several sets of hands were still on him. One at a time they each let him go. Victor let the collar of his jacket go, and immediately Jake came out fighting. Nothing in this world made Jake madder than being out of control. And this whole thing was totally out of control as far as Jake was concerned. At this moment, Jake was unable to contain his feelings of rage where these people were concerned. He had trusted them, and now to be pushed around and treated like—well, like an outsider.

At once Jake went to address Victor's actions. "Just what do you think you are doing? Do you think that this is funny?" But Jake was brought up short as soon as he saw that he had disappeared right off the street along with all of the others. He was now standing on the outside edge of a room. The room wasn't very big. It had no doors or windows. No, that couldn't be right. Making another quick survey of the room, he again confirmed that there were no entrances or exits. But how? There was little or no ventilation, so there was a real thick musty odor, not like anything Jake could remember smelling before. Jake wasn't sure what was in the air. At first he suspected smoke, but on second evaluation, it was more like dust. The only light that was in the room came from a small lightbulb hanging from a wire in the middle of the ceiling. There was a single string hanging from the bulb. Jake could tell that the light had just been turned on, the bulb and string were still swinging from its position over the people. And then there were the people. A whole lot of people all crammed into this very smelly, poorly lit, and poorly ventilated room. What on earth were they all doing here? And how the blazes did they all get here? For that matter, how the blazes had he gotten here? Jake noted that several people were watching to see what it was he was going to do now that he was off the street. Now that he was safe from being caught out after curfew. Jake also noted that it was very silent. All these people. At least sixty or so and not a single sound was heard. Except for Jake's voice and heavy breathing that was. Jake stood there. He was still shaking from being so angry, he thought that he might kill or at least do some harm to someone, but to whom? The people who just saved him from being arrested? Then on the other hand, he wouldn't have been in that position in the first place if it had not been for them. Then Jake heard a voice.

"Jake. Over here."

It was a voice that Jake was glad to hear; somehow it could bring balance to things in an unbalanced sort of way. It was Peggy's voice. Jake sought out the sound and at once began to follow it with his eyes to where he finally saw her. Peggy was standing there with her usual smile that she always seemed to be wearing even in the strangest of situations.

"Oh, Jake, isn't this so exciting? Come on in, it is just about ready to start."

Jake was on another emotional roller coaster. In his whole life, Jake had never encountered anything like the things he had during these last three months.

Here he was a stable man, from a good family, with a wonderful life and upbringing. He wanted for absolutely nothing. He had love, lots of it. And as far as material things, there was almost nothing that with a little effort he couldn't manage to get his hands on. He had often been hot tempered, but never had he been overemotional like this. What was it that was bringing out the worst in him? Why was he acting like such a fool these days? Perhaps he was so used to the environment he was brought up in that he was not a good candidate to go undercover. He seemed to lose his judgment so easily with these people. First, he felt a sense of belonging then of distrust. Then duty would call. Then friendship would win out. Jake had friends all of his life, but then again, he could never really be sure of why they were his friends. Was it because they liked him, or was it because of who he was? He could never know for sure. But these people were his friends, and so far as they knew he had nothing and he was no one. What was it that they wanted from him? Then again, what was it that he wanted from them? At first, all he wanted was information on them to shut them down. But now he really wanted to belong. Not be snuck in like some kind of thief. He wanted to be trusted. Perhaps this was the reality jerk that he needed. Something to set his mind back on track. These people never were going to totally trust him. For the first time since he had met them, this was probably one of the smartest things they had done so far as safety was concerned. But why did it have to be with him? Was there something different about him that would always keep him out, or was it just by chance that they chose to leave him out? Well, he was never going to know because from now on, he was going to do the job that he had been sent to do. If they think that making a fool of him was the end, then they had another thing coming to them. In two days, Jake was to drop off his first report, and with tonight's goings-on, he would have wonderful things to write about.

Jake did not move over toward where Peggy was standing, but instead, Peggy moved over toward him. Following close behind her was Sandy. This was the first time Jake had noticed her. Sandy hurried around going past Peggy so that it was she who reached Jake first. Sandy noticed Victor standing directly behind Jake. The look on Victor's face was one of regret. Both Sandy and Victor could see from the way that Jake was acting that they had taken a huge step backward where trust was concerned. Jake had lost any trust that had been won by them. Sandy knew that she must try and explain. "Jake, I am sorry if we hurt your feelings about not trusting you to know where this meeting is taking place. Please don't blame Victor. This is standard treatment for all newcomers. It is to help protect all of us. You can understand that, can't you?"

Jake knew that what she was saying might be true, but then again it might not. But none of that mattered now. He was here to do a job, and that was all that mattered. "Oh, Sandy, don't worry, it was that you caught me off guard. I understand now. I thought you were playing a trick on me or something. I don't like being tricked very much, okay?"

Victor could hear the words coming out of Jake's mouth, but he didn't think the look on his face was telling the same story. "You know, Jake, we can understand if you are mad at us. We can handle it, you know. Friendship is much deeper than ending it because someone got mad at you or you got mad at them."

"Victor, I said that I understand. Now let's just drop it, okay?" Jake wanted to not think about this anymore. He might decide that they were really his friends again, and that would interfere with his job. For now he just wanted to stay mad at them. But now he really needed them to think he was not angry. Jake turned and smiled really big at Peggy. "Besides, there is something exciting going to happen, right, Peggy?"

Peggy was excited now to be a part of this conversation. Up to this point, she was trying to figure out what Jake had to be mad about. When she had first moved here, no one told her about some stuff, and that didn't make her mad. But none of that mattered now. Jake was right, there was something real good getting ready to start, and she—no, *they* were going to get to be a part of it.

Victor and Sandy both knew that things with Jake were not truly worked out, but if he did not want to make it better, there was nothing they could do about it. It was up to him to be honest about how he felt. So for now, things would have to stay where they were. Perhaps in time, Jake would better understand what had happened and why.

Peggy noticed that Jake was holding his arms tight around his body trying hard to make his coat be enough to keep him warm. Yes, the day had been beautiful with its clear skies, but this night's temperatures were going to hit an all-time low. "Jake, I think that you need a better coat. That old thing does not keep you very warm, does it?" Peggy was often one to note the obvious and then to bring it to people's attention. "Jake, I have an idea, why not ask for one at the asking tonight? Remember how it worked for my boots?"

How crazy that sounded to Jake. Peggy thinks that God gave her the boots. That was what she has been talking about. This was what her thanking and praying conversations were all about. Peggy had asked God to get her boots, and she thinks that He did. What a foolish thing for her to think. How could she not know that it was someone else? Someone real that had done the giving. Jake was looking around now. Looking at all these people. He was wondering if all these people felt that this God of theirs could and would actually give them things. And this meeting was called? Yes, that's right, the "asking." Is that what they were all here to do? Were they here to ask God for favors? How crazy, how totally insane of them, if that was what this was all about. Didn't they know that if there were a God that he would be much too busy to be caring about their little everyday problems? To bring things like coats and boots to them. Why, that was just the craziest thing that he had ever heard of.

Victor looked over at Jake realizing for the first time that Peggy was right. Jake always had his arms crossed in front of himself. Victor had thought it a habit or being insecure, but no, Jake's coat was truly not nearly warm enough. "You know, Jake, that might not be a bad idea. You really could use another coat or at the very least a sweater."

Sandy was going over inventory in her mind, and no, she couldn't recall any coats left in the clothing bank back at the shelter. She could work on that idea tomorrow. But for now, it wouldn't hurt to bring it up. "What do you think, Jake?"

What did he think? Well, if they really wanted to know what he thought. No. If they really wanted to know what it was he knew for sure, it would be that these people were truly nuts. And this, along with all the other things he had seen, proved it. Three sets of eyes were on Jake now waiting for an answer. Jake had not a clue as to what to say. As Jake was about to speak, the lights in the room went out. Jake could hear the click of the light as someone had pulled on the string. Then he could hear a sliding sort of sound, and then a blast of colder air, and then the lights had come back on. There it had happened again just like it had happened back at the shelter. Lights out, cold air, lights on, and more people were in the room.

Jake couldn't stand it any longer; he had to know. "Victor, why do they keep turning out the lights when they open the doors? What does it mean?"

Victor was happy that Jake would think to open up and finally ask a question. "Well, it is an easy answer. We turn out the lights when people come and go so that the light shining out of the entry-way doesn't give us away. It is a safety precaution. So as not to draw any unwanted attention to the area. Do you understand?"

Of course. It was clear to Jake now. How was it that he had not seen it for himself? What a strange response Jake had received from Victor, almost one of relief. Jake had tried hard not to ask any questions in fear of giving himself away, but somehow his asking a question brought out a different response. One of almost comfort about him wanting to know. This was all so very strange, but Jake could feel that he was finally getting somewhere. "Thanks, Victor, I can see that now. How very smart."

The lights went out and then back on again. Only this time there was only one new arrival, and it was David. Jake had not seen or heard of him since the last time they were together at the communion service. But now here he was. Once again the room came alive with the mumblings of excitement. And again, it was David who brought on this response.

Victor noticed David's entrance, walked over, and exchanged their usual greeting, one of a handshake and half hug. Sandy was close behind with her usual greeting also. Now the room seemed to be settling in for whatever it was that was going to be happening. Jake was a little nervous but was sure that no one could tell because everyone thought that he was cold. And that was fine with him.

David and Victor walked to the middle of the room. Everyone gathered in a circle around the two of them. There was about a three-foot space left open all around the two in the center. Tonight there were no candles. Jake was relieved at that, he was not sure that there was really enough air for the people, so if they were to add candles, the smoke would have been unbearable. Besides, Jake was going to need every ounce of light so he could see enough to make out the people who needed to be placed in his report.

One thing was for sure, David was some sort of a leader. Of the two big events that Jake had been to, David was there, and things did not get started until he arrived.

As David took off his hat and gloves, he called the room to attention. "Ladies and gentlemen, I would like to thank you and welcome you to our asking tonight. I would like to keep this meeting very simple. We have a lot to go over, but I really do think that we should begin tonight with a testimony of thanks. Is there anyone here tonight that would like to start us off?"

There were a few minutes of quiet, and then it was Sandy standing next to Jake who was the first to speak out. "Yes, I would like to give thanks tonight for a government officer who was at the shelter over on Front Street a few weeks ago. I am not sure who he was. *Officer Hansen* was on his name tag. He helped us out and literally kept us from being shut down. I give both praise for him and also ask that prayer be given up for him to be kept safe from all harm."

As soon as Sandy was finished, one voice after another spoke up, each bringing up things that they thought that their God had done for them. From what Jake was hearing, these people thought that God had a part in even the simplest of matters. One man was thankful that his child was able to go away to a farm to live. What craziness. He was thanking God for sending his son away. One by one almost every man and woman had one thing or another to be thankful for. Someone even was thankful to God for the weather. This amazed Jake how very detailed these people thought their God was. Then Jake heard Peggy's voice. He thought for sure that she was going to talk about her boots, but now instead, he heard her say that she was thankful for her new friend Jake, for all of the help that he had brought to the shelter, and then she added how wonderful it was that he made her laugh. She added the fact that after all of the hard times she once had that she was now able to laugh again. Those were her exact words. "After all of the hard times she once had." Peggy had never once mentioned hard times to Jake. Why, as far as Jake was concerned, the only problem Peggy ever had was being poor and homeless. Although she never complained of that either. *Wow*, Jake thought, *these people even thanked their God for him.* The man who was just about to help shut them down.

But it was Victor himself who supplied the exact words Jake needed to hear. "I would like to thank God for the survival of the Knowing and for the safety of the people involved in it. It is truly an act of God that we have gotten this far, and it is only with His help that I know that we will continue to do our work."

There it was like a news flash. Confirmation of this being a part of the Knowing and that these people themselves were members.

There were other things brought up as well. How the rabbit holes and the farms had been kept from the government. That was two other areas that Jake would have to get into before this whole thing was over. Now he was feeling like his old self. Back on track using his instincts like he was supposed to do while undercover. Not doing dishes like some crazy kid.

The room had gone silent. David again spoke as the leader. "Now that we have done that. Let's each of us take this time to search our hearts for anything that needs to be dealt with before we go on to the asking." The room remained silent. Jake could hear a few mur-murings but nothing that he could make out. Almost everyone's head was bowed. A few were facing up to the ceiling, but their eyes were closed. Jake was watching. He was trying hard not to miss a thing. As his eyes scanned back and forth across the room, he couldn't help but feel uneasy. It was almost as though someone were watching him. He turned his eyes to his left, followed by his head, and then his whole body, and within seconds, his eyes locked onto another set of eyes, Sandy's. It was as though she could see right into his thoughts. It made him feel so uncomfortable that he thought his skin was going to crawl right off his bones and then find a place to hide. There was no looking away she had caught him analyzing everything in his head.

There it was, that look. Sandy was looking Jake straight in the face, and she could see it. No, she could feel it. He was not just learning about them, but he was investigating what it was they were doing. At this very moment, Sandy thought Jake looked more like an officer than he did a kid. She had seen a glimpse of this look in his eyes before, but it was never there long enough for her to be sure, but she was sure now, and she felt more confident than ever of her distrust in him. There was nothing that she could do now. If she were right and he was the undercover officer, then they were all in deep trouble; and if she is not right, then there is something very wrong with this young man. The same problem she had before was still with her. She had no real proof of her distrust in him. Truly, she really did like Jake, but all the same, she didn't fully trust him. Her feelings alone were not enough to make a move right now. She decided that there was nothing she could do except keep an eye on Jake and pray. What better place to pray than at a prayer meeting. Sandy wasn't sure if Jake had noted her evaluation of him, but she had a suspicion that he had. There was no need in trying to cover up the fact that she didn't trust him any longer. She would just wait, be careful, pray, and hope that she was wrong. With that decided, Sandy lowered her head and began to pray her heart out.

Jake wasn't sure of what Sandy was thinking, but he was sure of one thing, and that was that she didn't trust him completely. She was one he needed to be really careful around. She was easy to like, and he could fall into the trap of not wanting to disappoint her again.

Perhaps he should put in his report that she should be picked up and arrested so that she couldn't hinder his investigation any further. That was something he would have to think over. He didn't want her hurt, but possibly he needed to get her out of his way until he was able to finish his job.

David's voice brought Jake's mind back to the matter at hand. Breaking the silence. "Now with a clear heart and mind, let us now go onto the asking." David's voice was clear and steady. He truly believed in what it was he was doing. His confidence alone could make anyone want to be a part of this God of theirs. There was a peace about him. He was sure of what it was that he was doing. David was sure in what he was believing in. It was a fact that these people took what they believed very serious.

Now, once again the people started speaking. Each taking his or her turn asking of their God things that they felt needed to be done. One asked for a shelter for his family where they could all be together. Some prayed for the weather to be good. They asked for food, clothing, peace, good health, and a new job market for the chipless. One person, Jake couldn't tell who it was, said that the doctor was in the asking for a shipment of medicine. Odd, thought Jake, he would have never expected a doctor to be of the Knowing. With his education, you would have thought he could have made a better choice. They asked for protection for all who were involved in the Knowing movement and for those who were sympathetic to their cause. But then the most unusual prayer of all was lifted up by one of the three men who had helped Jake into the meeting place. If you wanted to call it that. He asked for the government, the officers, and their families to be lifted up by God. That they be able to find peace and that if there were any way that they could begin to know the truth that it would happen soon. Jake could hardly believe his ears these people were praying for the very people who were opposing them. The more he got to know these people, the stranger they seemed. It truly was a miracle that the Knowing was still in existence with the attitude that they were having toward their enemy. They seemed to have no fighting spirit at all, and yet even if they were not winning the war, they were still in the battle, to say the least. It seemed amazing that these people had avoided the government all this time. They just did not seem careful enough, and yet what they were doing was working.

Jake continued to listen to their petitions one by one. Each request was brought up with such ease. You would have thought that they were ordering at a restaurant. When the room had gone silent again, each having spoken his or her mind. There was a brief time of silence. Jake thought to himself half in jest and again half in testing, *Oh yes, and while You are at it, how about a warmer used coat?* Jake would never have asked for a new coat, not even their God could pull that one off. And truth be known, he never really expected to even get an answer, but then again just in case. It was rather cold, and a warmer coat would be nice. With that done, Jake stood there looking down at the ground almost afraid to look up just in case Sandy was still staring at him. She could make him feel so uncomfortable.

David again took the lead. This time it was in a prayer itself. "Dear Lord our God. Thank You so very much for all that You do for us. Please know that we want only Your will to be done in all of these matters, and we honor Your judgment in all of our petitions. May Your will be done. With glory, honor, and praise to You. We thank You. We love You. Amen." With that last word, the entire room said, "Amen." The silence again flooded the room. No one moved. It was as if there was one more thing left to do, but for the life of himself, Jake couldn't figure it out. As Jake was standing there waiting for something, anything to happen, he felt a small hand slip itself up past his folded arm and then into his hand. As he turned to look to see whose hand it was, he found that it belonged to his newfound friend Peggy. She was quiet, at total peace. She simply smiled up at him hoping that this action would be okay with Jake.

Jake's heart started beating. How very soft her hand was. Funny how until now he had never really noticed how very small her features were. Her whole build was small. Jake's build had always been on the smaller side for a man, but next to Peggy, he was huge. His whole hand engulfed hers when he held it. He felt that he needed to be extra careful so as not to hurt her. It felt good to touch her hand. This was a thought he hadn't allowed himself to think of until now. After all, he was here to do a job, not find a wife. Woah. There he went again jumping way too far ahead. He had now gone from holding hands to being married. How strange his thoughts had been lately. But not anymore. He was back on track, and back on track he was going to stay. Perhaps after this whole thing is over and everyone realized that what he was doing was for the best, then he and Peggy might have a chance to pursue a much different avenue other than just being friends. But for now, that was all he could afford to get into. Friendship was to be the safest way to stay for now.

As if a signal had gone off, people started to break up into small groups, visiting with each other. Jake could see that some of the people had not seen each other for some time and were happy to be reunited with old friends. While others seemed to have business to take care of.

Peggy was now looking over at Victor and Sandy. "Sandy, are you and Victor going to stay here tonight?"

Jake was still holding Peggy's hand, and he could see that this was making Sandy somewhat uncomfortable. "Yes. Hey, Victor, are we going to be staying here? Or should I look forward to being pushed through a wall again?" Jake was still upset about that matter, but he was trying hard to make a joke about it.

Victor realized what he was trying to do and decided to play along. "No, Jake, I thought we would try the floor next time. What do you think? Should we live on the wild side?"

Sandy was in no laughing mood, and she needed to have some time alone to think through what she had decided about Jake. This was not the time or the place to do anything about it. Anyway, she needed to be with Victor alone in order to tell him what it was that she was thinking. Remembering the schedule ahead, that might be some time away. All she could do was hope that Victor would stick to his word and not let Jake in on any more secrets than he had to. "You know, Victor, I am really tired, perhaps we should stay here tonight. What do you think?"

"Okay, Sandy, that would be great. I am not in much of a mood to go out into this cold. Besides, there are a few things I can take care of while we are here." With that, Victor headed off into another corner where he met up with several other people. Most of whom Jake hadn't ever met. Jake thought that one or maybe even two of them had been to the shelter, but he did not have any names to put to the faces. As Jake was watching Victor, he realized that he was still holding onto Peggy's hand. As he looked down to see what it was she was doing, he found that she had laid her head slightly onto his shoulder and was looking as though she were almost asleep. It had been a long day, and it must be well into the night. With that thought in mind, Jake pulled ever so softly on Peggy's hand, giving her a signal for her to follow him over to an area of the room where they could find space on the floor in order to sleep for the night. Jake was the first to sit down, and Peggy took her place by his side. Jake was sitting upright with his back against the wall, and Peggy sat beside him and leaned herself into his chest. "Jake, this will be a good way for us to sleep. This way I can help to keep you warm."

All Jake could do was to agree with the idea of keeping warm, but he couldn't help but be a little disappointed that keeping him warm was the reason she was being so close to him. Perhaps this was for the best anyway. Jake was not sleepy, or at least he didn't think he was. He kept his eyes on the goings-on in the room. Jake kept a special eye on David and Victor both. Making special note of all of the people who he recognized. Although he couldn't hear anything they were talking about, he knew from the way that they looked that it was all serious stuff. Without even realizing it, Jake began to doze off, and in no time at all, both Jake and Peggy were fast asleep.

As the night began to wear on, more and more people found what little space there was to sleep in and called it a night. All but three people were left awake, and they were gathered in one of the corners of the room. They had turned out the only light and had lit a candle in order to see by.

All three of the men were seated on the ground with their backs facing the middle of the room. The lit candle was up against the wall, so the light from the flame cast their shadows out onto the rest of the room. Jake stirred and then realized with a start that he had fallen asleep. As he opened his eyes, he could see the three men, or at least the backs of them. One was Victor, and one was David, but the third was someone he couldn't quite make out. Even if he was someone he had met, he could not make him out from where he was seated. They were all three sitting now with their heads bowed down. Jake now knew that what they were doing was praying. The room was quiet now, and Jake could make out most of what was being said. The men were asking for guidance in their leadership. They needed a clear sign of what it was that they were to do. Things were getting harder and had become more dangerous, and they needed answers as what to do next. Jake thought that this was an odd thing for leaders to do. If one of them was the leader, why didn't he just make a decision and get on with it? Jake was sure that this must be the head leader of the Knowing group. Even if he didn't have his name or really anything to base his decision on, this was to be the man Jake would call the leader of the Knowing in his report due in a few days. This was good. Really good. Jake could finish up his job with a success and not even endanger his new friends Victor and David. Of course, there would be some fallout from all of this, but at least they were not the head leader with crimes against the government. Who knew, perhaps when all of this is over, they could all still remain friends. *Now enough of that. I must have a name.* Jake listened very closely. He was trying so hard to hear that he even wished his breathing would stop so he wouldn't risk missing even one little piece of evidence. Well, their prayer went on and on. First with praise then with more questions and even a few quiet times thrown in. But finally, this prayer time came to an end. How strange it was for Jake to see three such strong and obviously intelligent men going onto their knees in order to speak to this God of theirs. It was just so very odd. Perhaps if they were not so strong, it could have been more acceptable, but with these three, it just didn't seem to fit. The three now stood from their crouched position and stretched out their legs. Victor picked up the candle, and all three men took a seat now and were leaning up against the opposite wall from were Jake and Peggy were sitting. Now instead of their backs, Jake could fully see their faces. Victor now passed the candle onto David, who in turn motioned for the stranger to take it and place it over to the one side. As the stranger took the candle, the light shone directly onto his face. And now there he was, and Jake now recognized him. It was the man who had brought the grape juice and bread to the shelter several months ago. But how could he be here? Jake was sure of one thing. This man was a chipped man. Why would such a man risk being found out? How could he risk being found with the Knowing? How could the Knowing risk being found with him? He could be tracked. It was so important to keep this place a secret from Jake, and yet they would bring a chipped person into their hiding place. That would be like bringing a wolf into the hen house. Crazy. Total craziness. Okay. That was their decision and their business. Jake's business was to get this guy's name, and he needed it real soon. The drop-off was days away, and Jake needed this information. Then there it was like a gift from above, or should Jake have said a gift to himself. The very answer that he needed.

David looked over at the stranger. "Michael, would you please get the light?" With those words, this Michael leaned over and blew out the flame. Jake sat there in total awe of what all had taken place during the last few hours. Perhaps this investigation was going to go better than he had ever hopped. With the lights out, Jake closed his eyes and let himself drift off to sleep. What more could a man ask for? A woman friend at his side and the information he needed to get the job done.

Jake was sure that he had only slept but a few minutes, and yet it was now time for him to be getting up. As Jake heard his name being called, he opened his eyes to find Victor standing over him looking down. "Jake, it is time for us to be going."

Jake noted at once that almost everyone had already gone out of the room. Boy, were these people sneaky. He had not heard a thing, but the most amazing thing of all was that Peggy along with Sandy were also gone. It seemed strange to Jake that Peggy could get up unnoticed and could leave without him even knowing it. But she had, and now it was his turn to leave. Was Victor going to trust him with the information of how they had entered this room? Or was he to be tricked again? One thing was for sure, and it was not going to be that easy for them this time. Jake quickly got to his feet and stood ready to go with Victor.

"Jake, this is going to be a real problem you're leaving and all. We usually don't let people into our meeting places until we are sure of their standing, but you are and have been from the start somewhat different from the rest. So, I am going to give you a choice. Do you want to know about the street entrance to this meeting place, or would you rather wait until later for this responsibility?" Victor had given his word to Sandy, but he felt that he owed Jake something also. And that something was trust. Victor thought Jake had earned it somehow. For now, he was going to let Jake make the next call.

Jake's heart was pounding. Was this some sort of a test? If he seemed overly anxious, he might give himself away, but then on the other hand, hadn't Victor almost seemed relieved when Jake had asked questions last night? Now what to do? The answer really was not that hard to come up with. Of course Jake wanted to know the entrance. He needed all of the information that he could get his hands on. With what he already knew, he could really close this case, so all the rest was icing on the cake as they say. Even if they do get suspicions of him, now was a time he could risk taking a few more chances.

"Victor, I think that I can handle the responsibility of knowing the entrance to this place." Jake looked directly at Victor while he was speaking, and to his surprise, Victor received it with a slight chuckle, acting as if he had already guessed the answer even before Jake had said it.

"Okay, Jake, if you are sure. Then let's get out of here before the streets get too busy." With those words, Victor walked to the wall directly behind where the three men had their prayer meeting the evening before. As Victor approached the wall, he raised his hands up and placed them on the wall in an open position about shoulder high. With a quick shove and a push to the right, the wall where the wallpaper had met the paint gave way, and with incredible ease and silence, the wall soon became an entrance. Jake was amazed at the precision of this false wall. It was definitely a work of art. Victor stopped the wall from sliding very far until he had a chance to look carefully outside to see if the street was clear enough for them to leave. The movement of this wall was so very quiet, no wonder Jake had never suspected that they had a secret entrance. Even standing right next to it, you would have to be looking right at it in order to know that it had opened or shut for that matter.

"Okay, Jake, now let's go. Quickly now." With those words, Victor saw to it that Jake was first to go out the door; he followed right behind. With the same movement as before, Victor now closed the entrance. The siding and all moved itself back into place. There were a few plants growing right next to the opening. If Jake had not seen it himself, he would have never thought it possible to create such an elaborate setup. No wonder these people had not been caught. The government had underestimated the Knowing. Jake himself had found a new respect for this group. Why, with their smarts and getting them headed in the right direction, these people had great futures ahead of them in the real world. "Jake, what do you say about getting something to eat? I am starved." Victor headed out down the alley with such ease it made Jake wonder how long Victor had been living like this. In the secret sort of way. It was just a way of life to Victor. Jake was sure that he could never get used to this. Not in a million years. And for sure not by choice.

"Yeah, sure, Victor, that sounds like a good idea. Shall we go back to the shelter?" Jake was keeping in step with Victor, which is why he noticed Victor's hesitation when he had mentioned the shelter. Jake looked up to try and read Victor's body language. He could see that something was wrong, but for the life of him, he had no idea as to what it could be.

Victor realized that Jake had caught on to the fact that there might be a problem with going back to the shelter, but he knew for sure that Jake had not a clue that he was the problem. Or at least a part of the problem. Victor had given Sandy his word. He had told her that he would be careful with the secrets of the Knowing when it came to Jake. Victor had never before gone back on his word where Sandy had been concerned. They had always had a trust in and for each other. But this was different. He had made a judgment call. As far as he could see it, there was no other way he could have handled it without losing Jake's trust altogether. So, what was the big deal? All he had to do was to explain it to Sandy, and then there would be no problem. But what if she didn't understand? They had been friends for a long time, and losing this friendship was unthinkable. Victor gave up a prayer asking God to give him guidance as to how to explain what he was thinking when he made this decision to trust Jake and to let him in on the secret of the entrance. Jake was smart enough to figure that there had to be more than one of these meeting places in town, but he would never be able to find them all even if he was found to be a…a what? What, Victor was not sure, but if he had to put it into words, he would have to say "found to be something other than he seemed." At this point, Victor realized that it was not he who was suspicious of Jake but Sandy. How very sure she was of her feelings. Perhaps after last night, she would see things different. Peggy sure felt as though Jake was truly one of them. Perhaps Sandy would now see it that way too. As Victor had worked that thought through his mind, he and Jake had rounded the corner and had the shelter in sight. To Victor's amazement, there was Sandy standing outside of the shelter. She was up on a chair, and she was washing the windows. "Prayer warrior by night, and window washer by day." Victor hadn't realized that he had spoken out loud until he heard Jake laughing. He now realized that his thoughts were coming to the surface.

"Victor, I had never really thought of Sandy in such a way before, but I guess you are right. Think I should tell her?" Jake was wearing an "I have something over you" kind of smile. As he ended his words, he started to run forward as to get ahead of Victor, acting as though he would get to Sandy first and tell her his news.

With very little effort, Victor reached out his hand and grabbed Jake by the sleeve of his jacket. Within an instant, Victor had passed Jake up and was well on his way to greeting Sandy first. Both men were laughing and were acting as though they had a secret between them.

Sandy, hearing all the ruckus, turned her head to see who on earth was making such an entrance so early in the morning. Seeing both Victor and Jake laughing made her heart sing. It seemed like it had been a long time since they had all had something to be happy about. Grateful, yes, but not really happy. This felt good, and Sandy wanted to very much be a part of it. "Okay, you two, what are you up to?"

"Well," Jake began to say, but Victor pushed his head down in a wrestling kind of way and then chimed in.

"We were just saying that it is going to be another sunny day. Isn't that right, Jake?" Victor was still holding onto Jake's head. But Jake quickly moved around so as to free himself and then again started to speak to Sandy. But this time it was Sandy who interrupted. "I can see that talking to you two is useless when you are in this kind of mood." Without a second thought, she handed Jake the bucket of water she was using to clean the widow.

Victor began to laugh teasingly at Jake about getting the job of window washer when with a second move, Sandy laid the sponge and towel directly into Victor's hands.

It came into Sandy's mind that these two men were more like little kids that grown men. No, on second thought, they could better be described as more of a father-and-son type of team. That was good for Victor. And without a doubt, it would be good for Jake too. Sandy was not sure of what Jake's background had been, but she was sure that this new friendship was good for him. Victor on the other hand truly deserved a good relationship of this kind. Sandy could not remember how long it had been since Victor's family had left him. It was a hard time for all of them, but for Victor, it was truly the worst situation Sandy had ever seen someone be in. Victor's wife and two boys had chosen to go the way of the new government. Victor had chosen the way of his faith. All it would have taken for him to get his old life back was to decide to go along with the new way of life. But instead he had made one of the hardest choices that any of them might ever have to make. His family or his faith. For Victor, there had been no choice. His faith had won out. Several months later, Victor was given divorce papers. In these papers, it was made clear that his family wanted nothing to do with him or his decision. It seemed so odd to Sandy that when it came to really knowing people and how they would react, reality showed its true self when it came down to living out what they say they believe. Sandy had known Victor's family. His wife and Sandy had even been friends. When things started to change in other parts of the world, it was easy for everyone to say what way of life they would choose to take, but as things began to change more locally, that is, when everything came out into the open, people started choosing up sides and ideas. So many people felt that this new way of life did not have anything to do with going against God. Still others felt that their choices were directly led by God. They felt that they had no other choice to make and could not go the government way. No matter how hard their choices would prove to be.

Sandy continued to watch the two men doing what they would call window washing. Victor looked the happiest Sandy had seen him in a long time. At once, a feeling of fear sprang up into Sandy's heart. What if her suspicions about Jake were true? She really did not think that Victor could stand being hurt again. What could she do? How could she tell Victor about what she had seen the night before, but then again, how could she not? If Jake was not on the up and up, then Victor was heading for a real bad experience. Whatever the answer was, now was not the time to get into this. It was a beautiful day, and everyone was feeling good. Sandy shrugged it off and gave a smile.

Victor had seen Sandy's smile and took it as a good sign that she had perhaps changed her feelings of suspicion about Jake. Why, she had not even asked him how he had gotten Jake out of the meeting place. With any luck, he would never have to address it. Victor decided to enjoy the moment and take the opportunity to get to know Jake better.

CHAPTER 8

The day had started off with window washing and then continued on like any other day. There was a lot of work to be done. With so many being gone from the shelter last night, there were things to be caught up on today. Both today's work and some of yesterdays.

Jake had finished all of his chores, it was late, and he was beat. The shelter was extra full tonight. A lot of new faces had shown up. It wasn't unusual for new faces to come, it simply meant more work.

Jake was really looking forward to a good night's sleep. He finished cleaning up and took one last check to make sure that everything was done and then left the kitchen. Jake didn't go very far but stopped just inside the main room. He stretched out and, within seconds, was fast asleep.

It wasn't unusual for Jake to sleep in the main room. It was warmer there than it was in the kitchen. Although the days had been warm and had given hope of spring coming, they had turned cold again, and there was even a hint of rain in the air.

Jake stirred a little and then realized that he could hear voices. He opened his eyes to what should have been darkness, but he could see flickering. Over in one of the corners, the women's side, there was a lit candle.

Several people were gathered around in a circle type of formation. Even though the main room was warmer than the kitchen, it was still very cold, so many in this group had blankets over their shoulders or heads. And they were definitely up to something.

Jake rose to his feet quietly so as not to alert anyone. Then he began to make his way over to the group. As he got closer to where they were, he could see that something was wrong.

Sandy had heard Jake as he got closer to the group; she turned and looked over to see who was coming.

Jake could see from her eyes that something was wrong, really wrong.

On seeing Jake, Sandy simply turned back to what she was looking at within the circle. Jake moved in a little more so he could see what they were all looking at too. But to his astonishment, it was not a what but a who.

There in the middle of the circle was a young boy. Jake guessed between thirteen and fifteen years of age. Some of these kids lived such a hard life that it was not easy to guess their age. It was obvious to Jake that the boy had come in from outside. Odd, thought Jake, that he would have had to have come after curfew. He was soaked to the bone with rainwater. Several of the ladies were helping to dry him off and trying to warm him up as best as they could. The boy was not very much help in getting dry as he just sat there on a chair shivering like crazy. It seemed to Jake that the shaking might be from fear as much as it was from the cold. Now that Jake was able to get a little closer, he got a real good look at this kid. Up close and personal. He had straight blond hair and big blue-green eyes. He was thin, but Jake could see that he was healthy.

Someone in the room asked if Peter wanted something warm to drink.

Okay, now Jake was getting somewhere. This kid's name was *Peter*. Now where had he come from, and what on earth was he doing on the streets after curfew?

Jake heard a noise behind him from the direction he had come from. As he looked over, he saw Victor coming out of the kitchen, but that was impossible. He had been sleeping right outside the kitchen door, and no way was Victor in the kitchen. Jake would have known if he was. There was defiantly no one in the kitchen when he left to go to bed. But he saw it himself. Victor had come from the kitchen all right. Jake made a mental note to himself. Another fake door? One to the kitchen? Was that how Victor had come in the other night when Jake had been waiting for him? Maybe Jake was not so crazy after all.

Victor came in the main room holding on to the door so that it would not make any noise. Then shutting it, he turned and walked over to where Jake and the rest were standing. Victor got over close to this kid Peter and kneeled down so that they were at the same level.

"Okay, Peter, what is this all about? I heard on the street that there was a problem over at the South Street shelter. What happened?"

Peter lowered his head and started to shake a little harder. Then he looked away from Victor with tears streaming down his already damp cheeks. "It is all my fault. I didn't think they would ever go through our stuff at the shelter."

Peter's words were so hard for Jake to hear. He was speaking in almost a whisper, and this was some upset kid. But why?

"All right, Peter, so they searched the shelter, what happened then? What on earth did they find that would shut the shelter down?" Victor had kept his voice calm and even, much like he had on the street the first day that Jake and he had met.

What a calming effect this man could have on people. What power it must be to have such a way about yourself, Jake thought.

Peter took a big deep breath. "Victor, it was awful. There was this guy who had been at our shelter for over six months. He was a real great guy. He was our friend. You know, almost like family."

"Peter, this guy, who was he?" Victor was showing a little sign of being worried now, but Jake could tell that he was trying hard to seem indifferent about the awfulness of everything that was going on.

"It turns out that he was a government undercover officer. Victor, he had been living with us a long time, he was our friend. How could he do that to us? To my mom and dad?"

Victor laid his hand on Peter's shoulder. "Now, Peter, what did he do?"

"Victor, he kept records on us. On all of us. He had names, dates, and even a list of things we did. Oh, Victor, he had the names of places that we meet."

"Peter, did they find out about the rabbit holes?"

"No. No, I don't think I heard them say anything about that." Peter closed his eyes. He was trying hard to rethink all that he had heard the others say before he left the South Street shelter.

"Peter, this is really important. A lot of lives could depend on the information you have for us. It is important that you tell us everything you heard them say. Do you understand? Everything!"

Jake wasn't sure of all the things that they were talking about, but one thing was for sure, and that was the fact that there was another undercover officer in the program doing exactly what he was doing. Trying to find the leader. Had he succeeded? Time would tell. And if he had, what was to become of Jake and his instructions? Tomorrow was to be the day that he would drop off the records that he had been keeping. Although it wasn't until this week that Jake had acquired some real information, it was looking like it was not to be a second too soon.

"Okay now, Peter, what was it that they found? And why on earth do you think that it was your fault?" Victor was searching Peter's face closely, trying to see if there was anything he could tell from his outward looks, but all he could see was a frightened young boy trying hard to keep himself all together.

Peter finally got his thoughts in order and began to fill everyone in on what had happened. "Victor, they found some of the Bibles. I was the one who showed him where they were. I really did not think that it would be any big deal. He had so many questions about God and the Lord. He needed answers that I just did not have, so I took him to the books. I am so sorry. I cannot believe that I did that. I am sorry, can you ever forgive me?" At that, Peter could talk no longer and just broke down and cried. Several of the others began to cry too. A few gathered around Peter and laid a hand or two on him in a way to reassure him of their continued acceptance of him.

As all of this was beginning to unfold, Jake again heard the kitchen door open. To his amazement, in walked David. The look on his face was one of great concern. For a moment, the way he was looking almost took away from the fact that like Victor, David had come from the kitchen, and his only way in would have been from a now-confirmed fake entrance. Jake now knew for sure that simply like it had been for Victor that David had not been in the shelter previously. The conclusion could only be that there was a secret entrance to this place like the one from last night. Just another bit of information that Jake could pass on tomorrow in his reports.

Victor looked up to see David coming over to where they were all gathered. Victor could see from the look on David's face that he had found out some news about what was going on. Victor stood up from the kneeling position in front of Peter and began to walk over toward David. They both met halfway in the room.

This was great for Jake; from where he was standing, he could hear almost everything these two men were saying.

"David, is it as bad as it seems?"

"Worse." David looked over to where Peter and the rest were standing to make sure that what he needed to tell Victor wasn't heard by Peter, not yet anyway. He would need time to adjust to all that he has already experienced before he received any more bad news. "Peter's parents and most of the leaders at the South Street shelter had been arrested, and it had been reported that all of the people found there had been chipped. They tore apart the shelter and found a lot of the stuff we had hid there."

"What things did they find?" Victor knew that he had to ask but wasn't sure that he himself was ready for that answer.

"Well, they found all of the study material that we had stashed. But I know that you are asking about the lists that were kept there. And well, no, they did not find them. In fact, we are not sure ourselves where they are. After the officers had left, we went back to see if we could retrieve any of the things that they had missed. They had found many of the hiding places but not the one where they kept the records of the Knowing. What was really strange was that when we ourselves went to the hiding place to get the records, they were missing."

"Missing? What do you mean missing?" Victor did not know if he should be grateful or horrified. If these papers got into the wrong hands, well, it could mean the end of the Knowing and everyone involved.

David had the same problem as Victor was having with this information. Where did the papers go? "Victor, I don't have any idea about the papers. I was hoping that Peter here might have an idea. Do you think he is up to a few questions?"

Victor looked over at Peter, he was a wreck; but perhaps if he could help in some way, it might make him feel better about things. "I am not sure, David, but I think that we should give it a try."

David and Victor walked over to where Peter had regained himself a bit. As David spoke to him, Peter seemed to almost get strength from this man he knew he could trust. "Peter, do you have any idea what happened to the records that were kept at the shelter where you lived?" Peter stopped to think about what it was David was talking about.

"David, I am not sure if this is what you are looking for, but my dad took a bag, and he and my mom taped it to me before they told me that I had to leave and come over to this shelter." As Peter was talking, he started to pull his shirttails out of his trousers. Then he lifted up his shirt and started to unbutton it. There taped to his middle with duct tape was a black-and-blue striped bag. There was so much tape around this young man, not even the rain could have found its way through. Someone pulled out a pocketknife and cut away the sides of the tape. The rest of the tape would have to be removed more carefully a little later.

Victor was the one to ask questions now. "Peter, how was it that your dad knew to do this? What did he tell you?"

"Well, he did not tell me what was in this bag but told me that he had gotten word that there was going to be trouble at the shelter tonight. That if there was anything real important there that he should get it out at once." Peter started to get a little anxious now that he was realizing that his dad had not only kept the stuff in the bag safe from the government but that he had also kept him safe too. "David, what about my parents, are they okay?"

David knew that he had to be upfront and honest with the boy, but this truly would not have been the time he would have chosen to discuss it, but Peter was asking, and so now he needed to know. "Peter, it has been reported that almost everyone from the shelter has been arrested and that many of them have been chipped. It sounds like most of them will be released, but, Peter, it is reported that your parents are going to be charged with who knows what. But for now, it looks like they will be the ones charged with the crimes against the state."

"But they are okay? I mean they are safe and they are not hurt, right?" Peter needed something to hold onto right now, so for him to know that they were healthy was important to him.

"Yes, of course they are safe. The whole arrest was a peaceful one. No one put up a fight, and so things were as good as could be expected. Besides, we all know that God is with them, and He has a plan. One that we don't know anything about. So, for now, let's do what we can to get through this, and let's remember that God will take care of the rest. Okay?" Although those words from David were meant for Peter, everyone who heard them were put a little more at ease by being reminded of who it was that was really in charge of this whole mess.

It was getting late, and tomorrow was going to prove to be a hard one. Many decided to go back to bed giving Peter a sign, word, or a hug of encouragement prior to finding their place for the rest of the night.

Two of the women took Peter in hand and led him to the kitchen in order to try and find something dry for him to put on. Another lady joined them expressing how she had an idea as to how to get the tape off of him.

David and Victor took the bag that had been taped to Peter, and they met up with Sandy over in one corner. David pulled the tape back from the zipper in order to find out if the lost papers were really inside. To all of their relief, they were. "Thank God they are here. I am not sure how it was that Peter's dad knew to do what he had done, but thank God he did. If these papers had found their way into the wrong hands, it would have been disastrous. We really need to destroy them—and right away."

Victor noticed that Jake was still standing off to the side of the room taking in everything that was going on. He at once decided that this goings-on had caused Jake to be afraid of what might happen to him. Victor's heart was full of compassion for him and wanted to reassure him that things would be all right.

"Jake. Jake, would you like to join us?" Victor asked Jake with a lowered voice but with a voice of lightheartedness and one of reassurance.

Jake was caught off guard by the question Victor had asked. "What, Victor, were you saying something to me?"

"Never mind, Jake, perhaps it would be best if we get together in the morning. Forget what I said. Why don't you go to bed, and we will talk in the morning."

Jake, feeling somewhat like he had been dismissed, did as he was told. His body went to bed, but his mind refused to give up. Those papers. Jake needed to get his hands on those papers. Jake continued to monitor the goings-on in the room as best as he could from over where he was bedded down. Again, his location gave him a better-than-okay position for listening to what was being discussed.

Victor saw that David was trying to return the papers back to the bag from which they had been removed. Victor lent him a hand while Sandy stood there not being a part of the goings-on but not willing to give in for the night either.

"Tell me, David, how on earth did this happen? How could anyone have gotten in so deep?" Victor was sick with the thought that this had happened to anyone, but the further worry of how much information this man had picked up was even worse. Would his findings lead the government back to the Knowing?

"Victor, God only knows what this is all about, but there is one good thing for sure, and that is that we finally know who the spy is. The information we received awhile back has proven to be true. There was a spy, and now we know who it was. At least we can live a little easier and will not have to be suspecting everyone new that we meet. As this comes to an end, perhaps we should have suspected the ones who had been with us longer also. We will have to remember these lessons in the future."

Sandy looked slowly over to where Jake was lying down and began to feel bad about the way she had not truly trusted him. Even though she still had reservations about him not being who and what he said he was, it is now clear that the spy they were looking for had been at another shelter all along. Perhaps in time she could share with Jake why it was she wanted Victor to be so careful about giving him information about the Knowing. That would take some of the heat off Victor and would make Sandy feel better too. By tomorrow, this misunderstanding could be totally fixed, and then Jake could feel the trust he now deserved. *Odd,* thought Sandy, *I usually am right about people and what is going on with them. But, boy, was I wrong about this one. Thank God. What if everyone had listened to me?* Oh my, what an awful thing it would have been to have turned Jake away. Maybe she was losing it. Perhaps her days as a leader were over. This was a second big mistake she had almost caused. First being caught out after curfew and now not trusting a boy like Jake.

This was a great thing for Jake being in the placement that he was in. With the other spy out into the open, it would free things up with the people. How was it that they even knew that there had been a spy on the streets in the first place? How was it that Peter's dad had been warned of the searching and closing of the shelter? It would have to have been someone from real high up to have let that information out. But who? Who on earth could be the leak? Before Jake was to finish writing out his report, he needed to get just a little more information. If only he could get his hands on those papers, that would be the greatest feat of all. But how?

*****

Victor began to realize that something was not quite right with Sandy. She was rightfully upset, but it was unlike her to take anything so meekly. It was not at all in her nature. "Sandy, are you all right?"

David also noted that there was a difference in Sandy's reaction to all of this. Victor was right, something wasn't right about how she was behaving. In the past, it would have taken the two men together to try and talk her out of some harebrained idea of how she could rescue the others or at least to try to regain some of what was lost, but not this time. This time, Sandy was just taking it. No fight, no spirit, and that wasn't like her at all.

"Yes, Victor, I am fine. I think that I am simply too tired. I think that I will go to bed. Things should seem better in the morning. I hope." With that said, Sandy headed off to find her spot to bed down for the night.

Victor reached out his hand and took Sandy by the arm in a very comforting sort of way. Both Sandy's and Victor's eyes met. As Victor tried to focus on Sandy in order to see what was really going on, he noted a sadness in her like he had not seen in a very long time. "Sandy, come on, let's talk."

Sandy was not in any mood to talk right now. All she wanted to do was go to sleep and to make all of this go away. She wanted her old life back. The life where she and her two girls lived together. Where the biggest decision of the day was what to wear or what to have for dinner. The life where believing in God was a way of life and not a crime against the government. Before all of this, Sandy had never broken the law. In fact, she had not even had a speeding ticket. But now, here she was, a felon if she were to be caught even praying. What on earth was she thinking? Perhaps she should just go away and join her two girls. She sure did miss them. The past few months had been hard. But they were somehow bearable when she could think somehow that they were all doing okay. But now knowing that at any moment someone could tell something, and without even a fight, their whole existence could be wiped out. Perhaps that might be for the best. Maybe. Just maybe this is what God wanted to happen all along. What if it was them that were out of the will of God and not the government?

Victor could see that Sandy did not want to talk right now. It was plain to him that she had thoughts all tied up in her head and that she was racing them through her mind over and over again. It was also clear that these ideas were not ones of a positive nature. Victor had learned from the past that Sandy was not one to get down very easy but that when she did, she did not have any idea about how to get back up. Emotionally Sandy was strong. In fact, one of the strongest people Victor had ever met. But even the strong need some help from time to time. And it was clear to him that Sandy needed a friend right now, even as much as Peter did.

"Really, Victor, all I want to do right now is to go and get some sleep. We can talk in the morning, okay?" Sandy had looked away from Victor's gaze. She was not sure how, but it almost seemed at times that Victor could read her mind. She needed some time and space in order to get herself together. She hated it when she was feeling sorry for herself. It was not what she wanted for herself, and she was sure that it was not what God wanted for her either. Space and time, yes, that would be the answer. Perhaps she needed to get away from the shelter. It was past curfew, but if she were careful, she could get to a rabbit hole and stay the rest of the night there. Yes, that is what she should do.

"Sandy, I think you might be able to sleep better if we talk about all that has happened today. It is awful, and it is scary too. I think we really need to talk or at least sit together for the rest of the night." The look on Sandy's face brought a strange feeling of uneasiness to Victor. It felt as though he were about to lose a good friend. But to what? Perhaps he was putting too much into his feelings. But he needed to try. "Okay, Sandy, can we just sit together for a while?"

"Actually, Victor, I think I have a better idea. I think I need to get out of here for a short time. I really need to have some time to myself. So why don't we plan to get together tomorrow." As Sandy was saying those words, both Victor and David noted that she was buttoning up her coat and reaching for her gloves and hat as if she were going to be going outside.

Alarm swept over both of the men. There was more wrong with Sandy than just needing to talk. She really was not thinking right if she was thinking about going out after curfew. Especially after the closing of the other shelter. Everyone would be on extra alert for violators.

David, who had been over to the right of Sandy and Victor, began to tune into what he thought was taking place. Sandy had always been the most levelheaded woman he had ever seen. David could always be sure that Sandy would somehow get things done and in the right and safest way. But this was not the woman he was used to working with. The Sandy he knew would have never thought of taking the chance of going out after curfew. Something was very wrong. At once David walked over to where Sandy and Victor were standing. If Sandy was determined to leave, it would take both men to convince her otherwise. "Sandy, what's going on? You are not thinking of going out before curfew is over?"

Victor was grateful that David had come alongside of him. He was equally glad to see that David was seeing and hearing what he was. As far as Victor was concerned, this was confirmation to him that something was wrong with the way Sandy was acting and that they needed to do something about it and right now. The morning might be too late.

Sandy quickly realized that she was about to be overrun with logic. She wasn't feeling too logical right now, all she wanted to do was get out of here. Sandy also knew that there would be no way she could out talk these two. She did not have the energy or the time as far as she was concerned. She would need to distract them and get them off her back before she could leave. "No. I wasn't thinking about leaving right now. But first thing in the morning. A short get-away. If that is okay with you two?"

"That's fine, Sandy, but why are you putting on your gloves and hat?" Victor motioned to Sandy's hands and then to the hat on her head.

Sandy looked down and had not even realized that she had put them on. She had though, and now she needed to explain herself. "I was cold, that's all. Now if you'll excuse me, I need to go and lie down before I fall asleep on my feet." Sandy spotted a space over near the front door. That would be perfect. After everyone had fallen asleep, she could slip out and get off by herself.

As Sandy was looking around for a place to sleep, Victor and David had exchanged glances, both noting that Sandy was not to be trusted. At least until they were sure of her state of mind. So much had happened to her over the past few years, and yet she of all people seemed to handle everything extremely well. Perhaps this was maybe all too much. Sandy had been in charge of a shelter some time ago that had been closed down due to "questionable practices." Exact charges were never filed, so Sandy was let go, but the way that it had happened was awful. In the middle of the night and without warning. Everything was searched, and everyone was arrested. All of their belongings were confiscated. Even the personal stuff. It was horrible for everyone, but for Sandy, it was even worse. She had been in charge, and she was the one who took the blame for its closing. Not only among the government people either but a lot of the chipless groups felt that she was to blame too. Sandy had seemed to have handled it without a single outward sign of remorse. She seemed to take it in stride and acted to everyone like she was okay with the whole thing. To everyone but Victor that was. She had not shared very much with him but enough for him to now realize that what he saw on the outside was not necessarily what was going on in the inside. Victor was not sure, but he was thinking that perhaps the closing of the South Street shelter was somehow bringing all of the old memories back. Perhaps some unresolved ones that were compounding the fears of what was happening now. Whatever it was, both he and David were not going to leave her on her own. They owed her that. They were her friends, and as they could see it, she needed them right now even if she herself didn't realize it.

Victor saw the spot where Sandy was thinking about bedding down, and seeing where it was only convinced him more that she was planning on leaving the shelter before morning. And alone.

As Sandy began to head off to the spot she had chosen, Victor made a fast move so as to be in front of her before she could even take a single step. He placed his arm around her waist and pulled her into his side. She did not fight the move, but she was not receiving it either. Sandy swung her head around to see who it was that was now in her space. A space she so desperately needed to keep void. She was not ready to deal with anybody or anything right now. Not until she had a chance to get her head on straight. At first glance she could tell it was Victor, and right away, she decided to explain how it was that he needed to leave her alone. But on second glance, she could see that he had his mind made up. About what, she was not sure, but whatever it was to be, he was determined. "Victor, what on earth are you doing?" Sandy pulled away slightly only to note that she was firmly in Victor's tender but immovable grip. "Victor, I told you that I need to bed down for the night. I need some rest. Now please let me go, and we will talk in the morning."

"Sandy, I could not agree more that you need to get some rest, but I think it would be best if you were to stay over here beside me for the rest of the night." Victor tightened his grip a little more, assuring Sandy that he had no intention of letting her go off by herself. Not in this room and for sure not out of the shelter. Together they both walked over to a space to the left of the door leading to the kitchen. Sandy sat herself down with the actions of one who was not happy but also like someone who had no other choice. Victor sat himself down on the floor, placing himself between Sandy and both the outside door and the kitchen door as well. Sandy laid herself out on the floor with her back to Victor, using her arm as a pillow while Victor leaned himself up against the wall. He was not ready to go to sleep yet. He had a few matters that needed to be addressed. The least of which was to have a prayer time with his God. If there ever was a time that they all needed reassurance that God was with them, this was it. Victor lifted up in prayer all of the people at both shelters and especially all of the leaders. He prayed for all of the government people who had been involved and for the spy that had tried to do them in. He asked God for guidance and for peace for all of those involved. A special request was sent up on behalf of his friend Sandy. She had been there for him so many times after he had lost his family. She was his pillar of strength when he had no hope or faith left. Now he desperately wanted to be there for her. A peace flooded over Victor. As he came to the end of his prayer time, he noted that Sandy had finally fallen asleep. Victor carefully lifted himself up off the floor and decided to seek out David's advice.

There were only two men still awake. David and another man who had once lived at the South Street shelter. He had met the spy. Jim had been filling David in on some of the details that he knew before he had moved over to this shelter. As Victor was approaching, David and Jim were finishing up on some of the last of the details and were saying their goodnights. David was glad to see Victor but immediately scanned the room to make sure that Sandy was still in the shelter. "Victor, what do you think is going on with Sandy?"

"I am not too sure, but if I were to guess, I might say that this was perhaps a last straw for her. I have never seen her without fight like she was tonight. It is like she has just given up."

"What do you think will happen tomorrow? I mean with Sandy." David was truly concerned. He did not know Sandy as well as Victor did, and so he was looking to him for confirmation that she would be all right. He needed her. They all did.

"I am not sure myself. I have never seen her act anything like this. But I will tell you one thing, if anyone had a reason to take a vacation, it is this lady." Both men knew that it was impossible to take a vacation from life, but if it could be done, they would truly send her. God says that you never get more than you can handle, and so both these men were banking on that for their friend Sandy.

The men had a quick prayer together and then decided that it was time for them to bed down for the night. A lot had happened, and tomorrow could prove to be just as bad. David placed himself over in the space close to the front door that Sandy had originally planned for herself.

Victor went back over by Sandy. He wanted to be there in case she woke up and wanted to talk. This time he stretched all of the way out and lay on his side so that he could face his friend Sandy. Somehow the word *friend* just did not seem to tell it all. Truly the word itself lacked something in describing their relationship. Victor had been married once, and this friendship—as he was choosing to call it—was emotionally more than that relationship had ever been. Perhaps it was because of tension in the life they were all leading, but then again, it might be something more. This life that they were living did not leave any room for an individual relationship. Or did it? Victor reached out his hand to lay it on Sandy's shoulder, he wanted to somehow reassure her, it was all he could think to do. She was still facing away from him. What a surprise it was for him to feel that her body was shaking. Victor raised himself up onto one elbow so he could see Sandy's face. She was not asleep like he had thought. But instead she was lying awake with tears streaming from her eyes and then rolling down the side of her face. She was crying, and yet she lay there silent. Barely moving. If it had not been for his touching her shoulder, he would have never known that she was in such an upset state. This lady truly was a silent warrior. Without even a thought to what others might think or of what Sandy might think for that matter, Victor laid himself alongside Sandy but closer this time. He put his whole arm around her and pulled her into himself. She did not even react to his coming into her space, but instead she settled herself back into his chest. And then she wept. Silently like before at first, but then as time went on, she let herself go ahead and cry. Along with the tears that came out of Sandy also came the fear, frustration, anger, hurt, and a total release from the pressure. As time passed, a feeling of peace overcame her.

Victor and Sandy did not say a word to each other, they did not require any. They were friends, and now they were a new kind of support mate for each other too. Victor had always been able to go to Sandy, and perhaps after this, Sandy would now be able to trust in Victor's support as well. As the tears from Sandy came to an end, both she and Victor fell into a deep sleep. Only a few hours of night left, but it would be a peaceful sleep, and it would be enough.

CHAPTER 9

The morning had come fast. Jake was so excited about today that he was awake before anyone else. The night had become colder. But even having a coat that wasn't quite warm enough was not going to get him down. Today was Jake's day. He would make a name for himself, and he was so excited that he almost forgot about how it was he was going to do that. He would make his name famous by deceiving his friends. For a second or two, that idea bothered him, but when he thought it through, he knew that what he was doing was the right thing. These people were good people, but they were misguided. By putting an end to the Knowing, they could all be placed back on track. Once they were chipped, they could quit living such gruesome lives, and then they would have the kind of lives they truly deserved. Jake was sure that at first, they would all be mad at him, but in the end, he had no doubt that they would someday thank him.

As Jake got up, he thought it was odd that Victor and Sandy were lying together, but he had always suspected that they were perhaps more than just friends. The sight of the two of his favorite people getting together was the icing on the cake. Jake could not think of two people who belonged together more. Just like his mom and dad. They had a great relationship. One Jake hoped to have with his wife if he were to have one someday. Thinking of his mom and dad made Jake feel sad that this was only the halfway mark in his mission. Perhaps with any luck, things might move along faster than they had hoped. Maybe the information he had gathered along with the information the other spy had turned in might be enough to bring the Knowing down.

Jake looked around to see if anyone was watching. Everyone was still asleep. He grabbed his backpack that he always used as a pillow, opened it, and took out the notebook he had been keeping. This was to be one of the greatest entries he would make. As he began to flip the pages, he realized that he had grabbed the wrong book again. Both books that were given to him were exactly the same. Except for the entries, that was. Now, on to making the final entries. Jake had decided that having Sandy arrested was really not necessary. From what he had seen last night, she would not be a problem for him for some time. She was so shaken up. This life was not good for her. She had so much she could offer the world. And yet she forced herself to live life as a criminal. The way Jake saw it, by him doing his job, he was not only shutting down a criminal group but he was also going to be helping a lot of really great people get their lives back together. Sure, they would be hurt at first, but in the end, they would be grateful. Perhaps his dad could help get them all jobs that would keep them in Jake's life. Wow, this was going to be a great thing. Now he needed to quit daydreaming, and he needed to get down to work.

Jake got all of his entrees made, and not a moment too soon. As he was returning the notebook to his bag, he saw that David was getting up, and then several others in turn started to move around. Jake was so happy that he hardly noticed the cold. He picked up his things and started for the kitchen. This morning was an odd way to start. Usually it was an all clear siren that got everyone up, but not today. It was as though Jake's excitement had given energy to everyone here at the shelter. The next exciting thing on his list this morning was that after the all clear siren, Peggy would come running into the shelter ready to start the morning cleanup. Her entering the shelter always made Jake feel alive.

Perhaps Peggy would be the one he would make his wife. Only time would tell.

Jake began to notice that several things were different this morning. First off, when the all clear siren went off, most of the people stayed at the shelter. Usually everyone would leave as soon as they could get out of the door, but not today. Instead they hung around as if they were waiting for something. The second thing he noticed was

Sandy. She was not up yet. She was always one of the first to get up and help get things going. But not today. She and Victor were still in the same position that they had been in all night. Even the all clear siren had not awakened them.

Many at the shelter saw that they were together and were pleased that the two of them had obviously figured out something that the rest of them had known for a very long time. All of the women smiled and made small talk about how they couldn't believe how long it took the two of them to get together. No one was judging, but rather everyone was excited about this happening. Perhaps a bright spot in the middle of hard times.

For the first time, Jake started to think about a few questions that had never come up. Like, how was it that couples got together? He was thinking in the "relations" kind of together. Even the married people slept in the same rooms. One thing was for sure, and that was that they were not all celibate. Too many babies had been born to these people. So how was it that they got together? Then there were the children. Where were they? Several would show up at the shelter, and after a few days, they would be gone. Where was it that they went? Jake had noticed a pattern. First the children would disappear, usually with the mothers, and then in a few days or so, the dad would be gone too. But where?

Some information for Jake to look into for the next notebook he would turn in.

The last of the odd things to happen, or should he say not happen, was the fact that Peggy had not shown up this morning as she usually did. It was odd, but Jake was not really worried. With Peggy, anything could be going on. She had a way of doing things that just "came up," as she would put it. Jake thought it funny how the things about her that used to drive him crazy he now found rather endearing. Almost normal.

There really was not any extra time to worry about much of anything though. Jake had other problems of his own. He needed to get away from the shelter by himself so he could deliver the notebook to the bus locker. Perhaps it was good that Peggy was not here today. She would have wanted to go with him for sure, and he could not for the life of him think of an excuse that could put her off. This day was working out to be a good one for him.

Several people gathered around David all wanting to know about the rumors connected with the closing of the South Street shelter. Once they had heard of the goings-on, off they would go carrying out the vital information.

Jake had seen Peter in the back part of the kitchen earlier this morning but had no idea of where it was they had taken him. He was gone just like all of the other kids. Jake was sorry about that. He would have liked to have talked to this kid and to have learned some information from him. It sounded from what he was saying last night like he had a true working knowledge of this God of theirs. He sure would have loved to have talked to him and found out some of the things that he was not sure of related to the religious practices. This praying thing still seemed odd to Jake. Whenever there was a problem, these people just prayed instead of doing something about it. They did not fight or do really anything until they all prayed. Jake smiled at the thought of his dad coming up against a big problem, and instead of setting up a plan like he usually did, to see his dad pray instead. Not his dad, he was too strong for something like praying. Jake looked over to where Victor was lying and then over to David. On the other hand, Jake would have never expected these men to pray either, but they do. How odd.

David had spoken to almost everyone who was left at the shelter. He was a caring man, so he wanted to answer as many questions as he could before he had to leave. He gathered his things and, noting that Victor and Sandy were still asleep, gave a nod to Jake and then left the shelter. Jake wondered where it was most of these people spent their day, but mostly he wondered where it was David spent his time away. There would be very long periods of time where David, for the most part, just did not exist.

Victor woke up with the full knowledge of where he was and of · whom it was he was holding. This night could have gone on forever, but it didn't. And now with the morning would come a whole lot of new problems. The least of which was the state of mind Sandy was going to be in. How was she going to react to his being there for her last night? Well, no time like the present to find out. With a gentle touch on Sandy's shoulder, Victor helped to usher her into the awareness of the morning. "Good morning, sleepyhead."

Sandy rolled over onto her back before she opened her eyes. Or at least tried to open her eyes. It was a disturbance to both of them to discover that Sandy's eyes had swollen shut. She sat up and at once began to rub at her eyes. Victor deflected her hands as best he could. It was his way of thinking that rubbing them could only irritate them more. "Jake, would you please bring me a towel and some cold water."

Jake turned to look at Victor and at once realized from looking at Sandy what was going on. Jake was as concerned as all the rest who had seen what was happening and started to quickly walk into the kitchen to do as he was asked.

"Jake, that will not be necessary. I can get the water myself." Sandy was getting herself up onto her feet. Or at least she was trying. Not being able to see, she stepped on someone's bedding and almost fell back to the ground.

Victor's hand was fast to react to her falling, and he caught her before she fell all of the way to the ground. "Yes, that is right, you can do it all by yourself. Now listen to me and sit down. For a while, okay?"

"Victor. I can't do this. Would you please help me to the kitchen? I don't want anyone to see me like this." Sandy was horrified. She had never in her life let herself get into a mess like this. She was a leader. She needed to be setting an example to everyone else. But here she was acting like a small wounded animal. Eyes swollen, and from crying of all things.

"Oh right, we wouldn't want anyone to know that you're human, would we?" Victor was angry at Sandy for putting such a high expectation on herself. She would have never expected from anyone else what it was she expected from herself. This needed to come to an end. This way of thinking was not good for her or anyone else. If Victor had learned one thing from last night, it was that his friend Sandy was a wonderful, sensitive, and delicate person. Someone that not only he but also everyone else had taken advantage of.

They did not mean to, it was just that Sandy seemed so strong. She was always there for everyone. I don't think that until now even Sandy knew how human she really was. But for the good of everyone involved, things needed to change.

"Victor, please help me, would you? I need to get to the kitchen and to get some cold water on my eyes. Now are you going to help me or what?" Sandy was looking in the direction that she thought Victor was standing. He did not answer, and so she decided that he had walked away. She started to reach up with her hand thinking that if she held her eyelid open, she might be able to see well enough to get around. As her hand was about to reach her eye, she heard a voice from behind her. It was Victor's.

"Oh no you don't." Victor took Sandy's hands in his. He was reaching around from behind her. So that all she could do was to lay her head back against his chest. "Good, thank you, Jake." Jake had done as Victor had asked. He had brought a towel and a bowl of water. "Jake, would you please put the towel into the water?" Jake did as he was told. "Now would you wring it out but not too much, it needs to be on the damp side. Yes, that is right." As Victor was speaking to Jake, he was leading Sandy back to where they had spent the night. As he started to lower her down to the ground, she became off-balance and was startled.

Sandy gave out a little gasp as she felt what seemed like falling. "It is okay. I've got you. Just relax, and we will get the swelling down, and then you can get on with your day."

Victor was seated, leaning up against the wall, with Sandy leaning back against his body. Victor had raised both legs up on each side of Sandy so he could better support her. "Jake, now please place the towel on her eyes. Yes, like that. How does that feel?" Victor could feel Sandy becoming tense as she was attempting to move away from him.

Sandy desperately wanted to be out of this situation. As if last night were not bad enough, first crying like a baby, and now she couldn't get on with her day because her stupid eyes were swollen shut. This had to be a nightmare. This couldn't really be happening. She was not some silly schoolgirl who needed to be taken care of.

"Victor, I can take it from here. So go away and leave me alone with my towel, my water, my swollen eyes, and bruised pride, all right?"

Victor motioned for Jake and everyone else to go on with what they needed to do and leave them alone. Everyone was sensitive to the situation and at once did as they were told. But not Victor. He had decided to see this thing through. He did not want to be mean to Sandy, but he cared about her way too much to leave her like this. "Sandy, I am not going to go anywhere. At least not yet." Victor was still holding onto her hands, and he could feel an old familiar shaking starting to come from her like he had felt late last night. "Now, Sandy, you listen to me. There is nothing wrong with needing help. Everyone does from time to time. Even you."

Victor transferred both of her hands into one of his and took his other and laid it across the towel on her eyes. "Now with a little time, and patience on your part, you will be up and running in no time at all. But for now, what you need to do is to sit here and let the cold water do its job. All right?" Sandy didn't answer. "All right?"

This man was making her crazy. What was it he wanted from her? If he wanted to see her fall on her face, well, here was his chance. She didn't know what she was feeling more—cold, ashamed, angry, or just plain tired. But whatever it was, she couldn't handle it right now. So if God saw fit for Victor to be here to take over, so be it. The fact was she really did not have any other choice now, did she. All she really could do was to do as Victor had suggested. "All right."

"Good. Now that is better. Now lean back and relax, will you?" Victor couldn't believe that she had given in so easily. Sandy was better after last night, but she was still not her old self. Victor wondered how it would have been if Sandy's eyes had been all right this morning. Perhaps they all would have fallen back into the old habits of thinking she could handle anything. Perhaps this was God's way of showing them that one of His children needed help. But for whatever the reason, Victor was not going to pass up this chance to help her. Even if she really did not want him to.

Sandy was sitting still, but relaxed was the farthest from the state she was in. Her trembling was even more noticeable. It was almost like she was going into shock. Victor was not sure, but he was beginning to think that Sandy was going to need more than he could do to help. It had been only a few minutes, and Sandy already had decided that her eyes were better. She lifted her hand up to the towel in order to remove it. Once she had, she became more discouraged as she found that things had not already changed with regard to her eyes.

Jake was walking past when Victor motioned with his head for him to come over. Jake leaned down so Victor could speak directly into his ear. "Jake, I think that Sandy may need a doctor. I want you to go and find David and ask him to get in touch with Doc. And hurry, will you?"

Jake looked at Victor. How could Sandy be so bad as to need a doctor? Why, just last night, she was fine. She was upset, but she was healthy. He was not sure of what was going on, but he agreed to do as he was asked. It could not hurt to have her checked out. Besides, this was exactly what he needed. An excuse to get away from the shelter unnoticed. He could learn how it was you got in touch with David. He could make his drop at the bus stop, and he could find out who this Doc was. What a great day this was going to be. For him anyway. He stopped to look at Sandy and quickly decided that he was right in his thinking that this was to be the best thing for her. Getting her off the streets and into a real home would do her a world of good. He was truly doing a good thing. "Yes, Victor, I'll be right back. Who do I ask to help me with finding David?"

"Finding David? Victor, why do we need to find David? Has something else happened?"

Sandy again began to try and get up. But Victor held onto her with his arms and began to rock her ever so slightly from side to side. He leaned his head forward, placing his mouth close to her ear. He then began to hum a familiar song that both he and Sandy knew all too well. A song from their past worshiping, which gave them both a sense of peace. He stopped only a moment to mouth to Jake to find Jim and that he would help him find David. Sandy was not so easily put off this time, and it took a little more effort for Victor to keep her down. Victor smiled. *Good, that's more like it*, he was thinking to himself. That's more like the Sandy he knew. Hopefully by the time the doc got here, she would not need him, but it would be good to have him look at her eyes all the same.

Victor was not sure as to how long it had been, but he was sure that Sandy was ready to move the towel and to see if her eyes were less swollen. They both were in a position neither had expected them to be in. Victor was taking care of Sandy, and it felt really good. He was worried about what was going on with her, but it felt good all the same. "Sandy, do you want to see if your eyes are any better?"

"Yes. Let's try it again." Sandy's hand was free to raise up to her eyes so she could remove the towel. Once she had, it did not make any difference. Her eyes were exactly the same. "Victor, what is going on? Doesn't God realized how much I need to do today? With the South Street shelter closed, a lot of the people who usually stayed there would be here tonight. Why is God allowing this to happen? Can't He see that I need to be up and doing His work?" Sandy was feeling desperate. What would God have her to do now? Delegate?

Victor was not sure what was going on in Sandy's head right now but decided he would share an idea he was having. "Sandy, I am not sure, but I am thinking that God may be putting an anchor on you. Slowing you down. Perhaps God wants you focusing less on the work for God and to focus more on the God of the work." He had heard that somewhere and felt it applied here."

Sandy stilled. "What?" In a situation like this, all she could do was to tell others what needed to be done.

That's it. She could tell the others what needed to be done. She could oversee. Well, kind of. That thought gave Sandy a smile inside that made its way to her face.

For a second, Victor thought that he had not seen right. Sandy was smiling, and in the middle of what seemed to be total distress. "Sandy, what is it? What are you smiling about?"

"Oh, Victor, I just had a thought. I can't do the job, but I can be the overseer. Without eyes." Sandy's voice trailed off, and she began to laugh.

Victor also began to laugh. But his laughter was with her and not about her. Victor couldn't decide if Sandy was crazy or just plain wonderful. Her ability to bounce back always amazed him, "Oh yeah. I get it, an overseer who cannot see. So who do you plan on bossing around this time?"

Sandy quit laughing. "Victor, where is Peggy?"

"What? What do you mean where is Peggy?" Victor thought that this was an odd question, but then this whole last few months had been that way.

"I mean where is Peggy? She should have been here by now. Have you seen her today?" Sandy wasn't waiting for any answers. She knew that if Peggy had been here, she would have heard her. "Victor, something is wrong. Peggy should have been here by now."

"Sandy, you know Peggy. She is a free spirit. She comes and she goes." Victor was sorry he had even asked the question of who. Things were getting better, and now this.

"Victor, will you please go and look for Peggy? She was to have met me here today to go on a gathering. I know that she would not have forgotten that. I need you to find her." Sandy was trying hard to act as if everything with her was all right. She knew that Victor would not leave her until he was sure that she would be okay. "Besides, Victor, I am not going to be much fun for a while. I was thinking of taking a nap. Sounds good, yes?"

Victor knew what it was she was doing. Sandy was one to always put other people first. Perhaps this was just what the doctor would have ordered. Get her mind off herself and onto other things. Victor was sure that sooner or later Peggy was going to show up with some crazy story about some thing or another. On one hand, they would all be so happy to see that she was all right, and then on the other hand, they would want to wring her neck. Victor had been at that place with Peggy before. She was a great person, but she also had a way of making the average person feel insane. "Sandy, if you think that it would do any good, I will go and look for her. But you know, I think that she is going to turn up just fine. You know Peggy has done things like this before."

"Victor, I know that it seems like that, but I have a feeling. Would you go now and make sure?" Sandy actually did have a feeling about this. Peggy had never missed a gathering in all of the times

Sandy had asked her. Peggy looked forward to going and thanking the people herself.

"Sandy, I said that I would go, but not yet. I want to wait here for a little longer and see if she shows up. Okay?" Victor was sure that he could find Peggy, but he wanted to wait and see Doc when he arrived. Victor was sure that he would have things to tell the doctor once he arrived. Victor knew that all Sandy would choose to share with him was that her eyes were swollen shut. Sandy's choosing to leave some of the other things out was not a game with her. She truly believed that people did not want to hear all of the bad stuff. What she had not learned yet was that sharing the bad stuff with friends was a great way to get through tough times. In time, she would figure it out. But for now, he would be there to make sure that the doc knew all that he needed to know.

Jake was still excited. He had found Jim and asked him to get a message to David about them needing a doctor. Originally, Jake had planned on going with Jim to find out how you got a hold of David, but the day had gotten away from him, and he needed to get to the bus locker and make his drop-off. So this was to be it. On the way to the bus station, Jake had to pass the South Street shelter, or what was left of it. Someone had gone into it with what looked like a wrecking ball. Nothing was left unturned. The floorboards were pulled up, and a lot of the drywall had been pulled off as well. This place would never be the same. No wonder Sandy was so upset. Jake was glad that she was not going to see this. It even made him sick to see it, and he was definitely not attached to it.

Jake was walking at an even tempo. In fact, he almost had a skip in his walk. He alone was going to be able to do good for a lot of people. Least of all for his career. His mom and dad would be so proud of him. He could hardly wait until they had their first dinner with all of the family together so he could tell his story of how he was a dishwasher in a chipless shelter. Jake knew that they would listen intently, and there would be a lot of questions. He would be in the limelight at last.

Jake had walked past the shelter and toward the bus station. On down the street and then up the steps into the building he went. He looked around for the lockers. There they were. Now to find #363 and to make his deposit. As he was looking at the lockers, he realized one thing was wrong. He did not have any change. All he had was a dollar that he had stashed in his coat pocket before he left for his last meeting with Mr. Diggings. Okay, now he had the money, but he still needed change. As Jake looked around, he noticed a change machine over in the far back corner of the building. He immediately walked over and got his change. As he reached down to get the money out of the change drop, he looked over to the lockers by one of the back walls, and for a second, he thought he saw David. But that was impossible, or was it? Jake stood up so he could get a better look. Yes, it was David all right, but what was he doing here? He was supposed to be helping Sandy get a doctor. David looked over toward Jake's direction, and Jake took a step back. He did not want to be seen here at the bus station just in case the other spy used this same kind of drop-off technique. Now that Jake had verified David's being here, the next thing he wanted to do, other than drop off the book, was to see who it was that David was talking to. Jake walked back over to the locker where he needed to place the book. He deposited two of the coins into the key slot and opened the door, double-checking that he was at locker #363. He then reached into his inner coat pocket and pulled out the notebook he was to leave. He quickly put the book in place then shut the door, turned the key, and removed it from its keyhole. Jake considered that he would be the one with the key but guessed that the officials would have had a second one like it. Jake checked the door to make sure that it was secure. It was. Jake considered this a job well done. Now on to see what it was that David was doing here in the bus station and who was it that he was meeting. Jake walked around the other side of the change machine this time so he could get a clear eyeshot of David and the other man. He was sure that he would not be seen from where he was but kept low just in case. Jake could only see the back of the man that David was talking to. He was not sure about it, but this man seemed somehow familiar to him. It was something in the way he tilted his head while he was talking. Every so often the man would raise his hand and sweep his hair back out of his eyes. One of the times that this man raised his hand, Jake was sure that he recognized the ring on his left hand. Jake had seen this ring before—but where, he could not even begin to guess. It simply wouldn't come to his mind.

As Jake was ready to give up trying to see who this man was, the stranger and David decided to part ways. The man handed David what looked like a newspaper, and then as the two of them shook hands, they moved in a semicircle, just enough so Jake could get a good look at this mystery man. "Oh my goodness! It was one of his brothers, Mark." Jake was talking to himself, but did he say it out loud? He was thankful that no one heard him. What on earth was Mark doing here at the bus station, and why on earth was he talking to David? Jake wondered for a moment if it was Mark who had been sent to retrieve his notebook. No, that would be nuts. Mark was not even on the force. One thing was for sure, and that was that he should not be seen by Mark. Mark had been told that Jake was off on some kind of training program.

Not in Jake's wildest dreams could he think of one single reason Mark would be here at the bus station and definitely not as to why he was talking to David. After all, David was a suspected criminal. Jake wondered if Mark even knew who David was, or perhaps it was only by chance they had met and started chatting? One thing was for sure, and that was as soon as this was all over, Jake would sit Mark down and explain a few things to him. Jake knew that David would not do anything to hurt Mark, it was that it could put Mark in a real bad position. What if when this whole thing came down, he was to be found with David when he got arrested? One thing was for sure, David would be one of the ones who would be arrested and chipped. That single thought gave Jake a chill down his back. But as he rethought it, he realized that it might be just as good for David to get off the streets as it was going to be for Sandy.

That is right, he needed to see if the doctor got the message and was able to go to the shelter. If not, perhaps he would be needed again to send another message. Jake looked down at his hand, and he noticed that he still had the key to locker #363. What should he do with it? He felt it was way too risky to keep it with him, and yet he did not want to just throw it away. Someone might find it and get to the notebook before the authorities could retrieve it. Jake looked around for a place to hide it. There it was, the perfect place. There was a planter over by the change machine. He could hide it in the potting soil. That way he would know where it was and, at the same time, not have to have it with him. As he put the key in the soil, Jake was thinking to himself about how easy this undercover work really was and that he was a lot better at it than he thought he would be. With that task done, Jake went out of the bus station's side door. He did not want to risk running into David, Mark, or anyone he knew for that matter.

*****

Victor had done like he had said and stayed with Sandy. He had let her believe that he was waiting for Peggy to show up, but he was also waiting to see Doc as well. About an hour or so into the morning, Sandy finally fell asleep. Victor slipped out from behind her and met up with a few of the helpers from the shelters. Victor saw that Jim had come in and was wanting to speak with him. "Victor, I saw Jake, and he told me that you need to see Doc, but the streets are so guarded right now that I cannot get word to him without putting him at risk. Who needs a doctor anyway?"

Victor looked over to where Sandy was lying. It was not only unusual for Sandy to be lying down but it was also against the rules. "Sandy is having some kind of allergy attack or something. Her eyes are swollen shut."

Jim, then, following Victor's gaze, saw what it was he was talking about. "What have you done so far for the swelling?"

"Well, we put some cold water on them, but with very little, if any, difference." Victor felt helpless in this situation. He had never come up against anything like this before.

"Victor, I am by no means a doctor, but my grandmother used to have problems with her eyes swelling. I can remember as a little boy that I would sometimes go into the house and find my grandmother with tea bags lying on her eyes. It was just about one of the funniest things I had ever seen as a kid. Anyway, she swore that the tea would make her swelling go down. I know it sounds like a crazy thing, but at least until the doctor can get here, I don't think it would hurt anything to try it, do you?" Jim had a look of excitement on his face thinking that he might have an answer that could help.

"Jim, I think that you are right. I don't think it could hurt anything. Can you help me figure out how you prepare the bags?" Jim was delighted not only to have an answer but also to be a part of the plan.

Several of the women helpers watched the two men as they prepared the tea bags and got them ready for Sandy's eyes. They were all chuckling at the two men and the way they were acting. One of the ladies said to the other, "Wonder if we should offer to help? They are handling the bags like they are alive."

"No, I think that it is good for them. Look how much fun they are having," said another. The ladies broke out in laughter at that remark. The joke was that anyone could tell from the faces on the men that they were having anything but fun.

The men finally got the bags exactly the way they thought they should be. They woke Sandy from her sleep and explained to her what they were planning. Sandy was ready to try anything at this point, so she was more than happy to let the men apply the bags. As the application of the bags was done, the front door of the shelter opened. Everyone in the shelter jumped and at once came to attention. It was not so much that the door opened but rather the way it had. The door opened, and then it just stood open. No one came into the shelter. Victor took the first incentive and walked over to the now-open door. As he approached, they could see that someone had placed a sack on the floor right inside the room. It was a large brown sack. It had the top rolled down only enough to hide its contents. The bag was full. But of what? Victor continued to walk to the door. He put his head outside just enough to look around. No one was there. Not a soul in sight. Only the sack.

Victor reached down to pick up the sack, but when he went to lift it, he was met with incredible resistance. Whatever was in the sack was very heavy. It slipped out of his fingers and remained on the floor where it had been placed.

Everyone in the shelter was watching. That is except for Sandy, who could be heard saying, "Okay, what's going on? Will someone please tell me?"

As Victor was about to take his second try at retrieving the sack, Jake came to the entrance of the shelter. Seeing the sack, he reached down and lifted it. At first he was equally as surprised about the sack being so heavy, but he put a little more backbone into it, and up the whole thing came. "What on earth do you have in this bag? Rocks?"

Jake continued to walk on into the room. He found his way over to the counter and placed the sack on the top of it.

Everyone was standing still looking at Jake as if he were a ghost or something. Jake took a quick scan of the room, and seeing that everyone was acting so strange, he thought that something must really be wrong with Sandy. He could see that her eyes were still not doing too well. In fact, he could have sworn that she had what looked to him to be tea bags on her eyes. "What's wrong? Isn't Sandy going to be all right? What did the doctor say?"

With those questions, Victor realized that they were all a little on edge. "Jake, no, Sandy is going to be fine. Well, we think so anyway. The doctor is not going to be able to come, so Jim here had an idea that we think might do the job."

"Then why are you all acting so weird?" With those words coming from Jake and the way he was looking around, several of the helpers began to chuckle. They were acting weird. Grown people afraid of a sack. With what had happened last night, they needed to be careful, but they did not need to act like scared rabbits.

"Well, what is going on?" Jake still wanted to know.

"Well, Jake, we are not sure. Did you see anyone out there when you were coming down the street?" Victor was asking Jake all the while he was looking at the sack on the counter and not directly at Jake, like he usually did.

"No, I did not see anyone on the street. Did someone leave the sack? I get it, you don't know who left the sack. You did not see them?"

Sandy was coming to the end of her patience. She was feeling much better now after her nap. Although her eyes were still not doing very well, she was ready to take charge and get on with what-ever this was that was going on. "What sack? Who did you not see? And who needs a doctor?" Sandy's voice was clear. It was direct, and it demanded an answer and right now.

Victor looked over to where it was that Sandy was now stand-ing. She had taken the scarf from her hair and had tied it around her head in order to hold the tea bags in their place on her eyes. "Well hello, Sandy. Nice to hear that you are doing better."

Sandy was now speaking even a little louder. "Victor, would you please tell me what sack? And for goodness' sakes, tell me what is in it."

Jake, being as eager to know what was in the sack, began to speak. "I will tell you one thing, Sandy. Whatever it is, it sure is heavy."

Sandy was now making her way over to the counter from the side of the room where she had been most of the day. She was doing well until she bumped headfirst into someone. That someone was David. During all the goings-on over the sack, David had slipped into the room and was more than halfway in before they noticed him. There was a climate of fear in the room. Not at all the kind of atmosphere he was used to seeing in these people. David was not sure what had brought this on but was quick to see they needed some encouragement.

"Oh, hello. Do I know you?" Sandy was feeling the tension same as David was. Things needed to lighten up a bit. Who she had bumped into was not important to her at this moment. She needed help to get around, so she took the newfound person by the arm and was led by him the rest of the way to the counter.

David leaned down to speak to her. "Sandy, I am glad to see that you are feeling better. Anything on the eyes yet?" David was happy to see that Sandy was doing better. Sandy doing better was good news on its own. They were going to need her even more after they all heard the news that he had to tell them. Oh, how David wished he could be the bearer of better news. Sandy was glad to hear David's voice and was happy that he was here while they were having a regrouping time together. These times helped to build the team spirit and the kind of family feelings that grow as you are with people. Leadership was hard, but it was times like this that you look back on during the hard times to help you keep going. Sandy knew that David was a strong leader but thought he could use some more of those together memories too. "Well, David, there is something new on my eyes. Tea bags." Everyone in the room went nuts at hearing what Sandy had said. Even Sandy did not think it was that funny but was glad to see they could all have a laugh together over it.

"I can see that you are feeling better. But seriously, what did the doctor say about your eyes? Is it allergies? And how long will they take to get better?" David wanted to see how bad things were with her before he decided how he would tell what needed to be told.

"David, you will be happy to know that I plan on being good as new soon. So what's up with you?" Sandy knew David really well. Over the years, she had known that one of the hardest things for him to do was to deliver bad news. In the past, anytime he had to tell her something that was wrong, he would always start it out with "How are you doing?" She had learned that when he said that, there would most likely be bad news of some kind or another that followed.

She had done it again. Victor was amazed at how Sandy could so easily shift attention from herself to others without them ever catching onto the fact that she had. She was a master at it. He now realized that for Sandy, true happiness in life was doing for others. If the focus was on her, then she could not do what she liked to do best. Victor wasn't altogether sure how healthy this was mentally. But until now, Sandy had done just fine. Perhaps this was how God planned her to be. Realizing all that, Victor let slide the fact that Sandy had misled David to think she had already seen the doctor. She did not lie, but then she did stretch the heck out of the truth. Seeing all of this made Victor smile at her. What a woman he had allowed into his heart. Not that he had any real choice in the matter.

Victor then looked over to see what it was that David was here to relay. He had not been scheduled to be here today, but then nothing about this day was as it had been planned. Although Sandy could not see, she was right, something was up with David. Victor could see it in the way he was acting. David was a strong man, but he was sensitive at the same time. Victor had always thought that this blend was what had helped to make David such a great leader. "David, was there any special reason you are here at the shelter? Or are you just dropping by to see us?"

David was not sure how he was going to break the news to these people that the closing of the South Street shelter was not the only bad thing that had come out of last night. Reaching into his coat pocket, he pulled out a newspaper. It was only a matter of time until someone from the street would bring this information back to the shelter anyway, and David felt that he owed it to these people to hear it from him first. He wanted to tell it as gently as it could be done. He unrolled the paper and laid it onto the sack that was on the counter. As he did, the paper draped itself over the sack, and there on the front page was a very large picture of Peggy. The headlines read, "Young girl arrested. Suspect in drug trafficking for the Knowing."

Everyone in the shelter came in close to the counter in order to try and read the article. David quickly realized that this was not a good working situation. Not only was it that not everyone could see the paper, but then there was Sandy. She of all of the people had the right to hear about Peggy firsthand. David picked up the paper and began to read,

> Yesterday a young girl was arrested. She would only identify herself as Peggy. Due to the fact she did not have a chip, there will need to be further information gathered in order to find her true identity. Formal charges as of yet have not been filed. Further information needs to be in place before the officials could go any further. She is being held at the local government station until further notice.

The entire shelter was quiet. Not a word was spoken by anyone. "Then the story goes on to say that the closing of the shelter over on South Street was a direct result of finding Peggy. They say that they found not only drugs but that they also discovered guns and ammu-nitions as well. The last of the article states that they need to retrieve some final information in order to fill in all of the unknown details." As David came to that part of the story, he rolled the paper back up and placed it into his jacket again. No use in continuing any further. They all knew what this meant. This was another setup in order to give them a reason to shut down chipless shelters.

Everyone was acting like they had been shot, but it was Jake who was the first to speak. "What on earth was Peggy doing over at a shelter that had drugs and guns in it? How could you be so crazy as to let her go into a place like that?" Jake was angry, but not at the government officials. But rather at these people. Peggy's so-called friends. Who would let her get herself into such trouble? Couldn't they see that she trusted everyone? Didn't they realize that she didn't think sometimes? What was wrong with these people?

Now everyone was staring at Jake. They could not believe his reaction. What kind of people did he think them to be?

Victor walked over to where Jake was standing. He took a deep breath and then let it out. Victor was not sure what he was going to do, but he knew one thing was for sure, and that was that he needed to set this young man straight and right now. "First of all, I think you need to know that none of us, not a single one of us, at this shelter or any other for that matter would ever do anything like being involved with drugs or guns. The one thing you need to know is that we fol-low all laws. God calls us to it in the Bible. We are told to follow the laws of the land."

Jake was getting irritated at these people. They are told to follow the laws, and yet some of the things they do go directly against the law. "Victor, you and I both know that is not true. What about going out after curfew? And how about having meetings where there are more than ten people at one time? What about those laws, or don't they count?"

Victor couldn't believe his ears; this young man was defending the government. What on earth kind of teaching had he received in his past? "Jake, you know that the only laws that we choose not to follow are the ones that go against our God. There are certain things that the government would have us to do that is specifically against what God tells us to do. But running drugs and going against gun laws is something we cannot do. Do you think if we were going to break laws to make money, we would live like this?"

"Well, if you have done everything that your God has told you to do, then why are you in this mess? Why don't you go to your God and tell him to do something?" Jake did not care if anyone knew how he felt at the moment. His possible future wife has been arrested and is going through heaven knows what, and these people stand here talking about keeping this God's law. "Yes, since you are God's people, why don't you go to Him and get all the answers? That is what you think, don't you? That because of your faith, you have all of the answers?"

Now it was David's turn to have a talk with this young man. Rightfully he was upset, but to take it out on God was going too far. "Jake, you are right. We are God's people, but God does not give us all of the answers. He gives us someone to go to with the questions. From there, we can get an explanation or a peace, but either way, we do find an answer."

Jake stood in a fighting position acting like if he could win the verbal argument, then he could somehow make everything come out all right. "Well, if our God is so great at saving us, how is it that he can't even save his Bibles?"

Sandy, having no eyesight, had been put into a very unusual situation. Not being able to see, she was somehow able to read between the lines of Jake's conversation. The most important thing she had picked up on was that Jake had gone from saying "you and your God" to saying "us and our God." Somewhere in all of this upset, Jake had switched sides. At least in his subconscious. Sandy was amazed at how God worked. She knew for a fact, if she had been able to see, that she would have missed the underlying truth. This battle of words was getting nowhere. Several of the people who had entered the shelter were starting to take up sides. Some could clearly see Jake's point of view and wanted answers while others felt as if Satan himself were speaking through Jake. Several arguments broke out in different places in the room. No matter what the people were feeling at this moment, it was not getting them any closer to helping Peggy. Sandy decided that with her new insight to Jake's thinking that it was time for her to speak up. With her first try at interrupting the conversations, Sandy found that she made not even a dent in the noise level. Thinking to herself that if perhaps she were to lift herself up onto the counter, they might see her, and then she would have a better chance at being heard. Finding the counter edge with her hands, she went to hoist herself up onto the top of it, but instead her knee met with the sack that Jake had placed there. As soon as her knee hit the sack, she lost her balance, and reaching out to grasp anything that would help to keep her from falling, she found the top of the sack. She grabbed hold of it. Although it was heavy, it was not heavy enough to keep her from falling. Sandy gave out a loud yell as she came flying off the counter backward with the sack following quickly behind her. Sandy went one way while the sack went the other. Unlike this morning, Sandy did not get caught but fell totally to the floor. Just seconds after Sandy hit the ground, she could hear whatever it was that she had grabbed on to hit the ground also.

Then there was silence.

Someone quickly came to Sandy's aid, but no one was saying a word. Finally, things got the best of Sandy, and she decided that swollen eyes or not, she needed to see—and right now. Without a second thought, she reached up and pulled the scarf from around her eyes. Tea bags and all fell away from her head. It was like a miracle. The tea bags had removed almost all of the swelling. Sandy had gotten the use of her eyes back but was still having trouble focusing. Sandy opened and shut her eyes several times, and finally she was able to see well enough to look around. As she scanned the faces of the people, she saw that they were all looking in one direction. Their heads were bowed but not because they were in prayer but because they could hardly believe their eyes. Sandy quickly followed to where they were looking. There on the ground having fallen out of the now-ripped sack were a pile of Bibles. Some were old, some new. They were all different colors and different kind of print. Some were even different translations. But the only thing in the sack was Bibles. As soon as Sandy saw what the books were, she remembered what it was Jake had said about God not being able to save His Bible, much less his people. Sandy's chest was pounding. If this was not a message to Jake from God, then Sandy did not know anything. Sandy quickly looked over to where she had seen Jake standing during her original survey of the room. Jake looked like he had been hit by lightning. His face was white, and his eyes were trying hard not to see what he knew he was. Jake's eyes met with Sandy's.

Everyone continued to stand still. Not a word was spoken. Everyone knew without a doubt that this was a special happening. First of all, to get Bibles but to also get so many at the same time. Only God could pull off such a task as this with such perfect timing, and they all knew it. Even Jake. Especially Jake. God had heard, and God had sent an answer.

Jake couldn't believe what had happened. This God, He was real. He had to be. But how? Everything Jake had been taught seemed so dumb compared to what he thought he now knew. He was not going to help these people. God took care of them. Oh no, what had he done. The notebook. It had the second part of the information that the officials were waiting for in order to charge Peggy. With that information, they could not only keep Peggy, but so many others would be in danger too. Jake knew that he needed to do something. But what? Get the book back? Yes, that is it! All he had to do was get to the bus station, get the key from the planter where he had hidden it, and get to the notebook before the officials had picked it up. He could make it right with God, all he had to do was get the notebook back. Jake looked up at the clock. Only a little time left until the first siren for curfew, but it did not matter what happened to him. What did matter though was God's people. Jake decided that he needed to go. And right now.

Jake at once headed for the door. David was quick to realize that this young man was about to leave the shelter. "Jake, you can't go now, it is too close to curfew. Besides, we need you to help get caught up for the dinner." David was thinking along with the others that Jake must be embarrassed by what he had said. They wanted him to know that even if he did spout off, they still thought of him as one of their own.

Victor walked over and joined David in talking with Jake. "Now is not the time to be out on the streets, even if you are not comfortable with us here. Don't worry, this will all blow over in a day or two. No one will even remember what it was that was said."

Jake stared at the two of them. Were they crazy? Of course, they did not know about the notebook full of information, but still he had said awful things about God. "You two don't understand. I really do need to go. I will be off the street before the second siren, I promise." With that he turned and ran to the door. As he was almost to the doorway, someone was coming in from the outside, so Jake had an uninterrupted exit.

Jake ran down the street. Somehow this same street that had given him such high hopes this morning was anything but a good memory now. What had he done? The information he had placed in his notebook was going to jeopardize the one he loved. Yes, Peggy. The one he truly loved. And it might be Jake himself who helped to send her to prison for what could be the rest of her life. All Jake could do was to run as fast as he could. Not to beat the curfew like he should be thinking but instead to get the book before the officials did. As he was coming past the South Street shelter, he could see, not for the first time, what total devastation had been done to it. The first time he had seen it with his eyes and now was seeing it with his heart. And then on top of that, all the lies about why it had been done. As Jake was on his last part of his trip to the bus station, all he could think to do was to pray. And so, for the first time he could remember praying, Jake called out to God to help with this whole mess. He knew that only God could fix the timing so that he would get to the locker in time. God could make it so he could destroy the notebook before it could do any damage. God could help Jake to save Peggy and all the others. Jake reached the steps. Climbing them seemed a hundred miles. As Jake reached the top, the warning siren for curfew began to call out. Jake could ask God to help him get back to the shelter safe before the last sounding, but at this point, he did not even care. All he wanted to do was destroy the book. Once inside the bus station, Jake ran to the planter where he had hidden the key. Yes, there it was. Right where he had left it. Running over to locker #363, he plunged the key into its place, and hearing the click, he gave a sigh of relief he was almost done. Jake opened the locker. Reaching toward the inside. But he stopped short.

Jake took a few steps backward. It was as if he had been hit with something. The notebook was gone. They had already picked it up. The officials would have all the information they would need to put Peggy away. Jake was in shock. He did not really know what to do next. Jake was not mad at God. Jake was mad at himself for being so blind. What on earth had kept him from seeing and feeling? Jake could not quite put a finger on it, but he somehow knew that these people had found a special something that he was now sure he would never have. Jake was sure that after having his hand in destroying some of God's people that there was not a chance in the whole world to ever be a part of their group. Jake was devastated. What would it matter now if he were arrested after curfew? His chance at a real life was over. Now that he had seen the light, how could he ever go back to his old way of living? Jake was no longer standing but was now on his knees right in the middle of the bus station floor. Nothing was going through his head except the fact of how he had gone against a great group of people. He had let them down, but the worst was that he had failed to see that there was a real God, until it was too late, that is. Nothing else mattered to him right now—nothing. Nothing.

All at once, Jake felt his arms being seized and felt himself being lifted up off the floor. Literally. Jake knew that this shouldn't be the officers taking a hold of him, not yet anyway, the last curfew siren had not sounded. Giving a quick glance around, Jake could see that it was Victor, David, and Jim who had lifted him up. Jake did not know whether to be happy or sad about this. So he did not argue when they insisted he come with them immediately. Jake noted right off that the men were not leading him back to the shelter but they were going in exactly the opposite direction instead. Victor looked to David. "Rabbit hole, right?"

David responded in the exact same tone of voice, "You got it."

Jim chimed in, "Let's do it then."

Without warning of any kind for Jake, he was turned down a residential street. What on earth were they thinking? Being out after curfew was one thing, but being in one of these neighborhoods could cause great trouble. Jake was not so concerned about himself, but for these men, it could mean prison. To think that they were risking prison for his safety. Especially since he really might not get into very much trouble at all.

The four men, first running and now walking down the street, turned off the sidewalk and were now finding themselves walking along the backside of one of the houses. Jake was concerned, but he also knew that these men had a God who would help them. He also knew for a fact that they were praying, and that was totally fine by him.

They stopped. Two of the men, Victor and Jim, turned to look out to see if anyone had seen them. Victor turned his head so David could hear him. "Coast clear." David reached out and pulled a trash can away from the house. There along the ground was an air vent. David looked again over his shoulder to see that the others approved of his next move. Doing so, David pressed hard against the wall. To Jake's surprise, the whole bottom part of the siding gave way and folded itself up and back. There before the men were a set of stairs. David entered first followed by a very stunned Jake, then Victor, and last to enter was Jim. Jim turned before coming down the stairs. He reached out and dragged the trash can back into its place. With that done, he then pushed on the inside of the wall, and they all stood as they watched the entrance disappear before their very eyes.

Before the entrance had completely closed itself, they could hear the final siren going off. Not a second to spare.

Jim coming on down the stairs was wiping sweat off his brow. "I know that this sort of thing is supposed to keep you young, but I think it is aging me."

Victor could sympathize with what Jim was saying. Cutting it close like that was not something he ever looked forward to doing again. It was one thing to be on the streets with a solid plan, but doing it like this was way too much for him. "I know what you mean, but we are here now, and we are safe."

David was here with the men, but his mind was back on Sandy and what it was that she must be dealing with. The only real information she had was what David had read to her. That would be enough for a while to keep people satisfied, but it wouldn't take long for some to decide that she was not doing enough to solve the problem. "You know, I think that we should take a little time to stop and thank God for helping us to get to safety, and I think we should ask for extra strength for Sandy tonight."

As David was finishing his statement, the thought of Sandy being alone at the shelter came to Victor's mind. There would be a lot of people there, but she would be the only leader planned for tonight. Originally, there were to have been two more. Jim and Victor as well as Sandy.

All three men quickly agreed that going to prayer was first priority. As they began to kneel, Jim noticed that Jake was standing over in one corner with his back to them. He reached out his hand and tapped both David and Victor so as to get their attention. When they looked up, he motioned for them to look over at Jake in a half-whisper, half-mouthed communication.

Victor was the first to offer an invitation for Jake to join them. "Jake, why don't you join us in prayer? I think that you will feel better if you do."

"No. That is okay. Why don't you just go ahead? Besides, I think God has heard enough from me today." Jake was not feeling sorry for himself, but he felt that even God could never get over all of the things Jake had done in all this mess. God had already shown him that he had enough of Jake by not helping him get to the locker in time enough to undo all the damage that he had done. Jake felt it was obvious that God wanted nothing to do with him. After all, Jake did not blame God one bit.

David was not sure what was going on in Jake's head. It really didn't matter about whatever it was that Jake was thinking he had done that was so awful. From David's point of view, Jake had some arguments with God, and God would lead him to the truth of it. It really was no big deal. After all, God could handle questions. In fact, David was sure that God could even handle Jake's being mad at Him.

But that was going to be something Jake would have to work out for himself. There would be help from all of them, but Jake would be on his own with his personal walk with God. "Jake, do whatever you think is best, but please join us if you can. We need all of the prayer power we can pull together."

Victor looked over at Jake. "Jake, we sure could use the extra help."

Jake was not sure what they were talking about when it came to prayer power, but the words "we need you" was all he needed to hear to give it one more try. "Okay, if you think it can do any good." Jake joined the men, and they all went into a kneeling position. This was something new for Jake. Every single one of them were on their knees. He had seen a picture of a child kneeling by a bed once, but he had not seen this done by everyone at the same time the whole three months he had been with the shelter. Perhaps because this was a big one. But whatever the reason and whatever the way, this was something Jake felt good about being a part of. He was somehow a part of the team. From what they were saying, he could make a difference. And he was grateful.

The men prayed for a time, and then one by one the prayer ended. Jake had knelt silently listening to these seemingly strong men go to God and confess their weaknesses and then ask Him for strength and support. Jake knew that God would not be here to listen to him, so he was just delighted to be near these men knowing that where they were, God would surely be. Now for the first time, Jake was seeing how it was that the government had not been able to get control of the Knowing. That was because God was in control of it all along. There was not a single man leading the group but God. And one thing Jake had seen was that God took care of His own. Jake couldn't help but wonder how it was that God had let him get so close to the group in order to do so much damage. How was it that God had not realized what an awful traitor he was going to turn out to be? Jake did not think he could ever feel as low as he was now. So many of the people at the shelter said that when they found God, it was a wonderful experience. How was it that his finding God was not so wonderful? In fact, it was just about the worst thing Jake had ever encountered. He found this loving God, and he now felt as though he could never be a part of the Knowing, or could he?

Jake decided that this was something he really did want in his life, so for the very first time, he was in the asking. *God, can I please be a part of Your group? Whatever the cost, please let me in.*

CHAPTER 10

The rest of the evening had gone without any incident. Jake had been told about the rabbit holes. Victor had even shared about how Sandy liked to rate them from bad to good on a scale only she understood.

Jake had not asked any questions. He did not feel like he had the right to after what he had done to his friends. The fact that they did not know what he had done yet really did not matter. Jake was sure that this God he had only just started finding out about and who he was beginning to believe in would have known though. As much as he wanted to get to know more about this newfound God, he realized that it was all too late. At least for him, but not for Peggy and the others. Perhaps there would be something he could do to stop the information he had provided from doing too much damage. Perhaps he could go and talk with Mr. Diggings. Jake had thought through that idea, going over and over what he thought could make a difference to someone like Mr. Diggings. Jake finally came to the conclusion that he was absolutely too tired to make any decisions right now. The only thing he could be sure of was that he needed sleep.

Jake was ready to lie down for the night when he noticed that he was warm. Really warm. It felt extremely good. Looking around the rabbit hole, he noticed that the people in this house had not only arranged this hiding place by digging in more space, adding stairs, and finishing off the area with real imagination, but they had also added a heating vent down to the crawl space. Jake felt a connection to the group when he found himself thinking that he was sure that Sandy would rate this place very high on the list. Hopefully, he would someday have the chance to ask her.

Jake was not sure what tomorrow would bring, but one thing was for sure, and that was nothing could ever be the same again. Not with the shelter, not with his friends, not even with his family. Speaking of family, what was Mark doing at the bus station? Jake's mind couldn't even begin to guess. It was odd how comfortable Mark looked standing with David. In fact at first glance, Mark could have been mistaken for one of them. Jake began to think back on how his mother often commented about how Mark chose to dress himself. With the kind of money Mark was getting from his trust fund, he should have been able to dress like a king. Jake had not considered until now that Mark never had lived as anything but a simple man. His apartment was very small, he dressed so modestly, he rarely bought himself anything extra, and now he did not even have a car. Jake was beginning to wonder what it was Mark was doing with all his money. Why, with the interest from his trust alone, he could live better than most. Jake was also remembering that in the last year or so, he had not spent very much time with his brother. Jake's career had been the most important thing in Jake's life for quite some time. Even over friends and family. Except for the family dinners that they all had weekly, Jake had little to do with the others in his family, even his favorite brother. That would be one of the things Jake planned to change in the future. He enjoyed being with Mark, or at least he used to.

While Jake was doing everything but sleeping, David and Victor sat off to one side of the crawl space, and by whispering as low as possible, they had a conversation concerning what the day had brought. "David, what on earth do you think the shutting of the shelter is really about?"

"Victor, I am not exactly sure, but it is my guess that this is only the beginning. They have been trying to shut down the shelters for a long time now, and with them not being able to do so, it is most likely making the government look bad, the fact that we still exist and all. As for Peggy, I haven't a clue what is going on with that whole thing. I can only pray that things will be okay until we get back and can help." David motioned his head over to where Jake was sleeping. "What do you think is going on with Jake here?"

Victor looked over to where Jake was now lying with his back to them. Jake looked quite at home. He had found one of the mats that had been left in the crawl space for sleeping on. All of the walls had been finished off with paneling, and the ground had concrete poured and then carpet placed down on it. In some ways, Victor thought this might even be better than the shelter. Even the bathroom facilities had been thought through. The owners of the house had placed a portable camping toilet down in the space. This was really a great place to hide.

As Victor was looking at Jake in this environment, he noted that even though it was warm, Jake still held his arms like he was cold. He had thought that Jake had held his arms gathered around himself the way he did because his coat was not warm enough. But from how Jake was lying now, Victor was thinking Jake's body language was yelling about how uncomfortable his being here with them was for the boy. "You know, David, I really am not too sure about Jake here. When he first came to us, I had been led to think he was a believer, but after what I have seen and heard today, I am not sure anymore."

"Well, Victor, the way I see it, many people believe in God, but for many of them, that is all it is, all they do is believe in a God who is out there somewhere. It is when God becomes God where you are that things really start to change. That's when people start to change. That's when instead of being a God you conjure up from time to time, He becomes a God who walks with you, in you, now that's when the real Christian life begins. Up until that point, somehow He is only a thought of life instead of being a way of life." David paused for a moment looking over at Jake again. "Give him time. He has got what it takes to be a true believer, I can feel it. There is something special about this young man. I am not sure yet what it is, but I have every confidence that God has sent him to us for a reason."

Jim had moved over to join the two and was now adding to the conversation. "I know what you mean. There is definitely something about him that is exceptional."

Victor had to agree also. He had gone out on a limb with Sandy about this young man. That was not something he was likely to do for just anybody. "I wonder what it is God plans for him? Judging from the way things have gone lately, the future should prove to be exciting, whatever it is."

The three men decided that this day had been way too long, so they grabbed mats and bedded down in this wonderfully warm hiding place. All of them were grateful tonight.

*****

Morning would never come soon enough for almost everyone. Everyone that was except for Jake. Fear of what this new day would bring was swelling up in him until he thought he would explode without some sort of release. Jake had thought of telling the three men of what his true story was, but somehow he could not bring himself to do it, not yet anyway. Whatever time he was to have left as their friend, he wanted every second of it, and who knows, perhaps there might be a way out of this. Only time could tell. Perhaps he could hold out hope that God had a plan better than anything he could come up with.

Whatever the information Mr. Diggings was going to use out of the book Jake had turned in would most likely be found out sometime today. Perhaps if Jake could have a talk with Mr. Diggings, he could persuade him that some of the things he had written were in error. This idea was not likely to work, but he had to try to do something. Okay, now Jake had his plan. Get out of here as soon as he could and speak with Mr. Diggings. He needed to go alone if it was going to work. Now he needed an excuse. He would tell them that he needed some time to himself to think things over. They would respect that. Then all he would have to do is to get word to Mr. Diggings that he needed to speak to him. Surely that would not be as hard as it sounded.

Victor woke up, and as he sat up, he noticed that Jake was already awake and had put his bedding away. It was obvious that he was planning on getting out of here as soon as he could. Victor thought that this was a good sign. Jake was obviously as worried as the rest were about the others at the shelter. It was however a great disappointment to Victor when Jake expressed how he wanted to go off and be by himself. The fact that Jake was seemingly not at all concerned about the others at the shelter was upsetting to him. Somehow, he thought that Jake would at the very least feel something about what was happening to Peggy, but by the way he was acting right now, that seemed to be the last thing on Jake's mind. How very disappointing Jake's actions were turning out to be. It appeared to Victor that Jake was still thinking of only himself and his own feelings. This was getting way too hard, Victor wanted desperately to be right about his first impressions of Jake. This situation needed more than blind faith, it needed God. Victor made a gracious effort at supporting Jake's choice in going off by himself.

Jake was never so grateful for anything in his life as he was that the rest of the men had not questioned him about where he was going. He hated not telling the truth, but having to lie to them was somehow even worse. As the opportunity to leave the rabbit hole had safely come, it was Jake and Jim who exited first. Each chose their direction to go and left with a simple wave of the hand.

Jake felt a chill go completely through his body. The weather had not only turned colder but had also become wetter. The rain was not coming down hard, but was steady all the same. Perhaps the contrast of going from the warmth of the rabbit hole into the outside was making it seem worse than it was, but Jake was feeling cold like he could never remember feeling. Jake was determined to get this new plan of stopping the damage his book could cause done and over with. Not even the weather was going to stop him.

Getting to the neighborhood where Mr. Diggings's office was would not be that difficult, but getting into the building and to his office was going to prove to be almost impossible. With a chip, he could go unnoticed, but without one, he would be detected right away. Perhaps that was what he was going to need to happen. But no, getting arrested would not do any good. Who would listen to him about needing to get a message to Mr. Diggings? Who would care that he needed to speak with him? After all, he could not tell them what this was all about, it was classified. Jake knew that even he would never have heard out anyone with such a crazy story, especially someone who did not have a chip, and on top of that, someone who had been arrested for trespassing in a restricted area. God, how was he going to pull this off? He was not sure, but he felt that he needed to try.

Getting to the right district did not take as long as Jake thought it would. Funny how far apart mentally these people seemed, and yet they almost live in the exact same neighborhoods.

Jake stopped walking. He had come to the building where he needed to try and change the mess he had made.

He did not move, he just stood there. What was he waiting for? His mind knew what it was he needed to do, but somehow his body would not move. What was he really doing anyway? Jake was sure of one thing, and that was that Mr. Diggings was not going to listen to anything he had to say. He was sure that he would accuse him of having been brainwashed. So then what? All of Jake's new friends would have been arrested, the shelter closed, and his career ruined too. What good was it going to do anyone for Jake to throw away everything he had worked for? It is a lost cause, and it just doesn't make any sense to ruin his life as well. Who knows, his keeping his position might somehow prove beneficial to all of the others in the future. Perhaps having someone like him in his governmental position would be better in the long run. Wait, was this Jake's idea, or was God putting this new idea in his mind? Did God work like this? Peggy seemed to think so, Sandy and Victor too.

Jake's heart was pounding. He had almost made a major mistake. Thank God he had come to his senses before it was too late. Odd, Jake thought the words "Thank God" had just been a way of speech before, but somehow they had a totally new meaning now.

Jake turned around and began to walk back to an area that he knew he would be safe in without a chip. He was not sure how long he had stood outside the building looking at it, but it was long enough for him to get his wits back. Jake was almost out of the restricted area when he realized that he was being followed.

Not wanting to look any more suspicious than he already did, he did not turn around to look at whoever it was following him, but he was somewhat sure that it must be government officers. He had only a half a block to go, and he would be home free.

That was the game plan, but that was not the way it was to turn out. Just as Jake was to take his last few steps into the chipless area, someone knocked his feet out from under him. The sweep came from behind him, so he fell backward and found himself lying on his back looking up at his pursuers. He did not recognize any of them, but he did recognize their uniforms. Just as he had suspected, it was the government officers. Jake somehow knew from the start of this that they were not planning on any official action. The look on their faces alone gave away their plan, but when they pulled him to his feet and dragged him off to the side of a building away from the sight of the everyday passersby, he knew that his suspicions were coming true. These were not officers like his family members or fellow officers he worked with, but these were radical officers. Only a few, yes, but that did not make the trouble he had gotten himself into any less. The officers were making jokes among themselves.

"What is it we have here?" One of the officers was circling Jake, making sure that he kept his face uncomfortably close to his. The others chimed in with answers. "No, not human. No chip." Another added to the heckling. "If not human, then what?"

Jake had counted from what he could see about nine men altogether. Far too many for him or anyone else for that matter to fight against. His only hope would be to do whatever it was they wanted and trust that they were the kind of people he had always thought his kind to be. Jake's optimism did not last long. It was only a matter of seconds before Jake felt the sting of a baton come across the side of his head. The blow made him fall to the ground, catching him totally off guard.

One of the officers stepped in and was objecting to the treatment that Jake was receiving. That only brought verbal wrath on him, so he decided it best not to protest any more than he had. Jake looked into this man's eyes and could see the desperate want he had to help him, but Jake also knew that this man had no other choice but to go along or become part of the battering line.

Finally one of the men realized that a small crowd of people were beginning to gather at the end of the walkway. "Hey. I know what we should do with this guy. Let's 'baptize' him. Isn't that what you people do?" Looking around, he saw a large pool of water that had gathered from the lack of proper drainage. The rain that had fallen most of the night and on into the morning had built up near the drain. It was this man's idea to place Jake into it to make some sort of point. Jake was not sure what it was that this guy was talking about, but one thing was for sure, and that was that this was not going to be pleasant.

Like a single-minded group, they each helped to escort Jake over to the edge of the pool of water. From what Jake could see, it could not have been more than one or two feet deep at the most. No matter how deep it was, it was not somewhere he wanted to go.

Jake turned to look at the small crowd to see if there would be anyone there who would help him by objecting to what was going on. To his disappointment, not only were they not going to help him but most of them seemed to be enjoying what they were seeing.

"Come on, my little chipless soul. Let's get on with it." Two of the officers grabbed Jake and flung him into the water.

Jake found himself totally covered in a water and mud mixture. Not only was this degrading, but it was also very cold.

Jake's first reaction was to get himself up and out of the cold water, but to his horror, he quickly discovered that he was now being held down just deep enough into the water so as not to be able to catch his breath. Now this was not funny. In fact, this was downright one of the most frightening things he had ever encountered. What was the matter with these people? His people, or so he had thought. Jake was not sure if he ever wanted to be a part of them again. Even if he was given the chance.

Jake's mind went blank. Then real clear and distinct thoughts started to come into his head. If he was going to die, then he wanted to do it with God understanding how it was he was feeling about what had happened. He wanted to make sure that this God of the

Knowing knew that he was sorry for his part in all of the anti-re-ligious plan. *Forgive me. I know that it is too late, but I need to ask. Please, I am sorry.* Jake could not speak the words out loud. *I do believe in Your Son Jesus. Jesus, help me.*

The hands that had been holding him under the water had let him go, but his mouth was still full of what he had been trying to breathe in.

At once he came up still trying to speak out his thoughts and then trying to catch a breath of real air. Choking, he pulled himself up to the side of the hole grabbing onto some tall grass that had grown up around its edge. Although no one was holding him down anymore, the weight of the water and mud along with the cold and lack of air made him feel so heavy that there might as well have been twenty people holding him down. Jake's survival instincts were starting to kick in. Somehow from down deep inside of himself, he found the strength to continue to reach out, hold on, and pull himself partway out of this mudhole. Enough so he could relax and catch his breath anyway.

Jake, for the life of himself, could not figure out what had happened to the men who were attacking him, but for some reason, they had left. Jake pushed himself up from the ground as best he could and was trying to pull himself over to the side of the building. People were walking by him, but no one stopped to help him. No one even stopped to see if he was going to be all right. How was it that these people had gone so far as to not recognize a fellow human being? Even someone without a chip was still a human being. When did this kind of response become a part of everyday life? Could fear be enough to make even the caring look the other way?

Jake finally made it to the wall and pulled himself up into a sitting position. He knew that if he stayed here, it would be just a matter of time until someone would have him arrested for loitering. He knew that he needed to get himself up and get to the safe zone at the least. Then in the long run get himself off the street. Perhaps to the shelter if he could.

"Oh, God, what now?" Jake shut his eyes and leaned his head back against the wall. There was no relief. His head was hurting from the blow he had received. He was cold, and he was dirty. There was warmth on one part of his body, and that was on the side of his face. He lifted his hand up to the warmth only to find that it was warm because there was blood coming from the wound on his head. What a mess this was turning out to be.

With short delay and seeming to come from nowhere, there arrived a man. Jake was startled at first from the man's attention. Becoming aware of this man's arrival, Jake opened his eyes to see an obviously chipped man kneeling down holding a cloth of some kind in his hand. He placed it on the side of Jake's face. "Here, this should help to stop the bleeding." He took Jake's hand and placed it over the cloth in order for him to hold it in place. With that done, he reached down and took Jake under one of his arms and began to try and lift him to his feet.

One of the first thoughts Jake had was that this man was going to get his clothing dirty if he got too close. As Jake was about to say something about it, he felt this man move his arm from under Jake's to a different position, coming around behind and helping to hold him up. Jake had no real strength of his own. All he could do was lean into this man and take all of the help he could get. Taking help from another was not at all something he could ever get used to, but at this moment, there was no choice.

"I don't know who you are, but thank you." Jake had finally gotten his breath back enough to speak.

"That does not matter now, but what does matter is that we get you off these streets and to a safe place. Got any ideas?" The man knew enough to walk Jake toward the chipless area. At least being arrested would not be so likely there.

"No. I mean, if you can just get me off to the side where I can rest a little, then when I can, I will get to where it is I need to go." Jake was not sure who this man was, and as grateful as he was to him for the help, he knew that he couldn't let him do too much. On the one hand, he could be trouble (working for the government officers), and then again on the other hand, if he were not against the chip-less, then the more he did, the more at risk he would put himself in. Either way, Jake needed to be careful.

The man did as Jake had asked. He made sure he was as safe as he could be. "I'll send help to you, just stay here and be still. Okay?" Then the man started off in the direction they had just come from.

Jake couldn't feel the cold anymore, but he knew that he was cold from the way he was shaking. Peter suddenly came to his mind. The kid at the shelter. Jake remembered thinking about how he had been shaking. Now it was Jake who was in the same condition. Jake knew that he was cold, but he also knew that he had experienced real fear. Not a place or a feeling he ever wanted to have to happen to him again. But then it wasn't over yet, was it? He was still out here on the street unable to help himself. The shaking of his frame worsened.

Jake closed his eyes not wanting to see what a mess he had become. Thoughts of what-ifs started to fill his head. They were not helping him at all. In fact, they were only making things seem worse, but at least they were keeping him awake. Jake felt he needed to at least do that much for himself.

At first Jake thought he was hallucinating. He felt something heavy and warm drape over his upper body. As he opened his eyes, he saw what seemed to be a another chipped man placing a very large and heavy coat over him. "What are you doing?" Jake was trying to say, but his voice came out only in a whisper.

"Shh. Don't try to talk. This should help to keep you warm until help gets here." The man tucked the edges of the coat around and under Jake as best as he could.

Jake looked down at the coat and at once remembered his prayer for a warmer coat. Warmth came over Jake, but it wasn't just from the coat. Part of the warmth was from down deep inside of himself. He could feel tears of gratefulness swelling up inside of him. He couldn't talk. All he could do was sit there and think grateful thoughts. What kind of God was this who would answer the prayers of someone who hadn't even believed in Him? What kind of God was this who would answer the prayers of someone who had been sent to destroy His people? Jake was not sure of those answers, but he was sure that He was this kind of God. The thoughts of what-ifs had now been replaced with thankful and hopeful ones. Jake's mind quickly went on to think that of all of the prayers that God had answered for him, why hadn't He answered the one about Jake getting back to the locker before the book had been picked up? That would have made more sense. But then so far as Jake could tell, this God had not necessarily been one of sense.

*****

News of what had happened to Jake hit the streets like a flash of lightning.

As word reached the shelter where Sandy was waiting, it was only that someone without a chip had been hurt and was in need of help.

Victor had received a similar story where he was at, but to his message was added that this person needed to be rescued and right now.

Both Sandy and Victor headed out from their separate locations to see if there was anything they could do to help.

It was Victor who arrived first. He did not go right up to Jake but took in the situation. For one thing, he did not recognize him. Jake was wet, covered in mud and blood and the coat he had over him Victor had never seen before. Victor stepped just out of plain sight to keep an eye on this man who was in need. Victor had heard stories of how the government officers could use a situation like this to get people involved in illegal actions in order to arrest them. Although Victor was not sure of how hurt this man was, he was totally aware of the need of being cautious in this circumstance. He would take a little more time observing, and then he would go and check things out. As Victor crouched down into a more comfortable sitting position to keep his eyes on this man, he noticed movement in his side vision. He turned his head to look and see what or who it was that was going toward this man on the street. It was Sandy. What on earth was she doing? She was not stopping to see if it was safe. Victor could see from the look on her face that she had already decided to help him no matter what the consequences. What on earth was the matter with that woman? Perhaps too many months living like they all had been? But whatever it was, Sandy was becoming dangerous. Not only to herself but to the others around her as well. What if she were to be sloppy one day and give up some important information? Victor knew one thing for sure, and that was that Sandy would never be able to live with herself if she did something like that. Victor would need to address this situation, but now was not the time.

Realizing that it was too late to stop Sandy, Victor decided to go and help her. From the look of things, this guy was going to need some real help, perhaps even a doctor, seeing all of the blood he had lost.

Sandy got to the man first and had already determined that it was Jake. Victor was quick to be at her side. Sandy was not sure what surprised her more, the fact that this man in need was Jake or that Victor had arrived when she was needing him most, but whichever it was, she was glad to see them both. Victor for the help, and Jake for the fact that she now thought he was not as bad as he had first seemed. There was a lot of blood, but from raising children of her own, Sandy knew that a head wound will bleed a lot, even a simple one. She could not be totally sure, but from how he looked right now, she would guess that he was going to be all right. All they needed to do right now was to get him off the street and back to the shelter. Hopefully word of this happening had also reached the doctor, and he would follow them to the shelter soon. "Victor, boy am I glad to see you."

Victor was now seeing who it was that they were helping. "Jake! What on earth are you doing here? How on earth did you get into this mess?" Victor was feeling bad that he had misjudged Jake. He had now concluded that Jake was in this situation because he was somehow trying to help Peggy. "You foolish kid. What on earth were you thinking?"

Jake was in a fog. He was sure that he must be dreaming about Victor and Sandy being here to help him. Wishful thinking. No. This was not a wish, but this was real; it was Victor and Sandy, just like he had thought. They were here now, and he knew that he would be okay. That was one of the last thoughts to go through his head before he passed out.

"Maybe his head wound is worse than I thought?" Sandy was concerned as she noticed that Jake was unconscious.

"Don't worry, Sandy, this kid is a lot tougher than he looks. I am sure that he will be okay." Victor was not a doctor, but he did think that right now things looked worse than they really were. "Now, let's get him out of here and find out what this is all about."

Victor and Sandy were able to get Jake up enough for Victor to pull him up onto his shoulder.

"Victor, do you think that carrying him like this is good for his head wound?"

"Sandy, I am not sure if it is good for him or not, but I do know that if we don't get him off the street, he is going to be in a lot more trouble than this."

Jake was not completely out of it. He realized he was moving and also realized that he was not in a normal position. He could feel the blood rushing to his head. As he forced his eyes open in order to take inventory of what was going on, all he could see was the backside of whoever it was who had him over their shoulder. He did not recognize this person from what he was wearing, but it really did not matter, did it? What did matter was that it seemed that he was getting off the street, and that could only be better than his situation had been.

Sandy was still concerned about the way Victor was carrying Jake, so she pulled back a few steps in order to get a look at Jake as best she could. As she bent her head down in order to see Jake's face, she noted that he had come to. She placed her hand on his back and smiled. "You are going to be okay. We are going to get you back to the shelter. You will be safe there."

Victor heard her talking and looked around to see who it was she was speaking with so intently. "Hopefully you are right. I just hope that we are not being followed. You know, you did not take the best of precautions back there. What were you thinking, Sandy? You know that the government officers sometimes take advantage of situations like this in order to get others involved as conspirators. You know if they are following us, we are leading them right back to the shelter."

Sandy knew that Victor was right, but she also knew that Jake needed to get off the street, get himself warm and dry, and if it could be worked out, he needed to see the doctor. "Victor, you of all people know that sometimes we have to take chances. I do not know about you, but I for one am sure that this is one of those times."

"Sandy, I know what you are saying, but all I am trying to tell you is that perhaps precautions on the front end of this mess would have been in order."

"Victor, I hate it when you talk like that. You sound like a worrywart." Sandy crossed her arms and rolled her eyes at him.

"I may sound like a worrywart, but I think you are acting like someone who is new on the street. You would never have taken a chance like that a few months ago. I don't get what's going on with you." Victor stated this while keeping his stride fast but consistent.

"Well, Victor, that makes two of us." Sandy was too tired to make up any excuses right now. She knew that he was right, but it was too late. All she could do was pray that this was not a setup and vow not to be so careless next time. Sandy was tired, she was worried about Jake and mad at him at the same time. What on earth was he doing out of the safe zone? If it had not been for his foolishness, she would not have been in a position to make such a mistake. Sandy stopped in midthought. She at once called an end to her pattern of thinking. She had been here before. This was a pattern that she would fall into when she was too tired or when she had not spent time alone with God. Right now she was in both positions. Anger, blame, and fear were all signs of her head and heart not being right somehow. Sandy called to God in her mind. *Help us through this mess. It seems so impossible. We need Your guidance. We need Your hand of protection. We need You.* Sandy did not feel the peace she had hoped to get after she was done praying, but praying did keep her from saying anything she would regret later. Sandy hated to make mistakes, especially around Victor. She wanted him of all people to think she was able to keep herself together. So much for that. Sandy felt a smile come across her face. Somehow she was feeling like a schoolgirl where Victor was concerned. Most likely it was because she was so tired and worried.

But whatever it was, for now, it was enough to help her get through this with a glimmer of hope.

*****

There it was again. Sandy had given up his questioning without even a fight. Somehow that was not like the Sandy he knew. She always had an excuse for everything; even if it was not a great one, she would usually conjure one up all the same. Now Victor was honestly getting worried. That was one time too many for Sandy to, one, make a mistake and, two, for her not to put up a fight. Something was truly wrong, and it definitely needed to be taken care of, and soon. Sandy needed to be taken care of. Victor was sure that he was the one to do the job.

Sandy had not taken her rotation out to the farm as she had been scheduled for some time now. In fact, it had been so long that Victor could not remember when it was she went last, but he felt that from the way she was acting, this was a sure sign of her needing a break. Being at the farm was a very different way of life. There was a freedom there that you just could not find in the city anymore. The families there lived a life very much like it was before all of the changes in the world because the farms were not patrolled by the government. There was too much for them to take care of in the city to branch out to the outlying areas. For now, anyway, the rules found in the city did not apply out there. Bible studies, talking about God, even singing was an everyday event. It was still kept low-keyed for safety, but it was an everyday thing to get to have a prayer meeting or communion. Even a baptism was known to happen from time to time. Time to pray, time to read your Bible. It truly was a place for gathering one's strength, and as far as Victor was concerned, that was exactly what Sandy was in the need of at this time. All he needed to do was convince her of that fact.

They reached the shelter door. Sandy hurried ahead of Victor, opened the door, and laid out some bedding for him to place Jake on. First on the agenda would be to get him out of his wet clothing. Sandy was trying to remove the coat that had been placed over Jake, but his hands were holding onto it for dear life. "Jake, you need to let me take this coat off so we can get your wet things off. I'll give it right back as soon as it is dry."

As much as Jake knew he needed to do what Sandy wanted him to do, he just could not let go. He was finally feeling warmer. Even more than that, this coat was his gift from God. He did not know how he knew it, he just did. He needed to keep it close to him. It was the only thing of God he had, and he needed it right now.

"Jake, let go of the coat, son!" Victor's voice boomed out with such authority that even Sandy stopped her actions to look at him. "Jake, you need to get your wet clothing off and then get dry, or you are never going to feel better. We need to clean you up so we can see how hurt you are. Now let go of the coat."

Jake looked up at Victor, who was now kneeling beside him. He thought for a moment, then handed him the coat. If anyone could be trusted with something of God's, it was Victor and Sandy.

It was the middle of the day, so there were only a few people in the shelter when the three of them had arrived. It would be some time before the curfew siren would sound, so there was time to get Jake cleaned up and make it as though nothing had ever happened. This was important in case they had been followed.

Sandy took Jake's coat from Victor and headed off to the kitchen. As she was walking to the door, she held the coat up to look at it. As she looked at the neck, she saw a sales tag hanging from it. She grasped the tag and turned around to speak to Jake. "Jake, how is it that you have this new coat?"

"What?" Jake was looking at Sandy now. She had walked back over to where he was lying and was showing him the tag she had found.

"The coat is new!" Jake was in total disbelief. Not only had God given him a warmer coat but He had also provided Jake with a new one. Not to mention it came when he needed it the most. Just how powerful was this God he had found? And of all of the people in the world, why would God have helped him? "Sandy, I can't believe that the coat is new. Why on earth would anyone give away a new coat?"

"God only knows." Sandy was shocked at what she had found, but after speaking to Jake, she realized that he was as stunned as she was. It was obvious to her that Jake had no hidden excuse, only a blessing.

Sandy continued to go on into the kitchen. There she laid out the coat to let it dry. She drew up some water and gathered a few towels. She then decided to look for some dry clothing for Jake. As she looked around in the kitchen, she saw what she knew was Jake's backpack. She thought it funny that he had not had it with him. He had carried it with him almost all of the time he had been at the shelter. Sandy was glad that this time he had not taken it. For sure he would have lost it, or it would have been taken if it had been on him during his encounter with whoever it was who attacked him. Sandy did not feel right going through Jake's bag, but she was sure that he kept his clean clothing in it. If he were ever in need of clean clothing, it was now. Sandy sat down the water and towels and pulled the bag over to where she was standing. She undid the hook and then unzipped the main opening. Reaching inside the backpack, she pulled out what she quickly confirmed to be clean clothing of Jake's. As she drew them out, a notebook fell to the ground. Sandy looked to see what had fallen out. The book had fallen in an open position. Sandy immediately reached down and closed it. It was not in her mind or in her nature for that matter, for her to be in someone else's private things. She promptly pushed Jake's things back into his pack, gathered it up along with the water and the towels, then she went back into the main room, finding not only Victor with Jake but they had now been joined by David and the doctor as well. Relief fell on Sandy at once. She was so happy to see the help that she thought for a moment she might break down and cry. But not this time. No, there was work to do (thank God) and people needing her right now.

As Sandy entered the room, the men all turned to see her coming. David reached out to take some of the things loaded up in her arms. "Here, let me take some of that."

Sandy was trying hard to simply smile at seeing the help that had arrived, but she was so overwhelmed with thankfulness that a few, only a few, small tears escaped from her eyes.

"It is going to be okay. You will see." David tilted his head and looked steadily at Sandy. He did not even blink. His words gave her even more strength. She was glad he and the doctor had arrived.

"Hi, Doc. Thanks for coming." Sandy did not look at the doctor as she did not want to take any chance of letting anyone else know how overwhelmed she was feeling right now. Instead, she simply knelt down and went to work trying to help clean Jake up.

Jake was helping as best as he could. His body was warmer, but it was still shaking. He had no energy to do anything. He wanted more than anything to figure out what was wrong with him, but not being able to keep a clear thought in his mind kept getting in the way.

After short of time, they had managed to get most of Jake's wet clothing off him. Sandy had turned her back while the men removed the lower part of his apparel. As Sandy was waiting for them to get the last things off and get him covered in a blanket, she again went into Jake's backpack to find something for him to put on. She knew that there were things for him, but now she needed to really take inventory. She found a shirt, sox, and even a tee shirt, but no pants. On her second dig in the bag, she finally found a pair of sweatpants she remembered giving him on one of the first weeks he was at the shelter. She noted how cautious Jake had been of all of his things. This truly was a special young man. Impulsive, yes. But wasn't that what people had said about her in her youth? As Sandy pulled out the pants, the notebook again fell to the ground, but this time it fell closed. Sandy reached to pick it up, but it was Victor who retrieved it instead.

Victor merely held the book in one hand and ever so gently tapped it into his other. There was no real rhythm to his tapping. Just a way to get rid of some pent-up tension.

The doctor was now looking Jake over to assess his wounds. "Mostly a few bruises. A scratch here and there, but his head wound is a nasty one. It is no wonder you feel so out of it. Jake, can you see all right?"

Jake looked at the doctor following his voice and then finally focused on his face. Boy, was he young. Not at all what Jake had expected of a doctor. Jake blinked his eyes several times and then came to view the doctor completely. As Jake was about to say yes, he could see okay, his eyes wandered past the doctor to where Victor was now standing. There in his hand was Jake's notebook. Panic flooded over Jake, but then Jake remembered that he had not added any entries in this book. There was no harm done. There was no way for Victor to know anything about why Jake was here. Not yet anyway. Or could he tell? No. No way. Jake could feel his racing heart start to steady again. This was getting way too much for anyone to handle. An emotional roller coaster, and it was far from over. Jake's eyes fell back onto the doctor's face. He had no problem focusing on him this time, and he had no problem seeing that this doctor was misreading Jake's reaction to seeing Victor with his book. The doctor was thinking that he was having a problem. Nothing could be farther from the truth. "Doc, I am going to be fine. Other than a raging headache, I think I am good." Jake started to raise himself in order to get dressed. Great idea he was having, but the body was not going along with what the mind had decided. Jake suddenly felt a rush of dizziness. He immediately closed his eyes in order to stop the room from spinning, but it was too late. His body was overcome with queasiness. Sandy knew exactly what was happening and at once came to Jake's aid with a wet towel. Motherhood had trained her well in such matters. It had been a long time since she had needed such skills. She was glad that she still had what it took to be a mom.

David and Victor were both surprised at Sandy's quickness in that matter. And as for Jake, he was extremely grateful for having been spared any more embarrassment. He had already had enough for a lifetime by his count.

"The book. Oh, God, the book." Jake was mumbling. His eyes were blurred, and he had become weak like before.

"Jake has a bad concussion. I can't really tell at this point, but I think he is going to be fine. I need to place a few stitches in his head. It really is a bad gash, but nothing we can't handle here. Sandy, like I said, I think he is going to be fine, but you will have to keep an eye on him during the next twenty-four hours. Wake him up every hour at least until night and then about every two hours or so. If for any reason you cannot get him to wake up, then you need to get word to me at once, okay?"

Victor walked over and placed his arm around Sandy. "That is great news, Doc. I think that between all of us, we will be able to do that. How long do you think it will be before Jake here can travel?"

"Travel? Where do you plan on taking him?" Sandy was the first to speak. They had only returned Jake here to safety, and now Victor was wanting to take him out again. Men! There was just no figuring them out.

"Well, I thought that perhaps it was time for Jake to take his turn out on one of the farms. Good idea, don't you think?" Victor had asked Sandy but was looking over to David for confirmation.

David was a quick study and promptly realized that Victor had a plan. "That sounds like a great idea. Jake could not only use some time to heal but perhaps the atmosphere at one of the farms would be good for his spiritual life as well."

The doctor thought for a while. "I think if you could give him a week or so, it would be safe for him to travel. That is barring any other complications."

"Great, then it is settled. Jake is to go to the farm, and Sandy will take him." Victor was fast on this one. This was a great way to get Sandy off for a break. Killing two birds with one stone as it were.

"Great! And, Victor, you can go with them too. That way I can stay here and work a few things out that I need to get done." David was in on the fast track too. He had already decided long ago that both Victor and Sandy needed to get off for some R and R. This was a great chance to make it happen. Neither could back out without the other doing so as well. They both needed the break. They both were going and with no argument from either one of them. This was remarkable. David had tried to get each of them to take their rotation out to the farm, but as usual, they each had a convincing answer as to why they couldn't go. But not this time. David was grateful. He cared deeply for both of these people. He knew that they needed a break, but he also needed them in the city doing their jobs. It was an awful dilemma. But now God had provided a way to get them off to the farm, and David was sure that God would provide the help he needed to keep the city shelters running. *How* was not his problem, it was God's, and he was glad of that fact.

Victor and Sandy looked at each other. Each knew that the other not only deserved but desperately needed a break from the stress of the city shelters. There was no way of backing out without jeopardizing the other person going. So for now, the plan was set. The three of them would head to a farm in about a week. No discussions. Just a plan.

The doctor, with David's help, started stitching up Jake's head. Victor and Sandy started about their daily business. They did not speak a word to each other but found themselves something to do separately. Victor walked over to where Jake's backpack now lay and placed the notebook back into it. Then off he went to do something he remembered needed checking on.

David and the doctor smiled at each other. They had discussed many a time about trying to get these two to take a break from their everyday stressful lives. And now with very little effort of their own, these men's concerns and prayers had been answered. Life had dealt its hand, and the job was done. Whoever would have thought that God could use such an impossible situation to answer such a long-awaited prayer?

*****

A few stitches and several hours later, Jake found himself leaning up against the wall in the kitchen. The risk of someone finding him lying around in the shelter was way too great. In case they had been followed, Sandy and Victor wanted to make sure that there weren't any more rules broken than had to be. No matter where they put him though, it would be difficult to convince anyone that he was working at the shelter. The spinning in his head had lessened, but he was still very weak. Jake knew the risk the people at the shelter were taking by letting him stay here like this. How hard this was for Jake. Not only was he a traitor but now he was also a risk. Wasn't it bad enough that he had been part of getting Peggy and some of the others into trouble? But now here he was risking the others the same fate. This was awful. Jake was way too weak to do anything but sit here and think about all of the things that have come to pass. The guilt he was feeling was so overwhelming. Even if God could forgive him, Jake knew that he could never forgive himself. Peggy was a good friend, and now look where that had gotten her. She was arrested. She was who knew where, and who knows what was to happen to her? This was not a comfortable position for Jake to be in. All he wanted to do was to run away from all of this. There would be no running today though. All he could do was stay leaning up against this wall and continue watching these people whom he now cared about desperately. Knowing that at any moment, because of his note-book, the shelter would be taken over, shut down, and everyone here arrested and at the very least chipped. What should he do? Should he tell them? Should he say something? Or should he simply ride it out? No answers. Just questions. Oh, God, wasn't this how he felt when he had first arrived at the shelter? Same feelings but for different reasons.

Jake closed his eyes, he could not bear looking at these people anymore. They were going on about their lives like always. They had things to do, and they were going to get them done. What a group of people this Knowing was. It was no wonder the government had not been able to catch them. They just didn't recognize defeat.

Victor saw that Jake was awake and walked over and sat down beside him. "How is it going? Feeling any better?"

Jake knew that it was Victor even before he opened his eyes. There was no mistaking that voice. "Yeah, I am getting better. Thanks for stopping the room from spinning." Jake tried to laugh, but it made his head hurt.

"You know, Jake, I think I know what it was that you were trying to do. You really should have come to one of us for help with the idea. We really do know the rules on the streets a lot better than you do. If you had asked, we would have told you that the best way to help Peggy was to pray and to wait it out." Victor was trying to be okay with Jake attempting to rescue Peggy, but Jake needed to know that what he had done was very serious. Getting in trouble put them all at risk. This needed to not happen again.

Jake's head was hurting, but he was getting the idea of what Victor was talking about. Although things had not worked out how he had planned, he still wished he had been able to talk to Mr. Diggings. Not that it would have changed anything but he would have felt better at any rate.

"Jake, what you did was real brave. Dumb but brave all the same. All I am trying to say is next time come to one of us first, okay? We know about these things. After all, that is what a family is here for." Victor patted Jake on the shoulder and got up to go on about his business. "Get some rest. There is a lot to talk about once you are feeling better."

Man oh man, what a mess. Not only did Victor think he was brave but he now referred to him as one of the family. There could never be a guilt worse than how he was feeling right now. Nothing. Nothing could ever make this mess all right. He did not think even this new God could make this turn out okay. Jake knew that it would be only a matter of time before the authorities would be coming to the shelter in order to arrest some or all of them or, at the very least, shut the shelter down for some of the things Jake had listed in his book. How could things have changed in such a short time? In just three months, Jake had come to know that who he thought was the enemy was now his new family. That the people he had always referred to as "his people" were now his worst nightmare. Jake continued to think about all that had happened. Jake had been moved back out into the main room. Every time the front door opened, he expected to see the government officers coming through with orders of some sort that would forever change his life. But time and time again, the door opened, and when Jake opened his eyes to see if his worst fears were to be realized, he would be left with a great relief. It was becoming so bad that Jake was almost wishing that it would happen and then it would finally be over with once and for all.

*****

The day passed as if nothing unusual had even happened. It was becoming closer to the time of day when curfew warning would be sounding. The rumors on the street were slow. As the people started to file into the shelter, very little, if any, information came with them today. Several had heard of Jake's incident and were happy to see him doing so well. As with most rumors, some of the ones about Jake had been blown up way out of proportion, but for the most part, what they had heard was that he had been rescued and was going to be all right. Jake was amazed at how the street network was used by these people. He couldn't believe how quickly word of what had happened had spread. Even Jim, who had been heading out to one of the farms, heard about it and had turned around and come back to the shelter to see if he could be of any help.

The five-minute warning was sounding, and then the door would be closed for the night. Jake was not sure if he was relieved or angry, knowing that sooner or later the dreaded coming was going to happen. Now it was just seconds before the door would be closed. Jake's heart was pounding. He was not sure about how he was feeling, but he was sure of one thing, and that was that he didn't like feeling this way. Anxious, guilt, fear, happy to be here and safe (for now anyway), dry, alive, warm (his new coat was dry, warm and Jake was now wearing it again), worried, hurting, and grateful. So many emotions and all at the same time.

Jim was now walking over to lock the door. He had the keys in his hand and was searching the key ring for the correct key. Jake was thinking that there were so many keys on this key ring and yet only one door? Something to think about. Jim had reached the door. The final siren was starting to blare. Jake was keeping his eyes on both Jim and the door. Jim was pushing the door to its closed position. All at once, a very loud banging came from the outside of the door. Jake knew without a doubt that this was it. The moment of truth. Jake's heart cried out to God for help. If there were ever going to be a time that he needed God, this was it. Again. To Jake's thinking, this was even worse than being beat up and being held underwater. When that happened, it was only Jake who had been affected, but this was going to affect everyone he had grown to care about. All of their lives were going to change and forever. Jake wanted to scream.

Jake screamed, "Oh my God, it's Peggy."

The entire room stopped and looked over at Jake. Some were thinking that perhaps he was having a hallucination brought on by his head injury, but as they saw his face and looked over to where it was he was now trying to go, they quickly realized that he was right. It was Peggy and several of the others who had been arrested. The whole room exploded with excitement.

Jake was not too successful at getting to where he had planned, but instead it was Peggy who ran to him to help steady him. "Jake, what happened to you? And where did you get that coat? It is great!"

Leave it to Peggy to make simple out of even the most complicated. This was a homecoming. And a very unexpected one at that. How was it that the only thing she could think to say was that Jake had a new coat? She truly could make Jake nuts if he were not so happy to see her.

Victor and Sandy looked at each other. Not needing to say a word but knowing exactly what the other was thinking. Same old young Peggy. Nothing could ever seem to get her ruffled for too long. She was quick to overreact and yet just as quick to overcome whatever it was that was sent her way. Some might say that it was a gift, but whatever it was, it was great to have her back. But how?

Several others had continued to enter the shelter after Peggy. Some were people Jake had at least seen, and yet others were completely new faces. There was such an excitement in the shelter that it almost seemed electric somehow. Within a few seconds of the entrance of these returning saints, the siren blare had come to an end. The door was shut and locked, and a reunion party of sorts had broken out. Everyone was excited and ready to accept their homecoming as an answer to prayer.

Except for Jake. This just could not be correct. The information in his notebook alone would have been enough to arrest and chip most of these people and at the very least close down the shelter, but if you added the information that must have been retrieved by the other undercover officer, this could in no way be happening. Not even God himself could have pulled this one off. Perhaps this was a trick in order to get more information about this group. No, that wouldn't make any sense either. The quicker they shut down the shelters and the Knowing, the happier everyone in the government would be. After all, this is an election year, and wouldn't that look great on the "now in office" list of successes?

Jake's thoughts were interrupted by questioning from Peggy. "Jake, you never did tell me what happened to you. Where did you get that incredible coat? By the way, did you miss me?"

If Jake's head had not already been hurting from his blow on his head, this sort of questioning coming from Peggy would have caused pain for sure. Jake's only defense right now was to hold up his hands in order to try and call Peggy's rambling to an end. "Peggy. One question at a time, will you? My coat came from a man on the street. My wounds, kind of the same, and as for if I missed you, well, that question is just crazy all by itself. Of course I missed you."

No sooner had Jake finished saying that he had missed Peggy, she gave out a squeal and threw her arms around Jake's neck, placing an incredible and passionate kiss on his lips. It lasted only a few seconds, but the dynamics of it would remain a lifetime for both Peggy and Jake.

Jake kissed her back, which was definitely an excitement for Peggy. "Wow, that was great." Peggy took a step back and looked at Jake. "Hey, Jake, you don't look so great."

Peggy was right. Sandy had overheard what Peggy had said and could see that all of this excitement was finally catching up with Jake. He was as white as a ghost. Sandy was hoping to suggest that Jake should lie down for the night when all at once he sat straight down, right where he was standing. "Victor. Could you please come here?" Sandy was calling out to Victor as she was going over to where both Jake and Peggy were now sitting.

Victor came immediately at Sandy's calling. He could see without even being told what it was he needed to do. Jake needed to get bedded down for the night, and from the looks of Peggy and the rest, they had a long day too. A long week for that matter. Perhaps there did need to be a party, but not right now. Victor was thinking that in due time they would send as many as they could out to the farms. Perhaps then there would be both time and energy to celebrate, but for now, everyone was safely tucked away in the shelter, from what he could see anyway. All the hellos were over, so now getting on with the business of eating and bedding down for the night needed to be resumed. Victor, seeing that Jake was gaining color back, patted Jake on the back, and giving him a reassuring look, he stood up and called out into the room, "Let us pray."

Almost like magic, the room grew silent. All heads bowed, and Victor's voice called out clear and direct to God himself. Jake was amazed at how this action brought unity out of insanity. In all of his life, he had never seen anything that could bring people to a halt like this calling out to their God. Whether it be having fun or in disagreement, the people all rallied around this one idea of prayer. Jake wondered if it had always been like this. It was not normal for people to not fight. It was not normal for people to care about each other the way these people did, and yet it was happening. Yes, the people disagreed from time to time, but in the end, a compromise was somehow always met. Could it be that because life was so hard for these people that somehow making things work out was a requirement? Or was this the way it was because of their belief in God? Most likely Jake would never know for sure. As much as he wanted to think that the future might hold better times, he of all people knew that even what they now had was going to someday soon be taken away. From what Jake had seen so far, he knew that they were tough, but could they continue once they had lost everything?

There were a lot of questions about the release that everyone wanted to ask and then hear the answers to, but with the prayer, Victor called them all into a time of silent praise. God had done a wondrous thing, and they only really knew the half of it. In the next few days, all of what had been accomplished would be known by everyone, but for now, silent praise and then sleep was to fall on this shelter where they were now gathered.

CHAPTER 11

The morning light brought with it a new excitement. So many of the people from the now destroyed South Street shelter had been released. Even Peter's parents had been allowed to return to the streets.

Victor and David had an extended conversation with Peter's parents, Frank and Martha. As usual, there were no last names used during the description of events. Jake had recognized that these were Peter's parents even before they were introduced to him. The facial features of both Frank and Peter were undeniable. Frank was simply an older version of Peter. From what Jake could tell, these were great people. They obviously loved each other, and as soon as they had seen David, they had expressed their concerns for their son's well-being. Jake thought that it was going to be interesting though to see how they reacted to Peter when they saw him. Although they loved him, it was Peter after all who had caused the shutdown of the shelter and originally had them all arrested, wasn't it?

Frank and Martha were able to explain about the undercover agent that had been with them at the shelter. They still could not believe that this friend of theirs could have done such a thing to them. But the fact that the shelter was now gone and the arrests had been made, what else could it have been?

"I still don't think that he was what they are telling us. After all, we are not in jail, are we? I can believe that perhaps he may have started out doing a job of spying, but maybe he changed his mind." Martha was desperately needing to think that this must be what had happened. She had lost her home, their way of life, not to mention having been separated from her son Peter in a traumatic fashion.

Frank placed his arm lovingly around his wife. "You know, Martha, not everyone has as a wonderful nature as you do. You know some people are not as we are, and they think of us as the enemy."

"You know, Frank, not everyone is out to get us either." The love between Martha and Frank was genuine, but they each had an obviously different outlook about what had happened.

If Jake had not known better, listening to these two discuss the issue, he would have bet anything that he was listening to Victor and Sandy. Each allowing the other their opinion even if they did think that the other's opinion was completely wrong. On second thought, they also reminded Jake of his own parents. Same loving relationship as this group. Only difference, these people had God and his parents did not, right? Boy, he missed his family.

As the story unfolded, it seemed to confirm that there was an undercover officer in the shelter. To the best of their knowledge, they guessed he had been there a little more than six months. While he was there, he had taken notes on just about everyone in the shelter. Both their comings and goings and everything that he had seen. It was not so much what they did know about him that was interesting to Jake, it was what they did not know. They were not sure how the information about the shelter had been transferred. They were not sure as to where this man had gone to now. And no one had any idea at all as to why they were simply released.

"Frank, do you think this could be some kind of trick or something?" David had to ask. Although he was the only one to bring it up, it was definitely on several of the others' mind.

"David, we thought about that, and that is why we all came here. We decided that it was not safe to even go near the rabbit holes." Frank was a very levelheaded man. Being careful was simply a way of life for him as it was for many of the others.

A sigh of relief came from Victor when he had heard that they had not gone to the rabbit holes for that reason. He was afraid that they had been found out and that was why they could not go there, but this was great news. The rabbit holes were safe, for now anyway. And for once, someone was using their head and being careful.

Martha was the next to speak up. "We were extra careful after we were released. We all walked around and then tried to wait until the last free second before we entered the shelter. We figured that anyone following us would need to get off the street like us."

"I was never so happy to hear those blasted sirens," one of the other men added from over in the corner.

"Yes, that was to be the signal for everyone to head to this shelter. The five-minute warning was a perfect way to tell everyone to move on to here. I really don't think that anyone was following us, but if they were, I am sure that they were confused when we all went sixteen different directions and then all ended up in the same place for the night." Martha was almost excited at the idea of giving the officers a runaround.

Peggy was back and in rare form. She was quickly moving around the shelter trying to bring some kind of order to this now very overcrowded shelter. It was obvious from how she was acting that she was only kind of listening to what was being said about the ordeal. Many had chimed in about some of their ideas as to why they had been let go, but it was Peggy who then decided to add her information to the story.

"I don't know what all this arguing is about. Like I see it, the book just didn't get there in time."

It was as if everyone had become speechless at the same time. Silence totally overtook them all.

Sandy knew that if there were going to be any sense made out of what Peggy was saying, it would require questioning by someone who knew how to ask the right questions. In order to glean any (if there were any) real answers from Peggy, one would have to hit on exactly the right question. "Peggy?"

"Yes, Sandy, did you want something?" Sandy was trying for a calm yet very direct approach now.

All ears were on this conversation.

"Peggy, what book are you talking about when you say it did not get there in time?"

"The one they were all waiting for of course."

"Who are *they*?"

Peggy was irritated by Sandy's lack of understanding. "You know, the officers. I really did like the one who brought us our food. Martha, don't you think he would have made an excellent helper here at the shelter?"

Sandy did not let this discussion get away from her. "Peggy! What book, and who told you about it?"

"The one with all of the extra information that was going to verify that we were in the Knowing."

"Peggy, who told you about this book?" Sandy was being extra careful to keep a steady voice.

"No one." Peggy was looking to see if anything else needed to be done.

"Then how do you know about it?" Sandy asked, getting right in front of Peggy.

"They were all talking one night. They thought I was asleep, but it was too hot in there to sleep. Do you think that it was actually hot, or do you think that I was used to the cold so much that being warm felt hot?"

"Peggy, I am not sure about that, but can you tell me more about what it was the men said when you overheard them?"

"Sandy, I do not know what you are getting so upset about. It was just that they were waiting for some book that was to be dropped off or something like that." Peggy walked away from Sandy and began to pick up things around the shelter again.

"And?" Now it was Victor who was asking the questions.

"And what?" Peggy was trying to figure what it was they wanted her to say. She sure wished they would be clearer about what it was they wanted to know.

"And what happened to the book?"

"They got it." Peggy was really tired of this conversation. She had not even been able to see Jake and find out how he was doing. She needed to get her work done so she could spend time with Jake, and they were definitely cramping her style.

"They got the book?" This time it was a number of voices that sang out the question.

Victor looked over to Sandy and decided this was not a battle he wanted to enter into with Peggy. It was now a matter of stubbornness that was going to get the answers they needed.

"Yes, they got it, but it was late I think. No, I remember now, it was empty. Yes, that was what that really mean man had said. It was empty."

The inquiries went on, but after the words "it was empty," Jake did not hear another thing. His heart was pounding so hard that he could not have heard anything even if he wanted to. He knew that he was breathing, but his whole body had gone cold. This cold had absolutely nothing to do with his having been wounded. This had to do with his needing to see his backpack to find the second notebook and to see what was on the pages in it. This was a threefold problem. One, where was the pack with his book? He had been so sure all this time that the pages were blank, so the need to guard it was no longer necessary. Two, Victor had the book last. Had he opened it and read any of it? And third, if he had turned in the wrong book, he was going to be in a lot of trouble when this was over. A lot of money had been spent on arresting and charging all of these people. Jake now knew for sure that they had been counting on his report in order to close the case. But he did not do that. In fact, he may have blown it altogether. Oh, what a mess this was going to be when he returned to work. Oh my God, he may not have betrayed these people. They would never have to know what it was he had been doing here. He was going to make it out of this mess and be okay. But then again, what about his career? They very well might understand him not turning in the right book but not turning in any book, that would never be accepted. These were decisions he could think over later. For now, what he needed to do was to get to his pack and find out what the real truth was regarding the book. Jake's head was swimming. Was it the situation, or was it his head wound? *Focus, Jake, focus!* He had to work hard to stay on task and pay attention to what was going on around him.

At the end of Peggy's questioning, the final finding was that there had been a book that was to have contained information on the Knowing. There was not enough evidence to convict the people who had been arrested, not yet anyway. And there was an angry man who was vowing to continue "hounding these people until he could put them away for good." A direct quote from Peggy.

That being the case, it was decided that as many as possible of the sixteen who had been arrested should go to one of the farms. Peter's parents would be going to meet up with their son. The others would be distributed throughout the area farms.

Jake was interested in this decision about going to the "farms." This was a new term to him. But at this very moment, what he needed to concern himself with was the finding of his backpack. "Peggy, would you do me a favor?"

Peggy was delighted. She dropped what she was doing (literally) and ran over to where Jake was sitting. "Are you feeling any better today?"

"Yes, Peggy, I am doing much better. Could you do me a favor?" Jake hated to use her like this, but she was the only one he could think to ask right now. "Could you please see if you could find my backpack? I know that it is here somewhere. Sandy got me some clothing out of it last night."

"Sure, no problem." And without hesitation, off she went to do her deed. Peggy quickly scanned the room and then headed off to the kitchen. Within a few seconds, she came flying through the doorway with her duty fulfilled. The smile on her face was one of great satisfaction.

Jake watched as she came closer to him. It seemed odd to him how much more mature she looked. Somehow, in his mind, she had gone to jail as a young girl and had now become a young woman. Perhaps she had always been as he was seeing her now. Perhaps he was just understanding her better. Wow, that was a scary statement, if Jake had ever made one, but yes, he really could understand her and cherished that fact.

Peggy walked happily over to where Jake was waiting. "Here it is, can I get anything else for you?"

Jake reached out and took the bag. "No, no, thank you," was all he said.

Peggy's feelings were a little hurt. She was wanting to visit with Jake, but from the sound of his voice, she had been dismissed. If he did not want to spend time with her, why had he even enlisted her help in the first place? Men! Peggy, not really understanding what had just taken place, made an excuse about needing to do something and headed back to the kitchen.

Jake could tell from the way that she was acting that he had hurt her feelings. This blasted lying was nothing but trouble. From the very start of all of this undercover stuff, there had been one misunderstanding after another. Where was it going to stop? Jake was not sure. In fact, he was not even sure if he would have the courage to stop it even if he decided to. Two days ago, life had dealt its hand and the book had been picked up, not even God could change that, or could He? Jake's thoughts returned to checking the notebook in his bag. He looked around to make sure that no one was watching him too closely. For the moment, that was not a problem. A lot of planning and activity based around them moving on to the farms was underway. Some of the people were for it, and yet others felt that it was much too risky for everyone. What if they were being followed, or worse yet, what if there was another spy?

Jake half laughed at that idea. Yes, what if there were another spy? What if? What if? What If? What if he had given the right book and this book was empty? What if he had given the wrong book and this one contained the evidence needed to complete his job? Then what? Jake pulled the book out and held it in its closed state for a moment. No time like the present. Again his heart was beating so hard he thought his chest might explode. He was anxious, but what was the answer that he wanted? Well, that did not matter now; whatever it was, it was. With that thought, he opened the notebook to the first few pages. They were blank. But that was not the answer to his question of which book was delivered. He had purposely started his paperwork a few pages into the book. He turned just a couple of pages at a time. It was looking more and more like he had dropped off the right book.

"What's that?" A voice came into earshot, giving Jake the startle of his life. Jake looked up and was met with a set of motherly eyes looking down on him. It was Martha, Peter's mom.

"Oh, it is just a notebook. I like to write down things that I am thinking from time to time. You know. I kind of keep my head cleared out. It helps me to think things through." Jake realized that he was rambling and decided to cut his explanation short.

"You know, Jake, the last time I saw a book like that, it was carried by the man who helped to shut down our shelter. I think that it might be best if you don't let some of the others see you with it. They might jump to the conclusion that you might be a spy too." For only a moment, that idea had occurred to her, but one good look at Jake, and she realized that a boy like this could never be a spy. Why, he could be only a few years older than her Peter.

"Oh, I didn't know. Thanks for telling me." Jake was amazed at how easy it was to keep his cover with these people. Even when they did detect him, they just never caught on to the idea that he was a spy. How these people never got caught was definitely a miracle. This God of theirs positively had to work overtime to keep them out of trouble. If that was something their God could really do, that was amazing. Jake wanted to heed Martha's warning, but he had to know what book he had even more. Martha had walked away, and so Jake again resumed his search of the pages. There it was. His report. The whole thing. Written in his very own handwriting. But how could this have happened? How on earth could he have turned in the wrong book? A feeling of relief suddenly came over him, but then it was followed by excitement. No, it couldn't have been, but then what other explanation could there be? He had called out to their God. Could He have actually have listened to him? This was the third time Jake had been surprised about the outcome of a situation. First, the coat; second, not drowning in the puddle; and now, the notebook not getting into the hands of the officials. This was getting way too much for it all to be a coincidence, or was it?

As Jake was sitting and thinking this over, he heard a commotion going on outside the shelter door. Jake did not recognize the voices, but he could tell right off that they were in dispute about something. David and Victor along with Frank headed to the door in order to try and determine what it was that was going on outside. The three men reached the door, and each slipped out one at a time.

The commotion from the outside did not stop, but it did not get any louder either.

Finally, the waiting got the best of him, and Jake decided that there was no time like the present to try and see if he had his land legs back again. Slowly using the wall to help steady himself, Jake lifted his body up from the floor. So far, so good. Now to go it alone without the wall? The shortest distance was as the crow flies, but the surest would be to travel along the wall to the counter and then over to the door.

Jake had almost reached the door when the door swung open and in flew—or should you say in was thrown a man. Several of the men from the shelter were helping this man into the room, where Jake was now trying to leave. The man came to rest on the ground in front of Jake. As he looked up and Jake looked down, any fool could see the look of recognition on both Jake's and this new intruder's face.

"What on earth are you doing here?" The words were out of Jake's mouth before he could even think about what he was saying.

"I guess the same could be asked of you." This intruder was now pulling himself together in order to make a stand for himself.

"Jake, do you know this man?" One of the men from the shelter was wanting an answer and right now. From the tone in his voice, everyone could tell that he was angry. Several of the others in the shelter were now also yelling questions with similar actions and vocal tones as well. It was quickly stated that they all thought that perhaps this man was a spy.

As Jake was about to speak, David interrupted the goings-on with an answer of his own. "I know him. He is here to meet with me." David pushed his way past the crowd in order to make his way toward where Jake and this man were now standing. David placed out his hand in a greeting sort of manner. The man immediately reached out and shook his hand in return.

A look of relief came over this man's face and was then quickly replaced by one of question. He looked over to where Jake had moved. Jake had found support by leaning up against the doorjamb.

Jake was trying hard to figure out what was going on. How on earth was this man here? And why?

"Everyone, I would like you all to meet a good friend of mine." David was trying hard to overshout the crowd in the room.

"A good friend of mine." Was that what David had said? No way. Jake was full of a lot of feelings, but trust was not one of the first to be coming up right now. Jake needed to figure out what he was going to do. What could he do? He stood there leaning so hard against the doorjamb that he felt as if his shoulder might have already become a part of the wood.

Once again David tried to overshout the voices in the room. "Everyone. I would like for you all to meet my good friend. His name is Mark, and he is here to help me figure out some of the things that have been going on around here. Although this was to be a secret meeting, I guess you all now know."

Yes, this was exactly what he had heard the first time. "This is my friend." Jake had heard him right. But to Jake, this was not a friend, it was his brother. His brother Mark. Suddenly Jake couldn't catch his breath. He was not too sure what was going on, but one thing was for sure, and that was that he was not going to be able to speak in order to explain himself if need be. In fact, right at this moment, he wasn't even sure if he could keep breathing. Was this being caused by his head wound, or was it from total anxiety? Jake did not have very much time to mull it over in his head. The very next thing he saw was black.

Jake's falling to the ground seemed to bring this upheaval to a stop. Sandy and Martha together decided that someone should get word to the doctor in order to have Jake checked out. Martha had only known Jake for a very short time, but she already felt a closeness to him.

Martha spoke up. "I think we might need to rethink Jake's medical condition. Perhaps he needs to go to the hospital shelter after all. I am thinking this might be worse than we all thought at first."

Mark used this idea as an opportunity to convince everyone that he should be the one to take Jake there due to the fact he had not had any known contact with the shelters and might bring less suspicion about how Jake had been hurt in the first place.

CHAPTER 12

When Jake came to, he wasn't at the shelter anymore. Where he was, he was not sure, but it definitely was not the shelter.

He was in a bed that was surrounded by a curtain about two feet from the bed on all sides, except for where his head was; there was a wall with his name "Jacob" written on tape stuck to it. There was no last name and nothing that gave him any idea of exactly where he was. From the smell and the sounds of things, his first guess was that he was in some sort of hospital or clinic. Jake had been to see his grandfather in the hospital several years back, but it was nothing like this. His grandfather was in a small room, but it was much bigger than this space Jake was now in. There had been a TV and a telephone. There were charts and name tags on almost every piece of equipment. But this place was not even close to what he remembered. Only the smell and the sounds were similar. From what Jake could see, he could only conclude that this must be a chipless hospital clinic.

Jake was feeling tired, and his head was still in pain, but he had enough of his senses to remember what it was that had happened before he passed out. Oh my God! That was right. Mark had come to the shelter, and the people there thought he was some sort of a spy.

What was he doing there? Was he looking for Jake? Had he thought that he needed to be rescued or something? Why else would he have come to the shelter where Jake was living?

Jake decided that it was time to get some answers. He not only wanted them but needed them as well. He lifted his left hand, only to find that there was an IV needle in the back side of it. The tape was so tight around his hand that Jake wondered if his hand hurt from the needle or the tape itself. Deciding that using his left hand was out, he then tried to lift his right hand, only to find that it was being held down by someone else's hand. Jake lifted his head so as to see who it was holding onto his hand. As he looked down to his right, he saw that there was someone sitting in a chair beside his bed. The person had laid their head down on the covers and was holding onto his hand. Jake may have mistaken his brother Mark for someone else at the bus stop, but not this time. This was Mark all right. But what was he doing here?

Most likely Mark had told the others at the shelter that he was his brother, and he was sure that the fact that he was an officer for the government most likely would have come up too. Oh well, if that were so, then everything was over, but then why had he been brought here and not to a government hospital?

As Jake had come to the conclusion that there must be some sort of mix-up, Mark stirred and raised his head. As he looked at Jake, Mark noticed that he was awake. "Jacob, you are awake! That's great. How are you feeling?"

Jake was amazed at how great Mark was at being a brother. There was no lecture, just concern about how he was feeling. And the name *Jacob*. He had not heard that name in over three months. How very off it sounded to him. "Mark, what happened? How did I get here?"

"I brought you. We all felt that you needed some medical help, and we did not think that the doctor would be able to come quickly enough. As it turned out, we were right, you were dehydrated. That was why you passed out. Sandy thought that must have happened because of your head wound. She said that you had been dizzy and couldn't keep anything down. But you are going to be okay. Just a few days, and you will be out of here, good as new." Mark had stood up from his chair and was now looking down at Jake in his bed. "Jacob, what happened to your chip? I had to bring you here because your chip can't be read. What happened to it?"

Jake was getting tired now. Even though he was feeling better, he was still so weak. "Mark, can we talk about it later?"

Mark put his head down close to Jake's. "Jacob, what happened to your chip?" He was whispering, but he was firm and very direct. Jake could see from the look on his face that Mark was not going to be put off. If Jake was going to get any rest, he had better give up the answer and now.

Jake shut his eyes and said, "You know, Mark, I should not be telling you this, but they took it."

"Who took it, Jacob? And how?"

"The government officials took it out." All Jake wanted to do was go back to sleep; there would be enough time in the future to discuss the particulars.

"Jacob, don't be crazy, no one can remove a chip. How did they disarm it?"

"Honest, Mark. They took it out. They have this new way of doing it. I am only one of two, or so Mr. Diggings said."

"Mr. Diggings. How do you know him?" Mark was getting a little too intense, so he stopped for a second and took several deep breaths. Jake was keeping his eyes closed. Mark suspected that the light from the room must be hurting his head. "Jacob, what are you doing? I mean, how is it you don't have a chip and that you now live on the streets? What is this all about?" Mark might as well have been talking to himself. Jake had slipped off into a deep sleep. The doctor had said that this would be normal for a few days until he got his energy back. His body not only needed to be rehydrated but it also needed to heal. The head wound turned out to be a really bad concussion. The doctor had said that head wounds were all different but that he thought it was something that was just going to take time. Mark, realizing that he had all of the information that he was going to get for now, decided that it was best for him to leave. Jacob was going to be okay, so it would be safe to leave him.

*****

Jake woke again, only this time there was no Mark at his side. Jake could remember talking to Mark, but he couldn't remember too much of the conversation. What on earth was Mark up to, and why on earth had he placed him here at a chipless hospital? With one call to their father, and Mark could have cleared this whole thing up. Or had he tried that and it did not work? Just too many questions and no answers. Jake was almost getting used to feeling like this. It seemed to be the state he stayed in most of the time these days. When Mark returned, Jake would get all of the answers he needed. Or so he hoped.

*****

An entire day had passed, and there was no sign of Mark. In fact, the only person he had seen was a nurse who came in and changed his IV bag. She told him about the bathroom facilities (a bedpan). He tried to question her, but it was evident that she had a chip and had no real time for someone without one. She did her job all right, but that was all. She did her job and no more. Someone brought Jake some dinner late in the day, but same as with the nurse, there was no real interaction between worker and patient.

Under normal circumstances, this would have been beyond frustrating for Jake, but he found himself sleeping more than he was awake. Perhaps someone else had come and he had missed them. Yes, that could have been it. This idea gave Jake peace of mind. Kind of.

*****

It was very late in the evening when Jake awoke from another long sleep. He could tell that it was a long time because the night had come. At least the lights had been lowered and the noise level was so low that it being night could be the only real explanation. Jake first noticed that his room or curtained-off area had been straightened up. The dishes were gone, and a new bedpan now replaced the other one. There was an extra blanket that had been laid on the end of his bed and a cup of ice chips, half melted, were on a very small table just to the left of him.

Jake was half startled and half grateful to see that there was a cleaning man now entering his cubicle. He was in a cleaning uniform. He had backed into Jake's cubicle through an opening in the curtain he had made with his body as he came in. Dragging along behind him was a mop and a professional mopping bucket. He bent down and squeezed out the mop that had been resting in the water in the bucket. As he had finished getting out as much of the water as he could, he shook out the mop and flipped it onto the ground. It was not until he had moved almost completely up the right side of his bed that Jake recognized him. "It's you! You're a janitor."

"Yes, I am a janitor." The man continued to clean the floor around Jake's bed, making his way up to where Jake's head was now lying.

"But I thought you were a doctor." Jake was completely confused at what was happening.

"I am." With that statement, he leaned his mop up against the side of the bed and took Jake's right hand in his and started to take his pulse.

"I don't understand. Either you are a doctor or you are not. Now which is it?" Jake felt he had the right to know.

"Jake, I am a doctor. A doctor without a chip. Thus, I am also a janitor in a chipless hospital clinic. Now hold still so I can check you out."

"That doesn't make any sense. If you are a doctor, you don't need to clean floors." Jake was uneasy about what he was hearing. This man had chosen to give up his career in order to not have a chip. This was just plain nuts. As a doctor, this man could do a lot more for his faith and his people than he was doing right now. All he had to do was to think about the kind of money that a doctor could make versus a janitor. It was not like he had to keep the money or anything. He could always give it away. And being in a position like he would by being a doctor, the influence he could make would be endless. But no. His choice was to do what was unexpected. Jake was feeling as though he had been here before. Wasn't doing the unexpected the way of life for these people? No sense, just the unthinkable, to Jake anyway. But to the people making the choice, it was more than a choice, it was a way of life. Life with God guiding them and not the government.

*****

214

The doctor slash janitor had finished taking Jake's pulse, and he was looking into Jake's eyes and watching to see if they dilated like they were supposed to. The doctor was satisfied with what he was seeing. He double-checked the IV needle and then adjusted the drip. "There, that will be better. Now what I want you to do is to rest as much as you can. Make sure you drink everything that comes your way, and try to eat whatever you can. It is important that you be up to snuff by the end of the week. It has been decided that you and several others are to go to the farm. So, be as ready to travel as you can, okay?"

Jake now realized that the doctor had not been caught up on things. Jake was sure that his true identity had been found out by the others and that all the plans that had been made before had to have been canceled. It was awfully nice of them to make sure that he was all right, but he would not blame them if they never talked to him again. "Sure, whatever you say, but if you should find that the plans have been changed, I would not be surprised."

The doctor had thought that Jake was hard to know all along, but the answer he got made his understanding him even more impossible. "Jake, why would things have changed? Just because you got hurt isn't any reason for you not to get to go to the farm. At the most, you might have to go later, but you will still get to go."

"I know how it seems now, but you will see. Just know I understand if things have to change. I don't blame anyone." Jake knew that the doctor was not understanding right now, but in a short time, he was sure that he would.

"Well, Jake, it is obvious that you know something that I have no clue about. But what I do know is that as of a short time ago, this was the plan. So stay here and wait for someone to come and get you." He reached out grabbed the handle of the mop, plunged it into the water in the bucket, and exited in very much the same manner as he had entered. Backing out through the curtain pulling the bucket behind him. Before he left, he looked Jake straight in the eye. "Remember to take care and wait for someone to come and get you, okay?"

As the doctor slipped through the curtain, followed by the bucket, Jake felt as if he were even lonelier than he was before he had been visited. Perhaps this was to be his very last visit from someone from the Knowing. Perhaps this was going to be the only goodbye he would have with his newfound friends. Jake laid his head back and tried hard to imagine what could happen to keep things from changing, but within seconds, he was fast asleep again.

*****

Several days passed, and Jake was feeling much better. He was trying to follow the orders that the doctor had told him to do. He drank as much as he could, ate anything he could get his hands on; the food was limited, but he was always fed twice a day. One day he even found when he had woken from a nap that there were two oranges left on his pillow. This was odd, people coming and going into his life without any detection of any kind. How very strange it was to Jake that each and every visit, except for the one from the doctor, food handlers and the nurses, were always when he was asleep. This sleeping so much sure was bothersome. Not to mention very tiring. On the fourth day of his stay, Jake decided that it was time for him to get back onto a schedule. Sleeping in the night and being awake during the day. Yes, that was the plan. That morning, the nurse had removed his IV. She said that he was doing so good that he would not be needing it any longer. She then looked at his head wound and said that it would be three or four days until the stitches would come out. Jake was surprised to see her doing the decision-making on his case. He had not seen a real doctor since he had been here. He had asked her if the doctor would be coming to see him anytime soon. He wanted to find out about getting out of here. But all she did was laugh. "You think that a doctor is going to come see you?" was all she said. She left the room roaring with laughter. Jake could hear her all the way down the hallway.

So much for getting information, but Jake had a backup plan. To get himself back on a schedule. Yes, that was the plan. Although he was able to stay awake longer than he had been, it was shortly after lunch that he found he could not keep his eyes open a single second longer. Jake couldn't stand this anymore, he needed to get some exercise. Yes, that was it, he had rest fatigue. Some fresh air might be just what the doctor should have ordered.

Jake swung his legs off the side of the bed. He took it slow. Not so much from caution as it was he couldn't seem to muster up the strength he had always been able to rely on. Jake looked down to note that he was in no way dressed to go wandering around. Where was his clothing? Jake looked around and saw that hanging from the back of the chair beside his bed was his backpack.

Jake regained his memory of his having a notebook that was full of information about the Knowing. How was it that he had not thought of it before this? That book could destroy lives. And here it was just lying around so anyone could get their hands on it. Jake needed his clothing, but more than that, he needed to get his hands on that book. Jake slowly reached out and grabbed the shoulder strap on the backpack. He lifted it off the chair back very carefully. As it slid off the chair, all at once the full weight of the bag fell with a jerk, slipping past his hand and then falling to the floor. *Great, that was real smooth work.* Jake was often irritated with his not being able to do things. But here he had been doing nothing but resting for days, and yet he still was not able to find the strength to even pick up his pack without dropping it. How long was this "getting better" supposed to take? He had things to do. The world was not on hold until he got better. No, it was continuing on at its very same speed, and it was leaving him behind, or so it felt anyway. Jake sat there on the side of the bed looking down at the bag. He was wishing that he could get it by doing anything but having to get down and retrieve it. A short time passed, and Jake realized that if he were going to get it, he needed to do it himself. With that thought set into his mind, he started to lower himself from on top of the bed. Letting first one foot touch the ground and then the other. So far, so good. Now bending over, he retrieved his pack. He stood up, only to find that his head was not at all in perfect working order. Just like before, his head began to spin. Not as bad as the last time, but spin all the same.

Jake closed his eyes, and let the bag drop. He took both of his hands and reached back to take hold of the bed. Finding the sheets with his hands, it was to be his plan to lift himself back up onto the bed. Things did not go as he planned. With no strength to speak of to lift himself up, he continued to hold onto the sheets, and then reaching for the pillow, he slowly slid down to the floor, sheets, pillow, and all. He did not drop to the floor very hard, but it was to the floor all the same. Now this was getting ridiculous. Jake moved himself around so as to make himself more comfortable. He laid his head on the pillow and then, with the other hand, pulled a sheet and blanket up over himself. Perhaps if he rested here for a time, then he could get himself back upon the bed. Jake went to pull the pillow up under his head when he felt his backpack. It was now under him and all of this mess from the bed. A smile came across his face. At least I have the backpack. With that thought, he slipped off to sleep.

When Jake awoke, he was still in the same place he was when he had last been awake. He had no way of knowing how long he had been asleep, but whatever the amount of time it was, he felt much better now. Jake sat up and decided the best plan would be to get himself up on the chair and to get himself dressed. First job. Get to the chair. Okay, that was done. Now find his clothing. Jake reached down and pulled up the backpack. But this time he went slower. So far, so good. Now he opened the pack and began to take inventory. Pants, shirt, socks. Great start. No shoes, but he was sure that they would be here somewhere. Jake took his time, making sure not to rush anything. Getting dressed was not usually a hard task, but he was a little weary from it all. Looking back into his pack, Jake decided to find the notebook and to quickly get rid of it. He could rip it into pieces so that no one would ever be able to use it for anything. Jake reached his hand down into the pack for the book, only to find that it was not there. Perhaps it was in another compartment. No, not there either. He had an idea. Perhaps it had fallen out when it had dropped to the floor. Jake began to lift the sheets and blanket. Not there. Now the pillow. No nothing there either. Perhaps if he placed the bedding back upon the bed, he would be able to find the book. But it was not there either. If it were not here, then where could it be? Perhaps Mark took it. No, why would he? Well, it didn't really matter now, did it? The truth was out into the open, and most likely, the information was as well.

Jake sat there in the chair. All dressed except for shoes. He was tired, but more than that, he felt numb, somehow empty.

Jake could hear a familiar sound coming down the hall. If he were right, the janitor or doctor, whichever you wanted to call him, would be coming to visit him. Perhaps not though, if he knew about Jake's real identity. He most likely would just pass him by.

Jake was right about one thing, and that was that the doctor was coming down the hall, but on the other hand, he was wrong about the other, he did stop by to see how he was doing. As the doctor pulled open the curtain in order to make way for his bucket and then himself, he saw that Jake was up and dressed. Jake was semi-sitting in the chair by his bed. "Jake, what on earth do you think you are doing?" The doctor rushed into the cubicle and at once took hold of Jake. Jake fell forward, putting his full weight onto the doctor. The doctor lifted Jake up and placed him on top of the bed where the only real part left intact was the fitted mattress sheet. He then found the pillow and placed it under Jake's head. "What on earth are you trying to do? Didn't I tell you to take it easy and to just get better?"

Jake was glad to see the doctor, an old friend of sorts. "Yes, I know what you said, but I should be better by now. It has been almost a week since this all happened. I should be ready to get on with things."

"So, Jake, when was it you became a doctor? I didn't know that we had so much in common." The doctor was trying hard to make light of all of this. He had often worked with discouraged patients who felt that they were somehow at fault in that they were not recovering as fast as they thought they should. "Jake, I don't think you have any idea as to how bad you were hurt. These things take time. And the timetable you think you know is not even close. In some ways you will be better in a week or two, but in other ways, it might even be months. So will you please just follow the janitor's orders and stay in bed and get better?"

Jake burst out in laughter. "Janitor's orders?" Jake closed his eyes and continued to laugh at what a mess this all was. Then he realized that he did not even know this wonderful man's real name. "Hey, what is your name anyway? You know, if I am going to take orders from you, then I think I should at least know what to call you. Don't you think?"

"Bill." The doctor was now real serious in his wording. "And now that you know who and what I am, will you do as I say and stay put? Somehow finding my patients lying on the floor is not the way I want to start my rounds." Bill was smiling at Jake.

To anyone else, Bill was washing the floor, but to Bill, he was doing his rounds. Jake thought it funny how it was all in the way you look at things as to how you feel about what you are doing. Could it all really be that simple? If you were doing the job you were called to do, could that be enough to not care about whether you are called doctor or janitor? Could there be a way to be both and yet neither and it still be enough to be fulfilled as a man? It sure was working for this man. Jake could only admire Bill. He had made a choice in his life. Not one most could live with. But then it was clear to Jake that Bill wasn't and never would be like most men. He was more somehow, and yet he has chosen the life of less.

Bill couldn't stay long. He needed to get on with his other work, but he promised Jake that he would see him again as soon as he could. Jake had a new friend, and he was excited at the chance to get to know him better. Although Bill felt Jake's getting better was coming along fine, it was in Jake's mind that perhaps he might be mistaken. Perhaps Bill didn't realize how very strong he had always been. It was not like him not to bounce back in these situations. But whether Bill was right or not, there was not a lot Jake could do about this whole thing anyway. So it had been decided for him. He would rest and wait for whatever it was to come.

Bill had finished his work for the day and was heading back to the shelter where he lived. He thought it best to look into the shelter where Sandy was and to see if there had been any more information about the closing of the shelter.

"Hi, Sandy, how is it going?" Sandy was in her usual mode. She and several others were making the final arrangements before the curfew sirens began to gather in all the people. The overcrowding due to the closing of the one shelter and the lack of one of her best workers, Jake, had put a pinch in things, to say the least. But it was always a pleasure to see Bill. "Hi, Doc. How is our very favorite patient?" Sandy wanted to stop and visit, but she knew that Bill would understand if she did not. There was simply way too much to do.

"Well." Bill reached out to help Sandy with one of the soup kettles. "Let me help you with that." Bill and Sandy lifted it up onto the counter.

"There, thanks for the help. Now what were you going to say about our patient?" Sandy had stopped working and was wiping her hands off onto her apron.

"Well, he sure is an overanxious one. You know today I found him completely dressed and sitting up in a chair. I think he thought he was going to be able to leave the clinic. But I tell you, he would not have gone very far. He is still so very weak. And rightfully so. With the kind of head injury and blood loss he had, and not to even mention being dehydrated, and now he's pushing himself and not taking the time to heal. Well, all I can say is that if he doesn't stay down for a while, it will take him twice as long as it should to get up and going. And as for his being ready for travel, well, we will have to see. Perhaps if you talk with him. Maybe you can bring some sense to him."

"You know, Doc. When it comes to you men, I don't really know if there is really any talking to you. But yes, I will give it a try. How soon until we can spring him from the clinic?" Sandy was again getting things prepared. "Hey, why don't you stay here tonight? I know that Victor would love to get a chance to visit with you. What do you think?"

"Sandy, I would like that too, but you know I was thinking to maybe stay at the shelter closer to the clinic. That way I can go and see Jake first thing in the morning. I am not too sure what it is, but I feel like he needs to be close to one of us for a while yet. But thanks anyway. I would love to see Victor too. I sure do have a lot of questions about all this stuff going on. Do you know anything more about what happened at the shelter and with all of the arrests?"

Bill was exactly like all of the others Sandy had seen all day. Everyone wanting an answer and all very disappointed to find out that she didn't have any to give. "No. We don't know any more today than we did yesterday. David even had his friend Mark come over. Of course you know all about that. So much for keeping a meeting a secret. That poor man. Coming to help and then almost being mobbed by the people he came to help in the first place." Sandy was sad, mad, disappointed, and angry at the whole situation.

"You know, Sandy, fear does strange things to people. Even Godly people like the people here at the shelter." Bill had always been amazed at how quickly people could change in different situations. Even the most loving and kind people could be vicious when backed into a corner. "Sandy, survival is a real strong instinct. I think that is what we are all trying to do right now, merely survive. Don't be so hard on them. They meant well."

"What good is it going to do all of us if we survive only to become like the very people we are fighting against? I can understand being careful, but being untrusting? Where will that get us in the end?" Sandy was tired. Still. Again. Going to the farm at the end of the week was sounding better and better.

*****

The day had finally come for Jake to be released from the hospital. All of the papers had been signed. He had been escorted from his room with all of his belongings. Jake had found his shoes but was quick to realize that his new coat was still missing. *Oh well, it was great to have it even if it were for a short time.* Now was to come the final answer as to what was going to happen to him. Who was it going to be that would come and take him home? And to what home? Where was it he was going to go? Only a little time, and he would have his answers. Jake was not sure who it was that he wanted to come and retrieve him. No matter who it was and where it was he was to go, it would definitely be both happiness and sadness all tangled up in one emotion. If he went to the shelter, it would be a chance for him to learn more about the Knowing. Not so much for anyone else as much as it would be for himself. Then there was Peggy. It would be great to see her and even to get to know her a little better. On the other hand, there was Jake's family. He really did miss seeing them. Somehow spending a little time with Mark made Jake realize how much he had missed all of the people he loved. So much had happened and so much had changed, not only in Jake's life but in Jake himself. What would it be like to go back? Could he even go back? Jake sat trying hard to think of how things would be in either situation. But not even in his wildest dreams could he have thought up what was to happen to him in the next few weeks.

Almost an hour had gone by when Jake thought he recognized a figure coming down the hallway. He was not sure at first, but he thought it might be Sandy. As the figure got closer, his recognition was confirmed. It was Sandy, and she was coming down the hall looking as though she had won a million dollars. She smiled a huge smile when she saw that Jake was ready and waiting for her. She picked up speed as she got closer to him and was almost at a full run by the time she had reached him. "Jake, how are you? I have missed you so much. Are you ready to get out of here?"

Jake was as glad to see Sandy as she was to see him. "Sandy, thanks for coming. I am fine, but, boy, will I be glad to get out of here." As Jake was about to get up, he saw that Victor was also coming to get him.

Victor had rounded the corner and was coming to where Sandy and Jake were now getting ready to leave. "Sandy, what on earth are you doing here? I thought we decided that I should come and get Jake." The look on Victor's face wasn't as pleasant as the words he had spoken.

"I know that was what we had decided, but I couldn't wait any longer. I heard that you had been tied up and that you were going to be late, so I decided that I would come and get Jake out of here." Sandy put her arm around Jake's shoulder and gave him a hug.

"Besides, it is still cold outside, and I thought Jake might need this." Sandy reached into a large bag she was carrying and pulled out the coat Jake so wanted to have for himself.

Not only was this a nice, warm coat but it was also the only gift God had given him, and he was glad to have it back.

"Thanks, Sandy. I thought it was taken. I am so glad that you took care of it for me, it really means a lot to get it back. Thanks." Jake stood up and took the coat. He immediately put it on and then leaned over and gave Sandy a kiss on her cheek.

Victor was watching the happy faces of these two. "Sandy, I never will understand you, but since we are both here, let's get this guy home. Jake, how does that sound to you?" Victor knew that discussing this further with Sandy was of no use, so he decided to get out of here and get back to the shelter as soon as they could.

The three of them left the clinic without any delay. The walk home was without difficulty at all. Once they were there, several of the helpers ran to greet Jake. This was a great homecoming. Not that Jake was not happy to be back at the shelter, but a small part of him was disappointed that Peggy had not been there to greet him herself.

Jake's homecoming was a big deal, but there was still a lot to be done at the shelter in order to get things ready for the evening. All the odder, thought Jake, for Peggy to not be here—if not waiting for him, then at the least to be working for the shelter. "Hey, Sandy, where is Peggy? I haven't seen her."

Sandy smiled at Jake's question. "Peggy is off on some errands. She will be back before the curfew tonight."

"Oh, just wondering." Jake was disappointed but was also glad to know that he would be seeing Peggy before the day was over.

The rest of the day went on like a great production. Each person going about his or her duties. And without fail, as usual, things were ready for the people who were coming to the shelter for both dinner and rest.

The sirens began to howl, and yet no sign of Peggy. There was still five minutes before the final closing of the shelter doors. Jake could hardly believe his eyes when he saw how many people were coming into the shelter tonight. There had to be at least double what they used to have before he went to the hospital. How on earth did they plan on accommodating all of these people? One thing Jake knew for sure though, and that was that if anyone could get this job done, it was Sandy and her crew.

The last siren began its warning, and then the shelter doors were shut. Jake couldn't believe how very disappointed he was at not getting to see Peggy tonight. But then that was just a part of this crazy life. Things hardly ever went as planned. Something Jake was not sure if he could ever get used to. Sandy and the others were way too busy to talk to Jake about what might have happened to Peggy. But he knew that if there were any reason for concern that they would be doing something about it. Jake had some soup for dinner and found himself a very small space over in one of the corners and took a seat. Jake couldn't believe how incredibly tired he was. He was better, but he was not 100 percent. Not yet any way. Jake was about to close his eyes for the night when he heard a noise coming from the kitchen. There was a slight commotion, and then Jake could hear Peggy's voice. It was not clear exactly what she was saying, but Jake could tell that there was some sort of altercation over something. The kitchen door opened with a bang, and Peggy pushed her way through. She stopped just inside the room and began to scan the area ahead of her looking for something or someone. Jake only hoped it was him she was looking for.

"There you are!" Peggy had found Jake and gave out a yell and worked her way through people in order to get to him. "How are you? I am so sorry that I was not here when you got here. I had so much to get done before I leave tomorrow. You know how crazy it is around here. Jake, you never did tell me how you are doing."

"Hi, Peggy, I am glad to see you too. I am fine. And I didn't answer you because you didn't give me a chance. Where on earth have you been anyway?"

Victor and Sandy were standing within earshot of Jake and Peggy. They both looked at each other when they heard the two of them talking. They gave each other one of those "can you believe these two?" kind of looks. "Victor, can you believe that there are two people in this world who can talk like they do?"

"You know, Sandy, I think that Jake might be one of the only people in the world who can keep up with Peggy and the way she talks, and with all of her questions." Victor and Sandy were having a great time listening and watching these two and the interaction between them. At the very least, they might learn something about communicating with them in the future.

Jake couldn't believe what it was he was hearing. He had finally come home to where he felt he needed to be, only to find out one of the key people he wanted to be with was not going to be staying. "Peggy, where is it you are getting ready to go?" Jake did not want to seem too interested, but then he was, wasn't he?

Peggy stopped for a second to think about the question Jake had asked. "Jake, you are such a kidder. You know very well where I am going." She paused. "Don't you? Well, you should. I think you should." Peggy looked over to where Victor and Sandy were standing. She caught Sandy's eye and turned to ask, "Shouldn't he?"

"Well, yes, I think you are right." Sandy looked at Jake. "I thought we had someone tell you about all of the plans for the next few days. About all of the changes we need to make?" Sandy in turn looked to Victor to fill in the blanks of what it was Jake needed to know.

Victor walked over to where Jake and Peggy were now sitting. "Jake, didn't Doc tell you of the plans that had been made concerning you?"

Jake thought hard about Victor's question. "Well, Victor, I do recall something about a farm. But what does that have to do with Peggy leaving?"

Peggy could not stand the excitement any longer. "Don't you get it? We are all leaving."

Jake not only did not get it, he was even more confused than ever. "Where are we going, and how can everybody leave?"

"Not everybody, silly. Just us." Peggy was having fun with all of this. She had absolutely no idea how very frustrated she was making Jake.

Victor noticed Jake's reaction to all of the confusion and decided the only humane thing to do was to step in and straighten him out. "Jake, not everyone is going to leave for the farm, only a few of us. Sandy and I, Peter's parents, and several others who have transferred in from the other shelters will all be going. As Peggy here has just told you, both she and you will also be going." Victor looked over to Sandy and Peggy and started to tell them plans about leaving; he had not had a chance to fill them in on until now. "There is a lot of things to get done before any of us can get out of here. There are a lot of things we need to get out to the farm, so everyone will have to wear a vest."

Sandy and Peggy immediately understood what Victor was talking about. "Do we really have that much to transfer out of here?" Sandy was trying hard to keep up with what Victor was planning.

"Yes, there is, but most of all, the Bibles that were left here need to be moved, and the sooner, the better." Victor and Sandy began to walk away going on with their conversation like it had only been the two of them talking all along.

Jake, being left with only Peggy to question, looked to her now for the next round of information. "Peggy, what are the vests that Victor was talking about?"

"Oh, Jake, there really is so much for you to learn, isn't there? Well, the vests are a netting type of material that have been sewed into a type of clothing. You put it on under your coat. They have large pockets. We wear them inside out so the pockets are next to us. We can fill the pockets with whatever we need to carry on long trips. They are covered by our coats, and that way, we do not look like we are going anywhere special. We can merely walk around empty-handed looking like everyone else. No one would ever guess that we were loaded up heading on a long trip. Great idea, yes?" Peggy was so proud to tell of such a clever idea.

All Jake could do was smile at this most wonderful, excitable young lady he was with. "Peggy, I am not sure I completely understand what you are talking about, but from what I do understand, it is a great idea. Thanks for telling me about it."

Peggy was beaming from satisfaction at pleasing Jake in such a way. She wanted to stay and tell him more, but she had way too much to get ready. Besides, Jake needed to get some rest. Even though he was mostly recovered, this trip was going to prove to be hard on everyone. The farm they were going to was way out from the city. By car, it would only take the most part of a day; but traveling on foot with all of the curfews and laws that had to be observed, it would take the most part of the week. Sleeping and eating arrangements would be rough going, so starting out rested was the least they could do for themselves. "Jake, I need to go now. You get some rest, and don't worry about anything. I'll see to it that all of your stuff is ready to go for you, okay?" Peggy reached for Jake's backpack. "That will have to go. I will help you get your things into a vest. That backpack would be a dead giveaway for you being a traveler. Not a risk anyone would want to take."

Traveling was allowed within a short distance of your living or working area, but any long-distance travel had to be approved ahead of time. It was easier and a lot safer to do it this way. The less questions and drawing attention to the farms, the better.

Jake was not sure that he totally understood, but he felt he knew enough to go along with Peggy on this. "Thanks, Peggy, that would be great." Besides, he was feeling tired now. God, how long was he going to be tired? Well, only time would tell that one, but for now, he needed to get some rest. As Peggy departed with Jake's bag, Jake laid his head down for a few minutes to get a quick nap. One of the last thoughts to go through his mind was that he was glad there was no book to worry about anyone finding. For the life of him, he did not know where that book had gone, but for now, it was out of his life, and he was glad to be rid of it. From this time on, he was going to take on this new life he so wanted to get back to. Whatever the future held, one thing was for sure, and that was that he could never go back. He did not want to.

*****

Jake stirred, and hearing the voices of the others, he opened his eyes. He could hardly believe that it was morning. He had only planned on taking a catnap. People at the shelter were gathering all of their things up and were preparing to leave at the first blast of the all clear siren. Jake looked around to see if he could see Peggy or anyone who would have answers as to exactly what the day was going to bring. There over at the end of the counter were a small group of people gathered together talking very seriously. Obviously from the looks on their faces, this was a very important meeting. No one was taking notes, but Jake could tell that each, as they were told, had locked the information away in their thoughts. "It must come from practice they're not needing to take notes and all." Jake had not realized he was thinking out loud until he heard an answer come from behind him.

Jake turned to look and to see who it was trying to explain things to him. It was Peggy. "What?"

"You said they don't have to take notes to remember, and I said it is because of the Holy Spirit giving them remembrance. You know, like in John 14:26. That's how." Peggy set her lips and set her gaze directly at him.

Peggy was so matter-of-fact about the whole thing that Jake was sure he would make a fool of himself if he even tried to question this any further. "Oh, yes, that's right, the Holy Spirit." Jake had not even a clue as to what she was talking about. In his pre-studies, he had not heard of this Holy Spirit. Definitely something to peruse in the future.

"Jake, are you about ready to go?" Peggy was really excited.

"Oh yes. To the farm." Jake was not sure if he could muster up any excitement about leaving the shelter. "Well, I am not exactly sure what it is I am supposed to be excited about." Jake began to gather his things up, only to realize that other than his blanket, there was nothing. *His backpack—oh yes, Peggy has it.* "Peggy, do you have my backpack?"

"Oh, that's right." With that, Peggy jumped to her feet and ran over to where the small group was still meeting. As she approached, they stopped talking and turned to honor her request. Someone in the group reached to the ground and pulled out a pile of netting-type clothing. It was white in color. Having retrieved it, Peggy thanked them and quickly returned over to where Jake was now slowly moving into a standing position. "Jake, take off your coat, will you?" As Peggy assisted him in removing his coat, she held up the netted garment. It was a vest. Just like they had said last night. It had very large and deep pockets. They were for the most part all on the back part of the vest. The tops of the pockets were held shut with what at first looked like zippers but, as it turned out, were Velcro closures. Some of the pockets were already full. At second glance, Jake realized that the stuff in the pockets were his things from his backpack. "Now let's try this on for size." Peggy helped to slide Jake's arms into the openings. And then helped him place his coat back on. "See, no one would ever guess that you were a traveling man, would they?" Peggy was quite pleased with being able to show Jake how this worked. "Sandy thought of this. Isn't she smart? She said God gave her the idea, but she did it."

Jake was amazed at how simple and yet how very clever this idea was. It was brilliant not using zippers. Not even a metal detector could find it out. "Thank you, Peggy. And yes, you are right, this is a great idea."

"Before you leave, you need to get some other supplies and put them into the other pockets. The plastic bags and any food should always go into the front pockets." Peggy opened up the front of her coat and showed Jake her supply of foodstuffs. "You know, if you think this is a great idea, you should see what we do in the summer." With Jake set up and almost ready to go, Peggy went off to get her further orders.

Jake decided that since it seemed he was definitely going, he should get his orders for himself. Jake walked to the outside of the small circle of people. Making a quick scan of the group, Jake took special note of the people he was going to be traveling with. Of course, there was Peggy, Sandy, and Victor, both of Peter's parents (Frank and Martha), and there was Jim. Jake had not really talked to him since that night at the rabbit hole, but he could likely fix that on this trip. Several of the other faces, Jake recognized, but he did not know them very well. Then again, some of the people going, Jake was sure he had never seen before, but all of that did not matter now. What did matter was that they were all leaving, and soon. Jake was not too enthusiastic about all of this. He felt as if he had just got home, and now he was going to leave. The fact that most of the people he felt close to were leaving with him was making it a lot easier to go though.

It was David who was giving out the traveling orders. "Oh, and yes, one more thing. We have all of these Bibles we need to get away from here. Who can carry some?" A few hands went up into the air. David at once began to pass out the Bibles. Jake noted that they were still being kept in the now-torn brown bag. Past feelings came rushing back at Jake. Jake realized that Peggy was one of the ones holding up her hand to be a carrier.

"Peggy, I don't think that would be a good idea. I am afraid that you have been in the spotlight too much, let's pass this time, okay?" David was sympathetic and yet was very decided. No one questioned his decision. Except Jake. Jake could see Peggy's face from where he was standing. He saw that she was truly disappointed. Perhaps if he got one, he could give it to her. "David, I can carry one."

David stopped and spent a second or two thinking that thought over. "Jake, do you realize what it would mean if you were to be caught holding one of these Bibles?"

Jake hadn't thought about that at all. No, he would not want to be caught with a Bible; for that matter, there was not a person here he wanted to take this kind of risk. "I know, David, but I have a lot of room, and after all, who would ever suspect me?"

"Okay then, here you go." David handed Jake one of the more-used Bibles.

Jake could not believe how tattered and worn this book was. Looking at it somehow gave him the feeling of unbalance. For the government to be making such a big deal about a book as to make it a sentence of a lifetime in prison to have one, and for these people to risk such an outcome for such a simple thing. Perhaps there was more than meets the eye in all of this. This gave Jake two reasons to not give Peggy the Bible. First, the risk it would take for her to have it; and second, the fact that Jake might have a better chance to read through this book. Hopefully he will be able to get a handle on the Holy Spirit thing. Mr. Diggings had said that this stuff seemed crazy, but this was even odder than he could ever have imagined.

Something had happened to him. Not bad. Not really good either, but definitely different.

After Jake had received the Bible, Peggy helped him place it into one of the very back pockets in his vest. She helped to make sure that it was closed safely in place. Jake looked to see if there was any anger in Peggy's face, but there was none to be detected. How was it that these people could roll with the disappointments? How was it that they could accept the negatives and yet still keep going? Where on earth do they get their hope?

CHAPTER 13

Everyone and everything was ready to go. All they needed was to hear the all clear siren, and they would be off to their new destinations. Those that would be staying would be going off to do a day's work while others, having been assigned jobs here at the shelter, would go about doing the Gathering and then preparing for the coming evening.

As for the traveling group, it was evident to Jake that they would all be leaving together, but how the traveling would be done was not yet clear. Jake knew very little about the plans, only what pertained to him, and even that was sketchy at best.

As the all clear siren began its cry, the front door was opened, and several of the people started heading out of the door. As quickly as the exit was usually done, today was not going as planned. A few had left, and yet the line was still not moving.

"Hey, what is going on? I need to get out of here, would you hurry things up please?" someone from the middle of the room was heard saying.

"Oh my God! It's the government officers." A lady at the front of the line had seen what was going on and had turned to tell the rest of the room what was happening. "It seems that they are searching and then looking to arrest people as they are leaving the shelter. I can't hear what they are saying, but there is a whole squadron of officers out there."

It was as if by plan that the whole room looked to David for advice on what to do. "Let's pray!" was all that he said and then lowered his head, as did all of the others.

Jake could not believe what he was seeing. Their very way of life could be at stake, and they want to pray. Oh yes, from what Jake had seen in the past, prayer had its place in life, but not now. Now they needed a plan, not a prayer.

"Father, guide us now. We need Your protection. Please, I ask for traveling mercies on this small group. Be with them and give them wings of eagles." David ended his prayer with "Amen." Followed up by the others repeating it too.

Victor reached out to shake David's hand. "Thanks for everything. We will see you in a few weeks."

"Victor, don't worry about anything. I will take good care of things here. And even if I don't, what are they going to do, fire me?" David gave out a small chuckle and motioned with his head for them to head to the kitchen.

Great. First, we pray, and now we will most likely do lunch. These people are nuts, and this time, they are going to take me down with them. Jake was trying as hard as he could to not be skeptical, but it was hard. Their lives were about to fall apart, and they all were acting like they were going to a party.

Victor turned and spoke to the small group. "Those of you who are packing, you need to leave first. Then the rest will follow."

"Packing?" Jake did not know anyone was armed. Why, this was the first time he had even heard of them having any kind of fighting power.

Peggy could see from the look on Jake's face that he was thinking about weapons of some sort. She reached out with her hand and slapped him on the arm. "Not guns, silly. Bibles!"

Jake's mind immediately went to the book he now had in his vest pocket. *Oh no, Peggy's right, this is worse than having a gun. This is a Bible.* He needed be one of the ones to leave first, but how to get out of here? There was no way out of the kitchen except back through the main room. Or so he thought. Perhaps now he would get his answer as to how people in the past had simply shown up in the kitchen.

Several of the men were standing at the door entrance to the kitchen. David was one of them. He looked out into the main room and then gave the okay for them to proceed.

Jake could not even begin to imagine what was going to come next. One of the fellow travelers bent down and pressed a plank in the hardwood floor. It gave way, and there was a handle now exposed. Reaching down, Victor took hold of it and gave a gentle tug. At once, very quietly and gently, the back wall of the building gave way and swung out, leaving an opening only large enough to walk through. Outside of the opened wall were a set of stairs. Where they went did not matter right now. For now, it was a way out.

Martha and Frank were motioned to go first by Victor. Jake guessed that they must be carrying something important. Like Peggy, they were not given a Bible, but they must have something that would put them over the Bible carriers.

They did not hesitate one second. They exited. Victor called to several others to follow, each doing as they were told and in the order they were called. Jake knew that he was going to be traveling with Victor and Sandy, so he was surprised when Victor called to him to go on ahead of them. Jake knew better than to question this. Time was of the essence. Jake took one last look at Victor and Sandy and then gave a half smile and started down the stairs. One last look into the room gave him a glance of Peggy, who was now over by the door helping to keep watch in the main room. Victor saw what Jake was looking at and at once realized that Peggy was not in place. "Peggy, your turn. Follow Jake. Then get him to Martha and Frank. Do not stay with them but go on your own plan. They know what to do with Jake. Understand?"

Although Jake heard what was said, this was not what he had bargained for. Leaving the shelter was one thing, but doing it with strangers, well, that was a whole other story. Jake would address that later. Now he needed to figure out where it was he was going. The stairs continue to lead down deep into the ground. It was damp and very dark. Someone up ahead of them had some sort of light. But from Jake's point of view, all he could see were shadows. The form in front of him stopped. Jake could see enough to not run into the back of them, but that was about all. Peggy placed her hand on Jake's back and leaned around to see what was going on in front of him. "Jake, don't worry, it will be all clear in a second or two. They need to make sure that we can get out without being seen."

"Peggy, how come no one ever told me about this exit? I should have figured it out, but it was hidden so well." Jake had remembered at least two times when Victor and Peggy had appeared in the past and that there was no way they had come in the front door, the only door. *Some officer, huh?* Jake was quick to connect the disappearing of the men on the street to the false walls too. Oh, and yes, the meeting place. Jake had thought one of these type of walls was great, but a whole setup of them. This was incredible!

Peggy smiled. "You haven't seen anything yet."

Jake was afraid to ask. This whole setup was simply amazing. The engineering behind this was brilliant. And so very well done.

Finally. The line began to move on out. But to where? Jake followed the person in front of him. He was soon to come to another set of stairs that led up this time. As he climbed them, he saw that he was going to be coming out into a room. He did not recognize it because it was in another building. They were in a house. It was a dining room. The cover over the stairs was put back into place. A carpet and a table were put over that. Several people helped place chairs around the table, and no one would have ever guessed anything else but a dining room. Jake knew he had traveled a long way in the tunnel, but he had no idea as to where he was now. He saw a window and walked over to see out. Perhaps he could get his bearings. As he pulled back the window curtains, he was surprised to see several officers standing on the lawn just outside of where they were. Jake could not begin to guess where he was in relation to the shelter. Martha walked up behind Jake. She pointed out that past all of the officers was the shelter. They were across the street and two or three houses down from where they had been. They had gone under the mess outside of the shelter. This was unreal. It was like something from a movie. The time and the talent it would have taken to pull this off. Well, it was a miracle. Man-made, but a miracle all of the same.

Jake was so excited about all of the goings-on that he had not noticed right off that both Sandy and Victor were missing. When he had inquired of their whereabouts, everyone smiled and told him that he would see them again later.

It was over half the day before the streets were clear. From what they could see, the shelter was searched, and nothing criminal was found. All of those arrested were let go and were able to go on their way. A spot inspection is what Jake would have called it back in his old days. A life-threatening invasion of his privacy is what he called it now. How could things have changed so much and yet not at all?

Jake was paired up with Martha and Frank. This was not bad, but he really did not know them now, did he? "Will Peter be there when we get to the farm?" Jake asked them both, but it was Martha that answered him.

"I sure hope so. I have so much to say to that young man when I see him." Martha looked over to Frank and shook her head as she was deep in thought about something.

It was Jake's guess that the meeting up of Peter with his parents was not going to be one of those warm fuzzy ones. After all, it was Peter who helped to close down their shelter. Jake wondered how Frank was going to handle it. How would Jake's dad have handled it? Jake was not sure about either but thought it would prove to be interesting. The homecoming would have to wait though. For now, they needed to get on the road. With the day half spent, Jake would have thought it a better idea to stay the night here and then head out in the morning, but that was not to be the happening. A few at a time were let out and went on their way. How on earth would they all join up again in order to travel together? So many questions. And no better way to find out than to live it out. It was now Martha's, Frank's, and Jake's turn to leave. They double-checked their vests to see that they were in place and covered. Then they went right out the front door into the very world they were hiding from. Off to their new home away from home.

*****

Getting to the farm was taking much longer than Jake thought it would. Over four days alone were spent getting clear of the city.

They all traveled in small groups but were always together in the same area by the end of the day. When they arrived at the chipless shelters, they never had conversations with the other groups but gave only a nod of recognition to each other. One night, one of the groups had not yet arrived. It was clear to Jake that everyone was worried, and yet they said and did nothing. Several hours into the evening, the group arrived at the shelter, coming in a secret door was Jake's guess. He had learned that there were some things you do not ask about. And the *how* was one of them.

This was to be their last night at a shelter. This shelter was different. It was on the outskirts of town. They had taken heated mini-storage units and had made apartment-type houses out of them. Many were inhabited by families. There were more children here than were in the city shelters, but still not the number Jake thought there should have been from the ones who came through the shelter these past few months. Where had they put their children? The rooms that remained open were for the travelers. This was fantastic. There was not any advertisement as to where these places were located. They had no maps or road signs, and yet everyone knew exactly where to go and where to meet.

Jake was feeling okay, but he was amazed at how tired he would become during the day. At night he could hardly eat from being so exhausted. Martha would see to it that he would have at least eaten something, but all he really wanted to do was sleep.

The next morning was to bring a new adventure. They left the city and headed out into the countryside. Jake had been camping only once in his lifetime. His first and his last time, and he had planned it to stay that way. He had hated it! Jake had gone camping with his brother Mark and some of his friends. They loaded Jake up with supplies and led him out into the wide-open spaces. Mark loved it. Jake never understood what the big deal about being in the out of doors was all about. Yes, sleeping under the stars was a great-sounding idea, but on the cold hard ground. With rocks, not to mention the bugs. After that experience, Jake had vowed that no matter how good the equipment was, he was not going camping again. Ever! Yet here he was with no equipment, heading out into the wilderness.

Mark? I wonder where he is right now. Ha, if he could see me, he would probably laugh himself silly.

*****

Most of the morning and well into the day, Martha, Frank, and Jake stayed on the road heading out of town. It was late afternoon when Frank led them off the main path and into a clearing. This was definitely a resting place used by many others before. Jake noted that not only was there a fire ring for a campfire but logs had been dragged over making a perfect seating place too.

As much as Jake wanted to end this road trip and to arrive at the farm, he wanted even more to stop and rest. "Martha, how long will we be here?" Jake was not sure if he should sit down and be ready for a long break or if it would be better to lean up against a tree and rest that way. Truthfully he was not sure if he would be able to get up once he got down. He was not wanting to make a big deal about being so weak these days, so he needed to be extra careful not to put himself in positions that would give it away.

Martha was not so easily fooled though. She had been around way too many "men" in her life. First of all, she had three brothers, then a husband, and next to follow was her son Peter. All were very wonderful but proud men. Many a time she had to read between the lines about what it was that was really on their mind, but in this case, she would have to have been blind and dumb not to notice that this trip was really getting to Jake. "Jake, why don't you sit down and make yourself at home. We will be here for a while. The others should be here soon."

"The others? Who all will be coming?" Jake felt a jolt of adrenaline run through his body. Perhaps Peggy was going to be one of the others that would be coming? Although Jake had seen several of the others off and on this whole trip, Peggy, Victor, and Sandy were continually not around. Jake was not sure if it were more about knowing where they had been or more about missing them. But whatever the true reason, it would be good to see them. Jake did not get any real answer from Martha. She simply gave him a smile and a hug. "Go get some rest." Jake walked over to a grassy area off to one side of the fire ring. There was a small patch of grass with a window of sun falling on it. Jake looked up to see how it was that this was the only real patch of sun to be getting through. There was a large tree—oak, he thought, that had a full head of leaves. It was where there had been an obviously fallen limb that was now letting this bit of warmth through. Jake was sure it had all been an accident of chance, but right now, it was creating the perfect dream come true. Jake stretched himself out onto the ground, first looking up and then over to where Martha and Frank were now gathering small pieces of wood in order to start a fire. Jake decided that he would take a short rest and then would chip in and help get things ready for the incoming guests. Whoever it was they would turn out to be. He then turned over onto his side so as to have his back to all of the goings-on, also trying to give the couple some well-deserved privacy. This life was hard on everyone, but it had to be hardest on people who really needed time to be alone together. That was something to think about. But for now, even thinking took too much energy, so Jake fell asleep letting the sun warm him deep into his very soul.

Martha and Frank got the fire going and proceeded to rummage through the pockets in their vests. Between them they came up with a tea bag, some water, and a metal drinking cup. "There you have it, the perfect makings for a cup of tea." Martha began putting this little feast of hers together.

Martha had been and would always be a real lady. She and Frank had been married a lot of years, and even though his wife could dig in and help with the best of them even in the toughest of times, there was always an added quality she brought to their life. Today it was tea. Not too long ago, it was a candle added to a table made out of an old cardboard box. She had called it atmosphere. He had thought it a bit dangerous. To her, it was romantic; to him, it was a fire hazard. But Frank had learned from experience that some things were worth the risk. Like using the last of their water to make tea. Perhaps tomorrow they might wish different, but for right now, this was what they were going to do. "You know, Martha. I never dreamed that we would be spending our retirement years living like this. Any regrets?"

Frank was sitting on the log beside his wife, looking to see if her words would match her expression.

Martha lifted her head up in order to show she was thinking about what he had asked. Thinking it through completely before answering, "You know, Frank, I do have one regret."

Frank's heart sank. *Well, you asked, so get it over with.* "And what is that?"

"Honey," Martha answered.

"Honey?" Frank had always found women hard to keep up with, and at times, Martha was the hardest of all, but what on earth was she talking about now?

"Yes, honey. I wish we had some honey for our tea." She smiled, and as he smiled back, his entire frame relaxed with her answer now out into the open.

"You know, Frank, I didn't plan on our life being like this either, but when you think of it, our life really is not as bad as one might think it to be. We have each other and a good marriage. Other than aging, our health could not be any better. We have a son that anyone would be proud of, even if he is a teenager. We have friends who we not only share our faith with but also our very lives. I think that all in all, we have done pretty well with our life, don't you?"

Frank loved this woman he was married to. He loved her for a lot of reason, but the way she looked at things, he knew that she was his blessing sent to him by God. He reached out and pulled his wife over closer to himself. "You know, woman! If I wasn't already married, I would marry you!" They both laughed and then shared their cup of tea.

The sound of a motorbike pulling out of the camp was what woke Jake with a start. At first, Jake did not remember where he was. As he opened his eyes, all he could see was underbrush and trees. He was cold. It took him a second or two to remember where it was he was at. He had done it again. He was planning on sleeping a short time, but here it was—dark. Judging by how dark it was, he must have been asleep several hours. As he began to stir, he could hear sparks from the fire. Fire, that meant warmth. With that thought in mind, he began to lift himself up off the not-so-soft grass area he had so longed to lie on. Funny how things look so different when you are rested. When Jake was tired, the thought of lying on the ground was a dream come true. Jake laughed at himself as he got to his feet.

"Glad to see you still have your sense of humor. What is so funny?"

It was Peggy. She was leaning up against a nearby tree with a cup in her hand. From the steam coming from it, he knew it was something warm. "Hi there. Where have you been? I thought that perhaps you decided not to come." Jake was walking toward where Peggy was standing when he noticed that not only she but several others had made it to camp.

"No, silly, I did not decide not to come. I came a different way. There were some things that needed to be cleared up before I could leave, and so Victor and Sandy helped me out, and here I am." Peggy handed her cup to Jake, offering him a drink.

"Thanks, what is it?" Jake reached out and thankfully took it from Peggy.

"Hot cocoa," Peggy said with a smile like she had a secret she wanted to share.

"Cocoa? Wherever did you get hot cocoa?" Jake drank some. He was so excited that he burned himself.

Peggy giggled. "It was a gift. We have some dinner too. Come join us. Guess what else we have? Jelly. And homemade biscuits. And—"

"Peggy, slow down. Where did this all come from? How on earth did you get it here?" Jake was looking around. Peggy was right, there was food enough for everyone. And not just any food. This was food he had not seen since he had left to go on his undercover mission. Boy, was that a long time ago and a long way away.

"How long have you all been here?" Jake was looking and trying to note all who had arrived. "When I woke up, I thought I heard a motorbike. Do you know what I am talking about?" Jake hated that he had missed so much while he was sleeping. Some detective.

"I am not sure how long we have been here. Several others have yet to come in, but I am sure that they will be here soon." Peggy was leading the way, talking as she walked back over to where all of the food and the fire were located.

Jake heard some rustling coming from the brush alongside of the clearing. As he looked up, his heart leaped with excitement. It was Victor and Sandy. Jake could not have been more excited if it had been his parents. He was not sure when it was that he had become so attached (emotionally) to them, but it had happened, and he was truly glad to see them, relieved too. "Victor, Sandy, how are you?" Jake forgot all about the food and was anxious to find out about their trip, about all of the food and where it had come from, and better yet, how much farther it was going to be until they got to the farm. Jake would eventually get it out of Peggy, but this would be a lot faster and a lot easier. "Check out all of this food. Where did it come from?"

"Nice to see you too. Food, food, food, is that all you men think of?" Sandy was smiling and gave a pat on Jake's back as she passed him by and joined up with Peggy, who was now heading over to get some of this wonderful-smelling food. The ladies joined up and immediately began talking about all of the things that had been going on.

Victor and Jake on the other hand merely stood back and looked at the ladies as they headed off together. "You know, Jake, as long as I have known women, and I have known some for a very long time, I will never understand them. The whole time we were on the road, all Sandy could talk about was if you were all right. But then the first thing she does when she sees you is to give you a bad time and then get together with Peggy to talk and eat. I just can't figure them out." Victor then turned his attention over to Jake. "How is it going with you anyway? Doc said that this trip might be rough on you. How did you find the travel? Any problems?"

Jake was amazed to hear what the doc had told Victor about his going on the trip. He had not thought of Doc since he had left the shelter. This man who had played such an important part in his life, and he had not even given a second thought about what would be going on with his life. Doc had not forgotten him though. In fact, he had gone to extra trouble to advise Victor about his health. *These people sure are a special breed.* "Wow, Doc, how is he doing anyway?"

"Jake, that is not the point. He is fine. What I asked is, how are you doing?" Victor was concerned. Jake was not one to complain, so when it seemed he was avoiding the question, his first thought was that there actually was something wrong.

"Oh, Victor, I am doing great."

Victor gave him a questioning look.

"Okay, not great. But I am doing fine. Just a little tired, that's all." Jake looked past Victor and then gave a childlike expression.

Victor turned around and saw what Jake was looking at.

"Food!" Both men exclaimed as they headed for the layout.

Someone had brought in fold-up tables. That alone would have been a task all of its own. But this food. There were biscuits and jelly, like Peggy had said. But there was also chicken, potatoes, all kinds of vegetables. Hot cocoa and coffee too. Real coffee! As the men dished up and found a seat over by Peggy and Sandy, several others had found their way into the camp. It was so strange for Jake to see all of this. These people were having a party in the middle of nowhere. Or so it seemed. There was no fear here. They kept putting logs on the fire, getting it as big as they could. The warmth from the fire reached the very outer edges of the camp. The light from the fire must have been visible for miles around. But again, no one cared. It was a fact that the laws in the cities were not enforced in the outside areas. But were they far enough away? Jake guessed that they were, or this would not be happening. Everyone was so lighthearted. Jake could never remember feeling so happy. How he wished his family could be here to share all of this. He wondered if they would approve. Mark? Maybe. But the others? He doubted it. Oh well, that did not matter now. What did matter was that this was wonderful.

Most of the food had been eaten, and several of the ladies were starting to clean up. Everyone had eaten so much that the thought of moving seemed unthinkable.

Jake was surprised to hear what sounded like music coming from somewhere in the dark. At first he thought his ears must be playing tricks on him, but as time moved on, he realized that he truly was hearing a guitar playing and people singing. The songs were getting louder because the group was getting closer. Just before the group made their appearance through the brush, there was a beam of light, and then another, and then people carrying children, blankets, sleeping bags, all entering the camp with greetings.

"Sandy, do you see Peter?" Martha was running over to the edge of the camp trying to wait patiently to see her son. "There he is! Peter! Come here! How are you? I have missed you. Come over into the light so I can see you. I think you have grown two inches."

"Mother, would you please stop?" Peter was glad to see his mom but all of this fussing. Well, it was seriously not welcomed. Not for a teenager and in public anyway. "Mom, is Dad here? Did he come?"

That's right, Peter had not seen his dad since the South Street shelter had been closed. Could Frank ever forgive his son for being so irresponsible? How does a man like Frank handle a situation like this? Well, Peter was about to find out. Jake was anxious to see Frank too. It would be interesting to see how things were to go.

Frank had not been in the camp but was now walking into the main area. He had an empty coffee cup in one hand and a flashlight in the other. Frank had obviously heard all the commotion and knew that something was up at camp.

Frank came in expecting to see people from the farm and was hoping to see his son Peter. He looked around; at first he could not see him. Just as he was about to believe that his son had not come, he saw Martha with her arms smothering someone. Obviously, their son. From the looks of things, Peter needed to be saved from this "mothering" ordeal. He walked over into earshot of his family. "Peter, it is so good to see you, son."

Peter swung around. Father and son met each other's gaze. For a split second, you could see hesitation in the young man's actions, but as soon as Frank extended his arms out into the direction of his son, Peter went directly to his father.

"Dad, I am so sorry. I never thought anything so awful could come of it. I am—"

Frank lifted his hand, causing Peter to stop speaking in midsentence. "Son, what has happened has happened. Learn from it and get past it. It was not intentional, I know, but remember that rules are for a reason. Even if you can't understand the why, know that they are, okay?"

Peter did not care if it were in the public or not, he was so happy to see his dad's reaction he took hold of him and received a fatherly hug. Seeing that his father practiced what he preached, as it were, was a gift Peter would never forget.

Jake either for that matter. Jake hoped that his father would be that forgiving, but in all reality, he was not too sure he ever could. For that matter, how could anyone? But these people who have God, they sure are able to overcome a lot. Jake stood watching for a while daydreaming about what was happening. Trying hard to see how all of this could ever fit into his life.

Introductions went all around. New friends, old friends reunited. Jake had learned that the farm was not too far away. Some people from this same group had earlier provided the food that had been brought to the camp. Questions from everyone about everything. The sound of talking was so intense Jake was amazed that anyone could hear.

As the evening went on, several returned to the farm, but some stayed out in the camp. All of the newcomers were kept at the camp for the night. Jake had been told that arrangements were being made for all of them to enter the farm in the morning. Things had to be settled and arranged. This confused Jake. What on earth needed to be arranged? Well, he would see soon enough, in the morning. Jake was surprised at how tired he was, even with a nap.

Only a few of the people remained awake. Victor, Sandy, Martha, Frank, and several of the people who obviously were in some sort of leadership position. They were working on something, but whatever it was they were doing, Jake was not needed or invited, so off to bed he went.

CHAPTER 14

It seemed that no sooner had Jake laid down his head, it was morning and time to get up. The camp was all in a stir. So much excitement and from so many people. Jake noted that several members of the group had already gathered up their things and headed out to their new destination.

It was a crisp but beautiful day. Jake could hardly wait to see what this farm was all about. After seeing the homes made out of shelters, Jake did not hold much hope of the farm being any place he would appreciate, but to hear these people speak of it, he somehow envisioned a heaven on earth. Jake felt that having the notion of heaven anywhere was an odd thing to find in his mind, but there it was nonetheless. Perhaps in this new place, it would be easier to find out more about their teachings and about the Knowing.

The walk to the farm itself was not far at all, and to Jake's relief, it was mostly on level ground. The main entrance to the farm was not more than a five-foot gate with only a single open lock now hanging from the sliding latch. Jake took a good look around and was amazed at how wonderfully kept and clean this place looked. There were many buildings. Most of them were old, but from the style of a few of the buildings, Jake could tell that some of them had been built not too long ago.

There was one very large barn-type building that stood out the most to Jake. It had large doors. The building had its doors open, and people freely came and went from it. Some of the other buildings were laid out somewhat like a neighborhood. These were obviously living quarters of some type. There were a wide variety of smaller barns and storage units as well as clothing lines and toolsheds. It was hard for Jake to imagine that a place like this existed, and the people—well, there were a lot of them. Many were watching the new arrivals, but then others went about their lives like new arrivals happened all of the time and were not a big deal. There was a lot of work going on too. Some of the people were obviously getting ready to go out and do farming of some type. They had gathered up their tools and were preparing to leave.

One by one the new arrivals to the farm were paired up with the people who were regular residents at the farm. They would be their teacher, guides of sort.

Victor and Jim (one of the previous leaders of the farm) were standing out of earshot of Jake, and the two men were in deep conversation about something. Victor saw Jake out of the corner of his eye and gave Jim a nudge on the arm, getting his attention; he motioned with his head in the direction of Jake. At that moment, both men nodded their heads as if to come to an executive decision. Then they headed over to join Jake. Jim looked around and called out, "Hey, Peter, would you come over here for a moment?" Peter stopped what he was doing and at once joined the other three.

"What's up, guys?" Peter was always quick to be of use in just about anything. His good attitude was almost overwhelming sometimes. Almost too eager. Jake chalked it up to youth.

"Victor and I were thinking that you would be the perfect guide for Jake, what do you think?"

Peter was excited about being able to be a guide for anyone, especially after the mess he had made of things in the past with the telling shelter secrets and all. Peter saw Jake continuing to walk their way. "You bet! That would be great. I will get started now. I mean, if that is okay?"

Both men knew that this offer was a special one to Peter. He probably figured that he would never be trusted again. Victor and the others felt that someone who had learned a lesson as hard as Peter had learned was just about the safest person not to do the same thing again.

"Hey, Jake, what do you think? Can I be the one to show you the ropes?" Peter was reaching out to help gather what few things

Jake had with him. Most of the stuff were in the vest, which he now carried.

"Peter, that would be great. Where do we get started?" Jake was not too sure how he felt about this pairing up. He had hoped for an older guide, one that could teach him more, but perhaps this was for the best. Peter had an ongoing knowledge of the teachings of the Knowing.

Peter headed out with Jake close behind him. Peter stopped and called to Victor, "Where is there room for Jake to bed down?"

This was to be a bigger problem than it sounded. There was only one bed left in the men's single quarters. The closing of the shelters had caused a rush on the farms in the area. Victor's best bet for Jake was to give him his bunk. That would be good because that would put Peter and Jake in the same area for living.

"Put Jake in my bunk, and I will make other arrangements for myself later." Victor had a thought hit him as he was finishing his statement. A very large smile came over his face, and he could not help but to let out a laugh.

Jim, Jake, and Peter all looked at Victor, trying hard to figure out what was so funny. Victor waved them off and went out on what seemed to be a mission of his own.

"Come on, Jake, I will show you where your new home is going to be." Peter led on.

Jake continued to follow Peter. Wondering about Victor's goings-on as Peter showed him the way. A few moments later, Jake came to his senses and tuned into what Peter was telling him. From what he was hearing, it was a fact that while he was thinking about Victor, he had missed some of what was being said to him about the farm. "I am sorry, Peter, but would you repeat that again? I was not listening too well, and I do not want to miss what it is I need to know."

Peter was more than glad to repeat all that he had said and a whole lot more. There were rules for everything. Where to get your clean bedding and where to drop it off when it's dirty. Who, what, where, when, and even a few whys. There was a special time to eat and a rotation for all of the work to be done here at Jake's new home.

This was so different than the shelter. This was more like going to summer camp.

"Hey, Peter. All of the other buildings that are laid out around the area, what are they?" Jake was very comfortable asking questions of Peter. What a wonderful pairing up this had turned out to be.

"Let's get you settled, and I will show you around if you are up to it. Then I can show you how the farm is divided up." Jake could tell that Peter was proud of this home.

Jake and Peter entered a very large building. There were bunk beds all over the place. There were two medium trunks at the end of each bed. Peter was quick to point out that as soon as Victor had moved his stuff out, that one of the trunks would be Jake's. Victor had a lower bed, and now this was to be called Jake's new home. As much as it was not a real home, it was so much better than the shelter had been, with only floor space for yourself. Each building had a shower unit in it and a bathroom setup much like the ones found in a public building in the real world. What a funny thought, that this was not a real world, and yet to all those living here, this was as real as it would get. Someday Jake would return to his real world and to his real life. Jake was not too sure how that thought was making him feel, numb sort of. But this was not the time to think about that, this was the time for gathering information. Jake still had not found his notebook. Funny how this was the first time he had thought about it since he had discovered it was gone from his backpack. Perhaps someone at the hospital had found it and thought it junk and thrown it away. Regardless of where it was now, all future information would have to be stored the "Knowing way." In Jake's head.

Peter had introduced Jake to several of the men in their building. All ages, races, sizes, with the one thing in common for all of them, they all were chipless. Jake was amazed at the introductions. Peter had given their name and shared some information about each of them. Most were called by their first name and then a title of occupation. There was a man from the higher ranks of a major corporation; there were engineers, mechanics, builders, contractors, designers, teachers, lawyers, and Jake had already met a doctor. And many more people in this situation who had knowingly given up any future they could ever hope to have by choosing not to have a chip. Plumbers, electricians, the list went on and on. Jake could hardly believe how naive he had been. He had been thinking from the start that only Doc and a few of the others might be educated but that most of these people would be homeless and without jobs. The occupations of the many helped to explain how very well planned and organized this farm was, the Knowing was. To say that Jake's old world had very much underestimated these people was to say the least.

As Peter took Jake around, it was clearer by every new thing pointed out to him that this was more than a farm, this was a city within the confines of a farm site. Peter took Jake off to one of the far sides of the yard to what looked to be an old cemetery. At first glance there was not really anything too extraordinary about the cemetery grounds, that was until Jake and Peter got closer to the headstones. Jake had noted that the headstones were rather large for such a small area, but it was not until he got a better look that he could see there were solar panels attached to the stones themselves. As Peter and Jake came around one of the stones, there were two young ladies kneeling down working on one of the panels. Both of them jumped up to their feet as soon as they realized that it was Peter. "Oh, hi, Peter, I had heard that you were back. How was it out in the real world?"

Jake could tell from the excitement and the tone in the young lady's voice that she was somewhat envious of Peter getting to go to the city.

"Mary, how many times do I have to tell you that the good life is here, where we are now? The city may sound exciting, but I am here to tell you that if it were not for the grace of God, I do not think I would have made it back this time. It is hard out there." Peter's tone was a little short with Mary, but then she had started this conversation out in the same kind of tone. Both Mary and Peter ended in a silent conversation. No voice, just a lot of body language.

With the absence of the others talking, the second of the young ladies noticed that Jake was confused by the goings-on of the two sparrers.

"Hi, I am Sally. I take it that you are new here? And new to these two going at it? Well, you will get used to it. They have been like this since kindergarten. They are harmless, just annoying at times." Sally had taken hold of Jake's hand and was giving it a friendly shake.

"Hi, I am Jake. Yes, you are right. Uhm, I am new to the farm I mean." Jake was sounding like a schoolboy. "What are you two doing?" Jake could see that the two had been working on some wiring of sort. Jake had not noted anything electric in all of the buildings he had been to, so what would they be doing wiring for?

"Oh this." Sally reached down and pulled up the wires that they had been working on. It was obvious to everyone that the wires had been cut. "You see this? The groundskeepers just don't get it. They go through here without a single thought as to what their equipment does to the setup here."

Mary added in, "Yep, Sally and I spent most of the morning trying to figure what was wrong with the computer lab, only to find out that it was messed up at the power source. Another day wasted, and we have assignments due in only three days."

Jake was taking everything in as fast as he could, and yet there was so much that did not make sense to him. A computer lab, assignments. What lab? What school? Jake was not sure if he should enquire about it or not, when Peter spoke up and mentioned that he had not gotten to that part of the presentation of the farm yet.

"Oh, then let us be the first to show you our prison?" Mary was reconnecting the wires together and hiding them in the grass. The wires then ran what looked to be into the ground. "Oh, not to worry, it will be fine now." Looking at Jake's face, she could see that he was confused. She thought it was about the wiring, but what she did not know was he was confused about the whole farm thing.

Mary and Sally headed off to one of the main buildings. Jake and Peter followed after them. He and Peter had already been to this building; it was one of the eating areas. Sally and Mary got to the building, entered it, and went to the back wall, giving it a small shove. As they did, it popped up toward them, then Mary gave it a slight shove to her right. The wall moved inside itself to give a view of a stairway that went down to what looked to be a root cellar. The girls both giggled as Jake gave out an expression of awe. "Cool, huh?" Mary loved to do this for the newcomers. "We have some guy who used to work at a theme park. He was great at illusion and special effects stuff. He has designed all kinds of fake walls and the like. Even if you were to think that there might be something here, most of the world would never guess what all is here at the farm."

As the day went on, what Mary had said turned out to be an understatement. As they went down the stairs, there was another wall at the back of the storage room; this led into what could only be called a miracle. There was a whole world underground. There was lighting all throughout and some of the finest decorated rooms that Jake had ever seen. There were classrooms, computer labs, even science areas. There was a very nice fully stocked medical area. There was an area for financial activities. Things so far over Jake's head that he did not even begin to try and figure what or how they were even doing it.

But why the underground? It was obvious to Jake that it was for security, but then it was explained to him that with all of the electronics being so deep into the earth, the satellite observation units could not scan and detect them. This was so much more than Jake could have dreamed up. Ever. Even if he had been told ahead of time, he would not have believed it. No wonder the Knowing was so effective. All along they were looking for a low-tech simple type of group, and here it was, a super-high-tech organization.

Jake saw that on one of the computer screens, there was a man monitoring the government station. Thank God that all of Jake's doings was never put into the government system. He would have been found out even before he had started. The ability of this group was unbelievable. Jake realized that he had just thanked God. Hadn't he?

The day continued on with one new discovery after another. Jake could not begin to take it all in as fast as it was coming at him. They had lunch on the run, as it were; they stopped off at a food center only long enough to grab a sandwich and some fruit. The food at the farm was so much better than the food at the shelter, and so much more of it was available.

Jake met so many new people and so many families. With lunch finished, it was time for some downtime for Jake. He needed not only the rest but also some time to allow all of what he had seen to sink in.

As Jake and Peter were off on their farm experience, Victor had decided to take his new idea and to try and make it become a fact. First stop was to find Sandy. Victor knew that there was no room for her at the farm either. His guess was that she would be with the younger girls in one of the dorms. After enquiring at all of the dorms and finding that his thought was true, no room and no Sandy. Where was she? Victor thought for a few moments, and then it came to him. Sandy's favorite tree. He guessed that is where she would be. Her favorite place to get away and think things over. Victor headed out as fast as his legs could carry him. Not running but as close to it as one can get without doing it. No one noticed him too much. That is except for a few of the ladies who knew exactly where Sandy was and now knew who was heading there at this very moment. They had no idea at all about what he was thinking, but from the look on his face, they knew that it must be a biggie. Several of the ladies spoke softly about it and gave out a laugh or two about how it was about time the two of them started realizing how very good they were for each other.

Victor could not get to Sandy fast enough. He had a great idea. A heartfelt idea. Would she be there? Would she be alone? That almost never happened. *Oh, God, let this work out.* Now that he figured out what he wanted out of this life, Victor was calling out to the one he truly knew would be of help. "Oh, God, help me to have the words and help Sandy to have the heart to accept what I need to tell her." Victor rounded the wooded area, and there she was. Sitting as beautiful as he had always thought her. And alone. "Thank God." April in the northwest is a very special time of year. The air is still cool and crisp, but the trees do not seem to notice it; they begin to bud and to bloom in spite of the crazy weather. Cool, warm, rain, dry, sun, and then it starts all over again. But it is oh so magnificent, and Sandy too, who was now sitting there relaxed listening to the breeze blow softly through the leaves of the tree.

Victor did not speak as soon as he got there but instead stood watching Sandy. What an extra wonderful person this woman was. He had known her for many years. They had been friends even before this crazy world had become all mixed up. They had been through so many things together. Good times, bad times, easy and really hard times, but always as friends. Just good friends. But now? What was it that he was wanting to say? What had changed that made this all seem so very clear? And why now? Victor was quick to know that he did not have any answers, but one thing he knew for sure and that this was right. This was the right time and that he wanted—no, that he *needed* for this to work out.

Sandy sensed Victor's being there. She was not sure how she knew when he was close, but somehow she simply did. She looked up, and sure enough, there he was. But the look on his face was so different than she had ever seen before. "Victor, what's wrong?" Sandy was not questioning in alarm, but more in a tone of wanting to be in on some kind of secret that he obviously must be keeping. The look on his face was giving it all away. But what was it.

Victor walked the rest of the way into Sandy's special spot. He knelt down and then sat leaning up against the tree where Sandy was also leaning. They were side by side but not eye to eye. "Hey, Sandy?"

"Okay, Victor, what's up?" Sandy was truly curious.

"Sandy, we have a problem…kind of…well, as I am sure you know by now, that we are out of room at the farm. For singles I mean." Victor was trying hard to figure out how to present his new idea to Sandy, and it was not going exactly as he had hoped.

"Victor, you can stop right there. I am not, and I repeat, I am not building another building with you. So you go and get someone else to work with. The last one we worked on together almost cost us our friendship. Do you remember?" Sandy crossed her arms in order to show how serious she was.

"Sandy, would you hold on for one second?" Victor was trying hard to get his idea back online. "Doggone it, Sandy." She could always keep him a little off-balance.

Sandy was determined not to get talked into another big project with Victor. Not now anyway. She was too tired to even think about it. "Victor, I mean it, not another building project. I need some time. Okay?"

"Sandy, if you will hold on for a moment, I assure you that I have no plan to do another building project with you. What I am trying to say is that there is an empty home in the married section, and well, I thought that—"

Sandy could not believe her ears. "Victor, we could never do that, it is against everything we believe. What would that say to all of the young people about what is right between adults? What would it say about how God feels about the meaning of marriage?"

"Well, I would hope that it would teach them that it is important to save yourself for the special one you marry." Victor did not move to look at Sandy's reaction. He almost knew what it would be without even seeing her face.

Sandy's mind was still racing about the fact that Victor would suggest that they live together when all at once it hit her that he had used the word *married*. "Marry? Victor, are you crazy? We can't get married."

Victor held his form, not moving as not to start a confrontation with Sandy. Victor was sure of the debate that was to come. Sandy had very strong convictions about second marriages. They had a conversation over a year ago about how they felt about that. But that was when Sandy's ex-husband had asked her to leave and Victor's wife had left him. At the time, they both still had great hopes that they would someday be reunited with their spouses. That was way before the other partners had each gone on with their own lives (chipped lives), and each had chosen to make a new life by marrying someone else. Victor believed that their marrying another person had relieved both Sandy and him of any vows or of any chance of reconciliation. But from this reaction, it was clear that Sandy had not thought about it any further than their last conversation. Victor kept his voice steady but firm. "Sandy, why can't we get married?" Victor stood. Still looking out away from the tree and still not eye to eye with Sandy.

"Victor, we have had this conversation before, remember?" Sandy recrossed her arms as she stood fully to her feet.

"Yes, I remember. But that was a long time ago, and a lot has changed since then." Victor stilled.

"Not God's word." Sandy also was keeping her position, but not so good was the keeping of her voice. This was making her nervous. What kind of a crazy person would risk a friendship like theirs for such an idea? "Victor, we talked about this, and we both agreed that we would remain single until...well, you know what we said."

"Until what, Sandy? Until we were reunited with our exes. Well, that is not going to ever happen. Both of them have gone on with different lives now. They are both married to someone else, and well, as I see it, that changes everything."

There was not another word from either one of them for a very long time. Victor knew that Sandy needed to work this out in her head. He only hoped that the love she had for him was enough to get her past her old decision and that it would help free her to see that things were not what they were when they had talked years ago. Victor loved Sandy, and he was sure that she loved him too. He hoped that their love would be adequate to help Sandy see that even God's word would not call them to remain alone under these circumstances. "Sandy, I know what we said, or decided, years ago, but things have changed, and well, Sandy, I love you." Victor reached out and took Sandy's hand. They were both still looking out away from the tree. Side by side. "Sandy, did you hear what I said? I love you, and I want to be with you as your husband and with you as my wife. Sandy, I need you."

"Victor, what about my girls? What would they think?" Sandy was running this thought of marriage through her mind over and over again. She loved Victor, but marriage, well, this was not even an option, or at least it had not been until now.

"You know, Sandy, I think your girls would be glad to know that their mother is happy and that she is not alone." Victor liked and was very much liked by Sandy's girls. He was sure that they would be happy for them to be together.

"Well, when?" Sandy still did not move.

"Sandy, did you say *when*?" Victor's heart leaped in his chest. He never in a million years thought Sandy could be persuaded so easily, but he was sure she had said *when*.

"Yes, I said, when would we do this getting married thing?" Sandy was mixed up some, but just as she knew when Victor was around, and just as she knew that she loved Victor, she also knew that this was the right thing to do. To marry Victor was right. Life had dealt her a hand of freedom. She had never asked God to do anything but to reunite her with her ex, but circumstances had given her the okay to go on.

She had made a choice long ago to follow God at any cost, even the losing of her husband, who she had felt had chosen to go against God. And for a long time while there was still hope, she had followed God's word, but Victor was right—things had changed, and all hope of ever being with her ex-husband was gone. And as much as that made her sad, the thought of marrying Victor made her oh so happy. God knew her heart; she had tried, and she was sure that this was a plan only God could have worked out.

Victor, overwhelmed with excitement, reached around and pulled Sandy toward himself. "What are you doing tomorrow?"

Sandy willingly moved into his strong but gentle arms. "Sounds like I may be getting ready to get married."

Victor had not dared to even let himself dream about how a wedding with Sandy would go. Yet here it was, his chance to have his dream come true. My, how God was blessing him. This was more than he had ever hoped to see in his life. "Well, I think it would be best if David did the ceremony. Don't you agree?" Victor held Sandy back so as to be able to see her face.

"Yes, that would make it perfect. David is due to come back to the farm in about two weeks. That would be fast, but most likely, it would be best for everyone involved, not to have to bring him out on a special trip. So let's say that we will marry when David returns. If you do not think that is too fast, that is?" Sandy was glad to be getting married but was also glad that she was going to have some time to get used to the idea of being a part of a couple again.

It would be a fact that her girls would not be able to make it to the wedding, but they would at least have a chance to know about it before it happened.

"Sandy, that sounds great. I am so excited. I do not think I could ever be happier than I am right now." Victor gave Sandy a kiss like he had longed to do so many times before. And to his way of thinking, this was well worth the wait. "Sandy, let's go and tell everyone. What a surprise it will be to them." Victor shook off his tension and quickly gathered Sandy alongside of him, holding her so close to him that they almost were walking as one person.

"Victor, slow down, would you?" Sandy was trying hard to keep up, but Victor's excitement had given him some extra adrenaline and was giving him extra strength. What a future they were going to have. God only knows why or how two such opposite people could ever come together like this, but the truth was that God did know.

Victor and Sandy were well into the farmyard, and Victor had found the rope that would ring the Gathering bell. Victor began to ring out with as much excitement as he had run into the yard with.

At once, people assembled to see what news was being passed on. Several of the ladies who had been preparing the evening meal joined them, wearing aprons and drying their hands. "This had better be good," one of the ladies was saying. "We have so much to do, I hope that this will not take too long."

Peter and Jake heard the bell ringing too. "What is that, Peter?"

Peter looked over to the yard area to see who all was gathering. "I don't know, but it must be something really big to get this much attention. Let's go and see what's up."

Jake was happy to get to check all this out. "I thought it might have been a problem or something."

As Peter and Jake were walking over to where the crowd was gathering, Peter turned to explain that there was another bell that rang if there was a real emergency. "Believe me, if it were an emergency, you and all of the county would know it, and I mean in a big way."

Jake was not exactly sure of what Peter meant, but learning so much about this place in such a short time had brought him to the decision to merely take in whatever he could learn and would get around to asking further questions later.

Peter and Jake were now a part of the group waiting to hear what was so important to disrupt everyone's day. Everyone quieted down so as to hear what needed to be said.

"Everyone, I wanted to invite all of you to a special get-to-gether." Victor was smiling from ear to ear.

"Okay, so what are you up to, Victor?" someone from the crowd called out.

"Well, like I said, there's going to be a special get-together when David visits us next time. Sandy and I thought that we would take advantage of his visit and have a wedding." Victor stopped talking and stood there like a kid who had just told a joke and no one got the punch line. "Get it? Sandy and I are going to be married."

One of the ladies from the kitchen was the first to speak. "Well, it is about time the two of you figured this out." She was smiling, as were all the rest of the crowd. "So when is David to be here next?"

Victor answered but was set back by this woman's response as well as the reaction of the rest of the crowd. Obviously the surprise was more to Victor and Sandy than it was to everyone else. "Well, David will be here in about two weeks. We will have the exact day soon."

"Do you realize how soon that is?" The woman enquiring reached out and took Sandy by the hand. "Well, we best get started planning this thing if we are going to be ready." Sandy was being led away by a group of women all with questions of their own. What color? Have you thought about a dress? And on and on. Not one person questioned about them getting married. Everyone thought it was a great idea. Victor was glad that the men were more matter-of-fact than the women were. What kind of preparation could possibly be needed? He would have a preacher, David, and a bride-to-be, Sandy. What a great day that was going to be. He was going to have a bride, a wife.

Everyone was happy. Some stopped to congratulate Victor, some shook hands, and yet others went on about their business with smiles and happy thoughts of two of their friends getting to start a new life together.

*****

Several days had passed, and Jake was continually amazed by all of the goings-on at the farm. From the information that Jake had gathered, there were several farms all across the state. They were linked together by computer as well as paper communications. Jake had never in his life seen such an organized group of people. There were a lot of meetings. Jake was astonished at how often and how openly they all talked about their leader. Jake spent most of his time trying to understand what it was that they all had in common, and to date, it was their leader. They all believed in God, but then they all talked about their leader here on earth. He was a man apparently born long ago. Jake was not sure how long he had been dead, but he was sure that no one here, not even the oldest, had ever met him. It was remarkable how everyone knew so much about someone they had never met. Everyone here believed that somehow this man Jesus, after his death, had sent a spirit or something like that back to earth. It was hard for Jake to get all of this together in his head. It did not seem to him that people of such logic and education could believe in such a thing, and yet there it was. Jake could not even begin to explain it to himself and so gave up trying. So from this moment on, he would continue on his mission of gathering more information about the Knowing and its leader. Why, he was not sure, but it was his job to do right now. Later he would decide what to do with the information he found.

Jake had not seen Sandy or Peggy at all today. To tell the truth, it was not until now that he had even thought of them. He was questioning where they might be when he became aware of some kind of commotion going on over in another area of the farmyard. Many others began to take note too. Each stopped and began to head over to where the goings-on were. Jake could not pass this up, so he looked over to where Peter had settled himself down to see if he had noticed. But no luck. Peter had found himself some old friends and was telling them about some of the things he had learned why he was in town. He was being very careful in his telling, not making it sound too exciting but not making it too bad either. Simply the truth.

Peter saw that Jake was watching and signaled with his head, expressing question as to what Jake was wanting. Jake looked at Peter and then looked over to where many had now gathered. Peter, now being aware of the activity, got up, excused himself from the others, and headed over to where Jake was standing. "Hey, Jake, what's up?"

Jake was glad that Peter had joined him and hoped that he was going to be able to explain. "Well, I was trusting that you would be able to tell me what all the fuss is about?"

Peter was quick to want to meet any needs Jake had. "I am not too sure, but let's check it out. Usually that is where they have board meetings. It must be a really big subject to get so many people to go. You know, they usually have trouble getting anyone to go to the meetings. Borrring!"

Jake knew exactly what Peter was talking about. The worst part of his old life was all of the meetings. People talking about doing things that usually never really happened. Or if they did happen, it was usually planned way before the meeting ever transpired. Jake was anxious to see how this group handled planning and such. Jake had been amazed at how great things went at the shelter. Everything seemed to happen and as planned. The whole three months he had been at the shelter, he had heard only a few disagreeing words expressed (usually between Sandy and Victor), but somehow they always quickly came to a decision. Everyone agreeing and doing their assigned part. But this was looking more like the meetings he was used to in his old world. The group was getting larger and louder as well. Peter tapped Jake on the arm and motioned for him to follow him. Jake was confused. Peter was heading off into the other direction. "Come with me, I know of a way that we can get up closer so we can see better."

Jake was surprised at how clever Peter was in this life of his. Being so very young and yet seeming to always be thinking ahead and knowing what seemed to be the right moves to make. Jake followed Peter to one of the rooming houses. They went to the back of the room, and Peter pulled a ladder directly out of the wall. It was fantastic. All of the hidden things scattered around this place. Jake was not sure how he missed most of them. It was that they were for the most part hidden right out in the open. The two climbed up to the top of the ladder that seemed to go nowhere except the ceiling.

Peter, leading the way, pressed on the top wallboard next to the ceiling, and a four-by-four square gave way to another ladder, leading to the roof. They then walked along the top of the building over and around to a ledge that led the way to another building. Peter and Jake passed over several buildings until they got to the one where all of the commotion was going on. Peter came to a stop, and they both sat down on the roof area where they both had a perfect view of the meeting. "Cool, huh?" Peter was more excited about showing Jake something new here on the farm than he was about what was going on with the people. Peter had pride in all of the special effects that had been added to the farm. He delighted in all that God had put into place for him and all of his people in order to keep them safe.

Jake smiled and settled down so as to hear what was being said. It was something really upsetting from the way everyone was looking. Voices were rising louder and louder.

Jake could see that in the center of all this was a family. They were dressed for travel. They had backpacks and suitcases, not the usual vests like Jake had been taught. Several of the people had surrounded the family and were making a wall so as not to let them leave. The oldest man, who Jake guessed to be the husband and the father of this group, was speaking, or trying to. "I told you that I—I mean *we* have made the decision to leave the farm and to stop this craziness. We cannot live like this anymore. We miss our families and our old way of life."

At these words, the crowd went wild. "How could you do such a thing to your children?" Several were asking.

The man reached out to his two young ones and pulled them in closer to him and his wife. "Don't you realize that it is because of my children that we make this choice? What future can we offer them if we stay here? What hope do they have of ever having a quality life?"

Again, voices of the group went up in protest. A few of the people who gathered were quieter and stood taking note of all that was happening. Among them were Victor and Sandy. Martha and Frank were there too, being just as quiet.

Victor stepped forward and held up his hand to motion to the crowd to quiet down so he could speak. "Now everyone settle down.

This is not a government society. If this family feels the need to go, then let them go. It is what we must do." Victor turned to the man and his family who were ready to go and asked them what their exact plans were going to be.

"We plan to go back to the city and to resume our old lives, if we can." The man still holding his family near to him looked to his wife for confirmation. She nodded her head as he spoke.

"And will you be getting the chip?" Victor was making it clear to everyone exactly what the choice was that they were making. "You know that once that is done, you may never return no matter what."

The man nodded in recognition of the agreement.

"And you agree before God, in the name of Jesus, to keep all that has been known by you and your family about the Knowing to yourselves?" Victor looked each parent straight into their eyes as he spoke.

"Victor, we know all the rules, and we agree now as we did when we first came to keep them. It is that we cannot do this any longer. I am sorry, but we have to do what we have to do. I do not expect you to understand since you are stronger than we are. We just can't do this anymore. I am sorry. We will miss you all, but we have to do this." The man reached down and picked up a suitcase. "Now please, let us go."

"Of course, but let us pray first. Okay?" Victor was hoping that this would put off the crowd but not a chance.

"Victor, are you crazy?" One of the men had jumped between Victor and the family and was now taking his turn yelling at Victor. "Do you have any idea what they can do to us if they decide to sell us out? Do you have any idea how many people would be chipped or imprisoned or even worse if they decide that the other side is right?"

Jake recognized this for what this really was. Fear. Real fear.

Frank now came forward and began speaking to this man, but he was actually speaking to the group as a whole. "Are we forgetting that it is not by our might or is it by our power that we are able to keep the Knowing safe?"

As Frank was speaking, Peter leaned over to speak into Jake's ear, "Dad got that from the Bible. Jesus taught us that. Don't you just love it?"

"But by the Spirit. And is it not the Spirit who led us here and has kept us safe all of this time? Is it not faith that makes this whole thing hold together? Then let's remember once more and ask ourselves what the Lord Himself would do in the situation?" Frank made eye contact with as many as he could one at a time.

The crowd settled down. Each notably in thought about the words that were said. Jake was not sure why these words would have such an impact on these people, but the fact of the matter was that they did. Jake talked to Peter to enquire as to what these words really meant. "I don't get it, what does all of that mean?"

Peter was taken aback. This question was not a question of a believer. A small feeling of warning came over Peter as he looked at Jake in order to make sure that he was serious. "The words are God's inspired word. God's word has power. Right?" Peter kept a firm eye on Jake in order to see if there was any recollection of what it was he was speaking about. "Jesus Himself when tempted by the devil used the Word of God to put him off. Right?" Jake was looking at Peter like he was speaking another language. "You aren't getting this, are you?"

Jake looked away from Peter's gaze. He was trying hard to get a hold on this, but there was not a chance he could come up with an answer. Perhaps the answer was to merely tell the truth. "Peter, I am sorry. But I don't understand. I don't know the story you are talking about."

"Jake, how it is that you are a believer and yet you do not know the basics?" Peter was feeling genuinely sad for Jake. He couldn't imagine trying to keep his faith without all of the teachings. The stories of the Old Testament alone gave him strength daily to keep on going. Peter could see in Jake that he was confused and afraid of what Peter was going to do or say with this information.

Peter shot up an arrow prayer asking God to give him the words to help Jake to understand the Word of God. This was a big prayer to be said so fast, but then Peter's God was truly a big God. "Jake, not to worry, I will explain it to you later when this is over. But for now, trust me, and trust God, this is working."

Peter quit talking, and both returned their attention to the goings-on in the yard. Everyone was bowing their head in prayer. Victor and Frank both spoke as they led the group into a united agreement. They prayed for everyone at the farm. They prayed for the family, and then Jake heard them do the most amazing thing—they prayed for all those who had chosen different than this group. They asked for God to be with them and to touch their hearts, to give them a better understanding toward the Knowing. This was nuts. But Jake had experienced it time and time again. These people did things that no other group would think possible. Whatever it was these people had, it was obvious to Jake that it was special.

Not everyone, but many shook hands with the family. A few gave hugs and good wishes to the family as they were leaving. It was obvious to everyone that some were much unhappier about the outcome than some of the others, but all agreed that this was the only thing that they could do. Let the people make their own decisions. No matter how hard it was and no matter how dangerous it could turn out to be for the whole group. This was the only thing that they could do in keeping with their faith.

Jake and Peter sat on of top the roof for a long time watching as the family was led to the gate and let out. It was so different here than it was at the shelter. "Peter, I don't get it. The people at the shelter all stuck together and almost never had a disagreement. And the life there was so much harder. But here at the farm, where things are so very wonderful, they fight and disagree. It all seems backward or something." Jake had not taken his eyes off the crowd that was now dwindling down in size, but was talking to Peter with all his honesty. He really wanted to know—no, he really *needed* to know.

"You know, Jake, I asked my dad about that one time, and he said that he was not exactly sure why, but for some reason, when things get easy, people begin to worry about their rights. When things are tough, all they worry about is each other. He did not say that it was right, just that it almost always seemed to happen that way." Peter got to his feet and motioned for Jake to do the same. "Come on, Jake, I want to show you something." Peter led the way.

It was a good thing too. Peter went a totally different direction this time. Soon they were back at their sleeping quarters. Peter went to his bunk and opened his storage locker. Once there, he pulled out his Bible. Jake knew it was Peter's because it had his name on it. Such a dangerous thing to have for such a young guy. If he had ever been caught with it, they could prove it was his, and to jail he would go. It was just a book to Jake, but from the way Peter was handling it, it was much more to him.

"Jake, have you ever had a chance to study one of these?" Peter was speaking softly so no one happening by would hear what it was they were talking about.

Jake was nervous. How should he handle this? What if his answers gave him away? But on the other hand, what if this was the door to understanding the Knowing? What if this was a way to their human leader? But even more than all of that, Jake really wanted to know for himself. His heart was pounding. He felt strange some-how, kind of like every one of his nerve endings were standing on end ready and waiting. But for what? No more thinking. He simply answered, "Kind of. I mean, well, once." This was the truth. He had one night back at the station, a quick overview of a Bible. From what he remembered, it was not such a big deal.

"Okay, once. And what happened?" Peter was not only hearing Jake's words but was trying hard to read his face also.

Jake shifted his weight and looked first to Peter and then away. "I don't know what you want me to say. I looked it over and found it to be a big book of words, I guess."

Peter's heart reached out to Jake. The sadness he felt for him was almost overwhelming. It was like nothing he had ever felt before. He liked Jake, and to think of him not knowing how it felt to have a life with Jesus, to know that Jake did not know how it felt to have the Spirit of God himself living inside, guiding him. Well, it was almost more than Peter could handle. Tears began to well up inside him. The heaviness Peter felt was indescribable.

"Hey, you two. What are you doing?" It was Peggy. Her voice shot through the two companions like a knife.

Peter was brought back to the reality of the goings-on of the room. "Hey, Peggy, you can't be in here." Peter wrapped his Bible back up and placed it back into its place.

"Well, I called to you two several times, and you were so deep into whatever it was you were talking about that you did not even hear me. So the best thing I could think of was to come on in and find out what is so important. So, what's up?"

Jake was so disappointed. He was so close to understanding that he could almost feel it. Understanding what, he was not exactly sure of, but it was important, and he knew it. From what he had experienced back at the shelter, with God helping him and all, he needed to know more. As excited as he was to see Peggy, he wished her timing had been a little later.

"Jake, what's the matter?" Peggy was feeling out of place now and her feelings were hurt by both of her friends' reaction to her arrival. "I am sorry if I got into something private. I will go and meet you later." Peggy turned in order to make her escape. She was now the one with tears in her eyes. She had missed Jake and wanted to spend time with him. Perhaps his feelings for her were not the same. Perhaps he did not feel about her the same way that she felt about him. She thought he did.

Jake reached out and gently took hold of her arm. "Wait a second. You startled us, that's all. Of course we're happy to see you. By the way, where have you been? I was looking for you earlier."

Peggy's face lit up at the thought of Jake's having been looking for her. "It's a secret. We are planning a wedding shower for Sandy. Great idea, yes?"

Both Jake and Peter looked at each other, smiled, shrugged their shoulders, and at the very same time said, "Great."

"Hey, Peter, do you mind if I steal this guy from you for a while? I have some things I want to run by him." Peggy was smiling all over. She was so happy and so excited. This was a state she was often in, but this time, it was almost contagious.

Peter was overwhelmed with gratefulness to Peggy. This was exactly what he needed. "Peggy, that would be fine. I mean if it is okay with Jake here?" Both Peter and Peggy looked for Jake's agreement with the proposition. And Jake was more than happy to be swept away by Peggy. So off they went.

Peter could hear Peggy talking even after they had left the building. If this shower was going to be a surprise for Sandy, it would take a miracle.

With Peggy and Jake well out of sight, Peter made an immediate attempt to find his dad. He needed someone to talk things over with.

*****

Peter was somewhat put out that it took him so long to find his dad. When he finally found him, he was glad to see that he had found Victor also. These two men were always good to get advice from. "Hello, Dad, Victor. I am so glad that I found you. I have a seriously big problem."

"Just a minute, son. I will be right with you." Victor and Frank were obviously deep in discussion about something important. There was another man with them. They stopped talking, and to Peter's relief, the other man needed to go as soon as their talk was finished.

"Dad, I really need to talk to you." Peter was upset. Anyone could see that, but it was Victor who was the first to sense the urgency in Peter's voice.

"Frank, I think this needs to wait. I think that Peter has more need of you now than I do." Victor turned to Peter. "Would you like me to leave so you can speak with your dad?"

"No, I mean I really need to speak with the both of you. There's a problem. At least, I think there is. Well, yes, I know that there is." Peter was so upset that he was hardly making any sense.

Frank went to his son and escorted him over to a nearby table where there were enough chairs plus one for them to be seated. "Now, son, what seems to be the problem?"

"Dad, it's Jake. He is the problem. Well, I am not sure, but I think that he is not exactly who he says he is. I mean, I do not think that he is what he says he is." Peter knew that he was not making sense even to himself, so he was sure that the other two were not getting it either.

Victor reached out a hand and placed it on Peter's shoulder. "Peter, slow down, take a deep breath." Victor was great in situations like this. He could somehow bring order to the most disorder and help to bring peace to where you would never expect to find any. "And take another deep breath again. This time hold it for a few seconds then let it out." Peter did as he was asked. "Good, now start over, and this time, go slower, okay?"

Peter had done as Victor asked, and yes, he was feeling better. Somehow with all of the running around looking for his dad, he got caught in thought about what had happened earlier that evening. "Well, like I said, it is Jake."

Victor was the first to respond to this statement. "Is Jake ill again?"

"No. Well, yes, kind of, but not how you think. It is more of a spiritual sickness. I mean… Dad, did you know that Jake doesn't know anything about the Bible?" Peter was now eye to eye with his dad. It was thinkable for Peter to have not caught on all of this time, but it was unthinkable for both his dad and Victor to have missed such an important thing. "Dad, I don't think he is a believer. Or at least I am not sure if he is. Can you be a believer and know nothing about your faith? Is that possible?" Peter was awfully upset about this. "Dad, can you imagine going through all that Jake has been through these past few months without the help of the Lord and the Word of God? Why, it must have been awful. I feel so bad for him. And to think all this time he was surrounded by people who could teach him. Dad, Victor, what are we going to do?"

"Well, how do you know that what you are thinking is true?" Frank was a well-organized man. His plan of attack was to always gather the facts.

Peter thought a moment. "He asked me to tell him about it. Well, more or less. He was asking questions that anyone with basic teachings would have known. Then when I questioned him about Bible study, he himself said that he had only seen and read parts of a Bible once. Dad, what are we going to do?"

Frank thought about it, gave Victor a look to see if he had any ideas of his own, and with none offered, he said, "Well, I guess since it was you that Jake went to, then it is you who will need to teach him."

"Me? Dad, are you out of... I mean, I don't think you are remembering clearly. Victor, you can tell him why I am definitely not the one to teach Jake—or anyone for that matter."

Peter's experience at being the direct cause for the closing of the shelter had wounded him more than anyone had realized. In the past, Peter would have been one of the first to volunteer to take on such an undertaking. But this was clearly not the case now.

Quickly Victor could see why it might have been God that had chosen Peter to be the one that Jake would confide in about his lack of faith teaching. A teacher for Jake, and a new and better experience for Peter in the teaching department. "Peter, I am not too sure what it is you want me to say to your dad about your teaching Jake. Personally, I think it is a great idea. Who better than someone he feels drawn to?"

"Victor, what if...what if he is another spy? What if it is like before? What would happen to us now? Oh no, I have shown and told him so much about our operations. What if it is already too late?" Peter was getting himself worked up about all of this. He got to his feet and began to pace around.

Frank once again retrieved the boy and brought him back to his place at the table. "Peter, if only you had the power that you think you do. Son, no one—and I mean no one, not even you—can take this or any other place down unless the Lord himself allows it. The focus you need to have right now is Jake. How can you teach him in such a way that he can be saved? How can you let him know that there is a peace for him that only comes from knowing the Lord?"

The two older men sat looking at Peter. Although they looked passive and calm on the outside, both men were praying their hearts out. Praying that Peter would rise to his calling and take on the challenge both for himself and for Jake.

Peter came to a thought that he decided to share. "You know, I start teaching a children's class tomorrow. I plan to start with Genesis and work my way through the stories of the Bible. Perhaps if Jake came along to help, he could learn without being embarrassed. Even the songs we sing would be good for him." Peter was slowly rising to the challenge.

Victor was curious. "Peter, what song do you think would help Jake most?"

Peter smiled. "'Jesus Loves Me,' what else?"

All three joined in with tender laughter. Each remembering what it was like when they first found out how very much God loved them. Not something many can ever forget.

Peter got up from his chair again, but this time, it was to walk away with a mission and not to pace in fear. He leaned over and took hold of his dad's neck and, giving him a hug, thanked him for listening. He reached out to shake Victor's hand, but Victor stood up and wrapped the boy in a hug of his own.

That night, Peter was loved by God through the arms of two Godly men. Men who were not afraid to show the love of God that dwelled deep inside them. "Good night, son. We will be praying for you and for Jake. Just remember it is your job to teach but the Holy Spirit's job to bring Jake to the real knowledge of faith."

Peter nodded in acknowledgment of what they were saying and headed off to spend some time preparing for what the next days would bring.

Morning came, and Peter had a good night's sleep. He felt that he was ready for whatever the day would bring him. Jake had come in late from his time with Peggy, so Peter had not had time to ask him to help with the class yet.

Peter sat up and looked around to see if Jake was awake yet. Good, he was still in bed. Peter walked over to Jake's bunk and knelt down so as to be within earshot of him. "Jake, Jake, wake up. I need to talk to you about something."

Jake felt like he had just gotten to sleep. Although Jake had fully recovered from his head injury, there were two leftover signs of his not-so-good experience. One, the scar that he now covered with his longer and curlier hair; and two, the not being able to sleep a whole night through. Jake often woke up with dreams of the attack. He knew that the event was over and only a dream, but that did not make getting back to sleep any easier. "Peter, can this wait until later? I got to bed so late last night, and even then, I didn't sleep so well."

Peter was not so easily put off. "Jake, I really need to talk to you. You can sleep later. Come on now and get up."

Jake pulled the covers up over his head, trying hard to make Peter disappear. "Peter, now I mean it, would you please go away."

Peter stayed in his exact same position looking at Jake. A small amount of time went by, and Jake had the oddest feeling that he was not alone. He lowered the covers just enough to get a full view of Peter kneeling down simply staring at him. "You are not going to go away and leave me alone, are you?"

"Nope." Peter gave Jake a small smile and raise of an eyebrow.

"So what you are telling me is if I do not get up, you are going to make my sleeping impossible?"

"Yep!" Same smile.

Jake let out a laugh and took his pillow and threw it at Peter. "Just you wait until you want to sleep or something. You'll pay." He had often had pillow fights in the past with some of his brothers. Usually it was Mark that would seek him out to give him such a bad time about sleeping in so late.

Mark? Jake hadn't thought too much about his family since he had arrived here at the farm. In fact, he had not really given much thought to anything from his past in a very long time. It would only be about two and a half months until his assignment would be over, and he would be returning to his old life. Jake was not sure about how he felt about that idea, but the best news was that it was still a way off. And for now, he was in a great place. The weather was getting warmer, and there was plenty of food and lots of great people. Information still needing to be gathered, but he was in a great spot to enjoy the process.

Peter gave Jake enough time to freshen up in the bathroom and to get dressed before he hit him with his new idea. "Jake, you know what we were talking about last night?" Peter could see Jake pulling back inside with his emotions, but this was not going to change the course he planned (with prayer and confirmation with his dad and Victor).

"Peter, can we not go into this right now?" Jake was getting ready to walk away when Peter simply stepped forward only enough to block Jake's escape. These people were good at this. Jake wondered if they give classes in such moves or if it was a natural bossy thing they all got into.

"Jake, I think this is the best time, and I think you are going to love my idea." Peter was filled with joy. Even with rejection from Jake, the joy of sharing God with him took over. Peter was smiling. He could not stop smiling.

Jake could not help himself. He began to smile, and then laugh. This was just about the strangest reaction Jake had ever had to opposition. Usually, in the past, Jake's first reaction to such bossiness would to have been to take a swing at Peter. But for some very strange reason, Jake got caught up in Peter's excitement and joy of the matter. "Okay, so what is your big idea?"

"Well, I am going to be teaching a children's class today, and I think you need to come and be my helper." Peter laid it out straightaway.

Jake, in a very humble and low-speaking voice, replied, "Peter, you do not get it, do you? I can't help you. I truly do not know all this stuff."

"Exactly." Peter reached out and patted Jake on the shoulder.

"So, let me get this straight, you teach, and I...do what?" Jake was now getting over the joy of all of this, and it was starting to bother him.

"I teach, you help, you listen, and you learn." Peter made it sound so easy.

"Just like that? Just that easy?" Jake knew that he had lost the battle, but perhaps in losing the battle, he had actually come to a place where he could achieve his goal. Learn about the Knowing and their faith.

Peter was not sure if he had won or not. Jake stood their looking like he had lost his voice. "Any questions?" Peter was hoping this would bring it all to a close, and so it did.

"Yes, where and when?" Jake was anxious about perhaps messing things up. What if someone else noticed that he did not have as much knowledge as he had led them to believe? Well, Peter knew, and it did not seem to make much difference to him. In fact, with Peter on his side, it might be possible to speed this learning thing up.

"After breakfast, we can leave from here." Peter set the plan into words.

"Great," Jake said halfheartedly.

"Great," Peter said, making up the difference in enthusiasm.

Over breakfast, Peter told Jake everything he could think of in order to prepare him for the day's class. Peter knew that teaching kids could be one of the bravest things anyone could do. They are quick to ask any question and at any time. And they expected an answer. Peter loved the kids for that. It somehow made him be a better teacher.

The next few weeks passed quickly. Exactly as Peter had planned, Jake was fast learning all he could about the faith of the Knowing.

Jake more than enjoyed the Old Testament stories, especially the ones about the little guy winning over the big one. David, yes, that was the kid's name. Killing a giant with a single stone. Now that kid had guts. Jake enjoyed talking over the teachings with Peggy too. She had many insights that Jake could hardly believe could come from her. She had a special way of looking at the small and almost overlooked parts of the big teachings. Jake was amazed at how well the stories could relate to everyday life. Examples of how they (the Knowing) could use these old stories in order to help them survive the world today. Jake also found Sundays especially good for learning. Each and every Sunday, everyone would gather to have a worship service. Jake could hardly believe the wonderful music. Somehow it helped him to understand the things that he had learned even more. There was no explaining it. It was very good.

*****

Word had gone through the camp that David the preacher would be coming to the farm before long, and so that also meant that the wedding would be soon too.

The wedding was just about the only thing anyone could talk about. Sandy had received word from her girls expressing their happiness about the news. As far as Sandy was concerned, that made everything perfect.

Victor was as happy as could be. Not a doubt in his mind about what was to take place in the very near future.

The countdown continued only weeks now. Things at the farm could not be better.

Everyone had moved on past the disagreement about the family leaving the group. Word had come back that they were doing fine and that they were still glad to have made their choice. They were chipped now, so they could not return for a visit, but they continued to remain in the prayers of many.

CHAPTER 15

Peter was a wonderful teacher. Jake had spent many days as his assistant. Jake had underestimated Peter, most likely because of his young age. Jake could not believe how it was that so many would seek out Peter for information on what they called the teachings of the scriptures. The stories that Jake had heard (by way of Peter's teaching) were so very simple, and yet each time he heard them, there seemed to be yet another level of teaching in them and a new level of learning from them.

Jake had learned a lot about this God of theirs and His Son Jesus. It was not long before Jake himself began to have a great admiration for this Jesus. If He had in fact done all that the Bible was saying He had, He was a much braver man than Jake had ever met.

Everything seemed to be going along great, and Jake was starting to understand how the people could follow such a leader. But then they came to the teachings about the indwelling of the Holy Spirit. This was way more than Jake could bring himself to believe in. Jake had heard a lot about this Holy Spirit but was sure that it was an area he would never want to or be able to understand for that matter. Jake felt that it was urgent to not get too caught up in something he did not feel the need for. So he continued on with his learning in all of the other areas he had uncovered, with Peter's help of course. From all that Jake had learned, the hardest part was not in the learning about the faith, but it was going to be in the applying the learning to his daily life. As the saying goes, easier said than done.

*****

Although the wedding was the major talked-about event to come, Jake started to hear word about a celebration that would be a week before the wedding was to take place. Everyone referred to it as Easter. When Jake was growing up, there were holidays that came around several times a year. Jake was not too sure what they were about, but one thing was for sure, and that it was good for business in his old world. The people at the farm explained to Jake that Christmas, or the birth of Jesus, had been changed to winter feast and that Easter, or the death and resurrection of Jesus, was known by the state as spring feast. At the farm, many were still calling the holiday Easter. Along with Easter was to be another meeting referred to as Good Friday. This was all so confusing to Jake, but it was making more sense to him than the Holy Spirit thing.

Between the wedding plans and getting ready for this Easter celebration, Peggy was almost never available for Jake to be with her. Sandy was around, but like Peggy, she was so busy overseeing so many projects that she might as well have not been there either. But Peter was someone Jake could almost always count on to be there, especially when he had any questions. Jake especially enjoyed it when other people had questions that they felt Peter might understand. They would often go off on a tangent expressing different points of view. Sometimes all at the same time. This was such an exciting thing to see people agree to disagree.

The Sunday before the Good Friday celebration was a big deal at the church meeting. They all called it Psalm Sunday. There was a parade made up of mostly children that came into the meeting with palm branches that they were waving. Such a celebration with songs. "Glory to God in the highest" was one sentence that caught in Jake's mind. This was such an exciting event. The story was that back in the day, this Jesus came riding into town on a donkey and that many came out to greet Him as their new king. They waved palm branches and sang honor to this man. It was hard to think that in only a few days to follow that this same man they were so happy to see would be beaten and killed as a traitor to the world.

Then there was Good Friday. This Good Friday wasn't good to Jake at all. In fact, it was a very somber event. The service itself was quiet and simple. People gathered and prayed, but at the end of the evening, everyone went quietly to bed. This was an opportunity for Jake to consider what this was truly all about. That night seemed to be extra-long and very sad, but for as sad as Good Friday had been, the morning of Easter was an over-the-top celebration. For the very first time, Jake had actually grasped what this holiday was really all about, and it was awesome!

Hearing all the details of the abuse that this Jesus took in order to give believers life was so much harder on Jake than he ever thought it could be. But Easter morning had brought it all to a full under-standing with the excitement that Jesus had risen from the grave. This man Jesus had beat death and that he was alive. The joy was overwhelming. Jake was very glad that he had a chance to experience Easter out here at the farm.

*****

With Easter over, it would only be a week until the long-awaited wedding between Sandy and Victor. Letters were arriving along with a few gifts. The grounds were all getting their last touches done to them. The trees and the plants at the farm seemed to be doing their part. Jake was in awe of how very beautiful the trees were this time of year. A lot of blooms of varying colors. The smell of the flowers were filling the air. Jake sighed to himself as he thought about how much his sister, Sally, would have loved getting to see this wedding. Thinking of her was making Jake feel lonely for his real family. It was strange that this wedding would bring them to the forefront of his memory.

The weather was wonderful. Not a cloud in the sky. It was pre-dicted that for the next few days, the weather would hold out. Perfect for the wedding that would be happening in the middle of the day tomorrow. A few of the people coming from a long way off had already started arriving. It was reported that there was no resistance to their traveling around. There would not be any room for them to sleep in the bunkhouses, but no one seemed to mind. Most had come with packs for sleeping. Several fell in along with the others in bunkhouses and made beds where they fell. Jake was amazed as to how many people knew Sandy and Victor and how many would risk coming to their wedding.

Food supplies came from what seemed to be nowhere. Jake tried to keep watch on how the food was being delivered but could not even begin to guess how it was getting here. As he watched several ladies carrying baskets of ears of corn. It came to Jake that there must be another entrance. But where? Peter was most likely the one who would tell Jake, but he was off on an errand of his own. This would be a task that Jake would delight in doing himself. Jake was excited at the thought of the discovery of another entrance to the farm.

*****

It was early in the morning. The sun was coming up. This would be a perfect day for an outside wedding. Victor and Sandy would finally be together. United in marriage. This idea was running again and again through Mark's mind as he was making his way down the highway on his motorbike. His helmet blocked some of the view of the sunrise, but not enough to keep him from daydreaming about the day to come. Mark had not seen Jacob since the hospital. Although he had been keeping track of his whereabouts, he had not dared to speak to him. Not until now that was. Victor and Frank had expressed how very good Jacob was doing at the farm. They both expressed that he had learned a lot about the way of the Knowing and that he was one of Peter's favorite students.

Mark had been praying for the people he knew to become believers, but Jacob would have been the very last one he thought would have come over to the other side of thinking. "God does work in strange and mysterious ways," Mark was speaking out loud. As much to himself as he was to God. Mark was still not sure what it was that Jacob was doing with the Knowing, but he did know one thing for sure, and that was that God was in control of it all. Mark had so many questions about Jacob's being out on the streets and without a chip. How? Why? Mark had to have his chip removed from the very onset of them being given. He had an allergic reaction to this chip

280

in his body. It was more than a good bet that if it had not been for his family's high placement in the government, then most likely he would have died. But somehow it was removed, and his chip had been placed on a medal medallion that he always wore around his neck. Mark was in awe as to all God had to put into place in order to set up a plan to make a way for him to be able to come and go anywhere without being detected. As Mark was thinking about all of this, he came to an underground tunnel. He pulled his bike over and removed his gloves. Placing them on the gas tank of the bike, he reached into his shirt and pulled his medallion away from his skin. He then reached into his pocket and removed a large folded-up piece of tinfoil. He opened the foil and placed it around the medallion. Poof, the chip's signal was now unable to be detected. He went into the tunnel a chippie and came out a Knowing. What a great way to be able to help the Knowing and to help himself too. He would have had to drop out of his Knowing family altogether if he had not been allergic to the chip. God's long-term plan in total action. Mark had been instrumental in helping the Knowing keep itself alive. They often called him God's secret weapon. But now there was Jacob. How was it that he also had his chip removed? Had he become allergic too? When did he decide to join the Knowing? And who would have been the one to tell Jacob about God? Mark was full of questions. He was excited about what was to come, but he was also embarrassed that he had not been the one to lead Jacob, his own brother, to the Lord. He had been so afraid of how he would have reacted. The chance that Jacob would have told the authorities would have been way too likely for him to risk. Not a risk just for himself but for many others as well. Besides that, he had always felt that God would lead him to know when and whom to share his faith. Jacob had often stood up for Mark when his parents would grill him about his money, or the lack of it. Perhaps Jacob had always known. Perhaps Jacob was as afraid to let Mark in on his faith like he himself had been.

Mark placed the foil-wrapped necklace back into his shirt. He placed his gloves back on and started his motorbike back onto the road. In a short time, he would be able to speak to Jacob himself. He would be able to get all of the answers he needed. This was almost more than he could stand. The excitement and the anxiety was almost overwhelming.

The highway had now come to an end. The choice to the average eye was to go one of two directions. North or south. Mark pulled to the stop sign, looked around, and then took his bike straight off the road. To an onlooker, it would look like he was going to hit a hill covered with brush. But just past the road sign. There was a small trail that preceded straight up onto the hill and then directly into it. Yes, that is right. There about one hundred feet or so was an old abandoned mining shaft that had been boarded up so many years ago that there was no one who even remembered it's having been there. Almost no one. Except for the Knowing that is. The first part of the mine shaft was long and very dark. Many parts of the mine had been braced up, and a motion-sensitive light system had been installed. Attached to that was an alarm system. Mark coasted his bike with the motor off on into the mine opening. Once inside a few feet, he stopped his bike, pulled it over to one side, and placed it so that it would be out of direct sight. With it well stored, Mark continued farther on into the tunnel past the opening. Making his way through the tunnel, he knew that the alarm would have sounded and was anxious to see who it would be to meet him. Perhaps even Jacob.

Mark continued walking, and soon there before him were two of his best friends. Victor, the groom, and Frank. "Hey there, groom, there is no escape now." Mark was making fun with Victor. He knew that this was something Victor had wanted for some time now.

"Mark, how are you? I was hoping that you would get here early." Victor reached out his hand and took hold of Mark's, pulled him into his side, and gave him a huge hug. Next to follow was Frank; he overlooked the handshake and went straight for the hug.

All the men were lighthearted. The thought of the wedding brought so much happiness to so many—and in such a hard time of life.

Mark looked around to see if there might be anyone else with them.

"Are you looking for someone special?" Victor was hoping that he was looking for Sandy, but deep in his heart, he knew that it was Jake, his brother, that he really wanted to see.

"I thought that Jacob might have come to meet me." Mark did not want to put a damper on this wedding day, so he shrugged it off. "I bet he is really busy getting things ready for the wedding and all." Mark was half stating it as a fact and half questioning.

Victor and Frank gave each other a look and decided that inasmuch as Mark had come for the wedding, there were some other things that needed to be taken care of.

Frank was the one elected to bring Mark up to speed as to where his brother was concerned. "Mark, there are a few things we need to fill you in on as far as Jake is concerned."

Mark's heart began to beat in a totally different time. "Jacob is okay, isn't he? I thought his wounds had healed. What's wrong? Where is he?" Mark was ready to break out into a full run in order to find his brother.

Victor reached out and took a hold of Mark's arm in order to slow down his mind. "Mark, Jake is all right. Physically that is. It is that there are some things that we found out about your brother that we think you need to know about." Victor looked around the area in order to make sure that they were still alone.

"What do you mean? What is there about Jacob that I don't already know?" Mark was sure that there could be nothing for him to learn. Jacob was always different from the rest of the family, but that was nothing new. Perhaps they had information as to how and why Jacob had come to join the Knowing. They might even know how it was that Jacob's chip had been, well, removed. Mark had to listen very carefully. Victor and Frank were talking in a very low tone of voice. Each took turns telling Mark bits and pieces of the information as it came up.

"Mark, do you know how it was that Jake came to be at the street shelter?" Although it was Victor who spoke, both men watched Mark carefully to see if there were any emotions that might tell them that Mark was familiar with Jake's goings-on. So far, they could tell Mark was as confused as they all had been. "Well, we have come up with a theory. We believe that Jake is perhaps an undercover officer. We think that he was sent here to gather information about the Knowing and all of its people."

Mark could not believe what he was hearing. He looked over to Frank, only to see that he was nodding his head in agreement with what Victor was saying. "You have got to be kidding. If you really think that, then why on earth did you bring Jacob out to the farm?" Mark was perplexed about a lot of things, but this was making no sense at all. He could certainly get behind the idea of Jacob being there undercover, but what he could not see was why on earth they would continue to give Jacob more information. "If what you are saying is true, then you need to get out of here and warn everyone right away."

"Mark, that was what we thought of at first, but then after getting to know Jake, and after we found out he was one of your brothers, well, we did not have the heart to turn him away. In fact, after praying about it, we decided that perhaps the best plan was to do exactly the opposite and to have Jake join us and truly get to see what and who we are about." Frank was speaking very carefully. He did not want Mark to feel responsible for Jake's being here, but he wanted him to know that some things (like family) were more important than safety. "Jake needs God. And that we know about and can show him what he is looking for. At that point, it will be up to him as to what he does with that information. It is our prayer that he will use it to come to know God better."

"But don't you know the risk you are taking? Jacob's word will be enough to convict all of you. Our family is so high in the government that on his word alone, you could all be chipped and shut down forever." Mark was feeling sick. It was one of his family members that was putting everything he believed in, everything he had been working to save, at risk. "What were you thinking?" Mark ran out of words. His mind was racing, trying to figure out how these two very bright men could have been so careless.

Victor's turn. "By the time we figured out that he was undercover, he had already gathered enough information about us to close us down." Victor reached inside his coat and pulled a notebook from his pocket. "Here, we found this."

Mark reached out and took the notebook from him. He began to flip through several blank pages until he came upon notes that were clearly in Jacob's handwriting. There it was. The information on everything about the Knowing that he had found. Page after page and name after name. "Where did you find this?"

"When Jake was hurt, we looked for some clothing for him in his backpack. While we were looking, we found it and took it from him. He never asked about it. We guess that he must have thought that he lost it." Victor reached out and took the notebook from Mark. He placed it back in his pocket. "At some point, I do not know when, I will return it to him. What we think—no, what we *pray* might happen is that Jake will decide that this assignment is not as important as what he has learned here."

"And if he doesn't?" Mark was in need of a sane answer and right away.

"Then it will be up to God, won't it?" Frank was straight to the point. They had done all that they could. At the least, a soul could be saved (Jake's). At the best, they could have another ally on their side, and at the very worst, they could learn another lesson about trusting God.

"So, who knows?" Mark was coming up to speed on the plan and was ready to get on with it.

"Well, just us three. Peter suspects, but has not really put it all together. My son is the last to doubt a friend. Even after all of his oversights in the past."

"And Sandy?" Mark was sure that they would tell her.

"No, we decided that Sandy would keep her mouth shut about this, but her heart would give her away. Besides, there has been so much going on. The timing was not right." Victor said all that with his words, but his mind was not going along with it. He hated to keep Sandy out of this loop but was sure that this was best, or at least he hoped that Sandy would be able to see it that way later. Starting off their new life together with dishonesty, or more like not full honesty, somehow was never in his plans.

"Okay, so now what?" Mark needed a plan of action.

"Well, now we go to a wedding. Continue on as if this conversation never happened." Frank gave a wink to Victor. "And if all goes well, this man here will be an old married man by nightfall. Meanwhile, you talk to Jake and see if he offers up any information. Perhaps you can find out what it is that he is thinking. We all have trouble in that area. He is very hard to read. You know him better than we do, maybe you can help. But don't give him any information that would or could legally tie you up in this mess. So far, all he knows is that you are our friend and that you came to a shelter, and now are at a wedding. Anything else he learns will come from you. But please be careful, okay? We need you in our efforts. You are too valuable to lose."

Mark hated that kind of talk. All he ever was or ever did never felt like enough. They had given him the knowledge of eternal life. How could he ever do enough for them? Someday he would stand with them, not just behind them. It felt to Mark that he always took the easy way out. He had talked to Victor and Frank about his feelings many times, but they always talked him into staying in the government world so as to be a link for them. They looked at him as a hero, but he felt that not being out in the open was somehow disloyal. For now though, as Victor would say, "it was not his time to stand up, but was his time to continue to support them from behind the scene."

Victor looked down at his watch. "Oh man, Sandy is going to be more than upset if I miss this wedding. I think we had best be going."

The others agreed and headed on down the mineshaft. Coming to what seemed to be the end, a shove here, pull there, and then there was a stairway into what looked like a root cellar. Tapping and pulling on the next wall and all three men were now entering into one of the main lunchrooms.

Jake had been on what he was thinking of as his big adventure. Finding the other entrance into the farm. As chance would have it, he had come into the lunchroom just in time to see Victor, Frank, and, if his eyes were not deceiving him, his brother Mark enter the room from what he remembered as the root cellar or hiding place. As excited as Jake should have been at being such a great detective by finding the entrance and all, he was way more delighted to see his favorite brother.

"Mark, is that really you?" Jake completely forgot his cover as he approached the three men.

"Jake, you know Mark?" Victor asked a point-blank question.

"Yea, well, I mean kind of…" Jake was quickly trying to recover from his obvious blunder.

Mark added into the conversation. "Yes, Victor, don't you remember that I was at the shelter the night that Jake here decided to take a nosedive? I took him to the hospital."

"Oh yes, that is right, I do remember now. Forgive me, I guess you might say I have a few other things on my mind. Like a wedding or something." Victor was trying so hard to not lie, but he knew that he was walking so close to the edge of this situation that he could easily be pulled out of a truly "Knowing" way of living. No matter what else happened in his life, staying true to his faith was utmost. And lying was definitely not the Knowing way.

Frank reminded Victor of the time by motioning to his watch. Both men excused themselves. Frank asked Jake if he would mind keeping Mark company and perhaps show him around while they got on with the wedding business.

Jake was more than happy to be alone with his brother. This was exactly the chance he was going to need to find out what on earth Mark was doing here. "You bet, I would be glad too. You two go on, and we will meet up with you later."

Frank and Victor headed out together. Jake and Mark stood for a few seconds before either spoke.

"So hello, brother, long time no see." Jake did not have a clue as to where to begin with all of this.

"The same could be said of you, Jacob. Last time I saw you, you were laid out on a hospital bed. I must say you look a lot better. Could I say that farm life agrees with you?" Mark and Jake had moved off into a more private area of the yard. This should prove to be a safer place to talk.

Jake thought he had remembered his brother being at the hospital, but until today, he was not sure if it was really him or just his dreaming. So much had happened since his time in the hospital. Not only time had gone by but he had learned a lot about the Knowing. And now here was his brother. Hanging with the chipless. "Mark, might I ask as to what you are doing here?"

"Same as you I guess, going to a wedding," Mark was saying this as much as a question as it was a statement. "You know, I have known Victor and Sandy for a long time. We met in college. It always amazed me how the two of them were so happy regardless of the circumstances. You know, even when they were being thrown out of school because they refused to get a chip, they did not seem fazed. In some ways, I seemed more miffed than they did."

"You mean Victor and Sandy were students at your school?" Jake thought they were perhaps too old to be going to school.

"No, Victor was a teacher, and Sandy, well, she was working on the school newspaper. And as I am sure you can guess, it did not take a lot of effort to find both of them a threat to the system. You know, I still can't figure out how they got out of being chipped." Mark had done it now. The word *chip* had come up, and it now needed to be dealt with. "Speaking of being chipped, Jacob, what happened to your chip?"

Jake was set back by Mark's question. It was one that was just as relevant to himself as it was to Jake. "Well, I was wondering as much about you. Brother?"

"My answer is simple. Back when we all first got chipped, I had a problem with it in my system. Don't you remember how sick I got?" Mark studied Jake's face, and as he noted that Jake was remembering it, so he went on, "Well, thanks to the fact that I was in the right family, they were able to remove it, and, well, the rest is history."

"But, Mark, I have seen you scanned myself, and you have a chip." Jake was confused.

Mark reached inside his shirt and brought forth the chain around his neck.

Jake saw that from the chain was a piece of foil that had been tightly wrapped around something. "What's that?"

Mark pulled back as Jake had been reaching out to take hold of the ever so important item. "Well, Jake, this is the answer to your question. It is my chip. They had it embedded into this medallion I always wear. *Always!*"

"So, why the foil?" Jake was sure he knew, but he needed Mark to say it.

"Well, the foil keeps me from being scanned by the satellite, or any monitor for that matter."

This was going better than Mark had hoped. Now it was his turn to get some answers. "Well, brother, how about you? What are you doing here, and what happened to your chip?"

Jake broke out into a cold sweat. These were Mark's friends. How could he ever tell him that he was here to help take them down? "Well, Mark, you might say that it is a long story."

"I have all the time you need. So let's hear it. This should prove to be a good one." Over the years, Mark had heard Jake talk himself into and out of a lot of situations. He was truly anxious to hear about this one.

Jake began to try and put order to his thoughts. Truthfully, they were so mixed up in his head he was anxious to hear what he was doing as well. "Well, it started a long time ago. Almost six months ago to be exact. Well, you know that special assignment, training program I was to be going on..."

Mark and Jake were both shoved from behind by an incoming person. Neither knew exactly what had happened, but both were being held on to. Both men said in almost totally identical voices, "Peggy, what are you doing, and where did you come from?"

They each rebalanced themselves as Peggy joined in on their conversation completely changing the subject direction. "Hey, I didn't know that you knew each other. Jake, did you know that Mark here is one of our VIPs?"

"No, Peggy, I did not know that." This was going great. Jake was going to be able to get information on Mark's doings from Peggy and without even asking.

Mark was not at all happy with where this conversation was going. And the fact that Jake was here was not the problem either.

Mark only did as God led him. He was so uncomfortable about getting credit for what God was doing through him. "Peggy, that is enough, okay?" Mark was noticeably irritated.

"Oh, Mark, you are so funny. Jake, do not mind him, he is always like that when anyone talks about all the things he does for us." Peggy was going to continue on with her telling, but Mark brought it to an end with a steady look at Peggy. "Okay, okay, I get it. Anyway, Mark, I am so glad that you could come to the wedding. I know that Sandy and Victor will be excited too. Hey, have you seen them yet?"

Peggy was so full of excitement about all of the activity at the farm. Not only the wedding but a lot of the people she felt dear to had already arrived or were on their way. This was going to be a great gathering. "Oh, Jake I almost forgot, Sandy sent me to get you. She said that she needed to talk to you."

Jake was disappointed about not gathering any more information about Mark than he had but was interested in what it was that Sandy would be needing him for. "Where is she?"

"Oh, she is over in the single women's housing. If you head over there, you cannot help but find her. There are so many people getting some of the last things ready for the wedding, she will be there somewhere. And I will take Mark with me, if you don't mind?" Peggy turned and gave Mark one of her "boy, do I have a secret" kind of looks.

Jake wondered what she was up to, but he was still more interested in what it was Sandy wanted. He had not seen much of her these past few weeks. He knew that she was busy with wedding things and all, but he really missed talking with her. "Okay, I will catch up with you two after I see Sandy."

The three of them went off to their preplanned directions. So much was going on and in so many different areas of the farm. Jake was amazed at how many people had come and how easily they had been adopted into the daily life. At first glance, it would be almost impossible to tell that there was an overflow of visitors.

Jake's thoughts came screeching to a halt as he came around the corner into full view of Sandy. What a sight he did see. This was a woman that he had not only learned to rely on but had also become as comfortable with her as he had some of his own family. And yet he had never seen her as the woman he was now looking at. She was beautiful. Her hair was washed, curled, and had been pulled up on one side. A small wreath of flowers had been placed on the crown of her head. They were small, delicate, and all pastel in color. They brought out the color in Sandy's eyes that Jake had never noticed before. Her dress was fitted at the waist, but the rest was draped and flowing almost as delicately as the flowers she was holding in her hand. This was unreal. She was a person. A woman. Just like anyone in his family. He had always looked on her as a survivor. And although she was that, she was also so much more. And now Jake could see that. Jake stood for a long time watching as everyone ran around getting things pulled together.

Sandy looked up and saw that Jake was standing in the doorway with the strangest look on his face. The first thought that came to mind was that perhaps his health was giving out again. "Jake? Jake, are you all right?"

It took a moment, but Jake finally realized that Sandy was speaking to him. "Oh what, yes, Sandy. Peggy said that you wanted to speak to me?" Jake walked over to be closer to Sandy so they could have a better conversation.

"Jake, if you are up to it, I was wondering if you would be one of the greeters at the wedding. With all of the planning, Victor and I both thought that the other had asked you, and it was not until this morning that we figured that you had been left out in the dark on this one. Would you mind?" Sandy felt bad that she had not thought of this earlier. Jake was an important part of their life now, and she would never intend to leave him out of anything. Why, he could almost be a son. That thought gave her a warm feeling in her heart. "You know, Jake, if I could have picked a son, I think that he could have been you, or someone very much like you." Sandy started to tear up. This day was so perfect. It was more than she had ever hoped, dreamed, or even prayed for. And seeing Jake in and having become a part of the Knowing family was the final touch of "great" on the day.

*****

291

"Sandy, you look amazing. I mean you always look good, but you look so different. I mean wow!" Jake was getting flustered. "Sandy, I would love to be a part of the wedding. I mean if that is still possible."

Sandy reached out and gave Jake a small hug. "That's fantastic. Find Victor, would you, and he will fill you in on what you are supposed to do exactly. And you had better get going or we will both miss this wedding." Sandy gave Jake a turn and shooed him out of the door he had come into.

Just as Jake was reaching the doorway, there came a head-on collision. Peggy had come flying around the corner with Mark close behind. All three collided. No one was hurt, but the sight of the accident sent the whole bunch into a roar of laughter.

"Why is it this wedding is starting to remind me of an old-fashioned TV show?" Sandy was grateful for the distraction from all of the important goings-on. "I think that this is going to be a great day for all. If you all live through it." More laughter rang out, and each parted their way. Jake leaving to find Victor. Peggy rushing in to see Sandy. This left Mark on his own, finally.

Mark was glad to have some time by himself. A lot had happened with getting to see Jacob and all. This was so much bigger than he felt he could handle. A quiet time of prayer was in order if he was going to be able to keep himself in control. A part of him wanted to put this all to an end and call Jacob out on what he was up to. Then the other part of him knew that God must have a mighty plan in the making for all of this to be going on. Mark did not want to go anywhere or do anything out of God's perfect will. Prayer would help with that. So Mark quickly slipped off to find himself a place where he could be alone. This task had turned out to be more difficult than he had first thought it would be. Finally he found a place off in the woods where the sun filtered through the trees. There was a log and the perfect place to sit. After some time, Mark having come to the end of his prayers, he lifted his head and opened his eyes only to find that his brother Jacob had sought him out and was now sitting silently beside him simply staring at him. "What on earth? Jacob, you scared me to death. I did not even hear you coming."

"Mark, it looks like you have done that a lot." Jake was floored at the sight of his very own brother praying.

"Doing what a lot?" Mark was not sure what it was Jake was referring to.

"Well, that praying thing that everyone does." Jake was asking as much as he was making a statement. "Does it help you?"

"Does it help me? What do you mean?" Mark was not exactly sure what Jacob was asking about.

"Well, so many people here do it, and they always say that it helps them?" Jake did not look away like he usually did when he asked for help from anyone, but continued to look directly at Mark, trying to get his answer from his body language as much from his words. "I mean that I am not exactly sure what it is that you do or what exactly it is that helps. Do you think you could explain it to me?"

Mark's heart was racing. This was his brother. His very own flesh and blood asking him about talking to God. This could only be the hand of God. Never could this have ever occurred on its own. "Well, Jacob."

"Jake."

Mark looked puzzled at Jacob.

"They call me *Jake* here. I like that better somehow." Jake was not comfortable with his new life and his old name being together.

"Okay, Jake. Yes, I often find talking with God helpful." Mark was intent on keeping eye contact with Jake the same as Jake was with him.

"Talking with God, is that how you describe this praying?" Jake was feeling somewhat dumb for not having figured that part out on his own. "And when you talk to God, how is it He answers you?"

This was going to be a tough answer. Mark was not sure exactly how much teaching Jake had actually had in all of this, so it was hard to know how far to go or even where to start.

While they were growing up, very little was ever spoken of religious goings-on around Jacob. And definitely not in a positive light anyway. Anything regarding God that came up was quickly downplayed in their household. From very early on Jacob had learned from a friend about how people of the Christian faith were crazy and an enemy of the modern world. And there was no changing his mind. Mark on the other hand could remember from his very early years some of the things his grandmother had referred to. She would often speak to Mark of such things as "speaking to the Lord." And about how answers often came from her Bible, or nature, or "even your dad," she had once said with a laugh. Those memories had stuck with Mark for years, and when he had heard about the Knowing, he somehow knew that it was a part of his legacy. Perhaps prayed down the line by his grandmother. That made it easier for Mark to accept some of the things of God. But this would be much different for Jake. He had never spent alone time with his grandmother. By the time Jake was old enough to learn from her, this friend of his had convinced him that she was crazy as well as anyone who called themselves Christion. It was easier for Jake to accept that explanation than it was for him to believe in anything he could not see for himself. "Well, Jake, talking to God is a lot easier than hearing from Him. I suppose that is because of how busy we and our minds are most of the time. Sometimes I get my answers from the Bible, sometimes they come from other people, and sometimes I know it inside somehow. I really can't explain it, but I know, in time and practice, you will understand," Mark spoke to Jake. All the while trying to pray at the same time. Jake looked like he was hearing what he was saying, but Mark could never really be sure if Jake understood anything or not. Jake usually kept this "Of course, I understand" look about him. Even when he was little, Jake looked as if he got the whole story about something, only to blow Mark away with all of the questions he would have for their older brothers as to what was going on. But this time would be different. Mark would say the words, and it would be up to God to deliver them.

The two men sat for a time looking at each other. Jake was trying hard to understand what it was Mark was saying. Of all of the people Jake knew, Mark would have been the last one he would have guessed would join the Knowing, and yet it all made so much sense now to Jake about how Mark had acted in the past years. Never having any money, always losing things (or more likely giving them away), never being at the expected place and at the expected time.

Mark was not irresponsible like he had thought. Mark was leading two lives.

As the two men sat, they heard someone calling out to them. "Mark, Jake there you are." It was Peter. He was all dressed up. Jake quickly noted that Peter did not look any older now than when he first met him. Like Jake, their youthful look was both a good and bad thing.

"Hey, Peter, how goes it?" Mark reached out and pulled Peter around, getting him in a brotherly headlock. In this picture, Mark was an older-brother type.

This was a move Mark had often used on Jake to make sure he had the big brother status that he deserved. Now here was Mark treating Peter in the same manner.

Peter resisted as both Mark and Jake knew he would. "Hey, watch the duds! I am going to a wedding, don't ya know." Peter was using a lighthearted tone, and all of the men burst into laughter at the interaction of the three. "And you know, Jake, if you value your life, you had better get to the wedding. At last I heard you were to be seating the guests, and Peggy was hopping mad that you were not there yet."

"Oh no, I lost track of the time. Mark, I will catch you later, okay? And, Peter, thanks a bunch for the reminder. I don't want to mess this thing up." Jake took off like his pants were on fire.

"You know, Peter, I think that is the fastest I have ever seen Jake go do something for someone else." Mark had noted and was pleased with the changes he had seen in Jake.

There was not an exact one thing but a difference all the same. He was somehow more relaxed. Not so quick to guard himself.

"Mark, do you know Jake very well?" Peter was noting a familiarity between the two.

This was a direct question. Mark did not want to lie to Peter, but this was not the time to share their brotherhood either. "Not as well as I would like to." Mark had not lied; this new Jake he really did want to get to know better. It would be nice to have Jake to share God with. This was a great thing that was happening (he hoped—no, he prayed).

"You know, we really should follow Jake and get to the wedding. I have waited too long for this day to happen." Mark led the way. Peter followed close after.

Everyone, or at least it seemed that everyone, had gathered at the planned wedding site. The wedding was being held outside, and the weather was perfect. Chairs and benches had been set up, there were lots of seats and standing room all around. The decorations were the natural landscape itself. There were blooms of all kinds. The cherry trees swayed ever so gently in a very slight and gentle breeze. The music was simple. A piano and a guitar. Peggy was dressed up in a very nice dress that looked as though it had been made just, and only, for her. She had pulled her hair up in a fashion much like Sandy's. Her voice sang out, and it only enhanced her beauty. Everyone was ready for the long-awaited moment. David had arrived and was beaming from ear to ear with happiness. As he stood up front with Victor and a few other men, things progressed from moment to moment.

Sandy came out from one of the buildings and was arm in arm with Frank. He would be the one to give her away. She only wore flowers and no veil, but that too only seemed fitting. Everything out in the open. This was a special occasion. Not just for Victor and Sandy but for everyone who knew them. This was a bright star of hope in the middle of what seemed continual loss. Things had changed a lot over the last ten years. What had always been a constant was now a forbidden. Who would have imagined that God would or could have become illegal? But today was a new and perfect day. Friends and family brought together in the name of God. Brought together for the beginning of a new life where two will now become one.

The ceremony went as flawless as any had ever gone. The people, the weather, even the music was perfect. After the ceremony was over, there was a huge party. Jake could not help but note how everyone acted as though they had not a care in the world. It would be hard to convince an onlooker that these people (most of them) were criminals. Most of them were wanted by the government for questioning and, if tied together with the accusations, they would be convicted of crimes. Yet here they were talking of the future like they had no care in the world, just living in the moment. How ironic it was that Jake himself, who was as much a part of all of this, was one of the only people in the world who could tie each of these people to their crimes. If they only knew how very dangerous this all was.

Jake's thoughts on all of this had brought a rather uncomfortable look to his face. As Peter and Mark approached Jake, they could not help but notice that something was wrong. Peter was the first to speak. "Jake, what's wrong?"

"Huh? What did you say? Oh nothing. Just thinking." Jake was full of discomfort by what his thoughts had brought to his mind. As he looked around, he was suddenly realizing that his allegiance had changed somehow. He had started off on this adventure to get his fame. He had started out to show the world how good he was at his job. What he had not figured on was finding a new family. Finding a new way of life that set God with him. This was not how it was to be. Mr. Diggings had said that these people had a special way of winning over even the most balanced workers, but how could this be? How could he now feel so very different than when he had first set out on his job?

Mark agreed with Peter's observation. "Jake, what's going on? Has something happened?" Mark was truly concerned. Perhaps Jake had not fully recovered from his accident.

"Would you two stop. I am fine. Just remembering something. Why don't we get on with this party?" Jake headed out to find Peggy. He wanted to have a dance with her. That would help to slow down his mind's excessive thinking. Peggy had been singing, so Jake kind of knew where to find her. As he went toward where the band had been set up, he saw Peggy in plain view.

Peggy was standing there putting together some music sheets when she looked up in Jake's direction. She gave out a loud yell and ran a few feet where she literally landed on the front of a young man about Jake's age. Jake, quickly realizing that Peggy was excited not about seeing him but this new man who Jake immediately did not care to like. Who on earth would bring about this kind of excitement? Peggy was easily excited, but this was way out of balance even for her. Unless this was someone very special. Perhaps a boyfriend or perhaps even more. Peggy went on and on about how good this man looked. Asking one question after another, not giving him any time to answer. Jake himself had been in this man's position. It would be interesting to see how he would handle this bombardment.

As Jake had decided to investigate this reunion for himself, the young man reached out, took Peggy into his arms, and swung her around. Causing her to let out a laugh and bringing an end to her questioning. He then placed her back on the ground, placing one arm over her shoulder and guided her off so that they could talk privately. Jake froze in place. *So this is how these people really are. Nice to you until someone else comes along. Then so long, good guy.* "Boy, am I a sucker. Perhaps Mr. Diggings was right all along," Jake said it out loud but didn't realize it.

Mark leaned in from behind Jake so he could speak directly into his ear. "I do not know what it is you are thinking, but Mr. Diggings has never been right about anything as far as I know."

Jake turned around, bringing himself face-to-face with Mark. Neither moved but stood staring at each other.

"So, how do you know Mr. Diggings?" Jake kept his voice low and steady.

"The same could be asked of you." Mark matched his brother's tone and expression.

"I think that we may have more in common than we know?" Jake was the first to throw in a white flag of sorts. This was most unusual for him. It felt strange to him, but somehow it felt good too.

Mark had noted the change in Jake as well. Jake was usually the one to come up fighting when he had been confronted on anything. And this was obviously a big something. "I guess that we need to talk. What do you say we go and compare notes?"

This was a strange choice of words for Mark to use. Wasn't it notes that had gotten Jake into most of this mess to begin with? But this was a good idea, or so he felt. "Yes, I think that you are right. But where can we go?"

Mark was getting ready to lead the way to a place where they could talk when he saw that Sandy was heading their way. "Jake, this may have to wait. Let's have a good time and get together again later, okay?"

Jake could see that Mark had the same respect for Sandy as he had. Both men wanted this day to be as special as it could be. And they were not going to be the ones to bring it down. Jake decided that his feelings about Peggy's new friend could wait as well. Besides, when he left the farm, it was most likely that they would never be able to blend their two lives together anyway. Perhaps this was for the best. Better that he figured this out now than after he had made some dumb choices based on a nonexisting relationship.

Sandy was having one of the happiest days of her life. The only thing that could have made it better would have been if her girls had been there. She had to remind herself that she had received a letter from them earlier this week. Also reminding herself that they were both excited about her new marriage and were glad to welcome Victor into their family.

Sandy walked over to the two men. "Hey you two. What are you doing just standing there when you could be dancing?" Sandy was amazed at how comfortable Jake was with Mark. She was happy and felt that this might be an answer to a prayer she had been saying regarding Jake. Someone for him to be friends with. Someone closer to his age than Victor or Peter. Not a brother or father figure but a peer of sorts. And Mark might very well be the one. She gave up a quick thanks to God. One of a hundred prayers she had said on this wonderful day.

*****

Mark was truly happy to see Sandy. This woman was one of the great people in his life. She had been what he called one of his spiritual teachers from his very first encounters with the Knowing. "Hey, Sandy, I am so happy for you and Victor. I do not think there has been a better day in years."

Sandy had a special feeling for both of these young men. They were the future generation of the church. They both had studied hard and learned fast. It was refreshing to see two who remain so very close to the truth. There had been so much false teachings going on in the world. And yet these two had stayed on track and not wandered into other ideas. It had been harder for Mark, and Sandy knew it. He was from a different world than most. His choice to follow God was constantly being challenged by the propaganda of the world. Yet in spite of all of the false teachings, Mark had remained true to his faith and for several years now. Jake on the other hand had not really been tested. He had been in what Victor called the safe zone. Surrounded by the Knowing. It was a hard life, yes, but he was not under attack like Mark. Perhaps this relationship could help Jake prepare for when he would be back out in the real world at the shelter.

"Jake, why don't you dance with me?" Sandy was determined to make sure these two were going to have a good time.

Jake was not one to dance. In fact, he never really learned how. Somehow to him it did not seem to be the manly thing to do. "Sandy, I do not think that would be a good idea. I am not really one to dance."

"Don't be silly, of course you are one to dance." Sandy was not going to let him off the hook that easy. What she guessed was that Jake would rather find some quiet place off in the corner by himself. But not today. He needed to include himself in the family. This was the time to become a part of the group.

Mark decided to be Jake's protector. "Oh, Sandy, you don't want to dance with this guy. Why, he will walk on the tops of your feet so bad that you might limp for a year." Mark gave out a laugh and met with Jake's grateful eye. Mark reached out and took Sandy's hand and was leading her to the dance floor. Mark looked back as did Sandy, and they both saw that Jake was about to make an exit. Mark called out. "Jake, you wait right there and take note of how we do this dance thing. Your turn is next."

Jake nodded in acknowledgement of what Mark had said. He was not very happy about this. He had hoped to get off by himself so he could think on all of the things that had happened. Like about Peggy and her new friend. What a fool he had been. Oh well, time will tell. Jake was wondering where Peggy was and if she was with her "friend." It did not take long for Jake's answer to come. The music changed tempo, and everyone stopped dancing and looked to the area the band was playing from. There on the stage was Peggy. She had a microphone and was getting ready to sing a song. And yes, right there beside her was her friend. He was playing a guitar, and it was obvious that he was going to sing too. They looked at each other and smiled as though they had some big secret of their own. Peggy was beautiful. She was dressed like an angel. This did not make it any easier for Jake to watch. She was truly happy with this friend of hers. As they began to sing, Jake knew that this was a good relationship. They somehow complemented each other with their voices. This could be called the perfect couple. They even had mannerisms that were much the same.

Jake heard his name called out, and as he turned to see who it was, he saw Victor and Frank walking his direction. Great. Just what he needed—another group of happy people. Victor could see by the look on Jake's face that something was wrong. He had seen this look before on Jake but not for a long time. Victor reached out to place his hand on Jake's back, only instead of receiving it like he had been, he pulled away and moved so as to resist any contact with anyone. "Jake, what is wrong? Has something happened to upset you?"

Jake realized what he had done. It was as surprising to him as it obviously was to Victor. He really was happy that Victor cared about him. But could he still trust it, him? He thought Peggy and he had something real but to only find out that he had totally misjudged the whole relationship. Perhaps this was the same with all the rest. Perhaps he had been brainwashed somehow, and this was his fortunate wake-up call. Jake needed a quick recovery from the way he had reacted to Victor. "No, no, everything's fine. You just startled me, that's all. What are you doing? Shouldn't you be dancing with Sandy or something?" Jake was desperately trying to get control of this situation and to get the attention off himself.

The music stopped, and Peggy's new friend was calling for Victor and Sandy to come up front. It was time for a toast and whatever else there needed to be said.

Jake had never been so relieved to be interrupted in his whole life.

Victor looked at Jake. He knew that something was wrong and that Jake needed some attention, but Sandy needed him also. "Jake, wait here, I'll be back as soon as I can. Will you wait here?"

Jake looked at Victor. This was his wedding day, and yet he was acting concerned about what was going on with him. Will these people ever stop? Jake nodded to Victor. "I'll see you later. Get over to Sandy." Jake pulled up the best smile he could gather under the circumstances. Victor headed up to the stage with Frank close behind him.

This was Jake's chance to make his great escape. Jake had remembered a place he had found that was out of the way and could be private. It was a loft in one of the eating houses. Yes, that would be a perfect place for him to find some time alone so he could get his head together. Determined to find this spot, he turned and walked away from the party. As he was leaving, he passed Peter. "Hey, Jake, where are you going?" Peter stopped and turned to see that Jake was still walking away from him. "Jake, Jake?" Peter was calling after him. But Jake still kept going. Just as Peter was going to go after him, Peter heard his name being called for him to join the others at the front of the party. They wanted him to give a blessing on the new couple. Not only was this his pleasure but also his privilege. So Peter sent up an arrow prayer on behalf of Jake and joined the rest of his family in the party.

*****

Jake had done it; he had made his great escape and was now up in a loft and all alone. What a strange last six months he had. He was definitely not the same person he had been when he had first set out to destroy the Knowing. This was not the enemy he had thought he was going to encounter. Not even close. Jake's head was spinning, but this time it was not from his head wound. This time he did not know what it was from. Confusion, he guessed. Jake sat there for a long time. He was not sure how long. He could still hear the music in the background, and from time to time, he could even hear the voices and laughter of the people. "God, this is a mess." There, he had said it and out loud. "You know, I do not even know for sure if You really do exist. But if You do. I need Your help. I need to get out of this mess. I need to get out of this mess now." Jake was so upset he could not hold two thoughts together for more than a moment or two. Ideas were traveling through his mind so fast that he was only getting more and more confused. What was he doing here? How was he going to get out of this? Could he get out without hurting his family? Without hurting his friends? Were these people really his friends? Or was this all just a game to win him over? Was he crazy? Had they brainwashed him? Was Peggy in love with the other guy? Did she ever love him? Was he lovable? Question after question, after question, racing in his mind. His heart was pounding faster and faster. "Peter said that You would never put people into a situation they can't handle. If that is true and You have put me here, then I think it is time for You to help me out. This is too much. I cannot do this anymore. I hate lying. I hate being in control. Please get me out of this mess." This was the last thought Jake had before he feel asleep. He had been talking to God when a heavy peace fell on him. He became so sleepy that he could hardly lie down fast enough.

*****

Victor and Sandy were having a wonderful wedding party. They could not ever remember having had such a good time together. Many of their longtime friends were there to celebrate their wedding. There was dance, song, and a lot of food. So many had helped to put this all together, and now all of the work had paid off. Only one thing had not gone as planned. That was Jake. He not only seemed to have a problem but had been missing most of the night. First, Victor was looking for him, then Peggy, now it was Mark asking if anyone had seen Jake. No one seemed to know where Jake had gone or why.

It was not until Peter showed up that he was able to tell Mark that he had seen Jake going toward one of the kitchen units earlier. He had remembered that Jake had once commented that the loft would be a great place to hang out. "Perhaps he might be there. I called out to him, but he seemed to have something on this mind, and he did not hear me. If you do find him, tell him to get himself back to this party. Peggy is getting mighty mad at him. He promised her that he would dance with her. And let's just say the night is getting late."

"Thanks, Peter. I will do that." Mark went off to see if he could find his brother. This kind of thing was not unusual for the old Jake. But the new Jake had somehow seemed so much more connected to the group. But for whatever reason he left, Mark felt that they should talk and perhaps get some answers from each other.

Mark entered the room. No Jake. The Loft. Maybe. Peter had said he thought he might be there. The kitchen was empty. Everyone was at the party. Mark climbed up to the loft. He did not call out but looked around. There he was. Mark could hardly believe his eyes. There was Jake. Sound asleep. This seemed odd to Mark. Jake was usually the last one to sleep when things were going on. He was not one to enter in on the activities but would usually hang out taking in as much information as he could get. Mark thought that was what made him such a good officer. And Jake was a good officer. On his own merit. He worked so hard to earn his own reputation. Perhaps too hard. But on second look, Mark noted something very different about Jake. Somehow, Mark would never be able to explain it, there was a peace about him. He looked so calm, at rest. Mark decided not to wake him. Mark had planned to stay for at least another day. There would be time then to talk. Perhaps that would be better anyway. So much had already happened. Mark backed down the loft ladder and went back to the party.

Mark explained to the others that Jake was sleeping. It seemed odd to them, but many decided that perhaps his head injury was still bothering him. Once they were confident that Jake was okay, the party continued on.

Several of the guests had gone home, but many were going to stay the night and head out in the morning. Victor and Sandy were in their new married housing. This new life was going to be so good. A place of their own. Privacy. This was a benefit all of its own. But to have all of this and a new relationship too. Well, it was almost more than Sandy could grasp with her mind. She and Victor had said all of their thank-yous and goodnights and were now to have time for themselves. This was not just a wedding night but a whole new beginning.

Sandy was tired and so was Victor. It had been a long day. "What a perfect day. I do not think things could have gone better. Did you see how nice Jake cleaned up? He sure is a nice young man. I really do like him. You know what I mean? Odd though."

Victor loved it when Sandy was nervous. She would ramble on and on and seemingly about nothing, but over the years, he had learned that if he listened closely, he would find out a lot of information. "What's odd?"

Sandy was pleased to find out that Victor was actually listening to her. "You know, Victor, if I did not know any better, I would have thought that Jake and Mark somehow knew each other. You know? From some other time or place. Did you see how easily they talked together? Jake has not been that close to anyone here, not even Peter, and he spent the most time with him."

Victor could not believe how intuitive Sandy could be. Should he tell her? No, it would make their wedding night nothing to remember. Perhaps in the morning he would tell her everything. No need to worry her. There was nothing they could do about it anyway. Except pray. Yes, she could be added to the group of prayer warriors. Tomorrow.

CHAPTER 16

Sandy woke up before the sun had even made its appearance. She was warm and safe in the arms of the man she loved. Her husband. She was trying hard to remember when it was that she first realized that she loved him and continued to wonder about when he first loved her. This *love* is such a strange thing and yet so wondrous at the same time. Sandy continued to doze off and on for what seemed to be a long time. She would wake only long enough to see if she had been dreaming or if this indeed was true. She thought of several of the people in her lives and wondered how it was that she was so blessed.

All at once there was a loud knock at the door of their one-room living quarters. Victor sat up with a start as did Sandy. As Victor was throwing on his clothes, the alert sirens began to go off. The sound was deafening. Victor reached the door. Opened it. It was Frank. He did not look good. "What's up?"

"Victor, I hate to do this on your wedding time and all, but we have a rather big problem. There has been a warrant issued at the station for the farm. We have begun to evacuate the children and are now getting the other things put into place."

"How many do you think we have here at the farm?" Victor knew that they were way overloaded as far as the number of people allowed here, but he was not sure about how bad it was.

"Well, we are fortunate there. Many of the wedding travelers left here early this morning, so there are not too many guests left. But as far as all of the families we have taken on here, well, we are in big trouble." Frank needed to get on with business. "I will go and take care of the computer room. If you will see to the electrical hookup and official papers for running the farm here. I think we will come out okay."

"Frank, I'll take care of that, but tell me, did your information tell you what it was they were coming after?"

"The information was not too clear, but I can tell you it had some big brass signatures on the paperwork. The word *retrieval* was on one of the forms. Victor, I think they could be coming to get Jake." This brought both horror and sadness to both of the men.

Sandy did not say a word but, in an instant, knew that she was missing some information that these men had about Jake. This was not the time for her to ask, so she sat still and took in as much information as she could get.

Victor had dressed, and he and Frank were heading out the door. Victor looked up to see Sandy sitting there on the bed with a sheet pulled up around her. She was obviously waiting for them to leave so she too could dress. "Oh, Sandy!"

"Victor, go on, I will be right behind you. I will gather the single ladies and get as many into hiding as I can. We will work on the supplies as well." Sandy could see the look on Victor's face. The one that said, "I love you, but I really have a job to do." "Victor, I said go on. I love you, but you need to go. Now go on."

Victor smiled. This lady was incredible. This was the perfect wife for him. She could read his mind. And man oh man did she love him. "Thanks, honey. I will see you at the roundup."

Victor and Frank resumed their talk as soon as the door closed. "What about Mark? Is he still here?" Victor needed to get a grasp of who and what was on the farm and quick.

"Well, I saw him late last night after you and Sandy went to bed. I think he is sleeping in Jake's bunkhouse, but I am not sure."

"Okay, that should be one of our first priorities. We need to find him and get him out of here." Victor was walking fast, but his mind was going even faster.

"Victor, I think we may have a problem with getting Mark out of here." Frank hated to bring up a problem that might not even come to pass, but he felt this was going to be a big one.

"I know what you are thinking, but we will just have to be the ones to make the final decision. My vote is that he goes." Victor and Frank both knew about how Mark felt. Mark wanted to make a stand and be known as part of the Knowing. They also both knew that Mark was a priceless player in their program and that he needed to be protected even if it was from himself.

"I agree. I will gather several of the men to make sure that it happens. You know he will not be very happy about this. Especially if Jake stays." Frank admired Mark, but the kid needed to wait until God called him into the line of duty and not out of some sort of guilt.

"Yes, I know, but he will just have to understand. Some things are greater than anyone of us. I'll meet you at the tunnel entrance. In say about five minutes? By the way, how long did they think we have?"

"About an hour, maybe two. I will see you at the entrance." Frank went to gather a few men to meet him at the entrance and then went to find Peter and Martha. He wanted to be with his family when the government officers arrived.

*****

Jake also heard the noise and came to a quick stance in the loft. As he looked down onto the main floor, there were literally forty or so people all running around each doing a task that was very much planned. Ladders were being tucked away in hidden slates in the walls. The light fixtures were being covered by wall hangings and lanterns. It was amazing how a very modern room was before his eyes being converted into what looked to be a backward and 1800 kind of look. The false wall was pulled into an open position. The children and a few of the older women were being ushered down the stairs. Jake could only guess as to where they were going. As Jake watched, he came to the conclusion that there must be some big evacuation going on. That could only mean one thing. The government officers were on their way. But why now? He was not ready. He had not decided what he was going to do.

As Jake was thinking this all through, he saw Victor and several others come into the room. People were checking in with Victor and relaying information to him as they themselves got it. Shortly thereafter, Jake saw Peter, Martha, and Frank come in. They quickly scouted out Victor and met up with him. Then along came Mark. Oh no, Jake had forgotten about Mark. He was so worried about himself that he had almost forgotten his own brother. Mark came in with determination, telling Victor that some of the chores had been taken care of. He wanted to know what he could do next. Everyone had a specific job and an exact person to check in with, but from what Jake was overhearing, Mark had never been in the plans for emergencies like this. "Victor, I need to know what it is that I am supposed to do next." Mark stood waiting for Victor to answer.

"Mark, I need you to listen to me carefully. Frank, several others and I are so thankful to you for all you have done for us, but we have decided that it is time for you to go." Victor stood looking at Mark praying that his answer would be a favorable one.

"No, Victor. I am not going to run anymore. This is it. I need to stand up and take my place as a believer. Who knows, having me here might be what we need to make a difference." Mark spoke firm and decisive.

Frank came alongside Victor and Mark. "Mark, I know that you think that what you are saying is right, but, son, you could not be further from the truth. The truth is we need you. But we need you out there. In the real world where you can be our eyes and ears. There will be a day for you to stand, but not today. So do as Victor said and get out of here. We will contact you later when things settle down."

"No." Mark had set his face and his body so that its language was backing up his words.

Jake could hardly believe what he was seeing. Mark was not one to speak up to authority like this, but here he was, the Mark that Jake never knew or had ever seen before.

Victor looked around. He nodded his head and motioned to several of the men in the room. At once, like clockwork, the men surrounded Mark and began to usher him to the hidden entrance (the one Jake had been looking for).

Mark was putting up a protest. "Please, Victor, Frank, don't do this. You do not understand. I need to stay. It is my duty. I am a part of the Knowing, and I need to stand up and take my place. Please don't do this."

Jake had been the victim of this kind of "man moving" before. It had happened to him on one of his first days on the street. It was hard to explain that a grown man could be moved so easily by a crowd, but here it was happening to Mark as easily as it had happened to him. Personally Jake was relieved to see this taking place. Mark should not be here when this all came down. It would be the end of his career at the very least, or his going to jail, or even the end of family relationships as they were. Why, in one moment of his being found here, he could lose everything. Unlike Jake. Why, he might even get a promotion out of this.

Mark continued to protest. Two of the men took ahold of Mark, one on each arm, and pulled him firmly but gently down the stairs to the entrance. They went through the back of the small storage room and then into the hidden tunnel. The wall was pulled to and locked. No one would ever have known that this was once a passage to safety. Mark was gone. He was safe. This all amazed Jake. If he had not seen it with his own eyes, he would have never believed it could be true. There really is an underground, and he knew about it.

Jake felt a sick feeling come over him. He was the one who knew about all of this, and he himself would be the very one to take it all down. Why was this happening? He was not ready. So much for God. Had he not just last night asked God to get him out of this mess? From what he was seeing, he was only getting into deeper trouble. He was going to have to make a choice. But how could he? He needed more time.

Peter happened to look up to the loft. "Hey, Jake, are you caught up there or something? I think you had better get yourself down and get ready for the mess to come."

Victor and Frank, along with many others, turned their view from where the goings-on with Mark had been to up into the loft where Jake was now watching.

"Jake, Peter is right, you will be safer if you join us." Martha was so glad to see Jake. She herself had wondered where he had been. She also had missed him last night.

Jake decided it best to join the rest of the group. He climbed down and found his way through the crowd so he could be with them.

As he walked into the group, it was Martha who received him. She pulled him to her and engulfed him in her arms, giving him one of the most loving hugs he had ever remembered receiving. Victor saw what was happening and was grateful to God that Jake not only accepted the love from Martha but he himself hugged her back. This was good. There had been a heart problem with Jake last night, but obviously God had corrected it. Jake was not as distant as he had been the day before. Granted he was still guarded and looked some-what uncomfortable, but he was notably better.

As Martha was holding onto Jake, he quickly realized what he was doing. This situation reminded him of a story Peter had told the kids of a man named Judas who before giving Jesus up to the author-ities gave him a kiss on the cheek. Would these people ever stop? Was there no trick they would not use in order to win someone over? Jake righted himself and gave a look around to see if Peggy might be there.

"Jake, where were you last night? Peggy spent most of the eve-ning looking for you?" Martha was more than concerned. This was so unlike the Jake she knew.

Jake could not believe his ears. It was almost as if this woman could read his mind. He so wished they would stop that. It made him feel uneasy somehow. "It is hard to explain. I needed to have some time to myself. Where is Peggy anyway?"

"I am sorry, son, but Peggy and her brother have already left. They have been in too many incidents lately. We felt that it was too risky for them to be found here, but Peggy told me to tell you that she was sorry that she missed you. She really wanted you to meet her brother." Martha finished her conversation, and then her attention was needed elsewhere. She reached out and squeezed Jake's hand. "I will talk to you later." And off she went.

"Brother?" Martha had dropped a bomb and then walked away. Didn't she have any idea what had just happened? Obviously not. Jake had never shared what he was thinking with anyone. Perhaps if he had, he would have found out earlier that Peggy was not the tease that he had decided she was. Jake felt so bad. What kind of person was he that he would always seem to think the worse of people? "Peggy was with her brother?"

Peter joined into the private conversation that Jake was having with himself. "You really did miss something great last night. Peggy and her brother sing together about the best of anyone I have ever heard. They seem to go together somehow. I guess it must be a family thing them being able to sing and all."

Jake was feeling dumb enough without Peter continuing to rub it in about how much alike Peggy and her brother were. If Jake had only taken the time to really look, he would have seen it himself. He was so busy jumping to conclusions.

The sirens had been turned off, but they were ringing once again. "What is that?" Jake knew that the first was for the evacuation of the camp, but what was this for?

Victor looked around to see if there was anything else that needed to be done in order to get ready for their uninvited guests. "The officers are only a few moments away. This is the last warning before they will enter the farm. Let's pray."

Everyone in earshot of Victor's voice bowed their heads and began to worship God with every idea you could think of. This was almost more than Jake could stand. One man offered up a prayer for the men who were to come into their farm. That they would feel the love that God had for them. Another asked for protection from the event but then went on to praise God for all that He had always done for them. He asked for faith to be strong and to help them to all remember that God had it all under control.

Was this group totally nuts? There was going to be no one in control around here except the government, and in a few minutes, they would all know what Jake already knew.

*****

Mark now found himself once again on the outside of the goings-on of the Knowing. How could they do this to him? This was to be his time to take his place among them, and he knew it. Didn't they think of what kind of effect he could have had on this whole situation? He could have been able to persuade Jake to remain faithful to the cause. But now Jake would be there all alone making decisions that he might not be strong enough to live with later. Of all people, Mark knew that Jake had a really hard exterior but that underneath all of that was one of the most sensitive men he had ever known. But what could he do to help now? Mark knew that it was useless to try and get back into the farm once the doors were locked down. Making noise could only give the entrance away. The only thing he could think of to do was to get back to the main road and get himself to the farm via the main entrance. Mark was quick to find his bike. He pulled it to its upright position and began to walk to the opening. No one was in sight. Everyone had vanished as if they had never even been there. Mark started his bike and headed for what he had now decided was his true calling. He wanted to be with his friends during their time of need.

First things first. Mark would have to go to the tunnel before he removed the foil from his chip. It was very likely that there was a close watch on the chips in this area. One popping up on the screen would definitely draw unwanted attention. As Mark reached the tunnel, he noticed a few of the Knowing along the side of the road. They were making their way to the main road that would take them into town. Mark pulled up and addressed them. "Hey, nice to see you out and about." Much care was needed to protect anyone he might come into contact with.

"Hey, same could be said of you. What are your thoughts on today's events?" The man he was speaking to knew Mark well but needed to keep his position as one who was chipless speaking to one with a chip.

"My thoughts are that I need to return to pick up a few of the pieces that I was made to leave behind. Has anyone of interest come by?" (He was asking about the authorities.) Mark was motioning to the road ahead of him.

"Why, I can say as a matter of fact that has happened." The man was still not comfortable to speak straight out in case they were being watched. "Is there anything I can do to help you?"

"No, I need to get my chip into place and get myself back to the farm." Mark was only a few feet away from the tunnel. As he began to move his bike in that direction, two of the men in the group walked closer to him so they could have a more private conversation.

"Mark, I think that perhaps it would be best if you just went back to town. Victor and Frank had a good reason for you not to be with them when this thing goes down." There was a man on each side of Mark's bike. They could speak directly to him and not have to worry about being overheard.

"I know that they think they know best, but not this time. I really need to do this." Mark began to engage the motor on his bike when one of the men reached out and took hold of the key and turned it off. He then pulled it from the machine. "What on earth do you think you are doing? Give me that key back."

The man quickly apologized to Mark for overriding his authority and threw the keys into the bushes nearby. His intent was not to abandon Mark but to slow him down. "Mark, you need to realize that God has Victor and Frank in charge for a reason. They know what they are doing. Trust me, I know. I have gone up against their ideas before, only to find out that they almost always have a good sense of what the right thing to do is."

Mark was so angry. Not only at the reaction of his friends but his not being more careful to be better in control of his situations. Only God knew what the right thing to do was. And God knew that Mark wanted to be with his people. Mark began to look for his keys. He was off the road and into the bushes when he heard the siren of a car coming through the tunnel. As the car reached the opening, he noticed right off that there were two familiar men in it. It was his two older brothers along with a few other officers, and they were obviously headed to the farm. Thank God they had not seen him. His chip was still covered. What if he had been in the tunnel when they passed by? Mark felt sure that this was God's work. Saved again. If his brothers were going to be there, things were going to be worse than even Mark had predicted. They were high-ranking officers. For both of them to be on the case, something really major was about to happen. There they were, his keys. Now to get his chip up and going. To the tunnel, foil off the chip, now on his way.

The road to the farm was loaded with parked government cars. There were three transport busses. There were also two TV crews and several newspaper reporters. Man oh man, this was going to be a mess.

Mark was stopped by a guard at the main entrance. His credentials were checked. "Mr. Singleton, go on in. Your older brothers are here too. I bet you are really proud of your younger brother, yes?" The man laughed and for sure was the only one of the two of them who knew what he was talking about.

Mark approached the main yard area. As he came up on the happenings, he saw that all of the people from the farm had been gathered up into the open area. They were all surrounded by the guards and were fully circled. One by one, each were having their paperwork checked. They were being logged in and then placed over to the other side of the yard for holding. Many guards were now going into the buildings. Everyone could hear the sound of breaking glass. From time to time they heard wood shelves being turned over. So far though, they had not found a single thing to report on. From what Mark could see, all they had on anyone was the fact that too many people were living at this facility.

Jake could not believe what he was seeing. The people of the Knowing were not resisting but were being treated as if they were. Everyone was keeping their temper under control, but no leniency was being shown by any of the guards toward the people. They were truly the enemy. Jake was not proud of how the people were being treated, but he was okay with it so far. Besides, they were simply doing their job.

Jake was still standing with Victor and the others when a few officers came over to address them. One of them grabbed Jake by the arm and swung him around.

"Hey, guys, look who we have here." The other guards who were with him took note of Jake as well.

Jake took a little longer to recognize them, but when it finally came to him, he couldn't believe who he was seeing. These were the men who had beat him up a few months ago. From one viewpoint, these were the men who almost killed him, and yet from another view, they gave him the million-dollar wound that got him the offer to go to the farm.

"Hey, you're right. Aren't you the one we helped to 'baptize'? I am so glad that you are up and about and doing so well. Are you ready for a little refresher course?" The officers broke out in laughter.

Sandy stepped in. "Jake, do you know these 'gentlemen'? And I do use the word *gentlemen* loosely."

The men were ready to have some fun. Being on the job and all, they knew that they could not get too rough, but this could be fun. Or so they thought.

As Jake was about to speak, he felt a weighty hand come down on his shoulder. He swung around in order to protect himself when his eyes settled on his two older brothers.

The brothers pulled back and gave out a laugh. "Boy, do you look like something the cat dragged in." Jake's oldest brother, Ben, reached out as he was speaking and brushed at Jake's unruly hair.

Jake shot his eyes around in order to see how his friends were receiving this reunion. "What on earth are you two doing here?" Jake could understand a raid on the farm, but how it was that these two were involved was a mystery of its own.

Marcus, the second brother in the family line, was so happy to see Jake he could hardly contain himself. "Why, little brother, we could not pass up a trip like this. We wanted to retrieve you ourselves. When we heard about all that you were doing. Well, we had to see it firsthand."

"Little brother?" Sandy had heard it herself and turned around, coming eye to eye with Victor. "Did you know about this?" Sandy was to the point and very direct.

"Sandy, we will talk about the details later. Let's just get through this, okay?" Victor was speaking with Sandy, but all of the while, he was keeping his eyes on Jake.

Jake did not have to look around to see Victor's gaze. He could feel it. "Hey, guys, what do you say we get out of here?" Jake needed to put some distance between himself and the Knowing.

"You bet, little brother. Wait until Mom sees you, she is going to have a fit." Marcus was having a great laugh about the appearance of his brother.

"You know, Jacob, I think that it might be a good idea for you to clean up some before Mom or Dad see you. I am sure they could handle the story of you being a chipless wonder, but to think that you could look like one. Well, let's just say, Marcus is right. You might give mom heart failure." All three men gave out a laugh. Humor was the best thing that Jake could come up with in order to get through the next few hours.

All three men began to walk to the main entrance. Jake stole a glance back at where his friends were still standing. The men who had beat him up were looking just as stunned as all of the Knowing. Both sides had thought he was something that he was not.

As Jake and his brothers came to the gate, one of the officers stopped Jake and began to announce that he was chipless and was not to be granted exit from the farm. Both Marcus and Ben produced their identification along with some written documents that explained that Jacob Allen Singleton had been on a special assignment and had been rendered chipless. They explained that his time in the field was up and that he was to be returned to full status as a chipped officer.

After a few moments of review, Jake was allowed to leave the farm. Jake had never felt so mixed up in his whole life. He knew what it was that would be expected of him in the next few months, but he was not sure if he was going to be able to live up to those expectations. Yes, he had plenty of information to share. But could he?

Mark, having found his keys and returning to the farm, saw that his older brothers had already retrieved Jake. They were loading him into the car as Mark pulled up on his bike. "Hey, guys, where are you taking that chipless lad?" Mark was adding lightness to his voice, in order to not draw attention to the concern he was having for Jake.

Mark could see from the look on Jake's face that he was not 100 percent sure of what all was going on or what all had really happened to him.

"We thought we would get him cleaned up before we took him to the office. Any ideas?" The older brothers both lived in government quarters and were hinting that perhaps it would be easier for everyone if Jake could go to Mark's place until he got rechipped. Mark's place was a mixed neighborhood of both chipped and chipless people. It would be a lot of red tape to get him in and out of the areas they lived in.

"Why don't you drop him off at my place? I think I have some of his things there. Then we can all gather at Mom and Dad's for dinner, and we can talk about what we will do next."

Mark was hoping that this was what they were thinking, and to his relief, it was.

"That sounds great. Do you think you could do something about getting him a haircut?" Once again, Ben gave a slap at Jake's curls. "Our little brother here could pass as our sister."

"Very funny." Jake was relieved and irritated at the same time. He was glad not to have to mix with people from the government yet. He needed time. But on the other hand, his being talked about and being decided over was not at all comfortable either. "You know if you don't watch yourselves, I will have to find my way back to the farm." Jake said it as though it were in jest, but a part of him really wished it were an option.

They all laughed. The three got into the car, and Mark rode along behind them on his bike.

CHAPTER 17

Arriving at the apartment, Ben and Marcus let Jacob out of the car and made sure he was paired up with Mark. They gave Mark Jacob's paperwork in case there was any problem and went on their own way. Mark gave Jake a pat on the back and gestured for him to head in the direction of his apartment. Mark got his keys out and opened the door. He and Jake entered the room and closed the door tightly behind them. Mark put his forehead to the closed door for a second or two. "Jake, what on earth were you thinking?"

"Excuse me? What was I thinking?" Jake was not going to be the bad guy in this one. "Need I remind you that *I* was on assignment." Jake stood his ground as Mark stood looking at him. What he saw did not sit right with him. On the outside, he was seeing this arrogant man with determination written on his very being, yet one look into his eyes, and Mark could see a very mixed-up man.

"Jake, how could you ever think to spy on our friends like that?" Mark was sure that Jake had likewise thought of the Knowing as his friends. Friends at the least and as a family in other respects. "Have you thought of what you are going to say or do to get out of this mess?"

"Mark, what do you think I am going to say?" Jake was hoping that perhaps Mark might have a plan that he could steal. Mark said nothing, so it was Jake that continued. "I had a job to do, and I did it. And when the time comes to report on my findings, well then, I will do that too. Who knows, with my point of view, perhaps a better understanding of the Knowing group might be just what is in order." Jake knew that this was most unlikely, but he could hope, couldn't he?

There was a knock at the door. Mark looked through the peep-hole to find that it was their sister, Sally. "It's Sally. Are you ready for one hundred and one questions from one of the government's best?"

Jake knew what it was that Mark was trying to say. Sally was not one to pull the wool over. She would be one of the best tests Jake could come up against when it came to telling exactly what he wanted to and yet not too much. "Sure, let her in."

Mark opened the door, and Sally entered with all of the poise and charm that her family upbringing had taught her. She was genuinely happy to see Jacob but kept perfect protocol. Sally went over to Jake at once and gave him a very soft, almost air-kiss on his cheek. "Jacob, how are you? Never mind that. Have you looked at yourself lately?" Sally was not one to beat around the bush about anything.

"I missed you too." Jake tried to brush the dark curls from his face, but it was of no use. His once tailored hair had not only over-grown but had a mind of its own as well.

"Jacob, you do plan on seeing to your appearance at once, don't you? Well, with all of the publicity this will bring, I would think that you would have the courtesy of not representing the family name looking…well, like a chipless." Sally should have been uncomfortable even being in the same room with Jake looking so much like the other side, but Jake was not getting the feeling to match the words she was saying. Jake thought that this was a strange idea to go through his mind. Too strange, so he dismissed it.

"Publicity?" Jake turned to look at Mark. "Mark, what is she talking about? Why would there be publicity about me?"

"Oh, Jacob, you are out of it, aren't you?" Sally was having great fun in being the one to tell Jake that he had now become a hero at the office. In fact, once word had gotten out that there was an operative who had penetrated deep into the Knowing everyone was calling and demanding to know who this person was. "And what a surprise it was for me to find out that not only did I know him but that he was my very own little brother." Sally was beaming from ear to ear. "You aren't planning on using your stupid middle name this time, are you? I should hope that with your big scoop on this case that you are now ready to rise up and secure the Singleton name." Sally had now moved farther into the apartment. She was not watching Jake anymore but was checking things out around Mark's place.

If she had only known some of the secrets Mark had been keeping from her.

Mark was glad that Sally had moved to investigating him and was not looking at Jake at this very moment. Jake had lost most of the color from his face and was standing staring out into space. Mark reached out and took hold of Jake's right arm, turned him in the direction of the bathroom, and proceeded to escort him on into the small room. After Mark led Jake into the bathroom and had him sit on the side of the tub. Mark reached under the sink, pulled out a cloth, ran some water onto it, and handed it to Jake, who was still staring in disbelief at all of the fuss that was being made over this case. Jake accepted the cloth but just sat there holding it. "Jake," Mark had lowered his voice so Sally would not get the idea that something was wrong. "Jake, listen to me. It is going to be okay. We will think of something. Just get through the next few hours, and then we will have time to figure things out."

Jake raised his eyes and looked at Mark as if he was starting to speak to him. He had not heard a thing Mark had said. Mark was about to repeat himself when Sally rang out with a stern voice, "And don't forget to get a haircut once you have cleaned up." Mark needed to speak with Sally and see if there was a way to clear her out long enough for Jake to have some time to compose himself.

Mark opened the door and exited running face-to-face with Sally. "Hey, Sally, could we ask a really big favor of you?"

"Sure, what do you need?" Sally was anxious to help so they could perhaps have some private time to talk with Jacob before his debriefing.

"Sal, we need some new clothing for Jacob. I thought I had some of his things here, but I seem to have misplaced them. Would you be a dear and find something for him? I would take him myself, but you see, he still has no chip, and it would be way too hard to drag him around with me explaining how it was he was chipless." Mark had a way with his sister, and he knew it. In fact, he was counting on it this time.

"Oh my. Mark, are you telling me that Jake had his chip removed?" Her reaction to the news was much like Jake's was when he had first been approached by Mr. Diggings. Seeing the look on Mark's face, Sally at once agreed to the task. "Jacob looks like he has lost weight since the last time I shopped for him, but I think I will get him the same size. He is bound to fill back out now that he is back in the real world." Sally was off with the mission laid firmly in her mind. "I will be back as soon as I can. Get him cleaned up and leave the rest to me." Sally was almost out the door when she whirled around to speak to Mark. "What will you do about Jacob getting his chip back?" She stopped and thought about their conversation. "I hope you have a good plan." With that, she made a graceful exit.

Mark, shutting the door behind her and checking to see that the door was secured, returned to the bathroom where he had left Jake. As he entered the room, he saw a sight that would forever remain in his mind. There sitting in total despair was his ever so strong brother Jake. He had not moved from where Mark had left him, but it was clear to Mark that Jake had heard Sally's and his conversation. "Jake, what is it?"

"Rechipped? How? When? What if I don't want…," Jake's voice trailed off, and he once again pulled back into his mind all by himself.

This scared Mark. He had never seen Jake like this. Jake was always the tough one. He was always quick to pull up some kind of a plan to make something work out. But not this time. This was different. Somehow Jake was more tender, more thoughtful, maybe even more real.

Jake was in trouble. He had choices to make, and Mark was afraid that this was perhaps more than even Jake could handle. "Jake, listen to me. You need to pull yourself together, and you need to get cleaned up. There is a lot to do today, and we need to be as ready as we can." There was no reaction from Jake. "Jake, do you want to pray?" Whether Jake wanted to or not, Mark needed to.

"Pray? Pray? Are you crazy? That is what got me into this mess in the first place. No, I do not want to pray. I do not want to do anything but take a shower. If that is okay with you?" Jake turned toward the shower and reached to turn on the water.

Mark took the hint. He was sad that Jake reacted the way he had, but he was glad that he had at least reacted. Mark said something to the fact that he needed to get some more towels, and he left the room. Jake began to undress and was anxious to get into the hot, endless water that awaited him. Perhaps after the shower, he would be able to be his old self again.

Jake showered and cleaned himself up. He put on some of Mark's clothing until Sally had returned with his new things. Sally did not stay but dropped off the things and went on her way. She expressed her excitement on all of the goings-on and voiced her being anxious to speak with Jake at dinner. She had a million things to do before their big day tomorrow. She was sure that photos would be taken of the family, and she needed to get her hair done. Before leaving, she pointed out once again that Jacob should remember to do the same.

Jake put on his new clothing. Sally was right—they were big on him, but they were clean and they were new. It felt good to Jake. He was trying to remember the last time he had something new. It came to him that it was the coat he so desperately needed when he was on the street. That time seemed like a hundred years ago. Here it was, today, a new day and a new life. He felt much more ready to get on with it now. Looking in the mirror, he noted that Sally was right, he needed to have his hair cut. "Mark, do you think we could find an appointment to have my hair cut?"

"Now?" With all they needed to talk about, Mark was somewhat surprised by Jake's request.

"Yes, now. I feel better with the shower and the clothing and all, but I think I would feel more like myself if I got my hair cut." Jake felt it odd that a story Peter had told him popped into his mind. Samson. A man who had strength in his hair. God made his hair the channel of strength. Perhaps if Jake got his cut off, he would be clearer on who and what he was. And that he was not one of the Knowing.

"Sure, Jake, if that is what you want to do, then that's what we will do." Mark made a few calls and set up the appointment so they would have it done before they went to dinner with the family.

It had been over six months since Jake had dinner with the family. This would be good. And for once, he would be the center of attention. Whether that was good or bad was yet to be seen.

Mark and Jake left the apartment with plenty of time for them to get the haircut and make it to dinner on time. Mark had two helmets so he and Jake rode on Mark's bike. Once again, Jake was out of the driver's seat. No matter how many times this happened, Jake knew he could never get used to depending on someone else. Mark made several turns and then pulled under an overpass. He took out his necklace with the chip and covered it with foil. Jake observed as Mark was careful to place the foil completely covering the medallion. Mark then placed it back into his shirt, and they pulled out and entered a chipless zone. Jake yelled to Mark, "Where are we going?"

"To get a haircut." Mark kept on going as he had planned.

Jake was not comfortable with this at all. "Mark, I do not think that this is a good idea. Let's turn around, and I will get it on another day."

"Don't be crazy, Jake, this needs to be done. It will only take a little time, and then we will get to dinner with the family." As Mark was speaking, he came to the place, pulled over, and parked his bike. He and Jake both dismounted the bike. Mark took off his helmet, and Jake did the same. "This way." Mark led the way to a door. He opened it and entered with Jake close behind.

Jake, not knowing what to expect, followed and did as Mark did. They entered the room and sat in two chairs by the door. A few minutes later, a man entered and greeted Mark with a smile. "So, your brother needs a haircut?" He reached out his hand and introduced himself to Jake as Bill.

Jake had seen this man before, at one of the shelters, but he did not recall where or even what his name had been. "Thanks for getting me in so fast." Jake could not think of anything else to say.

"Well, let's get to it." Bill took Jake into a back room and seated him in a barber chair. He placed a cape around him and began discussing his style. "Do you want it like you used to wear it?"

This was an odd question to Jake. How was it that he knew how Jake used to wear it? "That will be fine. Thank you." Jake was not in the mood for any more investigations as to how anyone knew anything. He sat in the chair and closed his eyes as the barber began to remove a tremendous amount of hair. Jake was trying hard not to think about anything. Just a time out from all that had gone on during this day, these last six months. He heard the door he and Mark had entered through open and then shut. Jake opened his eyes, only to see that both Bill and Mark were not in the least interested in finding out who it was that had come in.

It was not long before Jake looked into the mirror and saw his old self looking back at him. It was a good feeling. Now he could get back to his real life. Jake thanked Bill for such a good job. He watched as Mark paid him with some cans of food he had placed into his pocket. They said their goodbyes and were heading to the outer room. Jake was glad to be finished and was anxious to get back to his home territory. As he started toward the exit, he noted that there was a man seated in the chairs he and Mark had sat in. The man was looking down, and so he did not recognize him right off. As the man looked up, Jake's heart almost came to a stop. It was Victor. "Victor!"

"Jake." Victor was calm. He was genuinely happy to see Jake. "How are you?"

"I don't think that this is a good idea." Jake reached for the doorknob.

Victor stepped between Jake and the door. "I said, how are you?" Victor really wanted to know if Jake was all right. Victor knew that whatever the outcome and whatever Jake decided that it was going to be harder on Jake than even he realized.

"I am fine. What do you expect me to do? Fall apart because all of you were so nice to me? I was doing my job. That's all. And if any of you had half a brain, you would all come to your senses and realize that the way you are choosing to live your lives is plain crazy. I almost got killed living in your world. Victor, it is for your own good. The good of the whole group that you all come in and be chipped and get on with your lives." Jake was talking really fast. Ideas kept coming faster and faster. Then he stopped silent. He stood there looking at Victor. Expecting what? He did not know but not what would happen next.

"First of all, Jake, I am glad that you are okay. Next, as for your almost getting killed. Well, that was 'your people,' remember? As for us coming in and getting chipped. Well, I guess you could say that is in God's hands. Don't you think? Now, what I have come here for is to give you this." Victor reached into the inner pocket of his coat and pulled out a notebook. Jake's notebook. The one he had lost when he had gone into the hospital. "I believe that this is yours?" Victor extended his hand out, placing the book in Jake's hand. "I thought you might be needing this. Just in case that should be the way you decided things should go."

Jake opened up the book, and sure enough, it was the notebook with all of the recorded information about the Knowing. "Why?"

"Because it's yours. And you will need it if you decide to go through with your assignment."

Jake did not look up. He was confused. He had tears in his eyes, and he did not want anyone to know. He was not sure why he was reacting this way himself. And he for sure did not want to have to try and explain it.

Victor turned his back to Jake and reached out and took hold of the doorknob. He stopped. Not turning around. "Jake, whatever you decide. Whatever happens. God loves you, trusts you, and so do I." With those words, he turned the knob, opened the door, and was gone.

Jake stood motionless. He was numb. These people did not fight fair. They had him. They could have done anything to him, and yet all they did was support him and send him messages of love.

Mark came up behind Jake, reached around him, and opened the door. "Come on, we need to be going." Jake took the command and walked out to the street where the bike was standing. Each put on their helmets, and they headed out to meet with the family for dinner. Mark remembered to take the foil off his medallion at the underpass. Jake was impressed as to how good Mark was at his double life. This was an amazing side of his brother that he had never thought could exist.

*****

Arriving at their parents' house was all too soon for Jake. He and Mark had not spoken a word since they had left the barber shop. As they pulled the bike into the driveway, they both noticed that they would be the last of the family to arrive. Cars from the other siblings were already parked.

"Hey, Mark, how are Sandy and everyone at the farm?" Jake did not stop to talk but spoke as they made their way to the house.

"They are all doing okay. They are all under house arrest. No one in, and no one out." Mark smiled as he said that. This proved that Jake did care about the Knowing.

"Yes, that's right. No one in, and no one out. I saw the evidence of that about 30 minutes ago." Having just seen Victor at the barbershop. "Is Sandy mad?" Jake had stopped now, and he and Mark were standing and talking.

"Oh, you could say that." Mark lowered his head.

"Did you talk to her? Was she too upset?" Jake's voice was low.

"No, I did not speak to her myself, but Victor said that it was a good thing they were married because if they had been just friends, he thinks Sandy would have never spoken to him again." Mark was being lighthearted about this. "But don't worry about her, she is a good woman, and they will make up. Well, sooner or later. Most likely later though. She does have a temper."

"Tell me about it." Their conversation had brought back a lot of really good memories of Jake's life on the street. "I think I will miss knowing her the most." But that was not really a true statement. Jake was going to miss it all. He was going to miss them all.

Jake took a deep breath as he and Mark entered through the side door. The front door had always been reserved for guests.

Jake's mom was the first to see the men come in. She let out a very loving but calm welcome to both her sons. From her reaction, anyone would have thought she and Jake could have had lunch together that afternoon. "Well, Jacob, there you are. Come now and give your mother a kiss."

Jake did as she requested. "Hello, Mom. You are looking good as usual. How have you been?" Jake took his place in the living room exactly as it had always been done. Each sibling had their proper place in the room, and each in turn would discuss the important circumstance of their lives. As tradition would have it, tonight would be Jake's night to be the main topic. Each would have questions of him, but it would be done in an orderly fashion. Jake watched as the night unfolded. No surprises. Everything proper. Everything exactly as it should be. As the time passed, each informed Jake on what had happened while he had been away. And it had now come time for Jake's turn to speak (last because of his placement in the family).

A timer went off in the kitchen as it announced that dinner was ready to be served. As timing would have it, Jake never got to tell about his assignment. To the family's disappointment but to Jake's relief. As the food was placed on the table, Jake could not help but be disgusted as to the amount of food. This was not an unusual amount of food for the family, he was just not used to it anymore. This would have possibly fed most of a shelter with a full meal.

Mark watched Jake closely. He was trying hard to see if he could get any idea of what his little brother was thinking to do about his testifying about the Knowing in the morning. But Jake was closed and unrevealing.

Ben was the first to break the calm. "Jake, we heard that they found guns and drugs at the farm. Is that going to be in your report tomorrow? How big of a bust would you say it is going to be?"

Jake did not move. He did not blink. In fact, it did not look as if he was even breathing; he had stopped in midmotion.

Jake's mom was the first to answer. "I think that is enough of that kind of talk at the table. Tomorrow will be soon enough for all of the gory details of Jacobs's work. Tomorrow, Jacob will make his report. Just think, Jacob, you have finally reached your goal. I know that you will make your family proud." His mom was smiling, so very proud of her youngest son.

Jake's dream come true. But somehow this was not what he thought it was going to feel like.

"Let's make a toast." Jake's dad loved to make toasts on special occasions. "To the Singleton family. What a difference this family makes in our world."

"Here, here." Everyone raised their glass and expressed their agreement with what had been said.

Marcus, who had been anxious to hear details firsthand from Jake, raised his glass and agreed but raised his eyebrows and spoke to Jake in a whisper, "We will talk later, okay?"

All heard what Marcus had said but pretended as though Mom's final word was law.

The rest of the dinner went without a hitch. Everyone finished and left to recline in the living room.

"How about it, Jacob, now that dinner is through, how much armor and drugs did you see? And is it true that they really brain-wash people?" Ben was firing questions without giving any time for answers.

"As a matter of fact, Ben, the whole time I was with the Knowing, I did not see any guns or drugs. By the way, where do you hear what it is you hear about the Knowing?" Jake had an edge to his voice that made everyone stop and take note of his speaking.

Marcus loved to tease Jake. "Hey, Jacob, you had better be care-ful, you might make us all think that you have been brainwashed or something. It almost sounded like you were standing up for those, those Knowing. You weren't, were you?"

Straightforward. There it was—the question of the year, of a lifetime. Standing up for family and their way of life or standing up for the Knowing, God and their way of life. Which was it to be? Jake was not sure himself. He had thought he was being neutral, but his family had heard what his heart was trying to say. He did not think the Knowing were bad. But he did not think his family was bad either. What was he going to do? What could he do?

Mark to the rescue. "Hey, guys, leave Jake here alone. It has been a long day, and tomorrow will be even longer. I think it is time for us to go."

"Go?" Jake looked at Mark, wondering where it was Mark was planning for him to be.

Mark picked up on Jake's question. "Yes, I thought that you could spend the night with me tonight. That way we can get an early start in the morning."

"That reminds me." Sally had been quiet all night. "I almost forgot to tell you that I have several messages for Jacob. First off, you have an appointment first thing in the morning with the Chipping Office. They are ready to rechip you as soon as you can get there. Next, there was a Mr. Diggings. He feels that you two need to talk before the hearing. Oh, and did I say that the hearing is at 10:00 a.m. in the main courthouse."

"Courthouse?" Jake was lost as to why he would be going to court before he had made any of his reports.

"Well, yes, court. You will meet with the judge and give a report on the people who need to be arrested. They will issue warrants based on your testimony. Later, there will be trials, and then you will give your evidence against them, you do have the evidence, right?" Sally was really getting into this. "And just think, it is going to be broadcast on every station."

Mark wanted to say that was not a shock, because the government owned and operated all of the stations anyway, but he felt that pointing that out at this time would only add to the pressure Jake was already under.

"Why has this become such a big issue? When I went on the assignment, it was a 'no big deal' assignment. Since when did it become the story of the year?" Jake felt that he was entitled to a few answers before his whole life was broadcast to the world.

"Well, I guess if you had to have an exact reason, it would most likely be because of the elections coming up." Ben was the one to answer, but then the whole room agreed. "Mr. Diggings is wanting to nominate Dad here for a higher position in the government. And well, it looks like you are the son who will help put him there."

Jake turned to his dad. "Is that right, Dad? Are you planning on running for a higher position in office?"

"Well, son, that is one of the options that could come my way. Time will tell."

"And just think it is our little brother here that is going to help bring this family into its distinguished position in office." Marcus sounded so proud of Jake. They all did.

"Now, boys, remember, pride go before the fall." Jake's mom was proud, but it was not proper to boast about such things. At least until they were a done deal.

Jake listened to the conversation run on.

"You know, I think Mark is right. Jake, you look so tired. Perhaps you two should call it a night." Jake's mom reached out and took his hand and gave it a very appropriate squeeze.

Sally jumped in with supporting advice. "Yes, Jacob, and don't forget to get your chip first thing tomorrow. It is just too difficult taking you around town without one." Sally watched Jake closely as she was speaking to him.

"Yes, we will see to it." Mark had Jake rounded up, and they were on their way within a few minutes. This was a good escape. And his mother's idea to boot. *Way to go, Mom.*

Jake and Mark did not have far to go. In no time at all, they were back at Mark's apartment and once again found themselves all alone. Jake was beat. He was not sure if it had been the day or if the last six months had finally caught up to him.

"How long have you known that Dad was going to run for office?" Jake was wondering if Mark had been a part of the master plan as it now seemed so many others had been, even Mr. Diggings. Where had that man come from, and why was he now such a part of their life?

"Well, to tell you the truth, tonight was the first time I heard for sure that it was in the works. But you know we have heard about the Singletons coming into their warranted position almost all of our lives."

Jake knew that Mark was right. "I was just checking."

"Just checking what?" Mark was trying hard to understand where Jake was going with all of this.

"I was wondering about which side you are on." Jake was so tired. He wanted to talk this out, but he really needed to rest. "You know, Mark, can we finish this in the morning? I am beat, and I really want to lie down and sleep."

"Of course. We will talk again in the morning. By the way, Jake, do you have any idea about what you are going to say in court in the morning?" Mark watched carefully to see if he could discern from Jake's reaction as to which way he was leaning.

"In the morning, okay?"

"Yes, in the morning. Go on, you take the bed. You deserve that much. Good night." Mark turned to walk away.

"Hey, Mark?" Jake did not stop walking toward the bedroom but talked as he went.

"What?"

"Thanks."

"What's a brother for? You are welcome." Mark was glad that Jake was with him. He knew that the next few days were going to be hard on them all. Boy, was he glad that Victor and Frank would not let him stay at the farm. What would have happened to Jake if Mark had been arrested? What an awful thought. Thank God for the wisdom of Frank and Victor and the courage they had to stand firm on their convictions.

CHAPTER 18

Morning came slow and yet fast. It took Jake forever to fall asleep, but then once he had, it felt like he had never gone to bed at all. Jake heard the front door close and got up to see what or who it was coming or going. It was Mark, he was returning home. But from where?

"Where have you been, Mark?" Jake was rubbing his eyes, trying hard to see if perhaps he really had enough sleep and was only having trouble waking up, but to his anguish, he really was still tired. *Oh, would this ever be over.*

Mark held up a bag of donuts. "I thought you might want something different for a change? I got your favorite."

"What do we do first?" Jake was trying to make a clear plan of his day. What he would give for no surprises today.

"Well, I thought it might be best if we got your chip. How does that sound?" Mark was taking out the breakfast of donuts he planned and was making a pot of coffee to go with them, all the while keeping an eye on Jake in order to see his reaction.

"Get my chip? I guess that sounds about as good as anything else I can think of." Jake turned and went to get dressed. "I will take a quick shower, and then I will be ready to go." He reached over the counter and took hold of one of the donuts. "Breakfast of champs, right?" Jake was amazed at how Mark ate. Jake used to tease him about it, but now it somehow brought comfort.

Jacob dressed, and they had coffee with the rest of the donuts then off to their first stop. Get Jake's chip. Mark had barrowed Sally's car so they could have an easier trip. Jake was calm on the outside, but his insides were churning. He was not sure that he really wanted his chip back. He knew that he needed it to get on with his life, but if he took the chip, then he would never be able to be with his friends in the Knowing again. No matter what he decided to do in court.

Mark noted how quiet Jake had been. He was not sure exactly what it was Jake was thinking about, but he had guessed. "Jake, you are not sure if you want your chip back, are you?"

Jake turned to see Mark watching him. "How did you know?"

"I didn't. I just guessed." Mark kept his eyes on the road. With a quick glance at Jake, he addressed the situation. "So, what do you want to do?"

"I don't know. I guess I will have to get it. I am just being crazy. Those people, they got to me somehow." Jake could not believe that he was saying this out loud.

"I think I have an idea, if you will go along with me?" Mark did not wait for Jake to give an answer but turned on some music and began to listen. Jake was confused and tired. Mark knew that Jake would have too many questions. Jake would think this thing to death and then get upset and make a decision based on frustration instead of using his heart to guide him. It was Jake's way. It was Jake's pattern.

They had arrived at the chipping center. Both men went into the building together. "Mark, let's get this over with, okay?"

Mark could hear what it was Jake was saying with his words, but he could see something totally different with his body language.

"Jake, I am serious, if you will trust me, I think I can figure something out."

Jake was irritated. "Mark, there is nothing to figure out. I need to get this over and done with. Then things will get back to normal, and we can get on with our lives just like before." Jake went to the counter and rang the bell.

A man came through the double doors and looked first to Mark and then over at Jake. "Can I help you?"

Mark reached into his pocket and pulled out Jake's papers. Handing them over to the man, Mark leaned toward him and began to speak. "Can I please speak with you before this man gets chipped?"

The man noticed that this was to be a private conversation out of earshot of Jake.

The man nodded to the double doors. "We can talk in there." Looking over at Jake. "Will he be all right here by himself?"

Mark nodded to the man and made a gesture to Jake that he would be back in a short time to get him for the procedure.

Jake was too tired to argue with him, so he sat down on a chair nearby.

Mark went into the chipping room by himself. In a short time, he came out into the hall with a young man Jacob had never seen before. "Is this him?" the man asked Mark.

"Yes, this is him." Mark turned to see if Jake was still looking as bad as ever. And yes, as fate would have it, Jake looked awful. Life on the streets had taken its toll on him. Not to mention, the lack of sleep and his having been injured not so long ago. "Do you see what I mean? And when you add my problem of being allergic to the story. Well, I do not think it is a risk you would want to take. If you do this now, then once he is better, you can readjust it." Mark stood confident that this man was going to go along with whatever idea he was trying to convince him of.

"Okay, but just for now and just between the three of us." The man reentered the chipping room and let the door close behind him, leaving Mark and Jake alone in the hall.

"Come on, little brother, it is time for you to be rechipped." Mark had not disclosed any other information, and for all Jake knew, Mark's plan and conversation had nothing to do with him.

"You know, Mark, I think I would like some time to rethink this. Let's come back later, okay?" Jake was turning around and ready to make his escape. He couldn't do this. Not now anyway. Perhaps after he had made the decisions about all of the other stuff. Then he would be more able to make the right choice. But for now, he needed some air.

As he went to go, he found that he couldn't move. Mark had anticipated this. He was not sure how it was he knew Jake would try and leave, but he was right. The good news was that Jake had lost so much weight and was so weak from all of his events that Mark could physically have the upper hand on him. And this was a first. Mark had taken hold of Jacob from the back. He had him in a good old-fashioned officer hold. "Jake. Listen to me. This needs to happen and is going to happen now. Trust me. I have this worked out." Jake tried to get loose, but Mark held onto him.

"Mark, don't do this. I think I am not going to do this at all. Ever. I want the chance to decide later." Jake was still trying to get loose. "Now let me go."

"No, not this time, little brother. This time you will do it my way." With those words, Mark pulled Jake around so he had better control of him. He pushed Jake up to the door; as he did, he felt the door give way, and both men entered the room somewhat abruptly.

"Hey, is everything all right?" The man was at the counter preparing Jake's chip. He had all of Jake's paperwork and had entered all of the latest information on to it. There was over six months of information, so it had taken this whole time to get it ready. "Have him sit here, and I will take care of the rest."

Jake was sure now that this was not going to happen. He was determined to get away. At any cost. He was now being more verbal than it was safe for any of them to be. As Jake and Mark began to struggle, the man who worked in the office came across the room with the air gun that administered the chip. Jake had recognized it from before. What he did not see was the other medication that now needed to be given. He motioned for Mark to help him pin one of Jake's arms down so he could get a clear shot at the open skin. At once they all heard the sound of the air gun administering its product into the patient. Jake.

That was the last thing Jake remembered before he woke up in the recovery room with a massive headache. He reached over and rubbed his arm where the air gun had been placed. "Well, I guess that is that. It's done now. No going back."

"Jake, will you shut up!" Mark was really upset with Jake and the way he had not trusted him. Perhaps it was all that time on the street, but whatever it was, it was not something Mark wanted to put up with anymore.

"Do I have a chip?" Jacob already knew the answer but asked anyway.

"Yes, but not like you think." Mark reached toward Jake's neck. There on a chain was a medallion like the one Mark had. "I told them you were too weak to have a chip implanted. Especially with the family history we have. I almost died getting mine. And, well, with you being the son of an up-and-coming politician, he decided not to take a chance. Only we three know what the real truth is. Not even the higher-ups will find out. Why, it could mean this man's job. Well, you know what I mean." Mark simply smiled.

"Thanks, Mark, I guess you could say I overreacted. What was that he gave me with the air gun?" Jacob once again began rubbing his arm.

"Well, they do get some people who are not getting the chip by choice. So, they are prepared for resistance. He knocked you out." Mark was still smiling.

"You are enjoying this too much I think." Jake sat up and swung his legs over the side of the bed. "Whoo, I think I moved too fast." Jake had been here before. This brought back memories of being in the hospital after he had been wounded. "Mark, get me out of here, okay?"

"Sounds like a plan to me." With those words, the two men exited the building. They were both chipped men and could now go anywhere they wanted.

It was almost 10:00 a.m. by the time the chip thing was done and over with. "Time to get you to the courthouse. Any idea of what you are going to say?" Mark knew that Jake was as confused about testifying as he had been about his getting his chip. If the way he chose about the chip was any indicator, then Jake would never testify against the Knowing. But then this was going to be much harder than the other. All of Jacob's family would be there. Watching and waiting to see what Jake had to say. Mark thought of asking Jake if he wanted to pray, but then he remembered Jake's reaction the last time he had asked. So he decided to pray by himself.

Mark pulled up outside the courthouse. He let Jake off and went to park the car. He planned to join Jake later. As Mark was pulling away, someone in the press recognized the Singleton men, and at once, they all surrounded Jake. They were all asking questions and all at the same time. Jake could hardly get his bearings on where the main entrance was located. Jake began to hear a voice speaking over the noise of the crowd. Jake recognized it at once. It was Mr. Diggings. He was now addressing the media. He was stating that the Singleton family would have a press conference at a later date. As he spoke, some officers came to Jake's aid and escorted him into the building. As Jake entered the court, he could not help but notice that the room was clearly divided. The right section was made up of the lesser, the lower class, the chipless. The left of the room was made up of the known. Jake's family were definitely regarded as the known.

As Jake walked to the front, he was greeted by his two oldest brothers. Sally and their parents remained seated but noted Jake's entrance with a nod of the head. Jake was glad to see his brothers. "Hey there, little brother. We heard that you are now once again among the chipped. Welcome back." Ben was glad to see that Jake was looking a little more like the brother he knew. He still looked tired and thin, but his clothing and overall appearance, well, they were back up to snuff.

"Hey, Jacob, did you see all the reporters here?" Marcus was looking as good as ever. His uniform had never looked so refined. Jake took a good look at his whole family and noted that they all looked like they were ready for a family event. But was he going to disappoint them? He himself did not even know.

Jake could see both his family and his friends of the Knowing. They were all there. Even Peter. Oh, God. Where was God when he really needed Him? Jake was remembering that only two days ago, he was asking God for help. He had asked God to get him out of this mess. From that moment on, things had continued to get worse. How was it that the one time Jake had put his trust in God that things did not get better but had truly become as bad as they could get?

The courtroom had become a zoo. People were milling around and acting as if this were the party of a lifetime. What were they expecting? Jake knew the answer even if they did not really understand the whole picture themselves. For Jake to testify against the Knowing would be to end an organization that had a true faith. The one true God. A faith even unto death. To not go against them would be to destroy his own family singlehandedly. Their future was in his hands. And he did not want it. Peter said that God always gave you a way out. That you would always have a way to do what was right. So where was it? How would the way come this time? Perhaps the ground would open and swallow him up.

Jake looked at the setup of the room. There was an area that they called the bench. The judge would enter, and he would sit at this point in the room. There were two tables, one at each side of the front of the room. There were guards and a person who would record all of the evidence and keep track of all of the information that would be disclosed. There were officers of the court who were ready to gather up the warrants as they were issued and hand them out to make the arrests. The spectators were all behind the tables, and there were attorneys that represented both the government and the state. There were no defendants. Mainly because there would be no defending what had been done. On Jake's word alone, many people would be prosecuted and placed in jail or chipped or both. Jake had the power, and it was in his words. If he could just be struck dumb somehow.

Mark had entered the room and taken his place somewhere between his family and the Knowing. He chose this position on purpose but used the excuse of the crowd to make it okay. The Knowing looked good. They had been praying since the closing of the farm. Many had prayed, and several had fasted. They knew that God was in control of their lives. They were sure that whatever was to happen, God would see them through it. They had no fear. It was amazing to Mark, how the ones who truly feared were the ones who seemingly had everything and all the power.

"All rise," a voice rang out through the court. A hush fell over the crowd as a man wearing a long shiny black robe entered the room. Jake noted that the pleats in the robe were spaced perfectly. He was not sure if it had been laundered well or that perhaps this was a new robe bought for this special occasion. They announced the judge's name.

The judge was a man well in years, but the years had been kind to him. His hair was silvery white, and his style was perfectly balanced for his face and body shape. The contrast of the black robe and white hair were as different as the people in this room. All the same and yet as different as night and day. The judge had a very good manner about him. He demanded respect from the people in the room, and he got it. As he entered, he took special time to scan each and every person within eye view. Jake could tell that he was taking inventory of the people in his court. As the judge came to his seat, he picked up some papers, lifted a gavel, and uttered the words, "Please be seated." As he sat, the whole room joined him. The only other time Jake had seen such obedient respect was when Victor or Frank had called people to prayer. But then even that was different. The people in this court did it out of fear of the man. Where with prayer, it was out of respect for their God.

The court was then called to order. A man standing close to the judge quoted from a document as to what it was they were all doing here. There were numbers and reports listed. There were names given and the date stated. Things went very smoothly. This was not a trial, so there was no jury. Only a judge and Jake with his findings. These two men would change lives forever. Finally they came to the calling of Jake's name. He had a number as well and was tied in with several file names and numbers. He was asked to raise his right hand and to repeat an oath that ended in "so help me, God." Jake thought that this was a strange thing to have him say when they then wanted him to turn around and speak against these people of the very God they had him pledge to.

The judge had everyone sit down, even Jake. He then reviewed some documents and stated that he would not tolerate any disruption in his courtroom. He said that anyone who brought about such a thing would spend time in jail. No exceptions. He was fast to say that he was disappointed to see what a media circus this had become and wanted it to all be over as soon as possible. He then turned to Jake. "Son, you have been sworn in. Do you understand what that means?"

"Yes, sir." Jake looked at him. The sleeves on the judge's robe were perfect length. Not too long or short either. As he moved his hands over the paperwork and the books, they all but missed dragging on them. This judge was confident. He knew his job and was ready to get on with it.

"Let's go over some of the facts that have already been disclosed to this court." The judge opened up a file. The outside was blue, different than all of the others on his desk.

"This says that you are Jacob Allen Singleton. You are the youngest of the Singleton family here in Washington. Is that correct?"

"Yes, sir." Jake continued to look at the judge. He needed to not look at anyone else in the room. He knew if he looked at his family, he would have to go against the Knowing; and on the other hand, if he looked at Peter, Victor, Sandy, or any of the Knowing, then he would need to decide to go against his family. And that would destroy them.

"You were in the field undercover for six months. Is that correct?"

"Yes, sir."

"During that time, you were able to meet and join a group known as the Knowing. Is that correct?"

Jake froze.

"Mr. Singleton. Do you understand the question that I just asked you?"

"Yes, sir."

"'Yes, sir' what? That you met and joined the group the Knowing, or yes that you understand the question?"

No answer.

The courtroom started to buzz with noise. The judge banged his gavel and called the room to order. "If you do not remain orderly, I will vacate the room, and these proceedings will be done in a closed courtroom. Do you all understand?" Once again silence fell on the room. The judge turned again to Jake. "Son, now let's continue. Is it correct that you were able to meet and to join the group who call themselves the Knowing?"

Jacob could not answer. He knew that he had to make a decision. But he couldn't. Mark. Where was Mark? Jacob had seen where he was sitting. He turned to look at him; perhaps he would be able to calm him enough to help him make a clear choice. Jake scanned the room. No Mark. Mark had left along with several of the Knowing. Jake was alone. He had to make the only decision that he could. This was his life. He was on his own. He needed to survive. No one could hold that against him, could they? From what he had learned from the Knowing, God was on his side. God was going to be there regardless of his choice.

"Mr. Singleton. I will ask you one more time. Can you identify the leaders and the people of this cult group the Knowing?"

There was only one thing Jake could do. There was only one way Jake could answer.

CHAPTER 19

Cameras had been allowed into the courtroom. This was not usually done, but this was however not a trial but a gathering of information. Flashes were going off, and the judge was getting madder by the second. Jake was not too sure what was going on at that very moment. He had planed to keep his eyes on the judge but now found that he could not do that either. So many had expectations of him. His family, the Knowing, the judge, Mr. Diggings, even his brother Mark would have an idea of what he should do. Mark. Yes, Mark would have an idea of what he should do. Looking around the room again, he first saw his mother. He thought that she was looking frightened about what he was not saying. Then a look to Sandy; she looked frightened as to what he might say or do. Then a look to his father and then to Victor and then to Frank. They looked calm. Like they could handle anything. There were his two older brothers, Ben and Marcus, then over to Peter and some of the other men. David too. He had come. And then to Sally, and then there was Peggy. They were looking like they were feeling sorry for him for getting himself into this mess.

Jake looked back to the judge, and to his horror, he could not hear a word he or anyone else was saying. All he could hear really was what sounded like his own blood rushing through his body. He needed hope. He needed Mark. He needed God. "Oh, God, if You are real—no, I know You are real. I need Your help. I need Your forgiveness. I need You in my life. Now! Please help me. I do not know what to do." Jake was not sure if he had said this out loud, and at this very moment, he did not much care.

Sandy was scared. Not about what Jake might say or do, but from the look on his face, she was truly worried about what was going wrong with Jake himself. She looked to Victor and the others for confirmation that they too were seeing what she was. Jake was losing it. Something was truly wrong. He needed help. But all they could do was to sit and watch this young man suffer. Pray. Yes! Pray. "Victor, we need to pray!" Sandy grabbed Victor's arm.

Victor looked at Sandy. "What?"

"Victor, Jake is in trouble. We need to pray." With those words, she lowered her head and began to pray.

The others saw and heard her and began to do the same. They sat quiet with heads bowed and talked with God like they were all by themselves out at the farm.

Jake saw this and felt hope at first and then pure panic as he realized that if they were seen to be praying, they could themselves bring charges down on them. They needed to stop this. Not for him should this risk be taken; after all, he was the traitor. Had they not figured this out? Jake was about to stand up and say something in order to bring the attention back on himself when the back doors of the courtroom opened with a loud sound and in walked two men.

Almost everyone in the room turned to look at the sound, then the others who had not heard it turned to see what the others were looking at. Everyone that was but the Knowing; they kept their heads bowed and kept right on praying.

Jake looked up at the two men and at first was not sure who it was he was looking at. "Mark." It was Mark, and behind him was a man Jake knew that he had seen before. But where? Jake kept looking at the two of them as they continued to enter the room. Both made their way to the front where the judge was sitting.

The judge took note of the men entering and picked up the gavel in order to bring control to the court room. Cameras stopped flashing, the people took their seats, and the Knowing lifted their heads as if on cue.

Mark was almost to the judge when a security guard came to his side. "Your Honor, if I might have a moment. I think I can make some sense out of what is going on with Jacob here."

Jake could see Mark's lips moving, but all he continued to hear was the blood rushing in his ears.

The man that was with Mark came alongside of him, and Jake, for the first time, could see him in full view. It was the man on the street. It was the man who gave Jake the new coat. It was the very one who had saved his life by getting him off to the side of the street. But how? But who was he? Chipped? Yes. He had to be from the way he was dressed and from the way the people were reacting to him. Jake was quickly understanding from the reactions that this man was in fact a "someone."

The judge called order again, and the whole room came to a halt. He called out to Mark. "Now who in the world are you, and what makes you think we need your help in any of this?"

"Well, sir, I am Mark Singleton. And Jacob here is my younger brother. And well, sir, I think there is some information that this man"—Mark was pointing to the man who came in with him— "well, he has information that will help this out."

With that the man came forward and took off his coat and introduced himself as Dr. Harold Young.

With that statement, the room went nuts. This Dr. Young was very well-known among the upper society. He was the very best in so many specialties that they had difficulty introducing him.

The judge was delighted to have such a famous guest in his courtroom. Along with the other special visitors as well as all the media, this would truly put his name on the map as they say. "Well, hello, Dr. Young. I am glad to have you in my courtroom. I must say that it is a surprise to have you here. Please do come forward, to the bench, and let's see if we can make a judgment as to why Mr. Mark Singleton here thinks your services are needed."

The doctor strolled forward heading to the bench when he took a side-glance over at Jake. He reached out to touch Jake as he was coming past and noticed that this young man was now in a cold sweat. Jake did not move or react to his being touched. The doctor was touching his hair in order to pull it back off his forehead. This was to make sure that the judge would see the scar that was still very noticeable on Jake's head. *Thank God he got a haircut. It will make it easier to show the judge what I'm talking about.*

The judge took note of what the doctor was doing. "Doctor, what is going on? My patience is growing thin."

"Judge, I am here in order to set you straight on the health of this young man Jacob Singleton." He looked over to the Singleton family. "I am sorry to do this. I know that you are a proud family and that you are private in your family matters, but I think it only fair to you and your family that the world know what a sacrifice you and your young son Jacob here has made on behalf of the government."

With that, the doctor turned around to point out to the judge the scar that was found on Jake's forehead. "Your Honor, I need you to understand that this young man had been severely hurt while he was on an undercover assignment. Jacob Singleton was hurt and then spent another three-plus months out on the streets doing his job. He had spent several weeks in a chipless hospital."

That statement sent the crowd buzzing with disgust as they thought of the conditions this young man had endured.

"Judge, you need to know that even with his injuries, this young man stayed out on assignment in order to do his job. He was dehydrated, and he was under great distress in order to do so. But as all of us know, sometimes things go wrong, and we are not always able to do what we set out to do.

"Judge, if you would allow me, I think I can show you why Jacob Singleton here is not able to give you the answers you are requiring of him right now. Perhaps with time and some medical help, we can return him to duty so he can get on with his job." The doctor was still holding back the hair on Jake's head when Jake finally pulled himself together to see that things were going on in the courtroom without him.

Jake looked around like he had just awaken from a nightmare. As he looked over to his mom, he noted that she had pulled her hand up to her mouth in horror about something that this man had said, and this was making him angry at the man for scaring her. "What do you want?" Jake spoke out loud as he pulled his head back and took a swing at the doctor's hand.

The doctor stepped back and kept all but a hint of a smile off his face. Jake was playing right into the plan. And to think he had not an idea of what was about to happen. God was good, and He was taking over this courtroom. And the Knowing could feel it. Even Jake.

A peace fell over Jake like a blanket had been placed over his mind. He stopped midsentence and began to speak to the doctor, "Well, hello. You again?"

"Yes, Jacob, it is me Dr. Young." The doctor looked over to the judge in order to get confirmation that he could continue to work with Jake. The judge nodded his head so as to let the doctor know that he could go on.

"Jacob, do you remember where it was that you and I met?" The doctor locked eyes with Jake.

Jake looked back at the doctor and then closed his eyes for what he thought was but a second but was much longer to the room. "Well, yes, sir, I do recall. You bought me a coat. No, you are a janitor. No, I think I met you at the hospital. Yes, you are a doctor. Right?"

The people in the room laughed at the answer, and then some realized that this was not fun but was a very sad event going on. It was becoming clear to everyone that this man was hurt and needed some medical help.

The doctor kept a very calm voice. "Jacob, do you remember how you got hurt on the street?"

Jake thought for a minute. "Yes, there were some government officers who wanted to help me get to know God. They baptized me." Jake had no idea how strange and out of context he was sounding. He was telling the truth, but the way the room was hearing it, it sounded all mixed up. It sounded to the chipped like Jake had confused all of the stories in his head. It sounded to the Knowing like God had taken over. And He had. Thank God.

It was clear to the doctor that he was getting the idea of Jake's being mixed up over to the judge, but he needed to bring this performance to an end. The doctor looked over to Mark. "Mark, I am sorry to do this, but I think the judge needs to know how very bad your brother really is. I need to tell him everything about Jacob."

Mark was not sure what the doctor was talking about. His making Jake look mixed up was all they had planned. The doctor was to point out that Jake had been hurt in the line of duty and the extent of his head wound was not fully realized until he had been retrieved out of the undercover assignment. This plan was to get Jake off the hook as it were; it was to elevate the Singleton family by the mere fact that they had almost sacrificed their very own son—the youngest, they might add—in order to bring about a better government. "What?" was all Mark could say to Dr. Young. Mark looked to the doctor, to the group of the Knowing, where Mark was reassured by Victor, David, and Frank that this was a good thing and that he should trust the good doctor. Mark looked back to the doctor and then gave a nod of his head in order to confirm that he agreed to whatever was to be next.

"Jacob?" The doctor again locked eyes with Jake.

In response, Jake looked up and smiled. "Yes, Doctor, what can I do for you?" Jake could hear perfectly now but still was not sure as to exactly what was going on.

"Jacob, I want to talk to you about your chip." Jake blinked.

Mark felt panic come over him. No, this was not a place to take Jake in this state of mind. "Doctor!" Mark took a step in order to make sure the doctor understood his disapproval of this area of questioning.

The security guard stepped between the doctor and Mark.

The judge called out to Mark, "Mr. Singleton, as I am sure you remember, you are the one who brought Dr. Young into this courtroom in order to shed light on the goings-on of your little brother. Might I suggest that you have a seat and let him do what it is he came here to do?"

Mark stood silent and then took a seat over by one of the tables. Here it was, the moment of truth. It might be the very time God had planned for the truth about them being a part of the Knowing was to be told. So here it would be in front of the whole world. *Okay, God, if this is what You want, then so be it.* Mark sat down and watched as the story unfolded.

"Jacob, let's talk about your chip," the doctor continued.

"Just what do you want to know?" Jake looked fully in control now.

Jake's looking like he had it under control was exactly what needed not to happen for the doctor to finish this correctly. *God, help me ask the questions in such a way as to fix all of this.* The doctor sent up a quick arrow prayer. "Jacob, you had your chip removed in order to do your undercover work, right?"

Jake thought about the question, then answered, "Yes, I had to have it removed in order to be able to get into the Knowing group. They are really smart and can find out if you have one that has been disabled." Jake felt that he was doing good at delivering the answers.

"Jacob, how did you feel about getting it out?"

"Well, I really was not too happy about the removal of it. I felt that I was really putting myself into an awful place. Not being tracked and all. But it worked out okay." Again, Jake felt that this was a great interaction between the doctor and himself.

"Jacob, you got your chip put back today, didn't you?"

"Why, yes, I did." Again another safe answer.

"And, Jacob, how did you feel about getting it back?" The Doctor could see the look of confusion come over Jake's face. This was great. Exactly what the doctor needed the room to see. "Jacob, are you still with me?"

"Yes, Doctor, what are you getting at?" Jake was growing nervous.

"Well, Jacob, is it not true that in order to give you your chip—" The doctor looked back by the back door and motioned with his head to a man standing waiting to be called on. The man started to the front to be by the doctor and by Mark.

Jake looked up and saw as did Mark that this was the young man who helped Mark get Jake chipped.

"Jacob, is it not true that in order to get your chip back, you had to be sedated to make it happen? That you yourself were not sure that it would be what needed to happen?"

The courtroom went loud again, with total disbelief. It was a fact that if this was true, then this young man was even more mixed up than anyone could have guessed.

The judge called order to the room. He then spoke to the young man from the chipping clinic. The young man identified himself, and when asked if what the doctor had said was true, he confirmed it.

The cameras went wild again taking photos of everyone and everything. Jake sat there. Embarrassed. Not knowing how to react.

The judge called order and then spoke to the doctor, "What are you saying about this situation?"

"Well, Your Honor, I believe with all of my expertise that young Jacob here will make a full recovery. But it is my opinion that anything you hope to glean from him at this time would be inadmissible in a court hearing." The doctor had done his job. He had not lied, Jake had not lied, Mark had not lied. This was a way out, God had done it. The court hearing was over, and everyone was dismissed. The judge concluded that Jacob should have some time off and should be promoted (accommodated) for his sacrifice in the line of duty. The Singleton family was thanked and apologized to for the "airing of their personal matters as to the health of their young son" (in spite of the fact that it made great publicity for the election). The doctor was thanked. The young man who helped with the chipping was relieved that no one found out that he had put it into a medallion and was also relieved that he had not placed it into this young man who was obviously at-risk health-wise. The Knowing were let go in that they had no proof of any laws that had been broken.

The Knowing had to leave fast in order to beat curfew.

Mark had moved over to be with Jake, who was still not sure about all that had happened. He knew that it was over, and somehow it had all worked out. God had worked it out. Jake had found the leader of the Knowing. He had found Him. He knew exactly where the leader of the Knowing was. It was Jesus and Jesus was in Jake's heart.

CHAPTER 20

It had only been a few days since Jake had left the courtroom a hero. In some ways, it had only been days, but in other ways, it had been a lifetime.

Jake's mind still could hardly hold onto what had actually happened to end the trial. A doctor. A doctor he could hardly remember seeing had entered the courtroom and asked to speak on behalf of Jacob. At the time, Jacob was desperately trying to figure out how he could tell what he knew about the Knowing without selling out his friends. On one hand, he owed his family, his real blood family to do his job, but on the other hand, he owed his new faith family as much or even more. He did not figure it out. But God did. God gave Jacob a way out. Exactly like the Bible had promised.

The doctor had explained that with the kind of head injury Jacob had received, it had given him a lack of memory. That perhaps in time, he could regain his memory, but that he rather expected Jacob to be okay from now on, but most likely the past would remain forever lost.

The judge was so happy to get this whole thing over with that he did very little questioning and declared Jacob innocent of any wrongdoings and let him off. He declared that Jacob was to have leave with pay and was to undergo both a physical and psychiatric evaluation. Then he would be reinstated back onto the government force with a promotion for his good work.

Jacob had everything he wanted. So how come it did not feel the way that he had thought that it was going to? There was the appreciation of family and friends. There was the recognition for a job well done, and he was a celebrity, for a time anyway. He had made a name for himself and on his own without using the family name. There had been a family get-together, and he was the center of the story, but it was not even close to how he had dreamed it was going to be. He did not feel the excitement that he should have had for having been lifted up as a great cop who had gone undercover and survived the Knowing group.

*****

Fast-forward three weeks or so, and here is Jacob or Jake. He was having problems figuring out who he really was right now. Off duty for six months (with pay, mind you). Nothing to do but to remember how very different his last six months had been. He missed his friends. He even missed the chipless shelter. He missed Peggy. He so missed it all. But he did still have God. Or did he?

Jacob remembered how it was when he was at the shelter and what it had been like living with people who counted on God for every little thing. So far, being back in his old life was not at all what he had remembered it being like.

His family had been keeping their distance from him. All agreeing that he needed some time and space so as to get his life back in order.

His apartment was back like it had been before he had gone undercover, but everything he used to think was important now was just a reminder of how much he had lost coming back to his old life as a chipped officer.

He had not seen any of the people he knew from the shelter or the farm. He really wanted to see how they were all doing. He longed to sit and listen to the stories he had learned from the Bible and the nights of singing praise songs before bed. It was too dangerous for any of them to be seen with him for now. Even Mark, his brother, was having no contact with him. This was all for the best he was sure, but it was beginning to feel a lot like he had been removed from his saved family.

BEYOND KNOWING

"That's it," Jake was talking to himself. "It is time for you to pull yourself together and get on with whatever it is you are going to do with rest of your life."

Jake went to the bathroom to finish getting ready for the day. Looking in the mirror was still a shock to him, seeing the old, new Jake looking back at himself. His hair was short again, and his clothing screamed of a chipped officer for sure. The only telltale sign of the last six months was the scar on his forehead at the hairline. From the looks of it, he thought it would take a very long time, if ever, to go away.

Jake looked around the apartment one last time, making sure everything was in place, and headed out. Where? Not a clue as to where he needed or even wanted to go. Coffee. That was a great idea. Only a few blocks from his home, there was a coffee shop that he used to enjoy seeing friends and other officers in.

Jake got into his car and started it up. The sound of it was like the old days he remembered. A flip of a switch and instant heat. How great this was. How many times in his past had he taken this source of heat for granted? In just a short time, Jake had arrived at the coffee shop, parked his car, and went into the building.

As he entered it, he looked around the room only to see many faces that he had seen before but really didn't know. There was an empty table that would put his back to the wall. So he got a coffee and took a seat so that he could see the comings and the goings of the whole room. Jake was back home. He was back in his old life. And he hated it.

"God, is this it? I have gone through all of the learning about You and the Bible, only to be back to my old life where everything will be about me?" Jake had not planned on praying right now, but it was feeling right somehow to meet up with God about all of this. "I really thought You had big plans for me. I thought You were going to use me for saving the Knowing, but this feels as though You are done with me. So, I am asking, can You please use me again? I mean, I do not want to be famous or anything, I just want to feel like I am a part of something again. To feel like I make a difference. I cannot believe that this is all You have for me. Please show me what it is You

354

want me to do next. Even if it is only in a small way. I will be glad to simply get to be a part of the Knowing family again."

Jake had been sitting there long enough to drink one cup of coffee and to have a good start on another when every officer instinct in him was going off. A quick scan of the room did not give him any answer as to what it was his subconscious was telling him. He was being watched. He knew it. Another scan of the room. There it was—a very slight movement out of the corner of his eye. Low to the ground. A second look confirmed that there were eyes on him. There was a bench along the wall by the front door. There tucked all the way back to the wall was what looked like a small child. Dirty and, for sure, a chipless child at that. As he watched, he noted that the child looked up ever so quickly to another corner of the room. As Jake followed the direction of his look, he noted that there was another boy (older) standing in the room. He was tall and cleaner than the first child, but from the looks of him, he was also chipless. He had his arms pressed down at his sides so straight that Jake thought he might give a salute. As Jake watched, the older boy tapped out a beat with his fingers on his pant leg. Jake looked to the small boy, who was countering with a shake of his head no. You could not miss what was going on, but why? It was clear that the older boy was telling the young one to do or not do something and that they were disagreeing. For the life of himself, Jake felt like he was watching an old play of his brothers and himself. He was really enjoying the whole thing when there was a loud crash across the room in a totally different direction. Jake looked away from the boys for a quick second, and when he looked back, the young boy had come out from under the bench and gone to a wallboard and placed a paper onto it. The older boy was quickly walking to the board. As fast as the paper had been placed, the older boy had removed it. He reached out to grab the lad, only to miss him. The young boy turned and ran into the bathroom with the door swinging shut behind him. The older boy went to make chase when he felt a good grip on his right arm.

As he looked up, he found himself face-to-face with Jake. "Hey, what the heck do you think you are doing?" The boy tried to break free, but Jake had a really good grip. "Hold on. Now let me see that."

Jake took hold of the paper that the boy was now trying to place into his pocket.

A quick look at the paper told Jake that this was trouble in the making. It was a scripture printed out in bold letters, "John 3:16. For God so loved the world that he gave..." The boy reached out to retrieve the paper, but Jake countered his move and got the paper into his own pocket. Jake then pulled the boy closer so as to speak into his ear so only he could hear him. "What on earth do you think you are doing? Do you have any idea what could happen to you if you got caught hanging stuff like this up?" The boy then challenged Jake with a set look on his face. Not a word was spoken, but Jake got the message all the same. "Get away from me. Leave me alone. I have got this under control." Jake set his gaze back on the boy. Again, no words but a message of the same note.

"What's your name?" Jake asked with a quieter, kinder voice this time. His tone took the boy off guard, and without even a hesitation, he answered, "Marcus, now let me go. I have work to do." With those words, he pulled his arm away from Jake's hold. Jake felt a tug on his pocket. The boy Marcus had retrieved the note. He turned to follow the young boy into the bathroom. Jake again countered his move and suggested that he could get cornered in a one-door room. Marcus turned around and gave him a smug look. "Not likely" was his reply, and with that, he hit the bathroom door, it opened, the door closed, and then a locking sound clicked before Jake could open it.

Jake smiled at how very foolish this action was. He turned and walked to the counter where he asked for the key for the bathroom. The man at the counter looked at the bathroom door and then at Jake. Jake reached into his pocket where he pulled out his badge and ordered the man to give him the key. Which he did swiftly.

Jake went to the bathroom door and placed the key into the lock. As he entered, he had planned to give a lesson as to how this was not the best idea for getting away. Jake entered. No boys. Where had they gone? Jake stopped dead in his tracks. This was a Knowing setup. This was a hideout with a secret exit and entrance for getting off or on the street. He was sure of it. How clever these boys were after having been so dumb.

Jake returned the key, got his cup of coffee, and headed out to his car. Under the windshield wiper, he saw a piece of paper. He retrieved it and read the message.

"Hey, officer, thanks for the help. Better luck next time." It was signed *Marcus*. It had been written on the note from the board. There was John 3:16 fully written out on it. Jake smiled and placed it in his pocket.

As Jake drove around, he began to notice a group of people he had never noticed before. Young people. All boys from the look of it. Hard to tell as they all were dressed the same and were all dirty.

While Jake was at the shelter, he had noted that most of the kids were missing. He had decided that they had all been moved out to the farms, away from the city. But here they were. But how? Had they been there all along? Jake was tired of all the questions about his life and the life around him. He was lonely, and he really wanted to have friends again. Is this really what God wanted his life to be like now? Lonely and sad. Jake had stuff, so much stuff but was so much happier without it. Who owned whom? He the stuff or the stuff owning him?

As Jake's car rounded the corner, his heart almost leapt out of his chest. There on a park bench was his brother Mark. He was just sitting in the sun. His eyes were closed, and he looked so happy with peace all over him. That is what Jake wanted. And he wanted to spend time with his brother. He wanted to talk to him about God and for Mark to tell him about the chipless family he had to leave behind.

Jake parked his car and then set out for the park bench where Mark was. "Hi, stranger. Long time no see." Mark opened his eyes and smiled at Jake, truly happy to see him.

"Hey, brother, what is going on with you?" Mark gave Jake a gentle slug on his arm as he sat down.

Jake was so happy to see a friendly face. "Mark, where have you been? Have you seen anyone from the shelter or the farm? How about—"

"Jake, slow down. Take a breath and then we can talk." Mark was glad to see Jake too. He was worried how he would do being back to the chipped life and all. "Now, how are you doing yourself? Are you feeling better yet?"

"Mark, this is really hard. I feel like a traitor living such a good life like we do. Especially now that I know what others are going through. How do you do it? We are all alone. I hate it."

This was a new Jake. One that Mark was not used to seeing. It was not bad but such a different Jake. So sensitive, caring about others more than himself. God was really showing in Jake's life.

"Jake. You are not alone." Mark was trying to decide how to explain things to Jake.

"Mark, I know I have God, but it is not like it was in the shelter or at the farm. I need to be with people who know God. I am not sure what I am to do next. I think I need to make a difference, but how can I if I am safe and sound in my old job? They are taking all the risks, and I sit by and do nothing." Now the old Jake was back—mad, angry, and wanting to lash out at something or someone.

"Jake, stop for just one minute. Let me explain some things." Mark tried to make eye contact with Jake. "Okay, so let me give you a quick lesson about being a believer in a nonbelieving world. First, getting yourself caught or into trouble is not the way to help the chipless. Trust me, I have learned this the hard way. What you need to do is stay put and wait and see when you are needed. God has a plan and a way of getting you involved. Something will happen, or you will see a need. Maybe you will be contacted. So all you have to do is watch for the signal as to when you are needed. Then you do what you are asked. Only what you are asked. And then wait some more." Jake started to talk, and Mark raised his hand to silence him. "As to your being alone. Well, you have more than just God with you. You have believers everywhere. They are all around you."

"Oh, what a bunch of—" Jake did not want to be pacified; he wanted to go back to the chipless world and to get back to helping the real cause. He wanted—no, he *needed* to make a difference.

Mark interrupted Jake. "Okay. You got a haircut, right? Well, the barber reported to the group that you were doing okay and that your head was healing."

Mark had Jake's attention now. "And you have been out to dinner several times? Well, it is reported that you have not eaten much but that you have had it bagged up and then you gave it to someone on the streets to eat." Mark paused to give Jake time to connect the remarks. "Believers, Jake, they are all around you. They are everywhere. Just because you do not know them does not mean they are not there. Jake, God has a plan, and it involves all of us. Even when we do not see it or understand it. We all have a part. When I first started with the group, I was always jumping the gun as it were, sometimes still do, but time and again, God has shown me that I need to wait on Him, for Him to show me what to do.

"Okay, Mark. Let's say you are right and that there is work for me to do. How do I know what it is God wants me to do? How and who decides?" Jake was new to this faith thing. So many people talked about stuff like this, but they never quite explained how it worked.

"First, Jake, read your Bible. It is the one real way you can know what God really thinks about things. Then you pray. A lot. And one of the hardest things for me to do is to wait." Mark had a look of confidence about what he was saying. Like a man who had tested it out and could confirm that this was the way.

"Wait for what?" Jake was really trying to understand this stuff, but he was a black-and-white man. This limbo, gray sort of stuff was not for him.

"Wait for someone to get in touch with you." Mark needed to tell Jake as much as he could and as fast as he could to get Jake up and running in the group.

"Okay, so exactly how will that happen?"

"They will get to you one way or the other. A telephone call, a note, or even a person will bring you a message." Mark had lowered his voice so low that Jake was almost holding his breath so he could hear better.

"And how will I know who is from the Knowing and who is from another source?" As far as things had gone, Jake was obviously not aware of who was who in this game. He had not even suspected that anyone from the Knowing was around.

Mark looked around them to make sure that no one would be able to hear the next conversation. "Okay, so you will have a code word. It is yours alone. No one else will use it. When you hear it, it will tell you that they are a part of the Knowing. It could mean you are safe, that they have a message for you, or that they need a message from you. It is the one way for sure for you to know who you are talking with or doing things with is safe."

"That sounds like a good plan, but how will I get and know my code word?" This was so strange for Jake to be able to take teaching from Mark, but it felt right. It felt good. Not so lonely.

Mark handed Jake a piece of paper. Jake opened it, and one word was on it: ROCK.

"This is the word they will use to be identified as Knowing. And it will be used by you to let others know that you are safe for them too." Mark was glad to see that Jake had kept up with the conversation. "Any questions?"

Jake had a million questions, but for now, he had one important one. Mark handing him the paper the way he did reminded him of the events of the morning. "Mark, I do have a question. Kids? Young boys to be exact."

Now Mark was the one who was confused. "What are you talking about?"

"While I was in the shelter here in town, I hardly saw any kids. I thought they had all been taken out to the farms, but since I have been back to town, I have seen kids in the strangest places." Jake was surprised to see a really big smile on Mark's face.

"Oh, I take it you have run into Marcus or some of his group?" Jake was taken aback that Mark knew his name.

"Well, yes, I have met Marcus. And, boy, would I love to get my hands on him again. Someone needs to get that kid under control." Jake leaned in closer so as to not miss any information he could get on this kid.

"You know, Jake, he may look like a kid, but you need to know he functions like a man, as much as any of us. Do you remember in history about the pony express riders?" Mark had a half smile on his face.

Jake nodded yes but was interested to see where this conversation was headed. "Well, Marcus and his gang are the Knowing's underground pony express. The message takers. They are able to go everywhere. And I mean everywhere. It is like no one sees them. If they do encounter them or catch them, they are so dirty and so good at what they do that they almost always get away. No one wants to touch them. And if they do catch them, they just run away from the home they are put into." Mark had a look of appreciation and adoration for what these kids were doing. But it was clear that the best thing for these kids was to get them off the streets and to get them to Knowing homes or, even better yet, out to one of the farms.

Jake was excited to get this information. He had decided that this was what God would want him to do. Although the kids had good intentions, this was not a good thing for them. It was a matter of time before someone got hurt or, worse, got killed. Too young and too inexperienced. "So, Mark, you don't think it would be better for the kids to be in homes? Perhaps on farms away from the city and from all the goings-on."

"Jake, don't even go there. Trust me. This is not just any group of kids. They have a call on them. A God call. I have seen and heard things that would make you crazy. They are good at what they do. Really good." Mark could tell that Jake was already making plans to relocate these kids.

"From what I saw today, these kids are headed straight for trouble. I saw them enter a coffee shop and, in plain sight, place propaganda on one of the information boards on the wall. Two of them were there, and both could have been caught and put into jail." Mark was smiling. Not at Jake but with him.

"What is so funny? You did not see what happened." Jake was not at all happy as to how Mark was not understanding the urgency of the situation.

"Jake, what you saw was a plan gone wrong. Really it was not a plan. The young boy who did the paper hanging was doing it without orders. He jumped the gun and decided he wanted to make a difference. No matter what the outcome. Does any of this sound familiar? We have all felt that way from time to time. Marcus was there trying to stop or clean up the mess. I heard about it through the grapevine but did not know until now that you are the 'old man who got in the way.'" Mark was all but rolling around laughing about his brother being described as an "old man."

Jake was really trying to understand the whole thing. "Perhaps they should just get that kid off the streets and make things better for everyone. Think of him as the weak link."

Mark shook his head, not even listening to Jake's idea. "No, that will never happen."

"And why not? Because it is not your idea?" Jake was serious, and Mark was not even giving his idea a thought. "Give me one good reason why not?"

"Okay, Jake. Because they are brothers. Sam is like one of Marcus's little brothers. That's why."

Mark had Jake with "because they are brothers."

"And he can't control this little brother? Even more reason to get them help and off the streets." Jake felt that with things as dangerous as they were that extra effort needed to be taken to keep Marcus's brothers safe. After all, that is what he would do.

"And how well has that worked for us and our family?" Mark was not one to pull punches when he felt right about his ideas.

Both men sat not looking at each other but out across the park.

Jake was the first to speak. "Okay, maybe you are right, that would make it a problem."

"Did Jacob Singleton just admit I was right about something?" Mark was up on his feet. Smile on his face. "Well, if I had not known you were with God before, I sure do now. Jacob, you are a changed man, and I would have never thought I would have heard those words come out of that mouth of yours."

"Mark, knock it off. And don't call me *Jacob*, it is *Jake*. What are we going to do to help those kids? They are really not safe, and you know it." Jake was really upset about this situation with these kids being on the street doing God knows what.

Mark looked at his watch. "Oh man, I need to get going. I will see you again soon. Oh, that is right, we are all meeting on Thursday for the family dinner. You are going to be there, right? Right?"

Jake had not kept up with Mark's shift in conversation but was catching up quick. "Oh yes, I will be there. See ya then."

Mark left, and Jake sat out in the sun, eyes closed with his face to the sky. Jake was not the same person he had been.

"God, what now? What do You want from me? I was happy before. I thought. Now I know the difference of having a life with You. What do You want me to do now? Do I just go back to life as before? But how can I? I know You now."

Jake was thinking about what Mark had told him about not being alone. He felt alone. One thing he had learned from the Knowing is that you should never take things at face value. Perhaps he had missed something in his time back home. Tomorrow would be different. He would pay special attention to everyone that he had contact with. And what about those kids? Marcus's kids? Had God put them in his path so that he could do something with them or for them? So many questions, and the good news is that he now had the time to figure them out.

As morning came, Jake had a new burst of energy. He had a mission. Even if he had given it to himself. He really wanted to get the full skinny on the group of kids led by Marcus. There was a lot to find out before he could figure out what God wanted him to do. He was not sure how, but he knew without a doubt that he was a part of their world.

Jake got up and got dressed. He was ready for his adventure. He got a new small notebook to keep the information that he gathered in. The thought crossed his mind that the last time he used a notebook of any kind, he got himself into such a mess and ended up in the courtroom. "The past is the past," he said out loud. "This is a new day and a new job." He grabbed his keys and set off for the coffee shop.

This trip to the coffee shop would be different. This time he parked two blocks away and walked in. That way no one would know he was there by driving by. This time his entrance would be different in that he would make note of all of the people in the coffee shop. Both high and low. One quick scan of the room, and Jake was amazed at what he saw. First, there were all of the everyday people. Socializing and going about their business kind of people. Then within the same scan, he saw the young underground ones. Several as a matter of fact. There was no Marcus, but the young one that he had seen the day before was there. He was sitting right out in the open. Jake was stunned at how no one even took note of him. He could have been a houseplant for all it mattered. As he kept his eyes on the boy, he finally saw it. The pass-off. Two other boys had entered the room. They ran into the first boy and then kept walking. The one who had been there all along received a small envelope. He took off his hat and placed the envelope into it and put it back on his head. Jake continued to watch as the boy just sat. And sat. He chewed gum, he swung his legs and played with a straw he had found. The front door opened, and many looked up to see who was coming in. Including Jake. As Jake looked back to watch the boy, he was gone. Just like that. The boy, hat and all had vanished. Once again Jake scanned the room. No boy. In fact, all of the young people were gone. But where?

Jake got up and walked around the room. Looking as if he was stretching his legs. Refilled his coffee cup. Then he remembered the trick of the bathroom escape. He placed his coffee cup back on the table and headed to the back rooms. As he walked down the hall, a man saw him and called out to him. "Hey, sir, can I help you with something?"

Jake turned and saw that the man from the day before who had given him the key to the bathroom was now addressing him. "No, I was just looking around. I am fine."

"Well, there is really nothing for you down that hall unless you need the restroom, and for that, you have gone too far." The man was wiping the tables as he spoke.

Jake looked up and noticed that he had in fact passed the bathroom door and was well on his way to another part of the building. As he was getting ready to speak, the man had come over, very close to him. And in a lower tone of voice. "Officer, I think it might be a good idea for you to take a seat and finish your coffee. At least for now, if you know what I mean." Jake could see that the man was trying really hard to tell him something without using words. "So may I suggest that you rock back in that chair and have some more coffee, and I will be back with your order."

Rock? Is that really what he said? Oh my, a believer. Or was this just a misuse of his word, an accident or something like that?

The man could see the look of question on Jake's face. "You heard me. I said ROCK." Jake got it loud and clear. Get back to the table. Get your coffee and have a seat. He would be back to talk to him. Jake got the message. Jake did as he was told.

A very short time later, the man came over and brought Jake a breakfast sandwich. He sat it down and then sat down at the table next to him. "My name is Smitty. That is what everyone calls me. And you are Jake Singleton. You were undercover for a time in the family, but now you are our new secret weapon. How am I doing so far? My only question to you is, what do you want with the boys? Why are you watching them?"

Wow. Jake had been watched, and he had been found out. A countermove if he had ever seen one. "Well, if you must know the truth, I am fascinated by this kids group and how they function. I am not sure what it is they really do."

Smitty smiled and nodded his head. "Great question. They just showed up a few months back. No one really knows where they came from, but they have been doing a great job of getting messages and things from place to place and from person to person." Smitty leaned close to Jake and lowered his voice even lower than the whisper he had already been using. "You know, they can even get into the jail and courthouse? I even heard they got into the government station to get an order to someone."

Jake began to rethink this conversation he was having with this man. Who was he really? And why was he talking to him? "So, Smitty, it surprises me that you know so much about me—everyone for that matter—and that even though you know I am an officer, you would be so open with me. Would you like to explain that?"

"They said you were a smart one and that I should be careful with you." Smitty continued on talking as if Jake had not even been questioning him. "Well, Victor and Sandy said to watch out for you and know that you were one of the good guys. They also said that you were a bit of a hothead and that you might need some help to stay out of trouble."

"They said that, did they?" Jake was not too happy at being described as a hothead. "And what else did they have to say about me?"

"Not too much more. Just that you were on leave for about four more months and as you started feeling better that you might go nosing around and get yourself into some trouble. That is where I come in. I am to tell the kids, and they will get a message to Victor and Sandy, then they would get ahold of you." Smitty was so matter-of-fact that Jake had to like him in spite of the fact he shared not-so-comfortable news.

"So, Smitty, why don't we—" As Jake began to talk, the front door opened and in walked Marcus. There was no missing him. He had a leader air about him. As he entered, a few of the older people gave a very slight nod of hi to him. A kind of respectful gesture for a kid. Marcus nodded back but did not stop or say a word to anyone in the room. He gave a quick glance around the room and noted that none of his kids were there. Jake thought to himself that this kid would make a great officer. He had great natural instincts and good skills. Marcus continued on down the hall to the doors past the bathroom. No one stopped him or even gave a thought to what he was doing. This must be a normal routine. Jake was taking note of all the little details. This kid was good, and Jake wanted to know as much about him and what he was up to as he could learn. Only God knew why. Jake laughed to himself. For sure, he himself had not a clue.

Jake motioned over to where Marcus was walking. "Smitty, what can you tell me about that kid there?"

"Marcus?" Smitty was puzzled; he thought that Jake of all people would have known him. "Maybe you do not remember him? You of all people should know all about him. You are a Singleton, right?"

It was like Jake was back in the chipless crowd. Here he was again in total confusion like he had not been since he left the shelter. "What does my being a Singleton have to do with my knowing about Marcus?"

As Smitty was getting ready to speak, there came a very loud noise from the back room down the hall. Crashing of pots and pans and who knows what else. Smitty got up, excused himself, and left to go and see what was going on. Jake could see that he was concerned but did not want to draw any more attention to the situation than had already been done.

This was Jake's chance to have another face-to-face with Marcus. Or so he thought. He was right behind Smitty, so when he opened the door, he should once again have had a chance to see Marcus. But as they opened the door, there were only pots and pans scattered across the floor. Not a kid in sight. "What a mess, Smitty. Want some help cleaning up?" Jake needed to get a better look at this room to see where the entrance or exit was located. Jake entered on in and began to pick up. Checking for marks on the floor. Looking for a false wall or even a false floor. And there it was. A pull-away part of the wall. Very well hidden, he would not have ever found it if he had not known what to look for. Jake finished helping Smitty and gathered up his coffee cup and coat and headed for the front door. "Hey, Smitty," Jake called out to him, and getting his attention, he continued, "Tell my friends hello for me, okay? Tell them I hope to see them soon." Smitty smiled and gave a nod to confirm that he understood what Jake was saying. "I really need a meeting and soon."

Jake knew how to run into Marcus now. All he had to do was wait until he left out of the secret back way and then follow him back to where he lived. This was going to be way too easy. Or so he thought.

Jake waited for several hours, the rest of the first day in fact. Then he got up early the next day and waited. Jake had his first opportunity to set up his meet with Marcus. He saw him go into the front door, so he sat out back to be there when he left. But he did not leave out the back but used the front door instead. The one time he was seen inside, he must have used the back entrance. This kid was turning out to be impossible. He never did anything the same way twice. Except for one thing. He was always where the young ones were. If Jake saw more than two young ones together, then Marcus would always be there shortly after. Now finally Marcus was setting a pattern. Jake could begin to close in.

Jake was amazed at all the work this group was able to do. Communications were all over the place. The handoffs were so slick and so fast that often Jake would know that it happened but rarely saw the real handoffs themselves. Almost a work of art.

So this would be it. Jake went to the coffee shop and sat in his usual seat drinking his coffee. There were three of the young ones in the room. Jake kept a perfect lookout. Eyes on the kids. Marcus was sure to be there because it was getting late, and it would be curfew soon.

The front and back doors opened at the very same time. Both slamming into the wall as they fully opened. Jake quickly took his eyes off the kids but for a quick second so as to see what the noise was. No one was there. The doors were open and swung freely before they pulled shut. Jake looked to the boys. Again they were gone. "Okay, now that is not funny." Jake got to his feet and began looking for the boys who had been there only a second ago.

"Jake, why don't you have a seat so we can talk?" It was Sandy. Just as the boys had gone missing, Sandy had appeared.

"Sandy, where have you been? I really needed to talk to you and Victor. I think I have found something God wants me to do." Jake was so happy to see Sandy. He had been alone, or so he had thought for so many days that he had begun to wonder if he really was a part of the Knowing.

"Victor and I got word that you needed to see us. But we had, or thought we had, a bigger problem." Sandy was smiling at Jake. "We had gotten word that there was a stalker. A chipped man who was following Marcus's young ones. You are lucky that it was me who found you and not Marcus. I do not think you would have liked his way of handling someone who scared his crew."

Jake could see how very serious this could be. If someone scared a member of his family, there could have been a full-out war. "Sandy, I did not mean to scare anyone. I was just trying to get to meet Marcus. I think I am supposed to get him and his kids off the streets and into families."

Sandy was shocked that Jake had an opinion about someone he did not even know. "Jake, I am not sure what you think you are needing to do, but I think you may be way off on this one." Sandy lowered her voice and leaned in so Jake could hear her better. "Jake, Marcus has done and is doing a great job of running these kids. I know that his age could throw you, but you need to know that he is able and does function as good as any adult in the group. He has about fifteen kids, and all of them are taken care of. They are family to him, Jake. And to think about trying to break them up would, in my mind, be an awful thing." Sandy looked over her shoulder to see that Smitty was now giving her a go sign. "Hey, Jake, why don't you come with me tonight and meet Marcus and the gang? I have to deliver some things to them, and you can help."

Okay, God, now what? Jake knew in his heart or as deep inside as he ever was about anything that he was here to help this group even if his help and Sandy's help were two different ideas. But this was an opportunity to get to see for himself just what it is that makes everyone else think that this is all okay. To use kids in such a dangerous way. The thought brought up more questions than answers.

"Okay, Sandy, but I will need a few minutes. I will be right back." Jake went to the bathroom and went into a stall. He pulled out his medallion from around his neck. Once again he was so very glad that His chip had been placed in it and not in himself. Only God could have pulled that off, and Jake knew that was a fact. He took out some foil. (Foil had become a part of his new emergency kit.) He placed a rather generous amount of foil around his medallion and sealed it tight. He did this several times. Mark had shown him how to do this a few days ago, and yet now it felt like it had been a lifetime. Using foil should stop the tracking of his chip. The hard part was that he needed his chip to be with him all the time, but he also needed to be able to go where he was needed without being tracked. And this is what worked. He thought anyway. He had never truly tested it out. His chip was sealed up and back under his shirt, and he was now ready to go anywhere. Jake reentered the room and saw that Sandy was ready to go. There were four large shopping bags full, sitting on top of the counter where she was now standing. The tops were rolled down, but Jake could guess that there would be food in them. He motioned to them. "Dinner?"

Sandy smiled at him. "Something like that." She motioned for him to take two, and she herself retrieved another two. They headed out to the street. "Jake, we need to take your car. It will be faster if you drive part of the way."

Take his car? Hmm. They were going that far? Jake had thought that the kids' hangout would have been really close to their current location. "Sandy, how far away are we going?"

"You will see." Sandy smiled and shut the car door. "You know, Jake, things can go bad fast on the streets lately. The security is as tight as it has ever been. So it is important that you of all people stay out of the main stream of things. We need you. But we need you as a chipped officer. Do you know what I mean?"

Jake started to say something to protest the fact that he needed to stay out of the activity on the street. He very much wanted to be a part of the Knowing. He really wanted to be able to make a difference. Sitting on the sideline was not what he thought he should be doing. "Sandy, I really—"

But Sandy interrupted him. "Jake, you do not know the streets yet. Yes, you spent some time on the streets, but things are different now. The rules are always changing, and so we must be willing and able to change along with them. With God's help, we have been able to stay ahead of things so far, but it is getting harder every day. The government is growing tired of our resistance to the new way, and they find reasons every day to take us off the street. We may need you someday, and so for now, you need to really stay out of the street affairs. Okay?"

Jake was not happy. At all. He wanted—no, he *needed* to feel like he was making a difference. And he did not want to wait for another day. "Sandy, this is hard. I want to go back to work for the Knowing. I feel so—" He could not find the right words. God knew his heart, but he had no idea how to express it.

Sandy tapped Jake on the arm to get his attention. "Park over there, under the tree."

Jake did as she had said. The streetlight overhead was broken. Perhaps with a little help from friends. The thought made Jake smile. They parked and got out of the car. Quietly pushing the doors shut. They each had their hands full with the sacks and began to walk down the street. Jake noted that Sandy was keeping an eye on everything. She was being extra careful. "So, Sandy, how long has Marcus been here?"

"The nest."

"What?"

"Marcus's place, it is called *the nest.*"

Sandy was letting Jake in on some more facts about Marcus's group. "They have been here for about a year or so, but they did not work for the Knowing until about a month or two ago. A man named Reggie had gathered several kids up and taught them about life on the streets. He helped them learn how to pick pockets, steal, and cheat. The kids had become really good at working the streets when Reggie had been relocated, sort of. That is when Marcus got the new position as the leader of the group. He was the oldest. But, Jake, you need to know that he may be a kid to us, but you have never seen leadership skills like he has. God-given skills. At first, we all thought that it would be only a matter of time before they would be caught and placed in the programs somewhere, but as time passed, they not only stayed together, but they grew as a family and were able to do things no one else could do. They moved things around the street. In and out of places. They would find out things by hanging around the park benches. After a while, they had proven to be such a vital asset to the Knowing that we could hardly do without them. Their ability to steal a wallet and then get it back to the person let us see who and what they were and what they were up to. Believe me, we all thought as you do now, but, Jake, they do a great job. And we need them."

Jake heard what Sandy was saying, but he also knew in his gut that this was way too dangerous to keep going on. "You know, Sandy, as good as the pony express was in the day. It really only lasted about a year. Then a better safer way came along."

Sandy stopped dead in her tracks. "Really? And that applies how?"

"Well, the pony express was made up of kids. Most were orphans from the street. They did a great job, but a lot of them were hurt or worse. They were soon replaced by better communications. Don't get me wrong, they had their time, but then things changed. All I am saying is that with things as crazy and getting crazier, this may need to change." They continued to walk in silence. Jake knew that Sandy did not understand how he felt about the danger these kids were in. How could she? He himself did not fully understand it either. But as God lived in him, he knew that he was right. These kids were not safe, and God wanted him to help them. What on earth would that even look like?

As they came to a back alley, Sandy and Jake turned to go down it. They did not go to a door but to a wall on the side of a building. Sandy leaned with her back to the wall and motioned for Jake to do the same. Sandy looked carefully to make sure that there was no one around to see what happened next. Sandy used her foot and tapped on the wall three times and then paused and then two more times. There was a clicking sound, and then a crack appeared in the wall. A section pulled in, and a shiny clean face peered out at them. In a loud voice, almost a scream, "Sandy is here." Followed by a lot of shhhing. And an "I am sorry" and a "let them in," Sandy and Jake entered into a very large and very dark room.

Jake heard a voice saying, "I think they have food." And an "Of course they do. Why else would they be here?" Followed by a "Hey, who is that with Sandy?" And an "Oh no, it is that man. And he is an officer." Jake could hear the fear in the voices, and it made his heart hurt to think he had caused it.

The lights came up, and a voice, Marcus's, called out, "Everyone, freeze."

Marcus was standing in the middle of the room with his hands raised. In a very calm and very quiet voice, he began to speak to everyone in the room. "Now I want all of you to think about what you are seeing right now. Who is here and who brought whom? Sandy and Victor are both here. Sandy brought Jake the officer. What do we know about Sandy? In spite of what we are seeing?"

One of the really young ones spoke first. "We know that Sandy and Victor are our friends and that they would not do anything to hurt us. Even if they did bring that really mean officer with them."

Victor laughed to himself but let out a coughing sound and was hard-pressed to not smile at that statement. The description of Jake being a really mean officer was priceless. "Everyone, this is Jake. He is a chipped officer on the outside, but he is like us on the inside. I will tell you all that Jake is my friend, and your friend also. He is one of the Knowing just like all of us."

"A chipped officer? No way." A young man. From the looks of him about the same age as Marcus was, looking at Victor and then to Sandy and back to Jake. "No way an officer could be a part of the Knowing."

Sandy and Victor simply stood there. They let Marcus be in charge of the situation. "Travis, knock it off. I mean it. You are making trouble where there does not have to be any." Marcus and Travis locked eyes. They stood for a while, looking at each other.

Jake watched this whole thing play out. Travis had his hands clenched ready to strike a blow, but it was Marcus that most impressed him. He was relaxed. He kept his voice low and steady. He did not look away nor did he look Travis in the eye. He simply dismissed the young man with his working on the plans for the rest of the night. "Everyone, listen up. Sandy and Jake have brought us dinner tonight. Everyone, to their chores. The sooner we get everything ready, the sooner we get to eat."

Smiles and happy answers rang out in the room. Then action took over conversation. The place was quick to turn from a big room to a dining room. Table and chairs put into place. Plates and cups all piled up on one end of the table. The four sacks were brought forth, and an excitement about the food to come was evident. One by one the boys came to the table. They each stood behind their chair and waited.

Jake could not believe that these were the same boys he had been watching the past few days. They were clean. They had clean clothing, hair, and shiny faces. Not looking at all like the kids on the street. Jake loved to see the happiness that this was bringing to very grateful children.

"What do you think we get?" one asked. Another expressed, "Who cares, it is food. It is always good."

Jake noted that all sets of eyes were on Marcus, except one. Travis.

Travis had walked off to the area by the wall where Jake and Sandy had entered. He was mad, and his body language had let everyone know it. He was leaning up against the wall. Not paying attention to the goings-on about dinner.

"Let's pray." All heads were bowed as Marcus said a prayer over the dinner as well as over the guests and the boys. God was given all the glory, and thanks was offered up. "Okay, now let us see what is in the sack." Marcus reached into the sack and pulled up a pile of sandwiches. Meat, cheese, and all the fixings of a really great meal. There were chips and small apples. It was great. Jake noted that there were two sandwiches left. Marcus put one wrapped in a napkin into his pocket. He took the other with an apple and walked over to where Travis was sulking.

Jake was keeping a distance but was keeping in earshot of where Marcus and Travis were talking.

"I am glad that you are keeping watch over the entrance. Good job." Marcus was handing Travis his food as he spoke.

"Yay, like this is doing a darn thing. I watch over the entrance while you let anyone who comes by get in. A chipped officer? Marcus, you are such a fool. These people do not care a thing about us. They would sell us out in a moment if the need came up." Travis was up straight. He was getting into Marcus's face.

"Travis, what on earth is wrong with you? We are so blessed, and all you can do is be angry. When you talk like this, you upset the others. For that matter, you upset me. You need to be more thankful and work on trusting." Marcus was still relaxed sounding and looking.

There it was. Jake could hear it in Marcus's voice. It was slight, but it was there, a tremble in his voice. Marcus was upset. He was not kidding when he had told Travis that he was. "Travis, we are a team. I need you to be a team player. Quit stirring things up."

Travis was not going to give this one up. He was mad at Marcus, and he was going to have the last word or else. Jake could see it even if Marcus could not. "So, O Mighty Big Marcus, what are you going to do if I don't?"

Marcus backed up a step. He did not say a word. He gave Travis a surrender kind of wave. He turned and walked away.

"Big man you are, Marcus. Way to step up. What can you do to me anyway?" Travis was fighting with himself. Marcus had moved on to handle other problems over by the table.

Jake took his chance to have a little chat with his new buddy Travis. "Travis, why don't you and me have us a little talk."

Jake had startled him. Travis did not know what to say. So he listened. "You know, Travis, I do not know Marcus very well, but I think I like him. And from what I can see, he is doing a lot of good. And from what I see of you is that you are making trouble. So what if you decided to be nice? Why not decide to be part of the answer and not part of the problem?"

That was the last straw. No chipped officer was going to talk to him like that. Travis was clever enough to know that this was not the right time. But this officer was going to go down. And Sandy and Victor, they with their officer, they can go with him too. "Whatever" was all that Travis said. He walked back to the wall where he had been standing and began to eat his dinner. All the while giving Jake a warning eye.

Jake followed over to where Marcus was. He was anxious to see how Marcus was after his encounter with Travis. Jake was amazed as he watched the way this fifteen-year-old made decisions. One to go one place tomorrow, another to do a job for someone else. On and on it went until all but one problem had been solved. There was a small boy who had been crying. At the urging of some other boys, he came forward. "So what is the problem?" Marcus was a good listener. As Jake continued to watch, he now knew why the other adults admired him so much. He had a real talent for leadership. The boy had explained that he had been late and that he had missed dinner.

He was sorry, he was sad, and he was hungry. "Is that all?" Marcus smiled at the boy as he knelt down so to be eye to eye with him. "In the future, try and be on time. It is too dangerous for you to be out late. And as for the dinner, we happen to have an extra one right here." Marcus reached into his pocket and gave the child his own dinner.

That just about blew Jake away. He might have shared his food but never given it all up. The boy hugged Marcus and ran back to where the other boys were watching the goings-on. "Sandy, could we add another boy to our family count? It seems I have miscounted. Oh, and another blanket too please."

As Marcus spoke, all attention had gone over to Sandy and Victor. Victor had given Sandy a hug and a kiss. A few of the boys were making noises and faces as to how weird that would be for them. Sandy smiled and blushed some. She confirmed to Marcus that another food order would be added and another blanket as well. Marcus got a blanket from a shelf and handed it to one of the boys nearby with orders to find its new home.

Marcus went to take care of some doings in another room, so Jake walked over to where Sandy and Victor were. "So what do you think now?" Sandy was looking at Jake with an "I told you so" sort of look.

"Like you said, Sandy, he is a good leader. But he is still young. That is a lot of responsibility for one his age." Really any age is what he was thinking. "Not to point out the obvious but he has a real problem with that kid Travis. I think perhaps he should be asked to leave."

Victor put his hands in the pockets and looked as uncomfortable as Jake had ever seen him. "Well, Jake, you are right, he is going to be a real problem. But it is one that cannot be solved by sending him away. It can never happen."

"Why not? He is older. And more than that, he is and is going to be a problem. Trust me, I know kids like him. I have seen this before. Angry, full of hate, and always trying to stir things up. Give me one good reason he should be allowed to stay?"

"Well, Jake," he said, "because he is Marcus's biological brother." There it was. In a nutshell, the problem in the room was a brother.

Wow. That answer rocked Jake back on his heels. Never in a million years would Jake have guessed that one. "What on earth happened? How could they be so different?"

The evening went on like clockwork. Jake, Victor, and Sandy more or less got in the way. They observed everything from talks about fears and nightmares as well as their hopes and dreams. Lights out and everyone in bed. Everyone but the guests and Marcus that is.

Victor was the one to bring up the really important happenings of the next few weeks and about how important the orders would be to give and then to get back in return. "Marcus, are you and the boys going to be up for this?" Victor was not questioning their abilities as much as he was their willingness to do what needed to be done.

Marcus looked down to the ground. Then back up at Victor. "They are all trained, they have been told what to expect and what you expect of them. I cannot think of another thing I can do to help." Marcus was tired. He was in need of some good sleep, and as Jake knew, he really needed something to eat.

"Okay, Marcus. I was just checking. Sandy and I will go first, and then Jake can leave after us. If that is okay with you?" The choice was his. To leave him with a chipped officer could be uncomfortable to say the least.

Marcus looked at Jake. If Victor and Sandy trusted him with the boys, he guessed he should too. "No problem for us if he is okay with it." Marcus reached for a flashlight and spoke as he walked away. "I need to do rounds. Jake, can you let them out and then sit tight while I check things out and make sure we are all secure?"

Jake nodded. Victor and Sandy smiled at each other. "He likes you, Jake. Be honored. He does not trust anyone too easily these days. Lots has happened. Thanks, Jake, for coming." Sandy was patting him on the back with a loving touch.

Victor was right close behind with a direct question for Jake. "So, Jake, what do you think of Marcus and his leadership skills now that you have seen him in action?"

"He is a great leader, but he does have one major flaw. He does not take care of himself. He gives away his food, his blankets so he is not warm, and gives up sleep in order to get things done. That is dangerous for any leader, especially one so young. You are only as strong as your weakest link. And if he is not careful, he will become that link."

Victor knew that Jake was right. Over time, he could see Marcus was wearing out. Now that Jake had mentioned it, he could see that Marcus had lost a lot of weight too.

"Thanks, Jake. I will have a talk with him. But I think I may know why God brought you into this. I think you may very well be Marcus's answer to prayer."

Marcus made his rounds. It took about thirty minutes. Jake had let Victor and Sandy out through the wall. He had gotten two glasses of water and was sitting at the table when Marcus came back. "Are you ready to go? I can let you out now."

"Not yet." Jake motioned for Marcus to have a seat at the table with him.

"Jake, could we do this some other time? I am really tired, and we get up early around here." Marcus was not wanting to be rude, but it had been a long day, and tomorrow was not looking any better.

"This will only take a minute. Come have a seat so we can talk." Marcus did as he had been asked. Man, this kid was a good kid. And still only a kid.

"What can I do for you, Jake?" He had taken his seat and was now in his leader mode again.

"Well, for starters, you need to eat this." Jake had put a breakfast bar in his pocket that morning and had not needed it. He was more than glad to share it with Marcus now.

Marcus looked at it and declined the offer. "No, you keep it. You may need it later."

Jake smiled. "No, really, you should eat this now. You did not get any dinner."

"I am not hungry. I would rather just go to bed." Marcus looked down and away from Jake.

That was another problem Marcus was going to have. He did not lie very well. "Liar." Jake placed the bar into Marcus's hand. "And for the record, you really are a bad liar, you know. So now eat this and have some water and get to bed, so I can go."

Marcus was too tired to argue, so he took the bar and did as Jake had said. He let Jake out and went to do rounds one last time.

*****

Jake got to his car. He had his badge so he could be out after curfew. He was going home when he remembered his foil needed to be removed from his chip so he was safe on the street. Jake was in two worlds now. How weird for this to be his life now. He really liked Marcus. He was a good kid. But still just a kid. Jake knew it was not going to be popular, but he still believed that God had another, safer, get-to-be-a-kid plan for Marcus.

There had been talk all night of a big plan getting ready to come down. They all acted like Jake had known about it. He had not had time to ask with so much going on, but he might have a chance in the morning. Jake pulled into a parking lot of a food store and then went inside to shop. He had such a different world than the rest of the Knowing. He could come and go as they could not. He needed to be more grateful. Jake found himself asking, "What would Marcus do?" That kid influenced him in one meeting. Victor was right, he was an awesome kid and would make a great adult if he lived that long.

Jake bought four boxes of breakfast bars. They would taste good and had vitamins in them. He thought he could drop them off tomorrow, the kids would love them, and they would be good for them too. Jake was happy inside. He was back. He had a purpose. To help Marcus. Who would have guessed that one—or that he would be happy about it?

CHAPTER 21

Jake had a restless night sleep. He was so excited to have a call on his life. He was going to be able to make a difference. He was not really sure how just yet, but he knew that God would tell him eventually.

Mark had told him to pray and to read his Bible. He was trying to remember how Victor and the other men used to do it at the farm. "Wow, that was a long time ago," Jake was saying to himself as he got dressed. It was a little early, but he was excited to see the kids again and to bring them some extra food.

Jake finished getting ready and grabbed his keys when he noticed that the light on his answering machine was blinking. He listened to it. It was from his mom. She was reminding him that today was Thursday and that all the family would be together for the first time in a long time. "Oh man. Today is Thursday. I forgot. Thank God she reminded me." Jake loved his family a lot. Always had, but now somehow things were different. He really wanted to see them. To get to know them better. Bigger than that, he now wanted them to get to know Jesus and to go to heaven. He stopped. He prayed. "Oh, God, I really want them to go to heaven. More than that, God, I need them to go to heaven. And to know how great it is to know You. Help, God. I do not know what to do about my family. Or about how I miss my friends from the Knowing. Or what it is You want me to do with Marcus and his kids. I have the feeling You want them off the street and into homes, but then again, everyone thinks they are doing great. Please let me know what to do? Amen."

Jake locked the door of his apartment and decided that it was so early he would skip the coffee shop and go straight to the nest.

He could take the bars he bought last night to them. Jake thought he would do like Sandy had him do the night before. He would park the car and then walk in a few blocks to the nest. No harm in first driving past the front of the building and getting a look at it before he parked. As Jake was coming up the road, he could see from a great distance away that there were flashing officer lights. As he drove, it became all too clear that the cars, five of them, were parked in front of the nest. "Oh, dear God. No. How could this be? The kids. God, no." Jake's mind was racing. How could this happen? Perhaps the foil over his chip was not thick enough. Was he followed? No, he would have noticed someone following. There was no way this was happening. Jake passed the place and tried to view what was going on. He did not see any kids. Thank God. Okay, now he would park the car and walk in. That would work. So that is what he did.

Jake was almost half a block from the nest when he saw a dirty little face peer out from behind a bush at him. The kid was gone before he could get there to talk to him. Okay, what Jake knew for now was that the kids must be okay and had somehow not been found in the nest. But what to do now? Jake's heart was pounding. He was walking fast down the street toward the nest. He had his eyes fixed on the building and the activity when someone grabbed him by the arm and spun him into another direction and then into a doorway. "What the?"

"Jake, will you be quiet!" It was Mark. "Jake, what a mess. What on earth is going on? Do you know anything about this?"

Jake answered, "What would make you think anything like that?"

"Well, you are here, aren't you? So why are you here?" Mark was needing an answer. A fast version.

Jake came back with attitude, "What do you think I am doing here?"

Mark was keeping watch on the street down from where they were at. "I talked to one of the kids. He said that someone from the government department had notified them that a group of kids were living there. They thought it was an officer."

"And you all think it was me?" Jake was so tired of not being trusted. What did he have to do to prove his loyalty?

Mark took another quick look at Jake. He could tell that he was telling the truth, but to get the others to believe it was going to be a whole other thing. "So if you are not the one, then what are you doing down here?"

Jake stumbled over the words. "Well, if you need to know, I was going to visit the kids and bring them some breakfast bars. But when I got here, this is what I found. Do you know what happened when they got there?"

"No. I could not get very close. They said it was a crime scene." Mark was frustrated too.

Jake reached into his pocket and pulled out his badge. He was getting ready to walk away when Mark grabbed his arm again to stop him. "What do you think you are doing?" Jake pulled away from his grip but kept eye contact with Mark.

"They may not let a student get close to the scene, but they will let an officer." Jake smiled and placed his badge in his pant band like the other officers had theirs and walked toward the now empty nest.

"Hey, is that you, Singleton?" An officer from the group came over to greet Jake as he walked up. "I did not expect to see you for a few more weeks. How goes the hero life? What an undercover experience you must have had. Tell me, was it as awful as we heard? Were they all as bad as the ones around here?"

Jake did not know what to say or to think. This was his old life. He used to feel exactly the same way. Where had that idea come from? Not from experience, that was for sure. "Well, you know how it is, best to go on past the old news and move on. By the way, what's all the fuss?" Jake gave a nod toward the nest.

"Well, like you know, these people live like vermin. They just hit and then move on. We had it on good report that there was a whole group of the really bad ones here and that they would be here this morning, but as you can see, they got away." The officer was not happy about the results of this outing. "But one of these days, we are going to catch and chip every single one of them."

To Jake, that used to sound like a good idea; but now, it was a threat toward some of his own. "Do you think I could go in and take a look around?"

"Sure. Knock your socks off. The place is clean. Not even a piece of paper left to give us a clue. Just lock up after, okay?" With that, the officer gave the all clear signal. There was a buzz of movement, and then everyone was leaving.

Jake looked in. He could not believe how very good the kids cleaned things up, not to mention how fast they did it. Jake did not need long to look. One quick trip around the room and then out the door he was going when he ran smack into Travis. "Woo. What are you doing here?" Jake was careful not to say Travis's name out loud.

"Hey, Jake, get away from my informant." The officer he had been talking to earlier was still there and coming over to where Jake and Travis were standing.

Travis took this as his chance to get away, and he took off before Jake could even react.

"Man oh man, Jake. I am so glad that one is on our side. I sure would not want to try and control him." The officer was leaving for good this time.

Jake had hoped that Mark had seen what he did. But as he looked over to see if he had, Victor, Marcus, and Mark were watching him. Mark knew what he was doing, but the looks on Victor's and Marcus's face was one of hurt and distrust. *Oh no*, Jake was saying to himself, *this must look awful to them.* He needed to explain. He began walking over to where they were standing. He so must look like an officer from the look of fear on Marcus's face. He looked down and pulled his badge off and placed it into his pocket again. When he looked up, he only saw two. Victor and Mark. No Marcus. The one he really wanted to talk to was gone. Just like that, and in a flash, he was gone. Jake made a move as to look for Marcus when Victor took a step in front of him. "Look, Victor, it is not like it looks. Trust me. I did not do this."

Victor did not move but stood his ground. "You and I both know that you did not do this, but you need to leave Marcus alone. You are not his friend yet, and so he can't trust you like we can."

Jake was not so easily put off. "Victor, I need to explain things to him. He needs to know that not everyone in the chipped world is out to get him."

Victor persisted. "Why do you care so much about this? I do not see how this even involves you. These kids were here way before you and will most likely be here after you go on with your life. Why do you think they are any of your business?"

Mark was as interested in the answer as Victor could ever be. So both men stood looking at Jake. It was evident to both of them that Jake had an answer but was unsure as to how to say it. As the three of them stood quiet, a very young boy of the nest came running up to talk to Victor.

"Hey, Victor, sorry to bother you, but I have a message from Marcus." The boy was on a mission and was not put off by all the things that had happened this morning.

Victor knelt down so that he was eye level with the boy. "Hey, Jimmy, what is the message?"

Jimmy looked at Mark and Jake and then back at Victor with a questioning look about talking in front of them.

"It is okay. You can tell me with them here. I will vouch for them." Victor had a relaxed way of speaking with Jimmy, and that helped.

"Okay then. If you are sure." Jimmy, in a lower voice, recited the message; it sounded as if it might be word for word. "Marcus said to say that you should please remember that we have four more boys than last count. I am supposed to say *please*. I said that, right? Yes, I did. And he said to say that the crack in the foundation was found and taken care of. Okay, so you understand that part, right? 'Cause I don't, and Marcus said that was okay since you would." Jimmy was smiling. He was so proud of himself having done the job.

Jake interrupted the message with a question, "Jimmy, where is Marcus? I need to talk to him."

Jimmy made a face and turned his back to Jake. "I am not supposed to talk to you."

"Really? Why not?" Jake had knelt down beside Victor.

"'Cause Marcus says that you are bad. Because he would like you as a friend, and he said that he has bad taste in picking friends. So I am not to talk to you." Jimmy crossed his arms. Both Victor and Mark had to stifle their laughter. The look on Jake's face was priceless.

Mark patted Jake on the back. "Sounds to me, little brother, like you have a problem. Hey, Jimmy, is Marcus safe in the nest?"

Jimmy was stuck on the statement "little brother." "Mark, is Jake really your little brother?" His eyes were wide, and his face grew excited. "I bet Marcus would let me talk to Jake if he knew you were brothers. Don't you think?"

Victor jumped in, "We need to cut this short. The street is not the place for this. Jimmy, you go on and tell Marcus that I got the message. Tell him that I will see him at the nest tonight and that Mark will be the only one coming with me. Got that?"

Jake started to protest, but Victor raised his hand to stop him. Jake complied. Mark was shocked to see that Jake would give in so quickly. Ever since Jake had returned, there had been evidence of the change, but it still surprised him every time.

Jimmy ran off down the street and disappeared into a hedge by the sidewalk.

Victor and Jake both stood up now eye to eye with Mark. Jake was the first to break the silence. "Victor, I need to go with you tonight and to see Marcus. Mark, tell him."

Mark blinked at the request—or you could say *demand*. "Jake, I am not sure that is a good idea. Perhaps in time, but I think things are a little tense right now. Anyway, I am not sure you understand how important these kids are to the Knowing. Not to mention that it's clear from hearing you lately that you think the kids should not be here and should not be doing the things that they do."

Mark was right. That is exactly how he felt, but Jake still felt like Marcus was in his life because God had a plan, and that plan included him being a help to Marcus's life.

Victor chimed in with an agreement with Mark. Jake was outnumbered, so he listened to Mark and Victor make plans for the evening. The three men parted and would talk again another day.

As Mark was leaving, he turned to Jake. "See you tonight. Do you want to meet first and go together?"

Jake was once again reminded of the family dinner. What was wrong with him? He kept forgetting about the family plans, he really was excited to be a part of. "That would be great, Mark. Why not meet me at my apartment and we can go from there." This could so work. Perhaps if he had some alone time with Mark, he could convince him take him to the nest when he went. "See you at five?"

Mark agreed, and they went their own ways.

It was still early in the day. Mark would head on to school or whatever it was he did, but Jake really did not have anything to do. So he decided to go over to the park and then to the coffee shop and see if he could find Marcus or one of the kids.

Jake walked to the park and found a seat on a bench at one end of the park. From where he was sitting, he could see almost the whole area without moving his head. There it was, out of the corner of his eye, a movement at the tree edge. Yes, he was right, the kids were here at the park. He continued to watch, and one by one, he spotted and watched each of the kid workers. It was the young ones from the nest, and that meant that Marcus would be somewhere close. Somewhere he could see all of them. He watched for the longest time, and then a pattern showed itself. All of the kids would look to the right of Jake. Marcus had to be somewhere in that area. He was sure of it. In fact, so sure that he got up and began to circle around behind the area he thought he would find Marcus in.

As Jake came around a corner, there he was. Marcus was beside a tree acting bored. If he had not been looking for it, he would have never have guessed that Marcus was ordering at least seven boys in the park around. Marcus was using some kind of hand signals. He had some of the kids listening to the people talking on the benches. Some were hanging around people on the phones. While others were on the playground talking to the other kids about their parents. It was unreal how good this kid was at working a team. In fact, Jake could not think of a single adult he knew that could keep this straight and as organized as Marcus was. Jake walked up behind him. "Marcus." Jake saw him jump with hearing his name, but he did not turn around or take his eyes off the boys. "Marcus, I need to talk to you." Marcus did not move but kept his signals to the boys going. "Marcus, did you hear me? I need to talk to you."

"Get away from me. I need to watch the boys." Marcus continued with the signals.

"Call the boys back. I need to talk to you and explain." Jake was getting angry because he could not control this kid he so wanted to control. Only thing he could think to do was to resort to a threat. "Okay, here is the deal, Marcus. Call the boys back to the nest now and talk to me, or I am going to handcuff you and carry you out away from here, and then you will not be able to watch them at all."

Marcus stiffened and clenched his fists. He signaled the boys who did as they were told but were questioning as to why their jobs were being cut short. They had just gotten started and now were being sent home. As they looked over to where Marcus was standing, they could see that Jake had joined Marcus and that he must have brought information about aborting the job. They trusted Marcus, so off they went. Marcus did not turn around but, with a very slow and level voice, asked Jake what he wanted.

"Marcus, I didn't tell anyone about the nest." Jake could not prove it but hoped to at least explain why he was coming out of the nest this morning acting like a police officer.

"I know you didn't, Jake. Now go away." Marcus started to walk away, still with his back to Jake. Marcus never expected Jake to continue after him.

Jake took hold of him and turned him around so they could be face-to-face. As Marcus spun around, Jake was taken aback by two things. First of all, Marcus's face was bruised, and second, as he was turned around, he winced and grabbed his side in pain. "Go away, Jake, and leave me alone."

Marcus tried to pull away, but Jake held on. "What happened to you, and what do you mean you know it was not me?"

"Jake, don't worry. I took care of it." Marcus really needed Jake to stay out of this. It was hard enough without having someone adding to his grief.

"What do you mean you took care of it? How badly are you hurt? Who did this to you?" This was more than a little problem of Marcus not trusting Jake but had moved on to a matter of Marcus needing help. Now. "Marcus, talk to me."

Marcus stood with his eyes fixed on Jake. He did not make a move or a sound but stood there with a look of boredom. Jake could not read his body language. This kid was so good on so many levels.

As they stood there in the park, Jake heard his name from his other world being called out. "Jacob. What are you doing with this kid?" It was an old friend he had not seen since before his undercover assignment.

"Hey, Max." Jake was quick to let go of Marcus. He did not want Max to think that Marcus was in trouble. "Oh, this kid and I were just having a talk about how clumsy he has been to get such a bruised face and all." Max was looking at Marcus with an "ouch, that looks like it could hurt" sort of look when Marcus stepped back and then headed out of the park at a fast rate.

"Well, Jacob, I think he got the message. Look at him go." He was laughing at the sight of the kid running away.

Jake's chest was so tight. He felt an inner ache like he had never felt before. This young man was in pain, and he was in trouble. He needed to do something, but what? Jake felt like God was telling him to help Marcus, but he would not even know where to start. Even if Marcus were to let him. Jake sent up a prayer. Only God could fix this mess.

"Hey, Jacob, a bunch of us are getting together at my house tonight, want to come?" Max had been a good friend. Jake wanted more than anything to tell him about his new life, but this was not the time, and he knew it. Jake also knew that there would be a time and he would get to it. But not now.

"Max, I would love to, but I have family night tonight. You know how important they are to the Singletons. But another time real soon would be great." Jake looked at his watch and realized he was going to be late meeting Mark. "Max, I have got to go. I will talk to you soon, okay?" They parted ways, and Jake headed in the direction that Marcus had walked. There was no sign of him. He was gone.

CHAPTER 22

Jake went to his apartment. Mark was already there. He was waiting out in the hall. "Glad you decided to show up."

Jake sighed and pushed past Mark and went into his apartment. Mark followed and shut the door behind him. "So what's got you so upset?" Mark was sitting on the side of Jake's couch looking clueless to the happenings of the day.

"Mark, are you totally out of touch as to what has happened today?" Jake was changing his shirt and getting ready to go to the family dinner.

"Jake, I don't think that things are really that bad. No one got hurt, and the kids are all safe. Marcus said that they had found who leaked the information, and it had been taken care of. So what is your problem?" Mark was looking so calm. He had peace, and for the life of himself, Jake could not muster any up for himself.

"Have you seen Marcus today?" Jake stopped what he was doing and looked to see Mark's response. There was no sign of Mark knowing what Jake was talking about.

"No, why?" Mark was now fully engaged in what Jake was saying.

"Well, I did, and he looks awful. Someone beat on him bad. His face is messed up, and from the way he was holding his side, I think he is hurt even more." Jake could have kicked himself for letting Marcus get away. At least he was walking, but he might have needed a doctor. "Mark, I know that after the family dinner, you and Victor are going over to the nest. I really need to go. I think Marcus needs my help."

Mark was still shocked to see this new brother of his. He was truly thinking of people other than himself. It was strange to Mark, but he was getting it. "Jake, let me talk to Victor. Maybe tomorrow would be better though?"

"Mark, I know that I need to go tonight. I cannot tell you how, but I can make a difference with this kid. So please ask Victor. Please convince him that I need to go too."

Jake was almost pleading. That was a new side of Jake also. "Okay, I will see what I can do. But for now, let's get to dinner before we are late. Not to mention I am super hungry. I love Mom's cooking." With great big smiles, the men set off for their parents' home.

*****

Jake and Mark were the last two to arrive. Everyone was glad to see them. They had taken Jake's car; that way there would be no hassle about Mark's riding a bike. Not to mention they were more than likely to leave together and give Jake another chance to convince Mark he should take Jake to the nest tonight.

The night at the family house was great. Their two older brothers and their sister were so excited to see them. But Jake was the center of attention. It was good to be there together, but it was not at all what Jake had dreamed it would be. In the beginning of his going undercover, he was going to be a hero by taking out the Knowing group. All of the Knowing were to have been chipped and put into in appropriate locations. But this was not the way Jake had planned it. No, this was better. He had found God. He had found that he had a brother that had also found God. That was good. But it needed to be better. His other brothers and sister needed to know God too. The five of them had been talking over all of Jacob's adventures when Mom and Dad entered the room carrying a big cake with "Congratulations Jacob" on it. Jake could hardly speak. He was so touched by the love his family had for him. He was overwhelmed also by the memories of all the times he had not appreciated the love they had shown him. Thoughts came crashing through his mind of all the times he had been so mean when they had wanted to be a part of his life and he was offended by them.

Jake hurried across the room to greet and be greeted by his parents. "Mom, Dad, I am so happy to see you. Thanks for the cake. You didn't need to, but thank you so much."

Jake hugged his mom and went to shake his dad's hand but found his dad throwing his arms around him in one great big hug. "Welcome home, son. We are so proud of you." Jake could not recall a time when his dad had said he was proud of him, but this was one of the best gifts he could have ever gotten. It occurred to Jake that they had not changed but he had. Only God could have done this!

"Son, we were so worried about you. And to think you were in a chipless shelter right here in town. From the way you looked when you got back, I am not sure we would have recognized you." Jake's mom had hugged on him and was so glad to have all her family together once again. She was beaming with happiness. Their dad was too.

Jake's sister, Sally, was finishing her dinner when she decided that it was time to talk family business with Jake. "So, Jacob, did you get a call from the department about coming back to work early?"

"No, Sally. Why would they want me back now?" Jake was watching her as she finished eating the last bite of food.

"Well, they think you might be able to help them out with a new family that came to town. The family used to be a part of the chipless, and now that they have 'seen the light as it were,' the department needs someone to get information from them. There was talk that you might be the best one for the job since you know their lifestyle and all." Sally put another bite into her mouth, but it was Jake who choked on his food right in the middle of her talking.

Mark reached over and put his hand on Jake's shoulder, tightly squeezing. He was sending a message to Jake to get it under control. This information was good. The Knowing could be warned of the coming disaster. But could it be stopped? "So, Sally?" Mark was giving Jake time to pull it together. "Did the family say exactly what it was they wanted to tell?"

Sally shrugged her shoulders. "Well, they said that the people on what they called the farms needed some information. And that they did not know the truth about how good life as a chipped family could be. Also, that they had been told awful things about what would happen if they had been caught and chipped. They said they felt sorry for the kids especially. There was no education and no medical help for them. Why, it is dreadful, Jacob, did you feel the same way about what you saw?"

Okay, so here it was. The real question of the night was, to lie or not to lie? As a person of faith, Jake knew that he needed to tell the truth. But as a brother with a new life, the truth could cause so many problems that Jake was afraid to even imagine it. "Well, Sally, to tell you the truth—" Out of nowhere, a glass of water came flying onto the table. Jake's mom had been filling the glasses when one slipped out of her hand and fell to the table spilling water all over. They all jumped up to help clean it up. The subject was changed, and Jake was saved from his dilemma. All Jake could think was THANK YOU, GOD!

The rest of the evening went rather well. Jake and Mark did not get any more information about the family from the farm, but they did not get any more questions either. The two older brothers and Sally left first, then it would be Jake's and Mark's turn to go. But Jake's mom wanted to talk with Jake. "Jacob, are you really all right? I know that your head was hurt and that things have been tough on you trying to get back into your life again."

Jake loved his mom so much. He had always felt special here at home, but somehow things were better. He knew his mom was the same, but things felt different, more accepting, like family but more. "Mom, I am fine. Mark here has been helping me get back into the swing of things. I have only a few more months off, and I feel I will be ready to get back to work." He was hoping so anyway. She gave him a big hug and walked Jake and Mark to the door.

Their dad and mom walked them out to Jake's car. Dad addressed both the sons.

"Boys, if you need anything, and I mean anything, you know where to come, right?" Their dad was as direct as he had ever been.

Jake thought that was an odd thing for him to say, but it was nice at the same time. Both men confirmed that they had heard and understood what he had said, and they said goodnight and headed on their way.

Jake was driving away from the house. "So where do we go from here, and what do we do with the information we have about the family from the farm?"

CHAPTER 23

What to do? Mark had been told to come alone to the nest, but given the new information they had heard at the family dinner, Mark decided that he should take Jake with him. They parked several blocks away and came in down dark roads and even passed through a few doors to get to this new nest. Mark had explained that Marcus had moved the boys to the most secure nest they had. He had done it right after Jake had visited the last nest. Marcus was always extra careful with the boys. Lately, being extra careful had paid off.

Mark and Jake arrived before Victor. Mark went on in while Jake hung back by the false wall they had entered through. What a sight to behold. All the boys were studying. They had notebooks out and were writing sentences as Marcus was dictating to them. Marcus was walking around helping where help was needed. He called out to one of the boys to read back what had been read to them. "Okay, now I want all of you to do times tables by your age. If you are eight, then do eights and so on. Okay. Now go." Marcus took a seat and was reading a book. He had still not seen Mark. No one had.

As Jake was waiting back by the wall, it gave way, and Victor entered. "Jake, what are you doing here?"

"I am waiting for you." Jake stepped aside to let Victor in. From the look on Victors face, Jake knew he was not happy.

The wall made a noise, and all the boys came running. They had question after question for Mark. "Is Jake really your brother?" "Did you bring us any food?" "Is anyone else coming?" "Shh. Boys." Mark was trying to calm things down when Marcus gave out a very loud sharp call to order.

The boys froze. "Everyone get back to your study." The boys looked at Marcus with longing to visit with Mark. "All right, study is over for the night, but keep it down." The boys started to celebrate but at once lowered the noise level.

Marcus acknowledged Mark and then looked over to see Victor then turned and started to walk away when he saw Jake. Victor called out to Marcus. "You stop right there, young man. I need to have a word with you." Marcus stopped walking. The boys were speechless. They had never heard Victor talk to anyone like this, and no one ever talked to Marcus like that. (Except for Travis, that is.) Victor looked around the room. "Carry on, boys. Marcus and I are going to have a little chat, that's all."

The boys went about their business but all the while keeping an eye on the adults.

"Marcus, let's take this over there." Victor motioned over to a corner that was a little more private. Victor had not seen Marcus's face yet, and Jake was waiting for that to happen. There it was. Victor saw what Jake had seen earlier.

Victor's reaction was not what Jake thought it would be. "Where is Travis?"

Marcus looked down at the ground and turned his back to Victor. Marcus did not need words to answer. His body language gave his answer away.

"Marcus, where is Travis?" Victor was direct, but it was kind at the same time. It was clear that he was not going to go away without knowing the truth about what had happened.

Marcus stood up straight and set his shoulders. He turned to face Victor. It was obvious that he had made one of the hardest decisions he had ever made. "He cannot be here any longer. We can't trust him. I did not have to ask him to leave. He did not want to be a part of this life anymore. He thinks that life with the chipped would be a better one. And for him, perhaps he is right. I couldn't stop him. He had made up his mind." Marcus was trying to be strong, but he dropped his head and once again looked away.

"Okay, I get that part. Do you know why he turned the nest in?" Victor thought he knew but was not completely sure.

Victor was being very careful as he asked the questions. This kid was at a point of breaking. He had done such a great job with all of the boys, but his own brother was someone who risked the whole group. Victor knew that even a full grown man would have trouble with this kind of pressure.

"Your guess is as good as mine. I tried to talk to him. Well, let's just say that did not turn out so good." Marcus kept his voice low and his back to Victor.

"Speaking of that, are you okay?" Victor had walked closer so that he was standing right behind Marcus and was almost talking in his ear.

Marcus did not answer this time but nodded his head yes.

Jake had moved on into the room and was close to Victor and Marcus now. He was about to bring up the fact that he thought that Marcus had been hurt more than his face when the wall door opened and in came Sandy.

Sandy was carrying large sacks of food. You could smell it. And it smelled great. "So, what is up?" Sandy asked. There were two things she noted. First, the room was really quiet even with food in hand. Bringing food alone could bring about a buzz from the boys. Second, the men all looked at her and then looked away. Everyone that is but Marcus, he did not look at her at all. "So what happened? What is wrong?" She moved on into the room and placed the food on a table. She walked over to where Victor, Marcus, Mark, and now Jake were standing.

Mark was the one to answer her. "Sandy, there are so many things wrong I don't have a clue where to start."

"So let's start from the beginning. Why are all of you here?" Last she had heard, it would be only Victor and Mark. And they were all going to talk about Jake.

Mark jumped in to tell about how they had been talking at dinner. "Sally, my sister, said that there was a family who had left a Knowing farm around here. Anyway, she said that they were going to tell the secrets they knew so they could help the people who had been misled like them. She thought they were going to ask Jake to talk to them so they could get better answers."

Victor, Sandy, and Marcus all looked at Jake. "I don't know anything more than you just heard." Jake wished he had more information.

For the first time, Sandy saw Marcus's face. She let out a gasp and reached out to touch him. He pulled away like she was going to hit him. "Honey, what happened?"

Jake spoke up again. "I think that Travis is what happened."

This was all too much for Marcus. He wanted to be left alone. He needed some time to think about all the things that had happened this last week. Being found out by government officers would be one thing, but being sold out by a brother was a whole different story. Could any of them ever understand how this felt? "Sandy. Please, we need to figure out what we are going to do about that family. Victor, do you think that the nests are okay? Should I move the boys tonight?" Marcus needed to change the direction of this conversation.

That was a first. Marcus was not usually one to ask advice. He was not as sure of himself as he had been. Victor could hear it in his voice even if the others didn't. Victor looked up and saw from Jake's look that he had heard the same self-doubt. It could be a dangerous thing for a leader to not be confident of themselves. Second-guessing could cost time, and sometimes that time could cost dearly.

Sandy might have been put off for now about Marcus's wounds, but it was not over with, and Victor knew it. Marcus was not out of the woods with her yet. That was one of the things that made Victor love his wife more each day. She had great timing, and she knew how to help people and save their dignity too. Victor should know. She used it on him all the time.

They talked about the things they thought that they could control. They needed more information, and everyone agreed that they should be careful, but that for now, the nest should be safe. Dinner was served and cleaned up. It was time for them all to bed down for the night, but Sandy was not done.

Sandy had kept an eye on Marcus the whole night not letting him out of her sight for a second. He had eaten nothing and drank very little of the juice they had. He guarded his left side as he worked with the boys getting things in order and bedding everyone down for the night. She and Victor had exchanged looks to each other more than once in the evening seeing that their friend was in need of help. The hard part about this situation was that the trouble had come from within the family and not from outsiders.

There had been a Bible reading. Everyone was pleased when it was Mark who did the honors of reading to them. "I like it when Mark reads. He makes it sound different and exciting when he does it." This was a statement from one of the boys.

Jake was not at all surprised to hear that Mark had been here more than once reading and working with the boys. He was a good man, and he loved kids.

"Okay, lights out," Marcus announced as he turned the lights down but never completely out. Many of the boys had bad times already in their short lives. Sleeping with the lights low somehow made it feel safer even if it was a false security. "And I think it is a good time for you to go too." Marcus was addressing all the adults. They looked at him, and although they wished he had asked them to stay, they were impressed at his ability to bounce back and pull things together.

Everyone, but Jake, that was. "I am not going. I am staying the night."

Marcus raised his voice. "No, I don't want him here." He was trying then to cover what he had said. "I mean that today has been a long one and that everyone should go home now." He paused. "Victor, please make him go. Please."

Victor looked over at Jake, who was standing firm on his decision. "Victor, it is not going to happen. I am staying. Mark, here's the keys to my car. I will see you in the morning."

"Well, Marcus, it looks like you have a guest for the night. You will be fine." Victor was not going to get into the middle of this budding friendship. Marcus needed the help. Jake needed to be of help. Win-win situation is the way he saw it. But when he looked at Marcus and Jake, he almost laughed out loud at the looks on their faces. No happy looks on either of them.

Sandy interrupted the conversation. "Jake, could I speak to you please?" She motioned for Jake to meet her over where she had now moved. She wanted a private conversation with him. "Jake, do you know what you are doing?" Sandy needed Jake to know how hard this could get. He needed to be up for the long haul. This was not going to be a quick project.

"Sandy, you and I both know that Marcus is getting in way over his head for anyone, much less a kid. I know that he has done a great job, but, Sandy, look at him. He is worn-out. He needs a break."

"Jake, we know. But what you don't understand is that this is not the time. We have three really big projects for the boys to do. Then we are planning to take them all, Marcus too, out to one of the farms for a time." Sandy needed Jake to understand that there was really no other choice. Time was the problem, not them not understanding that Marcus was wearing out.

"Okay, so what do you want me to do? I want to help, but it looks like that sounds easier than it might be." Jake was looking over to Victor and Marcus, who were still deep in conversation about Jake's staying. Victor must have won because Marcus picked up a flashlight and went to do rounds and check the lockup of the nest.

"We are good for now, but do you think Marcus needs a doctor to look at him?" Sandy was not so concerned about his face, but the way he held his side worried her.

Jake looked in the direction that Marcus had gone. "Sandy, I am not sure, but I think one more change in his routine might make things worse. I am going to stay the night. If anything comes up, I will send a runner and get you. Okay? I think that if I get him to eat and drink something and have him rest, he will be good as new."

Sandy liked Jake's positive thinking. Perhaps he was right, but either way, she was glad to see that Jake was onboard. She had noticed Marcus's not eating and had a plan. "Okay then, if you are sure. I put an extra sandwich over on the counter, some juice too. Good luck. I really hope it works out. It would be good for Marcus to have your help."

Jake saw the others out. He closed up the area by the wall and put some tin cans by the opening. That way if anyone did come in, they would all hear it.

When Jake came back into the main room, he was shocked by the fact that Marcus was already back. There were two old over-stuffed armchairs in the main room, and Marcus had sat down in one of them. He had some papers in hand and was looking them over. As Jake came into view, Marcus only looked up and then went on with his reading. Jake did not say a word but went into the kitchen and got the things Sandy had left. Then he went back and had a seat in the other chair. Marcus did not look up at him. Jake handed him the sandwich first. "Here, eat this."

Marcus looked at the food and did not take it. "I am not hungry."

"I did not ask you if you are hungry, but I said you should eat it." Jake did not back down.

"I guess if I don't do what you say, you will not stop bugging me so I can go over the plans for tomorrow." Marcus still did not take the food.

Jake smiled and then made note to relax, both his body language and his speech. "That is right on so many levels." When he handed him the food, he also gave him the glass of juice.

Marcus's hands were full, and the papers he had fell to his lap and slipped to the floor, so Jake picked them up. Marcus overreacted to Jake having the papers and almost leaped over to take them back. Jake pulled them away from him. "Would you please relax? I will give them back. I was simply taking a look at what we are going to be doing tomorrow."

"We?" Marcus was not at all happy about the sound of this. "Jake, you cannot come with us. It would be too dangerous, and besides that, you would distract the boys while they worked."

There was a noise from one of the boys down the hall. They were calling out to Marcus for some help. Jake got up and put the papers on the chair. "I'll get this. You eat. I will be right back." Jake got up and went to find the boy in need.

It was one of the younger ones who had a bad dream. He wanted to tell Marcus because he always made it better, but Jake was able to persuade him that he would be able to do the same and that he promised to tell Marcus about it.

When Jake returned to the chairs, he found Marcus with sandwich in one hand and papers in the other. At least he was eating. "Hey, Marcus, while I am up, I think I will do rounds. If that's okay with you?" Marcus nodded his head yes and kept on reading and eating too. Jake smiled.

After doing the rounds and making sure the boys were all okay, Jake went to have a talk with Marcus. He paused before sitting back down. "Dear Lord, help me help this kid. Only You can make good out of all of this. I do not know where You want me to start, so I am asking for Your help. We all really need You and now." Jake muttered an amen. He went in and took a seat.

Jake noticed that all the food and all the juice was gone. Good start. He waited for Marcus to take a break from his reading and look up at him. He needed to go slow, but he needed some background information and some questions answered if he was going to help. "So, Marcus, how did you get this job anyway?"

Marcus was feeling better now. Not so anxious. "I am not really sure myself. All I know is that there was a need, and I filled it."

Jake was trying to keep things lighthearted. "So, Marcus, where did the kids come from? I mean, how are you all here?"

Marcus thought for a second or two and decided that it could not hurt anything to tell Jake about how the nest came to be. "Did you ever hear of the old program called foster care?" Jake nodded yes. Marcus continued, "Well, so many programs had to be cut, and one of the programs was foster care. Most of the kids in the program were sent to camps, but a few families tried to keep the kids they had taken in, even if they did not get any money. But as time went on, even they could not always afford to let the kids stay with them."

Jake watched Marcus and listened. Asking few questions but learning as much as he could. "But what about these boys?"

Marcus looked up from his paperwork. "The kids you see here now. Well, we are the leftovers. Victor and Sandy get as much information on each kid as they can. They try and find where their family is and get the kid to them, but some of us just need to be here and be a part of the nest."

Jake interrupted, "Slow down, you lost me on part of this. Victor and Sandy find the families of street kids and get them out of here and to where the families are at?"

Jake was really listening and trying to understand, so Marcus continued, "Okay, I will slow down for you."

That was a little brother jab at Jake, if he had ever gotten one. Jake smiled and said nothing but motioned with his hand for Marcus to continue.

Marcus did continue. "Well when children who are without a family are found, we try and help find their families. In the meantime, they are placed in several different places. The older boys come here. The girls and the brother/ sister sets and all of the younger ones are placed elsewhere until they are helped."

Jake was shocked. Of course, there would be girls, and there would have to be other nests. He had not even thought of that being possible. This was a lot to take in.

Marcus went on. "Not all nests work as we do. Most do schooling and work when they can. At least until they find their family and go to them, or sometimes the families come back and find us. There is also a chance sometimes for a group to be moved out of town to what they call the farm, but that is rare."

Jake was following enough to have questions. "So what about the group here? How did you all get here as a working group?"

Marcus looked around the room. "Well, we are family now. We are down to fifteen, still counting Travis." Marcus stopped talking at the mention of Travis, but Jake encouraged him to move past that thought and continue his lesson on the nests. "The kids that are here now, well, we are different. We are family. We have three sets of brothers. Travis and me. Then there is John and James, we call him *Jimmy* because of his age and the fact that we have another James. Their parents had to run away to not be chipped, they told the kids to stay here in town and that they would be back. So they are here until that happens. The other James, well, his parents are dead, and he has no family. Victor said last week they may have found an aunt who is in a camp, so James could go be with her there, but for now, it was best for him to work with us. James is almost fourteen, same age as John."

Jake was all in. He needed to know it all. "What about Jimmy? How old is he?"

Marcus smiled. He liked talking about the kids. "Well, Jimmy is nine, same age as Mike. Mike came with the other set of brothers Aaron and Zach. They had all been in the same foster home and were put out when the family decided to be chipped. The family thought it best for the kids to go back to the program they thought was still working. They sent the boys back, but when they got here, it was the nest that they found instead. Aaron is twelve, but Zach is one of our youngest at six and a half. He is only here because of his brothers. Sandy says brothers should always stay together. And I agree. We have two more boys who are eleven. Peter and Frank. Peter is really good at anything electrical. Victor said he would love to find him a home where he could lean more in that area, but Peter wants to stay longer because he thinks his mom might come back here to this town to find him. She said she would. He had said that he was not sure why she left, but for now, this was working out okay."

Jake thought he understood so far but needed some more details on the younger kids. *Six and a half is the youngest here?* "Marcus, where do the younger kids usually go?"

Marcus answered, "Oh, Sandy and Mrs. S. take them and get them to homes right away. They need to get to a regular life as soon as they can get them there. That is what Sandy says anyway. And I do not do well with little kids."

Jake almost laughed out loud. Here is this kid who is running this whole nest talking about not being able to work with little kids. Marcus had no idea how special he really was and that doing what he did was rare at best.

"What did your family do before you went to the streets?" Jake kept watch on Marcus to see if this questioning was making him nervous. So far it was good.

"My parents were both teachers. They got into trouble because they felt that history was an important part of our world. When the books were edited, they kept teaching the truth. That got them flagged, so when the opportunity came to get rid of them, that's what they did. The government officer arrested them and took them to have them chipped and then sent them to a camp. Mom and Dad told Travis and me to run so that we did not get chipped too." Marcus looked down. He looked so defeated. Jake did not want to overdo it with questioning, but he needed to understand Marcus better so he could help him better. "And then you and Travis decided to run?"

"Kind of. Travis did not want to run. He thought we should get chipped and all stay together as a family. That was our first really big fight. I wanted to do what Mom and Dad said to do, and Travis wanted to go with them." Marcus could not talk any more. He just sat there quiet.

"And you won?" Jake worked on keeping his thoughts from running too far ahead of the story. "What happened next?"

"Travis and I met a man named Reggie. He was good at living on the streets. He taught a lot of other kids street life too. For a price, mind you. Anyway, one day, things changed, and Reggie was not here, and we were. Then we met Sandy, and she liked that the kids knew things about the goings-on of the chipped. We started doing odd jobs for her, and here we are." Marcus sat thinking.

Perhaps Jake went too far with the questions. "What happened to Reggie?" Jake saw the change in Marcus right before his eyes. He had closed off to any more questions. They needed to move on. Jake reached over and took the papers and handed them to Marcus. "Okay, now why don't you tell me about the plan for tomorrow?"

Marcus looked at Jake trying to decide where this guy had come from, and what was he doing messing into his life? "Okay, Jake, this is how it works. We go out as a group. Tomorrow we are going to be at the park by the courthouse."

"In the park?" Jake was already confused.

"Don't talk, just listen. There is a lot of business done in the park. The people stay away from the adults, even me at my age, but they almost never bother about the kids." Marcus pulled out the plans. "If you look at this, you can see where each boy will be placed. I usually like to keep them in pairs. The ones that are paired up on this list are my very best combinations."

There was a map of the park. There were red *X*s on it to show where each group would be in place. Each team had a number, and the number by the X told them and Marcus where they would be. "See here, Jake, this is team one. They will work the morning, and team two the rest of the day."

Jake looked as Marcus showed him. "What questions are you looking for? Are there people you seek out? How do you get the information to and from the kids?"

Marcus stared at Jake hoping to stop the onslaught of questions. "If you could be quiet please, I will explain."

Marcus explained all the plans for the next day. Jake was amazed at how detailed Marcus was about the planning. Then in the end of the training, there was a very relaxed silence between them, no real need to talk about anything more.

Jake was thinking about all the things Marcus had told him about the nest group. It is unreal how this all came together. Perhaps God really did want it to continue. Jake looked over to Marcus just in time to see the papers he was going over slide from his hand. Jake caught them before they hit the ground, but this time Marcus didn't care or even know. He had fallen asleep. And that was a good thing. What a day this kid had survived. Jake prayed, "Oh, God, I need Your help. These are tomorrow's warriors. Do they really need to fight today? Couldn't we train them a little longer before we send them to war?"

Jake pulled his chair around in front of Marcus, took off this kid's shoes, and put his feet up so it was more like a bed. Marcus did not wake up, but he held his side and winced as he was moved. He stirred but went back to sleep just as fast. Jake did rounds one more time. He was able to intercept two of the kids from waking Marcus. At first it was hard to get them to understand that Marcus needed to rest, but then they let Jake help them.

Marcus slept well into the morning. He did not wake at all, not even when Sandy and Victor arrived with breakfast makings. All the fixings for a pancake feast. It was when Mark entered that the noise level came up enough that it woke him.

For the most part, no one was paying any attention to the sleeping Marcus. Except for Jake, that was. He had kept an extra watch on him in order to see how things would go today. He saw Marcus open his eyes and then close them in pain. Then Marcus moved his feet from the chair in front of him down to the ground. Jake saw him go white like he might pass out.

As Jake walked over to where Marcus was now sitting, he saw one of the younger ones come in view heading to jump on Marcus. Jake knew that this was the plan as he had received the same greeting on waking up this morning himself. He reached out and intercepted the incoming child and kept the attack from happening. The boy yelled out in excitement as Jake swung him around and then set him on the ground. All the attention was over on Jake, giving Marcus a chance to get up and retreat to the bathroom.

There was a lot of food. Pancakes and everything you could think of to go with it. The smell of sausage, bacon, and eggs along with the pancakes made it like heaven in the room. There was plenty of juice, butter, and syrup too.

Victor, Sandy, and Mark were standing together watching all the kids in the room. They saw that Marcus was up and had gone into the bathroom and that Jake was close behind him carrying his shoes. "Who would have thought you would have seen those two as friends like that?" Sandy was proud to see that they had worked things out.

Mark was eating a piece of bacon and popped the rest of it into his mouth. "What part are you talking about? The part where Marcus is letting Jake help him? Or the part where Jake is covering up the fact Marcus could hardly get out of the chair and walk to the bathroom?"

Sandy looked at Mark. "What?"

"It is hard for me to figure out why my brother who thinks these kids should be off the streets would cover up a fact about one of them getting hurt." Mark was so confused by Jake lately. "In the past, Jake would have gloated over the fact he was right. This sure is a new Jake." Then Mark went for another piece of bacon.

Victor and Sandy were both fast thinking that this needed to be checked out. Jake had come back into the room leaving Marcus alone in the bathroom.

"Hey, Victor. Hi, Sandy." Jake leaned over and kissed Sandy on the cheek. "The food looks and smells amazing. Where did it come from?"

Sandy was the one to answer. "We had a really good gathering this week. This is a special gift from one of the families. It was sent to the nest itself."

Victor got by Jake. "How is Marcus doing? Today is a big day. Can he do it?"

Jake did not want to lie, but the truth was he himself did not know if Marcus could. As he was about to give an answer, the bathroom door opened and out walked a perfectly looking Marcus. The kids were excited to see that the workday was about to begin. They had practiced this for a long time, and now the time was here.

Marcus called the gang to order, and they all gathered in a circle and took hands. The kids motioned for the adults to join them too. Marcus asked Victor to pray. Then Marcus called out the teams and their numbers. They had been given their locations. Marcus used a type of code with letters and numbers to give the orders. "Okay, any questions?" It was quiet in the room. "So let's dirty up."

The boys were excited about this part. They had a bucket of dirt, and they passed it around the circle. They put mud on themselves and on each other. Marcus called out, "Don't forget to do your shoes." And they all promptly got mud on their shoes too. Out they went. Some from the front door, others by the back wall door. All of them with orders as to where to meet.

Marcus was quick behind the last of the kid group. He turned and looked to Jake. "Well, are you coming?" And off they went, together.

Victor and Sandy needed to make a plan to have Marcus checked out, but first the cleanup and then off to the park to watch the work. "Mark, what are you doing today?"

"Well, I guess that I need to snoop around the chipped world and see if any news has come to the Singleton home." I think I will check it out and then see you all later.

Sandy tossed a towel at Mark. "After the cleanup, right?"

Mark smiled. "Yes, after the cleanup."

CHAPTER 24

Group one from the nest had arrived at the park by the courthouse. Jake and Marcus were the last of this group to arrive. Jake noted to himself to find out where the other groups stayed until it was their turn to work.

Marcus took his position on the top of a step only a few feet away from where all of the team would be working. The park was full of people already. So when each group came and got into their place, it was far from noticeable. Jake was wondering where he should be when one of the kids came over to him. "Hi, Jake. Marcus said you should stop looking like an officer and that you should stand over by that tree. You can see us from there."

Jake did as he was told, but for the life of him, he could not figure out how Marcus told this kid anything. As Jake was standing, he decided that being an officer right now might be a good thing. The park was full of chipped people, and not to mention he had been off the grid too long. So he reached for his medallion and took off the foil. Now he was back in his old world.

Jake stood keeping an eye on the boys and watching Marcus do his—what he could only call his work of art. Marcus would tap out a number with one of his hands. Then as he moved the other, an order was given. One tap. Group one. Moves to be made. More taps, another group, another order. Move here, get closer, move away, what did they say? How can you see? Join the other group. Break up the group. Get under the bench. Quick, get away. One of the boys was placed on a lower branch of a tree. Jake was amazed at all the fine-tuning this took to be a nest kid. This was a homemade code.

All the kids knew it, and they knew it very well. If Jake had not seen it with his own eyes, you could not have told him about how it was done. Jake watched for hours as the kids got close to people talking and making deals. Time after time they would all receive and send messages. Jake was truly in awe of Marcus and the kids.

The first hour or so of this event, Jake just had fun watching all of them talk together, but then he realized that he was learning the code. There it was, one of the boys heard about a family of the Knowing coming to town. The family was going to go to the courthouse and tell what they knew about the Knowing. Another said that there were two families. Oh yes, and another young boy who was going to come a different day and tell information about the Knowing. They were going to be heroes after they told because they would help get rid of the underground group that was trying to take over the government.

What a pack of lies, Jake was saying to himself. Then he looked at Marcus, who was now signaling him to stop looking so mean because he was worrying the boys.

Jake laughed to himself. I got it. I understood the message. Jake signaled for the first time. "Sorry, but this is so great." Marcus smiled and continued his work with the kids. The day was half over, and it was time for group 2 to get to work. Marcus replaced each group one by one. He was great at it too. First group got a signal. "Great job. Go get lunch. Second group. Good work." And so on. Group by group left the park only to have another set of boys replace them. Everyone got replaced. All but Marcus.

Jake was tired from the tension of the communication. Everyone had to be on task the whole time. As he watched Marcus, he noticed that he was holding his side as he stood. Just as Jake was about to signal him to take a break, he saw him step back and lean against the wall. Jake signaled, "Do you want a break?" *Oops, that was not received well.* This was Marcus duty, and he was very good at it.

Jake was surprised to see Victor and Sandy arrive at the park about 4:00 p.m. They gave him a signal to come talk to them. Marcus noticed them too and was signaling if there was a problem. Jake signaled that he would find out. So he walked over to meet the couple.

"Victor, this is the most amazing thing I have ever seen. They have their own language. Did you hear that the boys found out about some people who are going to tell all they know about the Knowing?" Jake stopped when he realized that they were obviously not there to talk about the information that had been gathered or even what he thought of the nest now. They had a plan, and it looked like he was going to be a part of it. "So, what is up?"

Victor checked around them to see that they could not be overheard. "You have got the code down now?" That was an answer of prayer as to how they could give Marcus a break.

Jake was shocked to hear that they had been watching them most of the day. "I think I have most of it. I can read it faster than I can send it. But yes, I do think I have it for the most part."

Victor and Sandy could see Marcus over Jake's shoulder, and he was signaling that they were distracting the boys. Victor covered a grin as Marcus was telling them to take their tea party somewhere else so the nest could do their work. "Jake, we need your help. We need you to take over for Marcus for about an hour. Do you think you can do that?"

Jake was puzzled. "Sure, but right now? Shouldn't we let him finish this job first? He is incredible at this. I am not sure I can keep up like he does. Do you see how he keeps each pair of boys in his mind at the exact same time? He knows exactly where each is and what they are doing all the time." Jake could see from the looks on Sandy's and Victor's face that they were not kidding about this. They needed his help. "Of course, I will try. What do I do?"

Victor knew he could count on Jake. "Okay, follow my lead." Victor was not very good at the code, but he sent a message to the boys that Jake would be taking over for Marcus to have a short break. All the groups signaled question about what he had said. Victor knew the signals, but he was sloppy with the moves, and they could not read him. The movements were so slight that they had to be exact or the message was lost.

Jake stepped in with the signal. "I will be taking over for Marcus while he goes with Victor and Sandy on a break. He will be back soon." Jake looked to Victor. "Did that say what you wanted?" The boys looked to Marcus, and he was signaling that this was not going to happen. Jake thought it could almost be funny because if you could yell a signal, Marcus was yelling it right now.

Victor signaled, "Enough." That was to Marcus, "Come here now."

Marcus got it loud and clear. He hesitated, but he complied. As he started down the step, he stumbled but caught himself.

Jake made a move to help him, but Victor stopped him. "Let him come on his own, or it will scare the boys." Jake looked to Victor for answers as to what is going on. "We are taking Marcus to see a doctor. He is in the building two doors down. It should only be about an hour at most. You okay with that?"

Jake was more than okay with it. He thought it was a great idea. As his friend Marcus was coming his way, he could see the look of rage in eyes. "Good luck with this. I need to get to work. Perhaps if he sees that we are okay, he will go along with it." He looked again at Marcus. "On the other hand, you may need the doctor."

Jake smiled at Sandy and Victor and went on to talk to the boys. He told them that things were okay. That Marcus had been hurt. They all signaled that they had noticed. Jake told them that he was going to see a doctor and he would be right back. The kids and Jake watched as Sandy and Victor talked with Marcus, who was clearly arguing with them. Sandy placed her arm around Marcus's waist, and Victor held onto his arm. Jake had been the receiver of this kind of takeover. It was with love, but it was forceful at the same time. Marcus looked over his shoulder back to the park to see what was happening. But Victor simply pulled him along the walkway.

Jake did not waste any time. He was slower at the signals than Marcus, but it was working. He was very glad that they had gone over the plans last night. It was time for people to be getting off work. The boys needed to be ready for a large number of people to be going to and cutting through the park. A lot of information would be gathered quickly. Jake wondered if Victor knew how bad of a time this was or if he even really cared. Victor was worried about Marcus, and that was good.

"Victor, Sandy, I am fine. Now please let me get back to the park and do my work." The two of them ignored their friend. They had no idea really as to what help he needed, but they were about to find out.

*****

Marcus was already in the building where the doctor was to meet them. They had his coat off and were getting ready to help him with his shirt when the doctor came in. "Hey, Marcus, do you remember me?"

Marcus reacted. This was a chipped doctor. This was not good, and he was not planning on going along with this any longer. He was reaching for his coat. Victor intercepted, pulling the coat back away from Marcus. "Victor, he is chipped. I need to get out of here." Marcus's eyes were set and locked on Victor's. All Victor did was place his hand on Marcus's left side and gently pressed. Marcus was caught off guard and doubled over in pain.

"Okay, now that we all understand, let's get your shirt off so the doctor can take a look at you." Victor felt bad for hurting Marcus that way, but sometimes you have to hurt people in order to save them.

The doctor was quick. He had his stethoscope out and was listening to Marcus's lungs with his shirt still on but unbuttoned. The bruising on his left side made Sandy hurt to see it. "Now tell me, how long ago did this happen?"

Victor answered, "Yesterday some time. Early I think."

"I am not positive without an X-ray, but I am confident that you have at least two—maybe three cracked ribs and maybe one broken one. I do not know how you are even walking around." The doctor lifted the back of Marcus's shirt and froze at the sight. Sandy and Victor walked around to see what he was seeing, and there was a bruise in the shape of a shoe print on Marcus. "Young man, you are lucky to be alive. Just a little lower, and you could have had internal bleeding from a ruptured spleen. Whoever did this, they knew exactly what they were doing. Lucky for you, they were off. Son, they were trying to kill you."

Before anyone had time to react to any of this, Jimmy hit the door of the building and came running up to Marcus. "Marcus, help! Some lady has one of the boys and has called the government officers. She is yelling that he tried to steal from her. Jake does not know what to do, and things are a mess."

Marcus pulled his shirt closed and headed to the door. "Emergency scramble! Run, quick, give the signal. Go on ahead, I am on my way." Marcus turned and looked with anger at the doctor and his friends. They had allowed this. He was not doing his job, and now there was a problem. This was not going to ever happen again as far as he was concerned. He did not need words. They knew exactly what he was thinking.

All three entered the park. Jimmy was right. There was a problem. The officers had arrived and were now gathering up the boys they could get a hold of. The signal was given. Then the real fun began. Two of the boys found some dog droppings and smeared their shoes in it. They ran over to the people who were holding on to the other boys and proceeded to wipe their feet on them. The smell alone caused a reaction, but with them getting it on the people, they let go of the boys and pulled away from them. Once they let go, it was over. These kids were so fast that no one could catch them. "Emergency scramble" meant they could not go back to the nest for at least an hour or two. Everyone was all over the street, taking a time out as it were, waiting to see how things settled. So far so good, no more officers came in. In fact, life on the streets returned back to normal.

It was hours before all of the kids were back at the nest. Everyone took extra precautions about getting home. One by one they had come in laughing and telling stories about how the people reacted to the dog droppings on their shoes.

"Marcus was right, this was a really fun way to get away. It was crazy, but it worked."

"Of course, it was Marcus's idea, who else could have thought up such a crazy escape?" Sandy was saying to Victor. As they were talking, they began looking for Marcus. He was still missing. They had gone back to where the doctor had been. They found the doctor still there waiting for them. He had Marcus's jacket and thought he might return for it. Sandy and Victor got to talk to the doctor about what to do with Marcus. From what he had seen, he thought Marcus would be okay if he took care of himself. He suggested two days flat on his back, only getting to get up to go to the bathroom and to eat. He gave Sandy some pain pills for him and said that Marcus really should take them because he would relax and he would heal faster. The doctor would like to have checked Marcus out more, but because of his chip, he could not go to the nest. He had told them that his wounds were bad and that if he got hit on that side again before his ribs healed, it could be fatal.

CHAPTER 25

Jake had met up with Mark on one of the streets. They both covered their chip medallions and were headed to the nest. Everything on the street looked back to normal. Curfew was about to sound, so they needed to move to the nest and quickly. They slipped in just before the siren started. Still there was no Marcus.

Jake was telling Mark about the day. "You should have seen these boys, man oh man, what a group they make. And you should have seen Marcus, even sick, he was so awesome. It was great until—"

The side wall door opened, and Marcus slipped in. He was cold. He was only wearing his shirt. As he entered, he saw his coat on a chair where Sandy had placed it and hurried over to pick it up.

Victor was so glad to see the boy. "Marcus, where in the world have you been? We have been looking for you?"

Marcus did not answer. He just wanted to put his coat on and get warm again. He tried to get his arms into the coat, but it took Sandy's help to get it all the way on.

Jake was so excited to talk to Marcus about the day's work. He saw him and went to talk. "Marcus, that was the greatest thing I have ever seen. You, my man, are awesome."

Marcus turned to meet face-to-face with Jake. "What on earth were you thinking? You risked all of my boys' lives. What were you thinking giving those orders to pick pockets?"

Jake was not following the conversation. "Marcus, what are you talking about? I sent no such order."

"My boys would never do that without orders, and you were the one giving them the orders." Marcus was as angry as he had ever been.

"Marcus, Jake did not give the order to steal stuff. It was Travis." Jimmy had moved closer so he could speak to him.

"What? Travis? Where? Why?" Marcus had lost his train of thought. He could not believe his own brother would knowingly put the boys in danger like that. "How did it happen? Where did Travis go after? Did he say anything?"

Victor knelt down to talk to some of the boys. "Okay, who wants to go first? What was Travis doing there in the park?"

One of the boys said that Travis had signaled that Jake was an officer and that you did not want us to work with him anymore. Travis also said that we would need money to get away from here and that we needed to get it now before Jake got us arrested and we could not get away. Victor talked to each of the boys who wanted to tell their part of the story. When he put all the stories together, the bottom line was that Travis had messed up the day's job.

Marcus stood silent listening to it all. If you did not look closely, you would have thought he was not even breathing.

Jake could see that Marcus was processing the information he had heard, piece by piece, and putting it up against what he had known from his past. Jake was amazed at how this kid could handle things like this without overreacting.

Mark was hearing all this and asked, "Did anyone see where Travis went after he left the park?"

Mike, one of the nine-year-old boys, said, "Well, I am not sure, but I think they arrested him. Maybe?"

Mark questioned the maybe. "What do you mean maybe?"

Mike looked to the other boys. "Well, we were talking about how it was strange that Travis did not put up a fight when they took him."

Marcus's head snapped to attention as he looked over to the wall entrance. He needed to go and find Travis and to help him.

Victor and Jake both saw the move and had figured out that Marcus was planning to try and find his brother. Marcus was halfway to the wall opening before they had intercepted him. By that time, Mark was onboard as to the next problem they were going to have. Mark joined Jake and Victor in order to box Marcus in.

Marcus's voice was not steady. "Get out of my way. You all know that I have to go and find my brother. He needs my help. I am all he has got." Marcus tried to step around the men, but they simply moved with him. Marcus was breathing really shallow and slow.

Victor was trying to get Marcus to slow down and to talk it through. "Marcus, I know that this idea of yours seems right at the moment, but trust me, as your friend, the timing is wrong. We need more information."

"Victor, you of all people know how fast they chip people once they get them from off the streets. There is no time to wait. I need to go now." Marcus was trying harder to catch his breath.

Sandy had joined the group of persuading friends. "Marcus, you know we want to do what is best for Travis, but we need to do what is best for you too. You are hurt. The doctor said that you have at least three cracked ribs, and one may be broken. You are going to be okay if you take care of yourself, but you need bed rest for a few days."

Marcus turned to her putting his back to the three men. That was a wrong move. A wall of friends were quick to move in and physically support Marcus and then move him back farther into the room. "Stop it. Now let me go. I will rest after I find my brother." Marcus was trying to twist his way out of the fixed hold they had him in.

"Enough!" Victor spun Marcus around and gave him one quick shake. Getting Marcus's full attention. "The last time you tried to help Travis, he tried to kill you. And that is *not* going to happen again. Not as long as we are around. Do you understand? And if you don't calm down and see how very wrong you are about going after Travis, I will take you to another nest away from your boys and keep you there until you come to your senses. Got it?"

Marcus was hit by full-blown rage and anger, then fear, and then a complete panic attack. Sandy was going to step in and try and calm him. Victor stopped her. Jake had a good grip on Marcus, who was now gasping for air. The fear of the day, fear for the boys, and fear for Travis, and now the fear of not being able to breathe fast overcame him. Sandy looked at Victor. "If we don't calm him down, he is going to pass out."

Victor gave Sandy a look. "And that would be bad how?" He put his arms around her. "He is in good hands. Jake and Mark will not let him get hurt when he goes down. We can get him to bed and get food and water into him. I don't think he has eaten all day. Then we can worry about Travis."

Just as Victor predicted, Marcus was overwhelmed with shortness of breath. He looked at Jake, then Victor. His eyes rolled back into his head, and he went totally limp. Exactly as Victor had said, Mark and Jake had a hold of him. Victor took his legs, and they walked him over to a cot and gently placed him on it.

The boys had seen the entire goings-on and were concerned for Marcus. "Is Marcus going to be okay?" Jimmy had elected himself spokesperson.

Sandy was the one to take the boys on. She left Jake and Mark with Victor to do what was needed for Marcus.

Victor looked to the other men. "Any ideas?"

They all considered the situation for a moment, but it was Jake that came up with a plan. "Hey, Mark, remember that time when we were kids that you tied me to the bed by wrapping the sheet and the mattress together?"

Mark smiled. "Sure do. I think that would work even better with the cot. I will be right back. I can see if Sandy can help me find some sheets." Mark went to find Sandy leaving Victor and Jake alone with the now resting Marcus.

Jake broke the silence. "Victor, back there when you were talking to Marcus, you said that you thought Travis had tried to kill him. What made you think that?"

Victor heard the question and thought about whether or not it was a good idea to show Jake the fact that Travis really had tried to kill Marcus. Jake and Marcus are friends now, and Jake could find it hard to help Travis in the future if he knew for sure he had tried to kill his friend. But "the truth can set you free" was his final thought as he motioned Jake over to help him with Marcus. "Here help me get his coat off and get him into bed." As they removed the coat, Victor had Jake help him turn Marcus onto his side so he could show Jake the footprint on his back.

As Victor lifted the shirt, Jake froze with the awareness of how very right Victor had been. This was not your normal brother fight. This was a true full outrage kind of fight. "Victor, this is awful. I can't believe a brother would do something like this. Not even a really angry brother." The wounds looked so bad that Jake couldn't believe that Marcus could even walk, much less do all of the things he had done today. "Victor, are you sure the doctor was right? Maybe he should go to a hospital. His having passed out and all."

Victor motioned for Jake to help get Marcus on to his back again. They got his shoes off and a pillow under his head. "Jake, he is going to be okay. He just needs some time. For the outside wounds anyway." Victor stood looking down at Marcus. He looked so young, and yet he had done so well as a man. "He has done well for his age for now, but he will need friends like us to keep him from hurting himself until he can figure it all out."

"Victor, I am not sure if I could figure this one out myself. A brother hurting a brother like this. This is a hard one for me." Jake felt so bad for Marcus. He knew that Marcus loved his brother like Jake loves Mark, but to think he could turn on him like this.

"Jake, have you ever heard of Cain and Abel? They were brothers in the Bible. Cain killed Abel because he was jealous of God's favor for Able. It was not right. But God gave us the story so that we can see that some people are born with a broken way of thinking. God knows about it. He doesn't like it, but He knows."

Mark had returned with some sheets, safety pins, and duct tape. "I got them. Jake, will you help me? I think this will help slow things down some." Mark took the top sheet, folded it into fourths long-ways. He tucked one end of the sheet under Marcus and passed the rest over him, under the cot, and then back over him. They pinned the edge of the sheet and put duct tape over the pins to keep them in place. "There, that should hold."

Jake was looking at the way Mark had fixed Marcus to the cot. He would be safe for now. Not only from Travis but also from himself. "Mark, do you really think that this will keep him down?"

Mark, with his arms crossed and a smirk on his face, answered, "It worked on you, didn't it?"

Victor watched as Jake obviously remembered the event. "Well, did it?" Victor asked him.

Jake answered, "Yes, as I do recall, it did. Now drop the subject and let's see about Marcus?"

Mark and Victor went to talk with Sandy and the boys. That left Jake to watch over Marcus. "Dear God, once again help me to help him. Help me to be the good friend that I believe he needs."

Jake was sitting in a chair by the now resting Marcus when he realized that he was being watched. As he looked up, there were two sets of eyes looking at him. It was two of the younger boys, Jimmy and Mike. They had come to see what was going on with Marcus. "Hey, boys, what's up?"

The two boys looked at each other then back at Jake and then at Marcus. They looked worried. Mike, the older of the two, spoke, "Is Marcus going to be okay?"

Jake could tell that they were really very worried about their friend and their leader. "Yes, we think so. But Marcus has to take care of himself and get some rest. He hurt his side, and it could get worse if he is not careful." Jake could see that they had concern about the sheet holding him on the cot. "See the sheet? Well, that will help him stay on his back until his ribs heal some."

Jimmy rolled his eyes and made a look. "He is not going to like that idea I think. But if it can make him better, then we think it could be okay." Jimmy moved forward toward Jake, holding a small black book. "Here, I think Marcus may want this." He handed it to Jake.

Jake looked at it. It was a Bible. "Thanks, boys. I think that he will be glad to have it when he wakes up. That was a great idea." The boys were still standing there. "Do you want something else?"

The boys looked at each other then at Jake. "Is Marcus going to go and get Travis? He is his brother, you know?" It was Mike who stepped up with the questions this time. "We think that he would come and get us if we were in jail. Isn't that right? I mean even if he was sick. Right?"

Jake could see where this was going. The one person they had always counted on was not doing what they thought he would do.

"Boys, you know that if Marcus were not hurt, he would have already gone to get Travis, right?" Jake felt the need to protect Marcus's reputation with the boys. He could see from how they were reacting that they were not thinking that this was right and that Marcus should do something. But what? "You know, boys, I think that you should know that if Marcus cannot go himself that he most likely will ask a friend to do it for him."

They smiled. Jimmy ran over to Jake and hugged him around the neck. "Thanks, Jake. Say hi to Travis for us." They both ran off leaving Jake and Marcus alone again. Jake was sitting looking at the Bible the boys had brought him. He opened the front cover and found a note to Marcus from his mom and dad. It had words of encouragement to follow God's word and to remember that he was always loved by God and by his family. It was signed, "Love mom and dad and Travis." There it was, love, and it always wins. Jake was guessing that in the end, it is the love of God that makes things work out. Jake began to read the Bible. He was enjoying looking at the things Marcus had marked. He could see from the worn pages which verses were his favorite. Jake thought to himself that Marcus was going to be a great man someday because he was already a great young man. As Jake continued to read, he noticed that Marcus was starting to stir. He had moved his hands to around his side slightly rubbing it. He began to slightly pull at the sheet trying to free himself. The pain he was feeling was all too real and sharp. Jake stepped over and knelt down by the cot so his friend could see that he was not alone.

Marcus's eyes flew open. He grabbed his side, and he began to sweat with the pain. He needed to sit up. That might make him feel better. He tried to sit up, but he could not get free from the sheets around him. "Jake, is that you? Help me get up, will you? It hurts me to lie down. I need to sit up."

Jake placed a hand on Marcus's upper chest and pressed him back into the cot. "What you need to do is to lie back and take a deep breath and relax. The pain is not from lying down, it is because you have been hurt, and moving around will not help the pain, so be still?"

Marcus was not listening. He was only making things worse by fighting the sheets. "Jake, please let me up. I can walk this out, you will see. So undo this wrap thing and help me up."

Sandy heard talking coming from the area that Marcus and Jake were in and hurried over to see what they were doing. One look at Marcus told her all she needed to know. He was in pain and that he needed to settle down and rest, but he was arguing with Jake.

The doctor had given her pain pills for Marcus, but she already knew he would never knowingly take them. "Marcus, good, you are awake." She could see that Jake was worried as to what he should do to help his friend in this situation. Sandy tried to put his pillow back under his head. "Marcus, you need to relax. Take deep breaths, it will help with the pain."

"Sandy. I need to sit up. Tell Jake to help me. It will feel better if I can sit up." Marcus was struggling again to get up off the cot. "Where is Victor? I need to see Victor."

Mark and Victor had heard the talking too. They were there in time for Victor to hear Marcus asking for him. "What do you need, Marcus?" Victor had entered the area with Mark close behind.

"Victor, I need to sit up. Then we need to talk about what is going on with Travis and about the families and the boy who plans to give up the Knowing. And the boys, where are my boys?" Marcus was in pain, and he was rambling trying to get past it. If he could get his mind on something else, perhaps the pain would lessen. "I need to get busy. It will make me feel better."

"What will make you feel better is time." Victor had slipped into where Sandy had been standing. She went to get juice and the pain pills. Jake had pulled back to let Victor get a face-to-face with Marcus. Victor seemed to have that respect factor that the rest of them did not. Whether it was age or relationship, it did not matter, it was needed now. "Marcus, look at me." And he did. "Now I want you to lie back and be still and let me check this bedding. It might be too tight." Victor proceeded to check how the sheet was, and no, it was not too tight, but it was the one thing that kept Marcus from getting up. "Well, it seems okay to me. Not too tight. Maybe if you don't pull against the sheet, it will not have so much pressure and will not hurt so bad."

Sandy had returned with the juice and the pills, one in each hand. Jake saw her as she entered the room. Jake met her and talked to her while Victor had Marcus distracted. "Are those the pain pills for Marcus?" She nodded yes. "How many should he get?" She held up two fingers. "He will never consciously take them, so I have an idea." Sandy was glad Jake was here. She watched as Jake opened two of the capsules and emptied the stuff inside into the juice. He reclosed the pill bottle and handed it back to Sandy. "Follow my lead."

Jake had the two empty capsules in his hand. When he and Sandy entered the area where Marcus was, the worry for Marcus was the same. Jake walked over to Marcus. "Here, I think these will help ease the pain." Jake held out his hand with the two empty capsules.

Marcus was not receptive to the idea at all. "I do not need pills. What I do need is to get up and get going, and then I will feel better. Let me show you." He tugged at the sheet again, bringing a sharp wrenching pain that almost made him pass out again. "Why are you making this so hard? Can't you see that I need your help?"

Jake was the one to address it. "Okay, you want my help, I will give it to you. You take the pills. Drink the juice anytime Sandy brings you some. Eat. And rest. While that occurs, I will go find out about Travis for you." Mark added that he would go with Jake and get information too.

Marcus realized that he was not going to win this argument, so the least he could do was make a good deal. "Okay, I will rest, eat, and drink the juice, but not take the pills. I don't need them."

Jake took the empty pills and handed them back to Sandy. Who then handed him the juice. "Okay, let's start with this. Drink it."

Marcus took the juice and drank all of it. He then handed Jake the glass. "There, are you happy?" Marcus was clenching his fists in pain but was trying to hide the fact that this was way harder than he thought it could ever be. He was totally depending on his friends for everything. "Now what do you want?"

Jake smiled. "There is nothing for you to do but rest and get better. Mark and I are going to go to the government station and check things out. Keep your promise to do everything Sandy tells you. Eat, drink, and rest. That's your promise."

"Jake, I need a promise from you too?" Marcus was still fighting the sheet some, which pulled against his side and made him catch his breath. "I need you to promise that you will tell me about Travis. No matter what you find out. You will tell me the truth. Promise?"

Jake had no problem with that. "I promise that no matter what I find out about Travis, I will tell you." Jake could not think of any reason he would withhold information from Marcus about his brother.

Victor and Mark were both in the dark as to why this deal would make Sandy and Jake so happy, but it was apparent to them from the looks on the two's face that they were.

As Jake and Marcus continued to talk about the information they had gathered earlier that day, it was notable how much better and relaxed Marcus was becoming. He had yawned a few times. His hands were relaxed and not in fists. The pain pills were working, and this was good.

Victor, Sandy, and Mark stepped back and let Jake do the questioning about what Marcus thought was a good idea to do next.

Victor whispered into Sandy's ear, "From the way Marcus looks, I would say he took some pain pills he did not know he was taking."

Sandy looked up at Victor and smiled. "Let's just say our friend Jake is really very good at deception."

As they were talking, it became very quiet in the room. Marcus had gone to sleep. Jake motioned for them to meet him on the other side of the room away from Marcus. "Okay, now that has been handled, Mark and I are going to go and see what we can find out on the streets." Jake looked at Mark. "Maybe even the government station." Both Mark and Jake left.

Victor and Sandy were the last adults left in the nest. What a day it had been. But this was good because they were here together. Sandy went over to Victor and placed her arms around him in a hug. "So what do you think about Marcus and his letting Jake go and help Travis?"

Victor hugged her back. "I think our young man Marcus just learned a new leadership skill called delegation. And about time too."

CHAPTER 26

Jake and Mark were now back in the chipped world. They had walked down the street toward the government security station. As they entered, they met several men and women who greeted them as if nothing had happened. But then in this world, nothing had. In this world, merely, every day events involving the unruly Knowing were happening.

"Hey, Singleton, is that you?" A man only a few years older than Jake had come out of an office to greet him. "I think I know why you are here. It is that weird kid, right?"

"Hi, Stan, do you mind filling us in on what is going on? We have been out of the loupe and need to be caught up." Jake had lowered his voice so it was clear that this would be kept between them.

"Oh, sure, Jake, this unchipped boy came in and said he had information on the Knowing, and he wanted to tell about them. He wanted to help get them caught and chipped so they could all get off the street and get on with their lives." Stan looked around to see if anyone was watching them. "That is when it got really crazy. This kid started saying how you and your family were a part of the Knowing." He laughed and gave Jake a slap on the back. "Like that could ever happen to a Singleton. The best part is yet to come. Are you ready for this? He said that your mom, of all people, was one of the leaders of the children's group they call the nest." Stan was laughing so hard he could hardly speak anymore. "Hey, do you guys want to watch this? Come in here and watch. I think you will get a kick out of this."

Jake and Mark joined Stan in a side room that was set up so you could view people without them knowing that they were being

425

watched. There was sound, and it had been turned on. As they watched through the glass, they could not believe what they were seeing or hearing. It was Travis. He had candy bars and wrappers on the table in front of him. There were several sodas, some open and some not, but it was obvious they had all been given to Travis.

"Okay, kid, what else can you tell us about these nests as you call them?" There was a woman in the room. She had a clipboard in her hand, and she was taking down notes as Travis was speaking.

This was not a good thing. Mark and Jake both knew the blessing in all of this is that the people thought that Travis was crazy and were having fun with him before they had him chipped and shipped him off to a camp. It would be checked out, but no one in their right mind would believe that a Singleton could be of the Knowing. Jake was worried that somehow he and Mark had gotten their mom involved. He would have to figure that part out later, but for now, they needed to get back to the nest and tell the others what they had found out. Jake felt sick inside. They needed to tell the others. But the others included Marcus. And Jake promised to tell him everything no matter what he found. Could Marcus take another hit like this? Only God could help this mess.

Jake and Mark said their goodbyes and thanked Stan for letting them hear the crazy kid. They were like-minded in that they thought they should stay away from the Knowing world for tonight. Things at the nest were safe for now, and they could tell Victor and the others what they had learned in the morning.

Mark and Jake stopped on the street in front of the station. "Okay, so we will go to our homes for the rest of the night. Then we will meet up at the coffee shop at, let's say, seven in the morning. We can decide what to do from there." Mark was doing all the talking. "Jake. Marcus will be all right. He has God. He has had him a long time. He knows how to get through tough times. God has helped him through before and promises to do it again." Marks words did not lessen the look of worry on Jakes face.

Jake nodded his head and agreed to meet in the morning. Jake walked to his apartment. The door was unlocked. He knew that he had locked it when he left. He entered and looked around. Nothing was moved that he could see. He saw the light on his answering machine flashing. There were three messages. He played them. One was from his boss, who wanted Jake to come to the station and talk to him about his coming back to work. It was still a few weeks away, but he had a special assignment for him while he was off. The second was from his mom. She had not heard from him and was thinking of him and that he should call soon. The third call was from a man who called himself Bill Thomas. They had never met, but he wanted to introduce himself and to see if they could meet sometime soon. He had a few questions for him about his time with the Knowing. That call could wait until tomorrow too.

Jake was still not sure about his apartment door being left unlocked. He looked around some more. But there was nothing out of place.

Jake needed a shower really bad. He could hardly wait to get into the hot flow of water. As he stood in the shower, he thought of the family of boys back at the nest. "Oh, God, help me to help them." Maybe he could let a few of the boys come and stay the night sometime. They could have the pleasure of a good shower and a real bed. On the other hand, would it be crueler to let them taste a better life that they might never get to have? They really needed to get off the streets and into families of some sort. But then what about the nest and the work it did? "No more thinking." Jake was talking out loud hoping it would stop him from thinking about the boys if he heard it.

"That should not be too hard for you." It was a woman's voice. He recognized it but could not place it at first with the water running.

Jake must have jumped ten feet. He was alone, and his apartment door was locked. As he pulled back the shower curtain, there sat his sister, Sally. "What are you doing in my apartment and in my bathroom? Get out of here. Can't you see that I am showering? How did you get into my apartment anyway?"

Sally was laughing as she left the bathroom. "Oh, stop it. I am not looking. Besides that, I used to change your diaper. It is not like I haven't seen you before, little brother." She left the bathroom and had a seat on Jake's couch.

Jake wrapped a towel around himself and joined her in the living room. "Sally, what are you doing here, and how did you get in anyway?"

Sally held up a keychain that had several keys on it. "Government keys."

Jake made a face. "To my apartment?"

Sally confirmed, "To all apartments." She put the keys away and looked at Jake. "As to why I am here, Mark called me. I am to talk to you and to convince you to blah, blah, blah. You know Mark, he is worried about you."

Jake blinked. Mark had called her.

"By the way, when I came by earlier, there was a man coming out of your apartment. I did a background check on his chip and found out that his name is Bill Thomas." Sally noted the look of recognition on Jake's face. "So I take it you know him?"

"Kind of." Jake looked at the answering machine. "He left me a message on my phone. He said he wanted to talk to me about the Knowing."

"Really? Anyway, the real reason I am here is that Mom and Dad are taking a lot of heat about that kid Travis. What are you going to do about him?" Sally was serious. "You need to figure something out and fast. Okay?" Sally got up to leave. She gave Jake a kiss on the side of his face. "See you later, little brother. I need to get back to work."

Jake was at the door holding it open so Sally did not shut it behind her. "Sally, wait. I need to talk to you some more."

"Later, Jacob." Sally reached around her neck and pulled on a chain. As she pulled the chain up, a medallion, like Mark and Jake had, was hanging from it. "By the way, Jake, welcome to the family." Sally winked. She put a finger over Jake's lips to stop the questions. "Not here, later. I love you, Jake, and I could not be happier." Sally looked down. "Jake?" She smiled. "Get dressed." And with that, she hurried off to work.

Jake went back into his apartment. He shut the door and leaned on it. Sally was going to go to heaven. Jake heard it, he saw it. His sister was a believer. How long? Why hadn't anyone told him? There were so many questions. He could not even decide where to start. Mark had said nothing. Three in his family were heaven bound. "Thank You, God. But I still need to ask for the others too."

Jake finished his shower and got dressed. He should have been ready to go to sleep, but he couldn't. He decided to call his mom back. He really enjoyed talking to her. Even if he could not tell her everything, she was good to listen to. The phone rang several times. No answer. Jake left a message. "I was just calling to say hi. I saw Sally today. She came to see me at the apartment. She looks great. I love you. Bye." Jake hung up the phone. He was a blessed man.

Sally said that he needed to figure out what to do about Travis causing trouble for their parents, but what? Tomorrow Jake was going to have to tell Marcus about his brother being a traitor. Jake was not anxious to get to the nest. This was going to hurt his friend Marcus. "Oh, God, could You please help us?"

*****

Jake got to the coffee shop early, an hour early. He saw Smitty and got a cup of coffee. He found his usual table and took his seat. This was going to be a busy day. He needed to go to the station and meet with his boss. He needed to meet with this Bill Thomas and find out what he wanted and why he had been in his apartment. He really wanted to talk with Sally. He was going to speak with Mark soon, but the real elephant in the room, as they say, is he needed to tell Marcus about his brother, Travis. Then they needed to figure out what to do about him. Jake was not paying attention and did not see Mark enter the room. He had purchased his coffee and was almost to the table before Jake saw him.

"Good morning, Jake." Mark sat down and had a smile that he could not contain. "What's new?"

"What's new?" Jake lowered his voice. "Sally is what's new. How long had she been...well, you know?"

"Sally will tell you herself later, but for now, we have got bigger problems." Mark took a sip of coffee, and Jake finished his sentence. "Travis."

"Mark, do you have any ideas?" Jake had a hope that Mark might have known a way to work this out because he himself did not have a clue.

"Personally, I would like to shake the kid until some sense comes to him, but we cannot get that close to him." Mark was serious, and he was sad.

"Do you have any idea as to what the government thinks they are going to do with Travis?" This was new territory for Jake; he had worked with adults but not with kids.

Mark looked even sadder. "As a rule, they are questioned, and then they are chipped and sent to one of the chipless camps. But that should have already happened. For some reason, they have kept Travis around and have kept him chipless. It does not make any sense, but what does these days?"

CHAPTER 27

Jake and Mark decided to go separate ways. Mark was going to go to the nest, and Jake was going to go to the government station and then meet at the nest later.

Jake got to the station just in time to see his boss enter his office. Jake's boss was a good man. Jake liked and trusted him a lot. He had not seen him or really talked to him very much lately, being that he was undercover and working for Mr. Diggings. Soon Jake would be back to days as usual, or could he? Things with him are so different now. All Jake could think of was, *Can I tell everyone about Jesus and how we can all go to heaven?* And as crazy as it sounded, even to Jake, it was a new goal.

Jake got a lot of information and fast by talking to his boss. First of all, that Bill Thomas was going to be going undercover on some new assignment, and he wanted some backup information about the Knowing. He had been trying to meet up with Jake to talk. That explained his being at Jake's apartment but not him being in it. Jake would choose to keep that part to himself for now. He found out that Travis was still being held there in town and that there would be more questioning soon. So far, all the information the kid had told was right on except the part of the Singletons, his boss had said. Jake was to start back to work in about five weeks but needed to see a counselor before he could. That was policy, after an undercover operation that had gone as long as Jake's had. Jake would set that part up. He offered to meet with Bill Thomas, but his boss said that it was too late because he had already started his case.

Jake left the station with a lot of information, but very little of it was going to help him tell Marcus about his brother. What Jake knew for sure was that Travis was okay, and it sounded like he was going to get what he thought he wanted. Chipped and off the streets. Their only hope was that he would not be able to take them down with him.

Jake did not go straight to the nest. He was worried that he might be under surveillance. He would have to be extra careful and alert. Jake went to the park and sat on a bench for a time and realized that there were no kids. That was odd. Not chipped or chipless. Jake decided to check it out and went to the coffee shop to see what was up. "Hey, Smitty, how goes it?" Smitty looked at him and smiled but did not say anything. "Anything new?"

Jake went to the counter where Smitty was alone. "Hey, where are all the kids today?" Smitty looked at Jake and did not speak but put a newspaper down on the counter in front of him. Jake could hardly believe what he was reading. The paper was about the chipless kids and how dangerous they had become. It reported that these kids had been accused of poisoning pets, and someone had reported that one of them had tried to poison their child. They were to have been a part of a shoplifting ring, and they were said to be pickpockets. It was said to have been on good report that there was going to be an overall takedown of this kid group. It also said that the officers were going to be taking out their hideouts and that they would be taken care of for good.

Before Jake could read any more, Smitty took the paper and rolled it up and handed it to Jake. "Okay, sir, can I get you your usual coffee?"

Jake became all too aware that there was someone standing behind him. He turned to see an officer with a chip scanner in his hand scanning Jake. "Yes, sir, this is a genuine Singleton. The famous one at that."

Jake did not recognize this officer but could tell from his tone of voice that he wanted trouble. "What can I do for you, officer?" Jake squared his body so he was face-to-face with him. "I assume that you men have been assigned to me to help me with my orders to round up the chipless kids?"

The officer lost his grin. "Why, no, sir. We were just funning. There is no way we want to have anything to do with those brats. And you should not either. Why, they stink, they are dirty, and"— the officer showed Jake his arm—"and look at this. They bite."

Sure enough, there was a deep bite mark on the officer's arm. Jake was trying so hard not to laugh. If this man only knew how very wonderful these kids really were. "Wow, how did that happen?"

"No matter about that. Just know that if there is any way you can get yourself out of this assignment, do it." The officer and his friends turned and hurried out of the coffee shop.

Jake turned back to Smitty so they could finish their conversation. But Smitty was far from ready to talk. As the officers left through the door and it closed, Smitty burst out laughing, joined by two other men in the room. "Jake, you liked to scare them to death. The thought of you making them go after the kids. Why, they are all scared to death of those kids." Smitty continued, "So what can I get for you?"

Jake lowered his voice, "Well, I am headed over to the nest. I can take the food if you would like."

Smitty's smile faded. "Jake, there won't be any food for a few days. The government are monitoring the food supplies. We all have to account for everything we buy and sell, or give away. They say until they get the kids, but they will get tired after a few days, and things will get back to normal. Sorry, Jake. Tell the kids sorry too."

Jake could understand it. But it was still hard to think the kids might not get breakfast. Perhaps Victor and Sandy had already worked that out.

With his newspaper in his hand, he headed out to the nest. Jake took a few extra minutes once he was outside to finish reading the news article. He read that the government had found three hideouts. That they found no guns, no drugs, and no people. But the report went on to say that there was evidence that guns and drugs had been there and had been removed just before the hideouts were found. The paper said that it would not be long before the group would be caught and chipped and dealt with due to the fact that they had a special force on the case.

Okay. Now that is why the kids were not on the streets working today. The article in the paper put the kids in trouble. It was like putting a bull's-eye on them.

Jake took extra precautions in going to the nest. As he arrived, he saw that Victor and Sandy along with his brother Mark were at the table looking at one of the newspapers. They had received one too. Jake looked around. No Marcus.

Victor saw him looking and guessed it was Marcus he was looking for. "Marcus is asleep. He had a long night. He was trying to wait up for you, but Sandy and I decided to give him some 'juice' as you call it. His pain was bad again."

Jake walked to the table and put his paper with theirs. "I see you know about this too. Does Marcus know yet?"

"No, it came after he fell asleep." Sandy was glad that Jake would be here to help them tell Marcus about his brother, Travis and about the need to shut down the nests. "Three nests have been found and two rabbit holes. Granted they were all old ones, but they were given up all the same. There were no arrests, but it was only a matter of time. We will need you to help us tell him about shutting down the nests along with word on Travis." Sandy hugged Jake. "I am really glad to see you." Jake hugged her back.

They went on for a few hours talking about all the options they had dealing with Travis and with the nest kids. They had a lot of ideas but no real solutions.

Victor looked at Jake. "Did you find anything new today? You were at the station, right?"

Jake thought. "Not really, only thing I can think of is that there is a Bill Thomas who was trying to find out about the Knowing. But it was too late for me to meet with him since he had already left for his undercover job."

Silence hit the room. Jake looked at all of them. "What?"

The answer to that question was never answered. Marcus was awake and fully dressed, except for his socks and shoes. He had walked into the room by himself but it was clear by how long it took him to get across the room that he was far from being well. Jake was about to inquire about who had let Marcus out of bed and as to how that decision had been made, when Marcus picked up the newspaper and was reading the article about the kids and the nests. "Is this article why the kids are not working the streets today?"

Jake walked over beside Marcus. "That would be correct."

"Did Travis do this?" Marcus did not look up but kept his eyes on the article.

"Maybe. We are not sure. But we are working on it. Jake was being so careful with his answers.

"Did you see Travis? Is he okay?" Marcus looked straight at Jake. "I trust you not to lie to me."

Jake nodded his head in agreement. "I will tell you what I know, but I will not guess at the things I do not know about, okay?"

"Okay." Marcus did not look at anyone while Jake and Mark told what they had seen and heard, but stared out into the air.

"We saw Travis," Jake started. "He looked good. Not chipped yet. They were feeding him candy and sodas. He had on new clothing and a fresh haircut. He looked happy."

"Did you talk to him?" Marcus looked Jake in the eye. He was trying to check and see if he was telling the truth.

"No, we did not." Jake motioned toward Mark. "We got to listen through a one-way mirror. Marcus, Travis was telling them about the Knowing and about people involved."

Marcus was soft-spoken. "What people?"

"He was telling about the Knowing people and the Singleton family." Jake felt that was enough information.

But it was Victor who commented on what Jake said. "Are you and your family going to be okay?"

Victor and Jake took over the conversation. "Victor, I am not sure, but I think it is going to be okay because they all think that Travis is crazy. They think that he is making things up in order to get attention. They are checking out what he says but not really believing there is too much truth to it. Not yet anyway."

Victor paced. "I think we might need to break up the nests sooner than we had planned, and as for you two"—he was meaning

Jake and Mark—"I think you had better stay away from all of us for a time at least."

They all talked about how that would work. Not even thinking to ask Marcus what he thought. Marcus walked up to Jake. Everyone got quiet. "Jake, I need to see Travis."

Without a second thought, everyone including Sandy said a loud and deliberate NO.

Marcus started to argue with them but only made a slight sound and then stopped. He noticed his coat on a chair and went to retrieve it. As he was putting it on, Victor questioned him as to what he was doing. "What are you doing, Marcus?" Marcus looked better than he had, but he was still very weak.

"I told you I need to see Travis. But for now, I need to get out of here. I need to think." Marcus was trying not to make anyone upset, but he needed some space and time. He continued trying to put his coat on.

As Marcus was working on his coat, Victor reached out and took hold of the collar of it and pulled it back off. "No. Not today."

Marcus had pulled away out of the coat and away from Victor. "What? I don't understand. I need to get away from here for a little while. You are not listening."

"No, young man, it's you who is not listening. You will not be going out of this nest anytime soon, and definitely not today." Victor saw that Marcus was going to continue to argue, so he beat him to it. "The streets are not safe for you or any of the kids. Not to mention you still need to heal some more."

"Well, if I can't leave today, when can I?" Marcus was dead set on getting out of here.

Victor looked down at Marcus's feet. "You can go when you can put your socks and shoes on by yourself." Marcus stopped talking and looked down at his bare feet, then he simply walked away from all of them. So angry that they would not help him in the way he wanted them to.

Earlier that day, Victor had seen Marcus try to put his socks on. He kept losing his breath when he tried to bend over. His ribs were still too painful. This would give Marcus a goal that would both keep him here for now but give him something he would work for later.

Jake went to follow Marcus, but Victor stopped him. "Let him be alone for a while. I think he needs some space and time to think about all this right now." Victor looked at Sandy and Mark then back at Jake. "There is a lot to take in, and a lot of changes are coming our way."

Sometime later, Jake found Marcus sitting on his cot doing schoolwork with a group of the boys. Marcus was reading out loud sentences from the Bible, and the boys were writing them down. Jake smiled to himself. He noticed that Marcus had one sock on. This kid was amazing. Jake and Marcus did not say anything to each other, but they gave a nod of recognition, and Jake moved on.

CHAPTER 28

A lot of decisions were made that last day in the nest. It had now been two weeks, and things were starting to settle down in the local area when it came to the kids. People get all worked up but are quick to forget when another big event comes along to take its place. This story about the kids had been no different. Some political person had been caught doing some crazy thing, and the heat was off the Knowing and the kids for now.

It was decided that the Singleton brothers would stay away from all of the Knowing. There would be a "no contact order" was what Victor had called it. Jake was not happy about the idea, but like Marcus, he had to go along with the plan for the good of the group.

Mark had gone back to school and continued his way of life. Jake was doing the counseling like he had been ordered and would be going back to work in about three weeks. Some of the smaller nests were being shut down. It would be just a matter of time until all of them would be gone, even Marcus's.

Since the article in the paper had come out, support for the Knowing had dropped tremendously. Jake and Mark would try and get information from Smitty about what was needed, but Smitty respected Victor's orders of no contact and answered them as if they had not said anything about the group.

Jake and Mark knew that there was a lack of food at the nests but could not figure out how to get food to them. Marcus's nest had been moved. Several times, from what Jake could figure out. Every day Jake would go to the coffee shop and spend some time there hoping that sooner or later he would run into one of the kids. He was sure that Marcus would get his kids back working as soon as he felt it was safe.

*****

It was the beginning of the third week after the article while Jake was sitting at his table at the coffee shop when he noticed a movement from under the bench. Yes, something had caught his eye. Yes, it was what he thought. It was Jimmy. He was signaling Jake. "Hi. We miss you. Are you okay?" Jake was so excited to see him he wanted to run across the room and take him up in a big hug, but this would have to do.

Jake had to really think about the signs. He had in fact only used it once, and that was weeks ago. "Yes, I am okay. Who are you with?" Jake had not seen a sign of any of the others yet.

"Mike, Zach, and Aaron are here too." Jimmy was not being careful, and his hand was almost stepped on.

Jake realized that he needed to back off and let them do their job. Jake also knew that it would be only a matter of time until he would get to see Marcus.

It seemed that time went on forever. Jake sat and watched the boys gather information. Smitty was up to his own work helping them. From time to time he would see Smitty give the kids food. They ate some and put some in their pockets. Smitty had put food in a backpack and left it on the floor by the coatrack. Jake kept an eye on that part of the project so he could learn how to pass things to the nest.

There it was. A large group of people had entered the room, and someone had slipped in behind them. Jake was not sure at first who it was, but when he got a glimpse of his side view, it was Marcus. Jake's heart sank. It was Marcus all right, but he looked awful. He must have aged ten years since the last time he had seen him. He was so thin, and he did not have any light in his eyes. What on earth had happened since he had seen him last? Marcus had entered and had snagged the backpack as he went by the coatrack. He then went down the hall heading to the bathroom. For one quick second,

Jake saw the old Marcus he knew. Marcus had seen Jake, and for a moment, Jake saw that he was glad to see him, but it was quickly covered by another emotion. There was a signal. "We are working, back off." Jake got it, and he did as he was asked. Clearly this "no contact order" was outdated, and it needed to be reversed. Marcus needed help.

Marcus continued down the hall and went into the bathroom where he closed the door behind him. Jake was close behind, but when he opened the door, there was no Marcus. Worse than that, when Jake went back into the room, all the kids were gone. And Jake still had no way to talk to them.

Jake was done with this craziness. He needed to talk to Victor *now*. How long could this "no contact order" stay in place? Obviously it had not been good for everyone. He himself did not like it, and from what he had just seen, it had not been good for Marcus either. Jake headed out to find Victor, or at the least Sandy. What day was it? It is Tuesday. Okay, Sandy should be at the shelter on Front Street cooking if her schedule was the same. Maybe Peggy would be there. That thought made Jake happy. Jake set out to find them and to get back into the Knowing life.

Jake went to Front Street and looked into a small window. Sandy was there all right. Jake needed a plan. If he went in the shelter by way of the front door, he would enter as an officer. But if he entered by the side wall, then he came as friend and would be in the kitchen where Sandy was currently. This was a no-brainer. He was a friend, and "no contact order" or not, he needed to talk to Victor even if it was through Sandy.

Jake went down the alley, covered his medallion with foil and used the side wall entrance to get into the shelter.

As Jake came through the wall, he was met with a "no surprise" look from Sandy. "Hi, Jake. I take it you saw Marcus?" She continued cooking and working with the food.

"Sandy, what on earth happened?" Jake moved on into the room and began to help her with the food. "Is Marcus still hurt? Did he not heal right?"

Sandy smiled at Jake and gave him a small side hug. "I have missed you. How is Mark doing?"

"I miss all of you too, and Mark and all of us are doing fine. I am here to talk about Marcus and his kids." Jake looked around the room. "Have they been here lately?"

"Jake, we are in a 'no contact' status. That means for the good of us all, we do not interact with anyone other than our group or nest." She wiped her hands and placed them on Jake's arms. "Marcus has been and is on his own for now. We had not seen him for almost two weeks. But when we did, we saw what you did."

"Sandy, Marcus is not doing well. Something is very wrong." Jake was pacing.

As he and Sandy were talking, Victor came through the side wall followed by one of Marcus's kids. It was John, and if Jake remembered it right, John was fourteen years old. Jake walked quickly over to the two new visitors.

"I see that you do not think the 'no contact order' included you, Jake." Victor was speaking to him all the while watching over Jake's back to see that Sandy was signaling him something. But he continued to talk to Jake. "I think you know John."

"Hi, John. How is it going over at the nest?" Jake wanted information, and he wanted it fast.

John looked up at Victor. He wanted to see if he had his permission to talk in front of Jake. Victor nodded yes, and John began to answer. "Things are okay."

Victor could hear the hesitation in John's statement. "Things are okay at the nest, but what?" Victor sat down in a chair that was handy. It would look less intimidating. God knows the look on Jake's face was enough to scare anyone. "So what is going on at the nest that is not okay?"

John looked down and thought for a few seconds. "I think that Marcus is going to go away." John looked up at Victor. "I think he is going to do something dangerous. And maybe get into trouble and not get to come back to us and the nest." There, he had said it.

"John, why do you think that?" Victor was trying to follow his lead but got lost on the logic. "Can you explain what you mean?"

John took a deep breath and then continued, "Marcus is upset all the time. He does not eat or sleep very much. When he gets to sleep, he wakes up, I think from bad dreams. And he pretends like he eats but, when he thinks no one is looking at him, puts the food back or gives it to one of the younger kids. He tells me all the time that I need to learn how to run the nest because when he is gone, it will most likely be me who takes over for him." John paused. Then he said, "And I really don't like his new friend. I think he might be mean to Marcus or something because he makes Marcus go with him sometimes when Marcus does not want to go."

"Marcus has a new friend?" Jake was quick to pick up on that one. "What new friend? Where did he come from? Where do you think they go when they go out? What about your kids? Who is with you when he goes out?"

Victor gave Jake a look of "say another word..." and Jake stopped his questioning.

"Hey, John, do you know what Marcus's new friend's name is?" Victor did not want to bring any fear to this meeting. "Do you know where he came from?"

John thought about it and then said, "I think his name is Will. And Marcus said that he came because Travis had sent him with a message."

Jake put his hands in his hair and pushed it away from his face. "Travis. What is it with that kid? Every time I hear his name, it is trouble for Marcus and the rest of us." Jake knew in his gut that this was all wrong. Something was not right with this whole setup. "Where is Marcus now?"

"I don't know. He said he would be back tomorrow, early." John started toward the wall door. "I need to go. I need to help with the younger kids. I told Marcus that I would take care of it for him."

Jake started to follow him, but Victor stepped close to him and motioned him to wait. "John, thanks for coming. It was a good thing to tell us your concerns for Marcus. We are going to help him. Okay?" Victor helped him open the wall and to slip out to be on his way.

Victor returned to two not very happy faces. Sandy and Jake looked set to pounce. "Okay, you two settle down. We need to make a plan. First of all, Jake, can you see if you can find out about this Will guy? And second, Sandy, I think we should stay the night at the nest and be there in the morning when Marcus returns."

Jake was going to offer to be at the nest too but realized he had really pushed the "no contact thing" too far already. "Victor, I will try to see what I can find out about this new friend of Marcus's. I will also try and find whoever it was that helped Travis get a message out and what that message was." Jake was ready to go out the wall door but turned to talk to Victor. "Hey, Victor, do you think you can stop this 'no contact order' now? Things are better, and we all know it."

Victor turned Jake around toward the door and gave him a slap on the back. "Like that ever stopped you from talking to anyone you wanted." Jake looked to get an answer. "Okay. Yes, it is off. Now go find out what you can. We will see you tomorrow."

Jake took off the foil cover from his medallion and walked down the street big as life. What a difference a chip can make. Jake needed to find out about this guy Will, but he was not back at work yet, so that was a closed door. Mark was at the school and off the street, so no luck would be there. Sally. That would work. If Jake could talk to Sally, he could get her to find out what she could about this Will guy. Jake's heart was so happy with the thought of his very own sister helping the Knowing. In fact, being a part of the Knowing. "Thank You, God." Off Jake went to find Sally. Jake did not get to talk to Sally very long because when he did find her, she was working. She could only speak to Jake long enough for him to give her "Will's" name and to confirm that there was a family dinner this Thursday. Only two days from now. He had agreed that would be soon enough for the information unless she found something really awful about him.

Jake decided visiting Mark at the school could be a good move. So he went over to the school and to the apartment building Mark lived in. Jake was glad to see that Mark was there. He could hear music coming from his room. Jake knocked, and Mark was quick to answer and to invite Jake in. "Hey, what are you doing here?" Mark looked down the hall to see if anyone had followed him.

Jake was not sure himself as to why he decided to come to Mark's place, but at the time, it seemed like a good idea. "I wanted to see if you had learned anything of value? I talked to Sally, and she said that she would talk to me on Thursday, at the family dinner." Jake would have forgotten the dinner again. Time was getting away from him. He guessed it was because he was not working. "I sure was glad that Sally reminded me of it."

Mark watched as Jake paced around his apartment. He was talking half sentences and going from subject to subject with no real conversation. "Jake, what are you doing here?"

Jake blinked. "Can't a brother visit for no special reason at all?"

Mark knew what needed to be done. "Hey, Jake, let's play ball." Mark took a basketball and tossed it to Jake. "Let's go, little brother. I think I am going to beat the pants off you." Mark knew that Jake could never ignore a challenge.

"You're on." Jake and Mark went straight to the basketball court there at the school.

Mark knew exactly what to do. Jake was all tied up in his mind about too many things. He needed to use up some energy so he could think straight. Mark had not needed to help Jake work through something like this in years, but he could see the pattern. Mark could see that Jake cared too much, and too deep sometimes. Having God in his life had made him even more aware of others around him. Jake had Christ's love now, and he did not recognize it.

Mark threw the ball way ahead of Jake and ran him all over the court. He made sure that Jake had few, if any, breaks during the game. When Mark was sure that Jake was good and worn out, he motioned for the two of them to take a break. They got a drink from the water fountain and stretched out on the grass.

Mark noticed that Jake was tired, but he was more relaxed. The trick had worked. Mark was smiling. "So, Jake, what are you really here for?"

Jake did not think about his answer he just spoke. "Mark, we have to get Marcus and all those kids off the streets and into homes of some sort. It is only a matter of time until someone gets hurt."

Mark was shocked to hear what Jake was thinking. "Jake, I thought you were Marcus's friend. That kid does a great job running the nest. The information he and his kids gather is priceless. Getting the information about what all is going on is such a big part of how the Knowing works. Not to mention what it would do to Marcus to have his kids taken away from him. Think about what you are saying."

"I am. I think we need to think of all the kids, even Marcus. They need to be kids, and they need to be safe. I am not trying to be mean but practical. I think that because of how good Marcus can run the nests, you all forget that he is still only fifteen years old. And that it is a lot of responsibility, for anyone, especially for a kid." Jake came to the end of the sentence and then realized that he had not even known that he felt this way.

Mark sat quiet thinking about what Jake had said. Perhaps Jake had a point. But so many people relied on the information the kids gathered. God only knows what would happen or how it could be replaced. "Jake, I really don't think you understand what you are asking."

Jake looked over at Mark. "Perhaps you are right, but I can feel it in my gut that something is going to happen."

Jake and Mark parted ways. Jake felt better even though he did not have any more answers than he did when he had arrived at the school.

Jake had hit a dead end in the gathering of information. But he did have a better understanding about helping Marcus and what that would look like. It looked like taking Marcus's job away and removing his kids. It did not look right, but somehow Jake knew it was the right thing to do. Perhaps if he talked to Victor and Sandy, he might get a better understanding of what he thought God was telling him. So with that in mind, Jake went to the nest.

CHAPTER 29

Victor and Sandy finished work at the shelter, and when all was set there, they got themselves over to the nest. Everything was perfect except one thing. Marcus was still not there. "Sandy, where is that kid? I could brain him. He of all people knows how dangerous it is to be out so late at night." Victor was now feeling some of Jake's concerns.

Jake entered the side wall and found Victor and Sandy sitting at the table having some tea. It looked like everyone else was asleep. "Hi, you two, I see there is still no Marcus. Have you learned anything else?" Jake sat down by them at the table.

Victor watched as Jake got seated at the table. "I guess from the look on your face you did not have any better luck than we did."

"No. I think it might be a couple of days before we know anything new about this Will character." Jake was discouraged, but he was not defeated.

As they were talking, there was a quick opening of the side wall door, and someone came in with such urgency that the three at the table were alarmed as to who it was and as to what was wrong. All three got up and went to see what was going on. The person had come in and shut the door and was leaning on it with his hands almost like he was holding it closed. His head was down, so it was hard to see who it was. They were surprised to say the least to find out that this was Marcus. He was dressed in an outfit they had never seen before. Victor got really close behind him before he spoke. "I sure hope you have a good explanation for this one, Marcus."

Marcus nearly jumped out of his skin when he realized that an adult was behind him. And even more surprised to see that there were three. "What are all of you doing here? Are the boys all okay?" Marcus turned, stood up straight, and continued to talk. "It does not matter why you are here, but since you are, we have a problem, and I think it may get bigger soon."

Jake was going to address Marcus about being on the streets after curfew, but Victor beat him to it. "Is it a problem bigger than the leader of this nest running around the streets late at night? Could it be bigger than the kids at this nest being left alone without their leader? Or is it the part that you are running around with someone who is a friend of Travis, who clearly wants to do harm to you? How am I doing, Marcus? Or could it be the fact that you have a new friend that the kids feel is dangerous. How am I doing so far?"

Victor was a man of few words, but when he did talk, he went directly to the point. This kind of conversation was a good way to get information quick, but it even made Jake uncomfortable for Marcus.

Victor continued, "And where is Travis? And what were you fighting about this time?"

Jake, Sandy, and Marcus all turned a direct eye onto Victor. Victor turned to Sandy and Jake. "Go ahead, ask him about the fight." Victor reached out and took one of Marcus's hands to point out one of his knuckles that clearly had been hurt, most likely by fighting. "Only this time you fought back. Marcus, what changed that would make you get yourself into a fight? This is not like you. Now what is going on?"

Jake was amazed at how observant Victor had been. He himself had not picked up on the fact that Marcus had been fighting. Victor would have made a good officer, maybe he already was in a way. He is like a God officer.

Marcus was upset. "I think Travis has a gun."

Victor's head shot up, and full attention was now on Travis and the subject. "What do you mean you think he has a gun? Does he or doesn't he?"

Jake could not hold back any longer. "You think he has a gun, and you went to fight with him. Are you crazy or just suicidal?"

The conversation was getting louder, and Sandy wanted to help calm things done some. "Okay, why don't we all go and have a seat and talk about this. We need to figure what is what, and it is not helping things by getting upset."

Marcus walked away and sat at the table. The two other men joined him, and Sandy made some more tea.

Victor's attention was now completely on Marcus. "So explain what is going on. You said that there was a problem. What is it?"

"There is a family who left the Knowing, you have heard of them. Well, they are going to be here this week sometime. There is a group who wants to make sure that they do not get to tell what they know. They want to stop them before they get to the courthouse and tell. I guess from what Travis said, everyone is getting tired of being loving and peaceful. They want to take action and not just stand around and wait to see what happens. Travis wants me to join them and to bring the boys along because they can carry things in and out easy."

Jake added, "You mean involve the young ones in a fight?"

Marcus did not answer but continued, "I thought if I hung out with them, I could change Travis's mind and get him to see how wrong he was. I swear I would never have let them use the boys. I just wanted to get Travis out of this group."

It was clear that everyone in the room knew that Marcus was telling the truth. That was the kind of man he was. But even though he had good intentions, he never should have been out with that group, for any reason, not even if it meant saving Travis.

The side wall opened very quietly. They all watched as it closed behind someone. This time it was Mark. From the look on his face, there was a problem. And it must have been a big one in order for Mark to come out like this.

"Victor, it is all over the news. They have arrested some of the Knowing. Victor, they say that when they picked them up, they all had guns." Mark had come over by the table.

Victor looked at Marcus. "What do you know about this?"

Marcus had stood up. "No. When I left, the group was going to go home for the night. Travis's friend Will was going to help them get rid of the guns. Travis was going to come back to the nest. He said—"

"It does not matter what he said." Victor was going into action mode. "We need information. All the information we can get." He turned to Jake. "I think this is where you are going to come in handy. Jake, do you think you can go to the station and see what is really going on? We cannot trust the news broadcast to tell us everything. Find out who and how many and how this happened."

Marcus got by Jake's side. "I am going to go with him. I can bring back the information if need be."

It was almost like a choir of voices in answer to Marcus's statement. "Oh no, you are not." The fact that Marcus was shocked by this answer was a dead giveaway of his youth.

Marcus went to argue. "Jake, you need to tell them that I need to go and help my brother. You know that I am right. You of all people must know how this is. What if it was your brother?"

This was a tough one. If it had been one of his brothers, Jake would have moved heaven and earth to try and save him. But it would be wrong to put himself in danger because of a brother's bad choice. In fact, Travis had put the whole Knowing in danger.

Jake put his hand on Marcus's shoulders and looked him straight in the eye. "Marcus, you want to be treated as a man and as an adult, so I am going to tell this to you like one. What needs to happen and what is going to happen are two and the same. I am going to go and try and get as much information tonight as I can. And you—" Marcus started to say something, but Jake gave him a slight shake and continued to speak to him. "And you, Marcus, are going to stay here and get the boys ready for tomorrow's gathering of information in the courthouse park."

Marcus stood looking at Jake. "You do not understand. I have to go. Someone else can take care of the boys. I have to take care of my brother and you."

The statement "and take care of you" caught Jake off guard. "What do you mean take care of me and Travis?"

Marcus was in a dilemma. "I can't explain. I just need to go."

Jake kept an eye on Marcus. "Why?"

Marcus, who was almost in tears, said, "I need to save him. And because Travis has a gun."

"And so do I." Jake pulled up his jacket in the back and showed him his handgun in the holster. It was government issued. And it was part of his everyday life. "And I will save him if I can. Marcus, you need to trust that God has a plan for you and your brother. Your going out and getting in a fight with him can only make it worse." Jake got in front of him. "I know that this feels all wrong, but trust me, it is the best choice we have for now. Your time will come. I promise. You need to stay here and let me do my job. Marcus, if you can't trust me, then trust God."

Victor walked over by Marcus and put his arm across his upper back. "Jake, you go and get all the information you can. And we will stay here, pray, and get ready for tomorrow. Right, Marcus?" Victor could feel the tension in Marcus. There was a war going on inside of him that only he could fight. But God needed to win, and the way Victor saw it, each had to do what they were called to do, and Marcus staying here was his part as much as Jake's going was his.

Marcus did not speak. He took a flashlight off the table and headed out to do rounds. He stopped partway and turned to speak to Jake. "Please, for God's sakes, help my brother...and be careful. Remember we are praying." He turned and went to do rounds.

Victor and Jake spoke briefly, and then Jake gave Sandy a kiss on her cheek and turned to leave. "Are you coming, Mark?" Both men went to find out what they could.

*****

Jake and Mark were only two blocks away when Jake stopped and motioned for Mark to talk with him. "Mark, I am not sure how we are going to pull this off? We need to be extra careful around this kid Travis. He knows us and has seen us with the Knowing. Both men uncovered their medallions and were now in the chipped world.

"Jake, what are you going to do if Travis pulls a gun on you?" Mark hoped that Jake had a plan.

Jake looked up to the sky. "You know, Mark, ever since I found out who God was and how He sent his son to save us, I wondered if He really did live in the details of our everyday lives. But time and time again, the little things keep happening that prove it to be true. So what I believe in faith right now is that God cares about all of this, way more than we do, and that He has a plan, even if we are not aware of it yet. So what I am thinking is that we should pray and then step out and discover the plan God has."

Mark was amazed at how much his little brother had grown in his faith. It was obvious that Jake had been reading his Bible more than he let on. "Jake, you really do surprise me in your planning on God being the one who is making the plan, but it is as good as any idea that I could come up with. So do we stay together or split up?"

Jake gave it some thought and decided that two were better than one in this outing. Perhaps if they went to the station hanging out as brothers, it would distract people as to what they really were doing. And what they were going to do is to try and see who it was they arrested and what they had done with them.

As the two men entered the government station, it was a buzz of action. The newspeople were there, and they were all over the fact that the Knowing had been caught with guns. The only problem they had was that all of the people they had arrested were adults, and none under the age of seventeen. Jake and Mark looked at the group on a monitor on one of the desks. There were faces that both Jake and Mark had never seen, and there was no Travis, or this new friend of his Will. Jake had looked over the paperwork listing all of the arrests and noted that two names had been blacked out. He thought it odd but nothing that would make him think anything was up. Not yet anyway. The two walked around and visited with some old friends, some of them they had known for years. It was different now. They both wanted to see these people get to know Christ the way they did. They figured that God must have a plan for that one too. But at the end of their searching, there was no Travis and no Will. The only thing they did know for sure was that all of these young adults were not of the Knowing they had worked with and that they had been chipped and were being sent away to a holding area.

Mark and Jake left the station and decided to cut through the park. It was a dark night with the moon covered by clouds. Many of the streetlights had been turned off to save energy, so it was a dark pathway they were on. As Jake and Mark rounded the corner, Jake saw Mr. Diggings. Jake reached out and pulled Mark off the path and into some bushes nearby. Mark started to question Jake about what he was doing when he himself saw the man. Then two others joined him. One was older, more Jake's and Mark's age, but the other was a kid. It was Travis.

Jake and Mark pulled back into the bushes, crouched down, and tried to listen as best they could. From the conversation, they concluded that Travis and this man both worked for Mr. Diggings and that he was very happy with a job well done. Mr. Diggings had slapped both men on the back several times showing his appreciation for the work they had done. All three men were laughing at how easy it was to set this up, making it look like the Knowing group was armed and dangerous and had expressed how very stupid this Knowing group was. Travis showed no sign of remorse; in fact, he was full of pride and joy over the matter. Mr. Diggings had talked about the fact that thirteen Knowing in all were removed from the street and had been chipped and sent away. He expressed at how excited he was that they were getting closer to taking out the Knowing. It was well into the conversation that Mr. Diggings pulled two guns out of his pocket and gave one to each of them. "You would not want to be found without these now, would you? Especially now that you are a part of the Knowing, you need to be armed." They all laughed. They were parting ways when Mr. Diggings called out to Travis's friend. "Hey, Will, great job. You know that you have accomplished more in a few weeks than Singleton did in six months?" They continued on their separate ways. Mr. Diggings one way, and Travis and the now named friend the other.

Jake and Mark stayed there well after the men left. Neither one of them wanting to talk about what they had seen and heard. Jake was not just mad, he was literally sick at the thought of what Travis had done. How could Marcus and Travis be such opposites? What on earth could have made things turn out this way? God only knows. That was right. God only knows.

Mark decided it was time to discuss their next move. "So, now what do we do? These men are clearly up to something, and from the sound of it, the something is to take out the Knowing by turning everyone against them."

Jake was speechless. He kept thinking about the conversation and how Travis really did not care about what he was doing to his brother or his friends. Jake shook his head. This was going to be an even bigger problem than any of them had imagined.

Jake was slow to speak. "Tomorrow is a big day of work for Marcus and the kids. I think we should wait and tell them what we saw after they finish their workday. But I think we have to tell Victor and Sandy as soon as possible. They need to know that Travis and Will are armed and that they work for the government."

They both agreed that this was a good idea but would need to run this by Victor and Sandy as what to do about telling Marcus.

CHAPTER 30

Marcus had finished his rounds, it was very early in the morning. Everyone else was still asleep. This was one of his favorite times of day. This was his time alone with God. Things have been so crazy for so long that he felt like he was bugging God about the same thing day after day. He prayed for the kids, the Knowing, Victor and Sandy, and so many of the other adults that were a part of his everyday life. He prayed for Smitty and about how he helped to make sure they got as much food as they could spare for all of them in the nest. He prayed for his parents, and especially he prayed for his brother, Travis. What had he done wrong to make him so angry? But today was somewhat different for him in his prayers. Marcus went to God for physical help too. He had come down with a slight cold about a week ago and had developed a cough. He did not need God to do anything big, but he was tired, and the cough was not going away. So many things had gone wrong, and now his body had become his enemy. He had been hurt some time ago and thought he had healed, but now his body was giving him trouble again. He was young and was supposed to be strong, so why now, of all times, would he be feeling bad again?

"God, please help me to be strong and to do the work You gave me. Help me to make good decisions and to be the kind of person that would bring glory to You. Help me to be a good friend and a good brother. Help all of us as we work today gathering information. Please keep us safe. I thank You for all of the things You have already done for all of us. Please help me to be strong mentally and physically. Whatever this cough is, please help take it away, but if not, then could You help it to not interfere with our working today? I love You, God. Thank You for sending Your Son, in Jesus's name. Amen."

By the time Marcus was finished with his prayers, the nest was awake and getting ready to go out and work the park. The weather was not warm, but at least it was not raining. Victor and Sandy had stayed the night and were up helping with morning chores. They all had breakfast and then lessons. Today was Bible readings from The Psalms. They were exactly what they all needed to hear. They had covered each other in mud and were gathering for the prayer before they went to work.

Victor and Sandy were meeting with Mark and Jake off to one side of the room. Marcus could tell from the way they were acting that there was news about Travis. He needed to get the kids ready and off to the park, but he also needed to know what was going on with his brother. Marcus walked over to the adult group and asked, "What did you find out about Travis and the rest of them?"

Victor looked at Jake so he would do the telling. "There were thirteen young men from this area that were arrested and chipped. Travis was not one of them."

Relief was all over Marcus's face. Not joy but relief all the same. "Do we know where Travis is now?"

Victor added to the story not telling a lie but not the whole truth either. "We do not know where he is exactly, but we do know that he is safe and that he has not been chipped." Victor looked at Jake to confirm what he had said. "Is that the way you would say it, Jake?"

"Yes, that sounds right." Jake made an exit from the adult group to go and help one of the boys put away his bedding.

Victor and Sandy went back to drying dishes. Marcus needed to talk to Victor. "Victor, I need a favor."

Victor turned to look at Marcus. "I need you to keep Jake and Mark out of the park where we are working today."

What Marcus did not know was that Jake had walked up and was standing right behind him. "I do not want them there today. They distract the boys when they are working."

Victor raised an eyebrow. "You mean they distract you, especially the part where Jake can figure you out. Marcus, this is not like you. What are you up to? What is going on in that head of yours?"

Marcus gave no answer. He turned and saw that Jake was standing behind him.

Victor continued, "Well, it is not going to happen. We need all the manpower we can get. Jake and Mark stay in the plan."

Marcus took a deep breath. He coughed a little. "That's fine then, if you are sure. I need to get ready." And he continued getting geared up for the job.

Marcus walked away. Victor looked at Jake. "Keep an extra eye on him today, will you? I think there is something that he is not telling us."

Jake rolled his eyes. "There seems to be a lot of that going on around here, don't you think?"

Jake was not sure if not telling Marcus about his brother working with the government was the right thing to do. After thinking about it, Jake wondered if there could have been a better way to handle this whole thing, but he could not think of anything.

They all gathered into a circle and had prayer. Victor was the one who did the leading of the prayer. Marcus was having a hard time talking with his head down, it made him cough more. The groups went out a few at a time. They would all meet up at the park sooner or later. Marcus stood watching as each group left. Victor noticed sadness in Marcus's face as they did. "What's wrong?"

Marcus did not hear him speak but kept looking the direction the boys had gone. Then he walked away, following the groups he had sent out.

Jake had seen the interaction between Victor and Marcus, or rather the lack of interaction. "What was that all about? I knew he would be worried about today, but I think this is more than a little concerned."

All Victor said was "Agreed." And he walked away after Marcus. As Victor was following after Marcus, he noticed that he stopped a lot and took a break or two. More like an old man than a fifteen-year-old kid.

Marcus arrived at the park. It looked like everyone was in place for the day's work. Jake was excited to see them work again. It was a wonderful sight to see. The signals were so slight but very exact. Jake watched as the gathering of the information was underway.

The park was full of people. Many had come out to see if they could get a look at the "bad" Knowing who had been arrested. A lot of people, a lot of talk, and a lot of information.

A signal was sent to John. Marcus coughed, and the signal was all messed up. Time and again the kids were misdirected because of Marcus needing to cough. Jake left the park for a short time and returned with a bag of cough drops. He found Jimmy and asked him to get them to Marcus. A signal to Jake, "Thank you, but please stay out of this. Jimmy is in the wrong place."

Jake signaled back, "You're welcome. Now take one."

Marcus did not want to be bossed around by Jake, but he really could use the drops. So he took one.

Signal sent to John, "Did Victor and Sandy get information about the families coming to court next Monday?"

John sent his answer, "Yes, but they need to know more if possible."

Marcus confirmed and continued to work the park. A new shift of kids would be arriving soon, and the chipped lunch crowd would be joining those already at the park. Marcus signaled that all of the teams were to stay in the park for the lunch crowd.

Jake had found himself a wall and placed his back up against it. He had found the perfect place to see the whole park all at the same time. Victor saw him and joined him. "Victor, this is the most remarkable thing to watch. It is hard to remember that these are just kids when I see how detailed they are when they work. What a team." Victor smiled.

All the kids were on alert. Something was wrong. Jake and Victor were both reading the signals when there was a new kind of signal coming from Marcus. Jake turned to Victor. "They have a different code, can you read it?" Victor shook his head no. The signals were all different. Jake and Victor could not read what was being said. John had moved to where Marcus had been. Jake scanned the park to locate where Marcus had gone. There he was walking out of the park with a man. But where was he going, and who was he with? Why would he leave his kids like this? Jake set out to go after Marcus. John and the boys were still using the new signals. Out of nowhere, there came three of the boys; they got in front of Jake and kept him from following Marcus. Jake tried to outmaneuver the kids, but they were really good at this. Marcus had disappeared from sight. This was a plan that Marcus had set up. But why? What were they up to? Jake looked to Victor for advice.

Victor, using the old code, called for a roundup and a return to the nest. *Scatter* was the team word. The boys looked to John, who then confirmed, "Scatter."

The boys left the park group by group, each going a different direction. Jake and Victor went in the direction that the man and Marcus had gone.

"Victor, what is going on?" Jake hoped that Victor had an idea as to what this was all about.

"Jake, I am not sure, but did you get a look at the man Marcus was with?" Victor looked at Jake. "Could it have been Will?"

Of course it was Will. That would make sense. Travis and he were friends. Will could promise Marcus a meeting with Travis. "It is a trap. Travis and Will plan on taking Marcus out of the Knowing."

Victor ended the sentence for him, "And Marcus is heading right into the trap."

Marcus hoped the kids would keep Victor and Jake busy. Marcus needed to get to Travis so he could convince him to return to the nest and the Knowing and be safe once again.

Marcus saw Travis. He was standing right where Will had said he would be. Travis smiled when he saw him. "Hey, little brother, how's it going?"

"Travis, what are you thinking? You need to come with me and come back to the nest." Marcus was trying his hardest to get Travis to see it his way.

"Marcus, you are such a weakling. What kind of a person do you want to be? It is time you man up and be a part of the New World. Marcus, come join us. Here, I have a gift for you." Travis reached down and took Marcus's hand and tried to put a gun into it. "Come and see what it is like to be your own man. No one will be telling you what to do. No babysitting those brats who keep holding you back. You can be a real leader with a real army."

Marcus pulled his hand back, and the gun fell to the ground. "Travis, you do not need guns, and neither do I."

Will had joined them. He reached down to the ground and picked up the gun. "Travis, it doesn't matter if he is found holding the gun or it is in his pocket, it will all be the same—he was armed and dangerous." Will tried to slide the gun into Marcus's coat pocket, but Marcus pulled away, and Will was left holding the gun. "Travis, your brother has more spunk than I thought he would. It is a sad thing to see that such a good mind is controlled by this Knowing cult. Not really a problem though. Once you get him chipped and away from the group, you will have your brother back as good as new." Will had grabbed Marcus by the coat collar and was holding him slightly off-balance.

Marcus broke out into a coughing fit. "Not now, God. I need to be strong and save my brother from this guy. Please give me strength. Help my body to be strong." Marcus felt like his prayers about his health had fallen on deaf ears. His coughing continued.

Will had let go of Marcus's coat collar. He had a look of fear on his face. "Travis, you did not tell me that your brother was sick. What is wrong with him?" Will was wiping his hand off onto his pants like he had touched something filthy. "Travis, if I catch something from this lowlife brother of yours, I'll have your hide." Without thinking, Will took the gun from his other hand and put it back into his own pocket.

There was a sound of cars coming from all directions. It was the government. It was true, Travis and Will were trying to set up and catch Marcus and his nest. Victor and Jake had just caught up to Marcus when they saw the officers pull into the area. All of the officers were out of their cars. They had their guns drawn. They were here to arrest Marcus and his gang, but there was no gang. Reports were coming in over the radios that the park was clear. There was not one single chipless kid to be found.

Jake pulled out his badge and had placed it into his waistband. Victor saw his move and overrode Jake's decision to show himself a supporter of the Knowing. "Not yet, let's see what happens first." Victor was right, but this could get bad and really fast.

Travis was hearing the radio calls about how the kids were not in the park. He had promised Mr. Diggings that at least thirteen kids and a few adults would be arrested. Travis was furious. "Marcus, where are they?" He grabbed Marcus and pushed him around, causing him to fall backward into a set of bushes along the side of a creek. It was only a slight hill behind the bushes, but with the push Travis had given him, Marcus slid down the small embankment and into the creek. It was not very deep, but Marcus was covered in mud and was wet to the bone. The shock of the cold water gave Marcus more strength than he had had in a long time. He came flying up out of the water and was heading straight for Travis and Will, who were now being arrested. They were chipless, and both had guns on them. Marcus was almost to the bushes and could see Travis being put into the government car. He needed to get his brother out of that car. He was ready to clear the bushes and get to Travis when he felt himself being pulled once again back down the hill and into the water. Only this time it was not a shove so much as a pull. Someone had grabbed him from behind, and they both slid down together. When they hit the water, it was to Marcus's surprise that it was Mark who had pulled him down.

Mark had been looking for all of them when he had seen Marcus and Travis talking. He was not sure exactly what was going on but knew that if Marcus had gone back to the clearing he would have been arrested also.

Marcus was wet, again. He was muddy, and he had lost his boys, and now his brother had been arrested. "Mark, what do you think you are doing? Are you out of your mind? Get out of here and leave me alone, will you?" Marcus was trying to get himself as dry as he could. The car that had Travis in it was gone, and his only chance to save his brother from being chipped was ruined by Mark. He was so angry. "I need to go and find my boys. I need to see if they are okay, and then I need to figure out how I am going to help Travis. So,

Mark, please get away from me. And while you are at it, keep your brother away too."

This was a mess, and there was nothing he could do about it. He felt a cough coming on, but when he went to get a cough drop, they were all wet and stuck together. He tossed them in a trash can as he went by, but then on second thought, he decided to keep them. He could dry them out, and they would be okay. As he was retrieving them from the trash, there was an officer walking by who took note of Marcus. "Kid, are you all right?" The officer sounded kind. He was middle-aged and had come over to where Marcus was. "You look a little wet and cold to me. I have a blanket in the car. Do you want it?" Marcus looked at this guy; he thought he had seen him before, but he could not remember where it had been.

"No, I think I just need to get home and I will be fine, but thanks anyway." Marcus went to walk away, but the officer asked him to hold up a moment longer. "Here, take this." When Marcus looked at what he was offering, it was a sandwich and a bag of chips. He looked at the officer and was grateful for the offer but felt that to take it would be wrong right now. He needed to get home. Marcus looked at the officer's badge. It had the name *Hansen* on it. "Thank you, Officer Hansen. But I will be okay now. But really, thanks anyway."

"Okay, if you are sure." The officer began to walk away but turned back and called out to Marcus. "Hey, kid?" Marcus looked at him. So the officer continued. "Take care of yourself too. You cannot help others if you get yourself into too much trouble first. Simply a word of advice." And like that, he was gone.

Victor and Jake had watched the encounter with the officer. Jake had seen him long ago at the shelter. He had in fact been saved before by this very officer. Jake made a move to go and join Marcus, but Victor stopped him once again. "Jake, I think it would be best if you stay away from Marcus for a few days. We need to all pull back and regroup. We have no idea about how much Travis has shared or Will has found out. Jake, one of the most important things I can think of for you to do is to stay clear and be distant from the Knowing for now. That means all of us."

"Are you going to make another 'no contact order'? Victor, I think you are wrong. I think Marcus needs us more now than ever. And I need to know what he thought he was doing trying to meet up with Travis like that." Jake wanted to be right, but he knew that Victor might be. So far Jake had kept his being among the Knowing a secret. And that was one advantage they had. Even Will had not seen him, and that was a bigger advantage. And he knew it.

Marcus was wet. He was tired, and he was angry. He was angry at himself for being so dumb to think that he could have changed Travis's mind. He was mad at his body for being so weak. Something was wrong with him, and he needed it to go away. He was so tired, and this dumb cough, what is that all about? "God, why don't You help me? I need to be strong now, of all times. I need help, God. I need You to show me what it is You want. Please help me and my brother. Give me wisdom and application. Help me to do everything You want me to do. Please?"

When Marcus got to the nest, everything was quiet, until he walked in, that was. The boys came from every direction with a lot of questions. Jimmy ran up to him. "Did you save Travis? We tried to keep Victor and Jake longer, but they took over from John and signaled for us to all go home. Was that what we were supposed to do?"

"Yes, that was exactly what you needed to do. Great job, everyone." Marcus was too tired to say much else. He told them that Travis had been arrested and that he would have Victor and Jake check things out and find out where he had been taken. He explained that they had done a great job today. They had gathered a lot of information, and it was going to make a big difference to the Knowing.

Marcus had them say a prayer of thanks, and he checked that there was enough food for the next two meals. It was a small amount of food, but they would not go to bed hungry.

CHAPTER 31

It was very late at the nest by the time everyone was cleaned up, had dinner, finished their studies, and were in bed for the night. Marcus had hoped that after the goings-on today that there might be a "no contact order" given, and so far, it looked like that would be the case. This would give him time to regroup. He needed to get the boys under control and to reassure them that they would all be okay.

Marcus needed to find out about Travis and to figure out how to help him. But for now, he needed to trust that Victor and Sandy were all over this. If anyone knew how important it was to get Travis back, it would be Victor. And perhaps even Jake might be on it too. "Oh, God, please help!"

Marcus was sitting in the chair looking so tired that John did not want to bother him, but he felt that they needed to talk. "Hey, Marcus, how are you feeling?"

Marcus looked up and began to cough slightly, cleared his throat, and began to talk to John. "You did a good job today, John. I think you will be good at running nests someday."

John's face lit up. "You mean you are not mad that we did not hold Victor and Jake longer? I was not too sure about letting Victor call a Scatter, sending everyone home, but it did seem to be the only choice at the time."

"You did great, John." Marcus was as sincere as he had ever been. "In fact, John, I think that your calling it that way may have saved our whole nest from being arrested. You did it perfectly."

John watched as Marcus had another coughing fit. "Marcus, are you going to be okay? Maybe you should get some help for your cough?"

Marcus reached into his pocket and pulled out the bag of wet cough drops he had saved. He held them up so John could see them. "Jake is already on it. He gave me these today, and they really do help. But thank you. I will be fine. So why don't you get some rest. We are going to move the nest early in the morning. We need to be someplace totally new for a time. I found a new place a few weeks ago. Even Victor does not know where we will be."

After their conversation, John felt that Marcus was not as ill as he had first thought. He was making plans. He was still on the job. "Okay, Marcus, I will see you in the morning." John was looking at how Marcus was still wet. "You might want to get out of those wet clothes. I think you will feel better if you do."

Marcus nodded his head in agreement. "I will. I just need to rest awhile." Marcus pulled his coat up around himself and lay back into the overstuffed chair he had been sitting in. John looked at him for a short time and then decided that Marcus must know best.

*****

The next morning, the boys moved the nest. As far as anyone knew, Marcus's nest was simply gone. He had moved his boys to safety, and no one knew where they were; and as far as Marcus was concerned, that was the way it would stay. Food was going to be the issue. There had to be one contact at least, and that person would need to know that he and the boys were still in town. So who could he trust? Sandy would tell Victor. And Jake knew about Smitty, but they were not really friends. Yes, it would be Smitty he would talk to about getting food. In the meantime, there was very little food, but they would make do until he could get it worked out. Marcus felt much better. He had a good night's sleep, and even though he still had a cough, he felt better than he had been feeling.

*****

Jake was not happy at all about his not being able to talk to anyone from the Knowing. This was not a good thing for Marcus or for the boys. He wanted to talk to Victor, but he was nowhere to be found. Sandy was at the shelter, but she was being watched, all of the shelters were. Jake had gone home last night to find a phone message saying that the family dinner this week was canceled. This did not make Jake happy. He wanted to talk to Mark and to Sally about the boys and what would be done with them. Jake knew that the kids were good at what they were doing, but he also knew that it was getting too dangerous for them to remain on the street. Travis had told so much information, that several of the nests had been found and put out of use. The question of the day was, how could he get to Marcus? Jake wanted to help. No one else could understand how Jake was feeling because he did not understand it himself. He just knew what it felt like to be alone on the street. He knew that Marcus and the kids needed help and that he was going to be the one to do it. But how could he if he could not find them?

Jake read his Bible, and he prayed. He had gone over in his mind several times about all the things he knew about the shelter and the nests. The only common factor was that everyone needed food. How would Marcus get food for the kids? Sandy and Victor were out because of the new watch placed on the shelters and the medical clinics. The news had reported that there might be an outbreak of some virus in the shelters. There had also been a report that there had been some more of the Knowing arrested but that the two they had caught had to be let go for lack of evidence. "That is a bunch of bull. They clearly had guns on them. So how did they pull that one off? Mr. Diggings. That had to be how they did it. He had helped them out, but why?" Jake was talking out loud to himself. He had stayed at his apartment last night hoping that someone would contact him. He hoped that he could come up with a plan that would help all the Knowing, especially Marcus and the kids.

Jake's doorbell rang. He opened it, it was Mark. "Hey, little brother, how goes it?" Mark had come with a bag of doughnuts and three coffees.

Jake saw the three coffees. "Am I going to have another guest?"

Mark sat down the stuff. "Yes, I hope you don't mind. I needed to have a meeting place, and this seemed as likely as any."

There was knock at Jake's door this time. He opened it to find that Smitty was standing very nervously in his apartment hallway. "Hi, Smitty, come on in." Jake shut the door behind him and motioned for him to have a seat.

Smitty acknowledged Mark. "Thanks for meeting with us, Smitty." Mark handed him a cup of his own coffee from his own shop.

"Not too subtle, Mark. What a note. Meet me at Jake's, now."

Mark smiled. "You are here, aren't you?"

Smitty knew where Jake's apartment was. "So, Smitty, how is it that you know where I live?"

"Oh, Jake, your apartment has been a drop-off spot for almost a year now. Didn't Mark tell you?" Smitty looked at Mark, and so did Jake.

Mark looked down and then over at Jake and gave him a smile and a shrug of the shoulders. "Whatever works, right?"

Jake was curious. "So why are we meeting here today?"

Mark got right to the point. "I think we can all agree that Marcus needs our help. He has taken his boys and gone underground. He is going to need food and supplies as well as communications for jobs we need him to do. But right now he is being so careful with the 'no contact order' that we have not been able to get ahold of him. So the way I see it is that he will sooner—more likely than later—get ahold of someone to get the stuff. I think it might be Smitty here because he is one of the only ones not being watched by the government."

Jake had to agree. He also thought it was a good idea but was confused as to how this involved him. "So where do I come in?"

"Well, I was thinking that when Marcus gets in contact with Smitty that he will be told that he cannot get any help unless he has a meeting with you in Smithy's coffee shop. That way you can meet with him, find out what is going on, and open communications up again." Mark looked pleased with himself for pulling all of this together.

"I have a few questions for both of you." They were quiet as Jake asked the questions he needed answered. "First of all, Smitty, what are you going to tell Marcus when he asks how I got you to call the meeting? And second, Mark, are you crazy thinking that you can use these kids again? They have a bull's-eye on their backs. Travis has seen to that."

Mark did the answering. "Well, as to the fact that Marcus has to meet with you or there would be no help, well, we are going to tell Marcus you said that if Smitty did not do as he was told, you would have him arrested. And yes, I do think we need the kids for the future as runners at the very least."

Jake did not like the second part at all but was sure the first idea was going to work. "Okay, so let me get this straight. If or when Marcus contacts you, you will tell him that if he does not meet with me at the coffee shop, then you cannot help him or the kids. And if he asks why, you tell him it is because I will have you arrested if you don't. It will make him mad at me, but it will work." All the men agreed that this would work, so now they needed to wait for Marcus to contact Smitty. The men prayed and parted ways. Now the next step was up to Marcus.

*****

It was two long days before Marcus contacted Smitty. During that time, things had heated up in the town. Rumors were everywhere about how dangerous the Knowing had become. Stories of them carrying guns and doing illegal things were being reported every hour. Marcus was not sure why Jake wanted to meet with him, but he did know that Smitty was afraid to help him unless he agreed to a meeting.

Marcus knew that he could not go on the street dressed as a Knowing, so he cleaned himself up, combed his hair into place, and put on what he liked to refer to as his chipped uniform. He looked into a mirror. This is how he and Travis used to look every day years back. So much had changed. Marcus had saved several of the cough drops. His plan was to take them before the meeting, that way he would be less likely to have one of his coughing fits. "Oh, God, please help me to be strong. Help me to get food today. Please help me to do what is best for the boys. Thank You for all you have done for us, but I really do need Your help. Amen."

Marcus had planned the meeting down to the last detail. He planned to take two of the youngest boys, Jimmy and Mike, with him to Smitty's coffee shop. They were all dressed up with instructions to act like a chipped child. Each of the boys had two plastic bags, a paper airplane, and one marker. Marcus inspected them over. They talked over the plan, setting up escape routes and signals. They had a time of prayer, and off to Smitty's they went.

Mark and Jake were seated at a table, each watching a door. Mark the front door, and Jake the bathroom door. They were not sure where Marcus would come in from, but the place was crowded, and they did not want to miss him. Smitty was behind the counter placing and delivering orders to the tables. He had some extra waiters helping that Jake had never seen before, but that could be expected with such a full house of customers. It was obvious that the news of the street people had brought a lot of nosey people out, but it was great business for the coffee shop. Mark looked at his brother. "Jake, do you think he will really come and meet with you?"

Jake did not move his eyes from the door he was watching. "He will be here. He would do anything to take care of his boys. He will definitely be here."

Marcus and the two boys entered the coffee shop and simply stood looking around for Jake.

Mark tapped Jake on the arm to get his attention and to direct it toward the boys. Jake and Mark were both set back with the sight of not just Marcus but Mike and Jimmy too. Jake did not take his eyes off the boys. "Mark, is that who I think it is? Those boys clean up good." Jake motioned for Marcus to come and sit with the two of them.

Marcus was a little sick to his stomach, but he could not tell if it was from stress or from all the cough drops he had eaten, perhaps even both. It did not matter now. What did matter was that this meeting had to take place so he could get the food needed for his boys. Marcus sent the two boys over to the bench by the door. "Mike and Jimmy, blend in and use new signals. Okay?" Both boys nodded and did as they were told. Marcus then proceeded to the table; he moved one of the chairs so he could see the boys from his seat and sat down. "What do you want, Jake?" He did not look at Jake or Mark but kept his eyes on the boys.

Jake was not at all right with the way Marcus was acting or talking. "Marcus, if I were you, I would drop the attitude and have the boys come and be here with us at the table." Even if they did look like chipped kids, it was not good for them to be alone by the door.

"The boys are working. You wanted a meeting, and so I am here. What do you want?" Marcus's tone was better this time, but his words undoubtedly told them that Marcus was mad at Jake and most likely at Mark as well.

Jake looked at the boys. "What do you mean that they are working? Are you crazy? It is too dangerous for any of you to be working the street."

It was like Victor came from nowhere, and he pulled out a chair and joined the group at the table. "Hey, I got word that there was a meeting, and I needed to be here." He looked at Marcus. "You sure do clean up good, the boys too. I guess it is safer for all of us to look chipped now." Victor himself was cleaned up and hard to recognize at first.

Jake thought about it. At first they dressed dirty and homeless so people would avoid them, and now they dress fine so they could blend in. That was brilliant. Once again, Marcus and the Knowing were ahead of him in being street-smart.

Smitty came over to their table. "Anything I can get you, gentlemen?" He looked at Marcus, catching his attention. "I see that the boys are raring to go. I think the two men at the counter may need help with sharing information, if you know what I mean."

Marcus was so cool at this street work. He did not look over at the boys when Smitty talked about them but kept his eyes at the table. He dropped a spoon off the table, and when he picked it up, Jake saw him scan the room and get a layout of the situation. He placed his hands back up on the table, bringing the spoon down on the wood hard enough to make a noise. Mike looked up at Marcus and smiled and watched as Marcus gave orders by signal to him telling him what to do. This was the new signal. He had his hands facedown on the table. He moved his hands and fingers so slightly, it was so slight that Jake could hardly tell that he was talking to the boys, and he knew that Marcus was doing it. Jake was so impressed with what was going on that it was a shock to him when Victor reached out and covered Marcus's hands with his. "Use the old signals please."

Marcus looked up at Victor. He did not use the old or the new signals but merely sat looking at Victor.

Victor leaned in closer so Marcus could hear him better. He was speaking slow and very deliberate. "You heard me. Use the old signals so we can know what is going on." As Victor got closer to Marcus, he picked up on a really strong smell coming from Marcus. "You smell like menthol? What have you been eating?"

Jake could hear Victor and was quick to remember that he had given Marcus cough drops the last time he had seen him. "Marcus, are you still coughing? Are you still sick?" Jake had assumed that his cold would be gone.

Marcus pulled his hands away from the table; he placed them facedown on the top of his legs. He began to talk to the boys again.

Victor was using what Jake could only call his father voice. "Marcus, I am not going to tell you again. We want to see the commands, and we want to know what is going on. We are a team, and even if you are mad at us, you need to be a man and not let how you feel right now interfere with the work." Marcus did not react but kept still. "Marcus, I am not going to tell you again. If you do not stop acting like a child and act more like the man I know you to be, then I am going to shut this whole thing down. Do you understand me, young man? And we both know that I can do it."

Marcus placed both of his hands on the table and used the old signals. Jake had not realized the last two times he saw the signaling that Marcus used his feet as well as his hands in the signals. Jake and Victor could both sort of read the signals; they were slow at it but could get the general information. Marcus signaled. "Boys, see men at end of counter? They are target. Look papers. See information. Separate. Airplane."

Jake thought he had misread the word *airplane*. He looked at Victor. Victor shrugged with an "I don't know" action.

Mike and Jimmy both produced paper airplanes. Mike got up from his seat and began playing with his airplane acting like it was flying around. He was walking over toward the counter. As he got close enough to ensure the plane's flight, he released the paper plane and sent it sailing on to the paperwork the men were looking at. They jumped and then looked to see who it was that interrupted their conversation. It was Mike who spoke first, "Mister, can you please give me my plane back?"

Mike was good at this; the man holding the plane was so impressed with this kid's manners that he melted with compassion for the boy. "Sure, son, but first come over here and show me how you made this very nice plane." Mike joined the men. There was a stool by the counter; Mike climbed up onto it, giving him a full view of the men's papers. "Wow, did you do all of this writing? And look at all those colors." Mike produced a felt tipped marker and handed it to the man and asked him if he could decorate his airplane like the paperwork he was now looking at.

Mike's hand was on his left leg. Signals began. "Papers are on farms, one with two barns? Time tomorrow, 2:00 p.m., 412 people, Knowing." Mike made a mistake. When he saw it was about going after the Knowing, he reacted to it and looked at Marcus with a look of terror.

Marcus was quick to react to the situation; he signaled something to Jimmy that neither Jake nor Victor could understand. "Jimmy, incoming."

Jimmy went across the room to where Mike and the men were. He slapped Mike on his back and said, "Tag, you're it." He then turned and ran toward the door. Mike jumped down from the stool and headed out after Jimmy. The boys were almost to the door when it opened, and both boys literally ran into a government officer. He reached out and took them both by the arm. "What is this all about?"

The officer continued to walk into the coffee shop, holding onto both boys.

Jake could not believe the bad luck of all of this. One of the men at the counter called out to the officer. "Hey, Hansen, do they belong to you?" The man then went across to where the officer and the two boys were now being held.

Marcus signaled for the boys to *run*. But before he could get off another signal, he broke out into a coughing fit that almost took his breath away. He sent up a quick prayer, saying it to himself, but in his heart, it was really loud. "God, help me. Not now. Make this cough go away. The boys need me. Help us."

Victor took over the signaling. "Boys, go with him. He is Knowing."

Marcus did not see the signal that Victor had sent. It was sloppy, not at all like Marcus's, but they got it.

Officer Hansen was smiling lightheartedly. "Yes, these two belong to me. I was to meet them for a bite to eat, but I got held up. You know how that is? Are they giving you any trouble?"

The man reached out to Mike and handed him his now decorated airplane. "Here, boy, you do not want to forget this."

Mike took the plane and looked to Marcus for advice as what to do next. Marcus was still recovering from his coughing fit. But confirmed that whatever Victor said, they should do.

Officer Hansen and the man talked a little longer, and then he and the boys got a seat at one of the tables that was open; they sat in silence not knowing what to do next. Victor signaled to the boys to eat lunch with Officer Hansen, and they in turn told him what was said. Officer Hansen was impressed with their ability to communicate.

Mark was totally in the dark. He could not read signals, so he had no idea what was going on or why the boys were doing lunch with a government officer. And he for sure did not know what was up with Marcus. Clearly Marcus had overreacted to the situation. But what was all of this about?

The color in Marcus's face had returned, and things were back to a settled-down state at best. Victor took this opportunity to address what he had seen with Marcus. "Marcus, are you sick? Why didn't you tell someone?"

"Victor, will you stop it? I am fine. I am so much better. It is better every day." Marcus tried to keep his coughing under control, but the cough drops had worn off.

Victor looked around. "Okay, Marcus, I want you to come see the doctor with me. Mark will take the boys back to the nest where they will be safe, and, Jake, you go and tell Sandy what we found out."

"I am not going to the doctor, and I am not leaving my boys." Marcus was speaking with a defiant tone in his voice. "The last time I did that, things did not go so well. Last time, you almost got my kids arrested, remember?"

Victor matched Marcus's tone. "No, that would be Travis that did that. Marcus, stop the attitude."

Marcus raised his head in a challenge. "Or what?"

"Or I will shut you down so fast you will wonder if you ever had a nest." Then silence.

Smitty came over to the table with plates of food. It looked and smelled good. The sight of the food made Marcus want to be sick. Smitty saw the reaction on Marcus's face. "Marcus, would you rather have soup?"

Marcus was going to answer that he was not hungry, but Victor saw that he was going to decline the offer, so he answered for him. "What kind of soup do you have?"

Smitty reported, "We have chicken noodle and clam chowder."

"Chicken noodle I think. Isn't that right, Marcus?" Victor was not going to give him another chance to control the people at this table. Marcus was a good leader, but Victor needed to be better at leading for this kid's sake. *Dear God, help me to not lose this kid. He is Your man, but he needs guidance. Help us to guide him. Please guide him through us. Amen.* Prayer always brought balance to Victor's life, and this time was no different.

There were four sandwiches on the table. The boys were eating a great lunch with the officer at the other table, and Marcus and Victor had found a silent agreement for now. They would all eat.

Smitty came to the table with a cup of chicken soup for Marcus. He almost turned green. "Thanks, Smitty." He took the cup and a spoon and began to play with the noodles.

Victor watched his friend Marcus, and for the very first time, he saw what it was that Jake was talking about. This kid was way in over his head. Marcus did not mind, but it was killing him. "Like I was saying, Marcus, you are going to come with me to see the doctor, and Mark can go with the kids to the nest. He can stay with them until you get back."

"No." Marcus was not going to play it their way this time. "I am fine. Just let me do my job. Just let me do my work. Then I can rest." Marcus began to cough a little.

Officer Hansen had left the two boys at the table and gone out of the coffee shop for a few minutes and had come back, to the delight of the two boys who were now enjoying an ice cream desert. Officer Hansen went to the table where Victor and the others were sitting. He handed Marcus a new bag of cough drops. "The boys wanted me to get these for you. They said that you are not sleeping very well because of your cough. I sure hope that these help." He smiled and joined the boys at the other table.

Victor looked at Marcus, who was taking one of the drops and getting ready to pop it into his mouth. Victor stopped him from eating it. "Not yet. You need to eat your soup first. It will not taste any good if you have that in your mouth."

Victor was right, but more than wanting to eat, Marcus wanted to not cough anymore. Marcus laid the drop on the table beside the soup. He picked up the spoon again and took some of the broth. It was good. It did feel good going down his throat. He was glad that he decided to eat after all.

They were all eating when suddenly beepers and pagers started going off. Officer Hansen got a personal call. Jake watched as many of the people in the shop began to answer and check on their electronics. Officer Hansen was listening on his phone. He looked up at Victor with horror on his face. Victor started toward him when he noticed that the officer was calling him off by a slight movement of his head and a motion with his hand. Jake scanned the room to see who else was being alerted. Jake saw John standing by the now open door. Many of the customers had left or were leaving the building, almost all of them officials in the government.

John was signaling Marcus. Jake tried to see what he was saying. "There is trouble in the park. Some of our boys are with Travis."

Marcus signaled back, "Where is Travis, and why does he have some of the boys?"

John was pushed on into the room. People were coming and going, and they were in a hurry. Another signal from John. "Travis is in the park, government too."

Both Jake and Victor were reading the conversation between John and Marcus.

Marcus was getting ready to get up. He signaled to John, "Go to nest, get other boys to safety in a new nest. I will get Travis and others. I will meet you." John turned, gathered both Mike and Jimmy up, and went out the door as fast as he had arrived. Marcus was not aware that Jake and Victor had seen the conversation until he went to get up and found both men, one on either side of him. Jake had a hand on Marcus's arm, and Victor had one across his back. He had planned to get up but found himself unable to.

Victor needed to get Marcus's attention and convince him that the only thing he was going to do was to get to the nest and to find the boys that were there and get them to a new safe nest. "Marcus, we saw what John said. You can't go to the park. It is too dangerous for you. Besides that, the boys need you."

Marcus was frozen in thought. "I have got to try and save my brother."

Jake squeezed Marcus's arm. "You have got to go and take care of the boys. I will go and find your brother for you." Jake saw this young man make a truly hard choice. He had a commitment to both his own brother and to the boys that he had taken care of for so long.

Marcus clinched his fists and made a frustrated sound. "Jake, are you sure you can do this? What if Travis makes it hard on you? He might give you up, you know."

"Trust me, Marcus, I can take care of this." Jake prayed that he could keep his word on this one.

Mark had returned to the table. The fact was that no one had even known that he had stepped out for a while. "Okay, we have really great news. Travis has been arrested with some people, but none of them are from our group. I found out that the people arrested were all chipped. I am not sure what that is all about, but our boys are not with Travis."

Jake saw Marcus sigh with both relief and worry at the same time. The boys would be safe, but Travis was still in trouble. A pattern was beginning to form. Whenever there was an arrest made, it seemed that Travis was a part of it?

Officer Hansen had returned to the coffee shop and was at the counter with Smitty. Whatever the information they had found out wasn't good from the look on their faces. Mark went over to talk to them. He came back to the table and sat down. Victor looked at him giving him a moment to figure out how to tell the news. "Okay, so what is it?"

Mark checked to see who was close enough to hear, and it looked clear for talking. "Okay, so here it is. We have got a break in our foundation. Information has been given to the government. They know about the nests and some of the safe havens. There is to be a citywide sting. They plan to take down as many of the Knowing as they can. To have them arrested and chipped, and once and for all to be done with them. They say that the Knowing are armed and are planning to take over the city. Victor, things look really bad. I am not sure what we should do. People are asking for a message as to what they should do, for themselves and how to help others. The Knowing has to stay alive." Mark's voice gave away the fact that he was worried. "Victor, what do we tell them?"

Victor looked Mark straight in the face and announced the battle plan. "Mark, spread it to everyone that they are all to 'pray, believe, and do.'"

Jake gave Victor a look showing that he did not understand. Of all the things he could think of to do, this was not it. Pray? Believe? Do? What was that?

Victor saw Jake's confusion, so he explained it to him. "Jake, we the Knowing are God's people. Everything we are is because of Him.

476

We would not even be a group if it were not for God. We go to Him for the answer this time. We should go to Him all the time, but this time things are too big for us to handle, so we take it to Him. We pray, thanking Him for what He has done already, for the things He is doing right now, and for all the things He will do in the future. Then we believe. We believe in his promises, in His Word, the Bible, and in the people He sends to do His work. Then we do. We do whatever God shows us to do. We do it with full awareness that God is in control and that He will make a way."

Jake looked at Victor. "And that works?"

Victor smiled and shrugged. "It has always worked so far." Victor turned to Mark. "That is the message: pray, believe, and do."

Mark shook Victor's hand and said his goodbyes and went to deliver the message.

From what Jake could see, prayers from all over the city would be hitting heaven like a huge tidal wave.

Marcus was the one who was frustrated about this too simple of an answer to the crisis. "Victor, I need to do more than just sit here and pray. I need to go and do something. I want to find Travis and get him back under control."

Victor stopped his talking by placing his hand over one of Marcus's. "Stop. This way of talking is not going to help. Marcus, you know better. So now you need to do better. Trust God, Marcus. He has never let you down, why would He start now?" Marcus started to protest, but Victor continued, "You know better than to go with what you see, think, or feel. Stay in what you know. It is the safest place to be right now. Actually it is the only place you can be. You know that you are to take care of the boys, right? So go do it. Do it the best you can and continue to trust that God will have the others doing what they are here for too. Believe, Marcus, even if it feels like it is not enough, believe that God has a plan, and it will work out like He has planned, in spite of us getting into His way."

Marcus reached for another cough drop. He would not be too happy, but he would do what God had called him to do and take care of the boys. He trusted God, but things had been really hard lately. His prayers about Travis and about his cough going away had not worked out too well. He could not see any reason God would let things be the way they are. He was trying to do what he thought God wanted, but it looked like he had it all wrong. In spite of how things were looking right now, he decided to take the advice of his Godly friends; Marcus decided to step out and *do* what he thought God wanted of him right now. "I am going to go to the nest. I am going to move the boys and get them settled. I will see you later."

Victor stopped him before he reached the door. "Marcus, look at me. Are you going to be all right?" He watched Marcus as he answered, "I am fine. I am not happy, but I will be okay. Can I go now? Please." Marcus turned again to go to the door.

Victor called out to him again, "Marcus, you are not alone in all of this. We are here for you, ya know? Where are you taking the boys? What number nest?"

Marcus looked so discouraged. "Where do you want them, Victor? I guess you have an idea?"

Marcus was showing attitude again. Jake was not used to Marcus ever acting like this with anyone, especially with Victor. "Marcus?"

Marcus was second-guessing himself again, and it made him so angry. "I am sorry, Victor. What number do you think?"

Victor wanted to be supportive of Marcus, so he gave him choices. "What do you think? How about twelve or six? Whichever one you think is best."

Marcus did not answer but nodded his head in agreement and left the coffee shop.

Victor, Mark, Jake, and Smitty stood looking at the door after Marcus left. Smitty was the one to make an obvious statement. "That boy is in some kind of trouble, don't you think? I have never seen him act like that before. I would have sworn I was looking at his brother, Travis."

The rest agreed that there was trouble coming, but none of them thought it would be from Marcus, not even after the way he acted. They knew him to be a man of God, and this battle he was waging would prove it to be true. But it would take time for him to figure out which side of this world he really needed to be on. Going with his brother was never going to be an option. He could never live that way, but they all knew that he had to think about it. Travis was family, his brother, at one time his best friend. To lose one of those relationships would be hard, but to lose all three, which was a lot to ask of anyone, even a good kid like Marcus.

Marcus would not like this decision, but he would do what he said, they were sure of that. The boys would get to safety. Marcus would see to that.

*****

Jake hit the streets looking for whatever information he could get about the takedown of the Knowing. There was not a lot to be found from the chipped groups of people. But whenever he encountered someone from the Knowing, they would just say, "Pray, believe, and do." Jake was amazed at how fast this message had hit the streets. Jake could not believe the peace these people had about what was happening. The news was reporting hourly about the Knowing group and the things that they were thought to have done. There were a lot of false reports. The Knowing had been made out to be this vicious underground group wanting to overtake the government starting with this town. On top of that, any and everything bad that happened in the town was reported to have been done by the Knowing. Jake himself had just heard that the "family from the Knowing" was going to go on live TV to tell what they know about the group. It looked to Jake like the Knowing was going to go down and nothing this side of a miracle could stop it. Between Travis, the family, and the false hysteria, things were going to be too bad to even hope for a return to normal life.

Marcus had returned to the old nest and had successfully moved the boys and their supplies to the new nest. He had done his job. They were all fed, had done their studies, and were now bedding down for the night. Many of the boys had expressed fear about what was going to happen to them, but Marcus reminded them that they were God's children and that God had a plan for them. Somehow in reminding them, Marcus found encouragement for himself. As Marcus lay in his bed, thoughts of Travis kept him awake. He was so tired from all the coughing, but that was not what was keeping him up this time, it was clearly Travis. Marcus started to think about what he should have done different concerning his dealings with Travis. He knew that if he could only talk to him for a while that he could show him how wrong he was about the Knowing. He was remembering that Jake had said that he saw Travis having a meeting in the past in the park late at night. That was an idea. Maybe Travis would be at the park. This new nest was only about three blocks from the park. The kids were asleep, and they were safe. He had done his job. Maybe he could get Travis too. Marcus sat up. His cough was still bad, but using the drops helped. He got out of bed and went to where John and James were. He did not have to wake them. His cough did it for him. As he was going to wake John, he had another coughing fit.

John and James both sat up. John asked, "What is the matter, Marcus? Are you all right?" He waited for Marcus to catch his breath.

"I am fine, but I need to go out for a while. I need you two to keep watch over the nest. I will not be long. Okay?" Marcus said it more like an order than an idea to be debated over by his friends, but they began to question the idea of him leaving alone late at night.

James also pointed out the fact that Marcus was sick and thought he could use some more rest. Marcus only waved them off. "I know what I am doing. I will be fine. I will be back really soon, I promise." At the end of his speech, Marcus turned without looking back at the boys. He knew that they might be right but that this might be his only chance to get to talk to Travis. "God, help me to find my brother and to get to talk him into coming back to the nest." He left the nest through a side door.

*****

Jake was at the park. This would be a long shot, but people were creatures of habit. Maybe Travis would be here. Jake thought about Marcus and was glad that he listened and went to the nest with the other boys. His cough was not any better, but at least it was not worse. Jake walked off the main trail so that he would not run into anyone he did not want to see him first. The night was cool, but the rain had stopped. It was wet enough to make things slippery.

Jake had come around a corner when there in the light just past the bushes was Travis and Mr. Diggings. They were arguing about what had been expected of Travis. "You, young man, were supposed to bring me the Knowing. And the brats that you knew about, where are they? And how about your leader brother? I don't see him either. Would you like to explain this to me?" Mr. Diggings was red in the face; he looked like he could explode at any time.

Travis tried to reason with Mr. Diggings. "This is not my fault. These groups are very good at what they do. Give me another chance, I am sure that I can get my brother to come and talk with me. Then you can get him and put him in jail. You will see, he is always thinking I care about him, he will come if I send a message. You know I gave you the nests and the safe havens, not to mention the farms. I would think that that would buy me some time to bring Marcus in."

Mr. Diggings threw his hand up in disgust. "I need to think about this one. In the meantime, you stay away from me. You could ruin my reputation by hanging around me. I will talk to you another day. Now leave me alone." Mr. Diggings stomped off leaving Travis alone, or so he thought. There was a sound coming from the bushes from across the clearing. It was a cough.

Jake heard it too. "Dear God, please don't let that be Marcus. What if he had heard what Mr. Diggings and Travis had been saying? Oh, God, don't let it be Marcus." It was a quick prayer but not likely one that would have been answered tonight.

Marcus now knew that his own brother was the one who betrayed the Knowing. Before Jake could decide what to do, Marcus had come out of the bushes and was questioning Travis as to what he had done. "Are you out of your mind? Travis, these are our people. They are our family."

Travis took up the challenge with Marcus. "These people of yours make you weak. You do not use your own mind anymore. How dumb of these people to put you, my brother, in charge instead of me. So how is that working out for all of you now? I bet you wish you had me on your side now."

Jake listened as Marcus stood there letting his brother rant and rave at him about everything he could think of. Finally Travis came to the end of all the telling and started out toward Marcus. Jake was not going to stand by and let Travis hurt Marcus again. But before he could interfere, two government officers came by to see what all the ruckus was about. "Hey, you two, what is going on there?"

Travis walked right up to the officers. "Thank God, you are here. I have someone for you to arrest. Him!" He turned to point toward Marcus, but he was gone.

Like before, Marcus was by the bushes that divided the flats and the hill that led down to the stream. Marcus was trying to get away down the hill, but he had slipped and landed in the water once again. "Dear God, this is getting ridiculous." He had pulled himself up out of the shallow water and again was trying to dry himself off.

The officers shined a light on Marcus. "And, Travis, you say that this is a leader of the Knowing?" They were laughing.

Travis was angry. "You go and get him. I tell you, he is a leader. Now you do what I say, or Mr. Diggings will have your badges."

Marcus was getting ready to walk the other way when he had a coughing fit that came so hard that he almost went down into the water again. The officers were laughing even harder. "Oh, Travis, we are so afraid, of you and of Mr. Diggings and of that great big bad leader down there." Travis reached out to hit one of the officers for laughing at him. He missed, but the action resulted in the officers hauling Travis off to the government station.

That left Marcus and Jake in the park alone. Jake waited for a length of time to make sure that the officers were not setting a trap of some sort and were coming back. Enough time had gone by, so Jake went down to the water's edge to see if he could find Marcus and help him out. But Marcus was gone. There was no sign of him anywhere. Jake listened to see if he could hear any coughing. There was none. The good news was that Marcus had not been hurt by Travis or the government officers, not physically anyway. Jake needed to see Marcus, but more than that, he needed to go and talk to Sandy and Victor and tell them what he had overheard.

CHAPTER 32

Jake used the rest of the night to continue gathering information about what was going on with the Knowing and to see if there was any information about where Marcus took the boys this last time. This kid was so good at running the nest that it was almost a shame to have to shut it down. But this was not his time to be leading kids in such a dangerous situation anymore. It looked like within a few more days, things were going to change forever. Travis was only one part of the takedown. "The Knowing family," who were about to tell the rest of the information on the group would take it out the rest of the way.

Jake remembered that the family was going to go on live TV tonight. He decided to go home and watch it there. He was tired, and he was worried. This was such a different life than he had before. It was a harder life, but somehow he was more alive and more at peace. God is in control, and that made it so much better to know that all of this was not up to him or any of them.

On Jake's way home, he took one more look around the park to see if he could find anything that could tell him where Marcus had gone. He was sure that he had gone back to his nest but not sure which one he was at and was not sure if he had made it all the way back there.

When Jake got to his apartment, he found a surprise waiting for him. Mark had come over and had let himself in. Jake was shocked to say the least but was glad to have someone to talk with about everything that had happened and what they thought would happen next.

"Mark, I am so glad you are here. What do you know? When was the last time you saw Marcus? Do you know how they number the nests? Victor said nest number six or twelve. What do you think would be the new one?" Jake had not even come into the apartment and shut the door yet but there were so many questions he wanted to have answered—no, he *needed* to have the answers.

"Jake, calm down. Get into the room and shut the door before you start asking questions. Now little brother, hello, I am glad to see you too." Mark had not seen Jake so upset in a long time. "So what has happened now?"

Jake did not take off his jacket or even act like he would be staying at the apartment tonight but paced and ran his hands through his hair, an old habit that showed up when he was most upset. "Do you know that the 'family from the Knowing' is going to tell their story tonight live on TV?"

Mark was trying to get information on what was really going on. "This family might not know anything. And even if they do, who will believe them anyway?"

"Mark, aren't you listening, the Knowing are in trouble. And we have to do something." Jake had raised his voice but not because he was mad at Mark but because of the fear of what was to come next. He loved the Knowing life and was horrified at the thought of it being taken away from him. His new friends meant so much more than he would have ever thought they could. He truly loved and cared about them. If only there were something he could do to help them.

"Okay, so let's pray." Mark put his hands together and lowered his head and began to pray for everything and everyone that came to his mind. He asked God to not only help but to let everyone see the hand of God in the middle of what looked to be a disaster.

Jake did stop and pray, but it did not help much. "Now what do we do?"

Mark smiled at him. "Now we believe."

"Mark, there has to be more that we can do. Everything is falling apart, and it looks like it is going to only get worse." Jake was pacing again.

"Jake, have you been reading your Bible?" Mark was serious.

"What has that got to do with anything?" Jake was so mad at Mark for his calm attitude toward all of this. Jake needed him to show that he was upset too.

"What I am trying to say is that in the Bible, there is story after story about believers who had to give things to God and then believe that He was working on it. All they could do was be ready when God told them what and when to do it. We are not so different. We know that we are God's people. We know that He loves us and wants the best for us, even when we are in our greatest hurting. We have to claim that promise. We have to believe that God can and will do what is best in this situation. It is no different than all the stories we have read in the Bible." Mark did not want to preach, but this needed to be said. Jake needed to see that he was growing in his faith and that this was only a test, a test of faith.

Jake sat down beside Mark. "This is so easy for you. I wish I could understand what this is all about."

Mark shook his head. "This is not easy for me. You have to remember, I have been doing this a lot longer than you have. It does get easier, but it is never easy."

"So what you are saying is we must believe for now and wait for God to show us what to do next?" Jake wanted something more he could do, but more than that, he wanted the peace that so many of the Knowing had in situations like this. "So, Mark, if I told you that I think God wants me to help get Marcus off the streets and into a home until he grows up, knowing that he would lose his kids, you would say that was okay?"

"Jake, if God wants you to do that, then He will clearly show you what and when to do it. Jake, in the book of John (6:6), there is a sentence that says, 'He asked this only to test him, for he already had in mind what he was going to do.' God knows exactly what he is going to do. We just need to trust Him." Mark got up and turned on the TV.

The family who had left the Knowing was going to be on TV in a few seconds. Things looked really bad for the Knowing. But having just heard what Mark had said, Jake was going to try and believe that God can make good of this, no matter how bad it looked to him.

The family came into full view. It was a live TV show, and the media were having a heyday with all of this. Jake could see Mr. Diggings in the background taking bows for having found this family and was stating that once and for all this group of Knowing were going to be taken down and put out of business.

The family entered the stage. Jake had seen them before, they were at the farm at the same time he had been undercover there. He did not remember the details, but he did remember them leaving. He also remembered how the Knowing people loved them and how they did not want them to go but respected their right to decide. What he could not understand is how they could tell the things they know, knowing that it would only hurt the group.

The announcer began by thanking the family for being so brave and for coming forward to help take out such an evil and dangerous group of people. It had been decided that the father of the family would do the talking. It was clear that the whole family was upset. The mother was crying as they stood to tell what they knew about the Knowing.

"So, sir, can you describe to us about how awful it was living with this group?" The man stood there. "Sir, can you tell us who is head of this organization?" The mother began to cry out right; and the kids, a boy and a girl, hugged her trying to help her not be so upset. The man finally spoke up. "I came here today to tell everyone about the Knowing and about how they needed to be taken out, but at this time, I feel that this was a great mistake and that my family never should have left the Knowing."

Jake sprang to his feet. His heart felt like someone had grabbed it and was holding on.

"Sir, are you saying that you are not going to give us the information you told us you could give us?" The announcer was on live and wanted to keep his calm, but this was so not what he was told it would be. He in no way wanted to be doing propaganda for the Knowing. "Sir, could it be that your family has been threatened by this Knowing group and that is why you are not going to tell us about them?"

The man lowered his head, and then he looked up straight at the camera. "Actually, my family have been nothing but loved by the Knowing. Since we have been in town, we have received many gifts and cards from them telling us how much they still love us. It has become clear to us that the mistake we have made is that we left them in the first place." He got closer to the camera. "Listen to me, hold on to the teachings of Jesus. Know that God is the only way and that it is harder to be without God and the family than it is to be in the Knowing on the run. This chipped world is made up of worldly treasures and can't bring you peace or happiness. Remember to pray, believe, and when it is time, do."

Before the camera was turned off, Jake and Mark witnessed a lot of yelling and upset people. The commercial came on, Mark and Jake could not believe what they had just witnessed. It was never going to be shown again, that was for sure, but with all the hype that had been given to this show beforehand it meant that a lot of people had seen it.

"Mark, what just happened?" Jake was so excited that he could hardly contain himself. "Mark, don't just sit there. Do something."

Mark was equally excited but found himself numb over the whole thing. "Jake, what would you like me to do?"

"Something, anything. Can you explain what happened?" Jake wanted to put some logic to this situation.

Mark took some time to answer. He wanted to use the right words. "God is what happened." Jake made a face at him, but he went on. "God always accomplishes what He sets out to do. A lot of the time, we do not get to see it, but times like this, all the glory goes to God."

"You can say that again. Not in my wildest dreams or prayers could I have seen this one coming." Jake could feel himself becoming emotional about what he had witnessed. This was so unlike him, but it did feel good to see God working in all of their lives. "Now what do we do?"

Jake looked at Mark, who was looking at his answering machine. There was a red light blinking. Jake had a message. "Hey, Mark, thanks for seeing that. It might be from Marcus or one of the kids."

Mark was smiling. Why would one of the kids call Jake? That was a funny thought for Jake to have. Mark watched as Jake played the recording. It was from Jake's boss. "Hi there, Jacob Singleton, tomorrow is your lucky day. I bet you can guess who gets to go back to work and help us clean up the streets of the town. The doctor says you are good to go, the shrink says you are good to go, and we need the help. So welcome back, we will see you tomorrow."

Jake went from high to low in one recording. "I guess that answered what we do next. I guess I get to be an officer again. I wonder why I am going back so early."

Mark reached for his jacket. "Who cares why you are going back early. Just remember that you now have your 'what to do next.'" He slapped Jake on the back. "So now go be an officer again. I will see you soon."

Mark left the apartment, and Jake was alone, but he did not feel alone. God had come so close to his life today that Jake knew that he was truly His. "Thank You, Jesus. Thank You, God."

*****

Jake had a good night's sleep. He got up to restart his life as an officer. This was an unexpected turn of events for now. He looked in the mirror and saw what he had seen a hundred times before. He looked like an officer, he had a job like an officer, but he was one of the Knowing now. Before his undercover job, being an officer had been his life, but now he had a life and then he was an officer. He now worked for God. It made all the difference in the world. And Jake liked it. "Dear God, thank You so much for my new life. Help me to be the man You want me to be and to do the job You want me to do. Keep the people of the Knowing safe. Help me to help them. Thank You for the miracle we had last night. Help the family do what they need to do to be safe and to know that they did the right thing. Please help me to find and help Marcus. Keep us safe. Amen."

Jake took the long route to work. He was watching the streets for any sign of the Knowing or the kids especially. He went back to work and was amazed at how fast things returned to the normal in this old life. Jake had moved from pray to believe and then to doing. It felt good.

Mark on the other hand had a long night. He had gone over to the shelter where Victor and Sandy had gone. The three of them stayed up all night making plans about what to do in the future for the Knowing. Things had to be different for the safety of the entire group. Many of the safe havens had been taken out. Some were left, but to know if they were still safe or might be used as a trap was impossible, so they needed to be used as little as possible, for now anyway. It was decided that all of the nests in this town would be closed for the safety of the kids, even Marcus and his group. This would be hard on Marcus, but there was no other choice any of them could see. Finding Marcus was going to be the problem of the day.

Mark was sad. "Victor, do you think Marcus will handle this decision okay?"

"He will not like it, but he will do what is best for his boys. He will do okay because he has God. It might take him a long time to adjust, but he will." Victor had seen Marcus handle a lot of things these past years and was sure he was right. There was a hint of concern about this though because of the last encounter at the coffee shop. But he thought with time and prayer, it could be handled.

Sandy handed the men a cup of coffee. "Okay, so now it is morning, where do we start?"

Victor looked at Mark for guidance about his brother. "So how do you think Jake is handling all of this?"

Mark smiled. "My little brother is growing. Because of what we saw last night on the TV, I think it will be a long time before he settles down. I think he is ready to do whatever God needs him to do even if it is hard."

Victor had an idea "Sandy, let's see if we can get the word out that there is going to be a general meeting this weekend. We will meet on Saturday. We will all meet out of town at site number seven. Let's have all leaders and their second-in-command be there. We need it to be after dark, so let's say eight p.m." Victor wrote it out for Mark and Sandy both. "Let's get the word out and pull all of us together. We need to regroup and decide what our future is going to look like."

*****

Days passed as Jake had fallen into his new routine. He went to work and was amazed at how easy it was to get back to the hum of his job. He spent most of his off-hours looking on the streets for any sign of Marcus's nest group. He had not heard anything about Travis or the Knowing family, who was by now safe in a camp somewhere, that he was sure of. There was one glimmer of hope for him to find Marcus, and that was that there was going to be a big meeting this weekend. Just out of town. All of the leaders were to be there, and that should include Marcus. Jake was sure that Marcus would not miss this get-together, and neither was he. He wanted to find Marcus and tell him that he was not alone and that he should let him help. Jake was sure that was what God wanted him to do. Thank God, it was Friday. The meeting was tomorrow. And tomorrow was just not soon enough as far as Jake was concerned.

*****

It was Saturday morning, and there was a new release of information about the Knowing and all the problems that they cause. The information was all over the news, and it could not have been further from the truth. Jake's week was long, but it felt good to be back at his job. He had missed helping people and getting the bad guys off the street. It was unfortunate that everyone wanted to blame everything on the Knowing. Jake would never get used to it. The reports of guns and weapons found in the nests were so crazy that Jake almost laughed when he heard it.

Mark and Jake were to meet up about noon, and then they would head out for the general meeting. They would have to take extra care not to be followed. Jake took time to pray for everyone, including himself. He added prayers for his family to find Jesus to his very long list. "Thank You, God, for listening. I now will believe and wait to hear what You want me to do. Amen."

They took Mark's motorbike to the edge of town. They hid it in the bushes and found another one, a dirt bike for them to continue on. They both covered their medallions, mounted the bike, and left for the meeting. It had taken them a long time to get to the meeting site. It was much bigger than Jake had expected. "Mark, how big is this place?"

Mark looked at Jake and realized that he had never been here before. "Well, it is bigger than you think. There are a lot of underground shelters and storage caves built into the hillsides." Mark saw someone he knew and wanted to go and visit him. "Hey, Jake, why don't you look around, and I will meet up with you later?" Both men agreed and parted ways.

Jake watched Mark as he found his friend and began a talk with him. Mark was a good man, Jake was lucky to have him as a brother. Thinking about that made Jake think of Marcus and his brother, Travis. How hard it would be to have a brother that you loved be a traitor. Jake kept an eye open for Marcus. He heard a voice behind him and turned to look.

"Hey, Jake, you made it." Victor took Jake's hand and gave it a shake. "Mark made it too, I guess. I heard his motorbike pull up. Bikes are rough to ride on, but it beats walking."

Jake was glad to see Victor. "Hey, Victor, have you seen Marcus yet?

"No, but he must be here somewhere because I saw two of his older boys walking around earlier. Both John and James are here." Victor was hoping to see the companionship between Marcus and Jake had been renewed. "So I am guessing that Marcus has forgiven you for getting in his business. How did you work that out?" Jake did not speak up but instead looked the other way. "From your reaction, I take it that it is still in the working?"

Victor was about to talk to Jake some more about the problem he had with Marcus when Jake saw the two boys from the nest going by. "John, James, come over here." Jake was so glad to see them. "Where is Marcus?" Jake was looking around to see if he was doing his usual sideline watching.

James gave John a nudge urging him to do the talking. "Marcus did not come today because he is busy, yes, that is right, he is busy." Both boys were lying, and Victor and Jake knew it. "He said that we are here for you to tell us what is going on and that he will meet up with you some other time."

Victor took the boys on in conversation. "Is something wrong with Marcus?" Victor's watchful eyes were fixed on the boys.

The boys both looked at Victor in shock. James answered, "He said to say that he is busy, and we are going to the meeting for him."

John said, "Yes, that is what he said, he is busy."

Victor continued the interrogation like a pro. "And what do you say?"

Both boys looked like they had been slapped. They both looked down and did not say anything. "Boys, you need to tell us what is going on. Is Marcus okay?" It was Jake that asked this time. The boys were clearly uncomfortable.

John decided that this was a good time to tell Victor everything. "Travis has been hanging around the park and has been asking Marcus to meet with him."

"When are they going to meet?" Victor watched as the boys looked sheepishly at each other.

James told this time. "Well, that is kind of a problem. We decided that Travis is bad for Marcus, and until things get better, we kind of did not tell him. We told Travis that Marcus was too busy and that he would talk to him later."

Victor was pleased with the boys' choice to protect Marcus. "I think you boys did the right thing. I do not think Travis has good intentions toward Marcus either."

Jake had heard something else in the conversation. "What do you mean until things get better? What things?"

Both boys got quiet again and did not look at Jake.

Jake continued, "Is Marcus all right?" Jake was concerned about the way Marcus had looked that last time he saw him, but the boys' being concerned worried him even more. "Did Travis hurt him more?"

James was quick to answer. "No, we would not let that happen. Marcus doesn't even know that Travis is looking for him. He is just really tired, that's all."

There was an announcement made that it was time for the meeting to begin, and everyone was to gather in the barn.

Victor told the boys that they could talk more later on but that they needed to get to the meeting. Both boys looked relieved. They hurried off in the direction of the barn.

"Victor, do you get the idea that there is more going on than the boys want to share?" Victor and Jake walked behind the boys far enough so they could not hear their conversation.

Victor's look of concern was evident. "I agree that there is more to this story than we know, but I also know the boys love and respect Marcus and would not do anything that would let him get hurt, but on the other hand, they are loyal to Marcus and would do what he told them, and if he told them to not tell us something, then they would try to do that for him." Victor looked at the boys. "I think we need to find out where our friend Marcus is and have a talk with him."

Jake was walking along with Victor heading to the barn when he saw something that made his heart stop. He reached out, grabbed Victor by the arm, and pulled him to the side, getting out of sight. "Victor, look, there's Will. What is he doing here?"

"I guess he is a part of the meeting today." Victor continued to walk toward the barn. "You might not want him to see you and Mark here, so why don't you stay in the background."

"Victor, are you crazy? Will is an undercover officer. He can't be here." Jake was trying to keep his voice down, but he wanted to yell at Victor for not realizing how bad this was.

"Jake, calm down. We know that he is an officer, and we know that he is here. We are only letting him know and see what we want him to. He came in the back of a windowless truck with some others, so he has no idea where we are. It is okay, we have it under control."

Victor was walking away, but Jake stopped him again. "What are you going to do about him?"

Victor turned and smiled at him. "We are going to do the same thing we did when we found out you were an officer."

Jake was shocked at the answer. "And what is that?"

Victor was having fun with this conversation now. "We will keep an eye on him, love him, and pray for him to see the truth about God."

This was the crazy stuff about the Knowing that made Jake irritated at the people. They took the chance of being brought down just to try and save one person. "Victor, is taking the chance of losing everything worth saving one person?"

Victor was at the barn door now. "It worked with you, didn't it? Now I think you and Mark should stay out of Will's view for now." He turned and walked into the room.

Jake was speechless. Victor and the others had risked their way of life in order to try and save him. But they did have one big secret weapon, and that was God. After all, He was in control then, and He still is. This was still crazy to let an officer into the meeting, but somehow there was a peace in all of this at the same time. Jake was smiling as Mark walked up to him and wanted to know what was going on.

"Well, Mark, I am not sure you would believe me even if I tell you. But we need to go inside and stay out of sight. Will is here, and Victor thinks that it is a good idea for him not to see us." Jake looked for Mark's reaction. There was none. "You knew?"

Mark held up his hand in retreat. "Jake, there are a lot of things I know, but you always find out sooner or later, right?"

Jake could hear the meeting getting started. "I guess we had better get in there now. We will talk about this later." Jake was not happy, but he understood, kind of, that some things just come up.

Jake and Mark slipped into the meeting room but stayed along the outer edge where it was dark. They could see almost everyone including Will, who was busy scanning the room for faces he could recognize.

Victor was not the first to speak. It was someone that Jake had never seen before, but he liked the man simply from what he was saying in the meeting. He talked about how God had set them apart for this task of keeping the faith. That being a part of the Knowing was to be a part of the family. He reminded all of them that the one true leader in this whole undertaking was God himself. That it was by the word, the Bible, that they had rules. And that the best any of them could do was to try to know and follow them. He reminded them that they have an enemy but that God wanted us to pray for all of them to be a part of the family. He wanted us to remember that we did not make them our enemy but they decided we were there's. We are all to do the best we could to love and respect the chipped.

There were a few of the people at the meeting who wanted to fight back. They wanted to use force. They spoke out and demanded that their ideas be heard.

Victor began to speak, and the room got louder as the night went on. It was evident that there was a split in the thinking of the Knowing. But Jake felt that it was clearly evident that the ones who wanted to do it the Bible way were ahead in numbers. The bad side of that is that it can take only a few to make things get bad quickly. This would need prayer, lots of it. The meeting went on for several hours. A lot of things were worked out. And a lot of changes were going to happen and very fast. The safe havens and the nests were going to be affected the worst of all the groups. They were going to be completely shut down. There was prayer, and then the night ended. Some were going to stay the night, others were going to head out for their homes, wherever they were.

Jake saw Will along with several others get loaded into the back of a truck. Exactly like Victor had said, there was a camper on the back that had no windows. It was confirmed by Jake that these people knew what they were doing when it came down to the underground street life.

James and John made a special effort to run into Jake. Mark and Victor were with him when the two boys began their talk with him. "Hey, Jake, John and me we want to say thanks for everything. Can I shake your hand?" That seemed a strange request coming from one so young, but Jake was glad to do it. But the surprise for him was that when he took his hand away, there was a piece of paper left in his hand. Jake gave a quick look of surprise at James, who at once looked away. "Come on, John, we need to get home and tell Marcus what is going to happen."

John joined James. "I think you should tell him. He likes you better, and I do not think he is going to be happy at all about this one." The boys walked to the edge of the camp.

Jake wondered how they got here but realized that there were so many mysteries about the Knowing that it could take a lifetime to figure it all out.

Victor and Mark walked up close to Jake. Victor was the one to ask. "So what did the boys give you?"

Jake reacted to the question. "What?"

Mark reached and took the paper from Jake. "This is what, now let me see it." Jake himself had not had a chance to read it. To all of their surprise, it was blank; it was just a piece of paper. They all thought *it odd for the boys to do what they had done. Perhaps they were practicing passing things.*

Jake waited until he was alone before he reached into his pocket to pull out the real paper from the boys. He had felt a slight tug on his pocket when James had slipped it to him. He read it. "Marcus is sick. Can you get us some medicine for him?" There was a number 12 on the paper and an address. "Thank You, God. This is what I need to help Marcus. This is my in with him."

Jake decided that tonight would be too late, but tomorrow would be the perfect day to find the nest and to see what was up with Marcus and the boys.

*****

It was to Jake's horror that it took him longer to figure out where the nest was than he thought it would. Most of Sunday was gone when he was finally able to figure out where the nest was hidden. This was one of the advantages of the Knowing, they were good at keeping things a secret. When he had arrived at the address on the paper, there was only a note with a second address on it, and so it went until finally he found what he was looking for. He found who he was looking for.

Jake had found the nest where Marcus and the boys had been staying. When he entered the secret door in the back, he could hear someone was having trouble breathing. They sounded terrible. It was Marcus.

Jake went on into the room. Several of the boys spotted Jake as he came on in to where they were all studying. The younger ones of the boys hurried over to Jake. They were trying to talk all at the same time. They wanted to know if Jake was here to help Marcus get better. They asked if he had brought medicine for him. They wanted to know if Jake was going to stay this time, or was he going to leave again? He motioned for them to be quiet. "I need you all to be quiet now and to go back to your studies. I need to talk to Marcus and see what is going on. Okay?"

Jake knew that Marcus would not ask for help himself, so this was an odd request to come from the nest. It had to have come from the boys. Jake was sure that Marcus did not know anything about the request, so he needed to be careful as to how he approached this whole thing.

As Jake continued on into the main room, it took him only one second to see what the matter was. Marcus was very sick. He was sitting up in a chair (barely). He was wearing his coat, his hat, and had a blanket pulled in tight around him. He had his head down so as to cough into the blanket to help stifle the sound. The coughing fit had stopped shortly after Jake had entered.

"So, Marcus, what is up?" Jake was glad to see that Marcus was reacting to his talking. He had looked so sick, Jake was not sure at first if he could.

"I am fine, Jake. Now get out of here so we can get some sleep. We have a really big day tomorrow and need our rest." As Marcus spoke, he ran out of breath and went into another coughing fit.

Jake reached out to Marcus but was shocked to only have his hand slapped away by him. "I said GET AWAY!" And then there was more coughing. Only this time Marcus held his chest, and Jake could see that he was having trouble breathing. He turned white and then red, and then almost a shade of blue.

This was not something Jake could take care of. Marcus needed to see a doctor. And he needed it soon. Jake walked away, going toward the door. He was going to need backup for this mess. As he walked to the door, Jimmy, one of the youngest of the group, ran to his side and pulled on Jake's arm. "Aren't you going to help Marcus?

You can get him some medicine, can't you? We really need him, and you need to help him not die." Jake's heart broke. This was a family. This was a very large and close family. And he had become a part of it. He himself was not sure when it had happened, but it had.

Jake knelt down, placed his hands on the Jimmy's arms, and gave him a face-to-face look. No words were needed. The boy could see from Jake's face that he was on this and was going to take care of it. "I will be right back. I need to make a call." Jake got up and went outside to make his call. His phone had a good signal in the building, but he did not want to take any chances that it would be tracked back to the nest where the boys lived. He walked a block or two away. He could still see the looks on the boys' faces as he left the door. They desperately wanted him to fix things but could only see him walking away. Jake was coming back. He knew it, and they should have known it too. How was it that they still did not have faith in him? He had helped before. Did that not count for some kind of trust on their part? Was this what real faith was like? Would there always be a question of loyalty? He heard the phone ringing, and then Mark answered. "Mark, I need you to get down to the boys' nest right away." It sounded like Mark had been sleeping, but Jake needed his help fast.

"Jake, what on earth are you doing? I told you to leave them alone." Mark was getting up and beginning to dress.

"Mark, we can talk about that later, but Marcus is really sick, and I need to get him some medical help. He will never leave if his boys are left alone. I need you for backup. It is the only thing I can think of." Jake heard Mark quickly come to an understanding.

"Hey, Jake?"

"What?" Jake did not want to talk, he wanted to take action.

"Where are you going to take him? He is chipless. Do you think the chipless clinic could work?" Mark knew that the clinic was lacking at best.

Jake had not gone that far in his thinking. "I have not thought that far yet. What do you think, any ideas?"

"I do have one, but it is a little crazy sounding. What about taking him to Mom?"

"To Mom? Are you out of your mind? I can't take a chipless boy into that part of town. And what could she do anyway?" Jake thought it was a crazy idea, but he could not come up with a better one either.

Mark was trying to decide how much Jake needed to know right now, so he continued to explain. "She did take care of all of us. And, Jake, she knows people who would help, medical kind of people."

"Mom knows people who would help a chipless kid? I really doubt it." Even though Mark could not see him, Jake was shaking his head.

"Jake, what other choice do you have?" Jake stood frozen in thought. That was a good question, what other choice did he really have?

"What about Mom and Dad? To have a kid like this at their house could be bad for them, you know, if anyone saw him there?"

Mark was smiling to himself. "Jake, you of all people know how to get into and out of their house without being seen."

Well, that was true. Jake had been doing it for years. Only thing that got him caught was the chip he had. And now that was on a medallion. "So, Mark, when did you get so smart?" Jake gave Mark the address.

"Okay, so I will meet you at the nest. Then you will take Marcus to Mom, and I will stay with the kids until we get better backup."

"Sounds great. I will be there as soon as I can." Jake was glad that Mark was with him on this but was unsure about getting his mom involved with a chipless kid. But even more problem than that was getting Marcus to go along with the idea. Leaving his kids, going with him in his car, then going into a chipped area, and then into a chipped home. Not to mention with a chipped officer he was mad at. Okay, so he has had bigger problems in the past. Not sure when, but he was sure he had.

Jake stood outside the door of the building. He had moved his car around the block closer to the nest; it would be better for Marcus not to have to walk so far. (If he could even walk at all.) He heard Mark's motorbike, so he knew he was almost there. Mark killed his engine and rolled the bike off the main street in silence. He placed it on the backside of the road and met up with Jake. "Are you ready for this?" Jake asked his brother.

"So, Jake, what is going on? Is Marcus that ill, or are you just looking for a way to get him off the street? You have made it clear that you don't like the kids being on the street, and you never have. You have always thought it was wrong for them to be living the way they are." He knew that Jake also thought that getting Marcus off the street was the door to getting them all off and into homes or on farms.

"Mark, before you jump to conclusions, let me tell you what happened." Jake wanted to get the kids off the street, but he would never do it like this. He had prayed and felt that God would give him the way, but this was not his idea. "Okay, so I get a note from one of Marcus's kids telling me that he is sick and that they are worried about him. Not sure what I should do, I decided to check things out for myself. So I get over here, and what I found was a really sick Marcus. Mark, I mean he is really sick. He is coughing so hard, and I am sure that he has a fever. I know that you think Mom could help, but this might be too bad for even her. Besides, I am not so sure we should get her involved with this thing. It could put her at risk."

This was such a new Jake that it was hard not to remember the old one. So for Mark to think Jake might have a bigger plan in all this would only be normal. But he could tell from the look on Jake's face that he was truly worried. "Okay, so let's go check this out and see if we need to get Mom involved or if there could be a better way."

Jake and Mark entered the nest and stepped quietly into the areas where the boys were.

"Jake did come back. And he's got Mark too," a young voice rang out as the two men entered the room. Both men smiled and moved on into the room. Jake looked over to where Marcus had been sitting and was not surprised that he was still there. But he was surprised that he looked even worse from the last time he had seen him. "Mark, it has only been about an hour since I saw him last, and he looks even worse." Mark looked over to where Marcus was sitting. Jake had not exaggerated at all. Marcus looked awful.

"Okay, Jake, let's do as we planned. You get Marcus out of here. I will stay until I get some backup, and then I will meet you at Mom and Dad's." Both agreed but then looked over at their young project.

Mark looked around the room and called out for a runner. "I need a runner to get a message to Victor and Sandy. Is anyone up for it?" Many hands went up to volunteer.

Marcus reacted quickly to the call. "No! Too close to curfew. Besides, we are all in for the night.

"Marcus, you send runners all the time after curfew, and you know it." Mark had talked back to Marcus, and everyone in the room became quiet. "Now I need to send a runner. Either you pick and plan it or I will." Mark stood his ground, looking Marcus in the eye, treating him like the man he was known to be. Marcus was a kid, but he ran the nest like he was a full-grown man. He knew who would be safe to send and who would not.

"I do not think this is worth the risk. We could do it in the morning, first thing." Marcus ran out of air and began to cough even harder and longer than Jake had heard before. When he stopped coughing and went to catch his breath, he just coughed more.

Mark took over. He called out to James. "Who would you send?" The boy looked at Marcus, who was not able to speak, and then to Mark. "I would send him. Peter, he is fast, and he is really hard to see in the night."

Mark looked over to the boy. "Peter, do you think you can get this message over to the shelter?" Mark was writing out a note and folding it as he spoke. The boy smiled and was more than happy to do this job. He was proud. Peter took the note and put it into his shoe. Just like that, he was off.

Marcus was not happy. No one could mistake the look on his face. Before Marcus could say anything, Mark spoke up, "Now everyone on with the regular chores, let's all get the nest ready for the night, get on with whatever you usually do." Mark was stumbling for the right words. But they all got the idea and began to do as they were told.

Now they moved on to the next hurdle, Marcus. Jake and Mark both went to address what was going to happen to the boy. Like it or not.

Jake started the informing. "Okay, so Mark and I have been talking, and we think it would be a good idea if you saw a doctor."

Marcus squared up to Jake. "Not tonight, maybe in the morning."

Jake and Mark were taken aback by the answer. "No, we think tonight is better."

No blinking and no holding back, Marcus answered, "No!"

Jake and Mark looked at each other. Jake leaned down so that his mouth was level with Marcus's ear. "Now you do have one of two choices. I can pick you up kicking and screaming and carry you out of here, which by the way will scare the young ones here to death. Or you can tell them that you are going to come with me to see the doctor and that Mark will be here and that you will return when you are feeling better. So what will it be?" Marcus was furious. He did not take his eyes off Jake for a single moment. Jake gave him a look that demanded an answer now.

Marcus motioned to James. He explained about his going with Jake and that he would be back soon. He told him that things should go as normal as they could and that Mark was going to be the one in charge (with James help) until Sandy or Victor got here. James looked worried but nodded his understanding of what was going to happen.

Marcus went to stand up but found that he did not have the strength, so Jake and Mark reached out to help him. Marcus reacted and pulled away from them, only to fall back into the chair he had been sitting in. Jake had seen enough. He reached out and helped Marcus out of the chair by holding him from under the arm. Mark grabbed the other side, and the three of them headed for the door together. Just as they had almost reached the door, Peter came running into the room announcing that there was a big problem and that they all needed to get out of the nest. Jake grabbed the doorknob and opened it with a firm hand. Marcus was trying to turn around and change his mind about leaving. But Jake and Mark did not let go of him or let him turn, but instead they walked him out into the cold night air. The change in the temperature of the air set Marcus off on a coughing fit. Jake and Mark took this as an opportunity to get him into the car and on his way with little or no fight from him.

"Okay, Marcus, in you go."

Jake was getting into the driver's seat, and Mark was getting Marcus buckled in. Before Mark shut the door, he looked at Jake. "Jake, you take care of this, and I will take care of the nest and the boys, okay?" Mark then shut the car door.

Jake pulled the car away from the curb and headed out to his mom's house. Jake was but a few yards away when he looked up into his rearview mirror. His heart almost stopped. There were officer cars completely surrounding the building with flashing lights. As fast as that, the government officers were at the nest. Should he go back or do what he was doing and get Marcus to his mom? Marcus was so sick that Jake was afraid that if he went back that he would be put into a chipless hospital and that they might not be able to take care of him. On the other hand, his very own brother Mark was also back at the nest. Mark might need Jake's help. What should he do? Who should be his priority? "God, help me. I need Your guidance about what I should do." Jake had no longer finished his prayer than he noticed that Marcus was trying to pull his coat off; he was gasping for air and was complaining about being too hot. Jake felt his forehead and realized that Marcus did have a fever. From the looks of it, the fever was really high. On top of everything else that was happening, it had started to rain.

Marcus was still trying to catch his breath when he reached over to grab the door handle of the car. "Oh, no you don't." Jake took hold of Marcus's hands with his right hand and continued to drive with his left. Marcus was weak, so it was not as hard as he would have thought.

"Jake, stop this. Let me out. Take me back. I need to do my job. Didn't you hear what Peter said? There is a problem. We need to go back now." Like before, Marcus lost his breath and could do little but hold his chest and cough.

Marcus had not seen the flashing lights or the government cars. Jake was thanking God for that. This was hard enough of a decision without adding Marcus's input.

Jake drove as fast as he could without drawing attention to them. As he came to a backstreet, he turned off his car lights and then killed the engine and let the car roll into a small turnout that could have been a parking place. Lots of bushes closed in around the car with only enough room to barely get the doors open. Jake got out and came around to help Marcus get out of the car. When he looked up, there was his mom, just standing there; she was wearing a raincoat that Jake had not seen before. She had a flashlight and was waiting for him to see her. "Oh gads, Mom. You liked to scare the heck out of me." His mom smiled, and then he realized that she had moved her attention to Marcus, who once again was trying to catch his breath. "Mom, we need your help."

She smiled. "I know. Mark called and told me you would be coming. Come on, let's get him out of this rain and get him inside."

Jake was so relieved to see his mom. This was going to be okay. Mark was right, she would know what to do. This was a good thing.

"Jake, let's get him into the house. Take him up to your old room. I put some sweatpants and a tee shirt on the bed. Get him to put them on, and I will take the wet things he is wearing now." She opened the door, and Jake took Marcus on into the kitchen, the plan was to take Marcus up the stairs to his old room.

But Marcus stopped and turned to Jake's mom and said, "Mrs. S.?"

Jake's mom smiled and placed her hand gently on the side of his face. "Yes, it is me. It is nice to see you again, Marcus. Now go upstairs with Jake and get the dry things on, and I will be up soon."

"Mrs. S., I can't be here. You know that. Now make Jake take me back to the nest. My boys need me." Marcus lost his breath again and was trying to hold onto something, but it was Jake that he got a hold of.

Jake was confused as to what was going on between his mom and Marcus, but his patience was running very thin. He reached down and lifted Marcus up off the ground and proceeded up the stairs and took him into his old room.

As they entered the room, he noted how very much the same it was from when he had lived here. His bed and dresser were the same as he had left it. They found the clothing on the bed like his mom had said. "Okay, Marcus, let's get you out of these wet things and get you into bed."

Marcus was not at all happy about any of this, but giving up his clothing was never going to happen. He reached a hand up to hold his coat tight around himself.

Marcus's reaction about getting out of his wet clothing and giving them over to Jake brought memories back of the time he had been hurt and was on the street and someone (Victor) wanted him to give him his things. His only coat and clothing being taken away was an awful thought. Jake stopped moving. "Marcus, listen to me. You will get them back. I promise you that. You need to get dry and warm now. So let's do this, and then we can move on to getting you better."

Marcus was trying to decide if he understood what Jake was wanting when he was overtaken by total exhaustion. He was cold. He was tired, and he didn't have any fight left in him. He did whatever Jake said. He was done fighting. All he wanted to do was sleep.

Jake was placing him into bed when his mom entered the room. She looked great to Jake. Why had he not noticed how beautiful she was? "Mom, thanks for this. I guess you want an explanation?"

"Not really. I am sure that you are doing what needs to be done." She smiled at Jake and gave him a hug.

"Hey, Mom, is Dad home?" Jake looked toward the hall.

"No, he is out of town for a week or so." She was looking at Marcus while they talked.

God had worked overtime on this one. Having his mom know about this was one thing, but bringing his dad in on it would have been a completely different story. "Thank You, Jesus," Jake spoke this under his breath.

His mom was picking up the wet things when the doorbell rang. "Oh, that must be my guest. Hold on, I will be right back."

CHAPTER 33

Mark was glad that he and Jake were working as partners. He had confidence that Jake would get Marcus to his mom and that Marcus would get the help that he needed. Mark was trying to remember how many years he had prayed for his brother, that he would become a man of God, and here it was. "Thank You, God." Jake's car had no sooner pulled away when government cars had surrounded the building. Out back, there were two vans; they were unmarked, but Mark recognized them right off. Mark went back into the nest. The boys were worried about a lot of things and were glad to see that Mark had stayed behind to be with them.

Mark entered the big room of the building and found all of the boys just standing around. Every single eye was on him, waiting for him to tell them what was to come next. "Okay, everyone, come and have a seat here on the ground. Get into one group, and we need to have a talk." Mark was glad to see that the boys trusted him and would do what he told them to do. This was going to be tricky, but if they did not fight him, things were going to go better for everyone. "Everyone, be quiet. I need you all to not talk or ask any questions. We are going to have to move really fast if we are going to make what is going to happen work." So far so good, all of the boys did as he said. They were signaling each other as he spoke. How he wished he could read what they were saying to each other, but for now, it was quiet, and that was good. "John, I need you to divide the boys up into two groups. James, you are to lead one, and, John, you lead the other." The boys did as they were told. "I need all of you to trust me and to know that God has a plan. Things are going to look scary for a short time, but I promise you all that by tomorrow, you all will be safe on a farm outside of this town, if things go as planned."

Jimmy could not stay quiet any longer. "Where did Jake take Marcus? Is he going to be okay? And I don't like it without him here."

"Jake took Marcus to get some medical help. I promise all of you that Marcus is in good hands. My brother is one of the best people I know to get around in this town, except for all of you, that is." That brought smiles to the whole group. They really did love the fact that they could move so well in and out of the area with anyone hardly knowing that they were there. They loved being a team. They loved being a nest family. "Now back to what I was saying. What I am going to tell all of you now is going to sound strange, but I need you to trust me and to do exactly what you are told. I need you all to promise that no matter how scary things look, that you will do what I say. I need all of you to trust me. Can you do that?"

Mark was surprised that there were no questions. So far, all of the boys seemed to be okay with the fact that he was going to lead them to safety. "Okay, here comes that scary part. Outside the building right now are a lot of government cars. They know that we are here and have all of the entrances covered."

James stood up. "What do you mean all of the entrances? This is a nest, there are at least three secret ways to get out of here."

"And the officers know them all. James, please just listen, we are all going to get out of here and get to safety, but you have to trust me and do exactly what I say." There was a noise at one of the side wall doors. A very tall man wearing what could only be described as a government wardrobe had entered the building. He was dressed in black from head to toe; he could have been a businessman at first glance, but with the shiny badge hanging from his waistband, there was no doubt that this man was a government officer, and pretty high-up too.

The boys were signaling each other. Their movements were not as subtle as usual. Mark did not need to be able to read the signals to be able to tell that they were trying to decide if they should trust Mark and do what he told them or if they should all do an emergency scatter and at least some of them could get away, maybe.

Mark needed to think quick—if these boys ran, they could get hurt, and the worst part would be that no one could help them then. He needed to keep them together. He needed to keep them calm. *God, help me to lead them. Help me to communicate with them.* "Boys, I think this would be a great time to pray." Mark lowered his head. He did not dare to look up for fear of what the boys might be planning. "Father, please give us wisdom. Help us to have the strength to do what You need us to do tonight. We need You help. Thank You for loving us. Help us to remember that in spite of how things look that You are in control. Amen." As Mark looked up, he noticed that none of the kids had bowed their heads, but that they were all looking at the officer, who had bowed his head and had been praying. Zach, the youngest, had stood up and was at eye level with the officer's belt. He was the exact height to be able to read the badge the officer was wearing. He was trying to sound out the words on the badge. "Si-ngel-ton. Hey, I think that his name kind of looks like Jake's." All of the boys checked it out. Yes, Zach was right. This officer had the same last name as Mark and Jake.

Mark was smiling. "Hello, brother."

The officer smiled back and gave a nod of his head to Mark. "Brother."

James was putting it all together now. "Brother, another Singleton? How many of you are there? And how many of you are officers?" The officer was older than Mark and Jake, but once you took a good look at him, you could see the family resemblance.

This officer needed to be clear as to what was what. "Jake and Marcus, where are they?"

Mark kept it short. "They are on the way to Mom."

"Does Jake know yet?" The officer had a small smile hinting a secret was to come to Jake.

"Not yet, but he will." Mark raised his eyebrows to note how good this was going to be. "But we need to organize this and get on with this plan for now."

Mark needed to get control of this. Time was running out, and they all needed to get out of here. "Everyone, this is one of my oldest brothers. This is my Marcus. Meet Marcus Singleton." They all stood there dumbfounded. They were quiet, and they were listening. Even the signaling has stopped. "So here is what is going to happen. I need all of you to get into your two groups. Each of you will go out of the door that Marcus just came through."

Mike spoke up, "Which Marcus? The big one came through the wall door, but the little one went out the other door."

Mark laughed to himself. Two Marcuses, this was going to be fun. "Okay, we will go out the one Big Marcus came through."

That statement got Mark a look from his brother. Big Marcus was not sure how he felt about being called by that name, but for now, it worked. "Mark, we really need to get a move on."

Both of the Singleton boys were shocked at how fast the boys had gathered their things and were ready to leave the nest. But then they had a lot of practice.

Mike and Zach were talking with excitement about how they had heard of the farm but had never been to one. Zach had to know. "Mark, are we really going to get to go to a farm, all of us, now?"

Mark nodded his head yes and motioned for the boys to start loading up in the vans. Then he shut the door to the nest and got in with one of the groups; the vans pulled away taking the boys to their new life.

Marcus Singleton had stayed behind checking out the nest; he was making sure that everything was cleaned up and that there was no personal property left. He found a cot made into a bed off to one side of the room and saw that there were personal belongings still on it. There was a book on the bed. He picked it up and saw that it was a well-read Bible. He opened the front cover and saw the name *Marcus*. "Hello, what do we have here? I sure can't wait to give this back to you, Little Marcus." He was talking and laughing out loud to himself wondering how the new name idea was going to go over with his namesake. He placed the Bible into his pocket along with as many other items he thought Little Marcus might want to have. Once this stuff was entered into the government files, he would not be able to get it back for him, so he would do his best to get it now. From what he had heard, this kid had lost so much already that he wanted to do what he could to make his life better. As Big Marcus had finished stashing as much stuff in his pockets as he could, there was a crash at the side door of the nest. Marcus looked up to see Travis flying into the room.

Travis had a great big smirk on his face as he walked over to Big Marcus. "So where are they? Are they on their way to the station? I bet Mr. Diggings will feel bad about how he treated me now. Will they all be chipped soon? I can't wait to see the look on Marcus's face when he sees that it was me who helped take him out of business. I am almost glad that I didn't kill him the other day." Travis was going on with his talking when he realized that this officer was not even listening to him. "Hey, I am talking to you."

Marcus was a tall man compared to the other Singletons. He liked to use his size to show that he was in charge. He had practiced it with his brothers in the past and found it to be most effective. He walked up to Travis and looked down at him for the longest time, not saying a word; he was simply looking at him.

All at once every single one of the entrances to the building opened, and officers from every door poured into the room. "Where are they?" One of the uniformed officers was asking.

Marcus spoke as he was still looking down at Travis. "Sorry, men, it looks like we were misinformed, again. There are none of the Knowing here. They had left before we got here. We need to check it out, but from what I can see, this is a bust."

Travis was angry. He took a quick look around and stormed out the building saying something about how this did not make any sense. He knew that they were all there only a few hours before.

Marcus loved it when God pulled off miracles especially when he himself got to be a part of it. *Now I am Big Marcus, very funny.* They closed down the nest and called off the hunt, for today anyway.

*****

Jake sat down in a chair by his old bed that Marcus was now lying in. Marcus had coughed so hard that he was having trouble catching his breath, so Jake placed him on his side, which seemed to help some. Marcus looked like he was asleep, but there was no peace in him. He would stir only enough to ask Jake about the boys, but before Jake could reassure him, he would go back into an unsteady sleep again.

Jake was thinking about how crazy this all was. His mom had let him come into her house and bring a sick chipless boy. Then what does she do? She invites a guest over to visit. Boy, she would never make it out on the streets. Jake laughed at the thought. Then Jake remembered that Mark was at the shelter where the officers had over-run it. "God, please help us all." And then there was his sister, Sally, his very own sister a part of the Knowing. Never in a million years had he seen that one coming.

Jake heard someone coming up the stairs; they were not talking, but they made noise as they walked. Jake looked up to see his mother's face and then her guest, who she welcomed into the room. It was the doctor who had helped Jake at his trial.

The doctor did not speak to Jake at all but put down the bag he was holding and took off his coat, tossing it off to one side. He quickly went to Marcus's side. "Hey, Marcus, do you remember me?" The doctor was checking to see if he could get a response. All Marcus did was cough; he did not even open his eyes. "Jake, hand me the bag, would you please?"

Jake did as he was asked. "He is going to be all right, isn't he, Doc?"

Jake's mom put her hand on Jake's arm motioning for him to give the doctor room so he could work. The doctor opened his bag, took out a stethoscope and a device that would read Marcus's temperature. The doctor simply ran the device across Marcus's forehead and down the side of his face. He was not at all pleased from the look on his face. He put the stethoscope in his ears and placed the other end on Marcus's chest in order to hear. "How long? How long has he been sick like this?"

Jake looked at the doctor. "I am not sure. He had a cold and a slight cough about a week and a half ago, but he was not like this at all."

Marcus had pulled the blankets up tight around himself. He was now trembling and trying to get warm.

Jake thought about what he had seen. "When I first got him into the car, he was complaining about being too hot, not at all like he is now."

"I think his fever must have been high before, but it is way too high now. We have got to get him cooled off and fast." The doctor turned to Jake's mom and asked her to run the bathtub with cool water. "Not too cold. I do not want him to go into shock when we put him into it." The doctor motioned to Jake. "Here, help me get his clothes off, down to his boxers."

Marcus was holding onto the blankets for dear life. "I am so cold. Please leave me alone."

The doctor was talking slow and very on purpose. "Marcus, you have a very high fever. That is why you think you are cold. We need to get you cooled off so you can get better. We are going to put you into a cool water bath and cool you off slowly in order to bring your fever down. Do you understand what I am saying?"

Marcus reacted like he was in fear of the thought of cool water. "No, didn't you hear me, I am too cold already. I don't want to get in cool water."

The doctor pulled the blanket away from him and motioned for Jake to assist him in getting Marcus into the tub of water that Jake's mom had run. Marcus was calling out for Jake to help him. "Please don't let him do this, I am too cold already. Please help me." Jake felt awful for Marcus.

The doctor saw that Jake was having trouble about not helping Marcus stay out of the cold water. "Jake, if we do not get his fever down, he could go into convulsions and possibly die. We do not have much time to lower his temperature before there could be permanent damage."

Jake was here to help Marcus. He knew that was what God wanted him to do, but this did not seem like he was helping him at all. This was not what he thought helping him would look like. "Dear God, give me strength to do what I have to do to help Marcus. Even if I have to hurt him to help him, give me strength."

Jake pulled Marcus up from the bed and carried him to the bathroom where he proceeded to place him into the tub. Marcus acted like they were putting him in acid. He begged them to stop and to let him get warm. Jake did not say a word but simply held him in the tub as deep into the water as he could get him.

The doctor was helping Jake. "Mrs. S., could you get some ice? I want to see if we can slowly cool the water some more. And if you have any cold juice, could you bring it too?"

Jake heard the doctor call his mom "Mrs. S." His mom was the Mrs. S. the kids had been talking about. Jake's own mother was a part of the Knowing.

His mom had done as she was asked. It took about an hour, but the fever was finally down low enough that the threat of permanent damage was over.

The doctor and Jake's mom asked Jake to help get Marcus back into the bedroom. They took over from there. They got him redressed and into the bed. The doctor had started an IV and said that he had added some antibiotics. "The medicine will work fast from here. I think he is out of the woods now. But you need to know that it is going to take a very long time for him to get all his strength back. This young man has a long road ahead of him."

The doctor gave Jake's mom some medication and instructions on how and when to use them. She was good at this kind of thing. Jake watched as she listened and noted that she did not need to write it down, she had a good 'Knowing' memory. The doctor needed to leave but promised to return tomorrow afternoon. "Or should I say later on today?" The doctor gave Jake's mom a light kiss on the side of her cheek. "Don't worry, he is going to be fine now. I will see you later." He gave Jake a glance. "And you, young man, good job. I know that was a hard thing to do, seeing your friend upset like that, but letting him be upset saved his life this time. You did the right thing. He will thank you for it someday." The doctor said he would show himself out.

Jake leaned up against the wall and slid into a sitting position on the ground. His mother was sitting in the chair beside both the bed and Jake. They were both looking at Marcus, who was still on IV fluids but was asleep and was looking and breathing so much better.

Jake was the first to speak. "Mom, can I ask you a question?"

"Yes, of course. What is it?"

"Well, Mom, are you a believer?"

"Yes, Jake, I am"

"I didn't know."

"I know."

Jake wanted to know so many things about all of this. "Mom, how long have you been a believer?"

"Jake, I have been a believer for a long time. Ever since I was a little girl, it is only the last few years though that I became a follower."

Jake reached out and took her hand and held it in his. "I love you, Mom. I am really happy that you believe too." She squeezed his hand back, and they both sat in the room in silence watching Marcus as he slept.

*****

It was early Monday morning, and Jake had to get to work. He and his mom had fallen asleep sitting by Marcus's bed. Jake shook his mom gently so as to wake her so he could tell her that he was leaving to go to work but that he would be back at the end of the day. He gave her a hug; she hugged him back but did not let him go right away. "Honey, I am so proud of you. I love you and will see you later, okay? Now get something to eat on your way out. I am going to stay here with Marcus for a while longer." She did not want Marcus to wake up in a strange place and not know what was going on.

It was several hours before Marcus did stir, almost midmorning to be exact. Marcus woke in a coughing fit. He rolled onto his side, so when he opened his eyes, he saw Mrs. S.; she was looking pleased at him, but what had he done? Where was he?

"Good morning, Marcus, are you feeling better?"

Memories all at once flooded into Marcus's mind. The boys, the nest, what about Jake, and was there a doctor in all of this? Why and how was he at Mrs. S.'s house? Was Mrs. S. really Jake's mom? Was this really Jake's old room? All of his memories were disjointed. Marcus tried to talk. "Mrs. S. What, who, how did I?"

514

"Shhhh, relax. It is okay. You were very sick, and Jake brought you here so the doctor could take care of you. Your boys are fine, you will be able to see them in a few weeks, but for now you need to get some rest. I am going to go and get you something to eat, so rest until I get back, okay?" She had pushed him back onto his back and fluffed his pillow to make him more comfortable. She gave him one last smile. "I will be right back." She left the room and went down the stairs. When she got to the kitchen, she stopped to pray. "Oh, Father, I thank You. Thank You, thank You. I know You love my boys more than I do, but, Father, I am so grateful for Jake being a believer. Thank You for Marcus getting better. Please be with the entire nest of boys today. They are all Yours, but I have a heavy heart for them. Give me strength to do what you want me to do next. Amen."

Mrs. S. made some soup and placed it in a cup. She made a half of a sandwich and put some chips on the plate. As she walked the food up to the room that Marcus was in, she had to laugh to herself, that this was like old times, another young boy needing food and love. She had missed her kids but was proud that they had grown up to be such wonderful people.

*****

Jake had gone to work that morning. He did not feel as tired as he should have. This God way of life had so many unknown factors about it. Jake had checked in and asked around the station if anyone knew anything about the Knowing. It was rumored that there had been some kind of problem last night, but nothing anyone could put a story to.

Jake walked down the main hall and ran smack into Mark. He was pleasantly surprised that one of his oldest brothers Marcus was there and had been talking to Mark. "Hey, you two, what's up?" Jake was happy to see Mark. He was even happier that Mark was walking the hall and not in a cell. "Mark, I need to talk to you about how things went last night? To say the least, I am somewhat surprised to see you here in the hall."

Mark could hardly contain himself watching Jake try and talk in front of Big Marcus like this. At some point, Jake needed to know that Marcus was a believer, but this was way too much fun watching Jake stumble around trying to figure out what to say. "So, Jake, how is Little Marcus doing?"

Jake shot a look to Mark. *What a shock to hear him speak of Marcus in front of Marcus... This is going to be crazy having two Marcuses in the family.*

Big Marcus was having fun with this too. "So you took a stray to Mom to take care of, I hear. And she gave him your old room? I get it, you do not want to be the little brother anymore, rounded up a younger one, did you?"

Jake was tired, but these two had lost their minds. "Mark, can I talk to you alone for a minute?"

Marcus stopped them from walking away. "That's okay, I need to go and check up on a few things. Jake, I will see you next week. Family night, you know. See you later. Oh, and tell Mom hi for me, would ya?" Marcus took off on his way.

"Mark, are you out of your mind telling Marcus about Marcus?" Jake shook his head. "You know what I mean." Jake continued, "Why would you tell him about Marcus being with Mom? What were you thinking?" Jake lowered his voice. "What happened last night? How did you get away from the officers, and where are the boys? Did the officers get them?"

Mark patted Jake on the back. "Little brother, tell you what, why don't we meet with Mom tonight, and we can go over a lot of your questions. But in the meantime, we have some really good news."

Boy oh boy, Jake could use some good news right about now. "So what is the good news, and who is it for?"

Mark checked to see if anyone was in earshot. "Do you remember James from the nest?" Jake nodded his head acknowledging yes. "I am not sure if you knew that his parents had been reported to be dead. Well, we found out that James's mother is alive. It was his aunt that they were reporting on as being dead. She has been looking for James ever since they had been separated. She thought he would be in one of the camps, so that is where she has been looking. Sandy and Victor found her, and she wants to get with James as soon as possible."

Jake did not know what to say. That was good news, for James anyway, but Jake was sad for Marcus; he would be losing one of his kids, but then they were all going to have to go sooner or later. "Wow, that is great news." Jake's tone was anything but happy.

"Don't overdo it with excitement, little brother." Mark was confused by the way Jake reacted to this news. "What is wrong with you? This is great news. We have one less kid to find a home for."

"I was thinking about Marcus. James was one of his leaders, he will be hard to replace." Jake was quiet then.

"Jake, you of all the people should think this is good. That is all you talked about, getting these kids off the streets and into homes, and now when we are about to do it, you are second-guessing it?"

Mark would never be able to understand Jake. Even when he thought he had him figured out, he would change.

"Mark, I am happy, but I was thinking about Marcus. When he finds out that all the nests are gone, and now James will be leaving, it will be hard on him. Just another loss, is all I was thinking."

"Well, I think this will help some. James does not want to go to his mom until he gets a chance to see Marcus. He has asked to have a visit with him." Mark looked around again. "I was thinking we could let him visit at home, that way Mom can say goodbye too."

"Mom knows James too? No, stop. Of course she does. Silly me, what was I thinking?" Jake had found out too many new things in the last few days. Both Sally and his mom were believers, what else could happen? Jake was excited about the news, but change was hard, even good change.

Jake needed to get to work; his radio was going off calling for his location. He made a plan to meet at Mom's tonight and then went to work.

Mark was almost giddy with the good news, but nothing was going to be as great as one of Jake's biggest findings yet to come. Mark needed to pull a lot of plans together before the night got here. He needed to arrange James being picked up from the farm and being brought to the Singleton house. Tonight was going to be a great night.

Jake had to work an extra-long shift, but when he was done, he went to his apartment to shower and get some clean clothing on. He thought to bring an extra change of clothing in case he needed to stay the night at his mom's.

It was almost 8:00 p.m. when Jake got to his parents' house. Jake found his mom in the kitchen making a tray of food for Marcus. Jake was surprised to see how much food she had placed on the tray. Jake gave his mom a hug. "Are you feeding Marcus or the whole nest? Is he really able to eat that much already?"

Mrs. S. rolled her eyes at Jake's comments. "I am as surprised as you are. In fact, he only ate a little soup but has asked for a sandwich every time he is awake. I guess he is just a growing boy. Jake, come on up with me and carry that juice, will you, it is time for his meds."

Jake thought he had seen Marcus do this before. He would ask for food for himself, but then he would stash it so he could take it to the boys at the nest later. This was hard for Jake to think about. Marcus still thought that he had a nest. Jake was going to have to tell Marcus before Mark and James got to the house. Jake stopped his mom in the hallway before she had a chance to go into the room. "Mom, I think we may have a problem."

Jake's mom placed the tray of food on the table in the hall. She took the meds from Jake and started to get them out of the bottle. "Jake, what on earth could be the problem now?" She had hoped there would be a break before the next problem came up.

"Mom, I don't think Marcus is eating the food. I think he may be stashing it so he can give it to his boys." Jake watched as his mom started to follow what he was talking about.

"But, Jake, he does not have any—" her voice trailed off as she became aware of what Jake was saying and what it really meant. "Oh, Jake, what are we going to do? Someone has to tell him. He doesn't know that the nests do not exist anymore."

When they entered the room, Marcus was fast asleep. They did not wake him. Jake sat the juice down on the bedside table and looked around for where the food might be hidden. He smiled and motioned for his mom to come and see the pile of food. It was all neatly wrapped in napkins and had been placed into a plastic bag. He had put everything except the soup in the pile.

"Jake," his mom was whispering, "we have another problem."

Jake gave her a look of questioning.

"This means that Marcus has hardly eaten a thing all day, except a little soup." She was not happy about that fact.

"When it comes to his boys, Marcus always puts them first. He is a good man, Mom, even if he is only a boy."

"Well, this is going to have to stop. But I don't have a clue as to what to do. Do you have any ideas?" Jake's mom did not like to be tricked, even if it was for a good cause. "I can see that taking care of Marcus is going to be a lot like it was with you. No more sandwiches for him. He will only get things that he cannot stash from now on."

Marcus had opened his eyes and was having trouble focusing on the two of them. It sounded like they were arguing, their voices raised some, but it did not look like they were. "What is going on? Oh, hi, Jake, did your mom tell you how good I am doing? I think you can take me back to the nest soon, maybe even tonight if you will help me a little."

Jake was going to answer, but his mom beat him to it. "Marcus, we need to have a talk. I am not sure that you are going to like what I am going to say, but let's be clear, this is not up for discussion. It is simply the facts, and that is all. So here is fact number one. You are not doing well, you are far from it. Better, yes, but not well. Then there is fact number two, the doctor has to give you the all clear before you go anywhere, and not to mention you have medicine that you have to finish before you leave."

Jake had seen his mom like this before in his life, and poor Marcus did not have a chance about changing her mind. Jake knew it even if Marcus did not. Marcus did not say a word but made a face, and a sound of irritation came from him before he broke out into a coughing fit. It was the first one in several hours. It seemed that excitement and his moving around set it off.

After Marcus caught his breath, Mrs. S. gave him his pills and some juice. She put her finger on the bottom of the glass, holding it in place on his mouth and tilting it back so Marcus had to keep drinking it or it would spill. Marcus, being the nice young man he was, followed the silent instructions given by her actions. She did not let up until the whole glass was empty.

Jake saw the whole thing and wondered if he should tell Marcus that he and Jake's mom were going to be at war over Marcus's not eating. It would make him laugh except for the fact he knew that his friend Marcus was going to lose this battle.

"Mom, do you think that Marcus and I could have a chance to talk alone for a few minutes?" Jake was not too anxious to tell Marcus about the nests and his boys, but he did not want Mark to show up with James before he had a chance to tell him about all of the changes. James's mom being alive was going to bring a big change in itself. James would be leaving the area, and maybe for good.

Jake's mom looked at Marcus and then at Jake. "I am not sure why, but the two of you talking alone makes me a little nervous. Jake, you can talk, but Marcus stays in that bed, do you hear me?"

Marcus was going to protest, but Jake answered first, "Mom, Marcus and I will be fine. I need to catch him up on some of the changes on the streets."

Jake's mom prayed as she left for downstairs; she gave one last glance at the two of them sitting and looking so innocent.

"Marcus, I need to tell you some things, but as bad as they may sound, you need to know that there is always a chance that things could turn around. Okay, so here goes. One of the most important things is that your boys are okay. Victor closed all the nests, and all of the boys are at farms or with families. Things will stay this way for a long while from the looks of it." So far, so good. Marcus did not even react to the news. "Okay, for the next news. James got a great report. Sandy and Victor found out that James's mother was not dead. It was her sister the authorities had reported on, and his mom has been looking in the camps for him ever since they were separated. Victor and Sandy want to send James to be with his mom. They will be together in a camp. The camp is not too close, but you will see each other once in a while. Good news, don't you think?"

Marcus looked like he was at peace with what Jake had been saying. "Jake, do you have any news about Travis?"

"No, but when James gets here tonight, we can ask Mark if he has heard anything." Jake was relaxed now. He had told Marcus, and the talk had gone well. Or so he thought.

"Jake, what are you saying? Why would James come here, and why would he come tonight?" Marcus was getting up from his lying position.

"Relax, Marcus. James wants to go and be with his mom, but he wanted to come and see you and to make sure that you are doing all right before he leaves town." Jake was not sure where this conversation was going.

"Jake, I can't let James see me this way. You need to tell him not to come."

"What is wrong with you, you do not want James to see you looking like what?" Jake was trying hard to track what Marcus was saying.

"Jake, you know what I mean. I need your help. Stop James from coming, please." Marcus was trying to get up out of the bed.

Jake got it. Marcus did not want to look weak in front of one of his peers. He wanted it to be reported about how good he was doing. He did not want to worry anyone.

Before Jake's mom had returned, Jake had Marcus sitting on the side of the bed, wearing a hooded sweatshirt with his hair combed. He had put on his socks and was getting ready to put on shoes when his mom entered the room. She was carrying some fruit and looked over at Marcus. "You look better. James will never know how sick you are by the looks of you now. But, Jake, no shoes. Marcus will not be leaving tonight."

Jake and Marcus both reacted to the statement. They had shocked and questioning looks on their faces. "You heard me, I said no shoes. Marcus stays in that bed until James gets here, then and only then can he get up and sit in the chair. Got it?"

There was no argument from either one of them. They looked at each other and did as she had ordered. Jake's mom has presented both of them with some fruit to eat, and neither of them even questioned her but promptly ate. Marcus was in the middle of eating as he and Jake talked about how bossy women were when Jake realized that Marcus was not keeping up his end of the conversation. He had fallen asleep. Jake took the leftover fruit and put it into a plastic bag that he had in his pocket (He had learned to always have a bag handy from being on the street) and added it to Marcus's stash. "So this is what it is like to have a little brother. It is hard, but it is good." He went downstairs to talk with his mom some about what was going to happen next. But really he just wanted to spend some time with her.

Jake took the dishes from the fruit over to the sink. He was glad to see that his mom had finished cleaning up the kitchen. "Here, I will do these." Jake put the dishes into the dishwasher.

"Is Marcus asleep?"

Jake nodded his head yes.

"How did he take the news about the nests closing?" Jake's mother was worried how Marcus would take it.

"He seemed to be okay with it. I think he may have suspected that closing the nests might be coming." Jake was not used to her asking questions this way.

"How about the news about James, was he okay with that too?" She looked concerned but not too worried.

"Yes, other than the fact he did not want James to see him sick, I think he was really okay with it, happy even. I think he agrees that in the long run, this is for the best." Jake took a deep breath of relief knowing that the telling was over.

Jake's mom looked suspicious. "Did he ask about Travis?"

"Yes, but I did not have any information about him."

"And how did he take that?"

"He seemed fine, why, what's wrong?" Jake saw that she was going somewhere with this questioning.

"Jake, I am not sure, but I think that Marcus is too fine maybe, do you know what I mean?"

Jake did not get what she was talking about, but he knew that in time, he would figure it out. "Mom, how are the kids doing out on the farms? Any word?"

Jake's mom stopped and wanted to deliver the information carefully. "The reports on the boys were good for the most part."

"What does that mean?" Jake was concerned.

"Well, they are all healthy, and they are good, adjusting, polite, and fit into the families they are placed in, but not one of them is settled in. They are all waiting for Marcus to come back and get them. No one can convince them that this is their new life. They are waiting for Marcus. No one can figure out how to change it." They were quiet for a while. They did not have an answer either. Jake and his mom talked for about an hour. Jake enjoyed being together visiting with her. This time was a gift from God, and they were both enjoying it.

There was a set of car lights that shone through the window. Jake's mom looked out and saw that it was them.

Jake headed upstairs. "I'll get him ready, so you stall them a little, okay?"

Jake got Marcus up and into the chair, redid his hair, and threw the bed together. They were ready. They heard a knock at the door; it opened, and James walked in to visit Marcus.

Jake was truly glad to see James. "Hey, James, I am glad that you could come by and visit. I know that it was a lot of work to get here, but you can fill us in on some of the things that have been going on with the nest." Jake started the conversation off because Marcus did not say anything at all.

James looked at the bed that Marcus had been sleeping in. "Marcus, is this your bed? It is a real bed. Wow. Look at all those pillows. I bet you sleep really nice in this thing. Can I sit on it?"

Marcus was glad to see that James was the same as always. "James, it is great news about your mom. When do you meet up with her?"

James was slightly bouncing on the mattress. "Well, security is tight right now. It took us over an hour to get here tonight. I think something big must be up. Did you know that they have closed all of the nests? Weird, isn't it? If you were not here, you would be on a farm or with a new family like us. Where are you going to go when you get out of here?"

Marcus had no idea. For now, Mrs. S. had told him that he was going to stay until the doctor told him he could go. But go where? "James, how are my boys?"

James gave out a great big smile. "Marcus, you should see the younger ones. They are so happy. Victor, Sandy, and Mrs. S. got everyone a family out by a big farm kind of far from here. We will get to see each other almost every day and will get to go to a real school. It is chipless, but, Marcus, we have books and everything. They even have computers for us to use."

"And you, James, how is it going for you?" Marcus was more relaxed now.

"Marcus, that is the great thing, my mom and I are going to be together. Victor says that we have to go away from here for a time but that we can end up by the farm too. We will get to be in the same area as the boys. I bet if you asked, they could find you a family out there too."

Jake saw what his mother was talking about. Marcus's reaction to information was the exact same thing, whether it is good or bad, he reacted the same way.

James was playing with one of the pillows. "Hey, Marcus, did you hear about Travis?"

Jake noticed that Marcus sat up a little taller. "Travis? What do you know about him? Do you know where he is? Is he okay, I mean?"

James now had two of the pillows and was trying to squish them down as small as he could get them. He was making a game out of it.

Jake's mom was by the door listening to the visit and watching the actions and the reactions between the boys. She found it funny to see that Jake was as much one of the boys at this moment as he had ever been. Jake sat down on the end of the bed and had been listening too.

Jake was the one to reask the last question. "James, what do you know about Travis? And do you know where he is?"

James quit playing with the pillow and looked at Marcus. "I think that Travis is in big trouble this time. I am not sure, but the last word I heard about him is that some really high-up government official had him arrested. I guess that he is in jail."

Marcus shot a look at Jake. "He is in your jail, and you do not know about it?"

There it was. For just a second, Jake saw the anger Marcus was feeling. "It is a big jail, and the program your brother would be in falls under a different set of rules. But I will find out what I can tomorrow, I promise."

Marcus composed himself. The relaxed "I am happy about all that's going on" was back. "So do you know what they are planning to do with Travis?"

"I am not sure, but from what I heard, they think he can give them some really big information in order to take down the Knowing. So, you remember that family that was on TV the other day?" James had all three of the pillows piled up on his lap and was pushing them down as far as he could. "Well, they told everyone that the Knowing was scared and had all moved out of the town to get away from the government because the town leaders were too smart and had been able to shut them down. That is kind of crazy, but it will help us to get back to work sooner. Especially if they think we are not here anymore. I just hope that Travis does not mess things up again." James made a quick look to Marcus. "I am sorry I said that. I know Travis is your brother, but he has really done bad stuff."

Marcus was under control of his reactions now. "James, it is okay, I have figured out that Travis was not making good choices for a long time now. So do you know if there is any way I can get in touch with him?"

The question shocked everyone in the room. Jake's mom entered into the conversation. "Hi, James, how are you doing?"

James got up and ran over to see her; he put a great big hug on her. "Mrs. S., I did not know that you would be here too."

She smiled and hugged him back. "James, I live here, this is my home."

"So Marcus gets to live with you?" James turned to Marcus. "We all thought we had it good, but you living with Mrs. S., you can't get better than this." James turned to look at Marcus. "Marcus, I need to know if it is okay with you if I go away with my mom? I know that I am supposed to take care of the boys until you get back, but it looks like we all have families now and that everyone is okay if I go. But whatever you think is best, I will do it, but I really think it is okay if I go."

"James, you need to go. I will be going out to the farm most likely tomorrow or the next day at the latest. So you go on with your mom. I will take over from here, and we will get in touch soon." Marcus was so convincing that Jake and his mom almost believed him, and both of them knew that it was not the truth.

"Marcus, if you are sure then?" James was so excited.

Jake's mom motioned for Jake to come with her and that they should let the boys talk by themselves. Jake was not too sure that this was a good idea. He kind of wanted to hear the conversation so he could know what Marcus was thinking. But his mom seemed to have a handle on the boys, so he went out of the room with her. When he came out the door, he was totally taken aback by the fact that both Mark and his brother Marcus were in the hall listening to everything that had been said. "Marcus!" Everyone shushed him at the same time. "Marcus, you are a believer too?"

Marcus raised an eyebrow and shrugged his shoulders. "What can I say? But remember that I did it first." Marcus rubbed his little brother on the back to show that he was happy about his believing. But brothers will be brothers, and he needed Jake to know that the game was still on when it came to family.

Mark was asking Jake, "So were they signaling the same information as they were saying?"

Brother Marcus was the one to answer, "You mean little brother here reads nest?"

Mark was proud of Jake. "Not only can he read it, he can speak it too. I think he even has the new one down by now."

Jake was not sure how his brother Marcus knew about the nest signals, but he felt good that this was looked at as a special thing to know. "They were signaling the same as they were talking. Marcus—I mean, Little Marcus was asking a lot of questions and getting nothing from James. I think James doesn't know anything. But Little Marcus told James that he had a plan and that he would get in touch with him soon. He wanted James to go to be with his mom. He told him that it would be good to have a camp contact in case when he left here he needed to run to a safe place."

That statement "when he left here and needed to run" grabbed their mom by the heart, and she felt a sad fear go through her. Marcus was like one of her sons. God had put him into her life and her heart for a reason, and it was not until now that she figured out that he was a gift for her, another bonus son, and the thought of him leaving and being alone on the run overwhelmed her. She could not figure out why she was reacting the way she was, but she felt that God had given Little Marcus, as they had started calling him, to her. "Okay, so what are we going to do about Little Marcus? He needs to get well, and he needs to get on with having a real life. So what are we going to do to help him?"

Big Marcus had an idea. "Someone needs to keep an eye on this kid. He is too smart for his own good. I would do it, but for some reason, the kids don't trust me."

Mark was looking at his big brother; he was dressed in his traditional government attire. All black with his badge hanging in full view. Mark laughed. "Really, big brother, you don't know why they don't trust you? Look at the way you are dressed. In fact, you scare me sometimes." Mark was making a point, but there was humor in his voice as he said it. "I personally think that you should let Sally take you shopping and get you some real clothing."

"I guess you want me to go to the chipless shelter and get outfits like you wear?" Marcus was not really irritated, but it was his brotherly duty to put up a fuss with the younger ones.

Mark countered with, "At least the people trust me."

Their mom was listening and watching them, and one of the amazing things to her was that not one of them thought different about Little Marcus being family or that his staying should go any other way. They all agreed that Little Marcus was family and he needed their help. God was a truly great and awesome God who was obviously way ahead of them in the planning.

They had all stood in the hall listening and hearing as much as they could. Jake kept looking at his big brother and trying to figure out how he had missed the fact that this many of his family were believers. Some detective he was. It was a short while when James came out of the room; he was shocked to find them all waiting for him in the hall. The men went downstairs with James to get him back to the farm where he would be united with his mom. "Thanks for letting me see Marcus. I know that he is a lot sicker than he wants me to know, but he is going to be okay, right?" James was as good at this life as Marcus, only he had not had to step up yet the way Marcus had. "I am worried about Marcus getting with Travis. You know that could be a problem, right? I don't mean to sell Marcus out, but he is really close to his brother and might trust him when he shouldn't." James stopped to wait for Mrs. S. so he could say goodbye.

Their mom had gone into the room to see if Marcus was okay. She was puzzled to see that Marcus was trying to finish dressing himself. He had decided that he needed to leave and go and find his boys and his brother, Travis. She did not dispute him but told him that she thought it was a bad idea but that he needed to do whatever he thought was best. She left him alone and went downstairs.

As she entered the kitchen, all the men and James looked up to see her coming in. She had a look of concern on her face. It was Big Marcus that inquired as to what was wrong. She stopped and looked at James. "James, I was wondering, if Marcus had asked you to stay with the boys and not go be with your mom until later, would you really have done it?"

James looked confused. "Did Marcus change his mind and decide for me to stay at the farm and not go with my mom?"

"No, I am sorry, James. I was just wondering what you would have done if he had asked. Marcus really does want you to go be with your mom." She felt bad that she alarmed him.

"Mrs. S., if Marcus wanted me to stay for a while, I sure would have, even if I did not like it. Marcus has done so much for me, for all of us. I guess you could say that he has saved our lives. And he did it more than once." James waited to see if she had more to say.

Mrs. S. walked across the room and put her arms around James and gave him a great big hug. "James, I am glad you are such a good friend to Marcus, he is blessed to have you, and so are we. You need to go to your mom, and we will take care of Marcus."

James's face lit up. "You really are going to take care of Marcus? I know that he thinks he can do it all by himself, but you know sometimes he needs help from other people."

She gave James one last hug and then let him go. "You know, James, that is exactly what we are going to do. Marcus…" She looked around the kitchen and saw the other Marcus looking at her. "I mean Little Marcus is with a family now. We will take care of him. And God will take care of us all."

It was time for James to go back to the farm. Big Marcus and Mark took James and left like they had come, leaving Jake and his mom alone.

"Hey, Mom, what is Little Marcus doing anyway?" Jake had realized that he had not even considered about him.

"He is getting dressed so he can leave." She was not looking at Jake but had a smile on her face because she knew exactly how he was going to react.

"He's what?" He looked at her with question. "He can't leave. He can hardly even walk."

"You know this, and I know this, but now he needs to find it out for himself." She was putting away the dishes. It was getting late, and they needed to get to bed soon.

Jake was on his way to the stairs as he was talking to her. "Well, I think I am going to go and see how our Little Marcus is doing. I will be right back."

She smiled to herself, all the while thinking that she knew that Jake would be right on the fact that Marcus most likely would need him right about now.

Jake literally ran up the stairs. When he got to the door, sure enough, Marcus was up, and it had taken all this time for him to put on his own shirt and his coat that he must have found in the closet.

Marcus saw Jake at the door. "Go away. You can't stop me." Marcus walked as far away from Jake as he could get in the room.

"I won't have to."

"What?" Marcus shot Jake an irritated look.

"You are not strong enough to get dressed and get yourself out of here yet. But go ahead and knock your socks off trying. You will sleep better if you get some exercise." Jake crossed his arms and was leaning against the doorframe watching Marcus.

Marcus was so angry. He would show Jake how wrong he was. He was fine, he was doing better, he was…he had prayed for God to heal him and to give him strength. He believed that God would give him an answer. He continued dressing. Marcus tried to keep on with his plan to leave. The adrenaline rush he got from being mad at Jake was wearing off. He sat down. "I'll just rest for a bit." Marcus started to cough. He bent over from his waist to try and catch his breath better. The fit ended. Was this answered prayer? He was dressed at least.

Jake watched as Marcus ran out of steam. He knew the time was soon when Marcus was going to need his help. There it was. Marcus slid to the ground. His head went face first into the bed. Jake walked over to Marcus, lifted him up, and sat him upright on the side of the bed. Marcus tried to protest the help, but Jake kept working. It took less than a minute to undo what Marcus had taken so long to do. "Off with this shirt and on with the sweatshirt." Jake was having fun about being right concerning his not being ready to leave. Marcus reached out to stop Jake from helping him, but Jake gently shoved Marcus onto his back on the bed. He undid Marcus's shoes and slipped them off. "Off with the jeans and on with the sweatpants too, the socks could stay." He grabbed Marcus like a rag doll and got him back into the bed. Marcus was exhausted. He tried hard to fight it, but he was asleep as soon as his head hit the pillow.

Jake stood looking at him; he looked so young and so frail. "God, why did You want him to be a warrior? Could his fight please be over? Can he be a kid again?"

Jake was not going to be able to get Marcus to not be in charge of the nest and the boys. That was clear from listening to James talk about how they would follow Marcus if he asked. And Marcus would do whatever it took to take care of the boys. But good luck convincing Marcus that letting the boys go was the right thing for both the boys and for him. He was still a kid. Marcus would have to decide to do it. *God, how can I get him to see that keeping the nests closed would be for the best? That he could finish growing up, get an education, and then go back to the fight and that the boys would be in families, safe from the street life?* Jake sat in the chair, his mind open to any ideas God might send his way. *That's it!* Marcus himself needed to send his kids away to the farms or to families where they could get a family life too. Marcus needed to send them, not Jake or anyone else taking them. *God, is that the answer? Is that how it can work?* It was clear to Jake that what he need to do was to convince Marcus to do that, send them away, give them permission to go. *But how? God, how?*

It was not an actual voice but a knowing from God somehow way deep inside. *Show him the love of a family.* This was the first time feelings like this had happened. Was it real, or just his mind playing tricks? It felt like it was right, but what did it mean? Marcus had come from a loving family. He had given love to the boys in the nest like a family. Marcus knew what it was to be in a family. *Show me, God, what You want me to do. I am listening.* Jake bowed his head.

Marcus was definitely out for the night. Jake went downstairs to see his mom. He left the bedroom door open so they could hear him if he needed them. Jake needed to get to bed; he had work early in the morning. There was a big meeting he had to be at. There was a message on his phone as well as one in his box at work. It sounded rather big from the way the orders were written.

"Hey, Mom, I think that Marcus will be out for the night. Boy, is he ever stubborn. Do you know that he was almost completely dressed?" Jake sat on a stool next to her. She was reading her Bible. She closed it and looked at Jake.

"I think the rest will do him good, and from the look of you, I think rest is what you need too. Did you want to stay the night? You can sleep in Mark's old room, or are you going to go to your apartment?"

Jake was so glad that his mom was a believer. "Mom, I was thinking about Marcus and the kids. You know how Sandy said that the kids are having trouble getting adjusted to the new families because they think Marcus is coming and that they will be going back to their old life? Well, what if we took Marcus to visit them, and they could see how good he is doing with us, and he could see how good they are doing with their families."

"Jake, I am not too sure if that would be a good idea right now. I think that it might be too hard on Marcus to see that his kids can do okay without him. He has been the leader over these kids for a long time, and the need to be needed can be a huge thing to have to give up."

"Mom, he can't keep going on like he has been. I am afraid for him to get hurt or sick again." Jake felt so strongly about Marcus not going back to the street that it even surprised him. He had not known this kid for very long, but he felt like family.

Jake's mom put her hand on top of his. "Honey, welcome to parenting 101. I have had this kind of talk with myself and God every time one of you kids leave the house. Sometimes I wish I could lock you up in your old rooms to keep you safe, but then I remember that God has a plan, and sometimes it is dangerous, but He is with you."

"But, Mom, he is just a kid." Jake thought this was different from her own children.

She squeezed his hand. "And you, my son, are simply a man, God is with you too. Just do your best to be there when Marcus falls, and remember that God loves him even more than we do or can ever understand. Marcus is a good man. He is a Godly man. And now he is a part of our family."

"Mom, I need to get to bed. I think I will take you up on staying the night. I have a change of clothing in my car. Let me go get them, and then we can close up the house for the night." Jake went outside to his car. The night was cool, but there was no rain. He thought about what his mom had said about being a Godly man. Marcus was a Godly man, and he felt so excited inside to know that he was a Godly man too. *Thank You, Jesus.* He was talking to God and had sent up an arrow prayer when he thought he noticed a movement off to one side of the yard. He stopped to look and see what it was, but it was not there anymore. He looked around; there was not any real wind tonight. He could not see anyone, but he knew that someone was there. He was glad he had decided to spend the night. In fact, he might be spending a few nights if he kept feeling like this.

The night went without any other events. Jake checked out the window several times during the night, but he saw nothing. Perhaps he was overreacting to the entire goings-on. But he would stay the night until his dad got back home.

CHAPTER 34

Jake got up early and went downstairs only to find that his mom was already up. She had made coffee and was waiting for him when he came into the room. "Good morning, Jake." She handed him a cup of coffee.

He smiled and thanked her.

"So, Jake, what were you looking for out the windows last night? Is something going on I should know about?" Jake looked at her questioning how she knew what he was thinking. "I heard you get up several times during the night. I was wondering if something was wrong."

Jake sat his coffee down and gave her a great big hug. "I wish you would stay out of my head." He had humor in his tone. "I am just being an officer. You know I need to check things out. That is all." He grabbed a breakfast bar out of a box and went to leave. "Hey, Mom, things are all right from what I see, but I need you to be careful. Keep the doors locked, okay?" He wanted to alert her but did not want to worry her about the fact he felt like something was up.

"Jake, we are fine, but I will be careful. Now you get to work." Jake gave her another hug, and off he went. As he went to leave, he stopped by the back door and turned to speak to her. "Thanks, Mom."

"For what?"

Jake smiled. "For everything." He shut the door and left.

His mom was so happy. Happy could not describe how grateful she was for Jake's being a believer. She was so glad that he had grown into the man he now was. She went to the door to make sure that the locks were set. She pulled back a part of the curtain to look out. She felt it too. There was a warning going off in her head. Something was wrong, and she needed to do something. She returned to the stool she had been sitting on and opened her Bible up. She knew exactly what to do. She needed to pray and read her Bible. She needed to visit with God.

*****

Jake entered the government station. Something was up. The whole place was abuzz with excitement. Jake checked in and went to the meeting. He got himself a cup of coffee and had a seat. Many of the other officers greeted him, and more than one had asked him if he knew what was going on. Jake was waiting for the boss to get things started; his boss had not come in yet. Jake looked and saw that his brother Marcus was walking into the room. He gave Jake a general hi and stood by the door. Jake's boss entered the room, and everyone got quiet. "Okay, some of you may not know this, but we had a super big bust last night. We caught a fairly large group of the Knowing. They were all at a shelter here in town, and the best news about it is that we think one of them is the leader we have been after for years. The media have not found out about it yet, but they should any time now. So to say the least, things around here may get a little crazy."

Jake sat up straighter in his chair. He shot a look over to where Marcus was standing. To his surprise, he got a nest signal from Marcus for him to remain calm. He signaled back to him, but no answer. He smiled; Marcus had learned a few signs of nest. That would be a conversation when things settled down again. Marcus signaled again. "I need help, you after." His signals were slow. "I look at you later." Jake had to figure out what Marcus was trying to say. Oh, he got it. *See me after.*

"Singleton, are you listening?" Jake's boss was looking at him. "You of all people should be about this. Your family is one of the ones on the list they are targeting."

Jake's boss had his full attention as well as the attention of his brother Marcus. "From the looks on your faces, I take it that neither of you were informed of the list and its danger? Okay then, see me after, and I will catch you up on it. But for now, everyone be careful. The media will be all over here. We do not want any information to get out that has not been given the okay by the top brass. So do your jobs, and please keep your information in-house. Okay, you can go now." He looked around the room as people were getting up. "Singletons, see me."

Jake and Marcus gathered together at the front of the room; they needed to wait until the boss was ready to talk to them. "Hey, Big Marcus, what do you think this is all about?" Jake thought a little humor might take the edge off things.

Marcus shot Jake a look. "Families on a list? Do you know anything about this?"

"Not a clue. This is the first time I have heard anything about it. By the way, nice nest talk, how did that happen?"

"Before all this crazy stuff started, we were taping the kids in the park trying to see how it was they worked. We noticed that they had signals, but lately they had changed, and we were lost again as to what they were saying. By the way, how is it that you can speak it so good?"

Jake shook his head in disbelief. "I am not sure exactly, I think God perhaps. All I know is that I picked it up fast, and now I speak it."

"Mark said you know the new signals too?" Jake confirmed it by nodding his head slightly and then gave the signal "yes" to Marcus. "Great. I need you after we meet with the boss. I need you to do something for me, okay?"

This was great. Jake felt that this was good to be united with his brother. He loved that he could be of help.

Jake's boss finally got to meeting with them. "Okay, Singletons, you may have a problem. When we picked up this last group of Knowing, we found a list of families in the area. There were nine families on the list. One of the names was yours, Singleton. We are not sure what the list is for, but we think the families were to be targets for something."

Jake asked, "Can we see the list?"

"Yes, I think I have a copy of it right here." He got out a file, opened it, and pulled it out and gave it to them to look at. "Do you see anything that we may have missed? Anything that would tie these families together?"

Jake and Marcus were shocked by the list. There were nine families of the Knowing on the list. They were well-known in the community, so the government thought it was a hit list of sort. What they did not know was they had a list of many of the families who were a part of the Knowing underground.

Marcus was the one to ask. "Can I have a copy of this?"

"Go ahead and keep that one. Let me know if you think of or find anything that can help us with it. In the meantime, we have everyone on the list being watched extra for their safety. The last thing I need around here is one of our top families getting hurt." He closed the file. "You two be careful, and I will see you later." He was looking at Jake when he said it. "Now get to work."

After Jake's boss had walked away, Jake asked Marcus what help he needed. "Jake, I think we had better get this news to Victor and the shelters. I am going to go and find Mark and see if he knows anything. You get to work here and see if you can get any more information about who these people are that they arrested. Oh, and if you get a break, do you think you should check up on Marcus and Mom?"

There was another Singleton in Jake's mind. "Yes, I was thinking to do just that. Any ideas as to when Dad will be home?"

Marcus was happy that Jake was thinking ahead. "Worried that Dad is going to let you have it for bringing home another stray?"

Jake looked down at the floor. "Well, there are a few other times in the past that might make me think that."

Marcus patted him on the back. "Not this time, little brother. Dad, like all the rest of us, think this was a real good call. Good job. Now get on with whatever it is you do around here, and I will see you later."

Marcus had talked to their dad. But when and what was said. The list of things to talk over with his big brother and family was growing. Jake called out to Marcus, "Hey, I thought that you needed my help."

Marcus stopped and turned, walked back to Jake. "I'll meet you at Mom and Dad's later. We can maybe get Little Marcus to help too."

"Okay, if you are sure." Jake was shaking his head in disbelief.

"I think it would be best considering everything else that is going on." Marcus turned and went on his way.

Jake went on to do his work like his boss had said to do. There were all sorts of calls all over the town, and almost everyone of them were blaming the Knowing for some or all of what was going on. Jake could remember days when blaming the Knowing would have made him happy, and now it is his family that they are talking about. In fact it is he, himself, they are talking about. He is now part of the Knowing.

It was early afternoon before Jake got to take a break. He would eat something at his mom's house. Her food was the best anyway.

When Jake got to his parents' house, his mom was in the kitchen, and so was Little Marcus. Marcus was still in the sweat clothes. His hair was brushed, and he had socks on his feet but no shoes. It was amazing how much better Marcus looked. The medicine and some rest had done him a lot of good. Marcus was sitting at the kitchen table with a bowl of soup and a glass of milk in front of him. His hands were by his side, and he was staring at the food. Neither of them was talking. It would not take a genius to figure out that the two of them were at some sort of a standoff. Not a fight but a standoff.

Jake went over to his mom and gave her a kiss on her cheek and asked how the morning had gone. He motioned with his head toward Marcus. "So how is our patient doing?"

She looked over at Marcus and then back at Jake. "You may need to ask him. I am not sure if he is talking to me yet." She smiled and winked at Jake.

Jake did as she suggested. He went to the table and had a seat across form Marcus. Marcus was not eating but still had his eyes fixed on the food that had been placed in front of him. Marcus looked up at Jake, who was signaling him about what was going on. "Is something wrong?"

Marcus used gestures larger than usual. "No. Can I go back to town now? Please."

Jake thought this a strange request since Marcus knew that the nests had been taken out of business. "Where would you go?"

Jake's mom had crossed the room to where the two of them were sitting. She brought each of them a sandwich and sat them on the table. She sat in the chair between them. They both had a hand they were using for signaling spread out on the table. They were using very slight movements, but they were there all the same. She stopped them both from signaling by covering each of their hands at the same time. "That's rude. If you two have something to say, then use your voice. It is not nice to talk in front of someone who does not understand the language."

Jake turned his hand over and took hers; he gave it a squeeze. "Sorry, Mom, I did not mean to be rude. I was practicing, that's all." Jake looked at Marcus, who had slid his hand out from under hers and placed it in his lap.

"So why does Marcus want to leave so soon?"

"Really? This is the first I have heard of it, but it does not surprise me. Marcus here is used to running the show. He is used to deciding everything that is going on in his life, so we had to have a little adjustment this morning, but I thought we had it worked out." She kept her voice light and easy. "Marcus wanted to get up out of bed right after you left this morning, and I made him stay there until now. He needed to rest, and there was no reason for him to get up. I took him up something to eat, and he would not eat it, so he stayed in bed until lunch. That was the deal. I let him get up, he eats lunch. And here we are." She took both plates of food and shoved them closer to each of them "Eat, so we can clean up and get on with the day." She got up from the table and went about her daily work.

Jake lowered his voice and leaned in closer to Marcus, "From my past experiences with my mom, I would eat if I were you."

Marcus shot him a look. He was so angry at Jake, Mrs. S., his mom and dad, his brother, Travis, he was mad at the world. "Fine." Marcus began to eat his soup. Jake joined him in silence.

A little later, Marcus's soup was gone and half of his sandwich. Jake had not seen him eat the sandwich, but he thought it was a good sign that he was so hungry. Jake's mom reentered the room. She walked up behind Marcus and reached out for him like in a hug from behind. She reached down into his lap and took the half sandwich now wrapped in paper and put it back on his plate. "There is no need to stash food. There is plenty, there should always be plenty. So eat." She walked away.

Marcus looked at Jake. Jake shrugged his shoulders and signaled, "You should eat." Both of them ate in silence. Jake could see that even the simplest act of eating was wearing on Marcus.

Marcus was more frustrated now than he was this morning. He was feeling good, but now it was as if someone had unplugged him. *God, where are You in all of this? I have prayed for strength and for my boys to be back with me, but no answer. I have prayed for Travis and for Mom and Dad to come find me, but no answer. God, please help. I need to be strong enough to get out of here and to go and fix things out there in the town. My boys are alone. Travis is making bad choices, and I sit here eating great food and sleeping in great beds with fantastic pillows. How can I love all of this when I know that the rest of the family may be in great need?*

Jake could see from the look on Marcus's face that he was in mental anguish over everything that had taken place. He only wished that he would talk to him about it. Jake might not be able to help, but he thought that Marcus would feel better if he talked about it. "So what's next?"

Marcus looked up at Jake somewhat anxious. He was caught in thought and did not get what Jake was saying. "What?"

"Some rest, maybe even a nap, and then a snack." Jake's mom was gathering the dishes and cleaning the rest of the kitchen.

Marcus shot her a look of total irritation. He was not used to being fussed over, and he did not like being treated like a baby one bit.

Jake's mom had not really looked at him. "Don't give me that look. You and I both know that I am right. You are exhausted and need to rest some more. Just the facts, young man, and neither of us can change them. Only time and rest will change it."

Jake's mom was good at this parenting. Jake's greatest joy though was that it was at Marcus and not at him. Jake's mom shot him a look too. "And you, Mr. Singleton, may I suggest that you get yourself back to work so this young man can get some rest."

Jake was surprised that his mom's statement made Marcus smile. Jake signaled him to not to be so smug. That he was getting to leave, but Marcus was going to go back to bed. Both of the men made faces.

Jake left to go back to work, and Marcus gave up the fight of not resting. From Jake's advice, it was clear that this woman was not going to change her mind no matter what he did. "Mrs. S., would it be okay if I went out into the backyard to rest instead of in here?"

She thought about it and decided the fresh air might do him some good. "Yes, but stay in the backyard so I can see you. And take your coat." She had moved his coat out of his room in order to launder it."

Marcus had not noticed his coat until now. This was hard and good at the same time. It was nice to have someone care about him, but it was hard to have someone in his business. He got up and reached for his coat. When he went to put it on, he was horrified at the fact that she had not only cleaned his coat but had taken off the extra pockets from the inside. He gave her a quick look of shock.

She was standing drying her hands, looking at him. "You will not need the pockets anymore. You are with us now, and we are going to take care of you."

Everything was changing and too fast. Even his coat was not street ready anymore. He did not say anything but took the coat and went out to the backyard as far from the house as he could get and still be in the yard. He did not want to argue with her anymore. But she really did not argue as much as she pulled rank on him. Jake was right, she was good at this.

Hours had passed. Marcus had spent most of the afternoon outside resting and getting fresh air, but it was cooling off, and he needed to come inside. Jake's mom walked outside to see what he was doing when she noticed that Marcus was awake looking up at the sky. He looked so young. *God, why did You not have me get him off the street sooner? This is going to be so much harder to get used to because of the amount of time on the street. Did I not hear You? Did You tell me to do it sooner? I know that You are in charge, please do not let me get in the way of Your work, but don't let me miss what it is You need me to do either. I love You, Lord.* Marcus startled when she got close to him. "Are you doing okay?"

He looked at her and nodded yes.

"I think—" She stopped and rephrased it. "Do you think you should come into the house? It is getting cool out here. Besides, it is time for you to take your medicine."

"Can I have a few more minutes?" He was not sure how long it would take him to get up from where he had been lying all afternoon.

When she had gone back into the house, Mark had let himself in and was sitting on one of the stools in the kitchen. He was waiting to talk to her about some of the information he had found out. Jake had not told her about the list, so Mark filled her in. That did explain the officer cars passing the house so many times during the day. She had noticed them but did not think too much about it. "Mom, I think it might be dangerous for you to have Marcus here." He was waiting to see her reaction. "Marcus is chipless, and the media will be all over this story. If they find out that you have a chipless kid in your house, not just visiting but living here, it could be trouble for both you and Dad."

Little Marcus had slipped into the house unnoticed. He was hearing what was being said. It was not really against him, it was merely the truth of the situation. He wanted to go away from here, and now he needed to get away from here for them as much as it was for himself.

Mark continued to speak to his mom. "Mom, you know that I am right. It will be only a matter of time until they come and get

Marcus and take him away, and there will be nothing we can do about it. We need to get him into hiding."

Jake had also slipped into the house by way of the back door. He was standing right behind Marcus unnoticed.

Mark and his mom were still talking when there was a noise from the living room and in walked two government workers. They could have been businessmen except for the fact that both of them had shiny badges hanging from their belts. They were talking together and laughing, which was odd to Marcus, but he knew when it was time to leave, and this was it. His adrenaline was going, and he turned to escape out the back door. He did not know that Jake was behind him and ran headfirst into Jake, knocking him off-balance. Jake caught Marcus before he hit the floor and was surprised when Marcus reacted like an alley cat and squirmed out of his arms and headed to the back door once again. Jake was the only one in pursuit of Marcus, but in his mind, the two government men were about to get him and have him chipped. He was fighting with all his might. Marcus sent up a silent prayer, *God, help me.* Marcus lost his breath and went into a coughing fit that took him down. He went limp and could not move. He was trying to breathe when Jake took him by the head with a hand on each side of his face. "Marcus, listen to me. You need to calm down. This is my brother Marcus and my dad. It is okay. They are family."

Jake's head jerked up as he looked straight at his dad. Then to his brother Marcus. Dad was here, and he had been smiling as he had entered. In an instant, Jake knew it. His dad was a believer too.

Marcus was still trying to breath but stole a look at the two government men who were still far across the room. They realized what had happened and knew to keep their distance. Mark and Mrs. S. had joined Jake by Marcus's side, also encouraging him to trust that this was not what it looked like to him. The coughing fit continued, but he was not trying to run anymore. The two men took off their badges and their outer jackets. They still looked like businessmen but not so much like government authority. The men who came to collect the Knowing and to have them chipped always came in groups of two or more, and they looked exactly like the Singleton men had when they entered. Both Mark and Jake felt bad about the misunderstanding because they should have known how it would feel to Marcus. Jake continued his banter trying to encourage Marcus to calm down. "Marcus, I am sorry that I had not warned you they were coming, I promise that next time, I will know better. I would have never done this to you on purpose."

Marcus's heart was racing; he was still trying to catch his breath. He could hear Jake, and it still felt like he should flee, but his body was once again his enemy, and he could not get his footing to run away.

Mrs. S. took a turn to calm him down. "Marcus, I want you to think about what you know. Not about what you see, think, or feel right now. God has your back. You know that, right? You know that Mark, Jake, and I are believers, right?" She kept his focus, putting herself between Jake's dad and Marcus, her other son. "Marcus, slow your breathing some, and you will be able to breathe better. Now follow me. Breath in slowly, and now out. No, slower than that. Slow it down. There you go. Okay, now that is better." Little Marcus was more under control of himself. He was embarrassed, but at least he could breathe.

With the skill only their mother had, she changed the whole tone of the room. "Okay, dinner is almost done. Let's get the table set." Without any conversation, the entire Singleton family went to work getting the table and food ready for a family dinner. Little Marcus was relieved to see that the Singleton government men sat together so he could keep an eye on them.

They had noticed that Little Marcus would almost panic if they came up behind him or if they separated and he could not see both of them at the same time, so they were working hard not to cause any more fear. This kid was not a coward. There had been so many years of being a survivor on the streets, not only for himself but for others too, that this reaction was as much a way of life as trusting their family was for them.

Jake was to one side of Little Marcus. He could not see his face but could see his right hand, which was signaling him, "Jake, please, you need to get me out of here." Jake did not answer but was praying about what to say or do.

There came another signal from Little Marcus, "Jake, your family is in danger because of me. I don't have a chip, and Mark was telling your mom that it will cause trouble for your family. Please get me out of here. Now. Soon. Please."

Jake's dad decided it was time to address the conversation that was going on at the other end of the table. "Would you two like to tell me what you are talking about?" It was a kind tone but was a command all the same. Both Jake and Little Marcus froze.

The room went quiet, and Jake decided that it was up to him to address the problem. "Well, Dad, Little Marcus was saying that for the safety of the family that I should get him out of here."

Little Marcus's head turned to look at Jake. He was being sold out by who he thought was one of his friends. Jake was signaling that it was okay and to give him a chance to work it out. Little Marcus was used to being in charge of decisions like this and did not need anyone's help or input.

Jake's dad thought for a while before he spoke. "Marcus." Both Marcuses looked up at him with attention. "Okay, two people with the same name is going to be hard, but we can fix this." He thought about it. Little Marcus had lost so much already that he really needed to keep his own name. "Marcus"—looking to his son—"we will call you Brother Marcus when we are all together, if that is okay with you."

"Not a problem, Dad. I do like it better than what Mark came up with." Shooting a quick glance at Mark.

Mark chimed in, "You mean you don't like *Big Marcus*?" He was teasing his brother.

"I am sure not any more than he likes being called *Little Marcus*. Am I right?" He was looking at Marcus, who had stopped signaling Jake.

Dad restated the question, "Will that be okay with you? You will be called *Marcus*, and we will call Marcus Singleton *Brother Marcus*."

It really did not matter because Marcus was not planning to stay in this house anyway. He would get out one way or the other, with or without their help.

"Marcus, it is customary for you to answer when you are spoken to." Their dad was a soft-spoken man, but his words were well planned. He expected respect and had a place of authority in this family. "Now is being called *Marcus* going to work for you?"

Marcus sat up straighter in the chair. "Yes, that would be fine. Thank you."

His dad needed to address the conversation that Jake and Marcus were having at the table. "First of all, it is rude to signal at the table when there are others around. We cannot understand, and it is uncomfortable to be around not knowing what you are saying. And as to you leaving this house for any reason, put that completely out of your mind. It has been decided that you are now a part of this family, and that is the end of it. You stay."

Marcus was not used to his kind of thinking. "But what if?"

All eyes shot at once to Marcus. He stopped in midsentence. No one at the table would allow him to talk back to their dad. The look on their faces told him that much. Marcus sent out another silent prayer, *Oh, God, what have I done to deserve this? Please help me get out of this mess. I am being smothered. I am putting them at risk. They are good people, but they do not understand.* Marcus had another coughing fit. He could not catch his breath no matter how hard he tried.

Jake's mom got up and went over to Marcus; she took his hands from behind and lifted them over his head to open up his chest, hoping more air could get into his lungs. It was working, and he was breathing better again. "I think we had better get on with this dinner. And no more talk about leaving or staying from anyone until it is over. Understand?" Jake's mom took her seat and placed her napkin back into her lap.

It was very clear. The dad had respect and authority but so did the Singleton mom. Brother Marcus agreed and lowered his head. "Thank You, Lord, for this meal we are having together. Thank You that we could all be together as a family. Help us to remember that it is You who is in control of this world. Amen."

Dishes of food began to circle around the table. There was more than plenty. Marcus's face showed the shock of getting to have anything he wanted and the amount of what he wanted. It made him think of his boys. Where were they tonight? What were they having for dinner? Did someone remember to make sure that there was enough food leftover for them in the morning?

Their mom took her fork and reached across the table and tapped on Marcus's plate, getting his full attention. "Marcus, don't think so much. Eat."

Marcus's eyes widened, and he blinked. How did she know what he was thinking? He wanted to signal Jake but was afraid of getting caught again, so he took some food on his plate and ate like the rest of the Singletons.

After dinner, their dad and Brother Marcus left the table and went into the living room. Mark and their mom cleared the table and went into the kitchen. That left Marcus and Jake alone at the table. Jake noticed that Marcus had not stashed any food. "I see that you are eating your food and not saving any."

"Your mom took all my bags. She took my extra pockets off my shirt and coat. She even took the extra napkins I had stashed in my pillow." Marcus looked at Jake knowing that he must know how difficult his mom was being to him.

Marcus was so whiny about this, that it almost made Jake laugh out loud. Marcus was so tired that he had become almost rummy. The excitement of the night must have taken more out of Marcus than he had thought. "I think it might be a good idea for you to get yourself up to bed, don't you?"

"No, would you please stop. I am tired of all of you thinking that you know what is best for me. I get to decide what time I go to bed, okay?" Marcus went to get up and leave the table but found that there were two hands, one on each shoulder, holding him in place. He turned to look up and to see who it was that was interfering with his escape from the table. It was Mrs. S.

Their mom had overheard the conversation between Jake and Marcus. Mrs. S. bent closer so her mouth was by Marcus's ear. She whispered something in it and then stood up. She gave Marcus a pat on the back before she walked away.

Marcus in turn bent to talk to Jake, "Jake, I am sorry I snapped at you. I think you may be right. I am going to go and lie down for awhile." Marcus struggled a little to get up but was able to do it on his own.

He went to go out the backdoor to get some fresh air. The only problem was that he met Mrs. S. in the kitchen, on his way to the outside. "I don't think so. It is too cold out there now. You can go and sit in the family room for a while if you do not want to go to bed."

Not again. More bossing, he was never going to get used to it. He put a hand up in defeat, turned, and walked to the family room where he found an overstuffed chair that reminded him of his favorite nest. He proceeded to sit in it and fell quickly asleep.

CHAPTER 35

Marcus woke up late the next morning; he was in his bed. How embarrassing. Someone must have carried him up to bed. Everything he had believed about himself had fallen apart. Maybe Travis was right after all. Maybe he was weak and needed someone to boss him around. One thing was for sure—that his body was not as strong as it once was. But as he sat up, there was a difference; he felt the best he had felt in a long time. His limbs were not so heavy feeling. *God, is this an answer to my prayers? Have I had a healing?* He gave thanks for it; even if it was not a complete healing, he felt better anyway. He prayed for his boys and for his own family. He especially prayed for Travis. Then he thanked God for all of the Singletons, and he prayed that they would not be so bossy in the future. He prayed that they would know that he appreciated them but that he could do things by himself from here on out. As he finished his prayers, he noticed that a box had been placed in his room while he had slept. There was a note on it to him. It read,

Dear Marcus,

I found these at the last nest you were in. I think you may be glad to get them back. Sorry to have caught you off guard last night. I am glad to have a new little brother to help me with Jake.

Always,
Brother Marcus,
also known as Big Marcus

The note made him smile, but the stuff in the box reminded him of the life in the nests that he had lost. Right on top of everything was his Bible. He had thought it was gone forever. Brother Marcus was right; he was very glad to have it back. He saw that there was a note in the pages. It was also from Brother Marcus. Jeremiah 29:11.

Marcus looked it up. He had remembered a teaching about it but needed to reread it for himself.

"For I know the plans I have for you." Declares the Lord, "plans to prosper you and not to harm you, plans to give you a hope and a future." (Jeremiah 29:11)

Okay, God, I really need to claim this one. Amen.

Marcus got dressed, even his shoes. He went downstairs looking for whoever was going to be home at the time. He went to the kitchen and found himself alone. The counter had a note on it telling him that they had all gone to work. Mrs. S. said she went to the store but would be back soon. He was to get something to eat and drink and make himself at home. This was great. He could explore the house. But he did not get very far. He found a room they called the study. And what a find he did make. There were almost three full walls of books, from the top of the ceiling to the bottom of the floor. He had not seen anything like this in any house. When he was little, his parents took him to a library, but this was right here in the house. There were so many books. Where should he start? The note said that he could make himself at home. He took about twenty books off the shelf. He was so excited to hold them and read the names and the front covers.

Marcus had no idea how much time had passed, but he was sitting on the floor reading when Mrs. S. found him. "Marcus, what are you doing?"

Marcus was startled but gave her a smile and waved the book he was reading to show her what he had found. "Look at all these books. You said it was okay to—"

"No, that is quite okay, but how long have you been in here reading?" She turned the light in the room on. The day had passed, and he had not even noticed it.

It was so good to see some excitement in Marcus's face. She was glad that he had found a project to do that made him so happy. She had prayed, but books? Who knew? God did. *Thank You, God!*

"Marcus, did you remember that tonight is family night?" She was leaving the room, stopped, and turned to look at him. "I think you might be surprised at what you learn from us all being together. Do you want to help me fix dinner?"

Marcus was hard-pressed to continue reading or be of help around the house now that he was feeling better. He decided he needed to help with the dinner, but he brought the book along just in case there would be a break and he could read a few pages. Having the access to all of these books was pure delight.

The two of them worked well together. They did not talk a lot, but occasionally Mrs. S. would ask questions to see how Marcus was doing. He would answer but was not one to offer any extra information. Dinner was almost done when they heard a motorbike pull up. "That would be Mark." She looked over at Marcus to see that he too had heard what she had. He was relaxed, and he was actually content. The back door opened, and Jake and Sally came in together. They had expected Mark, but these two had entered before him. Mark hurried in behind the first two. They were all laughing and giving each other a bad time.

Mark went over to see that Marcus was fully dressed and that Mom had him working already. "Hey, Sally, your prayers have been answered, Mom has someone else to help in the kitchen."

Sally went to join Marcus and Mark. "Hi, I am Sally, the only sister of the Singletons. And you so want to be on my team."

Marcus looked at Jake for an explanation. "What team?"

"Oh no, the boys have not told you about the family challenge, which by the way, Marcus, you and I are going to win." Sally had her arm around Marcus showing that they were united. "We are the winning team. Want to meet us?" She laughed and gave Marcus a hug. She whispered in his ear, "Stick with me, and we will mop the floor with them."

Jake joined in on the conversation, "Oh no, you don't. I get Marcus. I found him, and he is all mine."

They all noticed that Marcus tensed up some and then realized that Brother Marcus and Dad had come in through the living room. The men had taken off their jackets and badges, but they still brought a presence with them when they entered. Brother Marcus was carrying a box; he placed it on a stool motioning to Jake. "Do you think you and Marcus could help me with these a little later? I need to translate what is being said by the people on the tapes." Jake looked to Marcus, who shrugged and motioned yes with his head.

Their mom announced that dinner was ready and that everyone should help carry food into the dining room. The table was set; it looked great. "Ben will not be here but promised he would be here next month."

They all ate dinner with lots of happy conversations; they were telling Marcus all sorts of stories on each other. Everyone was all lighthearted and carefree. They acted like there was not a problem in the whole world. When the dinner was done and the table cleared, they pulled out a game board that looked like it was homemade. Jake was the first to the table. "Now let the games begin. I get Marcus."

Sally rallied with, "Oh, no, you don't, I get Smart Boy. I called it first when we got here."

Brother Marcus entered the conversation this time. "Did you say *Smart Boy*?"

Sally put her arm on Marcus's head. "Yes, and he is all mine."

"Sally, is Marcus really Smart Boy?" Brother Marcus was serious now.

"Oh, go ahead and act like you did not know who he really was." Sally looked at her brother and realized for the first time this evening they were all serious. "I am sorry. I thought you all knew. I assumed you all figured it out."

Marcus was watching and couldn't stand it anymore. "What are you all talking about, and who is Smart Boy?"

They all stopped talking and looked at Marcus like he had asked a wrong question. It was their dad who cleared it up for Marcus. "Marcus, you are Smart Boy. You got the nickname about two years ago when you first hit the streets without an adult. We were looking for the new leader of the nest group, but all we could find was this kid we named Smart Boy. You caused so much trouble in the agency with all of your new and clever ways that the agency has placed a rather large reward on you. We had only found out about a week ago that someone had identified *you* as being Smart Boy."

Marcus looked at their dad. "Mr. Singleton, who gave them my name?"

They all looked at Sally to answer that question. "Marcus, we are not sure, but we think it might have been one of your friends." She had not lied, really. All of the Singletons thought that it was Travis, but since they had no real evidence, there was no reason to bother Marcus with this detail.

Marcus looked down at the ground. He was searching his mind for the idea of someone who would do such a mean thing to him. And why would they? What had he ever done to anyone to make them be so awful? Mrs. S. once again was the one to move all of them away from the bad stuff and back to the game. "Okay, who needs a teammate?"

They all looked relieved to end this discussion, except for Marcus that was. He was frozen, stuck on the idea of finding out who would have done this to him. It was Mrs. S. who noticed that Marcus was caught in thought again. She placed her hands on his face and moved his focus from the ground to meet hers. "You listen to me. You cannot figure everything out yourself. You have a family now, and we have got what it takes to help you. So just relax and enjoy the moment. For now, this is what we have, so you need to enjoy it." For a split second, she thought she saw tears behind Marcus's eyes, but there was a quick recovery, and she was not really sure. *Oh, God, how much can any one person take? How strong can any one person be? Please help him and show us how we can help too.*

Sally got Marcus by the hand and took him over to be on her team. The game was full out crazy. There were questions and answers

553

and challenges, but in the end, it was Sally and Marcus who won. Marcus was glad to be on the winning team when he found out that the losing team had to clean the kitchen and do all the dishes. Brother Marcus and his dad were on the team in second place, so they also skipped dish duty for the night.

Brother Marcus was glad to see that Marcus had not gone to bed yet. "Hey, Marcus, do you think you would be up to helping me translate some signals and maybe even identify some of the people on the tapes?"

This was great. Marcus was as interested in the tapes as the Singletons were. Perhaps he could get some of the answers he had been looking for also. "You bet, I need to go and tell Jake that I am helping you so he can know where I am." He went to the kitchen to tell him.

Brother Marcus and his dad looked at each other like they had an inside joke or something. Jake's mom saw it and called them on it. "So what is up with you two?"

Brother Marcus gave his mom a hug. "It is nice to see that Jake has a little brother to take care of. I think it is good for him to see how worried you can get when you have a younger person in your care."

Mom was laughing. "I think it would take three Marcuses to cause as much worry as Jake did for all of us. But you are right, it is a good bond."

Marcus sat down in a chair by the TV. "Brother Marcus, where did all of these recordings come from?"

As he was loading them into the player, he read the outside cover of the one he was holding. "This one came from a table at a coffee shop, Smitty's."

There was no sound. But then Marcus did not need any to know what was being said. There were two men that he did not know, in a coffee shop using his language he had made up.

Brother Marcus had played these before, so he did not need to watch the TV but kept an eye on Marcus. He watched as his face went from confusion as to who these people were, and when he confirmed that they were in fact signaling nest, he was almost angry.

They were on the fifth recording when the TV went black, and they all turned to see what had happened.

Mrs. S. was holding the remote and had turned it off. "That is enough for tonight. Marcus needs a break, and you two need to go to work tomorrow, so we need to stop for the night."

Marcus had been almost asleep when the TV went off but was now totally awake and ready to continue. "I am fine. I want to help some more. I can do this." Besides, he needed to know what else was found on the recordings so he could figure out what was really going on.

Mrs. S. took Marcus by the arm and was lifting him out of the chair. "Yes, you are doing fine, and we are going to keep it that way. Enough, you can do more tomorrow, but for tonight, you are finished."

Brother Marcus looked at the time. He had not realized how long they had been at it. "Sorry, Mom, I had not realized how late it was. I will take these and bring them back tomorrow night, if that is okay with Marcus?" He turned and looked at Marcus in order to see his answer.

Marcus was not happy about stopping. He himself would keep going until the job was done. "I cannot see why we can't finish this up tonight. We only have about six more to go."

Brother Marcus raised his eyebrows and lowered his voice, "There will be no more recording translations tonight because Mom said so. That is why."

Marcus looked over at Mrs. S., and without a single word, she was showing that there would be no more recording tonight. Her body language said it all.

Marcus had an idea. "What if you leave them and I can go over them for you tomorrow?"

"Sorry, Marcus. Government property, they can't leave me. Besides, I am afraid that you would be tempted to do them tonight and get me in trouble with Mom."

That was exactly what Marcus was thinking to do. Tomorrow was a hundred years away, and Marcus was frustrated at being so close to figuring things out, and yet he was not able to do anything about it. "But—"

It was Dad's turn to give input. "Marcus, did you see anything that told you who these people were?"

Marcus thought for a moment and then realized he had. "The language was an older version of the one we now use. I had to change it to the new one because of the younger kids, and Jake." He smiled as he said that to tease Jake. "I have no idea who any of the people on the recordings were. They were all too old to be a part of my group."

Marcus began to rub his head and eyes without his realizing he was doing it. The family had seen him do it earlier during the game and while he watched some of the recordings. It was his *tell*, as they call it. Body language that you do and others can see. It often shows up when you don't want to say something, but can't really handle keeping it quiet either.

"Marcus, is there anything else you want to talk to us about?" Brother Marcus was gathering up the recordings but kept an eye on Marcus to see his reaction.

"Marcus, why don't you say what is on your mind and get it over with?" Their dad was a man to go straight to the point. "I can see from the way you are acting that you need something from us. Just ask."

Jake and Sally along with Mark had walked into the room as their dad had asked Marcus the question. They also thought he needed to come out with what he needed.

Marcus took a deep breath, coughed a little. "I need to see my brother, Travis. I think I can help him. I need to find him, that is all. Can you please help me do that?"

Wow, this kid did not pull any punches. The only thing he had asked for, and they could in no way let it happen.

The Singletons were silent. Mrs. S. stood in front of Marcus so she could speak to him. "Marcus, I know that you think you can help your brother, and in time, you might be able to. But for now, Travis has put himself into a lot of trouble. He is going to need to figure out which side he is on, and you cannot do it for him or make him decide to choose your way."

Marcus interrupted her, "You know where my brother is, don't you?"

Mrs. S. looked at her husband for his help in how to answer him. "Marcus, I am telling you that whether or not we know where your brother is, is not the issue. The real issue is that you need to give Travis space to make up his mind about what life he wants, and you need to take care of yourself."

Marcus looked at them all. They knew where his brother was, and they were keeping him from Travis. They were not going to help him after all. If he was going to save Travis, he would have to do it himself. "I think I need to go to bed now." He got up and turned to speak to them. "Thank you for the wonderful night. I had fun. Good night." He went to the stairs and started into a coughing fit. *Oh, please, God, not the coughing now. I need to be alone. I need to think.*

Jake was the one who went to Marcus this time. "Let me help you up to your room, and then you can be alone." Marcus nodded his head yes for the help. At least they were still on good terms about Jake getting to help him.

When they got upstairs, Jake tried to make small talk with Marcus. "Are you all right?" He looked to see if he could guess what Marcus was thinking. But he had his calm look going. "You do understand what Mom was saying to you, right?"

Marcus walked away from Jake and started to get ready for bed. "I need to get some rest now if that is okay with you."

"Sure, are you positive that you don't want to talk?" He waited for a reaction from Marcus, but he turned away and continued about his business. "Okay, goodnight then." He shut the door as he left the room.

Jake went downstairs only to find the family still in a discussion about Marcus. Brother Marcus was sitting on a stool across from his dad telling them something that they all should have thought of long before this.

"Okay, so what is going on now?"

"Brother Marcus was telling us that Marcus needs to be chipped like the rest of us. It is for the safety of Marcus as well as for the family." Their dad was recapping what was being discussed.

Jake needed to stick up for Marcus on this one. "Dad, there is no way that Marcus is going to go along with the idea of having a chip. I talked to Victor a long time ago about Marcus's parents having been chipped and then taken away. They ordered Marcus and Travis to run and not allow themselves to be chipped. Victor said that Marcus cannot even go on the street where the chipping station was built. Victor said that once they had to work on the very same street as the station and that Marcus had nightmares for weeks after. After all Marcus has been through, I think that this might take him over the top."

Brother Marcus stood up. He was passionate about this. "Dad, I know that it would be hard on the kid, but it has to happen, or he has to leave the house. It is too dangerous for Marcus as well as for the Knowing for him to live here with our family without a chip."

Dad was not happy about what needed to be done, but Brother Marcus was right, and Marcus needed to be chipped or move out of the house. He reached out and took his wife's hand. "Honey, what do you think? Can this kid be okay if we make him get the chip the family way?"

She looked up at him. "I do not know how he feels about getting chipped for sure, but I do know about how it would feel if he were to leave this house and family. He is here to stay, no matter what it takes."

They all agreed to meet late tomorrow afternoon here at the house to talk it over with Marcus. They knew it was not going to be easy, but they would pray about it and see what God was going to do. If things went well, then he could get chipped on Saturday morning early. Then they had a surprise for him on Sunday. They were going to take him out to the farm to see his boys. That might take the sting out of the chipping event.

Jake felt uneasy about the whole thing. He was not sure what it was that made him feel like this, but he was going to stay the night again, even with his dad here.

The night went without any flaw. Jake woke up that Friday morning with heaviness in his heart for his friend Marcus. He did not even get out of bed before he was praying for Marcus and for his whole family. He was thinking about how far he had come from his time undercover and that he was truly a blessed man to have God and the family and the friends he had. "Thank You, Father God. You know everything, and we know that. We need Your help now more than ever before. We are under attack and need to stay in Your will. It looks to us like the government is closing in on the Knowing, we have a leak in information, and we think it might be Travis. We have Marcus, who is so young, and yet it looks like he has so much against him. Help me—no, help us to help him. We are his friends, but today it may look like we are his enemy. It is yet another time that what will help him will hurt him. I know You have a plan, please show it to us and give us the courage to carry it out. Father, I pray to You. Now I believe that You heard me, and now I wait for You to show me what You want me to do, then I ask for the courage to do what You ask, in the name of Jesus. Amen."

Jake thought he heard a noise. He went downstairs to see what it was, and as he walked by the door of the study, he saw that there was a light coming from under the door. He listened before he opened it. When the door opened, he saw that Marcus was on his knees praying. There were books open to pages he had been reading. He had been studying, but what? Jake did not know how he knew, but he knew that Marcus needed this alone time with God, so he did not go any farther into the room but backed out quietly and pulled the door shut behind him. As he went to turn and walk down the hall, he almost had a heart attack; his mom was standing there beside him. She was fully dressed and motioned for him to stay quiet and to follow her to the kitchen.

When they got to the kitchen, she gave Jake a hug. "I know, we can all feel it. Today could be a very hard day for us all, and especially for Marcus. We are going to ask a lot of that young man when we ask him to trust us and to have the courage to get the chip. But, Jake, I know that this is the right thing for him to do. It is going to look like we are selling him out, but I believe that it will be the thing that makes his life safe."

"Mom, how can you know for sure that this is the right thing to do?"

"Jake, I don't really. But I have prayed, and I believe that if this is not the right thing to do that God will intervene and show us what to do instead. We have good motives, we have taken it to God in prayer, and now in the doing, we need to believe that He will show us what's right and provide us with the answers about what to do. Do you want to pray with me?" She sat on a stool and reached for her Bible.

Jake had always loved his mom. More times than not, he did not understand her, but he could see now that she was a good woman and that the love she gave to him and others was because of God. They prayed.

Jake looked at the clock and saw that if he left now, he would have enough time to go and talk with Victor and Sandy at the shelter. He was not sure what else they knew about Marcus and his family being chipped, but he felt that they might know something that would make this easier on Marcus. As he drove to the shelter, he felt a peace on him like he had not noticed before. He smiled. He decided that this was a God's peace. And since he thought that, he must be on the right track.

It would be nice to see Victor and Sandy. He had missed talking and being with them. He was anxious to hear if they had any more information about the closing of the shelters. It was only a rumor, but many rumors became facts these days. Jake parked almost three blocks away and walked into the shelter area. The all clear siren was starting when he had arrived at the door. A lot more people than he remembered were leaving the shelter, so he stood back and let them get out. As he walked in, he was pleased to see that Sandy and Victor were still there. His heart leaped with joy when he saw that Peggy was also there.

They were genuinely excited to see him, badge and all. He had dressed for work, and out of habit, he had placed his badge in his belt. Victor came over to him; Jake extended his hand in order to shake hands with Victor, but Victor wrapped Jake up in a great big hug instead. Jake was back with his shelter family, and it felt very good. Sandy and Peggy did likewise. When the greetings were over, it was Victor who asked about Jake's coming to the shelter to see them. "Is this about Marcus?"

Jake nodded his head yes, and looked down at the ground.

"Well, from the way you are acting, I am guessing the information doesn't look good?" Victor poured what they called coffee and gave him some.

"Victor, if I were to say that there is a lot going on, it would be an understatement. Marcus is doing real good, health-wise. He looks and sounds better, his cough is almost gone. He is worried about Travis and about his boys, but, Victor, we need him to worry about himself."

Victor was smiling at Jake. "Jake, you never do go for the easy stuff, do you? First of all, no one needs to worry about anything. I am sure that, like us, you are prayed up?" Jake confirmed that was true. "And I am not sure of too many things, but it is my guess that Marcus is too." And Jake could confirm that too. "So what you need is information so you can help Marcus get through whatever it is you think he needs to do. Am I right?"

Jake went for it. He simply said it. "We need Marcus to be chipped." After he had said it, he could see from the looks on their faces that they did not understand what he really meant. He at once corrected himself. "Not really chipped, but the way I am." He pulled out his medallion and showed it to them. He did not have it covered with foil because he could be there as an officer today.

"My advice to you, Jake, is to not tell Marcus what you want, the way you told us." Victor was even shook up by what had just happened.

Peggy threw her arms around Jake and gave him such a big hug. "I sure have missed you putting your foot in your mouth around here. You make me laugh."

Jake got it. How he presented it to Marcus was going to be critical. "Victor, what can you tell me about Marcus and the day his family was chipped and taken away? Would you remember the date, and I need Marcus's family's last name?" Jake knew that if he got the date and their last name, he could pull the recordings of the event, and perhaps he could see firsthand what had happened.

Victor and Sandy worked together trying to remember the date; they got as close as they could to narrowing it down, so when Jake looked it up, it would not take as long to find it.

"Did you hear that we are going to take Marcus out to the farm this weekend so he can see his boys?" Jake thought that would be a happier note to leave on, but from the look on their faces, he had missed something there too. "What?"

Sandy was the one to answer this time. "I think it might be hard on Marcus to see the boys." Jake gave her his full attention. "Will Marcus be getting back with his boys, or will he be saying goodbye to them?"

The thought hit Jake totally off guard. He had not thought of the leaving and coming back home, only the getting there and getting to see how good they were all doing. *Oh, dear God, even the good stuff's going to be hard.* Sandy patted his hand. "Just a thought you might want to be ready for."

Jake had to get to work. He left with a lot more to think about than he had arrived with, but the most important thing he had now was the date and the last name so he could find the recording.

CHAPTER 36

The morning went fast, and the rest of the day was just as busy. Jake had not had a chance to look up the recordings. He was running out of time and wanted to get clocked out and get to his parents' house before they started to talk to Marcus. He needed to give Marcus the information about what being chipped in the Singletons' house really meant.

When Jake got to the house, Sally and Mark were already there. He found them all in the kitchen helping make dinner.

Shortly after that, Brother Marcus and their dad joined them. Again they had taken off their badges and coats before they entered. Marcus looked at them as they came in. "You don't have to do that, you know?" He was speaking to both men. "I am okay with knowing you work for the government. I don't understand it, but I am okay now."

Dad put a hand on Marcus's shoulder. "Thanks. Glad to hear it."

Dinner went well, but Marcus could see from the way they were all acting that something big was about to happen to him. He was not sure, but he thought this might be his last dinner with them. After all, he was feeling much better, and they had done what they set out to do. He was well. He should be glad to get out of here. Why was he feeling sad about leaving? They were all about his business, and they smothered him by bossing him around. What was wrong with him? It was clear to him that he was going to be leaving and that he should be happy about it.

After dinner, they all went into the living room and had a seat. They made sure that Marcus was in his favorite easy chair that had his back to the wall. They did not want to give him the chance to run out before they could fully explain what was going on, and they also need him to be as comfortable as possible when he got the information they were about to tell him.

Marcus watched them and saw how uncomfortable they all were about what they were going to tell him. He felt bad for them. He did get it, that it would be too dangerous for all of them and for the Knowing for him to stay here with them. He needed to ease their guilt. "You all need to know that I know what this meeting is all about. And I am okay with it."

God worked in very strange ways, but this was a little too good to be true.

Marcus saw that they were still not off the hook. "I know that I am doing better health-wise, and I agree with all of you that it is too dangerous for me to be living here with you. I think it would be best if I go and stay at one of the shelters until things settle down some more. Do you think I can go and stay at Sandy's shelter? It is more central to the town, so I can get information from the streets as to what is going on."

They still didn't say anything. Mom and Dad looked at each other and then at the rest of the family. It was Mrs. S. that began the talks. "I am not too sure where you got the idea that you were going to go anywhere, but you, young man, are going to be living with us until God decides otherwise." She looked around the room to see that everyone was confirming what she was saying.

Marcus was confused. "Then what is going on if you don't want me to leave the house?"

Dad took a deep breath. "Marcus, I need you to promise us something?" Marcus looked at him then at Jake, who nodded his head that it was okay to trust his dad. Marcus turned back to the dad and agreed. "I need you to promise to not react to what you are going to hear until we are all finished explaining things to you. Is it a deal?"

Marcus slowly agreed. Jake wanted to be the one to tell Marcus that he needed to be chipped. After his trial run this morning, he felt he could do it the best. He reached into his shirt and motioned for Mark to do the same and pulled out a medallion. Marcus had seen it before but had not thought much about it. Mark in turn showed him his. "Marcus, you know that Mark and I have a chip, right? Did you ever wonder why it is we can go underground with you and the Knowing?"

Marcus had wondered but figured that they must have had them blocked somehow or the information erased. "Okay?" Marcus was not following.

"Well, Mark and I have our chips in our medallions. We can cover them with foil, and that is how we block the tracking of our chips." Jake thought this was going well.

Marcus summed it up. "Okay, you are chipped sort of, and why do I need to know this, and why now?" He looked at their faces and saw that they were all still so uncomfortable. "Jake, why do I need to know this, how does this affect me?"

Brother Marcus went straight to it. "You need to be chipped, that is why."

It felt like the air had been sucked right out of Marcus. Even if the chip was on his body and not in it, he could never be chipped. It would be against everything he had fought about his whole young adult life.

Dad reminded him that he promised to listen until he had heard the whole thing.

"Okay, I am listening." It was hard though because he could hear his blood rushing in his ears, and his heart was pounding.

Sally had the next explanation. "Marcus, you have been identified as Smart Boy. There is a bounty out on you. If Mom and Dad adopt you, then we can protect you from legal actions. The government will not be able to lock you up and have you really chipped. We can keep you safe, and you can continue to work on the streets, but as a Singleton, not as Smart Boy."

Marcus thought that these were his friends. They wanted him as family, but he had to be chipped in order for that to happen. *God, You always say that You will give us a way out of a situation like this. I so need Your help now.*

No one could tell what Marcus was thinking. He had a blank "everything is okay" look on his face. Brother Marcus did not get this kid. They were offering him a way out, a way off the streets, and he was thinking about it. "Marcus, you know we could have just picked you up and taken you down to the station and had it done, but Mom and Dad thought you should have the choice. So be smart about it, and let's get this done, for them as much as for you."

Brother Marcus was never one to beat around the bush as they say, but he did have a point. Mom and Dad were harboring a wanted kid.

Marcus sat frozen. He could hardly breathe, but it was not from being sick. He needed to do something to get out of this room so he could think and pray about this. "Okay."

Jake answered, surprised by what he had heard, "What did you say?"

Marcus looked at Jake. "I said okay. Can I please go to bed now? I am tired."

Jake looked at his mom. She was in nonverbal agreement that something was very wrong. There had to be more conversation before Marcus would ever agree to this idea.

Sally stood up. "Great, now that the bad stuff is over, did Mom and Dad tell you that we are going to take you to the farm so you can see your boys?"

Jake knew that his sister meant well, but something was too wrong with what was going on with Marcus. His reaction was too calm.

Jake got Marcus's attention. "You mean to tell us that you agree to be chipped and that you are okay with it?"

Brother Marcus was irritated at Jake for making such a big deal about this. "Jake, yes, he agrees that he is going to be chipped. Marcus, I will pick you up at seven in the morning. You have an appointment at eight to get your chip. I have it all set up. Is that going to be okay with you?"

Marcus could not talk at all. He just motioned with his head that it would be fine. He needed to get out of here. "May I go to bed now?"

What else could they do but let him go. He had agreed, and they had won the fight. Or at least the fight they thought they were going to have. Marcus left the living room slow and steady. They could see that he was upset, but they needed him to do this, he had to get the chip. After all, it was for the good of everyone, especially his own.

Brother Marcus was the first to address the situation. "You all know that this is the way it has to be." They were all staring at him. "Well, can any of you think of a better way to take care of this kid?" No one had an answer to the question, so they gathered together and prayed.

Jake was going to stay the night again. Tomorrow was Saturday, and he did not have to go into work. Brother Marcus said that he would pick Marcus and their dad up in the morning at seven. He wanted to be there to help Marcus make the right decision. Brother Marcus was right, there did not seem to be any other way. Jake had walked outside in the backyard. He was sitting in a chair out by one of the trees. He could see the upstairs window where Marcus had his room. Jake watched as he could see Marcus's shadow moving around the room like he was pacing. Jake started to pray again for Marcus when he noticed out of the side of his view there was movement. It was in the yard. It was someone sneaking around the Singleton yard. Jake moved slowly toward the person in the yard. Just as Jake was about to be in arm's distance from them, he heard a whistle, and the person ran fast to the fence and, without stopping, got a foot up and went over it like they had wings. The family inside the house heard the noise and came out to see what had happened.

Jake's dad was out the door first. "Jake, what on earth are you doing out here?"

"Dad, there was someone sneaking around the yard. I tried to catch him, but he was way too fast. He scaled the fence like it was only inches high."

Jake and his dad were walking out to the fence. "Did you get a good look at him?"

"No, Dad, it was too dark. But I think it might have been a kid. Maybe even Travis." Jake looked up at the window to Marcus's room and saw that he too had heard the noise. When he saw Jake look up at him, he pulled the curtain shut and walked away from the window. "Dad, something is wrong with all of this. I can feel it in my gut. Something is very wrong."

Jake needed answers, and sitting here in his parents' backyard was not going to give it to him. "Dad, I need to go and figure out something. Can you be okay here with Marcus?"

"Jake, I thought that you were going to be here with us in the morning to help with encouraging Marcus." His dad was worried that in the end, he might need Jake to convince Marcus to go through with the chipping.

"Dad, I am going to go to the government station and see what I can find out. I plan on being back before morning, but if I get caught up, I will join you and Marcus at the chipping station. Okay?" His dad confirmed that he understood and told Jake to be careful.

Jake went to the government station right away. He thought to go and talk to Victor some more but decided that he needed true hard facts. If he could track down the recordings of the day that Marcus's parents had been chipped, then he might be able to see how he could better help him. Jake spent hour after hour looking at recording after recording, but there was not a single one during the time frame that Victor and Sandy had given him. *Sally, she might have an idea as to where the recordings and records for Marcus's family might be.* He did not even look at the clock before he called her. "Sally, hi, it's me Jake. I need your help."

It was after 2:00 a.m., but Sally's advice to look under the Smart Boy case paid off. There were all of the recordings. They dated all the way back to when Marcus was little and with his family on the streets up to and including the new project that Brother Marcus had them working on now. He pulled the first ones dated over two years ago. Marcus looked so young. He could have only been about twelve or thirteen years old. There were tapes of his family in the park, on the street, going to work, school, and shopping. The family looked so happy and safe. But the next recordings told a totally different story. The parents were arrested right out in the streets. In front of a restaurant, Marcus and Travis were right there, and they saw it all. There was no sound on the recordings, but Jake did not need any to see the horror of it all. The two boys were running toward their parents, who were yelling at them to go and stay away. Two grown men had caught the boys and were carrying them away from the chipping station. Jake did a close-up and saw that one of the men was Victor. Marcus was small, but he got away from the man and ran as fast as he could to the chipping station where his parents had been. They were gone. Inside the building, and the door was shut and locked. The boy Marcus was pounding on the door when a tall man dressed in black opened the door and picked the young Marcus up around his waist and carried him back down the street and handed him to Victor. When the man turned around to the camera, Jake froze the frame and zoomed in. It was Jake's dad. Jake's dad had been the one to save Marcus from being caught with his parents. Jake followed on the recording showing Marcus kicking and fighting with his whole being to get away from Victor. Then it happened. Jake could see the very second that Marcus decided to be the leader he had become. He stopped, stilled, and turned to Travis and took a place by his side. Almost all of the recordings from that time on showed Travis and Marcus together. There were about six months' worth of recordings of the boys being with a street hustler who taught them lots of street smarts. Then he was arrested. Jake scanned the recording, and yes, Marcus saw that too. They had arrested the man and took him to the chipping station. Marcus sat outside the station for hours after the door closed. Jake froze the photo. "Marcus, what are you thinking?" Jake looked further and saw that the date of the first Smart Boy nickname had popped up. He looked closer. It was not Marcus but Travis that they suspected of being the Smart Boy. Jake smiled. "That information could come in handy." Jake looked down at his watch. Oh no, it was almost 7:30 a.m. And Marcus's appointment was going to be at eight. He was going to have to meet them at the chipping station. He was on his way immediately. "Dear God, get me there in time."

Marcus got up and was completely dressed when the Singleton men were ready to go to the chipping station. Jake was not there. Mr. Singleton had told Marcus that Jake had said he would be at the station if he did not make it to the house in time. They drove in silence to the station. They parked the car and were getting out when Marcus showed the first sign of having second thoughts. Mr. Singleton placed a hand on the middle of Marcus's back to give him moral support. Marcus got out of the car and went up the steps, slowly; he was doing okay until the door behind him closed shut. He stopped and looked at the now locked door. Brother Marcus wanted to help get this over with. The kid was being tortured by the wait. "Come on, Marcus, let's get this over with, and then we can go home."

Both Mr. Singletons were on either side of Marcus walking him down the hall to the check-in counter. Marcus had never seen this part of the station before but had seen it in his nightmares many times. This was harder than he thought it was going to be. What if they forgot to use the medallion? What if something went wrong and he really did get the chip? His mind was racing out of control. What did he really know about these two men other than they were Jake's family? Travis was family, and he did not represent Marcus and what he believed in. He had to go. He had to get out of here now. He turned to Mr. Singleton and began to whisper, "I changed my mind. I cannot do this. I need to get out of here please."

They could see that panic was about to set in. Mr. Singleton and Brother Marcus looked at each other; they had a choice to make. If they let him go, he would get arrested and be chipped for real. But if they made him go through with this, he would get chipped but not really, and they could keep him safe. Truthfully, there was no choice. He had to stay and get the chip. They each took one of Marcus's arm. He began to try and pull away from them. "Dad, there are cameras, be careful."

The security was watching the whole thing on their monitors. They were used to seeing this kind of reaction when some of the nutcases were caught and chipped. "Hey, you think we should go and help them with that kid?" The older man on the security team looked closer at the monitor. They read the chips of the men escorting the kid. "Hey, look what we have here, the very famous Singleton family. Maybe if we help them, we might get some kind of an reward or something." The security men were planning to assist with Marcus when they saw that another man had entered the scene. His chip read, "Jacob Singleton, Officer." "I think I would rather sit here and watch three cops take on that scrawny kid." And so that is exactly what they did.

Jake took hold of Marcus and turned him around so he could see that Jake was there. Marcus froze for just one second, giving the Singleton men a chance to get a better hold of Marcus. They were at the counter now and were greeted by a receptionist who was inquiring about their appointment. She stopped in midconversation and asked Mr. Singleton if he wanted Marcus sedated? The question brought Marcus back to some control. "Jake, please let me out of here."

Jake was talking very calm and very slowly on purpose. "Marcus, I promise that it is all going to be okay." From that moment on, Marcus kept his eyes fixed on Jake. They did not use words anymore, only signals from Jake to Marcus. "It is going to be okay. We have God on our side. This may look bad, but remember that God is in control. Remember sometimes God gets us out of the storm or trial, and other times he walks with us as we go through it. Marcus, this is a walkthrough. We are here with you, and I believe that God sent us to help you. I know that it does not feel like help right now, but believe me, it is true. God put us together on this one. And it is going to work out, you will see."

A technician came out of a door that was to a room for chipping. He walked over to the Singletons and greeted Marcus with a smile. "Let's get the paperwork done, okay?" He went behind the counter and pulled up the computer page. He found the account he was looking for. "Okay, here it is, Marcus, who is soon to be Singleton. He is an orphan, right?"

Marcus shot a look back at Jake. A signal came from Jake. "Just a word, we do not know anything about your parents." Marcus continued to listen.

The technician continued on with the questions. When they got to Marcus's birthday, it was a surprise to them all that Marcus was almost six months younger than they had thought.

Jake looked at him. He sent up an arrow prayer. "God, please help us stop his hurting over this. Help him to get through it with no more hurt."

"Mr. Singleton." The technician pointed to their dad. "Please state your full name and number for our records."

"Robert J. Singleton." When he finished speaking, the computer completed the form and made a copy for the files and one for Robert to sign.

Marcus looked down at the ground and then up to look at Robert. For the first time, he looked at him closely. *RS. Robert Singleton. Oh no. What am I doing here with this man?* He knew that name and those initials. This man was the man who had Marcus's parents chipped years back. And now he was about to get another member of his family chipped and off the streets.

The Singletons did not know what happened, all they knew was that Marcus became upset again and tried to get away.

Jake could not signal Marcus; he was not looking at him at all. He was trying to speak to him in order to calm him down. But while Jake was talking to Marcus, Robert and the technician spoke together, and then someone else came out of the chipping room door. He handed something to the technician who in turn joined Marcus and Jake. Jake was now in a one-sided conversation. "Marcus, it is going to be okay. You need to trust us. You will see it is going to work out okay. God will not let you down no matter how it feels right now." To Jake's horror, there was a loud click, and then a look of terror on Marcus's face just before his eyes rolled back in his head, and he fell forward into Jake's arms. They had knocked Marcus out.

The next thing Marcus remembered was that he was in the back seat of a car traveling down the road. Jake was beside him on the car seat, and Robert and Brother Marcus were in the front seat. Marcus pretended to still be asleep. He did not want to deal with these people. Especially with Robert, the man he now knew as the one who had taken his parents away from him.

Robert was driving. "Boys, we may have a problem. I think Marcus may have realized that I was the person who had his parents chipped."

Jake was caught off guard. "You did what?" He had pulled up in his seat and was demanding an explanation as to what that meant.

"Jake, I need you to listen to me. I did what I had to. There was a warrant out for their arrest with a shoot-to-kill order. I had to do it, or they could have been killed. Marcus's parents were my friends, and they got caught in a government setup. I could not help them any other way. I still think that God gave me the opportunity to save them, and I did everything I could at the time."

Jake trusted his dad, and yet this was really hard to hear and believe. *Oh, God, how is Marcus ever going to understand this? God, we need more help.*

Marcus was awake. Jake could see that his eyes were open. But he was not moving but staring out to nowhere. Jake knew from his own experience that Marcus was going to have one heck of a headache. He himself had been knocked out on the day he had received his new chip. It did not last long, but it did hurt a lot.

They had pulled up in the drive and were greeted by Mrs. S. Marcus was awake and moving, but he had not said a single word to any of them. Mrs. S. tried to give him a hug, but he stood there looking defeated. He had lost everything, and now he had a chip. They had put a chain around his neck before he woke up; it was heavy, and it contained his chip. It was a chain of shame to him. He has lost the fight, and now he felt like there was nothing left. He waited until they prompted him to go into the house. Mrs. S. suggested that he go up to his room and take some time to get used to the idea of his new life. Marcus could not get to his room fast enough. He shut the door behind him and slid to the floor blocking it so no one could get in. He was dead inside. He still believed that God had a plan, but it sure did not feel like Jeremiah 29:11. Marcus prayed. He wanted to give praise, but he did not know how to get past the hurt. So he told God, and he believed that God had heard him; he just wondered if God really cared. Then he remembered that things are not always what they look like, so he prayed some more. He did not know what else he could do.

Marcus did not know how many hours had passed since he had returned home. But it was getting late, and he had fallen asleep. His headache was better, but his heart was still broken. There was a knock at the door. It was Mrs. S. "Marcus, I think you have been alone long enough. I need you to come down and help make plans of what things we need to take out to the kids on the farm tomorrow." She did not wait for an answer, but told him she would see him downstairs and walked away. She knew that the one thing that Marcus would always do is take care of his boys. She was right.

It was not long before, Marcus had come down to the kitchen and was looking over all the supplies they had pulled together to take out to the Knowing farm. There were a lot of things going with them tomorrow. There was everything from clothing to food and medications. Not to mention the traitor Marcus with his chip. Mrs. S. was taking account of all the things they had and needed. "Jake, why don't you and Marcus load the first of the supplies into our car, and then you can pull your car into the garage and load yours up too. We can meet the others out at the farm tomorrow early morning."

Jake agreed that he and Marcus would do what she had asked of them. Marcus did everything he was told, but when he was done, he would stand around with a blank look on his face. After they had loaded up the things in the cars, it was time to get dinner ready. Tonight should have been a celebration of the new member being a part of the family, but it felt more like a wake. Their mom told Marcus to go and read some if he wanted. He looked at her and went into the study. He was not sure what he should do next. Brother Marcus thought it might be a good idea for Marcus to do something helpful and help translate the recordings with him. He brought the recordings into the study where he asked Marcus, and he agreed to do it.

They were all set up, and the translating began. Marcus did not know who these people were or why they had one of his languages and were using them. Marcus did not look away from the recordings even once. He kept his eyes locked on the TV. He would tell them what each of the men were saying to each other. Brother Marcus was writing it down as fast as he could get the details. Mark was in the room keeping an eye on Marcus. He was worried that he might not be okay.

Their mom called to everyone to come to dinner, but Marcus kept on translating the TV. Brother Marcus turned off the TV.

"Marcus, we can finish these later. Let's go eat now so Mom does not get upset."

Marcus looked at them with a blank look. He had not even heard their conversations about dinner. It was Jake who came to his rescue. "I bet your head is still aching from the sedative. Am I right?"

Marcus had the same dead face as before. "Sure." Marcus did not want to be with them or talk with them right now. "I need to go to my room now. Please?" He looked to Brother Marcus for the answer to his question, but did not wait for it but went up to his room.

The family did not know what to do. Perhaps time could heal old wounds, but could anything heal what felt like the loss of everything? "Maybe seeing his boys will make Marcus feel better." Mark was talking out loud more than stating a fact. The family went ahead and had dinner together. Only Ben and Marcus were missing. Little Marcus had become a true part of the family, even if he did not want to be yet.

It was late when they finished dinner and said goodbye. They had agreed to meet Mark and Sally at the farm. Jake would take Marcus, and Mom and Dad would go together. Brother Marcus planned to stay in town and monitor any orders given about the Singletons going out of town. With luck and prayer, they would go unnoticed. But just in case, he would be there to cover any problems.

Jake spent the night again in Mark's old room. He could hear Marcus walking around most of the night. It sounded like a caged animal was in his old room. "God, please help Marcus to heal. Help him to see that this was the only way."

When they got up on Sunday morning, they found Marcus completely dressed and ready to go. He was sitting on a stool in the kitchen. He had not turned the lights on but was sitting in the dark, looking out the window. Jake had run into his mom in the hall. They had not spoken but given each other a hug and headed down the stairs. They were startled to see Marcus when they turned the lights on, but they were happy too. Other than looking a little tired, he looked great. He was completely dressed and ready to go to the farm. He reacted normal to them when they entered the room by responding to them when they said good morning. Jake's mom was glad to see Marcus looking so good. "I can see that you are ready to go to the farm. How long have you been up?"

Marcus looked at her but gave no answer, he simply shrugged his shoulders and gave a slight smile.

"It only takes about an hour and a half to get to the farm. We planned to get there late morning, but we can go earlier if we want to." She had started coffee and was working on planning some breakfast.

Robert came downstairs and joined them. "Hey, good morning, everyone." He was also surprised to see that Marcus was up and ready to go. "I am glad that we are all up early. I think it would be good to take our time and have a Bible reading before we go. A lot has happened, and I really need some guidance from God for the next few days."

Marcus did not respond to the dad as he spoke. "Mrs. S., am I going to be staying here longer, or am I going to be staying out at the farm after today?"

She walked over to him trying to see if she could figure out where he was going with this question. "Marcus, the plan is for you to be living here with us." She got the feeling that Marcus needed something to hold on to, something that he could make a plan about. Coming back here and calling this his home could be one of the things he could work on in his head. "You have a chip now, you have to be here."

They ate breakfast and did the Bible reading, it was finally time to get on the road. Jake and Marcus got into Jake's car and were ready to back out of the drive when Jake's parents came to the car window and motioned for them to come back into the house. Jake was confused but turned the engine off, and he and Marcus joined them in the kitchen. "Marcus, what are you thinking?" It was dad who addressed him.

When Jake looked at his mom, she was holding Marcus's chain that had his chip on it in her hand. She joined in with Robert's question. "Marcus, you can never take this off. Never." She went to put it back on him, and he flinched back like it was a hot poker coming at him. "Marcus, I know that you do not like to have a chip, but you are not going to leave this house until it is on your neck and you agree to keep it there." She locked eye to eye with him. She knew full well that he was going to put it on and would go see his boys; he just needed to be the one to decide it for himself.

Marcus stood looking at her. She did not make a move but waited for him to decide he was going to put it on. This was a battle they needed to win. Without his chip, it could be too dangerous for him as well as the Knowing. Someone having a chip that is not in them would send up a red flag that they might not ever be able to repair.

Marcus felt sick. He so wanted to see the boys, but he could never wear that chip again.

"Mom, where did you find it?" Jake was hoping to lessen the tension in the room some.

She kept her look on Marcus but answered him all the same. "He had thrown it in the trash, but the chain was hanging out, and that is how I saw it."

Jake had a thought. "Mom, how did I get the real chip anyway?"

She smiled and rolled her eyes. "We had planned for all our family to be chipped like this." She held up the medallion to show him. "But you, my dear son, and Mark ran away from the school that day and marched yourself into the station and had your chip put in. We were horrified. Mark got sick and had his removed, but here we are years later, and God had you go undercover, so your chip was removed. You need to know that we had very long nights of agony about you having the chip. We so hate them and what they stand for. But always remember that what man can use for evil, God can and will use for good."

Their conversation hit Marcus like a rock. He heard *horrified* and that they *hated* them and *agony* about the chips. He felt exactly the same way, and he loved that they understood. He took the chain from Mrs. S. and slowly placed it over his neck. It felt awful.

Jake patted him on the back. "You will get used to it. I did. Now let's go." He turned and walked out the door. Marcus looked at the Singletons and gave a smile of apology and joined Jake in the car.

Marcus did not say one word all the way out there, but as they got closer to the farm, Jake could see that he was a nervous wreck.

Jake pulled the car over to the side of the road and could see Marcus was going to object, so he spoke first. "Before you get upset, let me show you something." Marcus took out several pieces of foil and reached into his shirt to pull out his medallion. He placed two pieces around it, pressing it hard to make sure that it was completely covered. He handed two foils to Marcus and watched as he did the same. "Now, we have one more thing to talk about. Today is going to be hard on you, I know, but you need to know that the boys think you are someday going to take them back to town and that you all are going to be in a nest again. Marcus, you need to tell them that is not true."

Jake saw it; for a split second, he could tell that Marcus had the same hope.

"You know that can never happen, right?" Jake was concerned that Marcus could not see the logic in all this. He was a smart kid. How could he not get that this idea was too dangerous for any of the kids to go back on the streets? Marcus did not answer but looked out of the window. "Marcus, you know I am right, don't you?" Marcus slowly shook his head that he understood. Jake gave it a time then started the engine, and they got to the farm.

The farm was beautiful. There were open fields, and the grass was green. It looked kind of like heaven on earth. There were several buildings and a lot of people. Jake's parents had already arrived. Jake knew that Mark and Sally were here because he saw Mark's bike.

They had barely climbed out of the car when they heard a young voice yell, "It is Marcus. Marcus is here." Young boys came from everywhere. They overran Marcus from every direction. There were questions and hugs. They were all so excited to tell Marcus about their new lives. They all hoped that Marcus could meet their new families; many had expressed that perhaps Marcus could come and live with them. Of course that was out of the question now because Marcus was chipped. It would be too dangerous for them to have him around them. Even his coming to the farm was a risk. *Dear God, I so love the boys, and I so hate this chip. Why did You let this happen to me?* Marcus sent up so many arrow prayers throughout the day, did God hear him? Did God even care that his life was such a mess?

Hours had passed, and Marcus had met so many nice people. They all expressed what a good job he had done in teaching the boys. All the boys were above their grade level in school. They were normal boys, that they had good manners, and that he should be proud of them. And he was. But he missed them. He wanted more than anything to have his family of boys back. But it was never going to happen, and now he knew it for sure.

Victor and Sandy had arrived sometime during the day. Marcus had seen them but had not had a chance to speak to them yet. How would they feel about him now that he was chipped? Did they know that he could never live at their shelter again? *God, this is too hard. Are You there? Do You care?*

Marcus was pleasantly surprised when Victor and Sandy came over to him, all on their own, and wanted to speak to him. Sandy gave Marcus a big hug. She patted him on the chest. "We know about the chip. And we are so sorry." Marcus almost lost it. He was so sad. He felt so alone. He felt abandoned by God. But he needed to keep it together for his boys; they were everywhere, and they were watching him.

Victor was the next one to get to greet Marcus. Marcus was going to shake his hand, but Victor grabbed him up in a great big solid hug. He put his mouth by Marcus's ear so only he could hear what he was saying. "I know this feels and looks like everything has gone bad. But keep trusting God. He really does have a plan." Marcus reacted to the words and wanted to pull back away from Victor, but Victor held onto him; there was more that needed to be said, and Marcus needed to hear it from a friend. "You feel like you failed because of the chip, but I am telling you that God is going to use it for good. I know that it is hard, but you have to believe and wait to see the outcome. A lot is going to happen in the next few hours, and it is going to be hard to do the right thing, but you are not alone in this. We are all here for you no matter how it feels, that is the truth, and you need to hold on to it."

All day the boys had been asking Marcus what he was going to do, and all day he had needed to know it himself, but now it was clear to him. He needed to not only let his boys go but he was going to have to send them away. *Oh, God, give me the courage. God, why did You give them to me only to make me give them back?* Victor wished he would never have to let him go, but Marcus had a job; and as hard as it was going to be on him, Marcus needed to do it. Victor gave Marcus one last word. "God is here. Never forget He gave His Son up too." Victor let him go.

Marcus stepped back away from Victor and caught his breath. One of the boys, Jimmy, had come over and taken Marcus's hand and was leading him to a stool by a firepit. All of the boys had gathered. Their new families had joined them. They were all so happy, all so family. It was exactly what the boys needed. They were safe here, and they were loved. This was exactly what they needed, and no matter how bad it hurt, Marcus needed them to go on with their new lives without him.

Marcus took his seat and began to talk. "I am so happy to see all of you, and I am so proud of every one of you. I need to tell you all something that is going to be hard, but you need to know about it. I cannot live with you anymore, and you cannot be with me either. I have been chipped, and it would be bad for us all."

The boys gasped and were horrified at what Marcus was saying. But he had to do something that would make the boys go away from him and to their own new families. "Please understand that the chip was not my choice, but it happened, and I cannot do anything about it. Remember what the Bible says about how God can make good out of everything? Well, we need to wait and see what the good God is going to do with this. But for now, God has given each and every one of us a new family, and we need to go and be the best family we can be. Do it for God, do it for you, and do it for me. Okay?" Zach, one of the youngest ones, burst into tears and threw himself on Marcus. Marcus gathered him up in a hug and sat him on his lap. "Look at me. You need to go and be with your brother and your new family. I need to get on with my new life too." It was not at all what Marcus wanted to say, but tough love was needed for this moment. "Now go on with you." Marcus placed him on his feet and stood up. "So now you all know what it is you need to do. I need you to go and do it now. He could not speak any more; his heart was pounding so hard, and he so wanted to run away. He signaled in nest for all of them to dismiss and to do it quickly. The families were grateful for what Marcus had done and for how he had handled it but were confused as to how very well the boys had listened and followed what Marcus had said for them to do. He was truly a good and powerful leader. They all thanked him with nods of their heads and with their body language. They gathered their boys up and headed to their new homes.

All of the Singletons, Victor and Sandy, along with many others had seen the whole thing. They were speechless. This kid had done a fantastic job of sending his boys off to the world. The boys were sad, but they would understand someday how much love it took for Marcus to do what he had done.

Marcus stood watching as the families left with his boys. Jake and all the others there stood beside him to give him emotional support. Marcus was the first to speak. "Sandy, they are good people, right?"

"Yes, Marcus, they are all good, Godly people."

"Victor, I did the right thing, right?"

"Yes, Marcus, you did the right thing."

Out of nowhere, Jimmy came running to Marcus's side. Marcus knelt down and let him speak to him. "Marcus, don't you love us anymore?"

It took every ounce of being for Marcus to answer Jimmy. "Yes, I do love you all very much, but they can love you better than I can right now. So you need to go, and I will see you again, okay?" Jimmy gave him one last hug around his neck and ran back to his new family. Marcus stood back up and did not move at all until they had all gone. He was alone. *God, are You really there? I need You so much right now. I need to feel You. Where are You in all of this?*

Mrs. S. was the first to get to Marcus. She turned him around and lifted his chin so to make eye contact with him. "You know, Marcus, I have sent every one of my kids away to school or on to their life, when they left home. And every time I had to do it, I felt like a part of my very soul was being ripped away. I can't even begin to imagine how it would be to lose all of my kids at one time. I am so sorry."

Marcus did not react at all, he only thanked her, turned and walked away.

Jake went to her side. "Mom?"

She answered him, "I know, Jake. I know."

The whole adult group did not know what to say to Marcus or what they could do for him, so they prayed.

They had lost him for a time but found him working with some of the others *restocking* the shelves with the supplies that the Singletons had brought out to the farm. Robert watched him for a while and noted that he was using up some nervous energy and determined that it was a good thing. The day had gone as well as could be expected, and it was time for the Singletons to go home. It was odd to them that Marcus was ready to go at the first mention of leaving. The cars were empty of the supplies, so Marcus got into Jake's car, but this time he got into the back seat. He stretched out and pretended to be asleep on the whole trip. When they got back to the house, Marcus shot out of the car and went inside so fast that they thought he might be sick.

Marcus was going to go to the backyard and spend some time outside. It was a good place to think and to talk to God. But he was sidetracked when he entered the house because Brother Marcus was there waiting for them, wanting to hear a good report about the boys getting their new homes. "Hey, Marcus, how did it go?"

"What?" Marcus could not think about anything but getting out of the house and not having to talk or listen to any questions or answers right now.

Jake and his parents walked in on the conversation. "Hi, how long have you been here?" Jake was trying to make small talk to avoid seeing Marcus get hurt any more than he already had been. This kid needed to get on with his life and let the past be the past. Sure he hurt now, but in time, he would be okay. *Right, God?* All Jake wanted was an answer from God about his friend's hurting. So many arrow prayers were sent up on the drive home.

Mrs. S. could see that they had a problem. Marcus wanted out of here, Brother Marcus wanted to be filled in on what had happened, and Jake wanted to fix everything he thought he could. She looked around and saw the book Marcus had been reading before. She opened it and thumbed the pages. She saw that he was on page 54 of the book. This will work. "Marcus, why don't you take your book out back and read for a while? It will be good for you to get some fresh air."

Marcus got a look of relief on his face. His eyes were not looking very lively, but he had thanked her with them before he took the book and went out back.

Brother Marcus waited until Marcus had left the house before he addressed the family group. "What on earth is wrong with Marcus? Did he not think the families were good for the boys?" It took some time, but they thought they had filled Brother Marcus in on all that had happened. There was so much lost in the telling of the goings-on, but they did their best.

A lot of time had passed, and they decided it was time for Marcus to join them in the house. Marcus came in at once when he was called. He placed his book on one of the stools and sat in a chair at the table. Mrs. S. looked where the bookmark was in the book and noted that it was still on page 54; Marcus had not been reading, he had just been sitting.

Brother Marcus had the idea. "Hey, Marcus, if you are up to it, I could use some help translating the recordings. I need them by tomorrow, so could you help?" He was holding the box the recordings were in.

Jake was so mad at his brother. Could he not see that this kid needed a break and not more work? What if some of the kids were on the recordings? Did his brother not think about how painful that could be for Marcus? "I don't think that is such a good idea," Jake was saying it to his brother, but it was Marcus himself who made the decision.

Marcus walked across the room, took the box from Brother Marcus, and headed out for the living room where they had worked before. He did not say a word but put the first one in the player and had a seat in the nice big chair in the room. He liked the safe feeling it gave him. The way the arms of the chair came around, he felt that he only needed to watch his front. It was strange to him that his street thinking was back. He had been feeling almost too safe here, but he was more or less acting like his old self, on guard again. But he could not figure out why. It was just a feeling he had.

The recording had begun to play. Brother Marcus had joined Marcus.

Sally and Mark had arrived, and they had joined in the watching of the recordings. Sally had been told about how fantastic this language was that Marcus had created and wanted to see how it worked for herself. She was amazed at how well it did work. She had remembered that Jake was excited about seeing this in the park; he was right, it was true art. The TV played, and Marcus told what it was they were saying. Brother Marcus would ask questions, and Marcus would fill in the blanks. Brother Marcus would write it down. So it went, recording after recording.

Jake's mom had stopped him from joining them in the living room. She needed to talk to him about his trying to protect Marcus too much. "Jake, you cannot keep him from hurting. You can only love him through it. You know that, right? You need to trust God in this too. God knows what Marcus can handle and what will make him the man he needs to be in order to be used by Him. And we are all here for Marcus. We just need to keep reminding him of that."

Jake knew she was right. He had never been a big brother before, and it was a lot harder than it looked. He needed to thank his own brothers sometime for all they had done in his life. He gave his mom a hug and thanked her and went to join the others in reading the recordings.

Jake went to the door of the living room and stood there unnoticed. Marcus was telling them all what the people were saying. Like Marcus had said, none of the people on the screen were people that he knew either. He was having fun reading the signals at the same time Marcus was saying them out loud. But something was wrong. He continued to watch the TV screen and listened to Marcus and realized that they had a problem. Marcus was lying, to all of them.

Jake really took a good look at Marcus for the first time. He was rubbing his forehead and his eyes as he was speaking. Jake looked at Mark and Sally and saw that they were aware that Marcus was leaving something out from the way he was acting. Brother Marcus was into getting the words down and had not seen what they had.

Marcus was telling the words, and Brother Marcus was asking questions. "The man says that—"

"Does the man have a name?"

"No."

"No name?" Brother Marcus thought this was strange.

"No name." Marcus rubbed his head more. "Maybe they call him T."

"Who are they talking about?"

Marcus answered, "I am not sure it might be someone who starts with an M."

"Marcus, what are you talking about, is it or is it not a name?" Brother Marcus hated to be confused, and it made him sound angry when really he was just frustrated and not understanding.

"Okay, he said, 'It was Marcus, and we need to get him out.'" Marcus needed to get out of this situation. He did not want to lie, but he could not tell them what they were really saying because it would make his brother, Travis, look bad.

Jake could not stand it any longer. He had promised his mom that he would not interfere, but this was different. He did not need to protect Marcus, he needed to call him out. "Marcus, you are lying."

Everyone in the room except Marcus looked at Jake. "He is lying to protect Travis. What the signal was really saying was that Travis wanted them to take Marcus out. That Travis wants them to make Marcus dead. The men are excited because not only would they get a reward for taking out Smart Boy, but that it would make their leader, Travis, happy with them."

Brother Marcus got only inches away from Marcus. "Is that true? Are you lying to us? Do you have any idea how dangerous it could be for us to not have this real information? Marcus, you could be in danger, not to mention the rest of us."

Their mom and dad heard the voices getting louder; they joined the others in the living room. One look at the way everyone was acting, and they knew that there must be a problem with something Marcus had done.

Dad took the lead. "So what has happened now?"

Everyone sat silent. No one wanted to tell on their new little brother. He had done a stupid thing, a really stupid thing, but he was their brother, and they needed to help him, not throw him under the bus.

Brother Marcus explained, telling the truth but not really the whole truth, "Well, Jake and Marcus are disagreeing about the recordings and what they are saying, that is all."

Marcus did not look up until he heard Robert speak to him. "Well, from what I know, I would think that Marcus here would be the expert in the room, isn't that right, Marcus?"

"Yes, sir." Marcus was still afraid of Robert, but he was more afraid of letting his new family down.

"Okay, why don't you go over the last recording again, and then we can all have something to eat when you are finished." He put his arm around their mom, and they left the room. But not before their mom had a chance to look at every one of them in the eye.

They waited until they had cleared the earshot of all of the others to talk. "Robert, you know as well as I do that they are all up to something."

"Yes, I know, but they are doing it together as a family. And if I am right, they are helping Marcus with something, and that will help him to know that he is family too."

Brother Marcus made Marcus reread the last recording word for word with Jake confirming that what he was saying was the truth. "Travis wants them to make Marcus dead." Marcus was beyond upset. He could not speak any more. He needed to get out of here and fast. "I am going to go outside for some air."

He was getting up to leave the room, when Brother Marcus and Mark both got in his way in order to stop him. It was Mark who explained it to Marcus. "It is too dangerous for you to be out of this house. Maybe you do not realize what you just saw, but there is a contract out on you. They want to kill you and get the reward. So—"

It was Brother Marcus who finished the sentence, "Until further notice, you are now under house arrest. Do you understand? You do not leave this house unless you talk to one of us and we are with you." They all agreed.

Jake had been quiet. But now he needed to say what they were all thinking. "Marcus, I know that you think Travis would never do anything to hurt you, but the evidence proves different. So until we figure this out, you need to think of Travis as dangerous for you and stay away from him."

Marcus spoke up, "But he is my brother. My blood brother."

And Sally answered, "And we are now your family, and we don't take kindly to someone threatening one of ours."

Marcus could not handle anything else. This was the last straw. His own brother wanted him dead and had really done something to make it happen; he had put a contract on him. Marcus went to leave the room again.

Brother Marcus stopped him again. "Where are you going?"

"I need to go outside for some air." Marcus was desperate to get away from them so he could think.

Brother Marcus was firm but kind with his next words. "I don't think so. You may go up to your room to have some time to yourself, but you will not be leaving this house. Do you understand?"

Marcus was being smothered. First, God had abandoned him and taken everything he had from him, and now this group God had sent him into was going to smother him to death. He did not answer but tried to walk away from the room. "Do you understand?"

He needed to get away even if it was only to a room in this house. "Yes, I understand."

"Understand what?" Brother Marcus wanted to be clear as to what Marcus was willing to do to stay safe.

"I understand I am to stay in this house, I understand that I have to have and wear a chip, I understand I have to give up my boys, I understand that Travis, my own brother—" He could not speak any more. There were no more words. He needed to go to his room, now.

He went up the stairs and into his room.

Jake positioned himself in the doorway in the hall so he could keep an eye on the stairs in case Marcus changed his mind.

Sally went straight to it. "Okay, so now what are we going to do?"

Brother Marcus looked to Sally and Mark. "I think we need Brother Ben for this one, don't you?"

The three of them all smiled. They knew that they were going to get a reaction from Jake.

"Ben is a believer too?" Jake was both excited and irritated by not knowing, at the same time.

"Sally, how soon can you get in touch with Ben?" Brother Marcus was reaching for his phone at the same time he was talking.

Sally showed him that she was already texting Ben as they were talking.

In a short period of time, they had told the parents what had happened and that they had called Ben to come and help. They gathered together as a family (minus two, Ben and Marcus) and prayed.

Marcus had made it to his room before he could really breathe again. He needed to get control of this. He was a leader after all. He was a good leader. So how did he get in this mess? "Father, I need You. Where are You?" He got out his Bible; he reread Jeremiah 29:11. He put the Bible down. "Father, why don't You love me?" He could hear God answer in his heart.

I have loved you. Didn't you see Me loving you through Victor and Sandy, in the Singletons, and in the boys? Didn't you feel My love with every breath you have taken? I loved you by the sun that shines on you and made you warm. I love you in so many ways.

"But, Father, I cannot do this alone."

I never asked you to. I have always been with you, and I always will be with you.

"But it hurts."

Then give Me your hurt, and I can make good out of it. Trust Me.

Marcus went to deep prayer, "Father, take it. I give up. I cannot do it. If You want things done, then You do it through me. I am too tired and too weak. Give me the strength and knowledge to do Your will. Amen."

At the end of the prayer, Marcus could not hold the pain back any longer. He started to cry. He tried to keep from making sounds, but even with his face buried into the pillow, sound was getting out. "Oh, God, please help take this pain away. I can't control it any longer." One tear was the beginning of a flood of grief pouring out from somewhere too deep inside for him to have even known it was there.

Jake heard something that sounded strange, so he went upstairs to see what it was. When he got to the hall, he saw his mom by his old bedroom door. She had her head on the doorpost, and she looked like she was praying. Jake realized that the sound he heard was someone crying. Although it was muffled like someone trying to hide it, they were crying really hard. Jake's heart broke, and he now knew why his mom was upset. It was Marcus, he was the one crying. Jake went to go through the door into the room with Marcus, but his mom led him by the arm down the hall so they could talk. "Jake, I need you to do me a favor. I need you to not go in there with Marcus."

"Mom, I need to go in there. Can't you hear he is hurting?"

"I know he is hurting, but if you go in there, he will not let himself cry in front of you. He will not let himself grieve, and, Jake, he needs to grieve and get it out. He needs to heal."

"But, Mom, he is alone."

"No, he is not, Jake, he has God, and he knows that we are only a call away. When he is ready, he will ask for us, but for now, we need to pray for him and let him have this time to be sad and to let it all out. I am not sure, but I bet he has not cried in years."

Jake thought back to the last time Marcus was sad like this, and she was right; as soon as Marcus knew that Jake was there, he pulled himself together. Perhaps she was right and this was the way to handle it.

Jake sat down in the hall right outside the door and prayed for his friend Marcus. "God, it always seems that when I help this boy, I am hurting him? Help me to help in the right way, God. I wonder, do You sometimes let us feel alone in our problems so we can grow, but all the while You are right there just waiting for us to call out to You?"

Time had passed. It seemed forever to Jake. He saw that his mother was getting ready to enter Marcus's room. "Mom, can I go in instead of you?"

She smiled and put her open hand on Jake's chest. "Jake, I think this is something a mother needs to do. Marcus has lost a lot, so it is important for him to not lose his dignity with you. Let me do this and know that there will come a day when it is your turn to help in a way only you can. But for now, he needs to finish what he has started in this healing process." She gave him a hug and turned and opened the door to Marcus's room.

All Jake could see was the chain and medallion lying on the floor by the door. The lights were out, and the room was dark. His mom entered the room and shut the door behind her. Jake heard her speak to Marcus with a soft and reassuring voice. He remembered that she had done this exact same thing for him once long ago. He wondered if she had been out in the hall waiting for the right time to come to him and to be his comfort also.

CHAPTER 37

It was early Monday morning when Jake came down to the kitchen to get breakfast before going to work. He could smell bacon, pancakes, and eggs for sure. The surprise of his life was when he walked into the kitchen and saw Marcus helping his mom cook.

Marcus had noted that Jake was there but had not made eye contact.

Jake walked over to his mom and gave her a hug and a kiss on her cheek. "Good morning. This is a shock to see the two of you up and making breakfast." Jake snagged a piece of bacon from a plate and got his hand slapped by his mom with the pancake turner.

Jake let out a whine. That made Marcus laugh in spite of how bad he felt for Jake to get caught. Marcus could teach Jake some lessons in lifting things.

"Jake, you should know better. Now are you going to stay and eat with us, or do you want me to make your breakfast into a sandwich and take it with you?" She hoped he would stay. It would be good for Marcus to learn that Jake did not think less of him.

"I have enough time before I have to go to work, I'll stay. Is Dad still here?" Jake looked around the kitchen to see if there were any signs of him still being home. "I need to talk to him about some stuff."

The back door opened, and Brother Marcus and Dad walked in together. They were talking like nothing had even happened.

Marcus was relieved that they were not acting mad about his lying to them yesterday.

They got coffee and juice for themselves and gathered around the table. Mom brought some of the dishes of food. Marcus helped her carry them and took a seat between Jake and Brother Marcus. He felt safe, for the first time in a long time.

There was a lot of light conversation. Marcus looked amazing considering what he had been through. The whole family noticed a difference in him right away. They saw that Marcus still looked sad, but he was no longer broken. They had also noted that he had the chain with the chip on his neck. Somehow Marcus had made peace with his new life. Without words, they all knew it was a God factor. God had somehow answered their prayers. It was a new start for their family.

Several days had gone by, and the streets were so quiet that it made many people nervous. The government was quiet. They were acting like the Knowing did not exist. That fact made the Knowing nervous because there was no one looking to do anything about them. Things were quiet, too quiet.

Jake had gone back to his apartment and to doing his job. The calls he made at work were back to the everyday variety. Seldom did he hear anything about going after the chipless.

Mark had gone back to school and was doing his normal going between the groups and gathering information. There really was not any information to speak of when it came to the chipless. In fact, it almost looked too good. Everyone was going about their own business. Living in peace with each other is what it looked like.

Sally and Brother Marcus were also back to their jobs; both were getting the same feeling, that everything was great and no one had a problem with the chipless anymore.

Brother Ben had not been seen by anyone in the family, but they had received word that he had made some things happen and that the hit on Marcus was almost completely eliminated.

Marcus was the one with the big changes. He made it so his new life was busy, he did not give himself too much downtime to think, it was easier on his heart to do it this way. He had made a schedule for himself and kept to it as tight as he could. He read every day, and he did math from some old college books of the Singleton kids from back when they were in school. He would exercise regularly, and he worked around the house doing anything he could find that needed doing. He got up early to study and went to bed early so he could read some more at the end of his day. Mrs. S. and Marcus did Bible studies every day, and whoever else came by at the time would join them.

From time to time Marcus would get a letter from one of his boys; at first they made him sad, but lately he had found them to be encouraging to him.

Robert had to go back out of town on business. Like everyone else, he could feel that things looked great about the chipless but that something was wrong. He would check it out at his level in the government.

Saturday morning had come. Marcus did not realize how different the weekends were going to be from the rest of the week. When he came downstairs to the kitchen, Jake and Mark were already there. They greeted him as he came into the kitchen with a cup of coffee, or milk with a little coffee, as Jake liked to tease him.

Mark and Jake could not believe that this was the same sick street kid they had once brought over to their parents' house. He had on clothes that were his own. They fit, and they matched. They could tell that their mom had helped with cutting Marcus's hair. That would be one intervention that the boys would work on. She meant well, but her barbering skills were lacking.

Jake felt good about how Marcus was looking. "Marcus, I would ask how you are doing, but I can see that for myself. So, I will ask, what have you been doing?" He smiled at Mark. "Or should I say, what is it Mom has got you doing?" He was making fun and being lighthearted.

Jake's mom had walked into the kitchen and was standing right behind Jake as he was attempting to tease Marcus. Mark and Marcus smirked at Jake as he finished talking. He did not need to turn around. He knew she was there. "Mom is standing behind me, right?" Everyone but Jake laughed. Then he did join in on the fun.

They had a light breakfast, some cereal and toast. They had conversations about so many normal and regular things; it felt good to Marcus to be a part of this family, but there was still a kind of sadness deep inside he could not shake. From time to time the family noticed that he would get a sad and lonely look on his face but for the most part felt like he was adjusting to his new lifestyle. Marcus had gone up to his room for something. Mark was the one to bring it up. "Mom, how do you think Marcus is really doing?"

She thought for a moment. "Well, from the looks of things, I would say he is great. He is definitely past the deep pain he was in, but I have to tell you something is up. I can feel it. I just do not know what it is or even where to look."

Marcus had come back into the room carrying a book. "What are you looking for?" He had only heard part of the conversation.

They just laughed. He did fit into the family.

Mark noticed that Marcus had brought a book to the table. He looked at it. "Hey, is that my old math book? What are you doing with it?"

Marcus opened up the book to one of the pages to show Mark that he was having trouble figuring out some of the problems. "If you don't mind, do you think you can help me figure out what part of this I am missing? I am kind of stuck."

Mark looked at the book a little closer. "Marcus, this is one of my college books. I can't believe that you get any of this." Jake and his mom both confirmed that he was in fact doing college-level work.

Marcus did not get the big deal. "Okay, I get that, but can you help me with this part?"

Their mom sat down beside Marcus at the table. "Marcus, I think that you may need to get into a school. I am not sure what or where, but I think we should put that mind of yours back to learning." She looked at the book again. "Not that you are not doing good on your own, but I think you might like to have the challenge."

Jake rolled his eyes. "Now you have gone and done it, now you have to go back to school." He was teasing Marcus. Having to go to school were not Jake's best memories, but he could tell that Marcus would be excited to get to learn. Jake could also see that Marcus did not have a clue about what Jake was teasing him about, and that made him laugh. "Marcus, what school did you go to before?"

Marcus looked blank at him and then answered, "I was taught by my parents, they homeschooled me until they had to leave."

"Then what happened? How did you learn so much?" Jake was fascinated that Marcus was so smart and did not even have a clue as to that fact.

"I got books and some help from people when I could." Marcus went back to looking at the math book. "Mark, could you show me this, if you don't mind."

Mark and Marcus went to work on the math problem. Jake was glad that he had asked Mark and not him. He did not have a clue as to what they were doing with the problems nor did he care. He was happy to see that Mark did. He got up and helped his mom clear the table.

Brother Marcus and Sally had joined them in the kitchen; they saw that Mark and Marcus were doing schoolwork. They were with Jake on this one. School was not a fun time for them either.

When Mark and Marcus had finished their schooling, they all sat around talking. It was good to be with family. They could tell from the way Marcus was acting that he needed to ask a question. He had rubbed his forehead several times and started to say something but stopped many times. Brother Marcus was the one to address it. "Marcus, why don't you do yourself a favor and just spit it out?"

Marcus looked at Brother Marcus. "What are you talking about?"

"We can all see that you have something to say, so why don't you just say it?" Brother Marcus was nice about the question, but the fact that Marcus still did not trust them had him concerned. "So why don't you say it and get it over with? Besides, how bad can it be?"

Jake loved that they were picking on the new little brother and not him. He drank his coffee and stayed out of it.

Marcus looked around the room and decided that he should get it over with. "Mrs. S., I was wondering if I could do the yard work around here."

Jake choked on his coffee, almost spewing all of it from his mouth. "Oh gads, Marcus, I thought you had something really big to say. You are asking to get to do chores? Are you crazy, or are you trying to get on Mom's good side? In case you haven't heard, you are already in the family." Jake started to clean up the coffee mess he had made.

Everyone in the room thought it was funny to see Jake overreact, but it was their mom who confirmed that Jake was right. "Marcus, first of all, why don't you start by calling me *Nancy*? Second, I cannot see any reason at all for you to not get to do the yard work if you really want to. In fact, the fresh air might even do you some good. But do it because you want to, not because you feel you have to."

Marcus shook his head that he understood. "Thank you. Do you think I can start today?"

Nancy loved this kid already. "Sure, and I bet if you asked, Jake here would love to help you." They all laughed, even Jake.

Jake and Marcus went out to the backyard to talk over the things that needed to be done.

Nancy called out to Mark and to Brother Marcus to stay. "I saw the looks you two gave each other when Marcus asked to do yard work. What is up with that?" Neither of them said anything. "Oh, never mind, I will find out sooner or later." She went upstairs to get on with the day's work. She trusted that they would take care of whatever it was that was going on with Marcus and that God would take care of them too.

Mark and Brother Marcus looked to see if there was anyone around. Mark asked his brother if he thought Marcus was up to something. They answered each other at the same time. "Absolutely." The fact that the Knowing used the excuse of doing yard work in order to make rabbit holes had not escaped all of the Singletons. Mark and Brother Marcus were all over it.

Two more weeks had passed with pretty much the same thing happening every week. Weekends were all about the coming in and out of family members. Marcus was getting used to people just popping in unannounced at any old time of day or night, especially Mark and Brother Marcus.

Marcus had added more exercises to his exercise program. He had found some old weights and had been running with them around the yard. He increased how many laps he did every day. He did sit-ups and pushups, adding to the number each day too. He did his pull-ups from a tree branch. Sometimes the family would watch Marcus work in the yard. He did funny things, like the fact he never went around anything in the yard but always went over it. Or the fact that he never did anything slow but worked as fast as he could; he worked long and hard at the yard and at his life. If he took a break, which was rare, he always had a book to read.

*****

Family day was here, and they were all going to have a cookout in the backyard. Marcus had done wonders with the yard. It had never looked so good.

Jake had been teasing Marcus since he had arrived to the family home, giving him a bad time about everything. So when he had made himself what he called the Perfect Hot Dog, it made him the perfect mark for Marcus. Letting everyone else see him so they could be in on the joke, Marcus took Jake's hot dog, had it wrapped, and tossed it to Mark before Jake had found it gone.

Jake took one look at the smirk on Marcus's face and knew that it was him and that he must have it in his pocket. Jake happily went after his new little brother in order to retrieve his property. He was laughing because he had Marcus trapped on the deck against the railing. There was no place for Marcus to go.

Marcus in one single move did a backflip over the deck railing and landed solid on the ground below. As much as that move shocked Jake, he continued to pursue Marcus by jumping over the rail also but using his arms to let himself down. Marcus was fast, but what happened next took everyone by surprise. Marcus ran full out toward one of the trees in the yard. When he got to the trunk of the tree, he placed a foot right on the trunk and sprang up into the air, catching the lowest limb, and swung himself up with great ease. By the time Jake got to the tree, Marcus was almost to the top in the most upper limbs. Jake could not reach the lower limb and could find no foothold in order to boost himself up into it.

The family could not believe what they had seen Marcus do. Nancy went to the edge of the deck and called out to both Marcus and Jake to stop playing around and to come and eat dinner.

If it were not for the looks on his family's faces, Jake would have missed Marcus's next moves. Jake turned around just in time to see Marcus throw himself from the top branch of the tree, catching some lower limbs that had leaves on them and sliding down to the ground. It was because of his weight that the foliage gently lowered him to the ground. He had almost landed on Jake, but ran back to the deck where he proceeded to retrieve Jake's hot dog and gave up the challenge.

Jake did not care about the hot dog anymore. He was scared by what he had just witnessed. "Are you out of your living mind? What were you thinking? You could have been killed." Jake wanted to grab this kid and shake him for being so reckless.

Nancy handed Jake his plate. "Jake, settle down, Marcus has been doing this all week. Wait until you see how he gets over a fence."

Marcus did not mean to scare Jake. He felt bad. He was only having fun. "Travis, I am really sorry. I did not mean to scare you. I was just having fun."

They all looked at Marcus. Jake corrected him. "You called me *Travis*, you meant to say *Jake*, but that is okay."

Marcus felt even worse. "Sorry, I will get us some drinks." He left the deck and went into the house. How could he have been so stupid? He should have never showed off like that. What was he thinking? He needed to be more careful about using his maneuvers around the family.

Jake turned to his other family members. "So what was all of that?" He noted that none of them were startled by the fact that Marcus was so good at getting away.

Brother Marcus was the one to address it. "I think little brother here has been practicing his street skills. I think he may have a plan that we need to find out about." They all agreed but kept it to themselves until they knew more.

The rest of the day went easy and without any big happenings. Marcus and Sally won the family game, again. So the winning team still held their position.

It was a few days later, and there was not going to be any yard work for sure; it was raining so hard that you could hardly see out from time to time. Marcus was at the kitchen table reading and studying when Jake arrived. "Hey, Marcus, I was going to go and get a haircut. I thought I would take you with me, and we could both get one. No offence to Mom, but we all try and not let her do our hair. It is not her best skill."

Nancy had overheard the conversation and was not offended at all. She was glad to see Jake and thought it was an excellent idea that Marcus get out of the house for a time. "I think that is a great plan." She startled them. She went to the cabinet and found a food list. "And while you are at it, you can go pick up some food at the store."

Marcus got all nervous. He dropped his book and was acting anxious. "I think I am okay with my hair the way it is, but thank you anyway." He did not get up but was acting like he was busy with what he was reading.

Nancy walked over to Marcus and gently pulled the book from his hand. "Marcus, you cannot stay at this house the rest of your life. Sooner or later you are going to have to go out into the real world and live your life." She was not going to take no for an answer. She should have realized that part of the reason he was doing so good was because he felt safe here at home, but he needed to get back out there and learn he could be okay there too. "Now go get your coat and go with Jake, get a haircut, and bring back some food."

Marcus wanted to argue with her, but she was too good at putting things in such a way that you couldn't say no. He looked at her and then at Jake. "I'll be right back. Give me a minute, okay?" He went up to his room. He would have to put on that stupid chain and chip. *Oh, God, I hate this.* But he knew that if he did not wear it that it could be dangerous for them all. He had worn it for the first few days, but after everyone thought he was okay with it, he found that he could keep it in his upstairs drawer and no one even thought about it. He put it on over his head and got his jacket. He looked at the inside to check the pockets he had sewn back in. They were gone; someone had removed them. Again.

Nancy was standing in his doorway. "You should have never taken it off, you know." Marcus gave her a questioning look. "I am talking about the chain. You have not put it on for days now, and about the pockets in your coat, you don't need them anymore. You have a chip now." She could see that he was uncomfortable. She felt for him, but this would be good for him to get out.

Jake had come upstairs to see what the holdup was. He looked around Marcus's room. It was in perfect order. Not a single thing out of place. Even the book he had been reading was put back on the bookcase. "Marcus, what is up with your room? It never looked like this when I lived here."

Nancy smiled. "And that is a fact." She went to leave the room to go downstairs. "Jake, do not pick on him about his room. It is his, and he can keep it the way he wants."

Jake rolled his eyes. "So are you ready to go, little brother?"

They left the house and went to the barbershop first. Jake had noticed that Marcus was rather quiet. He had slouched down in the seat of the car like he was hiding. Jake could tell that he hated everything about this. He was not comfortable being in this part of town. "Have you ever been in this area before?"

"Not when they did not chase me out. Jake, I think I would rather not do this today." Marcus did not want to look weak, but he also hoped he could be honest with Jake.

"I would love to get you off the hook for this one, little brother, but if I do not bring you home with a haircut and some food, Mom will not be happy, and as much as I like you, I like Mom happy more." Jake knew that his mom would not mind if he used her as an excuse in this situation. Jake was keeping it lighthearted. He never thought for one second that Marcus would be this uncomfortable out in the real world.

They parked the car and went to go into the barber shop. Jake opened the front door and motioned for Marcus to go in first. Marcus looked like a lamb going to the slaughter. When they entered, the barber acknowledged them right off. "I will be right with you two." He smiled and locked eyes with Marcus. Jake could see that there was some sort of exchange of thought even though he could not see what it was. Marcus had seen the barber's reaction when he realized who Marcus was, but Marcus had given a very slight signal with his head saying no. Jake and Marcus sat off to the side until all of the other customers had left the room.

The barber rushed over to them when the door shut. "Marcus, as glad as I am to see you, and I am, what are you doing walking in here and right through the front door and with an officer to boot?"

Marcus did not stand up to this man but looked down ashamed. "I have been chipped." It was all he had to say.

The barber looked like he had been told that Marcus had died. "Oh, Marcus, I am so sorry. Travis did this to you, didn't he? Well, it doesn't matter now, does it, what has happened has happened. So what are you going to do now?"

Marcus realized that he was being dumb. He was not taking advantage of this situation. "Hey, Frank, speaking of Travis, what do you hear about him?"

Frank shook his head. "It is not good, Marcus, that brother of yours has caused so much trouble. I almost think it is good that you got away from him. He is really bad news all around."

"Frank, I did not get away from him, he ran." Marcus needed to change the direction this conversation was going.

Frank motioned for Jake to get into his chair, and he draped him for his haircut. Marcus and Frank continued to talk. "So, Marcus, where have you been anyway? There was a lot of talk that you had been put into jail, but we later found out that it was Travis and not you." He was cutting Jake's hair as he talked. "Is it true that you sent all of your boys away to be with families? Marcus, I think that was a real good thing to do."

Marcus had not done any of this. He had not had a choice in any of it as a matter of fact. But he was glad that Frank thought it was good. "Frank, back to Travis being in jail, what do you know?"

The door of the shop opened, and two men walked in to get their haircut. Frank acknowledged these two the same as he had them earlier. The opportunity to get information was over. Marcus felt helpless again. Jake saw Marcus's hope fade but thought it was good that he not know any more about Travis right now. He needed to heal some more before he took that back on again.

When their haircuts were done, they paid and left for the food store. Jake's family liked to go to the one only a block or two from Sandy's shelter. As they drove down the road, Jake saw Marcus look down the street to see if he could see anyone they knew. No luck, the street was empty, maybe too empty?

"Jake, can I please stay in the car?" Marcus had enough for the day. He wanted to get back to the house where things would be easier. Not having to explain anything.

"Nope." Jake had learned this tactic from his mom. No extra words, just an answer. "You are staying with me." Although Jake thought it was a good idea, it was Brother Marcus who made the rule that Marcus was never to be alone when he was away from the house. He thought it strange that his brother had even thought about it, but right now, he was glad he had. Marcus did not argue but got out of the car and went into the store with Jake.

The store was big. There was lots of food everywhere. The list had a lot of produce on it. Jake read it out loud so Marcus could get the idea of what they were there for. No one even looked twice at Marcus. He looked up into the mirror in the vegetable section and saw what they all saw. A chipped kid, he was chipped, and he definitely looked chipped. Jake called him back into the moment. "Hey, Marcus, why don't you get the apples? Mom put down to get ten." Marcus was feeling very confident. He was chipped, and he was shopping just like the rest of the other world. Funny he can be a man of two worlds. *God, was this Your plan all along?* Maybe it will not be so bad after all. He was reaching for the third apple when a large walking stick came down hard on the back of his left hand. Marcus turned around in pain, and the man was coming after him again to hit him in the head.

Jake had reacted to the noise and was between Marcus and the man before the man could give another hit to Marcus. "What on earth are you doing to my brother?"

"Your brother? Don't be crazy. This kid is nothing but trouble. He is a thief. Check the inside of his coat, you will see. There are extra pockets where he puts the stuff he steals." He reached out around Jake and pulled Marcus's coat open. To his horror, there were no pockets. "Well, they usually have pockets. Just because they are not there now does not mean that he is not a thief."

The store manager came over to see what was going on. Jake's family had a good relationship with him. "What on earth, Mr. Thompson, do you have a problem with these two young men?" He looked at Jake and then at Marcus, who was holding onto his hand trying to stop the pain by rubbing it.

"That one, that one there, he is a thief, and you need to keep him out of your store unless you want those kids to rob you blind."

Marcus had never stolen anything from this man or his store. He would get things out of the garbage out back almost daily for his boys, but he never once took what was not in the trash. Marcus often thought that the food he found in the trash looked almost too good sometimes to be thrown away, but he was grateful no matter what. They needed the food, and God had provided it.

The store manager looked at Jake. "Mr. Singleton, is there anything I can do for you and your brother Marcus?"

The man turned white. "Mr. Singleton? Oh my, I must have made a mistake. I mean, this kid looks a lot like a street kid...and..."

"Mr. Thompson, I assure you that this kid is no street kid. Look at him. Really, what were you thinking?" The manager took Marcus by the arm and was escorting him to a section of the store away from where Mr. Thompson was still standing. "Let's get some ice on that hand. I think it will be okay, some bruising, but I don't think it looks broken."

Jake wanted so bad to get back at this man, but he was remembering a time not so long ago that he himself might have reacted the same way to a chipless teen hanging out in a chip store.

The manager took the list of food and gave it to one of the baggers he had working for him. He had him get the food and bring it to Jake. Jake and the manager talked some, and then the food was bagged, and they started to head to go home. The manager stopped Marcus before he left the store. "I am sorry this happened to you."

What did this man have to be sorry about? He had not done anything but stop that man from hurting him more. "You have nothing to be sorry about, you are a good man, and I thank you a lot for all the good trash you set out for us in the past." Marcus had figured out just now that some of the food must have been put out on purpose.

The manager looked sad. "I wish it had been more now that I know you."

Marcus squeezed his arm. "It was exactly what God had ordered for us. Thank you." Marcus wanted to get out of here and get into the car. He wanted to get to the house and go to his room. He needed God time.

Jake and Marcus were driving home. "Marcus, are you okay?" Marcus still had the ice on his hand. He was quiet and looking out the window.

Marcus did not look at Jake. "Can we not tell Mom and the others at the house about what happened? They would just worry about me, and as you can see, I am okay."

Jake agreed to do his best to keep it from them. Marcus was not experienced at the fact that his family had ways of finding out about everything. He also wondered if Marcus had noticed that he had used the word *Mom* and not *Nancy* when he had asked. He truly did like having a little brother.

When they pulled up to the house, Brother Marcus's car was there as well as Sally's, and Mark's bike was parked in the drive. Jake looked at Marcus. "Something must have happened."

Marcus agreed. "You don't think they heard about the market, do you?"

"No, with everyone here this fast, it must be something else. But what could it be?"

When Marcus and Jake entered the house, everyone was in the living room. Robert was there with a man Marcus had not ever seen in person but had seen in photos around the house. It had to be their brother Ben.

Robert got up and went to the two of them. "I am glad you are back, we need to talk." Robert looked at Marcus. He could tell that something had happened. He looked at Jake. "Did something happen I need to know about?"

Jake looked at Marcus and then at his dad. "No, not really. But what is going on here?"

Nancy was glad to see that all her family was here together. She hated the why, but she was glad all the same.

Brother Marcus started the conversation, "Ben has some news that is going to affect all of us. Marcus, this is going to be hard on you, but I think if you look at the big picture, you may realize that this might be a gift from God."

Marcus sat down on the floor by the chair that Nancy was sitting in. There were not enough seats for everyone to sit in. Jake had done the same over by Sally and Mark. "Okay?"

Ben began the story. "The reason that everything was so quiet is that they were working on some news about one of the leaders in the Knowing. He was to be a young leader, and so it would be a big takedown if it happened." So far everyone was onboard with the conversation. "There is an undercover officer, you call him Will."

Marcus looked at Jake. "You knew that Will was an officer?"

Jake talked to Marcus. "Victor and the others knew it too. They were keeping him in the know just enough to not have him get suspicious."

Ben continued, "Will was the one who had gathered all the information for them to catch this leader." He looked at Marcus. "I read the reports, and they say this kid went around calling himself Smart Boy and that he was building a following of men to take over the government. He had taught them the nest language, and they were teaching it to Will. Marcus, I am sorry, but the man he was reporting on was Travis. And that is who they have arrested along with many of the other men. They were not going along with the Knowing way. They had guns, and they really did have plans to do harm. Marcus, they are giving the Knowing a bad name. They need to be stopped."

On the inside, Marcus was screaming, *Tell them it was me, that I am the real leader, that I am Smart Boy, that I am the one who really did all of this! That way Travis could get another chance. What have I gotten*

Travis into? How will I get him out of it? On the outside, he looked as calm as he ever had.

Ben, not knowing Marcus thought he had done such a good job presenting this story and that Marcus understood, went on to the rest of the news. "Now here is where it is going to mess with the rest of us. There is going to be a news event released tomorrow morning telling about the arrest and about how Smart Boy was taken out with his whole gang. Then there is a follow-up story about how we, the Singletons, have taken in and rehabilitated Smart Boy's brother, Marcus. So we have to decide how we are going to handle it."

This was great. This was going to be Marcus's way out of this house. "I think that the best thing for me to do is to get away from the rest of you as soon as possible. Perhaps to a farm. That way when the news reports start coming in, you will all be free of me."

Robert was speaking in a firm voice, "I think that the best thing for you to do is to realize that God put you into this family and that this family does not ever let a member go it alone." The others agreed.

Marcus wanted to scream. What was wrong with these people? "So do you think we should tell them that I am really Smart Boy? That way Travis would not take such a big hit, and they might go easier on him?"

Ben looked at the others. "Marcus is really Smart Boy?" He had a very big smile on his face at the thought. They all confirmed it was true. "Well, welcome to the family. I can hardly wait to know you better." Ben was honestly happy about it.

Brother Marcus saw Marcus's calm reaction and heard his question. There was going to be trouble with Marcus; he wanted to save Travis, and he would make a plan to do it. Jake and Mark had picked up on it too.

Robert was the one to answer Marcus's question. "I think that your brother, Travis, has made his own bed. I think that God might be using it to give you a new start as a Singleton without a record or charges. I think you should be grateful at the chance given you."

Marcus had pulled the sleeve of his coat down over his hand several times, and Nancy noticed. Once when she had seen him do it, she looked at Jake, who was looking guilty about something. She would address that later, but for now, Marcus needed rescuing from the family and their opinions. He needed time to think about all that had happened. He needed his God time, as he had called it once when he was talking with her about devotions. "Marcus, why don't you go to your room and read some before dinner? We have some boring family things to go over. Okay?"

Marcus was so grateful. He could have kissed Nancy for the chance to get away without looking like a coward. "It was nice to meet you, Ben. Thank you for the information." He was so polite. Too polite as far as Jake, Mark, and Brother Marcus were concerned. He was up to something, and they knew it. He got up and was getting ready to leave the room. He turned to Nancy. "Mom, if you need any help with dinner, just call me."

Nancy knew that he had not realized that he had called her *Mom*, but it felt good to hear he was connecting with her. "Marcus, I think it might be a better idea if you take the ice out of your pocket and put it back on your hand, it will help with the swelling and the bruising."

Marcus shot a look at Jake. How could she know? Jake was never alone with her for him to tell her. "Don't look at Jake, he did not tell me, you did. Now go on with you and do as I said with your hand." Marcus gave Jake one last look and did as he was told.

They all watched as he left the room. Mark went to the hall to make sure he was going to his room. When Marcus shut the door, they all tried to talk at the same time.

Jake was the one addressed most, so he went first. He told them about what had happened to Marcus at the barbershop and at the market. They all sat silent for a while, then Sally shook her head. "Can't this kid catch a single break?"

Robert interrupted, "Marcus has a good break in that he has God and that God has put all of us in his life."

Brother Marcus stood up to pace. "Did anyone else get the fact that Marcus is blaming himself for this trouble. And that he is going to try and save his brother, Travis, out of this mess he got himself into?"

They all confirmed that what he was saying was true. They did not know what to do with the knowledge they had. This kid was so good at the street life, how on earth could they stop him? So they prayed, and they reconfirmed the plan to never leave him alone away from the house. They would keep an eye on all the kinds of books he was reading, and they would check his room daily for any written plans he might have made. They talked about putting his chip on a short locking chain so he could not take it off, but he had been wearing it, and that seemed too extreme of a move. They would limit access to the phones and keep him away from the computer unless someone was right with him. They told Ben about the habit he had of rubbing his head when he tried to lie. It was almost funny that he was so clever about so many other things, but when it came to himself, he gave away information by his actions.

Ben was having trouble believing that his family thought that it would take all seven of them to keep this kid from doing something stupid. On top of that, they were still not sure they could do it. "I can't imagine that Marcus is really as good as you think he is at street life."

Sally patted her big brother on the back. "You will see, just hang around some, and you will see."

The family had dinner without Marcus. When they went up to get him for dinner, he was fast asleep, and they could not wake him up. Or so they thought.

Marcus had to get to work fast if he was going to save his brother. He did wish he could include the Singletons in his plans, but if things went bad, he did not want them to go down with him. It would look to the world like their family had done everything for Marcus and that he had been ungrateful and had gone astray.

Marcus needed God time. He needed to sit before God and get guidance for his planning. He thought he had heard from God before and that God wanted Marcus to wait and to trust Him, but things were looking so bad that he was sure that God would want him to do something about helping Travis. He was his brother after all. "God, help me to do what is right. Help me to help my brother and the people I now call family. Don't let them get hurt because of me. I love You, Lord, I thank You, God."

Marcus got out paper and started to lay out his battle plan for the next week or so. He needed to get the yard finished. Mark and

Brother Marcus were right. There were hideouts in the yard now as well as storage places and supplies. Some of the window screens were already on springs, so they could be pulled out, and he could slide in and out without being noticed. More of those needed to be added. Marcus had moved things around in the closets and cabinets so someone could hide in them if need be without any problem at all. He had left a note at the barbershop for a contact from the Knowing to get a hold of him for information even before he had found out about Travis getting arrested. He needed a reason to go to town daily. He needed to go to school. That would work.

Marcus went downstairs really late to go out back but was surprised to find that the whole family was all still here. "Oh, I am sorry, I did not know you all were still up. I needed to get a book."

Nancy motioned for Marcus to come on into the room. "Jake told us about your market experience. Let me see your hand."

Marcus did not move. He did not want to look weak in front of his brothers.

"Oh, stop it and come over here. They have all had me look at their wounds at one time or another. Haven't you?" They all looked at him with sympathy because they knew that he was going to lose the battle, and she was going to see the injury and decide what needed to happen about taking care of it. "Take off your coat. I do not think you will need it to get a book, now, do you?" She handed it off to Jake, and he took it out of the room.

Marcus could not look at her. He had lied and felt bad because of it, not even realizing that he had been caught. He rubbed his head with his right hand, and she was going over the left hand with her thumb. He pulled back at one place she pushed on. She did not let go but continued to examine it. "I think we may need to go to town in the morning and have a doctor look at this."

Going to town was exactly what he needed to have happen. Going to the doctor was exactly what he needed not to happen. "I was thinking more along the lines of starting school."

She looked at him and the faces he was making as she moved the fingers. It looked like it could be broken to her. But an X-ray would tell it all. "Does it hurt? I could give you something for the pain?" What she needed him to do was to think about the now and not be planning tomorrow just yet.

"What?" He looked at her confused. He had an agenda, and she was not going along with it at all. "No, it is fine. I need to know if I can start school tomorrow or soon anyway."

"No, you are not fine, and no, you cannot start school until this thing with your brother is cleared up. Now do you want aspirin or Tylenol, or should I decide for you?"

The family was having fun watching the master mom work with the street master Marcus, who was about to lose the battle. Boy, was she good, and was he going to be surprised when she won the battle.

Marcus was confused at what had happened. He did not accomplish a single thing he had planned. Nancy had walked out of the room in order to get him something for the pain he told her he did not have. "Jake, can I please have my coat?"

Their mom called out from the kitchen. "And you can forget about getting your coat back, you will not need it until we go to the doctor in the morning. May I suggest you have a seat, and I will be back with the aspirin and some ice for your hand?"

Marcus looked at Jake. He shrugged his shoulders. "If I were you, I would do as she says. It is not good to push it past where you are at right now."

Mark chimed in, "And Jake here would know all about that for sure. He always pushed Mom to the end. And remember, Mom always wins." They all laughed. "Remember the time she took all of Jake's pants and locked them away so he could not leave the house?" They all had a laugh remembering it.

Marcus did not find any of this funny. He needed some space so he could figure out what he was going to do in order to help his brother, Travis. Nancy had come back exactly like she had said. She had ice, water, aspirin, and a pillow to prop his arm up with. She wanted to fuss, and he did not want her to. Marcus put his right hand up to protest, and she locked her left-hand fingers into his right-hand fingers and held on. Then with her right hand, she placed the pillow on his lap, put his left arm on it, and placed the ice on too. She held it in place putting only enough pressure on it that it would hurt only if he tried to move it away. Then she let go of his right hand and handed him the water. She took two of the pills she had already taken out of the bottle. "Open your mouth and take these." He did not comply with her order; he was getting angry. She on the other hand was not. "Marcus, open your mouth and take these, or I will get the boys to help."

Marcus looked over at the others who were shocked that anyone would defy their mom. Then he looked at Robert, who had gone back to reading the papers he had been looking at. There would be no help from any of them. He had met his match. He opened his mouth and took the pills in; he put the water glass to his mouth and began to drink. She did the same trick as before with the juice, holding the glass up to his mouth, making him drink until it was all gone. "Now that will feel better. And I know you will sleep better too. Stay here at least fifteen minutes, and then you can go to bed if you would like. We will go early in the morning, less traffic." She left the room without any gloating. She won because she had to, for his own good. When she got to the kitchen, she stopped and prayed. *Dear God. What am I going to do with this kid? It is a fine line to take care of him and to not break him or make him angry. Help me to keep him safe from himself. God, if it is Your will, let his hand be broken so it can slow him down. Could it be an anchor? I praise You for whatever it is you are going to be doing in our lives, help us keep our eyes on You. Amen.* She went about doing her work and closing down the house for the night. She was closing the curtain when she thought she saw someone in the backyard.

She went to the living room to make sure that they all knew that Marcus was out back; when she entered the living room, she saw that he was sitting right where she had left him. The look on her face told them that something was wrong.

Jake was on his feet. "Mom, what is wrong?"

She looked around to count heads. "Well, I thought that I saw someone in the backyard sneaking around."

Brother Marcus and his dad went to check out the yard. Ben went to do a once-over of the inside of the house. The others stayed in the room together, with Jake having been told by his dad to watch out for them.

It took Marcus a time to figure out what was going on. Did he need to tell them that he had asked someone from the Knowing to meet him? It could have been them, or it could be someone else altogether.

Dad and Marcus came back into the house having checked things out good.

Ben was close behind them confirming that everything was good inside.

Marcus was as interested in what they had found out as any of them had been.

Nancy went to her husband. "Did you find anything?"

"No, nothing, but we need to keep an eye out anyway." Robert hugged his wife.

Sally brought up the fact that the media might have wanted an interview with the family before the breaking news tomorrow morning.

Marcus was sitting holding his head again. He was quiet, and he had not shared an idea as to who it might have been. Robert addressed him, "Marcus, would you like to share who you think it might have been?"

He was on the spot. "I kind of left a message for the Knowing to contact me. I am sorry, I did not mean to cause trouble I just needed some information." How much more was this family going to take before they tossed him out of their house? He had now caused them to fear.

Brother Marcus went to Marcus's side. "What information?"

Marcus looked up at him.

"Your heard me. What information do you need?"

Marcus guessed that he needed to trust them. He had no other choice. "I need to know where they are keeping my brother and if he is all right. I need to know if my boys are really all right, or is it just a lie to keep me away from them so they can get information from them? I need to know if there really is a second group of the Knowing, or is ours changing? I need to know where I fit into all of this, or did I blow it and I am out of the group?" There it was in a nutshell.

The Singletons owed Marcus an apology. They had the information he was asking for and should have not only guessed he needed to know it but should have shared it with him. They looked at each other and decided that Mark would speak to the situation. "Marcus, we are sorry. We should have guessed that you would need to know the answers to these questions." They spent the next thirty minutes or so telling him anything they knew about his questions.

Nancy was right; his hand did feel better, and now with the truth out and his questions answered, he was as relaxed as he had been in a long time. The family was talking about ideas for keeping the media away when they realized that Marcus was not in on the discussion. He was asleep. Nancy and Sally pulled up the footstool and placed his legs on it. Nancy put another pillow under his arm to raise his hand even more. She took the ice off and looked at it again. Ben took the opportunity to check it out too. "Ouch, that looks awful." The bruising had become worse and the swelling as well. "Mom, that hand has to really hurt, this is one tough kid."

Jake saw what was going on and came to look also. "Ouch, that hand does look bad. But, Ben, if you think this is something, you should have seen this kid work with broken ribs. It was unreal." They walked out of the room with Jake telling Ben all of the things that had happened to Marcus in the last few months, including pneumonia.

Sally and her mom had a laugh. "Men."

CHAPTER 38

The next morning came fast for everyone. They had all stayed up way too late for a workday. Jake had spent the night in Mark's room, and Ben slept in Jake's old room because Marcus was in the chair downstairs.

Marcus woke up later than everyone else and was embarrassed because he had fallen asleep and because he slept in too. Ben was at the table having coffee. Marcus sat down beside him wishing his hand would be feeling better than it did. He saw that it looked worse, so he hid it in the sleeve of his shirt. "You do not need to hide it. Mom already saw it and called the doctor's office. You have an appointment before lunch." He watched as Marcus took in the news. He wondered which was worse, his hand or the fact that his mom was going to win again?

"Where is everyone?" Marcus had not seen anyone except Ben since he got up.

"Mom is upstairs getting ready, and everyone else has gone to work." Ben smiled. "I guess you could say that I have the Marcus watch."

"I do not need anyone to watch over me." Marcus was irritated that anyone would even think that way.

"Yes, you do." Ben's eyes darted up. "I saw the escape plans for this house. I slept in your bed last night. I found your stash. It took me a long time to find them. You are very good, you know. I am impressed at the things you have been able to do without us even catching on to it."

Marcus loved the compliment but hated that he had been snooped on. This family had the knack of telling you something good and bad in such a way that you don't even see them coming. "So where did you put them? The plans, I mean?"

"Dad and Marcus—I mean, Brother Marcus took them with them to show someone they thought should see the kind of work you do."

Marcus moved and hit his hand. It sent a sharp pain up his arm and into his shoulder. He reacted silently to the pain. "I wish you all would stay out of my business."

"We are family, which makes you our business." Ben went back to reading his paperwork.

Marcus sat at the table trying to figure out how he was going to get his hand working better sooner and not later. This being a wimp was getting old. He needed to figure out why God would keep him weak, when he really needed to be strong. He was thinking so hard that he had not heard Nancy come into the room.

She had made him some toast for breakfast and put coffee and juice in front of him. "Eat something, and then I will give you some more aspirin for the pain."

"My hand is better today. I will not need the aspirin." Marcus picked up a piece of toast.

Ben looked over his paperwork at Marcus, who was not aware of his incoming mom.

Nancy gently took hold of Marcus's chin and put her face into his. "Now let's be clear about something." She was speaking softly but very deliberately. "We are not going to do this anymore. You do not lie or keep things from family. Do you comprehend? We are family. We give help, and we take help in return." She let go and took a step back. "Now, does your hand still hurt?"

"Yes."

"Does it hurt today more or worse than yesterday?" She was watching every move he made.

Marcus hesitated, then started to lie, and thought better of it. "More. But—"

Nancy put her hand up to stop any addition to the *but*. "That is enough information. "Now eat so we can go."

To Marcus's relief, Ben had not laughed but acted like he had not seen what had happened. He wondered if Travis would have had a mom like this if he would have turned out different. He would never know. If there was only a way he could trade places with Travis.

They went to the doctor; he had taken an X-ray of the hand and found that it was broken, but it was still in place, so it did not have to be reset. They could not put a permanent cast on it because of the swelling. It would take time and patience first for the swelling to go down so he could get the permanent one, and then more time for it to heal.

Nancy felt bad for Marcus but still thought that it might be God's way of slowing him down so that they could keep up with him.

When they got home, the family were all there, again. It was hard to keep things from one Singleton, but when you come up against seven, it is impossible. They all wanted an account of what the doctor had said. They were discussing that the pain pills that they gave him said that he could take one or two pills for the pain. They were trying to decide which.

Marcus went to Nancy. "Could I please have two aspirin and go lie down for a while? I am not sure why I am so tired, but I think it will help me feel better."

Ben joined his mom and Marcus by the sink. Marcus was taking his coat off, and when Ben tried to help him, he pulled away and did it himself. "The pain will wear you out, especially when you don't admit you have pain and still try to do everything yourself."

Marcus was tired and needed everyone to go away and let him think. He appreciated that they thought they were doing him a favor, but he had done good for a lot of years by himself.

Sally carried over the pain pills and suggested he might find them more effective than the aspirin.

Marcus was done with family help. "Aspirin, please."

Nancy saw that Marcus needed to be the boss of something right now, so although she agreed with Sally, she let Marcus make the decision about what he was going to take. "Marcus, you can take aspirin for now, but if your hand is not feeling better in one hour, then you agree to take the pain pills, promise?"

Would he ever get the last word again if he was in this family? He breathed deeply. "Yes, if it is not feeling better." He took the aspirin and went to go upstairs, but Sally and Mark headed him off and made him go and sit in the chair he had slept in the night before. They could keep a better watch over him, and he could keep his hand up easier in the chair. He had no war left in him, so he did what they wanted.

Sally and Mark had reentered the kitchen. The family was talking very quietly about what had happened while their mom and Marcus were at the doctor's.

*****

The reports of Travis and of the Singletons had hit the news. They were on every TV and radio station. They had taken the phones off the hook to stop all of the calls.

Nancy looked to Sally. "Is he okay?"

"Yes, he is, but I wish he had taken the pain pills. I am afraid he is going to wake up and find out what is going on."

"Find what out?" Marcus was standing right behind Sally. "I forgot to tell Ben something about the paperwork I had put together, so I came to tell him, but what is going on that you are afraid I am going to find out about?"

They stood there for the longest time looking at each other and then back at Marcus. Jake decided Marcus needed to know. "Travis broke out of jail and has a warrant out for his arrest. They say that he is armed and dangerous, and they have a shoot-to-kill order out on him."

Marcus kept his very cool manner. "When?"

Jake used the same tone to speak to Marcus. "The report said that he escaped yesterday afternoon. But we got the report on it about an hour ago."

Marcus did not move but kept looking at the ground. No one else moved either, but it was a sure thing that every one of them was praying. This was a turning point for Marcus; he could go either way. He had always chosen the right way, and it seemed that he always got hurt by doing it. He used to have the boys to give him a reason to always do the right thing, but this time it was between him and God. The only reason to stay good was because of his relationship with God. They had not known Marcus long enough to say what way he would go, but they did have prayer.

Marcus was already upset because they had gone behind his back and kept the news about Travis from him. He was used to being treated this way by the chipped society, but now it was happening by his chipped, Knowing family too. "So is this the part where you tell me you did not tell me because I am a kid, or how about because you care about me so much that you would not tell me about my only brother being hunted down by your friends, or how about the one where you think I am so weak that I will make a bad choice and go with Travis?" Marcus's head shot up with the awareness of last night. "Oh no, what if it was Travis in the backyard last night? He may have come to me to get help. Maybe he feels bad about what he has done and wants to come back to the Knowing. Oh no, he came to me for help, and what did I do? I went to sleep in the chair." He needed to think. He began to pace. If anyone tried to speak to him, he would get angry and put up a hand and tell them to be quiet and that he needed to think. "Where would he go? I need to think. Where would he go?" Marcus froze. He knew exactly where to look for him. And he was definitely not going to tell the Singletons.

Jake went to Marcus's side but did not dare to touch him. "Marcus, let us help you."

Marcus turned and walked away. He needed his coat, and he needed to get out of here. He would only need a quick distraction to get past them, and then he could outrun them, even with his bad hand. Forget the coat. He could steal one when he got away. Guilt hit him. He almost lost his breath when he realized exactly what he was thinking. *God, what is wrong with me? I do not want to be an angry person. I need time, I need space. Oh, dear God, I need You. Help me make the right decision.*

The family was not sure exactly what had happened, but they saw the fight go completely out of Marcus. Marcus put his hands up on the wall with his head against them, forgetting all about his bad hand. "Help me to help my brother, Travis, please?" His voice was muffled, but it was clear he needed and wanted their help.

They all knew that this could be a trap for Marcus with Travis as bait. But he had asked for their help, and they all wanted to give it. Jake seemed to be the one that Marcus listened to the most, so for now he began to tell Marcus what else had happened since they had been given the report. "Ben has been working on where the report had come from. I found it in my inbox at work. Sally has instructions to change the shoot-to-kill order, but we need to leave the 'armed and dangerous' so he cannot hurt someone else, they need to be on guard. You do understand that, right?"

Marcus had put his arms down and stepped back from the wall but kept his eyes on it. He did not speak but slowly nodded his head yes. His hand had hit the side of his leg, and he pulled it into himself trying to stop the throbbing pain. "Can I please go outside and be alone for a while?"

Panic was a mild word to describe how the family was feeling right now. They thought that Marcus was okay with them helping him, but he was so good at his street skills that they were not sure.

Nancy needed to talk to Marcus. He knew her to be a direct person, so she felt she could pull rank on him a little and that it would work. "Marcus, you can be alone, but you can do it in your room. Not outside. The newspeople are everywhere, and we do not want them thinking you are Travis, now do we?"

Marcus shook his head that he understood. He took his coat and went to go up the stairs.

Nancy tapped his arm to stop him. "First, promise me you will not leave this house, and then you can go."

He did not look at her. "I promise not to leave this place. Okay?" And he went upstairs to be alone. They again looked to see that he did in fact go into his room.

"Mom, Dad, what are we doing? Travis looks like a bad seed. Are you sure that you want to risk Marcus to save him?" Ben was trying to be gentle with the question, but it needed to be asked.

Jake stood looking up the stairs. Something was not right. Marcus took his coat. Then he said it out loud. "Marcus took his coat." He ran up the stairs and tore into Marcus's now-empty bedroom. The only thing they could find missing other than Marcus was his Bible. They looked, and on his bed was his chain and his chip.

They had all run into Marcus's room. Ben, Jake, and Mark were ready to hit the streets and bring Marcus back.

Their mom was the one to call a halt to the hunt. "Everyone, wait a minute. What did Marcus say when he promised that he would not leave?"

Jake was mad at Marcus for lying. "Mom, what does it matter? He lied."

"No, Jake, he did not rub his head." They both remembered at the same time. "'I promise not to leave this place.'"

"He did not say *house* but *place*." Nancy was going over to look out the window. "Sally, will you please turn off all the houselights?" Sally went from room to room turning out the lights.

Robert and Nancy stood looking out the window to see if they would find Marcus. Nancy squeezed her husband's arm and pointed to the top of a tree. "Look, I told you, there he is. Just like he had said, he did not leave this place." The boys and Sally looked out the window, and there he was almost to the top of the biggest tree in the yard.

"Okay, so who is going to go and get him?" Jake was the one asking. "We all know I can't catch him. I have proven that already."

"Jake, do you remember the old saying that if you let it go and it comes back, it is yours, and if not, then—"

"Yes, yes, yes, Mom, I get it." Jake hated waiting. "Okay, we wait until he comes back, and then what?"

His mom patted him on the back. Then she gave him a great big hug. "Then we will see."

*****

It was almost two hours later when Marcus decided he could return to the house. They would never have to know he had left, so they would not be mad at him for leaving. He really did keep his promise though; he never left their place. He simply needed some God time. He got down out of the tree and hurried across the yard. He went up the side of the house, with only one hand. So far things had gone good. He pulled the screen that was on a spring that he had put into place and slipped in through the window into the dark. There was only one thing he did not count on, and that was that the screen would pull back tight and catch his bad hand. The pain brought him to his knees, and he sat in the dark holding his arm hoping to stop the pain. It was not working. He spoke out loud, "God, I really need Your help right now. Please."

A light came on in the room. Marcus was shocked to say the least to find the whole family sitting in his room waiting for him to return. He could hardly believe his eyes. They did not make a move nor did he.

"I really do think God wants me to work the streets. I work for God, and you can't stop me." Marcus was trying to explain his not staying in the house.

Robert led the conversation. "You are right that we can't stop you, especially if you work for God, but the truth is that even if we can't stop you, we can help you."

Marcus was silent.

"And if we do work together, then we need to have rules that we all follow. When we are in the chipped world, you follow and do what we say. In return, when we are in your world, we will follow you and you get to be in charge. Deal?"

Adult partners had always been hard to work with, even one-on-one, but to work with seven of them, and them all being Singletons?

They had to wait for Marcus on this one. He needed to decide and not to be persuaded to be a team. "What kind of rules?"

"Nope, either you are in all the way or you are out." Robert knew that he was making his side of the deal tough, but he could not let a fifteen-year-old, no matter how smart, run the show. They were still the adults and did know what was best.

"Okay, it is a deal. Could I please have one of the pain pills?" Marcus was done with being the boss right now. Maybe tomorrow he would feel different, but he believed that even tomorrow he would love not having to make all of the decisions.

Nancy spoke up; they might as well test the deal. "I think you should take two. It looks to me like you are hurting pretty bad."

Marcus gave her a half smile and looked her in the eye for the first time this evening. "Yes, two, and some ice too, please."

Brother Marcus had his chain and chip. He slipped it over Marcus's head and placed it inside his shirt. "And this does not come off again, understand?" Before Marcus could speak, he added, "And to let you know what will happen if you do take it off, there would be a shorter chain, and it would lock on. Understand?"

The new partnership went well from that night on. Marcus taught the Singletons about the street life. They thought they had known a lot until he began teaching them, and they now realized better how much work Marcus had done to keep all those boys safe.

In turn, Marcus kept the house rules. He did not fight too many things, and he was as happy as he was going to be with his brother still in trouble. They had not heard from or about Travis since he had run away. It had been almost three weeks. And not a single word about him in either world. The swelling in Marcus's hand had gone down, and other than the hard cast and some bruising across the top of his hand, there was little sign of his being hurt.

It was family night at the Singletons. Even Ben would be there. They all talked about everything. He would ask questions, and they gave him true answers; and in return, when they asked him, he would tell them the truth, when they asked him. There were some things a street leader had to keep to himself; if they had asked him, he would have told them straight out, but they had never thought to ask, so some issues did not come up.

They were all at the dinner table waiting for Dad to say grace. When he had finished, they all dived into the food. It looked great. Marcus reached for the potatoes. "I know that you have something you need to tell me, so how bad is it?"

Their little brother had started to know them better. He had a new edge on them; he could read their body language even when they were trying their hardest not to give it away. Mark liked the game. "So how long have you known we had news for you?"

Marcus and the family would play the game of reading each other. It was good practice for everyone. "Sally gave it away. She asked me if I had talked to anyone today." He smiled. "And Ben has something in his pocket to show me. He has double-checked it three times by patting his pocket since he has been here."

Ben reached to get the papers. Marcus laughed and told him to look in his side pocket. Marcus had lifted them and put them back in a different pocket altogether.

Ben pulled them out. "Did you have a chance to read them?"

"No." Marcus looked at Nancy. "That would be against the house rules."

It had been a tough three weeks. Each side of the leadership had to learn what was and what was not going to work in this relationship. Marcus taught them street etiquette, and they gave him house rules as each problem came up. He had snuck a paper out of Nancy's sweater and read it and put it back; when he told her about what he had done, that became another house rule. No lifting and reading other people's papers. The house rules were odd, exclusive to only this family. It was odd, but it was working for them.

Ben got a kick out of the way rules worked around here. "Okay, so I get it, it is okay for you to pick our pockets as long as you put it back and don't read it."

Marcus looked at Nancy and then back at Ben; both Nancy and Marcus were nodding their heads yes.

"Ben, the paper that you have, may I see it?" Marcus did not want to look too anxious, but this was family, and he cared less and less each day how he looked to them. He could be himself, and it was nice. Ben passed the paperwork over to Marcus. He unfolded it and read the report. "Okay, they have caught Travis, is he okay?" The paperwork did not say anything about how he was or how they got him, just that they had.

Brother Marcus told Marcus what little they knew. "They say Travis is thin but that he is overall in good health. There may be some sort of plea bargain in the makings." He looked to Sally to fill in that part.

"Yes, there is some paperwork with a code on it and no name, asking for a special situation by the top brass. I am not sure, but it could be about Travis." She took a roll and offered one to Marcus.

Marcus did not react to her offer. A tell that he was processing the information he had received. Marcus picked up his glass of water and went to the kitchen with the pretense of getting some ice. This information was lacking at best, but it was only the second he had received in three weeks. Travis was okay—that was good.

The family conversation while he was away was different. Sally brought it up to Ben. "I think Marcus knew about Travis being caught."

Brother Marcus added, "He knew that we had Travis but not that he was okay or where he was. How does that happen?"

Ben thought, "Maybe he really did read the report."

Nancy shook her head no. "If Marcus said he did not read it, I am telling you he did not."

Marcus returned to the table. "Did any of you want ice? Sorry, I did not think to ask."

Jake watched Marcus as he spoke, "No, we do not want any ice, but we do want to know about how you knew that Travis was caught? You were not surprised?"

"You are right. I had heard about it, but I had not confirmed that Travis was caught." Marcus sat back down.

"Who told you? You did not leave the house, did you?" Ben was concerned about who Marcus would be hanging out with.

"No, I found a note in the backyard." Marcus was not defensive.

"Did you know who it was from?" Brother Marcus was acting like a full-out interrogator.

"No, but they do know where I live and that Travis is my brother. So I think it must be someone who knows me." He was quiet. He put his hand to his brow but stopped himself, not wanting to give away the fact there were more notes. He did not want to give the family more to worry about.

Sally added, "Maybe it is someone from the Knowing?"

Marcus was sure that was not true. "No, it is definitely not anyone from the Knowing."

Brother Marcus watched him closely. There was more than he was telling, and they all knew it. "Marcus, look at me. How do you know that it did not come from the Knowing?"

Nancy was done with all the officer talk. "Enough. I do not want another word about anything to do with notes. I want us to have a family dinner, and you all can talk about the other stuff another day. Besides, I have some good news."

They all sat down and dropped the subject of the notes. They were all looking at her to hear about the good news.

"We are going to have a birthday dinner. Can everyone make it on Friday of next week?" She was aware that they could not figure out whose birthday it was going to be. "Marcus is going to be sixteen on Friday, and I think we should take him to dinner out in town."

Marcus was notably flustered. "I do not think we should go out, couldn't we stay at home and cook outside?"

Nancy loved to go out with her family. She liked it when they all dressed up and went together. "No, for your sixteenth birthday, you should get to go out to dinner. Can everyone make it?"

They were all smiles. They made comments like they always forget he is only fifteen and that they could not wait to get him a gift.

Marcus was upset with the idea. He almost knocked his ice water over. "I do not really think that going out is a good idea. The reporters will be all over this."

Nancy placed a hand on Marcus's arm. "We are all going out to dinner on your birthday, and that is the end of it." She pulled rank. "Remember the house rules."

Marcus was more upset. "May I go to my room and get the note to show Ben?"

Robert came to Marcus's rescue this time. "Yes. Go and then come back to finish your dinner."

Marcus was grateful to get a little time to himself. He went to his room and sat on the bed giving his heartbeat time to slow down. He slid off the bed and turned and faced it. He got on his knees. He prayed, "Father, I am so tired of being afraid. I am not sure why I am the way I am, but if this life is the one You want me to have, then I guess I am going to do it, even if I have to do it afraid. But I cannot do it alone. I have tried, and I can't do it. So if You want me to do this, then please give me Your strength. My own strength is not enough, it never has been. Father, I thank You for the outcome, no matter what it is. I am going to believe that You are the one in control. I give my everyday life to You to use me the way You think best. Please help me to not get in Your way, but to be Your tool, use me the way You see best. I give up. Amen."

Marcus got up. He felt a new boldness come over him. He was still afraid to go to the restaurant, but a strange feeling that it was going to be okay had replaced his panic. "Thank You, God." He smiled all the way down the stairs.

At the table, the family was confused as to what had happened. Jake could not stand not knowing. "So what is up with Marcus not wanting to go out to dinner? What is the big deal?"

Robert told them, "It has been three years since Marcus has been out to dinner. It was the night of his thirteenth birthday dinner that his parents were arrested and chipped. It has been three years of him taking care of himself and the other kids."

Jake saw the problem. "So let's stay at home and have his birthday here."

Nancy took Robert's hand. "I know that it would be more comfortable for Marcus to stay here in this house with all of us, but as his new family, I think it would be better if we take him and show him what a good life can be like. Let's help his face his bad memories so he can grow up and have a full life."

Mark needed to say something. "On that note, I think we need to be careful not to overdo the gift-giving to Marcus on his birthday. Our first thought is to give him everything he has missed out on, but I think it could overwhelm him a lot."

"Oh, Mark, you are such a shrink." Jake did not like shrinks; they made him nervous, and to think his brother had become one was more than he could handle. "Oh, that is right, you are still in school. Does that make you preshrink?"

Marcus came back into the room carrying the paper note. He sat down by his dinner plate and placed the paper in his pocket to share with Ben later. He began to eat and did not want to think about his birthday anymore, but doing it afraid was better than living in fear. "What time?" He was looking at Nancy.

She smiled at him. She did not know exactly how she knew, but she could see that Marcus had some God time. He was prayed up. "Would six thirty on Friday work for everyone? Let's all meet here." She placed her hand on Marcus's arm and squeezed it.

Marcus loved that she was so good at knowing what to do to reassure him; he did not look up for a long time, he was still building his courage. It was good that he still had a few days to prepare for the thought of this outing.

Marcus kept the fact that there were other notes to himself. Having one note kept them busy the rest of the evening.

Marcus was helping with the dishes, and he thought he was alone in the kitchen. He turned and was startled to see that Ben was on a stool watching him work. "What are you doing, did you need something?"

Ben did not change his look at all but simply asked a question, "So what did the other notes say?"

The question caught Marcus off guard. He had not told them there was another note. How did he know? Maybe he was guessing, or did he find them? "What other notes?"

"The ones you are not talking about." Ben had not changed a single expression on his face or in his body language. "Are they really that bad, or are you just letting them beat you up in your mind?"

Marcus looked back at the sink, not wanting to make eye contact with Ben. "They think I am a traitor." There it was, out in the open.

Ben did not react but sat perfectly still. "Who thinks you are a traitor?"

"It is some of the people from the Knowing. I know it looks bad, like I sold out, but they should know me. I was a leader for a long time. Why don't they know that I would never give up the Knowing?" Marcus continued to dry the dishes.

"I will never understand people myself. Just remember that your true friends will never need an explanation, and the people who demand an explanation will never believe you anyway, so don't even bother trying. All I can say is that you need to know in your heart what is right and do the best you can to follow through on it. When in doubt, ask God, and He will show you, but I guess you already knew that, right?"

Marcus turned around and looked at Ben. He was smiling a big confident smile. He had persuaded Marcus to not only admit there were other notes but to tell him what was on them and then help talk through them. These people were good.

"So do I get to see the other notes?"

Marcus put down the towel. "Sure, let me go and get them." He passed Brother Marcus, who was going into the kitchen as he was leaving.

Brother Marcus went over to Ben. "So did he tell you about the other notes?"

Marcus stopped in the hall. He had overheard their conversation. "God, these people are good. I wonder if I have a single secret that they don't know about." He smiled. It was comforting to know that they cared about him even if it was hard to have people in his business; it was nice at the same time.

When he showed them the notes, they were angry, mean, and ugly; but somehow they did not seem as bad as they had been once he had shared them with the others. He had been torturing himself over them for days now, and they were really no big deal.

Friday had come. Everything was a big deal from the time Marcus got up; there was a special breakfast, all of his favorite foods. Nancy and Robert had given him a birthday card that told him they were glad he had joined the family. That was one of the best gifts he had ever received from anyone. He was a part of a family again. Nancy had brought him his lunch outside while he was working on a new yard project. She had raved about how great the yard was look-ing and thanked him more than once. That was a second best gift.

The day had passed so fast that Marcus had not noticed that it was time for him to be getting ready to go out to dinner. He was dig-ging one last hole when he looked up and saw Sally standing there. "Wow, do you ever look nice." She was all dressed up in a beautiful blue dress that made her look, well, not like a sister.

As they were talking about the yard, he realized that she was dressed up—and here at the house. "What time is it?" Panic hit him. It was 6:00 p.m. He had only thirty minutes. He could do it; he did not want to be late for his own birthday dinner.

He jumped out of the hole he was digging and ran full out into the house. He slid across the floor of the kitchen, ran up the hall to the outside of the stairs. He did not take any time to go up the stairs. He ran to the wall. One foot on the stool, one on the outside landing and flew over the railing and into his room. He did not see that his brothers had arrived and that they were watching him acting like a cat. He found that new clothing had been set out for him; it was a nice dress suit. "Thank you, Mom." He jumped into the shower and quickly got dressed in the bathroom, ran back to his room, and found that there had been an invasion of brothers. All four brothers were in his room waiting for him to come back and finish dressing. They made a big deal, teasing him about how good he looked when he was cleaned up.

Jake was excited to see that Marcus was not bothered by the fact that they were going out to dinner anymore. In fact, he looked com-fortable about the whole thing. "We have a birthday gift for you." They were all smiling. Jake motioned for Mark to give it to Marcus. "We thought that this might help tonight." Mark handed Marcus a folded-up piece of paper.

As Marcus unfolded it, he could not believe his eyes. It was a layout of the restaurant they were going to. It was complete. The exits were noted, and all of the tables were shown. They had made reservations for a special table so that they would be back away from the main door where their backs would be to a wall. At the bot-tom of the page, there was a small map showing the streets and the surrounding buildings. They even had an emergency meeting place marked in case they would need it.

"This took a lot of work, thank you." Marcus was overwhelmed. "It is a great birthday gift. Thank you." He took time to go over everything on the map with them. It was perfect. "You know, you all make great street people. You are all very good at this." He was so happy to be in this family. He refolded the paper and placed it into his coat pocket. "Thank you. It is really nice."

They were all smiling at the compliment that had come from Marcus. For him, the street master, to think they did well was a gift to them. They were all having a great time and went downstairs.

Their mom and dad as well as Sally were waiting for them. Sally looked at all of her brothers. "Why does it scare me to think all of you were together upstairs?" She was teasing them. "Mom, Dad, be afraid, I think they are up to something."

Robert stood up. "Okay, let's go. Jake, will you drive one car? I'll drive the other." They all headed out the door.

Marcus stopped. "Go on ahead, I will be right there." He ran up the stairs; using the stairs this time, he knew that they would be watching him. He ran into his room and shut the door. He got down on his knees. He spoke out loud, "God, thank You. I would love to have a better way to say it, but thank You." It might have seemed dumb to take the time right now to talk to God, but he had to do it.

He thought they would all be in the cars waiting for him, but when he got up and turned around, they had been concerned about him and followed him to the room. They thought that they would find a boy who was upset, but what they found was a man of God on his knees. Robert took Marcus's lead. "I think Marcus has a good idea." So they all gave a prayer of thanks.

*****

The dinner was great. They all laughed and had great fun. The map to the restaurant was exactly what Marcus needed to be comfortable. Coming from the world he had been in the last few years, the map was a perfect gift.

They were eating and having a good time when a family who knew the Singletons came in and were going to be at a table right beside theirs.

Robert stood up and shook hands with the man. All of both families greeted each other as well. The man from the other family, obviously the dad, went to introduce a young girl to the Singletons. "Hi, this is our new daughter, Rachel." She was being polite, but they could all see that she was uncomfortable being here. She was not looking up at the people at first, but they all noticed that her head locked into place, and her eyes showed shock when she saw Marcus sitting at the table. "Marcus." She had recovered quickly. "It is nice to meet all of you."

Jake watched as Marcus and Rachel switched over to nest talk. He was fascinated at how fast they could exchange information.

"Chipped."

"Me too."

"Not my choice."

"Me too."

Rachel asked, "Are we safe?"

"Yes, my family is good. And what about yours?"

"Not sure yet."

"Think so."

"How—" They were interrupted. The family went to take a seat.

Marcus let some time pass before he excused himself from the table and went to the restroom to wash up, he said. The family watched him as he passed the table where Rachel was sitting. He had bumped into the back of her chair as he passed, but they saw no action between the two of them. Marcus had returned another way around the tables. He was trying to look normal, but they could tell he was on guard now. It was only a few minutes when they noticed that Rachel was unfolding a piece of paper. It was their map they had given to Marcus; he had passed it to her. But how had he passed it? They were all watching him the whole time. These two were good. They did not see the handoff, and they were all looking.

Rachel looked at the paper and smiled. It was perfect. She thanked him in nest. And he answered her that he needed it back because it was a gift. She sent him a question in nest. "A gift? Who from?"

"My brothers made it for my birthday," Marcus was proud to tell her this.

"Travis?" Rachel sat up straight and looked around like she was looking for someone.

Marcus did not know how to answer. He froze. He loved Travis, but these men here, with him now, were his true brothers. They cared about him and help take care of him. How do you explain this, how can you? But in God's world, it just works.

Marcus did not have to answer. Jake put his hand on Marcus's shoulder and signed to Rachel in nest, "No, his Singleton brothers."

Rachel was concerned to see that Jake had been reading their conversation all along. But she guessed that if Marcus was okay with them, then she could be too.

They all went back to their family dinners. Rachel and Marcus were stealing a look at each other from time to time. Marcus's family kept smiling at him. This was really irritating having them in his business. He guessed that there would be conversation about all this later.

Marcus looked up and saw that Rachel was on alert. She had fear on her face. He looked the direction she was looking and saw what she was looking at. He froze too.

Jake saw the reaction between the two of them and also looked at the door. There were three men dressed in black suits. All of them had badges hanging from their belts. They were talking to the manager, and he was acting like he had no idea what they were talking about. They were pointing all around the room, but Marcus could see that Rachel was going to panic and thought they were going to come after her. If she panicked and ran out of the restaurant, she would bring unwanted attention to his new family. He needed to do something. Marcus was signaling for her to calm down. That it was safe. He told her that his family would take care of them. But she panicked and stood up, getting ready to run. Marcus in turn stood up and went to where she was at. He took her by the hand, and the two of them casually walked out of the main room and back into the hall. Thank God, Marcus had seen the map. There was a storage closet right down the hall before the bathroom doors.

Robert and Ben saw what happened and were confused but decided to follow Marcus and Rachel out of the room. Robert gave Nancy a reassuring hug and said he would be right back. "Jake, you are with us, we may need an interpreter."

Jake joined Robert and Ben. They got to the hall and stopped. There was no Marcus and no Rachel at all. It was like they had vanished.

The three men had seen them all leave the room and had quickly followed them into the hall. Jake went into the bathroom to see if Marcus was there. No Marcus. Ben asked a woman coming out of the women's bathroom if there was anyone else in there and was told no.

The men stood there trying to figure out where they went to. "Singleton, what on earth are you up to now?" the man was addressing Robert.

"Having dinner with my family, and you?" Robert was known in the government world as a good man who was not very social with the other officers.

"There was a report that some chipless kids were eating here, and we were told to come and check it out. Did you see anything suspicious?" He was talking to Robert but looked at the others too. As he was talking, he saw the closet door. "Wait a minute." And he grabbed the handle and opened the door. As the door opened, the Singletons were as surprised at the sight as were the government men.

Marcus and Rachel were hugging each other, kissing full out. They both turned, and Marcus stayed in front of Rachel so the government men would not get a look at her face. She looked down and turned away acting embarrassed.

The government man looked at Robert. "I take it this is one of yours?" He pointed to Marcus who was trying not to run. "You really need to keep your boys under control. Good grief, man, no wonder you have so many kids if you are anything like this one here." They turned and walked away disgusted by having their time wasted.

Rachel's family, not knowing what had happened, had joined the men in the hall. They were as confused as the government men were.

Rachel started to cry and put her hand over her face and went to her parents. As she walked by Marcus, she reached out to grab him, but her mom pulled her away, but not before Rachel had a chance to grab Marcus's hand and pass the map back to him.

Robert in turn took Marcus by the coat collar and escorted him back to the table. Jake and Ben followed. They all took a seat. Marcus looked at the direction that Rachel and her family had gone. Robert tapped on the table, getting Marcus's attention. "Don't you even think about it."

Marcus took the map from his sleeve where he had slid it and was going to put it in his pocket, but Robert took it from him. "Let me see that." He unfolded it and saw that it was floor plans. It did not escape his notice that the handwriting on the map was from all of his sons. He looked around the table at each of them, folded the paper up, and handed it back to Marcus. "I do not even want to know."

Sally was totally confused but knew that she would find out what had happened. "Is anyone ready for the birthday cake?" Quickly the party was back on.

The ride home was really very quiet. It had been a good evening even if there were a few surprises. Jake, Sally, and Marcus were in one car, and the rest of the family went in the family car. They all got home about the same time, and all had joined together in the living room. Marcus was deep in thought. He had something on his mind, and he did not know what to do. Jake and Ben retold about finding Marcus and Rachel in the closet and about how they were kissing. Marcus turned away not from embarrassment but from sadness. The family did not understand at all his reaction to the situation.

Jake added, "Marcus, that was so clever how you thought to take Rachel out of the room."

Marcus spoke up for the first time since they were home. "I think you are all crazy for not realizing how I could have gotten all of you in trouble. It was a stupid thing to do. I should have let Rachel handle it without my help. I am so sorry." He looked at Robert and Nancy. "I am sorry that I put your family at risk. I should have known better."

Robert had thought to say something to Marcus about how he had handled the situation, but this was not it. They did not have to be hard on Marcus, he was already too hard on himself. "Marcus, what else could you have done?" Robert did not say another word and quieted anyone else who tried to answer. This was for Marcus to discuss with their dad.

Marcus looked at Robert. He did not know what he wanted him to say. He struggled with the idea that if he helped Rachel, he put the family at risk; but if he had not helped her, a young girl could have been sent away to Jail. He knew that she was wanted. How she was chipped and with a family in town was an impossible thing to happen anyway. He could not think of another answer. He looked at the other Singletons, but they were staying out of it. Marcus was on his own with Robert. "I am sorry. I can't think of anything else I could have done to save Rachel and not risk all of you."

"That is right. There was nothing else you could have done. In fact, I personally think that was the best 'on your feet' thinking I have seen in a long time." Robert was smiling at Marcus. "Why don't you not be so hard on yourself and realize that sometimes the best answer is not always the safest. All God ever expects of you is your best."

Marcus started to say something, but Robert cut in, "No, no more thinking. All you need to do is to realize that you did excellent with what you had to work with. And for the record, young man, we do not need you to take care of us. We are all grown up and can do a good job taking care of ourselves."

Marcus was so confused. As smart as these people were, how could they not see how dangerous he was to their family? He needed to think. God had given him this lovely family, and they did need his help even if they could not see it.

Marcus was so deep in thought that he did not see Nancy cross the room until she was right in front of him. She put her hand out and had him stand up. He was the same height as she was, so it put them eye to eye. "Marcus, you need to trust that God gave you this family not for you to take care of but for us all to work together help-ing and taking care of each other. And so far from what we have seen, you are doing a great job." She gave him a hug. That seemed to be a cue for the rest of the family to tell him a final "happy birthday" and to get on to their homes. Marcus truly loved this family. He would have some God time about all of this, but for now, he was going to enjoy every bit of the family time he could get.

CHAPTER 39

There was one more birthday surprise. When Marcus got up on Saturday morning, the family was all gathered at the house to have breakfast. They were surprising Marcus by taking him out to the farm so he could see all his boys. The family had heard that there was to be a local meeting added to this day, so many of Marcus's other friends would also be at the farm. It was going to be a great day. The weather was going to be warm, and the whole family was going to be there.

After breakfast, the Singleton family divided up in two different cars. The two older boys went with their mom and dad. The other four traveled in Sally's car, which meant that she got to be the driver. Mark yelled "shotgun," so he was the other rider to be in the front seat. Jake and Marcus were loaded up in the back seat and ready to go.

The cars had traveled down the road for about an hour. The conversations between Sally and Mark jumped from one subject to the other so fast it was hard to keep up. Jake was used to this kind of bantering but guessed that Marcus was being so quiet because he was not. But as Jake looked over at Marcus, he could see that he was distracted by something. He was going over and over something or someone in his mind, and Jake could not help himself. This was a perfect opportunity to get in some brother teasing.

When Jake could get a word in edgewise, he started a conversation with Marcus, hoping that the others would join him in the teasing. "Hey, Marcus, why so quiet? Thinking of something in particular? Perhaps a pretty little thing named Rachel?"

Marcus looked at Jake with the strangest look on his face. "Actually, yes. As a matter of fact, that is exactly what I was thinking about. But not like you think. Jake, something is wrong."

That was not the reaction Jake expected to hear from Marcus. By this time, both Sally and Mark had tuned into the conversation.

Sally looked up into the rearview mirror briefly to see the look on Marcus's face. It was exactly the same as his voice. Confused. "What do you mean something is wrong?"

Marcus shook his head and restarted the conversation. "Rachel should not have been there last night. It does not make any sense."

Marcus looked at Jake. "Jake, Rachel always travels really close to Travis. It does not make sense that she was caught and chipped and Travis was not. Another thing. How is it that she was placed into a family here in town and not sent off to one of the holding facilities somewhere else?"

Mark looked back over the seat taking up a discussion with Marcus. "People change. Maybe this is a new Rachel. You of all people know that being chipped is a hard thing to get used to."

Marcus shook his head no. "Not Rachel. She is a fighter to the end. Her acting like she was going to run away in fear last night was all wrong. I should have figured that out. I think that there was some kind of a scam going on and that I may have played right into it. I am just not sure what it was all about yet."

They arrived at the farm late morning, and Marcus's boys, like before, came to greet Marcus. They all had so much to tell him. They all wanted to talk to Marcus at the same time.

Jake had noticed that James was standing off to one side. Marcus saw him and gave him a quick look in his direction. James signaled to Marcus in nest, "We have a big problem. I need to see you."

Marcus signaled back, "I will come talk to you as soon as I can." Jake had seen and read the conversation.

Robert and Nancy had not seen Marcus signaling, but they did see Jake's reaction to it. They went to see Jake and find out what was up. Their reaction caused Brother Marcus and Ben to join the small Singleton group that was now forming.

"Is there a problem, Jake?" Jake's dad kept his voice low but said it loud enough so the immediate family were all in on the goings-on.

"I am not sure, Dad. I saw James tell Marcus that there was a big problem of some sort."

They had not seen that there was one of the younger boys hiding in the tree they were standing by. He decided to chime in and catch the family up on what was happening. "It is only a big problem if you think that Marcus getting caught kissing Travis's girlfriend is a big deal."

It was not clear as to which was more surprising—the fact that the boy was in the tree talking to them, that Rachel was Travis's girlfriend, or that the people at the farm had known about the Rachel and Marcus goings-on from last night.

Jake lowered his head and was kicking the dirt with his shoe. "Travis's girlfriend? Boy, I sure didn't see that one coming. Marcus knew that something was wrong. He had said as much on the drive up here."

It was Mom who asked the next question, "What do you mean he thought something was wrong?"

Mark decided to add to the rest of the story. "Marcus was telling us that he thought that something was wrong with Rachel being in town and the fact that she had been chipped and not Travis. It appears that Travis and Rachel usually travel together. Marcus never said anything about her being Travis's girlfriend."

At this point, the boy in the tree jumped down to join their group. "That is probably because she was Marcus's girlfriend first." With having said that, the boy took off in the other direction and joined Marcus and the other kids. He tapped Marcus on the arm and talked to Marcus, who had leaned in to hear. Marcus in turn looked over at the Singletons. Marcus sent a message in nest to Jake telling him that he would be over as soon as he could to explain some of the things going on. Jake in turn signaled that he understood.

The boy's last statement left the Singleton family speechless.

Mom was quick to point out that this could not be true because Marcus had just turned sixteen.

Jake and Mark looked at each other and smiled. They so loved their mother but were quick to remember what it had been like when they were Marcus's age and also remembering that Marcus had functioned as an adult for a very long time now.

Jake was going to say something, but it was Dad who took it from here. "I am not sure about all of that, but if this is going to be a problem for Marcus, I think we need to find out all the details we can and remind Marcus that he is not alone in all of this but that he has a family and we are here for him."

The farm was in full movement. People had gathered up into groups, some groups small and some large. There were many ages of people at the farm at this time. The Singletons felt that they were completely out of place. They wondered if this was the way Marcus felt when he was forced into their world. They tried to stay silent and watch and see what they should do, but Robert felt it was time to address Marcus as to what was going on. Robert called out to Marcus from where they were all standing. "Marcus, may I talk to you please?"

Marcus looked at the Singleton family and sent Jake another signal of "Just as soon as I can take care of this next group." Jake translated what he had said.

*****

Marcus was true to his word; he came over as soon as he had finished with a small children's group.

Robert began a conversation with Marcus. "Marcus, is there anything you would like to tell us?"

Marcus looked at all of them with a puzzled look. "I am not sure what you want me to say."

Brother Marcus felt that he might help get this going faster by letting Marcus know what they already knew. "How about starting with the fact that you did not come to us and let us know that you felt that something was wrong with Rachel being at the restaurant last night?"

Marcus figured it out. "You all think I have kept something from you. Not at all. Truly I had not even thought about Rachel being a problem until I was riding here in the car."

Ben stepped forward. "That might be true, but how about the fact that Rachel is Travis's girlfriend. Not to mention the fact she was your girlfriend first. You did not think that might be important information to share with us?"

This having a family who cared about you was so much harder than Marcus would have ever guessed. "Actually, no, I did not think it was any big deal. She was only being interested in me so she could get to know Travis. I was only her stepping stone. Sorry, I didn't think to tell you. I am used to taking care of things myself."

The family knew that this statement was true. Ben continued, "Is there anything else you would like to tell us about what seems to be going on?"

Before Marcus got a single word out, Sally came hurrying up to this meeting the family was having. She had slipped off to visit some of the people she knew here at the farm, and with so much going on, the family had not even noticed. "Marcus, is it true at you are being challenged by Travis for your position in the Knowing?"

Marcus looked at all of them watching him. "I did not know for sure, but I had suspected that he might. And now with the story of me being with Rachel there will be a lot more opinions about all of this. I can't believe I walked right into this."

Jake was totally confused. "What position in the Knowing? I thought that with your boys put into families that you would automatically be out of leadership."

Mark gave Jake a look. "I think I should explain things to you later, but I think for now, it would be good if we can figure out what is coming next. The fact that Travis has been into some trouble should count him out or at the least slow him down. Don't you think?"

Marcus thought for a short time. He looked at all of them as they were waiting to hear what he was thinking. "I need a really big favor from all of you." He looked to Robert and Nancy as they were, after all, the head of the family. "I know that this might be hard to explain, but I need to go and check on some things. I know you all want to understand this right now, but truly I am a little confused myself. If you will let me go and check this all out, I will come back and tell you what is up."

Jake was the first one to react, "No way. No way we are going to leave you by yourself to take on Travis."

Marcus turned to Jake. "That is not how this would work. There will be a formal meeting and then a competition of some sort. But not now and probably not even today."

Robert stepped toward Marcus. "Marcus, I am going to believe that you are true to your word when you say that there is no danger for you to go and do what you are asking. So go and do what you need to do, and we will be waiting here for you to return. This is your world, and although we are a part of it, we do not have the understanding that you have in how to live it."

Nancy stepped into Marcus's view. "But remember one thing, young man. We are family. And that in this family, that means you don't do hard things alone, ever." With those words, Nancy gave Marcus a hug and a kiss.

Marcus simply nodded that he understood, then he turned and walked away.

Jake did not like the idea of Marcus going off by himself. "Dad, are you sure about this? It sounds to me like Travis has been up to something in all of this."

"Jake, trust goes both ways. We have asked Marcus to trust us in our world, this time it is for us to show that we trust him in his."

Victor was coming over to the Singleton group. "How goes it?" No one spoke to him. They just looked at him. "I guess that you have heard that there is going to be a problem with Marcus holding his place in the Knowing. Travis has challenged that since Marcus no longer has a group that his leadership should be transferred over to Travis and his new formed group in this area."

Jake could not stand it any longer. He needed some teaching on all of this. "Could someone please explain all of this to me? Leaders? Groups? What is this all about?"

Victor was more than delighted to explain the origination of the Knowing. "The Knowing has a leadership in each state. Under the leadership, there is an area leader, and under each area leader are five subleaders as it were. I am one of these. Then there are the small groups in each area that are under the five. Each small group, there were originally only twenty-one groups, has a leader that teaches and leads that group. Sometime ago there was a small group of boys that appeared and started helping all of the other groups when they could. They were young, but they were very helpful and soon became a vital part of these area groups. It was decided that this area could add another group to the setup. As I am sure you can guess, that was Marcus and his group. Over time, Marcus had earned the respect of all of the other leaders. I think that this should bring you up to date on the layout of the Knowing. Where the big question now lies is what happens to Marcus next? He no longer has his boys and thus leads no one. Travis on the other hand has come into play with a new group who wants to take over Marcus's position. I can't say that I am very happy about this. Travis's group look at our future different than most of us. We believe that a peaceful approach to all of this is the right way to go. Others are leaning to the idea that we need to be of the fighting way of life."

Jake was all in. "So what happens next? Who gets to decide?"

From the look on Victors' face, the family could tell that the next part was going to be difficult. "Well, the leaders higher up have decided that this area has always been faithful to the Bible teachings and that we should do whatever seemed best. I must tell you a lot of prayer and thought has gone into this decision. Travis has a good size following, and it could cause problems if we simply discount them altogether. Because of this, it was decided that the boys could have a challenge if Marcus could come up with a group to lead."

Jake was quick to answer, "Why not give him back his kids and let's get this over with."

Victor smiled at Jake. "Aren't you the one who wanted Marcus off the streets and not in leadership? Things aren't as easy as they look now, are they? If Marcus goes on with his life as a kid, then Travis gets to have a group, but if Marcus stays in leadership, he will be giving up the chance to be a kid. A lot of prayer has gone and will continue to go into this one."

Jake interrupted, "Okay, what happens next?"

Victor saw that Marcus was coming their way. "I think we are about to find out firsthand."

The family looked at Victor with question.

Victor motioned over to where Marcus was making his way toward them. "I think the best answer is for us to let Marcus decide what he thinks is going to be the best. He is prayed up, and he has a heart for what he thinks God wants him to do with his life."

The family saw Marcus, and all of them could not help but notice the look of determination on his face.

Marcus reached the group. "Victor, may I have a word with you?"

Victor noted that he was ready to speak with Marcus.

Marcus did not hesitate to speak in front of his new family. "Victor, I would like to present you to my new group." Marcus pointed to his family. "They are a group of chipped Knowing. I believe they are all an asset to the Knowing, and that with permission, I would like to be the go-between for them."

Victor smiled. "I thought as much. You know what this means? You will have to go up against your brother in a challenge, I think he called it that."

Marcus looked at his family. "I think that it is worth it to try. I need you to recognize them as a group. And with your permission, I think that they should be able to join us in the meeting today."

It was obvious to the family that the last part was a surprise to Victor. "Well, yes, if you are sure that you want to get back into leadership again. You know that you could go on with your new life and no one would hold it against you."

Marcus thought on it for a moment. He looked to the Singletons and saw that they were somewhat confused but could tell from the way they were all standing that they would be behind his idea. Nancy and Robert were both smiling, and the rest were ready for whatever was to come. He looked to them for confirmation. "Are you all in to be a chipped group of the Knowing with me?"

Robert spoke for the family, "Like I told you before, we are here for you, and we are behind you. Just tell us what you need us to do."

Marcus looked back to Victor. "Will you take care of setting up the time for us in the meeting?"

Victor took time to look at the Singleton family as well and saw exactly what Marcus had seen. A family who totally trusted their new son and brother and who wanted to support him in his calling from God. "Okay, if you are sure that this is the way to go, I will let the others know what to expect. I am guessing that some of your older kids from your old group will want to be an unofficial part of your new group? I think that would be a good idea if you are okay with that addition?"

Marcus gave out a huge smile. "Thank you, Victor, that would be great. I could really use their help right now."

Victor nodded his head. "I will see to it that things are clear to the groups. I will assume that the challenge request will be at the end of the meeting. Perhaps that will give you even more time to work some details out."

Victor then turned and walked over to a large group of people clearly waiting to hear what was to come.

*****

Many of the older kids from his old group came up to Marcus where they received orders and then went on their way. James was across the way from Marcus and signaled him if things were contained and was told yes. The Singletons had moved over to a picnic table and watched as best they could to the goings-on. Jake was trying to keep up with all of the signs and the groups and who they were, but everyone was nervous and was signing way too fast. He could catch a question or answer from time to time, enough for him to know that the Singletons were the main subject. No one wanted to trust them. But they did because Marcus had.

Victor had delivered the information and came back to the area where he saw the family sitting at the table looking dazed to say the least. "Robert, I guess that you and your family are the ones learning now. I am both surprised and delighted that things have gone this way. I think it will be good for all of the area groups to have a chipped group as part of the Knowing."

Robert was talking to Victor all the while keeping an eye on Marcus. "Victor, I cannot believe that you put Marcus in charge of a group at his age. I know what I have heard, but it is hard to think he can lead like you are saying."

Victor gave a small sigh. "First of all, we never put him in charge, he earned it. Second thing is that you have not seen anything yet. I think after you see what happens in the future, you will better understand the true gift God has given this kid."

Marcus saw that Victor was talking with his family and went over to join them. Marcus did not speak out loud but nested to Jake if things were okay. Jake confirmed that it was all good with the family. Marcus simply nodded his head ever so slightly. He was deep in thought about something.

Victor decided to address the situation. "Anything I can do to help?" Everyone was quick to take note of the conversation.

It was clear that Marcus had come to some kind of decision about God only knows what. "Victor, do you think Sandy can be with my group today so they can get any answers that they need from her?" Marcus was worried about his family.

Victor smiled. "I think that I should be able to arrange that. Anything else?"

"Well, I was wondering will my group be in the same place as usual, or are we in a different position?"

Victor was quick to answer, "I think you have earned the position, so until further notice, your group will be in the same place by the main floor."

Marcus was clearly pleased. "Thanks, Victor. How long till the meeting?"

Victor looked at his watch. "We will be starting in about an hour. I cannot see any delay. I will be off now." He turned to look at the family. "I will see all of you at the meeting." He smiled and shook his head in disbelief. *A chipped group in the Knowing. Only God could have pulled this one off.*

CHAPTER 40

As nice as the farm had looked for a celebration, it had now quickly been turned back into an old-fashioned farm. Any sign of a party was gone.

It was clear to everyone that the meeting was about to start. Many groups began to enter the largest building here on the farm.

Sandy came over close to Marcus. They greeted with a smile and a hug. "Marcus, I have a message for you—everything is secure, and that everyone has arrived. Anything else you need before you go in?"

"Sandy, will you please be with my family?"

"Marcus, I would be delighted to join your group. Will we be in your original place?"

Marcus noted yes but lowered his head as he spoke, "Victor said that was what was to be, but there is a chance that there might be a change in plans, so do not be surprised if we get bumped by Travis's group."

They all walked to the meeting place. It definitely was the largest building on the farm. It was a barn that had both an upper and lower level, with piles of hay and bags of food organized so that it made an arena-like setup. There was a table in the middle of the area.

Jake, along with the rest of the family, was overwhelmed as to how many people there were here in this one building. There were groups of people that they had seen earlier that now filled the room. Marcus and his group joined along the side of the main floor right by the edge of the center of the room. Things were exactly how Victor had described the leadership layout. There was a table in the center of the room. There was one man, who was clearly the one in charge.

Jake was pleased to see that he had recognized him as David from the shelter. Jake had been right—he was one of the main leaders. Then there were five other men sitting beside David. One of the five was Victor. Jake felt that was no surprise. Behind the table of these men were twenty-one other men.

David was looking back at the group to see if everyone was here and quickly noted that there was someone missing. "We seem to be missing one leader." He looked to the side of the room where Marcus's group always stood and saw that Marcus was with his group. "Marcus, we are ready to get this started. Don't you think you should take your place on the floor?"

Marcus was not comfortable assuming that he was to be in the leadership group but was quick to comply to his calling him up. There was a round of applause as well as a small sound of boos in the room as he joined on the stage. Marcus took his place last in line of the group leaders, now making the number 22.

David smiled and noted his delight as to the fact that all of the leadership was now in place for the meeting.

A voice came from the upper level. "David, there are strangers in the meeting, who are they?"

David kept his head down with his eyes fixed on the paperwork on the table. "They are a new family group and friends. We will call them the New Group, and Marcus is their lead. They need to be here."

The voice spoke again, "What guarantee of safety do you offer for them being here?"

Marcus raised his head and stood tall. "I offer my life for them." Leader Marcus was clearly back. He spoke bold and with authority.

David then took over the speaking about this new group. "We have come to the conclusion that this new group of Marcus's will be as much of an asset as his boys have been. Leadership has unanimously voted this new group of people as a group under Marcus."

The room was silent for the longest time.

David called the meeting to order, and roll call began at once. As he called out each group by a number, a leader would come forward. David would ask each group what was going on with them.

They all had a code that the new family group could not follow, but they were fascinated by the whole goings-on.

David would call out, "Group one, how goes it?"

Book of John was the reply.

Group two, book of Mark. Group three, book of John, and so on it went for twenty-two groups. Only once did David question a group when their reply was the book of Romans, but they repeated the answer twice, and David stated that they would meet together after the meeting.

By the end of the calling out of the twenty-two groups, it was clear that this was a very organized group of people.

Jake looked around. So this was the Knowing. His eyes fell back onto Marcus, and he could not help but be proud that his very own little brother was a part of the leadership.

After roll call, there was a discipline review. As each group was called up with the charges against them, it was their small group leader who addressed them and their subject. It was finally Marcus's group to review their discipline. But it was not his new group but rather some goings-on of his old group of young boys. Marcus called out for discipline review. Two young boys, both who had been in his nest, came forward and stood before Marcus. "Erin, it is reported that you have been talking back to your new family. Is that true?" Erin did not speak. "You are ten years old now, and you are not keeping the way of the Knowing family. You need to learn from this and not do it again, all right?"

Erin spoke up, "But they want to help me all the time. I can do things by myself." Marcus smiled. "Being a part of a family means you have to help sometimes, but it also means that sometimes you have to let others help you. It is called family. Do it better, learn how to be helped. It will make your life better, I promise."

Marcus turned to Jimmy. "Jimmy, I hear that you are fighting. You are nine years old, you should know better, what do you have to say for yourself?"

"Marcus, they were being mean to the other kid, someone had to do something." Jimmy was frustrated, and Marcus could hear that this was not a fight of pride but of protection.

"Jimmy, look at me." Marcus was eye to eye with him. "Can you think of anything else you could have done to make that situation better?"

Jimmy tried really hard but could not think of a thing he could have done different to both not fight and take care of whoever it was he was defending. He shook his head no.

"Then you did your best. That is all God asks. Learn from the situations, and if you can, do better next time, but all that you can do is your best, and know that God promises to do the rest." Marcus snuck a look at Robert, who recognized that Marcus had used the same teachings he had used on him only last night. Marcus smiled a smile of gratefulness to Robert. And Robert felt proud to be a part of this kid's life. "You need to keep up the good work and always try to stay out of fights, but if you must fight, then do it with honor and with the help of God. You may go back to your group."

There were over two hours of meetings. Problems brought and problems solved. They talked over everything—from storing food to how to stay out of the government officers' way. David addressed an older group of young men. "The undercover officer Will, what is the status on him?"

One of the men stepped forward. "I think God is working on him. He is reading his Bible, but he is also writing out reports to hand into Mr. Diggings."

Jake was shocked to know that they all knew about Mr. Diggings, and the fact that they handed in reports should have been a secret too.

"Is there anything in his notes that is going to be a problem?" David asked as he was keeping notes on this meeting as they were having it.

"Well, there is only one thing that we are not sure of. He thinks Travis is a leader, but he is not sure yet." Then he stood silent for a time.

David was thinking. "Does he write in pen?" The young man nodded yes. "Then I think that there needs to be an accident and the notebook needs to get wet. Can you arrange that?" The young man smiled that he in fact would love to do that.

"I would love to take care of that. He always carries that book with him. All I need to do is give one shove into the pond, and I would be cooling off his hot temper and taking care of the notebook at the same time." Others confirmed that they felt the same way.

It had been reported that Will had a temper, and although they could handle him, it would be fun to "adjust his attitude." David had inquired as to where Will was just now. They had told him that the younger kids were putting on a play for the new families and anyone who was not in a group at the meeting, and that Will was in charge of the security. David smiled. "I think that is like putting a wolf in charge of the chicken house, don't you?"

"Yes, but it is fun to watch him think that all the families are the leaders of the Knowing." He thanked David and moved back to be with his group.

The meeting was coming to an end. A voice from one of the groups called out to Marcus. "Marcus, we hear you have a challenge, a full-out one. Do you need help?"

Marcus was getting ready to answer when an older boy from a group off to the side came forward and stood before him. "That is right, a full-out challenge. And I am here to represent Travis, who is challenging for Marcus's position."

Noise of people talking to each other was in the room. Sandy was quickly trying to tell the family what was going on. "Travis wants to be leader instead of Marcus. He is calling him out. This is going to be a game the nest kids play in order to determine if Travis or Marcus gets to decide where the real challenge will be held."

Jake questioned, "You mean where the fight will be?"

"Kind of." Sandy went on to explain that this game is something she had only seen once before but that it was one Marcus was reported to have made up. So that chances are good that he will decide the place for the challenge, and that could give him the advantage he might need to win.

Two chairs were brought in. They put one on either side of the table. Marcus turned his back on the table. He was facing the family although he was not looking at them. He was taking off the brace he had been wearing on his arm since he got his cast off for his broken hand. He looked like he had lost some of his confidence. His weak hand gave him doubt in himself. They all watched as Marcus looked up to the rafters and then looked down. He lowered himself to one knee and bowed his head in prayer. Everyone but the challenging group did the same. Marcus stayed in the position for some time before he got up and went back to facing the table, but he stopped and turned to the new family group. He went over to Nancy; he handed her his brace, but when he put it into her hand, he squeezed her hand telling her it was going to be okay. Nancy gave Marcus a kiss on his cheek. He turned and went to the chair on his side of the table. Another young man, Fred, was now seated in the chair on his side of the table.

The whole challenging group that were there to support Fred entered the arena. There were about twenty-three of them in all. They stood in a semicircle behind Fred.

Some of Marcus's old group entered the arena and stood behind Marcus. Jake wanted to go too and made a move to go. Mark stopped him. "Those are Marcus's commanders. They are invited to join him, they have earned it."

Jake looked at the commanders. He recognized James and John; they were boys from the nest, but there was one older boy and two grown men he had seen but did not know.

Jake and the others were anxious about what was to be next. Fred reached inside his coat pocket and pulled out a gun. He laid it on the table beside him.

Victor had walked over to stand by Sandy and the family. Jake started to react when he saw the gun. Victor placed a hand on his arm to stop him from doing anything. He motioned very slightly for Jake to look in his hand where he was showing him some bullets. "Jake, one of the boys bumped into Fred earlier and helped to rid him of these by borrowing his weapon and removing them and then putting the weapon back. It is okay."

Jake whispered, "Does Marcus know?"

Victor whispered back, "No, he would never have agreed to do anything involving a weapon. But he is here now, and he will play this out. He trusts God, and I believe that is why God gave him us, so we can have his back."

Marcus reached inside his coat and pulled out his Bible and laid it on the table opposite the gun. The challenging group was laughing and making fun of Marcus and his Bible. "What you going to do, read him to death?"

Marcus did not look at his men but spoke, "Commanders, I need you to please stand down." His men looked at each other and then back at Marcus. "I said that I need you to stand down please." The men did as they were told. They left the arena. It was clear to everyone that Marcus was protecting his leaders. He did not want them in the direct area incase the other side decided to start a fight, especially with the gun showing.

Sally had been quiet during the meeting and was now getting irritated that all of these people would let a young boy have such a position as Marcus had. "Sandy, this is insane. You mean to tell me that this game puts Marcus against Fred and his entire group?"

Sandy smiled. "It may look that way in the arena, but look around. Marcus is surrounded by supporters, and don't forget he has a secret weapon." Sally looked at her like she had lost her mind. "Marcus has God, his secret weapon. I have seen this kid do things that only God could make happen. You watch, and you will see what I mean."

Victor explained to the whole family, "This is a game that the nest kids play. I cannot figure it out. I am not even sure what the rules are exactly. This game consists of taps and hand movements. One challenges the other somehow, and the other counters. They tap and bang their hands on the table, and the one part that I do know is that when they put their hand to their head, that is when they score a point. When the game is almost over, one player will have both hands on the table, one facing up and one facing down. Then there is a type of playoff, and at the end, the winner will put both hands facedown just before the other one does, and then everyone gets excited, and it will be over. They are playing for the right to choose where the challenge for the leadership will be at. On whose ground you might say. If it is Fred who wins, it will be on Travis's ground.

The people deciding would be followers of him, but if Marcus wins, then it would be Marcus's group who would decide. Either way, the challenge will not be over tonight, but like in football, when they toss the coin, it will decide which team will start."

The family had so many questions. If this had been a story in a book, they would have to sell it as fiction. But with God, things never are at face value, and raising this kid Marcus was going to be a faith-building project for sure.

Fred started the game off. He pounded his fist on the table making a very loud noise. The game was off and running. They used their hands like Victor had said they would. Tapping and banging their hands all around—sometimes one at a time, and at other times, they were matching movements at the same exact time. Marcus would throw his hand up to his head, and his group would go wild with yelling and whistles. And when Fred would place his hand to his head, his group in the arena would go wild. Something happened, and Fred got flustered. You could almost feel sorry for the man. Marcus put his hands in the air like he was surrendering, but it was a way to take a time-out.

Marcus stood up and addressed his group, "We will celebrate our victory, but we will never rejoice at another man's failure. I need all of you to please remain quiet until the end of the game." He sat back down, and the game was back on.

The adults realized how brilliant this action was. Fred was getting angry about losing this game. Adding embarrassment to it could only escalate the situation. This was to be a game and not a fight. The war right now was between two people, and it needed to stay that way, or someone could get hurt.

The two of them went on for what seemed forever. The hand movements got faster and faster. Fred stood up but kept his hand movements going just as fast. Marcus matched Fred's position and stood up also; this was getting to be long and drawn out. Obviously both men were good at the game. But it was clear from the way Fred was acting, along with his group, that the end was near; the hand movements were getting louder and stronger and faster.

Nancy voiced her concern about Marcus's bad hand and how this could not be good for it. It had healed but was not 100% yet.

Fred let out a curse. But Marcus never changed his expression once during the whole game. Fred's face was getting red. All at once Marcus laid both hands out on the tabletop. His left hand turned down and his right hand facing up. Frank was doing some more movements. He hesitated and then started to tap again, and then his hands froze. Marcus turned his right hand over, and the room exploded with excitement. The game was over, and Marcus had won.

The family saw when it happened, the game was over and Marcus won and the other side lost. Anger welled up in Fred; he saw Marcus's open left hand on the table. He knew that it was weak from having heard about his injuring it before, and with all of his anger and wrath, he took his fist and came down on Marcus's bad hand.

The family, Victor, and Sandy saw that Marcus's legs almost buckled. No one else would have noticed. The rest of the crowd heard the noise and saw both men turn from the table, but they were all so busy celebrating they did not see the physical attack on Marcus. That was good because a fight could have started, and this was not the time or place. Someone could get hurt.

Marcus turned to face his family. They could see that he was in pain, but he was not giving in to it. He shut his eyes. They knew he was praying, so were they. Strength came over Marcus; his back straightened, and he placed his bad hand in his pocket. He walked back to the table and picked up his Bible. The whole room became silent. He looked at his opponent. "We will be in touch. Now we will celebrate."

David entered the main floor again. "This meeting is over." The whole room exploded with excitement.

Marcus turned and looked at his family. "Can we please go and take a break? I am done." He literally fell between Brother Marcus and Ben; they caught him with Jake closing in behind him. They got him seated. "Please don't let them see me weak like this. I just need a minute."

Victor took this as his cue. He and Marcus's commanders headed off anyone from getting close enough to Marcus to see he had been hurt.

With a bottle of water and a short time, Marcus was able to compose himself enough to make it look as though nothing bad had happened.

David called out for security. "Please follow Fred and his group and see to it that they are safely off the grounds. Commanders, please report on your groups in one hour. We need to pull things in security-wise for a while. Victor and Sandy, I think this is going to need to be a good party, so let's get things back to normal as soon as possible. I do not want us to look like we care about the challenge."

Victor almost laughed out loud. The looks on Marcus's new family's faces was priceless. Victor had forgotten how it threw him the first time he had seen God work through Marcus like this. Victor addressed Marcus, "What do you need me to do?"

Marcus looked at his family. "I have some business to take care of." He turned to Robert. "Thank you for being here. I needed the help. Thank you. If it is okay with you, I need to make some plans."

Robert thought for a moment then nodded yes. Marcus headed off to take care of things. He still had his hand in his pocket. He had not taken it out at all. He was acting like nothing had happened. People fell in behind him as he walked away. It was unreal.

Even if Marcus had regained his strength, his brothers were not going to leave him alone right now. Not after they had seen him physically attacked. They started to head out after him, but Victor stepped in. "Gentlemen, I wish you would not do that. Marcus needs his space right now. Besides that, you need to trust me when I tell you that he will not go too far from all of you. He is feeling protective of you. So why don't you go and have a seat." He motioned to the area they had all been in earlier. "Marcus will come and join you later."

The family did let Marcus go out on his own like Victor suggested. Not because they thought he was right but because they needed a family meeting about their little brother Marcus.

Robert was in awe of what he had seen Marcus do. "I cannot believe that this kid is one of the leaders of this order of the Knowing. The one thing I do know for sure is that only God could give power and respect like this."

Jake was shocked. "You mean that this is not the only Knowing? There are more of them?"

Ben patted Jake on the back. "You have a lot to catch up on, little brother, but for right now, let's focus on how we can help Marcus. Better yet, how we can convince him that he needs to let us help him."

Mark took the opportunity to point out some facts about Marcus. "The pressure of the meeting alone would have taken anyone out. They were in the game for over an hour, but to add pain to the mix, it is anyone's guess how he was still able to be thinking about anything but resting right now."

Brother Marcus looked around and saw that Victor was right, Marcus was still in the area. He had not gone too very far away from them. "Let's let him wear himself out, and then we can gather him up and get him home, at that point we can decide how we are going to contain this kid so he stays safe. I think with God's help and with all of us, we can let him do his job but safer."

All Nancy knew was that this young man was working for God, and as much as she knew that was a fact, she also knew that he needed to not continue to do it on his own anymore. "God has placed this kid in our family for a reason. Marcus works for God helping as a leader in this part of the Knowing, and we will continue to work for God helping him, even if it means that we have to do it with him kicking and screaming all the way." It was amazing to have this many people all agree on the same thing, but then this was a God matter, wasn't it? So they prayed.

They had just finished their prayer when Jimmy came running up. "Mrs. S., Marcus wants to know if he can please have his hand brace? He said I should bring it back to him."

They all smiled. This was their opening to get to Marcus. "Jimmy, where is Marcus right now?" Jake was glad that he had been with all these kids before because it would be easier to get them to trust him.

Jimmy looked across the yard at a building by the old barn they had the meeting in. "He is having a meeting there." And he pointed to where Marcus was at.

Robert had a plan. "Okay, we divide and conquer. I am going to find Victor and tell him what we have decided. Jake, you and Mark take the brace to Marcus, get him to let you help him if you can. But in case he will not accept your offer, then when you leave, Ben, you and Brother Marcus take over by staying out of his sight and keeping him under surveillance. Let's get him through today and get him home, there we can regroup and figure out what comes next." Everyone agreed.

Nancy and Sally decided to talk to Sandy and see if she had any ideas as to how they could be of better help to Marcus. Sandy smiled. "I think your family might be the answer to the prayer that Victor and I have had for Marcus for a long time. He is good at what he does, but he can be reckless, not with others but with himself. Perhaps with you all attached to him, he will be more careful."

That was the answer. He would stay safe because they were with him. Even if he would risk himself in a situation, he would never risk them or anyone else.

Sally summed up their little women's meeting. "So let's get this day over with and get him back home and teach him about his new team, called family." Now the women also had a plan of their own.

Jake and Mark went with Jimmy to find Marcus. Marcus was sitting with the group with the code of Romans from the meeting earlier; they were all discussing something real serious.

Mark and Jake noticed that Marcus still had his left hand in his pocket. Marcus looked fine at first, but as they watched him, he was rubbing his head and holding his upper left arm from time to time. Whether he admitted it or not, he was in pain. They did not want to interrupt his meeting, so they stood off to one side and watched as Marcus finished tying up loose ends.

Marcus's meeting came to an end, but there were many more people with questions also waiting in the sidelines. But later rather than sooner, the line of people waiting for Marcus ran out and he was alone. This was their chance. Jake and Mark took their turn to see Marcus and to see how bad that hand really was.

Jake was glad to see that Marcus was happy to see them. "Hey, Marcus, Mom sent us to bring you this." He held up the brace for

Marcus to see. Marcus was glad to have it, but they could tell that the thought of putting it on right now was not something he was looking forward to. "Why don't you let us help you get it on?" Jake reached for Marcus's arm, but he pulled away.

It was instinct to protect his hand from more pain. "I am sorry, Jake, but I think I had better do it myself. It is kind of hurt bad."

That was good news. Marcus recognized that he was hurt. That would make things easier later. "You asked for the brace, you must think it will make it better."

Marcus looked down at his arm. "Yes, I did earlier, but I am not so sure now, for now I think that if I leave it alone, it will be better."

James and John showed up as they were talking. They announced that dinner was ready and that they should all come and join the group to eat. Mark explained that they would be there shortly but that they should go on ahead. James and John waited to get a confirmation from Marcus that they should do just that. Marcus nodded his head yes. He was not in any mood to argue with anyone right now. So they left for the dinner area.

Jake waited until they had left. It was Marcus, Mark, and himself there. "Okay, Marcus, let's see the hand."

Marcus stood still for a moment and decided that it could be a good idea to put the brace on to support it. With the help of Jake and Mark, he began to pull it out of his pocket. It had been there for some time, now and even his arm did not want to work. They could see the pain was even greater than they had thought, but he did not cry out at all but held his breath as he moved it.

When they saw it, they almost lost their breath. It was black and blue and had swollen up to twice its size. Jake was the first to speak, "Marcus, this brace will never fit. Your hand is too swollen. You need to see a doctor and real soon. That thing looks terrible, even worse than last time."

Marcus looked at Jake. "We have been here before. It is broken, that is all. So let's not make a bigger deal out of it than it is, okay?" He gently put the hand back in the pocket at a great cost. He almost passed out from the pain. Mark and Jake steadied him until he had caught his breath and regained his balance. "Let's get this dinner over and done with, and then we can go home, if that is okay with you two?" Marcus looked over to one side of the room; there in the shadows were Brother Marcus and Ben. "And you two might as well join us." They had been watching from afar and were glad to see that their little brother was not so easily followed. They were good at following in secret, but he was better at spotting them. This was going to be a good team.

When they got to the dinner, there were so many people that Marcus was glad to see that there was a family table. There was a place for him between Nancy and Robert. They had motioned for him to join them, and he was so glad to do it.

Robert reached to help him slide in on the bench, but Marcus reacted in the same way as before, flinching back to protect his arm. "I am sorry, I am just afraid to hit my arm on anything right now."

Nancy looked him in the eye. "How bad is it?"

Marcus looked down at his arm. "I think it is broken like before. I am not sure what God is doing that I am always so broken all the time."

Nancy smiled. "You are not broken, Marcus, you are human. The body can only do so much before it rebels. You will learn." She looked at him trying to adjust his sitting to lessen his pain. "You will learn, even if you have to do it the hard way." Of course, Marcus did not understand.

Mark came over to Marcus with a small bag of ice. "What if you slipped this down in your pocket with your hand? It could stop the swelling at least."

Nancy looked at Mark. "How bad is it?" But before she could get an answer, Victor had called the group to be quiet, and they all had prayers together. He asked God's blessings on all of them. Anyone who had not been at the meeting earlier would have thought for sure that Victor was the leader of this Knowing group.

The party began. There was plenty of food. Nancy noticed that Marcus drank little and ate even less. They needed to finish this day sooner than later. Although Nancy was making plans for Marcus after she got him home, it was his brothers who had decided that there was no time like the present to get help for Marcus. They met with Victor and Sandy. Mark started the conversation, "Victor, we need a doctor right away for Marcus."

Jake added, "We saw his hand, and it is way worse than last time, and last time was bad enough."

Victor looked around. "Let me see what I can do. I knew he was hurt, but I did not think it could be that bad." Victor excused himself and went off to see if he could get some help.

That left Sandy with the brothers. "So you think you can handle Marcus, do you? Do you realize that it could take all four of you to keep up with him?"

Ben gave it a shot to explain, "Marcus is our little brother, and whatever it takes to keep him safe, we plan to do it, even if he hates it. After all, we had a lot of practice with Jake here."

Sandy needed to let them know exactly what they were dealing with. "The Marcus you all see here is not the only side he has. I have seen Marcus do off-the-wall crazy things when it came to protecting family and friends. Even with as smart as he is, he will throw all reason away in order to save a friend. He will protect his own, and you all have become his own. He will think himself responsible for all of you exactly like he did with the boys in the nest. He will rarely outright lie, but he will if he thinks he has to in order to protect you. So watch for it."

Nancy had walked up behind the family group and had heard everything that Sandy had said. "You mean like he says that he is doing okay when he is clearly not?"

Sandy nodded her head yes. "I have seen Marcus fly off the roof of a house to take out a man who was going after Travis. It took us two days to find out that he had messed up his shoulder. We only found out then because we saw him try and chop wood for the shelter with one hand. He was only thirteen, and it took three of us to hold him down so the doctor could check him out. We have all wondered how on earth you got him to go to the doctor with his last broken ribs and hand. We could have never have pulled that off."

Jake, not remembering that his mom was there, said, "You have never seen our mom in action. Marcus is good, but Mom is better."

"Why, thank you, Jake." She gave him a hug. "So what are we going to do with Marcus this time?"

As she was speaking, she noticed that Victor was coming with the doctor in tow. "Never mind." She said, "I know exactly what we are going to do." She spoke with the doctor for a few minutes. Then she and the doctor joined her boys in order to make a plan.

Robert had been sitting with Marcus and watched as Marcus put on the best act of his life. Many people came over and visited with Marcus, but not one person even suspected that anything could be wrong with him. The fact of the matter was that he himself began to think that Marcus's being hurt was perhaps overblown by Jake and Mark, although he knew that it was unlike them to do so. As he looked up, Robert saw that Nancy was motioning for him to join her across the way. He did not need to know what was going on yet, but he did know that he was going to be a part of a plan. As quickly as Robert got up, Ben and Brother Marcus each took a seat beside Marcus. Jake took a place behind Marcus.

Mark had called for Marcus's commanders to keep people out of and away from the area the family was now in. They would need some privacy for the next few minutes.

When Marcus looked up, he saw Sandy, Nancy, and the doctor heading right for him. He reacted in order to leave before they got there, but his brothers expressed physically a different idea. Jake pressed in from behind, and Brother Marcus and Ben pressed in on both sides in order to pin Marcus in his seat. His chest was up against the table that Mark was now holding securely in place.

The doctor, along with Nancy and Sandy, took a seat at the table across from Marcus. That relieved Mark from needing to hold the table any more.

The doctor did not address Marcus yet but called out to Mark. "Mark, would you go and get my bag out of the bunkhouse? It is the same one I had last time." Mark was glad to go and to not be in on this bullying Marcus into seeing the doctor. It was going to make Marcus not trust them in the future, and that was the last thing Mark wanted to have happen. He hoped that the risk of losing Marcus's trust was necessary, and this was worth that risk.

The doctor was looking at Marcus to evaluate his reaction. It was so far so good, as they would say. "So, Marcus, they tell me you may have rebroken your hand."

Marcus tried to move but had found that he could not even budge with his brothers around him. This was a nest trick he had taught them, and they were using it on him. "It is fine for now; Mrs. S. will bring me to see you in the morning." He looked at Ben and Brother Marcus, sending a "get away from me" look to both of them, but they did not move away but pushed in closer to him. That move made him pull up his left arm to protect it from being crushed by them.

The doctor smiled at Marcus. "Why don't you let me see it now, and we will save everyone time tomorrow?"

"And why don't you mind your own business and leave me alone?" was what Marcus was thinking, but he only said, "No, thank you."

Nancy stood up and reached across the table and started to undo Marcus's coat, motioning for Brother Marcus, who was on his left, to assist her in her plan. "Marcus, put your hand on the table now." They locked eyes.

Marcus answered, "I am thinking that this needs to be taken care of tomorrow. So no, thank you."

Ben summed up how they were all thinking with his next statement, "And you are our brother, so put your hand on the table before we do it for you." Marcus tried to get loose. "Now!" Ben raised his voice slightly to show Marcus that he was not kidding.

Marcus started to get his hand out of the coat. "You are all going to feel real silly when the doctor tells you that the hand is broken and that the swelling needs to go down before he can do anything." Marcus first took out the ice in the bag Mark had given him, and then he removed his hand and placed it on the table in front of him.

The doctor reached out and tried to pull Marcus's hand closer so he could see it. The doctor stood straight up and did not even try to cover up how upset he was at seeing Marcus's hand. "How long has it been swollen like this?" Mark was back, and Jake and Mark both looked at it again.

Mark answered, "It looked like that before dinner, but before that, I have no idea. Why, what is wrong?"

The doctor needed Marcus to stop pulling his hand back and resisting him. "Marcus, it looks like your hand is dislocated, and the blood flow may be pinched off. We have got to set it and real soon, or you could lose the use of your hand."

Marcus did not understand. "What does 'set it' mean? How do I do it?"

The doctor knew that Marcus was a man who needed information so he could make a decision, an informed one. "It looks like the bones in your hand are pressing on one of the veins and nerves in your hand. That is why you have so much pain. The pain is worse than last time, am I right?" Marcus confirmed with a nod of his head. "So if I slide the bones back in place, the blood will flow again, and the hand will be okay, but if we don't, you could be paralyzed in that hand for the rest of your life."

Marcus answered, "Are you sure?"

"Marcus, I am as sure about this as I have been about anything else in my life. Your hand needs to be reset." The doctor looked at the family to see if he was going to get support from them. But to his surprise, he did not need it.

Marcus looked up at him. "Then would you please set it?"

The doctor blinked and then took a breath. He reached for his bag and took out a syringe and a bottle of liquid. "I am going to give you something to stop the pain first. It will make you sleepy, but you will not remember the pain that way."

Marcus took his good hand and stopped the doctor from filling the needle. "You can set it, but I do not want any of your drugs. I will be okay without it."

"Marcus, don't be crazy, the pain would be more than anyone could or should handle." The doctor did not even want to try to do this with him awake.

Marcus willingly pushed his hand toward the doctor. "I do not want any drugs, but would you please set it now? It hurts too much to leave it any longer."

The doctor looked at the family wanting anyone to say something or anything to talk this kid into some sense. But not one of them was willing to override Marcus about this one. To do so would risk all the trust they had built in the past few months. "Okay, if you are sure, but once we get started, there is no turning back. Do you understand?"

"I will not change my mind. Please just do it." Marcus took a deep breath and closed his eyes. He did not move, he did not flinch, but kept perfect peace about himself as the doctor felt around in his hand to see where things needed to be moved to.

The doctor wanted to ask one more time, but when he looked at Marcus, he could see that he had readied himself. "Okay, here we go, on the count of three. One, two, and—" He did it before three. They all heard the pop and saw Marcus stiffen up and then begin to relax.

They all watched as Marcus rolled forward and placed his forehead down on the table. He was breathing hard, but it was over, and he did great. The doctor reached out to touch the back of Marcus's head. "You did great, son. Take a few seconds, and then I need to wrap the hand up to keep it stable until the swelling goes down." He looked at those around Marcus and shook his head in disbelief. "I truly have never seen anything like this kid in my life."

Nancy had Ben and Brother Marcus help pull Marcus back up into a sitting position. He was white as a ghost, but color was beginning to return to his face. "Marcus, we need to get home soon. Are you about ready to go?"

Marcus was trying to focus on his breathing. He blinked. And nodded his head yes. But he had no words. The doctor put a pressure bandage on the hand and gave instructions for what to look for in the next twenty-four hours. He kept shaking his head in disbelief. "I will see you two in town on Tuesday." The doctor motioned for Nancy to follow him over to where Marcus could not hear him. "Nancy, I have never seen anyone so pigheaded as this kid. You need to keep an eye on him and keep him quiet." He gave her some pain pills for Marcus and reminded her how to use them. He wished her luck and went on his way. He stopped and called out, "Make it two at a time for the next two days, okay?" They all thanked him, some with looks and others with words.

The commanders realized that the doctor was finished and those at the party did not know that anything had happened at all.

Marcus was sitting in the same place; he had pulled his left arm into his lap in front of himself. His color was still getting better, but he had a dazed look about him. One of the younger boys had come over to him to show Marcus that he had lost a tooth. Marcus looked at it and smiled. He showed the boy by smiling at him how happy he was for him but did not speak to him at all.

James and John were signaling Marcus from the side yard, but Marcus did not respond. Jake answered for him that things were going to be okay but that Marcus was tired and needed to go and get some rest. They took it that it was their duty to help that happen and started to intercept anyone who wanted to speak to Marcus.

Brother Marcus and Ben gave Marcus some space but had not left their places one on each side of him. They did not talk but sat silently showing their support and approval of Marcus. Robert and Nancy had been talking to Victor and Sandy about the day's events. They needed information about what a challenge was and what to expect in the future. Jake and Mark had done much the same information gathering and had met the others back by Marcus.

Jake needed to talk to Marcus. He sat across the table from him and waited until he could see that Marcus had realized that he was there. "Listen, buddy, do you know how Travis is going to get a hold of you?"

Marcus did not answer, but he took his good hand and began getting up from the seat at the table. Brother Marcus and Ben helped him. But not before they shot Jake a look of "Now is not the time." Marcus was met by his whole family on the way to the car. It was time to go. The day was over, and everyone knew it. Marcus did not care how he got home, he only knew that he needed to go there. Jake opened the back door of his mom and dad's car and did not even have to tell Marcus to get into it. He was getting in when one of the younger boys was running to him, calling out, "Marcus, don't leave us again." They thought they would have a fight getting him in the car, but to their surprise, Marcus simply looked to see that John had intercepted the boy and that he had been taken care of, then Marcus simply got into the back seat and pulled his left arm up and closed his eyes and went to sleep.

CHAPTER 41

When Marcus woke up, he was at the Singleton home; he was in his sweats again, no sox and no shoes. He was not in his bed but was in the chair that he felt comfortable in. His hand was propped up with ice on it, and he had a blanket tucked in around him. His hand hurt, but it was much better than it had been yesterday.

When he had opened his eyes the first time, he saw that Robert was sleeping in a chair across from him, but not now, there was no sign of him. He stirred himself slowly to see if his body was going to be his friend or his enemy today. He felt better than he thought he would. He could not remember the end of last night at all. Somehow, he was here and had changed his clothing; he hoped he had done it himself but doubted it. How embarrassing. He heard noise in the kitchen, the sound of papers, and there was the smell of coffee. He ventured out to see what was going on. He looked at the clock to see that it was late, around ten thirty to be exact.

When he looked at the breakfast table, it was Ben sitting there like before. Marcus gave him a look of good morning. "Good morning, Marcus, you look much better today, glad to see it."

Marcus figured that Ben must have had Marcus duty again. Marcus slowly poured himself a cup of coffee; he did not even bother to put anything in it but walked over to the table by Ben and took a seat. He sat there playing with the cup as it cooled so he could drink it. Ben did not engage in any more conversation, and neither did Marcus. The others had returned and had expressed that they were glad that Marcus was up but, like Ben, kept conversation toward him to a minimum.

Nancy went over to the table to look at Marcus's hand. "Here now, let me see that hand." She gently pulled it away from his body and began to move the fingers around some. Marcus did not react one way or the other to the movement. "It seems like it is doing okay, the color looks good, and the fingertips are warm. I think you are going to be good as new. We will see for sure tomorrow, you have a doctor's appointment at noon."

Marcus looked at her with an emotionless expression. She reached up and placed her hand on the side of his face. "Marcus, look at me, everything is okay, do you understand me? It is all going to be okay." For one quick second, she thought she saw tears start to form behind his eyes, but then it was gone, and he was just still. Something was very wrong, she could sense it, but she could not put her finger on it.

Jake and Mark came into the room and were talking about how crazy the news was. They stopped long enough to address Marcus, but Nancy motioned for them to back off and let him come around to them.

She had made some toast and placed it in front of Marcus. He looked up blank faced as she instructed him to eat some of it. He did as he was told. After he had one whole piece of toast, Nancy brought Marcus two pain pills and a glass of juice. She did not have to tell him to take them, he opened his mouth, she placed the pills in, and then he took the juice, drinking the whole glassful. She did not have to hold on to the glass to get him to drink it all this time. He just did it.

Marcus got up from the table and went into the living room and got into the chair, pulled the blanket up around him, and went to sleep. He slept most of the day away. They did not disturb him except to check the circulation in his hand and to give him some more pain pills when the time was right. If they gave him something to eat, he would do his best to eat it, but when he was finished, he would pull the blanket up and sleep again.

They talked among themselves about how he was acting, but they were not shocked at all that he needed time to heal. Nancy and Robert had discussed the fact that Marcus had made peace with his deep sadness the night he had let himself cry, but Robert agreed with Nancy that there were some things he still needed to work out. That night, they all gathered in the living room before everyone went home and had Bible devotions. It was a good one reminding them that God was the one who was in control. They all said goodnight and left for their homes.

*****

Tuesday morning came and went. Marcus had found a set of clothes on the table next to the chair he slept in. It took him a very long time to get dressed with one hand. He had done everything except button his pants. They were newer, and the stiffness made it harder. He decided to go upstairs and see if he could find an older pair that he could fasten better. No one expected him to be upstairs, and what he found was almost heart-stopping. His brothers were all there. He had not seen them and assumed they were at work. They were going through his room pulling all of his important papers from their hiding places. Ben saw Marcus and was angry at him. He came to Marcus's side and spoke to him roughly. He was carrying papers that had plans on them of all sorts of events. Events to meet with people outside the house. They were not illegal but were secret from the family. "Marcus, this stops now." He looked at his brothers and back at Marcus. "Your running around having meetings about the Knowing. It is not only dangerous for you but for our family as well."

Marcus did not understand why they were all so upset. Sally came hurrying into the room. "Is Mom okay?"

Marcus looked at the men; he did not have any idea what had happened. They could tell from the look on his face it was a real reaction. Jake told Marcus the story. "Mom was threatened this morning." Jake looked at Ben. "We think it might have been Travis."

There it was confirmed. Marcus had now brought trouble to his new family. He needed to do something, but he knew that they would never let him do it alone, and his biggest problem with them is that they are not street-smart enough to help him. *God, help me.*

Marcus finally spoke. "I am sorry that I have brought trouble to your family." He turned away in shame.

"Our family." Mark had been the one who said it, but they were all thinking it.

Marcus did not turn around at first but froze in place and had quit speaking for a long time. He was thinking. He lowered the level of his voice. "I promise you I will take care of this. They will never hurt one of your—I mean *my* family again, not even emotionally." Marcus was leaving the bedroom when he was headed off by his brothers.

Jake got Marcus by the arms and turned him to Brother Marcus, who towered over him. Brother Marcus and Ben were in his face so fast he did not know what was happening. Ben started the conversation. "No more secrets. We work together on this one and anything else that comes up in the future. Got it?"

Sally took a turn. She pulled Marcus in front of her and grabbed him by the waistband on his pants and proceeded to button them for him. "We are going to help you, and you are going to help us. Got it?"

It was Brother Marcus's turn to talk. "Now where were you headed just now?" He looked around at the others. "And don't lie, we will know."

Marcus was caught off guard by all of this. "Out back to see if I had any messages." He could not believe he was telling them this. They could get into trouble if they knew too much, but they could make his life harder if he did not tell them.

Ben grabbed Marcus by the collar. "Okay, let's go. You can finish getting dressed downstairs, and then we will go outside, and you can show us how they leave messages for you."

When they got downstairs, Marcus told them he had to go to the bathroom. They let him go in by himself, but they were in the hall waiting for him. Sally was the one to realize that Marcus had not asked for help with his pants. But when she said something about it, they almost all said "Window" at the same time. Jake and Mark ran to the outside of the house while Ben and Brother Marcus broke into the bathroom to find Marcus going out of the window. Ben grabbed

Marcus and hauled him back inside. Mark and Jake saw the retrieval and went back into the house.

Marcus was physically fighting them and demanding that they let him go so he could take care of business. "I do not need you or all of your help. Now please let me do my job and take care of this so Mom or any of my family doesn't get hurt."

They thought once he was inside his room, he would let up, but he kept trying to get away. With four grown men in the room, one would think Marcus would have figured out that they of all people could detain him. But he had to try anyway.

He reached for the door with his good arm, so Ben got it and gently placed him on his back with his arm pinned. Marcus was so upset that he was not thinking of his bad hand, so Ben had to hold that arm down too. Marcus then kicked his legs so he could get away (he almost did), but Jake and Brother Marcus each took a leg and pinned them to the ground. Marcus arched his back and fought them with all he had for the longest time. They just held onto him letting him wear himself out. He was angry, he was scared, he was young and thought things should be fair. He had a lot to learn. Mark tried to reason with Marcus, but he was not ready to listen yet. At one point it looked like Marcus was giving up, but when they let him go, he tried to get away again. They got him down again, but this time they held on for dear life. They needed to win so they could save this kid as well as themselves. He really gave up this time. They knew it when his body began to shake all over. He was so angry that they had not let him get away, but at the same time, he was so glad to not have to do this by himself.

He had quit fighting them, and when they let him go, he rolled over with his face down. Mark motioned for them to not let him hide the fact that he was giving in to them, but to turn him around and make him talk things out with them. They could help him work through his thinking, out in the open. Mark was thinking that Marcus should share his weakness so he could see that he was not judged or liked by his strength but by who he was.

Mark was talking loud to Marcus. "What are you thinking to do?"

The brothers had never seen Mark do his shrink thing. He was pretty good at it.

Marcus looked at Mark with question. "What do you want to do if we let you go?"

Marcus was loud back. "I want to go and find Travis."

"And then what?" Mark was still firm but not so loud. "And then what?" Mark was being firmer and had closed the distance between Marcus and himself.

"Then I would talk to him and... I don't know... I would tell him to stop being so..." Marcus was stuck on what he was feeling.

"What would you say, how would you change what you have not been able to change in the past?" Mark kept his voice loud and fast. Tapping into Marcus's anger that he never wanted to admit was there.

"I would tell him that I should have never taught him all the street stuff so he could use it for evil. I would tell him that I almost got my boys hurt because I let him do wrong things." Marcus stopped to catch his breath.

Mark did not let up though. "You did not let Travis do wrong things, Marcus, he made a choice. You could have never have stopped him. He could have stopped himself, and he does not want to."

Marcus came back with a vengeance. "But he will. If I have another chance, I can maybe convince him to do good and not evil. All I need is another chance to talk with him."

Mark took another step toward Marcus, backing him into the corner. "The last time you tried to talk to Travis, he tried to kill you. Don't you remember? What can you do to stop that?"

Marcus took a deep breath; he was trying to calm his anger. Mark went at him again, not giving him time to cover up what he was starting to feel. "What can you say or teach Travis that you have not already done in order to stop him from hurting other people? Just how much power do you think you have?"

"You don't understand, it is all my fault. I should have never let him get this far... I should have done something different, he was so angry, that is all. I should have never pushed him like that, I made him angry, and so he hurt me, that's all."

"You are angry at me now, are you going to hurt me?" Mark was in his face. He was almost screaming at Marcus, but his brothers could see that his anger was on purpose and under control.

Marcus screamed back at Mark, "I am not angry at you, and no, I would not hurt you even if I were."

Mark countered even louder, "You are such a liar, you are too angry, so why don't you just admit it and let yourself off the hook."

"I can't be angry. What if I become like Travis and hurt people? What would happen then? I ask you what I would do then." Marcus was screaming full out now; he was shaking, and he was completely off guard now.

All Mark had to do was to walk him through one of the hardest realities he would face, and that is that Travis chose to be mean and to do evil and to try and kill him. "So because you made him mad, he hurt you."

"Yes. That is right." Marcus was getting all mixed up in his mind.

"So if we let you go off by yourself and you get mad, you could hurt someone?"

"No. I mean yes." Marcus was shaking his head and pacing in the small amount of space left between Mark and the wall. "You are putting words in my mouth."

Mark lowered his voice just a little in order to calm things, but only a little. He needed Marcus to keep working this through so he could learn to trust himself and then be able to trust others as well. "No, I did not put words in your mouth. That is what you said. But never mind that. Tell me why you can go see Travis and we can't go."

"Because I might get mad at Travis for trying to hurt one of you, and I might have to hurt him to stop him." He was yelling and pacing and shaking. He needed them to understand. He needed to keep this under control, and the way he was feeling right now, he could not control himself, much less Travis and them too.

"So, you are saying you might get mad and have to hurt Travis in order to stop him from hurting others. Marcus, don't you know that Travis would not think twice about hurting you, whether he was mad or not?"

Marcus turned to square off with Mark for that statement, yelling full out, "But I am not him. I am not Travis."

Mark lowered his voice and slowed his speech down. "Exactly, you are not your brother. You are not like your brother."

Marcus had said it: he was not like his brother. He would never hurt someone even if he was mad at them. Marcus was emotionally shaken. He was not sure exactly what had happened, but he felt better somehow. He turned his back to his brothers.

Mark walked up behind him. "Marcus, I do not know everything, but I do know that you did not cause this, and you alone can't change it either."

Jake entered the conversation. "So let's do this together, and maybe we can help keep Travis alive."

Marcus still did not look at them. "But what if Travis hurts you because I let you come with me?"

It was Ben's turn to speak up. "Here is the deal, we work as a team on this, or you don't work on finding Travis at all. And you know that we can keep you from it if we decide to, now, don't you?"

Marcus had given it his all to try and get away from them but had failed to do so. What Ben had said was true, but he would still be putting their lives in danger if he joined with them. He did not know what to say. He was exhausted right now and was confused as to how he had ended up here in his thinking.

Marcus did not say a word, but when Nancy came into the room to see what all the talking was about, Marcus began to tell her how sorry he was about her being threatened. "I am so sorry. I never thought he would do this to your family. I am so sorry."

Nancy and Robert had heard most of what had happened. They were glad that the outcome was such a good one but needed to put in their two cents' worth. Nancy started off, "Marcus, you need to trust that God has put the right people in your life in order to help you, and you need to stop thinking that you are always to look out for them. Also, trust my boys and Sally. They are good people, Godly people." She looked at all her family and continued, "I know that you trusted your brother, and he hurt you."

"It doesn't matter." Marcus was putting his guard back up.

"You are right, it does not matter, but it still hurts." She did not go on until he agreed to the hurt. "It is only natural for you to wonder who you can trust after something like that. But you need to decide to give it a try and trust again or to go through life by yourself. And for the record, with all of us in your life, there is no chance of getting to do it alone."

He looked at all of them one at a time. Then he looked down and said something they could not hear. Robert was the one to ask what he had said. Marcus looked up and said, "I think I would like being a part of the family, but what if I can't do it?"

Robert spoke for the whole family. "It might take time, but we are going to help you through it. But for now, you need to get to the doctor. Ben and Brother Marcus are going to be taking you." Marcus's head shot up when he heard that. "Do you have a problem with that?"

Marcus looked at Nancy. "You are okay, aren't you? Did they scare you too much for you to go out?"

Nancy saw the concern Marcus had for her and was touched. "Marcus, I am okay. I have other things to do today with Robert. And the boys here, well, they were going that way anyway. So you go and get ready, and when you get back home, we can talk more." Marcus did as he was told. Jake and Mark stayed with Marcus while he went downstairs and finished getting ready, Ben and Brother Marcus talked with their parents to go over some details.

Robert made sure that Marcus could not overhear their conversation. "I know that things with Marcus look good right now, but be on your guard. He has been a street kid too long to not fall back into old habits. Do you remember what Victor and Sandy said about how Marcus will do crazy things in order to protect his own? Well, I did some checking around on Marcus here, and the stuff he has done in order to save one of his own is unbelievable."

Mark came upstairs to tell them that Marcus was ready and to see if they had any other ideas for the rest of Marcus's day.

Robert was glad to get to talk to Mark alone. From what he had seen and overheard Mark do with Marcus showed him that Mark had an inside sense for this kid. "Do you think he is going to run, or do you think he is really okay with us helping him?"

Mark gave it some thought. "You know that there is no chapter for this kind of kid, but it would be my guess that he will stay and work with us if for no other reason than that he thinks Mom might need to be protected. That works in our favor until we can prove to him and he can prove to himself that this is a good thing. Why, what are you thinking?"

Ben hesitated to say it. "We are thinking that we may need to put a locking short chain on Marcus with his chip. If he could not get it off, he would not have to worry about the temptation."

Mark did not need to think about this one. "No, his not being able to trust us is one thing, but his not being able to trust himself is a whole other thing. We need to send him the messages that he can do it and that he will make good choices, as best we can. If we lock it on him, the message he will get is that he can't do it, and he will find a way to get it off, and we will never see him again. He would not want to risk hurting all of us or letting us down."

Ben patted his brother on the back. "Mark, you are really good at this shrink stuff." He gave him a warning smile. "But don't you go thinking to use it on us because we will have words."

Mark gave a smile to Ben. "Where do you think I got all my practice to do this?" They had a big laugh and went downstairs to get on with the day.

*****

For weeks, things went great. Everyone went back into their usual schedule. Marcus was doing great. In fact, this Marcus they had never seen before. He was confident, he had fun and was relaxed. What a difference dealing with both his grief and his anger had made.

Marcus was teaching all of them a lot of street life skills at the same time he was learning and embracing his new life. Jake and Marcus had become even closer friends, and yet at the same time, there was a silent contest going on between them. They made a competition out of everything. Both were winners in their own world, but Marcus was catching up fast.

Only once in the last few weeks had Marcus shown a worry. It took them some time to get it out of him, and that was that he thought his left hand might not be healing as strong as it should be. One trip to the doctor and a physical therapy referral, and things went back to normal.

Marcus had a family, and he fit in somewhere. They all knew his weaknesses, and they accepted him anyway. This was as close to true happiness as he had ever been in a very long time, maybe even ever.

Marcus's hurt hand turned out to be a miracle. Only God could have turned things out so well. Marcus's physical therapy appointments sent him to the college campus where Mark was going to school. Mark has suggested that Marcus could use the gym and get more of a workout than in the backyard. Mark was more than right. Marcus loved the gym and the challenge of working out with other people.

Marcus had wandered off one day to a class on physics. He went into the class and sat quietly in the back row listening to the lecture. He was fascinated at hearing about all the things he had read in books put into application. It was great. So he made it a habit to be in the class every day it was offered. He did not have a book of his own, but the teacher noticed that he used one from the library, going there every time, looking things up to do his homework, so he gave him one of his own to use for class. The teacher had asked Marcus his name, but Marcus was able to avoid the answer so far. Marcus would do the homework but never turned it in. It was not until the last test he took when he went to put it in his book, the teacher asked if he could see it and the other homework he had not turned in. He only wanted to keep it until the next class. Marcus thought it was the least he could do since the teacher was letting him come to class and ask questions and even gave him a book.

Marcus had talked Robert and Nancy into agreeing that he could have a job and let him work at the store where his hand had been hurt. It was close to the campus. But they said he could do it only two days a week. They had discussed that it might be hard on

Marcus to be so close to Sandy's shelter but had decided to try it out, and so far, it had worked.

*****

It was family night at the Singletons, and everyone was there. Marcus had come in as they were setting down to eat. He had his physic book with him and had set it on the table, but Nancy made him move it off to the side. Marcus was so excited about everything. He had not stopped talking from the minute he had come in. He talked about the gym, about the library and all the books, and about the physics class and how it was, and how great it was that other people liked it as much as he did. He stopped talking. The whole family was smiling at him. He felt bad that he had not realized that he had made it all about himself. He took a roll and put a bite in his mouth, and went silent.

The family was super happy for Marcus and his new life. It was a blessing for them to see what God had done. But it was hard to imagine what he would have been like if he had been in a family all along.

The silence was killing Marcus. Jake was to the rescue. "Marcus, you are such a geek." He shot him a smile. "No one really likes physics."

Nancy was happy to see Marcus adjusting so well, but there were still some problems to work out. She pulled some papers out of her pocket and placed them in the center of the table. "Marcus, we need to talk about these."

Ben picked the papers up, and they turned out to be paychecks. Several of them, and none of them had been cashed. Ben showed the others, and they figured that there had to be several hundreds of dollars when they were all added up.

Marcus had not realized that this was going to be a big deal, so he kept eating. "Oh, those, I wanted to give them to you but was not sure how. I read a book on banking, and I think all I have to do is sign the back, and you can have them as money."

Mark saw the problem. Marcus was happy. He had everything he had ever dreamed of and more. What money was to some, life was to Marcus.

Sally was excited. "Marcus, I could take you shopping if you want. You could get almost anything you would like."

Marcus was serious. "Like what?"

"Like stuff you always wanted." Sally was catching on and starting to get it. "Marcus, isn't there anything you want to have, something that would make you happy?"

Marcus thought for a long time. His face lit up. "Maybe I could get the second physics book, and there is a math book I saw. But I can look at them in the library."

Jake said it again, "Marcus, you are such a geek."

Nancy signaled Jake in nest to stop picking on Marcus. That was a gift in itself when Marcus saw it. They were learning to speak his language. He felt loved.

CHAPTER 42

It was several weeks later when Jake had given Marcus a ride home that they got to the house and found Mark with several men in business suits waiting to see Marcus.

One of the men was the physics teacher. They were all gathered at the dining room table and had a recording and papers in their hands. Marcus was panicked to say the least. At first the look on his face was one of pure fright, but he recovered quickly. Only the family had seen it.

Right after they're getting to the house, Brother Marcus and Ben had come in too. Someone had tagged Marcus's chip, and a warning had been sent to both of them showing that someone was looking at Marcus. They came in quietly. They were shocked to see that the others were already there. One look at Marcus told them that he was on alert. He had already moved over to one of the side doors. He had double-checked the placement of the windows, and the screens were ready if he needed a quick exit. For the life of him, he could not think of a single thing he had done.

One of the men turned around and pointed to Marcus. "That's him." But he was not upset. He was excited to see Marcus. Everyone but Nancy and Robert were confused. They had already been talking to the men and had found out that Marcus had made such an impact at the college that these men had come to the house to fight over which one of them could get him to come to the college under a scholarship.

The physics teacher was going on. "Imagine how I felt when I found out that my best student was a sixteen-year-old street kid. I would be so excited to have him in my department. He is amazing."

The other two men were not happy about what the teacher had said. "We have been looking for this kid for weeks now, ever since we saw him working out on the field that night. We pulled the recording of his workout, but until we could scan his chip, we were not sure who he was." The man turned and started to walk toward Marcus, who by instinct started to back up in order to get away. But to both his horror and delight, he found his brothers lined up behind him. He could not move anywhere. He was stuck, but they had his back also. "Young man, we need you in our track and field department. With your talent, we could take championships in every field." He thought Marcus was playing hard to get. "We can get you scholarships with signing bonuses, I am sure. Once they see this recording, they will give you the moon."

Ben interrupted, "Recordings, what recordings?"

The man motioned to Robert if he could show the recordings on his screen. Robert helped him to get it started. There big as life was Marcus fully dressed doing all kinds of stunts on the equipment on the field. He was running and jumping with no effort at all. They saw him use the bars and swing from them and then walk on top of them like a circus act. He ran full out around the track clearing the hurdles with ease. Even with what they had seen Marcus do before, the family were surprised at what they saw. This had brought attention to Marcus and the Singleton family.

The man concluded, "So, as you can see, we cannot waste this kid on the science department, we need him in the sports department."

Marcus was still trying to back up. Ben took a hold of Marcus's arm from behind to give him mental support. Brother Marcus whispered in his ear, "It is okay. Don't panic, they want you to go to school, you are safe." It did not help though. Marcus had brought attention to his family, attention that could get them hurt, or worse, they could be found out. He felt so bad, so ashamed. He was not trying to show off. He was just being happy and having fun. This chipped life was dangerous for him and those around him. He needed to get out of this and now.

Nancy knew what to do, Mark too. They could see the panic on Marcus's face and needed to help him through it. "Marcus, I have an idea, why don't you tell the sportsmen why you were on their field and what you were doing there?"

Bringing Marcus back to something he knows, and that would settle him down. Marcus was thinking. His whole body changed. "I was working on a physics theory. I needed to see if it would work. And it did."

The men all laughed. Marcus did not know why. He did not care.

Nancy went to Marcus and put her hand on his shoulder. "Why don't you go and get cleaned up for dinner. We will call you when it is ready."

Marcus nested her, "Thank you." And he thanked the men and left the room.

The teacher addressed Robert and Nancy. He was showing them his test work. "You have got to see the work this kid can do. It is like nothing I have ever seen. And to think that he has had no real formal training."

The brothers all saw it. Marcus was going to run. They also excused themselves, leaving Nancy and Robert with the school representatives. They all ran outside except for Mark, who went into the bedroom. They were right; he was out the window and onto the roof by the time they got to him. He was lowering himself down from the roof when Ben, Jake and Brother Marcus snagged him before he could hit the ground running.

Mark came out the window behind him and was slowly walking on the roof to the edge. "Oh, God, Marcus, how do you even do this?"

Marcus saw that Mark was going to have a problem if he did not help him. He jumped up and took hold of the roof's edge and swung himself back up onto the roof by Mark.

"What do you think you are doing? You could get yourself killed, you know."

The two of them sat on the roof together looking down at the brothers on the ground. They could not get up and did not want to either. They stayed there until the men from the school left. The men's leaving was one of the best sights Marcus had seen in a long time.

Nancy called out from the window for the two of them to get off her roof and to quit acting like monkeys. They smiled at each other.

Marcus helped Mark off the roof and back into his window. "Thanks, Marcus."

Marcus looked at Mark. "No, thank you for risking your safety for me. I am sorry."

Nancy had convinced her boys that Marcus might need some time to pull himself together, so they all met in the family room first. There on the screen was a frozen recording of their little brother doing a backflip off a high bar he had just walked across. Jake looked at the screen. "He can do that because he knows science and math? Who would have ever guessed?"

Nancy and Robert laughed and went into the kitchen leaving the brothers alone.

Mark went to turn the recording off but had hit the play button instead. They were all having fun watching Marcus on the screen. They all stopped having fun when they saw a hooded figure enter on one side of the screen and grab Marcus and shove him up against the wall. There was no sound, but it did not take sound to see that this figure was planning on harming Marcus. They watched as Marcus tried to talk to the figure and were horrified that Marcus pursued him even after he had been pushed to the ground and was kicked several times in the side. Marcus did not let up, but he continued to go after him until the figure put a choke hold on Marcus, and it looked like Marcus must have passed out. Marcus would have never stopped otherwise.

Mark turned off the recording and then the screen. They all knew now why Marcus had overreacted to the recording. He knew what they might find out.

Brother Marcus stated what they were all thinking, "Would anyone want to put a wager as to who you think our hooded figure is?" They all agreed that it must have been Travis.

As brothers to Marcus, they needed to keep what they saw from their parents; but as adults, they needed to help protect this kid from Travis. For now, they decided to keep this among themselves until they could figure out what to do. Mark pulled the recording and placed it in his coat. They all went into dinner. This was going to be interesting to watch. Nancy had asked Jake to go and get Marcus. "Tell him I said to come down now." She smiled and thanked Jake.

Marcus did not want to come down to dinner. So when Jake came to get him, he was not excited to go. "Could you please tell them I am not hungry or that I was asleep, or make something up for me?"

Jake gently took Marcus by the arm. "Sorry, little brother, being a part of this family means you have to get your backside chewed sometimes. And today is your turn."

Jake thought it was strange that Marcus was more afraid of their mom and dad than he was a brother who tried to kill him. Perhaps fear was the wrong word. Maybe *respect* would be a better one. Marcus truly respected their parents. Perhaps that was it, Marcus was afraid of letting them down.

Marcus came into the room so much different than he had at the last dinner. He took his seat but did not look up at any of them. Jake felt sorry for Marcus.

Robert said grace, and they all started to put food on their plates. "Marcus, was that really you in that recording?" Robert kept working on his food as he asked.

Marcus cleared his throat. "Yes, sir, it is."

Robert stopped to look at Marcus and then continued, "If I am not mistaken, that recording was made late at night, I believe it was about one a.m.?"

"Yes, sir, it was." Marcus kept his head down.

Robert stopped what he was doing. "How did you get there?"

"I ran." His voice was strong but not defiant.

"You ran to the campus and back in one night, and you did all that running around while you were there?" Robert was hard-pressed to believe Marcus, but he had not ever really lied to him before.

Marcus was confused. "Yes, sir, but I took all night."

The rest of the family was having fun watching the interrogation of Marcus by their dad.

"And you did it without permission and at night? Why?" Robert needed to hear the motive of this young man.

Marcus answered, "I did it at night because I did not want anyone to see me. And I did not get any of you involved because I could do it myself."

Robert continued, "Well, that did not work out so good, did it?" He was thinking out loud. "Okay. Let's go over this. You left this house without permission, and you were out after curfew when you were seen by the coaches at the college? How am I doing so far?"

Marcus did not answer as to the fact he really did not know what the question was. He looked down in his lap.

Robert looked at Nancy and back at Marcus. "Look at me when I talk to you please." Marcus looked at him, and he continued, "Did you go out your window?"

Marcus did not know what that mattered but answered, "Yes, I did."

Robert thought for a very long time about what they had discussed. None of the other brothers said a word at all but kept eating dinner like nothing was going on.

Robert had come to his conclusion about Marcus going out alone at night. "Next time you need to go out at night, you ask one of us to take you. And you need to know that if you ever go out of your bedroom window again when we send you upstairs, we will nail your window shut, and you will not be able to use it in an emergency. And I am sure that you do not want that." Robert stopped moving and looked at Marcus. "Say it."

Marcus spoke up. "Yes, if I need to go out at night, I will ask one of you to take me, and when you send me upstairs, I will not ever go out of the window."

Robert added, "Or?"

Marcus added, "Or you will nail my bedroom window shut."

The brothers picked up on the play of words Marcus chose. "I will not go out of the window when you send me upstairs." He quoted their dad. But what he did not promise to do was to not go out the window whenever he went upstairs by himself. Marcus had been clever but not clever enough for this family.

Robert continued to eat. "Okay, enough of that, now what are we going to do about you at the college?"

Marcus was not happy about what needed to happen, but he had brought it on himself by bringing attention to himself and the family. "My hand is better, so I do not need to go there to do therapy anymore. I can get back to doing more things here around the house. But can I still use the library? I promise to not draw attention to us again. I know better now."

The whole family was trying to figure out what Marcus was talking about.

Marcus lowered his head. "I know I messed up, and I am sorry. I did not mean to show off in the class. I just liked doing the work, that is all. I did not give the teacher the papers, he had asked for them. I was not thinking. I really like my job at the market, and the owner said I could become manager someday. I do not know how to fix this, but I think in time they will forget about me. I pray anyway." Marcus was really nervous. "Please let me keep my job though, I like to work and I get to talk with the people."

The family caught on to what Marcus was thinking one at a time; as they figured it out, they each got a smile they were trying to hide on their faces.

Robert was almost the last to figure out that Marcus did not get the good news about the school opportunity. He thought that he was in trouble for bringing attention to himself. "Marcus, I want you to look at me."

Marcus was afraid that if he looked at Robert and the family, they might see how disappointed he was at not getting to go to the college anymore. This was on him though, he was the one who messed up. He was trying to pull it together before he did what Robert asked, but the disappointment was there, and he could not hide it very well. "I am sorry, but I can't talk about this right now, it hurts too much. I messed up, and I know it. So, can we please just not talk about it anymore?"

Robert thought he should be tough on Marcus, but no one could be tougher than Marcus was on himself. "Marcus, I think you must not see the whole picture. What you are in trouble for is sneaking out at night and running the streets. Not getting recognition for you and for the family. Marcus, this school opportunity is a blessing. You, in the middle of all this world mess, are a bright light. You have a God-given gift, and you need to glorify God with it. Marcus, you need to go to school and do as good as you can."

Marcus was the confused one at this moment. "What, you want me to show off?"

Robert took a deep breath. "No, but we do want you to do your best with what God gave you to do."

Marcus had a new hope. "You mean I can go to school?"

"The biggest problem you have as far as school goes is to decide which department you want to be under, the science or sports?" Robert continued to eat and let Marcus feel the full impact this was going to have on his life. "And since you have until the next school year to decide." Robert pointed to Brother Marcus and Jake. "These two have an idea for you, and I agree with them that it is time for you to do some additional training."

Marcus looked to Jake and Brother Marcus. "What kind of training?"

Robert finished his last bite of food before he answered, "They have asked to train you in self-defense, and I agree that you could use some help in that area. Although we all know that you are fast and are good at getting away, when you want to, learning to defend yourself is always another need in life."

The way their dad had said "when you want to" almost made the brothers think Dad knew about Marcus being attacked. But how could he? They tried not to react, but looks between them did not go unnoticed by their mom.

Nancy reached for a roll. "So why do I think that there is something else going on?"

Marcus interrupted before they had to answer. "Thank you for the offer, but I don't want to learn how to hurt people."

Robert continued the conversation. "Marcus, you need to stop being afraid to stand up for yourself. You wanted to go to school, but you were going to back down because you thought you messed up. You do not want to hurt someone, so you don't want to protect yourself. God gave you the ability to be a full person, so why don't you step up and do it."

Marcus used Robert's own words against him. "Okay, so I am stepping up and telling you that I do not want to learn self-defense."

Robert got up from the table to go and get something more to drink. "Too bad, your training starts tomorrow, after you get off work." And he left the room.

Jake and Brother Marcus could help Marcus with self-defense from bad guys, but no one could teach you how to counter their dad's parenting.

Jake leaned over and whispered to Marcus, "You should never try and use Dad's words back on him, he always wins."

Robert had put Marcus into a position where he could not get to argue his side of the story, it wasn't fair. It was...parenting.

Marcus hardly ate anything. The rest of the night was quiet. Everyone helped clean up and left to go home. But there was going to be a brother meeting after they left. "Let's meet at my apartment," Jake had said as they left the house. All agreed.

*****

The brothers needed a plan. "So, what is our goal?" Ben was the best at organizing thoughts.

Brother Marcus put it into words. "We need to keep Marcus safe, we need to get Travis off the streets, and we need to keep the Knowing safe from being found out."

Mark wanted to know why they had not told the parents about Travis and the college event. They explained that they were sure that their dad would lock Marcus up and that they would never be able to get Marcus free from Travis. This needed to come to an end. Travis needed to be a part of the game plan, or he needed to be taken out as the enemy. It would be Travis's choice, but Marcus needed to see that for himself so he could move on.

It was decided that night that Jake and Brother Marcus would teach Marcus self-defense and keep him busy every afternoon for the next week. Mark was going to hit the street and gather any information about Travis, and then there was the challenge that was coming up. Ben would contact Sally and tell her what had happened. He got the recording from Mark, so he could show her and see if she saw anything they had missed. Sally was really good at that kind of thing. They had also decided that they needed to get a short, locking chain ready for Marcus in case he decided to go it alone with Travis. They did not want to lose him by his taking off his chip.

*****

The next year was going to be so different for Marcus. He would be going to school with a name and, perhaps soon, to real classes and with his own books. This was going to be great. But before he could move on in his new life, he had to finish this thing with Travis. He had given notice two days ago about where and when to meet. He was not going to share that information with anyone. He did not want anyone else hurt. Besides, if he went to see Travis alone, and if Travis changed his mind about the challenge, then he would not be embarrassed, he could just tell everyone that Travis had won, and Travis could live here with Marcus. Who knew, maybe Travis could get to go to school also. Marcus could not wait to tell Travis the opportunity that the two brothers could have. This could change everything in Travis's eyes now that they could go to school. Maybe it would give Travis the hope he needed to change.

*****

Mark had found Victor and Sandy to ask if they had heard anything out about the challenge. They had heard nothing but made it work out so Mark was given the chance to talk to some of the nest kids. They had expressed their concern for Marcus. They told them that the meeting with Travis had been set up but that he was not going to tell anyone because he did not want anyone hurt or to get into trouble. Marcus thought he could handle it and that he had a new idea that might bring Travis around.

The only thing Sally could find from the recording was the fact that Travis meant to hurt Marcus, and they had a date from it.

Ben and Brother Marcus were at the office checking on some recordings from around the market when an officer came in to talk to them about their little brother.

"Hey, did you hear that Will's cover was blown?" The officer was not a friend of theirs, but he was a good guy and not prone to gossip.

Jake had joined them in time to hear only part of what he had said about Will. "What happened?"

The officer lowered his voice. "You know that kid you took in? Well, he has a brother I am sure you know about. Well, anyway, this kid Travis told everyone that Will was an officer. But that is when it gets really weird. Some of the older Knowing were going to teach our Will a lesson and were going to give him a beating. But this kid Travis literally stepped in the way of a bat and stopped them from hurting our own. Will said that Travis used his arm to stop the bat, and the only thing that kept this kid from getting hurt was that he had a brace on his arm. We pulled the rap sheet on this Travis, and he is a real bad seed, so it seems strange that he had changed the way he did. All I can say is thank God for the brace on Travis's arm."

Jake brought up the question, "What about Travis having a brace?"

The officer shook his head and repeated again what he had been told. "Will had said that one of the men was going to take a bat to his head when this kid Travis stepped right in front of the bat and used a hand with a brace to stop it. Will said that the only thing that kept his kid from getting hurt was that he had the brace on his arm. Travis then yelled at the men to stop, and they did what he said. It is all so strange, but anything about the Knowing is strange." He repeated this to make sure they all were clear on the story.

He was leaving the room when Ben had a question for him. "How did you know it was Travis?"

"Well, truthfully at first we were all told that it was your little brother Marcus, but when we did the chip scan, this kid did not have a chip, so when we pulled the records on Marcus, that is when we found out that it was Travis (without a chip), his brother, and not Marcus after all." He was leaving but stopped to say one more thing. "If I were you, I would keep my little brother as far away from this kid Travis as I could. First reason would be because he is mean. I know he saved Will, but he is bad news, and second reason is because the boys look too much alike, way too much alike for it to be safe for Marcus."

When the officer left the room, the men pulled up the files on the beating that did not happen. Sure enough, there was Marcus; they saw this dumb kid do exactly what the officer had said and had put himself in front of a bat for Will the officer.

Jake pulled up a photo of Travis and put it side by side with one of Marcus. They had not seen it before. They did look a lot alike. They pulled up the latest recording of Travis. Travis's hair was shorter, and his clothing was looser than Marcus wore, except for the brace they could pass as twins. They were all thinking it, but it was Jake who said it out loud. "I think we just got an answer to our problem. What if we use Marcus to get to Travis? We can follow Marcus when he goes to meet for the challenge. We can get Travis and have him arrested."

Ben thought it was a good idea but needed to think it through more. "But how will we keep Marcus from being arrested?"

Jake smiled. "Because he will not be there. There will be two Travis's there. One with a chip (our Marcus) and one without. We call it in and before the officers arrive, we grab our Travis (Marcus with the chip) and get him home."

Jake, Ben, and Brother Marcus had a plan even if they had not fine tuned the details. Ben set things in motion. "Jake, you get Marcus a haircut, I will get Sally to work on the clothing, and Brother Marcus and I are going to work on a new chain for our little brother for his chip."

"Jake, you and I are going to start Marcus's self-defense classes right away. Let's go." All three of them went to do their part and to fill Sally and Mark in on what they had found out and what they were planning to do about it.

*****

When Marcus had arrived home from work, he found both Brother Marcus and Jake were waiting for him. Marcus had hoped that they would forget about the self-defense classes. He was tired, and he needed to work on the plans he had for the day of the challenge.

Jake saw Marcus first. "Hey, Marcus, are you ready for your first class?"

Marcus sat down in the chair. "About that, I *really* do not want to learn how to hurt people. So, if you do not mind, I will just skip it."

"Not a chance. And get Dad mad at us because you did not get your training? Come on, this can be fun." Jake was turning his chair in order to coax him out.

Nancy was cooking dinner and had overheard the conversation. "Marcus, get yourself up from there and go out back with your brothers and let them teach you how to defend yourself now."

At this point, Marcus knew that it was useless to argue with Nancy, but he needed to get out of this. "Nancy, I don't think that—"

She turned to look at him. "You are right, don't think so much, and do. Go and learn what you can from them." She pointed to the door where the two of them were waiting.

The three of them went out farther into the yard, to a grassy area.

Jake crouched down and told Marcus to come at him. "Come on, geek, let me teach you something you cannot get from a book." He was trying to rile Marcus, but he was not going to go for it. Marcus sat down.

Brother Marcus was up for his turn. "Let me explain how the physical part works." He turned to Jake. "Hey, don't we have a book on self-defense? That might be a better way to train Marcus."

693

The two brothers used each other for practice showing Marcus how it was done. But Marcus sat looking at them not even pretending to learn anything.

Over an hour had passed, and every time Nancy looked out the window, she saw the two men showing and explaining things to Marcus, who was bored out of his mind listening. She was laughing to herself when Mark entered the door.

Mark went over by the kitchen window and looked at what she was looking at. "I do not get it, what is going on?"

His mom answered, "Your brothers are trying to convince Marcus that they should train him in self-defense. And as you can see, it is not working and has not been working for over an hour now."

Jake had come into the kitchen. "Mom, that kid is so stubborn. I do not think he can be taught anything about fighting."

Mark needed to know something. "Jake, is this important for him to know, or is this just an exercise?"

"Mark, he needs to know how to take care of himself. All he knows now is how to run or, worse yet, to stay and take it." Jake was truly concerned.

Mark thought about what he could do. "Mom, will you help me get Marcus to do what they want?"

"Sure, Mark, but how can you get him to do what they have not been able to do for over an hour now?" She looked at Jake and shrugged her shoulders.

Mark talked to Jake. "I need you to not let Marcus come into the house no matter what you hear coming from us. You do that, and I will guarantee you Marcus will fight you."

Jake shook his head no and laughed. "Do you want to bet on this? Mark, you are crazy, this kid will never fight." He looked at Mark. He was serious. "Okay, if you want to try, I am in."

Jake headed out the door to go back to the teaching as it was. "Oh, and, Jake, tell Brother Marcus to keep him out of the house too."

Mark waited until he saw Mark tell Brother Marcus, who looked at the window and nodded yes.

Nancy opened the window and yelled out, "Marcus, come here, I need your help!"

Marcus's head shot up, and he looked at the house. He started to get up, but Jake gently pushed him back down. "No, you stay here with us."

"Jake, didn't you hear her? She needs our help." Marcus got up on his feet before Jake could touch him again. "I need to go. I will be right back, okay?"

Brother Marcus got between Marcus and the house. "No, you stay here."

Marcus looked at the two brothers and then back at the house. Nancy said she needed him. He had to go.

Marcus clearly was not making these two understand that he needed to get to the house to help their mom. "I am going, and you are not going to stop me."

Jake teased, "Want to bet?"

Nancy called out again to Marcus. "Marcus, please come and help me." But this time, she sounded angry and even a little scared.

Marcus was getting anxious. "Look, I really need to go please. I need to go now."

"No. And if you really want to go, you will have to go through me." Jake was crouched down expecting Marcus to come straight at him.

But to the brother's credit and surprise, Marcus did the unexpected. He ran the other way and went over the backyard fence. Both brothers went into the house to head him off at the front door. When they went flying through the kitchen into the living room, Marcus came back over the fence, came up on the deck, and into the house. "Nancy, what do you need help with?"

Mark and Nancy were laughing so hard they could not catch their breath. When the two brothers came in to join them, they began to laugh too. Marcus looked at all of them and thought they were crazy.

Robert had arrived home, and Sally had come with him. They were as confused as Marcus. Robert gave Nancy a kiss on her cheek, and she told him she would explain later. Dinner was almost done.

It was not a planned family night, but it was turning out to be one as they were all sitting down to dinner. Ben had arrived, but he did not look like he was there for dinner. When he came in, he had a very official look about him. Marcus had never seen him look like that before, but he had seen it on the faces of other officials in the past. He had bad news. "Dad, Mom, can I talk to you alone for a minute before we eat?" They did not go into the study but went up to their bedroom to talk.

Jake was the one to speak about it first. "It must be really bad news if they went upstairs."

Mark agreed with Jake and asked everyone else at the table if they knew anything, but they had not heard a word about anything bad happening. The three of them came back down the stairs and went right to the table. It was a quiet meal. Some talk but mostly quiet. It was at the end of the meal that Robert talked about Marcus's defense classes and asked how they were going. Nancy and Mark both started to chuckle when they heard about it. They told Robert the whole story, and they all had fun with it.

It was Robert who changed the tone. "Marcus, diversion is good, but you need to learn how to defend yourself. Tomorrow when you get with the boys, I expect you to learn how." He looked at Jake and Brother Marcus. "Things out in the world are starting to heat up, and we need to be spiritually and mentally as well as physically ready for whatever comes."

Jake had to ask, "Dad, has something happened?"

Robert looked at Ben, who slightly nodded his head yes. "There have been some attacks on some of the chipless shelters lately. Not just around here but all across the United States. Reports are coming in that these are planed events."

Marcus was on full alert. "Was anyone hurt?"

Ben was the one to answer. "Yes, there were people hurt, and some even reported to have been killed. We have a good life, and God takes care of us, but we are going to have to be more careful than ever. The word is out that we have a group of Knowing who are armed and dangerous, so none of you should be seen with anyone from the chipless community. If they are chipless, it could be as dangerous for them as it is for us."

Robert looked around the table. "Marcus, I mean you too. I know it is your world, but that is your past. For now, you are in this world, and you do not under any circumstances interact with any of the chipless."

Marcus needed to tell them that they did not understand how it worked in the underground. "Robert, I need to get to go and tell someone about the information. This could be important for them to know. If you would let me get a message to Sandy or Victor, I could—"

Robert leaned into the table in order to get better eye contact with Marcus. "Marcus, no. That is not going to happen, you are out of it until further notice. As far as the information getting out, you can trust me it has happened."

Ben looked at Marcus. "I talked to Victor, and he told me to give you a message. I don't understand it, but he said to tell you that a 'no contact order is in place.' He said that you would understand. Do you?"

Marcus could hardly swallow the food he had in his mouth. This was not good. He had a meeting in only a few days, and he needed to be able to follow through on it. Travis was still out on the streets, and he needed to make sure that he took this seriously also. Here he was all safe and sound in a great home with great people, while many of his friends were out there on the streets and in danger.

The table was quiet, very little eating and even less talking was going on. They cleared the table and decided that it was a great time to have a devotion time. Robert got out his Bible and began to read from one part of the book of Exodus; there was a part where God's people had been kept slaves for many years, but God heard, and God had taken care of His people. Robert pointed out that it was still the same. God hears, and God will take care of His people. At the end of the study, they moved into the living room, all of them; they had to have a family discussion about what was to happen in the next few days. At first, Marcus thought it was about the challenge but quickly realized that what was going on in his small world was nothing compared to the big picture. People needed to hear about God, but now it had become even harder.

Robert and Ben looked even more upset, but whatever was going to happen needed to be done. Robert looked at Marcus and decided this was the time.

"Marcus, Ben tells me that you have some kind of a meeting with Travis getting ready to happen. You need to consider it canceled." He looked at Nancy and took a deep breath then continued, "Marcus, this is going to be hard, but it has to be done. We know that you are under a lot of pressure to decide what you should do with your two worlds always pulling at each other, so we have decided to take part of the temptation off you. The fact that you can remove your chip at any time would be a temptation on anyone, but with someone as young as you, it could be way too much responsibility. Marcus, it is not that we don't trust you, but we need you to not be able to take off your chip. We have a new chain for you to wear your chip on. It is shorter and cannot go over your head, and it is a special chain that cannot be cut, and it hinges and locks on. Marcus, what I am saying is that we are going to have to do that with your chip."

Ben pulled out what looked like a cable and not a chain at all. To say that he felt disappointment was an understatement. But the fear of not being able to get away from this chip was unreal. Not to mention the fact he had planned to do exactly that in a few days. He needed to not have a chip when he met Travis. He could not offer them his word that he would not decide to take it off, but he needed to do something. But what?

Marcus's thoughts were interrupted by Robert. "Marcus, please give me your chain so we can change it out." He held out his hand. "Son, I am sorry, but please don't make it any harder than it has to be."

Marcus took off his chain and handed it to him. Ben and Robert put his medallion with the chip on it. "Stand up and come here please."

Marcus did not say a word but did as he was told. He put his back to them, and they placed it on him and locked it into place. Marcus felt like it weighed a million pounds. This was going to mess all of his plans up. *God, now what am I going to do?* All of his plans for him and Travis had been around him being able to give Travis his chip so Travis could be a part of this world and take Marcus's place. But now, what could he do to save Travis? What could he offer him? Maybe he could tell the family what he was up to, but then whatever hope he had to save Travis would be lost. They would never understand his trading identities with Travis to give him another chance. They were right to think he was going to take it off; how they figured it out was unreal. But even if he could not give Travis his chip, once he showed up, they could transfer it to Travis; they had the ability to do so. Marcus just had to set things up, so they would have no other choice.

When they were done, Marcus did not say a word or even look at any of them. He needed time to rethink about what had happened. He went to go outside.

Robert called out behind him, "Marcus, stay in the yard. Understand? And be back in the house by ten."

Marcus kept his eyes on the now open door. He nodded his head yes, showing that he did understand, and went out to the tree he liked to sit up in and found a branch that he thought would put him out of sight from the people at the house. He needed some God time.

Nancy and Mark were watching him from the kitchen window. "Mom, he is going to be all right, I promise."

They watched him and saw that he wiped his eyes several times. "Mark, I think he may be crying."

Mark gave her a hug. "And that would be a good thing. He is learning to let his feelings out. It will be better for him in the long run, you will see."

*****

Everyone had gone home. Nancy and Robert were in the living room reading when they heard a noise from Marcus's room upstairs. When they looked at the clock, it was 9:59 pm; he was in the house on time, but he came through his window.

Robert looked at Nancy. "That is it. I am going to nail that window shut."

Nancy smiled and laughed. "He did not break his promise to you. You said he would promise to not go out of the window if you sent him to his room, not that he would not come in through the window." They both shook their head with disbelief of how smart this kid really was. And they thanked God for him in their life.

CHAPTER 43

The next day was a gift for Marcus. He was going to be working at the market most of the day. He would be off at four and would not have to deal with any family stuff until then.

Marcus had worked most of his day without incident. With the no contact order, there was no communication from anyone about anything dealing with the Knowing or the chipless people. Marcus was sweeping up before he got off work. A young boy ran though the store and bumped into him and then continued on his way. Marcus looked up to see where he went and then double checked to see if he could tell where the boy had come from, but there was no clue.

Marcus scanned the store again, only to see that Jake was standing off to one side of the room. He was leaning up against the wall and from the looks of him he had been there for some time. Marcus was sure he had seen the run in with the boy, but Jake did not show any awareness of the note that passed between them. Marcus had it in his hand and had slid it into his pocket. As soon as he was out of sight from Jake, he would look at it. Marcus gave a sign asking Jake why he was there, and Jake told him he was going to take him for a haircut. Marcus thought this was an answer to a prayer, with shorter hair he would look more like Travis and every little bit would help. Marcus signaled back that he would be off soon and went on about doing his work.

Jake had in fact seen the hand off. He would deal with that later. Things were going along well as far as the plans had gone. Marcus had his chip secure on his chain, he was going to get a haircut, shorter hair would make him look even more like Travis and he was no lon-

701

ger wearing his brace. Mark had called and said that he had found an extra-large jacket that looked almost exactly like the one Travis had been wearing in the last recording they had seen of him. It had a black hood and cuffs on the sleeves. They would give it to Marcus tonight and put away his old one to ensure he started wearing the right one.

"Hey Jake, are you ready to go?" Marcus had come out of the back room taking off the apron he had been wearing. He hung it up, told everyone good night and they both got in the car.

Jake did not start the car but turned to Marcus. "So, what did the note say?"

Marcus looked down. "You saw that did you?"

"Don't change the subject. What did the note say?"

Jake did not move.

Marcus pulled out the note from his pocket. It was a note about John, one of Marcus' commanders. He had been arrested. And they were asking for Marcus to help him. There was no signature so there was no way to be sure who sent it. "Marcus, we need to tell Dad about this and show it to him. I think he can help."

Jake picked up his phone and dialed his dad. They had a very cryptic conversation. Jake told him about the message and that they would be right home after the haircut. Jake started the car and they went to the barber shop they had been to before. This time was very different. When Marcus tried to have a conversation with the barber, he acted like he had never seen Marcus before. This was the no contact order in action. And Marcus hated it.

Jake and Marcus drove home in silence. Jake felt sorry for Marcus but more than that he felt scared for him. So, he prayed in silence for his new little brother, asking God to help him, help.

When they got home Brother Marcus and Mark were there. Marcus hurried out of the car and into the house. He went to where Robert and the others were. "Do you have any news yet?" Marcus was hoping for a miracle.

Jake was close behind Marcus. He had seemed fine in the car, but he was completely worked up now. "I mean, do you know where he is, is he ok, they did not chip him, did they?"

Nancy had overheard most of the conversation. "Marcus, slow down. Let them tell you what they know."

Marcus took a deep breath. "I am sorry."

Robert told Marcus what they had found out. John had been with a group of boys, led by who they think was Travis and they were arguing about something when the officers arrested the whole bunch of them. They think it was a setup done by Travis to get John off the streets so he could not help you at the challenge.

Marcus turned his back to them again. A new pattern that Mark noticed, whenever Marcus felt out of control of himself. Marcus turned back around. "What can I do? Can I go and see him?"

Brother Marcus had the rest of the information about John. "Ben is working on it; he has called Sally to see if she knows anything. They are going to call us as soon as they know something."

Robert interrupted his talk. "And you are not going to do anything, except have dinner with us and wait for them to call."

Marcus looked like the air was knocked out of him. There had to be something he could do.

Nancy put her arm around Marcus and led him to the dinner table. She squeezed him on his arm to reassure him that he was doing the right thing. They all joined them at the table.

Dinner had been a quiet event. Marcus had taken a baked potato wrapped in tin foil and fixed it up but hardly ate any of it. The longer they sat there the more nervous Marcus got. He needed to get out of here. He needed to do something. "May I be excused?" Marcus was looking at Robert.

Robert thought hard about what he should do to help Marcus wait this out. "What are you going to do?"

"I thought I would go out back and do some of the yard work, if that is okay?" Marcus had not thought that far ahead.

Robert looked at Nancy who agreed by nodding her head. "All right, but I need you to stay close in case we get a call."

Marcus had not considered that if he left to go out on the streets that he might miss some of the information about what was going on with John. Marcus looked at Robert with frustration. "Okay, thank you." It was all he could think to say. He was so angry at not being able to do something. Marcus went out the back door.

Robert continued to eat. "Boys I think it might be a good time to practice self-defense with Marcus. I think you might be able to get some fight out of him now."

Brother Marcus and Jake smiled at their dad. Jake raised his eyebrows and looked at Mark and then back at his dad. "Now who is the shrink around here?"

Brother Marcus and Jake got up to follow Marcus when Mark called out to them. "I think you might want to check his right pant pocket, he had the foil from his potato in it, I think he might be planning on covering his chip."

Jake answered again. "And look who is the officer now." They all had a good time being a family that worked together to help each other.

By the time the brothers had arrived to the back-yard Marcus was by the back fence. Marcus was so deep in thought that Jake was right beside him before he realized anyone was there. "May I suggest that you don't even think about it?"

Brother Marcus reached into Marcus' right pocket and took the foil he had stashed. Marcus tried to stop him and then tried to get it back. "Please give that back to me, I need it." The whole time they were working with Marcus they were leading him away from the back fence and onto the grassy part of the yard.

Jake was ready for a self-defense class. "Okay Marcus let's see what you have in the way of defending yourself. Try and remember what we taught you yesterday."

Marcus did not want to deal with Jake right now. Brother Marcus had the foil he needed, and he wanted it back.

Marcus turned to speak to Brother Marcus about getting his foil back, but Jake interrupted him. "Come on geek boy." Jake took the foil from Brother Marcus and put it into his own pant pocket.

Marcus saw him and tried to get it before he got it in his pocket but it was too late. "Jake please give me the foil."

Jake smiled at Marcus and crossed his arms. "No"

Marcus reached for the foil; Jake countered him by grabbing him and putting him in an arm move they had taught Marcus how to get out of the day before. Jake had Marcus locked into a holding position.

Marcus was being polite and asked Jake to please let go of him. Jake gave out a sigh and only held him tighter. "We can stay here all night if you would like."

Jake felt Marcus go limp. He knew this trick from being on the farm. They were taught that if they were being held that they should go limp and drop to the ground and then get away without any fight. But not this time, Jake was ready for Marcus' move. When Marcus went limp Jake held on tighter and he still had hold of him. "That is not going to work little brother. You know what to do so do it."

"Jake, I do not want to hurt you so please let me go." Marcus had tightened up again and gone limp several times only to find that Jake was serious about not letting him go. Marcus threw his head back against Jake's chest but found that he could not move at all. "Jake, I mean it, let me go."

Jake laughed and without another warning Marcus pulled his leg around and countered with the moves that his brothers had taught him the day before. Jake flew over Marcus' hip and landed on his back in front of Marcus who then reached into his pocket and took back his foil. Marcus was horrified when he realized what he had done. "Oh God, Jake I am so sorry, did I hurt you?" He felt so bad. But it was to Jake's surprise that the rest of the family had seen the whole thing. They were on the deck getting ready to call out to them telling them that they had some news about John when they saw Marcus take him out.

Jake got up and was laughing. "Little brother, you are a good student or we are good teachers. But yes, I am fine." Jake got serious. "Marcus sometimes you have to fight because there is nothing else you can do but fight back. Remember if you have done everything you can do to not fight, then you must do everything you can do to fight to win. You must fight to win even if it hurts someone else. If they bring the fight to you, then you must protect yourself. Got it?"

Marcus did not talk but shook his head that he understood. His attention was now on the deck of the house. They were calling out for all of them to come on inside. Marcus looked to Jake to confirm that he in fact was ok. Jake motioned for Marcus to go on ahead and see what was up.

As Marcus was walking across the deck he looked inside the house and saw that Sally was here and she was talking to someone. As he looked closer, he saw that it was none other than John. He went through the door and across the room and stopped short of flying into John physically. "What were you thinking? Do you have any idea what trouble you are in? I thought I taught you better. You, you, you should have been…" Marcus went the rest of the distance and put a hug on John, realizing how this might look, he backed off. "John what were you doing with Travis?"

John looked around at all the Singletons. Marcus told him that they were family and that it was okay to talk in front of them. But he signed that John should be careful so not to scare them. "I was trying to make a deal for you."

Marcus did not understand the statement. "Why would you represent me in a deal?"

John shook his head that Marcus did not understand him. So, he said it out loud. "No, I mean that I was trying to make a deal for you, your life for something else."

That statement sent an alarm off in the entire Singleton family. Ben reacted first. "What do you mean for his life?"

John went to speak to Ben and put his back to Jake so that Jake could see his hands. He was signaling Jake things different from what he was telling Ben.

Mark saw what was happening and made sure he kept Marcus from seeing the signaling that was going on.

John was telling Ben and Marcus that it was Travis who put out a hit on Marcus but that he now only wanted him hurt. But at the same time, he was telling Jake to keep Marcus away from Travis because he planned to kill him outright. Marcus had told John to not scare his family and on the outside view he was following the orders that Marcus had given him, but he was telling Jake what was really happening.

Ben asked John. "Do you know where the meeting is set?"

John turns to Marcus. "Is it set?" He forgets about the family in the room. "Do you know when and where you are going to meet Travis? You know we are with you no matter what, right? We all know about the large army, but we are with you."

Marcus shook his head no. John signaled to Jake that he was sure that Marcus did know. He sent an urgent message. 'Please help Marcus, he trusts Travis too much'.

"Marcus please look at me." John was trying to keep it cool but he was scared for his leader and friend right now. "Marcus you need to promise me that you will not meet with Travis alone." John stepped closer to Marcus. "You have got to tell them everything so they can help." John looked around the room nervously. "Marcus if you do not tell them then I will."

Marcus started nesting to John to be quiet or he would remove him from being a commander in his nest. John answered out loud. "I would rather lose my position than lose a good friend. This is crazy, you cannot save everyone"

Marcus was upset that his friend would betray him like this. He was upset because his family would never understand why he had to do what was next. He needed to do it for them, his new family and for the Knowing groups.

Robert could see that as long as Marcus was in the same room with John, that John was going to hesitate to talk freely with them. "Nancy, you and Sally please take Marcus into the kitchen for a while and we are going to talk with John."

Marcus shot a hand motion to John that shut the whole room down. John would not say another word after Marcus' last signal. Jake tried to use nest with John, but he would not even look at him. John hoped he had said enough for the Singletons to get the fact they needed to keep Marcus away from Travis. Marcus was the leader that God had given him to follow all of these years. And he would continue to do so out of honor.

After about an hour of trying to get more information out of John and Marcus the family decided that it was time for John to go back to the shelter for the night. Marcus sat quietly as they were getting John ready to leave. Marcus got up from the chair and went to the coat closet and gave John his old coat. Marcus explained to John that Mark had given him a new one and he wanted to give his old one to him. John accepted it without question. John thanked the family for getting him out of jail and was leaving with Sally when he turned to Marcus. "Marcus, please be smart."

Marcus' only answer was. "John I will do what I have to do. God will take care of us all. I will see you again." They did not even shake hands. The family thought it was strange that after the greeting was so close that their parting was so abrupt. Marcus got the new coat that Mark had given him, then he put it on and went out into the back yard for some God time.

Something was not right. All of the family felt it, but it was Jake, who was now keeping his eye on Marcus out of the window who had to say something. "The meeting is tonight." The family looked at him. "I really think the meeting is tonight. Brothers I think we may be in for a long night."

The brothers had planned to meet up later at Jake's apartment and that they would discussed things that they needed to do in order to get ready for tonight.

Brother Marcus had a question for everyone. "I think we may have a loophole for keeping Marcus here tonight." He had the family's attention. "Did anyone notice that Marcus was favoring his left hand? I think it is hurt again. We could use that as a reason for him to not to go."

Robert interrupted. "You know I am thinking that it is time to get this over with. We have been blessed with the fact we may know when it is going to be. If we put it off or stop it now it will happen later, and we might not have the advantage we have right now of knowing."

They all agreed that felt right. But Nancy who was looking out the window was confirming what Brother Marcus had suspected. Marcus was not using his left hand. He must have hurt it in the defense class. "So, what are we going to do about the fact that Marcus is hurt? Do we let him go meet with Travis while he is hurt?" She motioned out the window towards Marcus.

Ben who had been talking to Jake joined her, looking at this kid who had changed all of their lives. "You know mom I think we could use this as a fleece. If Marcus' hand is as bad as before, we shut this whole thing down, but if it is not as bad, we brace his hand up and then let him do what he needs to do." When he had said 'brace it up' he shot a look to Jake, who then left the room to go out to his car to get something. They all agreed that this was a good idea. Mom called Marcus to come inside.

Marcus had heard her call him and he came in at once. When he walked in the door she called to Marcus. "Here catch this." She threw an apple at him which he caught with his right hand. She tossed another which he also caught with his right. He really was good with his hands but when she tossed the third apple and he tried to use his left hand he was unable to hold onto the fruit. "That is what I thought. Let me see your hand."

Marcus was unsure what was up. They all acted as if nothing had happened with John. He had expected that they would drill him into the night with questions, so this questioning was a relief. Marcus looked around for Jake who was still out getting something from his car. "I hurt it when I flipped Jake. It is not nearly as bad as before, but I do not want Jake to know."

Mark found that a strange statement. "Is that because Jake will make fun of you for doing it wrong?"

Marcus looked at him with a frown. "No, because I do not want him to feel bad because I got hurt. I am a brother too and I know how it feels when your brother gets hurt, that's when you know you could not have stopped it, but you still feel like you should have somehow. I don't want him to feel like that because of me."

Nancy tried to look at Marcus' hand, but the new coat had a cuff on it, and she could not pull it up. "Marcus, I need you to take off your coat so I can see your hand." Marcus did as she had told him. He was right. The hand was hurt and was showing signs of bruising, but the swelling was not near as bad. It looked like it was only a setback and not a break. They put ice on it and Nancy gave Marcus some Aspirin. When she had gone to get the Aspirin, Nancy had seen the pain medication and thought for one moment to give them to Marcus and simply knock him out for the night, but when she prayed about it she felt that Robert was right to want to get this over with and not put it off any longer.

Jake had come back in and was asking about the hand. "I am sorry Marcus, I did not mean for you to get hurt."

Marcus shot him a smile. "It was worth it to get to throw you to the ground."

They all found the humor in this. But it was hard, knowing what might be coming up later on this night. Jake handed his mom Marcus' old brace.

Nancy looked at it. "I was wondering where this thing had gone to." She unfolded it and dried off the ice water from Marcus' hand and then she placed the brace around it. Brother Marcus and Jake had a special interest in the fact that the brace was tight and that it did fit alright. "Marcus, promise me that you will not take this off? No matter what you are doing you keep it on. Now promise?"

Marcus gave Nancy an extra-long hug thanking her for helping him again. "I promise to not take it off." They could all see that his not telling them about what was going on was not easy for him and that helped them to not be too mad at him. "If it is okay, I think I will go to bed early."

Mark loved to watch Marcus use his play on words. He was remembering how Marcus had promised to not go out his window if he was sent to his room, not if he went on his own. Mark thought he could write a paper on this kid someday. He smiled to himself, but it was his brother Jake who saw him smiling. "What?" was his only response to his look of question?

Marcus went to his room and the brothers went to Jake's apartment to make plans for the rest of the night. Time was short, they figured it would be after midnight before Marcus would leave the house.

Nancy and Robert went to bed like usual and peeked in on Marcus. He did not hear them because they had found him kneeling by his bed deep in prayer. They noticed that he had letters lying on his bed. It looked like he had one for each of them. This kid was a good man.

Robert and Nancy went to their room and did the same, they prayed.

It would be time for Marcus to go. He was glad to have this over with but was afraid to find out the outcome. He looked up. "God, You know my heart. You know my life, You planned it. Please let me be doing what You want me to do about this. I believe You have a plan, may I be totally in it. Amen." Marcus went to put on his new hooded coat and had trouble getting the cuff over his brace. He thought about taking the brace off but thought better of it because it did help make the hand stronger, not to mention that he had promised not to. So, he worked the cuff over it and then he was ready.

It was almost one o'clock in the morning when Marcus finally left the house. The brothers were all in a van just outside the back fence. They were parked so that Marcus would not see them even though they were in a van that Marcus had never seen before. This kid was good, and they had to be extra careful not to be seen by him. "There he is." Mark was pointing to the roof of the house. Marcus was like watching a cat. Even one handed, this kid could get around good.

Marcus disappeared for a time then he came into view when he cleared the fence like it was only inches high. He cleared one more fence and he was gone.

Mark panicked. How are we going to follow him? He isn't using the road." Brother Marcus smiled and pulled out a device and turned it on. "Jake put a bug with a tracking device in the brace that Marcus is wearing."

Mark took a deep breath. "Oh, thank God." Mark thought about it. "Hey, how did you know he was going to need a brace?"

Jake and Brother Marcus had asked themselves the same thing. They had decided it was a God thing and continued on. They did not answer but motioned for Ben, who was doing the driving to start out. They watched the direction that the signal was heading and had decided that the meeting place was the park. That only

made sense. They all knew the park and it was local enough that they could all get to it. Jake was the one to point out that Marcus had not been to the park in a long time so Travis might have an advantage because of that, but then they talked about how Marcus had a good memory. And Mark added. "Not to mention Marcus has God with him." They all found comfort in that statement. "We all do." Brother Marcus added.

They parked the van on an off street and sat in it to wait until they heard the meeting start. Each of them could hear the sound from the bug on their radios. They had given Mark one too. Right now, all they could hear was Marcus breathing from time to time but for the most part their radios were quiet.

"Jake, do you have the phone number ready to dial?" Ben was asking Jake but there was no time for him to answer because they began to hear a conversation start. It sounded like it was between Marcus and Travis. Then it was confirmed.

"Hello Marcus, it was so nice of you to come." They could hear the mocking tone he was using with Marcus and it made them all mad.

"Hello Travis, good to see you. I think you will like this meeting if you will listen and give me a chance." Marcus went right to the point. He wanted to make sure he got to make his offer before anything could interfere with the meeting.

"Marcus what makes you think I want to hear anything you have to say to me?"

Marcus and Travis had stepped out into an open area, from the van they could only see shadow figures so they decided to get closer so they could see what was really going on.

"Travis, I know that you think things have not been fair with you, so I have a deal to make you. You stop this building an army and I will give you the life you always wanted." Marcus was being direct.

"Little brother you have lost your mind. You do not have anything I could ever want." He stepped closer to Marcus.

"Listen Travis, I will switch places with you. Look at us. We look so much alike. Only the Singletons' would know the difference and I am sure they would go along with this once they got used to the idea. I have scholarships, two of them to go to college; you are smart, you can do the work too. I have a great family that I live with. They are great people and they love me, and you can have that too. It is a great thing God has done for me and I can give it to you, all you have to do is say yes."

The brothers had found a place to hide just off to the side of the clearing where the two boys were talking. "Mark can you tell which one is Travis?" Ben was asking.

They could not tell because they both looked so much alike. This was going to be tricky; they should have thought about that.

Ben turned to Jake. "I think you might want to make that call now." Jake agreed and did so. He let the phone ring and only said 'it is happening in the park now' and hung up.

Mark was out of the loop. Only the brothers who were officers knew what was really going on. But he was okay with it because he trusted his brothers and knew they were doing their best at whatever was going on.

Marcus had to try and explain it again. "Travis listen to me, we look so much alike I think you can slip into my life. The Singletons will be okay with helping you to be in their family. They are good people. You will like them, they are smart and kind and they can offer you a good life. Don't you see? You could get another chance; all you have to do is decide to take it? Let me help you." Marcus was right in front of Travis.

Travis was not hearing Marcus. He was laughing at him. Travis raised one of his hands and many men with weapons appeared all around the area. Travis had come with an army. Marcus had come with a hope.

When Marcus saw the other men, he did not feel fear but felt disappointment. "Travis, I trusted you. You said you would come alone."

"Marcus you are so stupid. And for the record I heard your plan the first time. I don't need you to give me your life, I have my own. And also, for the record I am planning on taking yours, for a while anyway. I do not want to go to school or work; in fact, I never want to work. Once I take down those weak, simple minded Knowing families you like, who don't want to stand up for themselves. I will never have to work again. All I have to do is hand them over to Mr. Diggings and I will have it all. You are such a fool."

Marcus did not say a word or move but stood looking at his brother. He had given him a chance and now Travis had made a choice. "Travis, this battle belongs to the Lord." Was all Marcus said and then he continued to stand there not moving but simply looking at Travis.

The power of his doing nothing was unreal. The brothers could not believe how angry Travis was getting at Marcus. Travis pulled out a gun and held it up for Marcus to see. "Wrong again little brother, the battle belongs to the one with the gun and the army." He laughed.

Marcus did not move, but he stood his ground. He did not advance or withdraw when Travis got even closer.

The brothers were watching and hearing it all. When Travis got closer to Marcus with the gun, they almost had to sit on Jake to keep him from reacting. There was a noise behind them. Mark was startled but the rest of the brothers were not. It was the undercover officer Will.

He addressed Ben when he got to them. "I got your message. What has happened so far?" Ben did not answer but handed him a radio and asked Will. "Did you bring back up, looks like we are going to need it."

Will looked at the two boys. "How do you tell them apart?"

Brother Marcus answered. "Scan them; the one with the chip is our brother." Will did the scanning. He said. "This thing must be broken. Neither of them have a chip."

All four brothers turned to look at Will. Marcus had his chain on and they knew it because it was locked on him. They all remembered the tin foil from the potato. He had taken it back during the defense class. Marcus had covered his chip.

This was not in the plan. Marcus was right, this battle did belong to the Lord.

Marcus had to try one more time to talk Travis into making a right decision. "Travis listen to me, I will give you everything I have.

You can be me. The Singletons have a way of fixing this. I can give you my chip."

Will was hearing all of this on the radio. It made the brothers nervous but what could they do. Will talking to Ben. "I need to help Travis if I can be the one." Ben did not speak but raised an eyebrow to show question. "After all it was Travis who saved me from a beating or maybe even saved my life."

Ben felt the need to explain that it was Marcus and not Travis who saved him but there was no time.

There was more talking on the radio. "Travis I will tell them I am you and you will not have to go to jail. You can live my life." Marcus was within arm's length of Travis.

"Marcus you are such a wimp. I love the thought of you going to jail. In fact, the only thing keeping you alive right now, is the thought of you rotting away in jail and all because they think you are me." Travis laughed. Travis waved his gun at Marcus and said, "Now give me that brace."

Marcus was confused along with everyone who was listening. "What?"

Travis had lost his patience. He took the gun and hit Marcus across the side of his face with it. Marcus fell to the ground but used his good hand to catch himself. That put his left hand in the air so Travis could get to it. "I am not sure how. But I know that you have your chip in your brace somehow, and I want it. I do want your life, for now anyway. And you little brother get to go to jail as me Travis, Smart boy." Travis took the gun and hit Marcus again, as he reached for Marcus brace.

Will told Ben that they needed more time for the officers to get into place. But there was nothing they could do to buy time.

Travis had a hard time getting the brace off because of the cuff on the coat. "Marcus you have to give me that brace."

Marcus talked back to him. "Wait, I will give it to you, but it is stuck on the cuff of my coat.

"Marcus this is taking too much time, I want you to give it to me now." But he did not wait and grabbed Marcus arm and continued until he had pulled it off. At the end of the struggle Travis had pulled off Marcus's brace and put it on himself. "I do not know how little brother, but your chip is in this thing and now I have it. Call me Marcus." Travis kicked at Marcus who was sitting on the ground in front of him. "Have a nice day Travis."

The struggle with the brace took enough time for Will's team to get into place. Travis and his army were surrounded.

Travis was feeling his victory. "By the way that is a really nice sister we have. I wonder how she would feel about doing a dance with me." Marcus flew off the ground and went at Travis. "You leave my family alone. They are good people and do not deserve being treated bad by the likes of you." Travis countered Marcus' moves and Marcus was once again lying on the ground. Marcus did not give up. Marcus pulled himself up and went at Travis again. But this time it was the officer Will that Marcus ran into.

Will took a hold of Marcus and flung him into Ben's direction. Ben and the Brothers took Marcus by the arms, pulled the hood of the coat over Marcus head so his face could not be seen and pulled him into the van, they took out his chain from under his shirt and removed the foil from it. As far as the officers were concerned this was a van of chipped brothers out for a ride. The government cars had arrived as the van was leaving the area. The bug was still picking up the sounds of the goings on in the park. They could hear Travis talking to Will.

Will had Travis who was now standing in front of him yelling how he was Marcus. "I am Marcus, here I am, and you need to catch Travis, hurry he just left in that van."

Will was confused at what he was seeing. This Travis was not the one who had saved him but the Marcus that the Singletons had was the Travis who saved him. His Travis was their Marcus. Will was thinking that only the God they talked about while he was under cover at the farm would be able to pull this off, and he was not even sure of the half of it.

The next voice sounded like Will's. Hello Travis."

"Will, you know I am Marcus, quick scan me, you will see, I am Marcus, call Mr. Diggings he needs the names of the families who support the Knowing. I need to tell him everything."

Marcus was sitting in the middle of the van that was moving down the road. The doors of the van had been closed and were locked. No one was speaking at the moment. One of the brothers had given Marcus some kind of cloth to put on the side of his head where he had been hit by Travis's gun. It had been bleeding but was slowing down now.

Ben was driving but he kept looking in the back of the van in the rear-view mirror. This was too dangerous and was too close for any of them. The brother's emotions were high and went from so proud of Marcus they could hardly contain themselves to how totally dumb he was to take such a risk with his life. Marks radio was still on and was next to Marcus. They could hear many conversations going on around Travis. The bug that was in the brace was still transmitting.

Will and Travis were having what sounded like a conversation between just the two of them. "Travis what were you thinking? Marcus is your brother, isn't he? And the Knowing are your people, aren't they?"

When Marcus had heard Travis wanting to tell information he sat up staring and looked at the brothers. "Oh, now what are we going to do?" He shook his head. "They still think he is Travis, they were supposed to think he was me now. I don't understand."

There was evil laughter on the radio. "Marcus is a weak link in my family. Do you know that he will not touch a gun?"

Mark reached to turn off the radio and Marcus stopped his hand from doing so. "Please leave it on, I need to make sure Travis is ok."

Mark looked at his brothers and it was Brother Marcus who motioned with a nod that it was ok to leave it on. What could it hurt now?

Travis was going on and on about how he was chipped with Marcus' name and that he would be famous after all of this. "I will go down in history as the one who took down the Knowing and the families who supported them. Look here Will, I have the chip right here in the brace."

They heard rustling from the radio and then they heard Will speak. "Travis, I think you are you out of your mind. They cannot put a chip into a brace." More rustling and then Will again. "Travis you are under arrest for being the leader of an army with weapons, you are charged with fighting and you are charged with being the Smart boy we have been looking for."

Travis was angry; they could hear it in the tone in his voice. "You know Will, it is only because of that weak link brother of mine that you are even alive. If he had not interfered, you would have been eliminated a long time ago. So, smarten up before it is too late and get on my side, the winning side. By the way. Mr. Diggings is going to love it when I show him this chip here."

There were some more rustling sounds on the radio. "You mean this? I am not sure what you think this is but be assured it is not a chip, in fact I don't even think it belongs in here, let me help you with that." And the radio went silent.

Jake adjusted the volume on the radio. "I am not sure, but I think that Will must have destroyed the bug." Jake looked to his brothers. "Could we be that blessed?"

It was Marcus who answered. "Yes."

Mark had to ask. "Ok now what do we do?" He was talking to everyone and no one in particular.

Marcus was quick with giving an answer. "Take me to the government station where I can talk to Travis. Maybe now he will be ready to make a better choice."

There was a chorus of "No "from the van. Marcus called on Ben. "Ben you of all people… "No Marcus." He looked to Jake. "Jake you…" "No Marcus." And so, it went to each brother. Marcus had "No" as his only answer.

"Mark took this moment to talk to Marcus. You don't still trust Travis, do you?"

"Mark, I don't trust Travis, but I do trust God. I need to convince Travis to keep all of you safe to not tell everything he knows. We need to save the Knowing from Mr. Diggings and Travis."

Ben was talking while he was driving. "Marcus you are right we need to protect the Knowing but your part is finished. You are done. As of right now you are off this case, we are going to take it from here. I am going to drop you and Mark off at home, we are going to go to the station and see what is going on, then we will see if there is anything we can do. But your part is over. You did good Marcus, but you are done."

Marcus was going to argue but he could see from the looks on all their faces that he was not going to change their minds. His head was starting to hurt and as he stopped to think about it so did his hand, although not as bad as before. His hand really was not happy about the brace having been pulled off by Travis.

Ben pulled the van up to the house. "Mark you stay with Marcus and do not let him out of your sight."

Marcus shot a look at Ben, but it did not matter because Marcus was out of it from here on out.

Mark asked Ben. "Are you afraid of getting arrested?"

"I am more afraid of walking into that house this late at night with Marcus hurt and no brace on right now." Ben smiled. He was making light of what they all knew could be coming. Ben looked at Marcus and quoted something he had heard him say earlier. "This battle now belongs to the Lord, right Marcus?" Marcus shook his head yes.

The three of them got to the station and were amazed at all the busyness that was happening.

Jake talked to one of the other officers and asked what was going on. "You know that cop Will? Well he just made an incredible bust. He took out an army of armed Knowing, and he caught their leader, who turns out to be none other than and that Smart boy. Why Will is a true hero." Jake, brother Marcus and Ben continued to walk down the hall towards the interrogation rooms. As they went around the corner, they saw that their sister Sally was there waiting for them. They gave her a hug and looked to see that no one was listing.

Jake had to ask. "So, what is up?"

Sally smiled at him. "Relax we are not arrested, not yet anyway."

Ben leaned over to speak directly into Sally's ear. "So where is Travis and have you talked to Will?"

Sally was not sure about Will, but she knew where Travis was. "Will is your job but Travis is in room 2. For some reason they have called for a psychiatric evaluation on him." Sally lowered her voice. Be careful. There are more cameras installed around here."

As they were speaking there was a commotion in the hall down from them. They saw Will walking toward them. People were stopping him and giving him a real hero's welcome. Slapping him on the back and telling him how great he had done. As he got closer to them, they thought his face lit up in delight when he had seen them. They gave each other a slight glance to note if the others were feeling funny about his reaction to them. It was confirmed.

Will was walking up to Jake in particular. "Hey, did you hear what happened tonight?"

Another officer was walking by and added that it was unusual that for the first time in a long time that none of the Singletons had been involved in a big bust like this. Will looked around. "I think it might be better if we talked in here." Will had gone to a door and opened it for them to enter. It was a door to that lead to the observation part of room 2. When they all four had entered the room, they could see Travis thru a one-way mirror. He could not see or hear them. Jake personally wished he could get a hold of this kid Travis for just five seconds. Will had shut and locked the door behind them. Brother Marcus looked at Sally. "Are there any cameras or voice recording in here?"

It was Will who answered. "Not until next week."

Sally crossed her arms and rocked back nervously on her heels. Her brothers had not told her how nice looking this Will was. And smart too from the sound of things.

Ben went straight to the subject. "So, what happens next?"

Will turned and was looking at Travis through the mirror. "Well we seem to have a problem. This Travis in the room here seems to be different from the Travis who saved me from a beating a few weeks back. Everything had happened so fast that night and I thought that this Travis had a change of heart. But from the conversations I have had with this young man, it is this Travis that called for my beating and still would like to see it happen. He seems to think that your little brother, this Marcus was the one who saved me." Will was looking at each of them to see if they would like to fill him in on the details. But no one answered him. So, he continued. "Well this Travis here thinks that your Marcus had a chip in his brace?" Will reached into his pocket and pulled out two small evidence bags. He opened one and poured out the bug into his hand. He handed it to Jake. "Here I think you might need this back."

Jakes first thought was that Will had messed up, and by his touching the bug he had made the evidence void. But on second thought he knew that this officer did better work that that. Something was up, he knew it and so did the rest of his family in the room.

Ben went straight to it. "Will, what do you want?" Their time alone could be short, so they needed to figure out what was to happen to all of them.

Will did not mix words either. "I want what that kid Marcus has."

Ben looked at him confused. "You think our little brother has something?"

Will wanted to get straight to the point and to be clear. "You know that I was under cover for a few months." They confirmed they knew with slight nods of their heads. "Well when I was out there I saw a lot of things that I could not understand and I read the Bible they had, but I did not get it. But from what I have seen your Travis, I mean your Marcus do. I want in. Only a real God could give the courage that your Marcus has to him. I want that too. More than that, I want to know the God he does."

"Will we are not exactly sure what you are saying." Sally was good at gathering information, but this was not tracking. "What courage do you think Marcus has?"

They all knew exactly what Will was saying but they needed him to say it.

"Well first off, the fact that Marcus stood up to Travis here more than once from the information I have gathered, but the night he physically got between me and that bat. Well that was more than courage, that was crazy, but tonight that kid going up against Travis and his army. Did you know that there were one hundred and twelve of them in Travis's army and they were all armed with weapons?"

Brother Marcus had to keep the record straight. "Marcus did not know about Travis's army or the weapons before he got there. He thought Travis was coming alone."

Will took the other evidence bag and removed a paper from it. "Oh yes he did, and I can prove it to you." Will unfolded the paper and read it out loud. "Dear Travis; I know that you want to meet with me to fight tonight but you need to know that if you do come with your army of armed men then you will lose. The God side is always stronger. You have a choice. I have a good plan that will give you everything you want except the power you are demanding. Come alone and make a good choice and you will win but if you come with your army of over one hundred armed men then you will lose. The choice is yours. I am praying and believing that you will come alone. It was signed, your brother Marcus."

Brother Marcus took the letter and showed his family that it had been dated the night John was at the house. "How did Marcus get this note to Travis? He was with us and there was no way he got it out."

Jake started to laugh. "He gave John his old coat, the letter must have been in the coat and John had it delivered."

Ben folded the letter up and put it in his pocket. "I am glad that Marcus and his men are on our side. But putting that all aside, Will, what do you want us to do?"

"I want what that kid has. I want in. I want God in my life too. I can do that right? The Bible says all I have to do is ask, but I am not sure how, can you show me?" Will was nervous.

"You know we are not all like Marcus, not many of us are as bold as he is or really ever need to be." Ben was being extra careful to make sure that Will was seeking God and not what looked to be an exciting lifestyle. This was a choice of faith, a choice to follow God and not the excitement of a situation.

"Ben, I want to know the God I heard about out at the farms and on the street, I want to know the God you have that can give someone the courage to do the things this kid Marcus has done." Will's expression and body language did not change; he stood there waiting for them to help him become a believer.

Ben looked at his family and then at Will. "Ok if you are sure? But your life will never be the same. Remember it is not an easy life, but it is a very good life."

Will was not put off one bit. "I want to have your God, Please."

Jake had never seen anything like this before. He had heard at the farm meeting that God was working on Will, but this was nothing like he had ever seen or heard a grown man do or say."

Sally stepped in. "Okay Will, I need you to repeat after me."

Jake interrupted. "You are not going to do it now, not here are you?"

Sally smiled at Jake. "Yes, we are, now be quiet please. Will repeat after me, Dear God, I believe in you, I believe that you sent your son Jesus to die for my sins, I am a sinner and I know that only my faith in you, Jesus can save me. Please forgive me of all my sins. Thank you, Lord, thank you God. Amen."

Will repeated after Sally and everyone in the room was happy but they could see that Will had a question. "That is, it? It is that easy?"

Sally put her hand on Will's arm. "It is about the decision and the faith and not about the words or the works."

Will was still confused. "I don't feel any different."

Jake patted Will on the back. "You will. Just wait until God has an issue with something you are doing, you will feel it, and then you will know what it is to be one of God's people. It really can't be explained you just have to live it to know."

Will's face lit up. "So that is why you all call it the Knowing?"

Jake walked over to the mirror and spoke as he watched Travis. "Yes, that and so many other things. You have only the beginning of the ideas."

Will's pager went off. He looked down at it and explained to the family that he had to go and get Travis transferred.

The family watched as Will entered the room where Travis was being held. There were two officers right behind Will when he entered. The family recognized them right off as being the same two officers they had met at the restaurant some time ago. Travis looked up as Will entered the room. "Here you are gentlemen, this is Travis. He is all yours."

The one officer questioned what Will had said. "Don't you mean Marcus?"

Will gave a slight smirk to the mirror knowing full well that the family was watching everything that was going on. "No this is Travis who thinks at the moment that he is Marcus Singleton."

"You mean the Marcus Singleton?" The officer really was mixed up about this.

"No, their little brother Marcus Singleton, this Travis could never pass as their older one." Will was having fun at the expense of the officer.

The officer started to transfer Travis's hand cuffs from the table to his other wrist in order to take him out of the room. "As much as this does not make any sense, leave it to the Singleton family to have so many kids that they have to start reusing names. Of course, they have two Marcus's what was I thinking?" He let out a laugh as he took Travis with him.

Will called out to the officers. "Hey where are you going to take Travis anyway?"

"The judge ordered a mental evaluation on this kid. And from the sound of things I am guessing that it is not far off to think he has lost his mind." The officer led Travis who had thought better of resisting, when he saw that the officers had brought some mental health people with him. He did not want to do anything that could be considered crazy right now. And Travis had to admit to himself that the story he was trying to tell them did sound crazy.

Meanwhile back at the Singletons house there was an accounting going on there too. Mark and Marcus walked through the front door. When Robert and Nancy saw them, they reacted much the way they had expected them too.

Nancy took one look at Marcus and seeing the wounds on the side of his face, she went over to speak to him. "Marcus what on earth happened to you? Are you alright?" She turned to Mark. "Would you like to explain this to us?"

Marcus was the one to answer first. "This is on me. I met with Travis and I lost him, he decided to choose the other life and to be angry and to do mean things."

Robert heard what he had said and felt he needed to address this thinking right now. "First of all, you did not lose Travis. He made his choice. You simply do not have the power, none of us do, to make anyone choose a God life. Robert could see that Marcus had heard his words and was seeing the point he was making.

Marcus headed to the living room. "Is it ok if I go to the chair in the other room? I need some time to think."

Robert thought that was a reasonable request. "I think that might be a good idea. We can get more of the information from Mark right now. You go ahead, but I want your word that you will not leave the house, and no play on words either. You do not leave this house under any circumstances." Marcus started to walk away. "Marcus, I need your word."

Marcus did not turn to look at Robert. "You have my word I will not leave the house." And he went to the living room to be alone.

Mark stayed with his parents and to the best of his understanding tried to explain what had happened. He also explained the hope that he had that God was going to continue to protect the Knowing as well as all of the families who were apart of the group.

When they had finished talking all three of them went into the living room expecting to see Marcus sitting in his favorite chair but instead, they found him in front of it on his knees praying. They all joined him, kneeling beside him and placing a hand of encouragement on his back. Marcus prayed and they all supported his request to God. "Father I thank You for Your being in my life. I am asking You for another favor and that is that You will be with the Knowing people again today. Please be with Travis and keep him safe. Please be with my Singleton family and with Victor and Sandy too? Please be at all the shelters and farms, as only You can be today. I have to tell You that I am very angry at how this thing with Travis came out, but I am going to believe that You know what is best and that you will take care of it. Be with that officer Will; help him to feel your love. Please forgive me for all the doubts I have right now. Help me to keep my eyes and mind on You, Father. Thank You for what You have done, for what You are doing and for all that You are going to do in our lives." And the four of them said "Amen".

CHAPTER 44

It was weeks later and a lot had happened since the big bust.

Travis had in fact been taken to a mental hospital but after being there only a few hours there was a mix up and somehow Travis was transferred to a chipless facility where they had lost track of him. The paperwork was messed up and a lot of people were working on figuring it out.

The newspapers had reported at first that the big bust had nothing to do with the Knowing, but as the report was reprinted and passed around the words in the report had gone from nothing to do with the Knowing, to it was expected that they had something to do with it but that it was under investigation.

Mark went back to finish his schooling and had been offered a debriefing job with the police department. The job would be to help those officers who would be dealing with the chipless. The officials felt that his work with Marcus was an asset and that he would be able to get information that would help officers in the field.

Jake got a new partner. Who turned out to be Will. The officials thought they would make a good team because they both had done undercover work with the Knowing.

Will and Sally had started meeting together. They made a good couple but the fact that she had so many brothers kept their getting to know each other at a very slow pace. Will liked the family but was very aware of the fact that this was their sister and they expected a lot from him. Sally was concerned about the fact that she was seeing a man who had a chip. It would keep him out of many parts of her life with the Knowing if their relationship went any further, but she was going to let God figure that part out. So for now she was going to simply have fun getting to know Will.

Robert and Nancy had fallen back into their old routine. They were glad and thankful that things had worked out so good with their family and friends. They were excited to have Marcus in their family but often discussed that if they were going to have any more kids, they should think about having a girl the next time. Perhaps it would be easier.

Because it had been reported that the Knowing had left their town it was easier for Sandy and Victor to move around. The shelters had been left open but many of the other programs for the chipless were discontinued for financial reasons.

Brother Marcus had been called back to Washington to be on a committee to discuss the chipless situation in the United States. It was reported that he might be gone for some time due to the fact there was a lot of things to discuss about the group.

Just like Ben had come into the family's daily lives he had disappeared. When Marcus asked exactly where he had gone back to work at, no one discussed or said anything about it, he was merely gone, again.

Marcus had decided to take school off for the summer. Then in the fall he would accept the scholarship from the science department but had also accepted a work program with the sports group. He would work with their team members, helping them to use science skills to improve their playing abilities.

Jake and Marcus spent a lot of time together. Often when Marcus got off work, he and Jake would go and hang out in the park together. Today they had gone and gotten haircuts and were headed to the park. Jake and Marcus often discussed a lot of things that would make the Knowing way of life better for the group. They had been victorious this time at keeping the Knowing people safe, but tomorrow was a new day with new challenges.

As they were across the street from the park Jake noticed that all five of Marcus's commanders were waiting for Marcus to arrive. It looked like they needed to have a meeting with him. Marcus looked at Jake and motioned without words if it was ok for him to go with his commanders. Jake gave out a sigh. "Go on, like we could ever really stop you from leading. After all we know the real leader and His name is God and we know your partner in all of this and His name is Jesus."

The End. Or really a new beginning!

ABOUT THE AUTHOR

CP loves to tell and write stories. She has a supportive spouse of forty-three years along with two fantastic daughters.

CP's writing partners comprise of two very spoiled house cats rescued from the humane society who often give comic relief to writing time.

CP was a hairstylist for many years and enjoyed getting to know about the people and their adventures. So much of what she writes about comes from getting to know them and hearing their stories.

She is grateful to both God and to friends for being such a big part of her life. If there was one goal of her writing, it would be that everyone will be encouraged to read their Bible and get to know God better. Thanks to all!

CPSIA information can be obtained
at www.ICGtesting.com
Printed in the USA
LVHW020201131020
668649LV00001B/1